THE
# SAINT-FLORENTIN MURDERS

Also by Jean-François Parot

*The Châtelet Apprentice*
*The Man with the Lead Stomach*
*The Phantom of Rue Royale*
*The Nicolas Le Floch Affair*

# THE
# SAINT-FLORENTIN MURDERS

JEAN-FRANÇOIS PAROT

Translated from the French by Howard Curtis

GALLIC BOOKS

London

Ouvrage publié avec le concours du Ministère français chargé de la
Culture – Centre National du Livre.
This work is published with support from the French Ministry of
Culture/Centre National du Livre.

MYS Pbk

A Gallic Book

First published in France as *Le crime de l'hôtel Saint-Florentin* by éditions Jean-Claude Lattès

Copyright © éditions Jean-Claude Lattès 2004
English translation copyright © Gallic Books 2010

First published in Great Britain in 2010 by Gallic Books, 134 Lots Road, London SW10 0RJ

A CIP record for this book is available from the British Library

ISBN 978-1-906040-24-6

Typeset in Fournier by SX Composing DTP, Rayleigh, Essex

Printed in the UK by CPI Bookmarque, Croydon, CR0 4TD

2 4 6 8 10 9 7 5 3 1

*For Arlette and Richard Benais*

# CONTENTS

Background to *The Saint-Florentin Murders*          xiii

Dramatis Personae          xv

The Saint-Florentin Murders          1

Notes          413

# Background to *The Saint-Florentin Murders*

For those readers coming to the adventures of Nicolas Le Floch for the first time, it is useful to know that in the first book in the series, *The Châtelet Apprentice*, the hero, a foundling raised by Canon Le Floch in Guérande, is sent away from his native Brittany by his godfather, the Marquis de Ranreuil, who is concerned about his daughter Isabelle's growing fondness for the young man.

On arrival in Paris he is taken in by Père Grégoire at the Monastery of the Decalced Carmelites and on the recommendation of the marquis soon finds himself in the service of Monsieur de Sartine, Lieutenant General of Police in Paris. Under his tutelage, Nicolas is quick to learn and is soon familiar with the mysterious working methods of the highest ranks of the police service. At the end of his year's apprenticeship, he is entrusted with a confidential mission, one that will result in him rendering a signal service to Louis XV and the Marquise de Pompadour.

Aided by his deputy and mentor, Inspector Bourdeau, and putting his own life at risk on several occasions, he successfully unravels a complicated plot. Received at court by the King, he is rewarded with the post of commissioner of police at the Châtelet and, under the direct authority of Monsieur de Sartine, continues to be assigned to special investigations.

# DRAMATIS PERSONAE

NICOLAS LE FLOCH: a police commissioner at the Châtelet

LOUIS LE FLOCH: his son, a schoolboy

MONSIEUR DE SARTINE: Secretary of State for the Navy

MONSIEUR LENOIR: Lieutenant General of Police in Paris

MONSIEUR DE SAINT-FLORENTIN, DUC DE LA VRILLIÈRE: Minister of the King's Household

DUCHESSE DE LA VRILLIÈRE: his wife

PIERRE BOURDEAU: a police inspector

OLD MARIE: an usher at the Châtelet

TIREPOT: a police spy

RABOUINE: a police spy

AIMÉ DE NOBLECOURT: a former procurator

MARION: his cook

POITEVIN: his servant

CATHERINE GAUSS: a former canteen-keeper, Nicolas Le Floch's maid

GUILLAUME SEMACGUS: a navy surgeon

THIERRY DE VILLE D'AVRAY: First Groom of the King's Bedchamber

MONSIEUR DE LA BORDE: his predecessor

CHARLES HENRI SANSON: the public executioner

LA SATIN: Louis Le Floch's mother

LA PAULET: a former brothel-keeper

MONSIEUR DE GÉVIGLAND: a doctor

MADAME DE CUSACQUE: the Duc de La Vrillière's mistress
MONSIEUR DE CHAMBONAS: her son-in-law
MONSIEUR BOURDIER: an engineer
MONSIEUR D'ARRANET: Lieutenant General of the Naval Forces
AIMÉE D'ARRANET: his daughter
MONSIEUR TESTARD DU LYS: Criminal Lieutenant of Police
ANSELME VITRY: a gardener
MARGUERITE PINDRON: the Duchesse de La Vrillière's chambermaid
JEAN MISSERY: major-domo to the Duc de La Vrillière
EUGÉNIE GOUET: first chambermaid to the Duchesse de La Vrillière
JEANNE LE BAS, known as Jeannette: second chambermaid to the Duchesse de La Vrillière
CHARLES BIBARD, known as Provence: a valet
PIERRE MIQUETE: a Swiss Guard at the La Vrillière mansion
JACQUES BLAIN: a caretaker
JACQUES DESPIARD: a kitchen boy
GILLES DUCHAMPLAN: the late Madame Missery's elder brother
NICOLE DUCHAMPLAN: his wife
HÉLÈNE DUCHAMPLAN: the late Madame Missery's elder sister, a nun with the Daughters of Saint Michel
EUDES DUCHAMPLAN: the late Madame Missery's younger brother
RESTIF DE LA BRETONNE: a writer and pamphleteer
OLD LONGÈRES: a cattle farmer
LORD ASHBURY: an English spy
RICHARD: a gardener at Trianon

# I

## PROLOGUE

The dark night drained things of all their colour.
MAURICE SCÈVE

*Sunday 2 October 1774*

What was the meaning of this unusual rendezvous? She should
have been able to wean him off such whims by now. The idea of
it! The servants' floor offered sufficient opportunities, so there
was no real need for him to force her into these pointless
nocturnal escapades. It was a good thing her chores in Madame's
apartments kept her away from her fine suitor for much of the
day. He often took advantage of her slightest foray into the
common parts of the La Vrillière mansion to . . . He was
insatiable. But how could she refuse him? She owed him her
position, and a kind of security. Still she waited, and the piece of
candle, which cast a parsimonious light on the roasting room,
would not last much longer. It was a large, dark room, with
chimneys of blackened stone looming over the spits, trammels
and dripping-pans.

She laughed at her own cleverness: every day she filched
pieces of candle from the apartments on the upper floors to
replenish her stock. Several times, she had come close to being
caught. She had to beware, not only of her mistress's constant

vigilance, but also that of the other servants, her competitors in this pilfering: they, too, were always on the lookout for anything to feed this lucrative trade in candle wax.

A metallic clinking broke the silence. Her heart pounded so hard it hurt. She held her breath, waiting for what was to follow, but nothing came. Another of those rats, she thought – impossible to get rid of them. One of those fat grey moth-eaten rats that fed on scraps from the kitchen, and from what had been left in the big adjacent larder. The best pieces from the larder were also regularly resold to a few taverns, and as for the scraps, they ended up in a soup which, sold for a few coins from a steaming carriage in the streets, provided momentary sustenance to the poorest of the poor. She had tried it herself, not so long ago, after fleeing her father's house, and still had the bitter rotten taste of it, which no seasoning could ever mask, in her mouth. Just the thought of it made her retch.

She was still listening hard, hoping to hear her lover's heavy steps. But all she heard was a distant miaow. She laughed: cats were no use here – they were too well fed on the leftovers from a rich table. Only their eyes, gleaming in the darkness whenever a ray of light struck them, scared off the most faint-hearted. Sometimes, you would see a big rat, in the peak of condition, rise up and bare its yellow teeth, defying a cat, which would slink off without a fight. As for her, she was not afraid of cats. She had seen some really formidable cats in the cowsheds belonging to her father, who raised cattle for milk in Faubourg Saint-Antoine, where they were attracted by the mice hiding in the straw and grain.

She preferred not to think about that. Better to wipe out the past. But she couldn't help remembering those last days spent with her family. Her father had been adamant that she marry a neighbour's son, a gardener in the *faubourg*. The boy was well enough built, but he had bulging eyes and did not appeal to her. His method of courtship involved listing the different kinds of lettuce, as well as the rules for cultivating plants under cold frames, the whole lecture embellished with observations on the best way to line paths with quickset hedges, trellises or picket fences. The preliminary visit she had made to the Vitry household had confirmed her in her rejection.

Their house had one room on the ground floor, looking out on the marsh. It was here that the family lived and ate. The floor was of beaten earth, a long way from the waxed tiles of her own house. Straw chairs, a large, worn wooden table, a porcelain stove, a copper fountain and an ugly dresser were the only decoration. On the first floor, two bedrooms, with straw mattresses and bunks, one of which was the son's and would be the young couple's when they married. Old Madame Vitry, a tall, thin, dark woman with soiled, worn-down nails, listed for her, in a severe tone, the duties of a gardener's wife. She would have to get up at five in the morning, in all weathers and all seasons, and work until eight in the evening, pausing only briefly for a little soup or a crust of bread. She would have to obey her in-laws as if they were her own family.

Her revulsion increased when they started discussing the marriage contract and the contributions of the bride and groom. Hers consisted, apart from a silver dowry large enough to bring a gleam to the old woman's eyes, of a supply of fresh manure for the Vitry family's gardens, to be provided in instalments spread out over several months. When the day came for the engagement to be certified before a notary, appalled by the prospect of a life with this oaf, she had yielded to a sudden impulse and decamped, leaving behind calves, cows, oxen, manure and lettuces, a stunned fiancé and two disappointed families. Fearing that they would search for her, she plunged into the great city, hoping to lose herself in an ocean of people. Appalled at his daughter's actions, old Pindron made no attempt to search for her. She had dishonoured the family, she was no longer of any account, and he immediately disowned her. He took to his bed and died four days later, leaving a widow who retired to her native Burgundy after selling off the farm for a good price to an important family who raised cattle in the *faubourg*, and who committed themselves before a notary to pay her an annuity until she died.

For months, Marguerite Pindron roamed the streets of Paris, sleeping on the *quais*, finding hiding places in the pyramids of the Port au Bois on Quai Saint-Paul or amid the casks on Quai de la Rapée. It was here that the wood carried on the river accumulated in piles as high as houses. Some were well organised into pyramids, but most were heaped up haphazardly, creating a kind of mysterious city made of detours and alleys, underground passages and inner rooms from which, early in the morning, there emerged, wild-eyed, a strange and varied collection of human beings. The few *louis* she had stolen from her father did not last long, but, being able to read and write, she used this skill among the poorest of the poor, and managed to hold out until winter. It was then, one desperate evening when she could no longer bear the hunger and cold, that she met a well-dressed young man who took her to his dwelling, washed her, and made her an object of his pleasure. He dressed her and fed her, then introduced her to his brother-in-law, who was the major-domo in the mansion of the Duc de La Vrillière. Her joy at finding a position was short-lived. She was only the latest in an army of servant girls who emptied the pots and buckets, doomed to the most repulsive chores and the harshest reprimands.

It did not take her long to realise that the brother-in-law also expected to have his way with her. The man had been a widower for two years, could not bear the solitude, and chased anything wearing skirts in the Saint-Florentin mansion. At first, she resisted his advances, but she was desperately afraid of finding herself back on the streets. She opened her heart to her original benefactor, who laughed in her face and urged her to yield: he had started making her small loans, to be repaid when she was able. Her new lover immediately conceived a genuine passion for her beauty and youth. She found it increasingly difficult to escape a bond that was proving burdensome and the constant attentions of a greybeard to whom she had been forced to yield out of necessity alone. She tried every stratagem she could think of, including brief dalliances with other, younger servants, in the hope of putting him off. The only result was to strengthen his desire for her. He was obsessively jealous, and some terrible scenes ensued.

Tears welled in her eyes. All that was nothing compared with what had happened three days earlier, which she could not get out of her mind. Her young benefactor had come looking for her in the evening after she came off duty, and had made her leave the building through a concealed door and join him in a cab. After a long journey, he had led her into an unknown house and made her put on a highly indecent costume. Why had she agreed to it?

She tried to dismiss the images of what had followed. How had she come to this? She had not protested, as if the frenzy and outrageousness of all that was happening had left her too stunned to react. Her 'friend' had appeared to her in such an ambiguous light that she found it impossible to regard him again as part of the natural order of things.

The candle flame suddenly flickered in a draught of air, sputtered a moment, then went out, giving off an acrid odour. That was all she needed! She had nothing with which to relight it. She felt suddenly anxious at being alone in this deserted place. She imagined presences around her. It was early autumn, a time when animals and insects often sought warmth in the kitchens of houses. Something creaked behind her, and she was aware of a furtive movement. She forced herself to turn round, but could see nothing. She was finding it hard to breathe: it seemed to her that there was not enough air in here. She was starting to panic. She was just about to rush madly to the staircase leading to the upper floors when she felt herself seized firmly by an unseen arm and pressed against someone's body. A terrible pain went through the base of her neck, and she collapsed without even realising that she was dying, in a stream of blood.

Early the next morning, a kitchen boy discovered two bodies. One was Marguerite Pindron, whose throat had been cut, and the other Jean Missery, the major-domo, lying unconscious and wounded. A knife lay on the tiled floor beside him, in the middle of a scarlet pool.

# I

# THE PASSING OF THE DAYS

Time uncovers secrets; time creates opportunities;
time confirms good counsel.
BOSSUET

*Sunday 2 October 1774*

Nicolas was surreptitiously looking at his son's face. He was the
spitting image of how he himself had been when he was young,
with that dashing air his grandfather, the Marquis de Ranreuil,
had had whenever he rose to his full height and looked his
interlocutor in the eye. As for La Satin, her presence was felt in
the gentleness diffused through his fine, if not entirely formed
features. The boy's noble but casual bearing showed none of the
awkwardness common to his age. He was talking to Monsieur de
Noblecourt, and his conversation was full of Greek and Latin
quotations: from time to time, with a smile, the former procurator
would correct his mistakes and solecisms. The presentation
dinner for Louis Le Floch at Noblecourt's house in Rue
Montmartre was at its height. Nicolas was happy and relieved to
feel the warmth emanating from his friends, Semacgus, Bourdeau
and La Borde. He himself did not take part in the discussion,
wanting Louis, who in fact seemed quite at ease, to find his place
here naturally. The role of father, which filled him with both joy

and anguish, was still new to him, and he had to learn it step by step.

The year was ending better than it had begun. The rumours circulating about the plots and criminal investigations that had followed the death of his mistress, Madame de Lastérieux, were gradually dying down. He still carried his grief for the late King in his heart, muted but painful. This troubled period of his life had had one fortunate consequence: he had discovered the existence of a child born of his liaison with La Satin fifteen years earlier. La Paulet, alerted by a first encounter and the impression of a conspicuous resemblance, had decided to intervene. Leaving her house in Auteuil, where she led a comfortably devout life, she had come running to see Monsieur de Noblecourt to plead La Satin's case and the importance of giving Louis a father he had never known. The former procurator had taken the matter very seriously and had agreed to intercede and advise both parents.

There had been misgivings, however, on both sides. La Satin feared Nicolas's reaction, recalling that he had once questioned her as to the father of her child and had declared himself ready, if need be, to assume responsibility. Being a sensible woman, well aware of the demeaning nature of her situation, she dreaded the consequences that might ensue, for both father and son, of recognising Nicolas's paternity and thus bringing this dubious lineage out into the open. At the same time, Nicolas, who still felt a great deal of tenderness for a woman he had known when he first arrived in Paris, was fearful of hurting the new mistress of the Dauphin Couronné by taking steps to remove their child from a pernicious, corrupting environment. Nor had he any desire to loosen the natural ties binding a son to his mother.

It was left to Monsieur de Noblecourt to resolve this thorny issue. He took up his pen and, as if setting out the points for a closing statement in court, undertook to bring the interests and feelings in question, delicate as they were, into alignment. La Satin was to readopt her birth name of Antoinette Godelet and abandon her present occupation. With Nicolas's help, she would buy a shop selling fashion and toilet articles in Rue du Bac from a couple who wished to retire. The hardest part was to convince La Paulet, who, seeing her carefully laid plans for the succession of the brothel collapse, raged and cursed like a fishwife in a manner with which Nicolas had been familiar in the past. Monsieur de Noblecourt waited for the storm to pass and, making full use of his mollifying influence on the good lady, dispensed so many compliments and displayed such a benevolent ear that his intervention worked wonders, and she gradually calmed down. The unexpected arrival of La Présidente, whose English adventure had ended in disaster,[1] made it possible to overcome the last objections. La Satin's friend jumped for joy at the idea of resuming her duties at the Dauphin Couronné, but this time as mistress and manager. Grudgingly, La Paulet agreed to everything. Indeed, she went even further. Her establishment had prospered, acquiring an elegant tone that belied its reputation. In order to show her gratitude to La Satin, she decided to complement her move to Rue du Bac by buying for her the little mezzanine apartment attached to it.

For his part, Nicolas recognised his son before a notary – the boy immediately took his name – and used his influence to make sure that anything relating to La Satin's former activities went missing from the police archives. All that remained was to inform

Louis of these events which would have such consequences for his future: a delicate operation which might well distress the young man. Monsieur de Noblecourt offered to take care of it, but Nicolas wanted to begin his career as a father by being completely open and telling the whole truth. In any case, he had nothing with which to reproach himself, having been unaware of his son's existence until quite recently. But the question remained as to what the young man would think of these decisions about which he had not been consulted.

Nicolas thought about how he himself had been at that age. Whenever he talked to Louis, it was indeed that distant image of himself that he strove to convince. Their first encounter reassured him. Under the trees in the garden of La Paulet's house in Auteuil, he told the boy his life story, omitting nothing, and taking care not to offend the love the child bore his mother. Louis listened seriously and naturally, and immediately launched into a long series of questions. Their encounters continued through the summer, mostly at Dr Semacgus's house in Vaugirard, and before long their relationship blossomed into affection. Having gained some idea of his son's knowledge, Nicolas decided to have him admitted to the College of the Oratorians at Juilly: he regretted that his Jesuit masters had been expelled from the kingdom, but the education, both classical and modern, provided at the college corresponded to the ideas the Marquis de Ranreuil had drummed into Nicolas throughout his adolescence at Guérande, with modern literature and foreign languages being particularly prominent. Louis would come back and spend his holidays in Paris, sharing them equally between Rue Montmartre and Rue du Bac.

'When will I see the King, Father?'

Nicolas gave a start, and again became conscious of his surroundings. The meal was starting. Marion and Catherine had just brought in a piping hot calf's-kidney omelette.

'I'll take you to Versailles one Sunday,' he replied. 'We'll attend Mass and you'll be able to observe His Majesty at your leisure, and then at even closer quarters in the great gallery.'

Louis smiled. His expression brought a pang to Nicolas's heart: for a moment, he had been reminded of his half-sister Isabelle.

'How is Monsieur Lenoir?' La Borde asked.

'From what I see, the Lieutenant General is doing well.'

Those present noticed the bitterness of his reply.

'If truth be told,' La Borde resumed, 'he's a man extremely well disposed to everything concerning opera.'

'I fear,' Semacgus said ironically, 'that our friend's desire to be noticed has influenced his support for the successor of the late lamented Sartine.'

Nicolas shook his head.

'It's one of those phrases,' Noblecourt said, 'that suggests too much or too little. I find it a somewhat laconic remark to make about someone in such an important position. Sartine actually increased the powers of the office. What will this man do with them?'

'Oh,' said Bourdeau, 'he's become as important as a minister, even though he doesn't have the title of minister. You know how much influence he has behind the scenes. He strikes down or he saves. He spreads darkness or light. His authority is as tactful as it is extensive. He elevates and humiliates as he pleases.'

Nicolas shook his head. 'The last one liked wigs, this one richly bound books.'

'Which suggests,' said Louis timidly, 'that neither one of them can entirely cover up his own emptiness!'

They all applauded. Nicolas smiled.

'As our late King used to say,' observed La Borde, 'like father like son.'

'He gets it from his grandfather,' said Nicolas. 'The marquis was never at a loss for a witty remark.'

'Gentlemen,' resumed La Borde, 'allow me to abandon you to the aromas of this delicious omelette. I salute in passing the tenderness of these kidneys. In honour of young Louis, I lent a hand myself, as I used to at Trianon. Catherine and I are about to put the finishing touches to my surprise. Semacgus, prepare our host to resist temptation! Louis, come with me, I need a kitchen boy.'

The boy stood up, already tall for his age. How many things there were to teach him! thought Nicolas. Riding, hunting, fencing . . . He was a Ranreuil, after all. He resumed his reflections. Naturally, the new Lieutenant General of Police had received him quite promptly. Following Sartine's counsel, he had asked for an audience as early as possible. He had found Lenoir standing behind the desk where, so often, his predecessor had played with his wigs. The man was tall, with a full figure and a distinct paunch. He had a strong nose above a mouth with a fleshy lower lip which, when it moved to express dismissal or disdain, drew the eye to his double chin. His own eyes were lively and penetrating, with a hint of arrogance, a marked scepticism, and an undisguised self-satisfaction. A powdered wig with ringlets added to the magnificence of cambric bands falling in a dazzling stream over an unadorned silk gown. The interview, cut short by the arrival of a visitor, could hardly have been classed as a genuine meeting of minds.

'Commissioner,' Lenoir had said, 'my predecessor recommended you. I myself, Monsieur, had the opportunity to assess the skill and expertise with which you handled a delicate case. On the other hand, experience has taught me that personal methods, however useful and effective they may be, tend to get out of control and become a burden to those in authority. You cannot play with me the same role you played with Monsieur de Sartine. I intend to revise the rules and bring a new order to our methods, one more in keeping with my own conceptions.'

'I am at the King's service, Monseigneur.'

'He appreciates you, Monsieur,' retorted Lenoir, somewhat ill-temperedly. 'We know he appreciates you. But the rules must be the same for everyone. Some older commissioners might be offended . . .'

They probably hadn't held back, thought Nicolas.

'. . . that one of their younger colleagues should get all the attention and be allowed such independence. Can we entrust you with a district? That would hardly be appropriate. You have treated your colleagues very badly—'

'Monseigneur!'

'I know what I'm saying, don't interrupt me. Many complaints and grievances have reached my ear. The sensible thing, Monsieur, would be to take things easy, relax, go hunting, and wait for more auspicious times to return. A position as police commissioner at the Châtelet can be sold at a good price and with excellent interest. There is no shortage of candidates, as you can imagine. I have the honour to bid you good day, Commissioner.'

Nicolas made no effort to counter this fall from favour. His upright nature balked at doing so, and he was unable to feign submission. Absorbed as he was by his discovery of Louis, he was more worried about what would happen to his deputy, Bourdeau, who had been dragged into the same storm and who, with children still young enough to require support, now found himself reduced to his basic allowance without the profitable extras to which his position usually gave rise. Nicolas took steps to have substantial sums passed on to his friend, justifying them, in order not to offend the man, as payments of long-forgotten debts, expenses incurred during past missions. As far as his own condition was concerned, he approached it with an almost religious fatalism: his future would be what it would be. The only people in whom he confided unreservedly were Monsieur de Noblecourt and La Borde.

The former approved of his determination to rise above the temporary vicissitudes that marked any career devoted to the King's service. Time was a great master which arranged things well, and, in these circumstances, the only obligation that imposed itself upon an honest man was to keep up appearances. In this way, he would show that he regarded as of little account what most men would have taken for a catastrophe. Monsieur de Noblecourt, with his experience of the century and of the ways of men, was convinced that Lenoir would overcome his initial prejudices. His first reaction had been perfectly understandable, the action of someone who wished to impress others and himself. Nicolas should not forget that Lenoir was the protégé and friend of Monsieur de Sartine, who had intrigued to have him appointed in his place, hoping thereby to keep some control over this important cog in the machinery of State, this privileged instrument of influence with the monarch. The talk that had reached Monsieur de Noblecourt's ears about the new Lieutenant General of Police painted quite a different picture. He was said to be clear-headed, a good conversationalist, a man of lively perception and exquisite judgement. He had studied long and hard, but this had not, it was said, in any way blunted the graces and ornaments of an amiable wit. He was, in addition, a discriminating lover of the arts and letters. In short, the most sensible thing, for the moment, was to wait, for it sometimes happens that our salvation comes from the very same sources from which we expect our ruin.

Monsieur de La Borde's argument, although different, pointed in the same direction. He had, immediately after the King's death, decided to forget a past that had been happy but was now over and done with. They had to accept it: they were both 'old Court', and would stay that way for a long time, if not for ever. He himself had resumed a number of activities which his duties to the monarch had caused him to neglect. Swearing Nicolas to secrecy, he confessed that the late King had promised to compensate him for a financial sacrifice to which he had once consented in order to enter his service. He also revealed, much to Nicolas's surprise, that he had decided to turn over a new leaf after a life of superficiality and dissipation. He had recently married Adélaïde-Suzanne de Vismes, nineteen years his junior. The ceremony had originally been set for 1 July, but, because of the public mourning, had been postponed to September and celebrated discreetly. His wife, sorely tried by these events and the dashing of their expectations, had fallen into a terrible state of languor, inflammation and weeping. Still in the mood for confession, and no doubt inspired by Nicolas's recent fatherhood, La Borde revealed to him that he himself had legitimised, four years earlier, a daughter born of his liaison with La Guimard, the famous actress. Saying all this seemed to relieve him of a burden and, putting his own troubles aside for the moment, he returned to those of his friend.[2]

He tried fervently to make Nicolas forget his gloom. After all, he had been granted leisure. By God, he should make use of it and devote himself to his son! A man who had studied the world knew when to wait and when to take advantage of opportunities. He had to adapt his means and make his thoughts serve his loyalties. His counsel could be summed up in the Italian phrase *Volto sciolto e pensieri stretti*: Open face and secret thoughts. Dissimulation and secrecy were to be cultivated: the commissioner should stand aside for a while in favour of the Marquis de Ranreuil. He should use the disadvantages of an apparent fall from favour, don them like a suit of armour in a society where the slightest weakness was noticed and provided ammunition to those who wished to mock or crush you. He should be seen in all the right places and make sure that the King, who already knew him, noted his regular attendance and expertise on hunts and at shooting parties, to which he had free access thanks to the favour of Louis XV. That would give others nothing to seize on as evidence that Monsieur Lenoir was keeping him on the sidelines. Nothing would be gained by arguing. La Borde noted sadly that times had indeed changed: a witty remark by Monsieur de Maurepas was considered of greater import in royal circles than protecting a good servant.

Nicolas was inspired by his friends' good counsel. He judged that salvation lay in the deliberate ambiguity of his conduct, which would lead commentary in different directions and, in the long run, drain it of all meaning. Despite the rumours, the cold hearts and false minds of the city and the Court would struggle in vain to spread gossip about him. Everyone might well have his own opinion about the case of 'young Ranneuil', but it wouldn't matter. All that remained to complete the picture were a few touches intended for the chroniclers, who were always on the lookout for things that might convince the less credulous: a gratifying flirtation with an indiscreet lady, a touch of condescension in his courtesy, and, most important of all, being noticed by the King. He had the opportunity to note, with some amusement, how he excelled in the career of courtier. In August, when the Court was at Compiègne, he had several times found himself in at the kill just after the King, and had benefited from his master's simple good humour. Subsequently, they had conversed merrily about the qualities of the animal or the episodes of the hunt. At shooting, he deliberately missed, much to the satisfaction of Louis XVI, who, as a mark of his esteem, resolved to present him with the rifles which the late King had lent to Nicolas on one of his last excursions, just before his illness.

All this caused much comment at Court, his supposedly fallen star suddenly shone again as brightly as ever, and the very people who, a few days earlier, had looked at him without seeing him now came running to compliment him. He had no doubt that news of his renewed success would reach the ears of Monsieur

Lenoir, who was informed by his spies of the smallest details of life at Court. When all was said and done, he realised, the last few months had passed quickly, with a great deal of agitation and a flood of impressions and feelings. A great cry drew him from his reflections.

'*Gigot farci à la royale* accompanied by mushroom rissoles!' roared La Borde, who was carrying a silver tray from which fragrant wreaths of steam were rising.

'Doesn't he look like the herald of arms?' exclaimed Noblecourt, his eyes already gleaming greedily. 'All he needs is the tabard.'[3]

'What do you think this is, then?' asked La Borde, indicating the white apron with which he was draped.

Now it was Louis's turn to appear, his face red from the heat of the ovens, carrying a porcelain dish filled with a pyramid of rissoles arranged on a cloth.

Nicolas decided to join in the mounting gaiety. 'And what are we going to drink with all that?'

Bourdeau produced two bottles from under the table. 'A plum-coloured Saint Nicolas de Bourgueil!'

'Gentlemen, gentlemen,' said Noblecourt, 'while Poitevin carves, I propose that Monsieur de La Borde gives us the usual descriptive and appetite-whetting speech.'

'May I enquire, Monsieur,' said Louis, 'as to the reason for this custom?'

'Young man, ever since your father brought joy back to this house, a joy made all the greater today by your presence among us, it has been a tradition which I would not dream of not respecting on this feast day. The delicious dishes concocted under this roof should be tasted not only by the palate but also by the ear.'

'And the eyes!' exclaimed Semacgus. 'In any case, that is the one sense I allow myself to indulge.'

'Well,' retorted Noblecourt, 'I'm going to disobey my doctor this evening. I shall satisfy those three senses to the full!'

'Gentlemen,' said La Borde, 'may I first point out to you that I had the honour to make this dish for the late King, and that Madame de Pompadour was very fond of it in spite of a weak stomach?'

'The good lady was quite lenient,' said Semacgus.

'On the contrary, she asked for more.'

'Gentlemen, stop this foolery,' begged Noblecourt. 'It's going to get cold.'

'Imagine a fine leg of lamb,' continued La Borde emphatically, 'kept cool for several days until it's nicely tender. First you must break the knuckle to get inside and take out the meat while keeping the outside intact. To do this, I called on the skills of a master!'

'A meat roaster from Rue Saint-Honoré?' Nicolas asked.

'Not at all. A naval surgeon, adept at cutting and digging.'

'It's true,' said Semacgus, closing his eyes with a show of solemnity. 'My knives proved very useful.'

'Good heavens!' cried Nicolas. 'Do you mean to say you used the instruments that are normally for—'

'I'd like to have you believe it, just to take away your appetite!'

'I'll never finish if you keep interrupting me,' moaned La Borde. 'The meat that's been taken out has to be chopped up very small with a little bacon, marrow, fine calf's-kidney fat, mushrooms, eggs, salt, pepper and spices. Keep kneading it all, making sure that each part absorbs the taste and seasoning of the others. Then fill the skin with it so that the leg reappears in its natural form and tie it all the way round with string, in order to maintain its consistency. Let it get nicely golden, then cook it in a pot with a good thick stock and a thin piece of beef, half roasted, which will fill it with its juices and give it more taste. Add onions stuck with cloves and herbs. A good hour later, turn it in the pot until it's baked. Check it with your fingertips, to make sure the flesh is soft. As the sauce is now reduced, add some sweetbread, and, once you've carved the leg, pour this succulence over it.'

Cheers punctuated Monsieur de La Borde's recitation. Everyone proceeded to savour a dish that required a spoon rather than a knife and fork. Nicolas watched his son out of the corner of his eye, happy to see that he was eating with that nimble elegance which, once again, recalled not only the bearing of the Marquis de Ranreuil, but also his mother's innate grace.

'Now there's a dish,' said Noblecourt, 'that's well suited to my old teeth.'

'The crustiness of the wrapping and the softness of the filling go together perfectly,' said Semacgus. 'And how well this purple beverage matches the lamb!'

'Doesn't it?' said Bourdeau, delighted. 'I find that the mushrooms in this fine mixture retain their softness and all the flavours of the forest.'

Noblecourt turned to Louis. 'This is a dinner you'll remember when you're at school, one with which you'll be able to enliven your dreams.'

'I shall think of it with gratitude, Monsieur,' the boy replied, 'when I'm eating hard-boiled meat and worm-eaten herring. It will strengthen my resolve.'

They all laughed. Catherine placed a dish of crystallised quince fritters sprinkled with sugar on the table. Noblecourt smiled and made a sign to Poitevin, who went out and immediately returned with two small packages.

'Young man,' said the former procurator, opening the more voluminous of the two, 'I was a schoolboy once, and had to suffer, like you, both harsh discipline and hunger. My mother took pity on me and made sure I had a supply of quince jelly, which I sucked every evening to calm my hunger pangs.'

He took from the packet a series of small round, flat deal boxes.

'These objects, which are called *friponnes*, contain quince jelly with a little added white wine. Not only will they assuage your hunger, but they are an excellent remedy for stomach aches. They will also help to combat whatever harmful effects the school food has on your health. You will just have to conceal them carefully, as theft is all too common in schools. You have enough here to last you until Christmas.'

The conversation then turned to more general matters.

'Are they still wearing mourning for our king at Versailles?' La Borde asked with that feigned indifference that ill concealed his sadness at being separated from the centre of the world.

'The recommended attire,' said Nicolas, 'is a cloth or silk coat, depending on the weather, black silk stockings, swords and silver buckles, with a single diamond ring. Last but not least, braided cuffs on the shirt. That's all until 1 November; after that everything will be simpler as Christmas approaches.'

'For someone who is out of favour at Court,' observed La Borde, 'you seem to be well informed!'

'I still have my place there, having followed my friends' counsel.'

'I am assured,' said Noblecourt, 'that the King has ordered Monsieur de Maurepas to put right certain abuses. Have we seen the first fruits yet?'

'A hundred and thirty horses and thirty-five grooms have already been removed from the royal hunt.'

'Can you imagine?' said Bourdeau, sardonically. 'Horses are done away with, while at the same time the King yields to the Queen's whims by increasing her already well-stocked household. Why did she need a grand chaplain on top of everything else, not to mention an official to heat the sealing wax?'

'Clearly, Bourdeau is equally well informed of matters at Court,' said Semacgus.

'Not at all!' the inspector replied. 'But I keep a close eye on how the people's money is dissipated.'

'It's been quite a while,' said Semacgus, 'since we last heard your caustic criticisms.'

'In my opinion,' said Bourdeau, becoming heated, 'the creation of Court positions is putting a strain on a budget that's already increased thanks to the military operations on the island of Corsica. Just imagine, the natives don't know how lucky they are to be French! Rebels and bandits are ravaging the countryside and extorting money by menaces.'

'As a matter of fact,' said La Borde, 'that's becoming a bigger problem. Our commander in the field, Monsieur de Marbeuf, has just pacified Niolo. Rebels have been put on the wheel outside churches in the presence of the populace. Six hundred rifles were found in a tomb at the monastery, and there was a terrible reprisal: two monks were hanged on the spot. It's to be expected that this business will continue. God knows when we shall see its end!'

'Enough of sad matters,' said Noblecourt. 'La Borde, I have no doubt you attended the first performance of Monsieur Gluck's *Orpheus and Eurydice*. Tell us what you thought. Such things hold no secrets for you.'

'In truth,' replied La Borde, impervious to the hint of irony in the procurator's tone, 'the audience were enraptured by that tragic opera, and its success surpassed that of *Iphigenia in Aulis* last April.'

'That indeed is what I observed for myself,' said Noblecourt, savouring the surprised reaction of his friends, who all knew that the former procurator almost never left his house. 'Oh yes! In the absence of Nicolas, away chasing both lovely ladies and the beasts of the field, I called for my horse and carriage. Poitevin donned his newest livery, and off we set!'

He looked at Nicolas out of the corner of his eye.

'On my arrival at the Opéra, Monsieur Balbastre,[4] who was all smiles, helped me to my seat. He was very friendly . . . if a trifle unctuous.'

Nicolas shrugged.

'Anyway, I attended the performance and can confirm its success. But what kind of success? And with whom? Apart from you, who are able to judge, even though in this case I do not share your taste. What did I see? An auditorium three-quarters full of old would-be gallants and young fops, the kind who spend their time making paper cut-outs in fashionable salons. This pack goes wild every time something new appears, provided it stands out more or less from the ruck. As for what I heard, it was nothing but a stew of very diverse ingredients. A disastrous mixture of sounds and impressions that bombards and paralyses the understanding to cover the lack of fecundity of an author who ought to prostrate himself before Saint Greluchon.[5] Oh yes, I'd prefer to go and hear the Tenebrae sung by the nuns of Sainte Claire at Longchamp. In my opinion, gentlemen, Gluck is beyond the pale.'

Taking advantage of the astonishment into which his energetic outburst had plunged his audience, he grabbed a slice of lamb with one hand while nimbly emptying his glass with the other.

'My dear Noblecourt,' said La Borde, 'please allow me to contradict you. For my part, I consider that even the finest brush would not have been able to render the details of that unforgettable performance. Yes, Monsieur, at last we have something new. Enough of Italian-style vocalising! Enough of the traditional machinery of the genre and all that monotonous recitative!'

'To be replaced by what? Wrong notes and high-pitched twittering? That's all I heard from the *haute-contre* who sang the role of Orpheus.'

'Monsieur,' said Louis timidly, 'may I be so bold as to ask what an *haute-contre* is?'

'I commend you for asking the question. One should never conceal gaps in one's knowledge. It does you honour, and we will always be happy to instruct you, dear boy. It is knowledge rather than brilliant but empty wit that makes the honest man. Whoever is master of his subject will be attended to and esteemed everywhere. Monsieur de La Borde, who himself writes operas, will answer you: it will permit me to catch my breath.'

'Your breath, yes, but no more lamb or Saint-Nicolas,' said Semacgus. 'The Faculty is strongly opposed to such things.'

Noblecourt assumed a contrite expression, while Nicolas's cat, Mouchette, put her little head above the table and sniffed the tempting aromas.

'An *haute-contre*,' explained La Borde, 'is a French tenor, the highest of all male voices, producing high notes from the chest, a powerful, resonant sound. To get back to our discussion, I am surprised to hear you criticise this choice for the role of Orpheus. It was a bow to the French habits which you love. To be replaced by what? you asked.'

'Yes, by what? I stand my ground.'

'Even with your gout,' sighed Semacgus.

'By a natural way of singing,' resumed La Borde, 'always guided by the truest, most sensitive expression, with the most gratifying melodies, an unparalleled variety in the turns and the greatest effects of harmony, employed equally for drama, pathos and grace. In a word, true tragedy in music, in the tradition of Euripides and Racine. In Gluck, I recognise a man of genius and taste, in whom nothing is weak or slapdash.'

'Listening to both of you,' remarked Semacgus, 'I seem to recognise the same kind of discussion that so often arouses our host on the subject of new habits in cooking.'

'How right you are,' said La Borde. 'Except that our friend supports the natural and the true in cooking, while defending the artificial and the shallow in music.'

'I'm not admitting defeat,' said Noblecourt. 'I don't need to justify my contradictions. I certainly maintain that meat should be meat and taste like meat, but in art I'm delighted by fantasy. A well-organised fantasy that makes us dream.'

'But the depth of the new style,' said La Borde, 'stimulates our imagination by combining the emotion of tragedy with the pleasure and delight of melody.'

'I see nothing in it but faults and pretence. A kind of deceptive mishmash of meat and fish.'

'You are talking just like the directors of our Royal Academy of Music, who ignore foreign art for fear it will bring down theirs.'

'Peace, gentlemen,' growled Semacgus. 'I'm sure you're both right, but you seem to take a perverse pleasure in forcing your arguments, with even more bad faith than the Président de Saujac.'

'Oh,' said Noblecourt, laughing, 'that's the whole pleasure of the thing. To maintain the unmaintainable, push your reasoning beyond the reasonable and put forward exaggerated arguments – all that is part of the joy of the debate.'

'You admit it, then?'

'I admit nothing. All I'm saying is that we should increase the controversy and put some bite into our presentation. The alternative would be like defending a dull thesis to the academics of the Sorbonne.'

Marion approached Louis, who was starting to doze off, and gave him a bag of fresh hazelnuts from a tree in the garden. Nicolas noticed his son's tiredness.

'My friends,' he said, consulting his repeater watch, which sounded softly, 'I think it's time to bring this memorable evening to an end. Our host needs to rest after this royal feast and his excesses.'

'So early?' said Noblecourt. 'Do you really want to interrupt this delightful interlude?'

'Tomorrow has already sounded, and Louis's mother is waiting for him. He is leaving for Juilly at dawn on the first mail coach.'

'Before he leaves us, I want to give him a gift,' said the procurator.

Monsieur de Noblecourt undid the second package, took out two small leather-bound volumes bearing his arms, and opened one with infinite care. Everyone present smiled, knowing his fanatical devotion to his books.

'Here,' he said with blissful solemnity, 'are Ovid's *Metamorphoses*, translated by Abbé Banier, of the Royal Academy of Inscriptions and Belles-lettres. These fine works are decorated with frontispieces and illustrations. My dear Louis, I offer them to you with all my heart . . .' He added in a lower voice, as if to himself, 'The only gifts that matter are those from which one parts with sorrow and regret.' Then, raising his voice again, 'May these fables, with their gods made flesh, stimulate your imagination and instil in you a love of literature.

*All is enchantment, each thing has its place,*
*With a body, a soul, a mind and a face.*[6]

May reading them persuade you that what is elegant in Latin is not necessarily so in French, that each language has a tone, an order and a genius peculiar to it. Whenever you need to translate, remember to be simple, clear and correct, in order to render the author's ideas precisely, omitting nothing of the delicacy and elegance of his style. Everything should hold together, in fact. Just as, in life, one becomes hard and heartless by being too attached to the letter of a principle, so in translation, the tone can become dry and arid as soon as one tries to impose one's own ideas in place of the author's.'

'Monsieur,' said Louis, now completely awake again, 'I don't know what to say. I certainly wouldn't like to deprive you of a treasure to which I know you are attached. My father has told me all about your great love of the books in your library.'

'Not at all, it is a pleasure for me to offer them to you! Don't worry, I still have Monsieur Burman's large folio edition, published by Westeins and Smith in 1732, with splendid intaglio figures . . .'

'Many thanks, Monsieur. These books will be dear to me, knowing they come from you.'

While the former procurator looked on approvingly, Louis opened one of the volumes and leafed through it carefully and respectfully.

'Monsieur, what are these handwritten pages?'

He held out a piece of almond-green paper covered in small, densely packed handwriting.

'Quite simply, translations made by yours truly of the Latin quotations in the preface. You will be able to check their accuracy.'

'Louis,' said Nicolas, 'it is a true viaticum our friend is giving you. Follow his counsel. I have always benefited from it. He was my master when I first arrived in Paris, when I was only a little older than you are now.'

They all rose from the table. The farewells took a while longer.

Semacgus, who was returning to Vaugirard, would give Louis a lift and drop him at his mother's in Rue du Bac. Nicolas made his final recommendations to his son. He was particularly insistent that the boy write him a letter, however short, every week. He opened his arms and Louis threw himself into them. Moved, Nicolas had the curious feeling that he was reliving a distant past, as if the Marquis de Ranreuil had reappeared in the person of his grandson.

The guests having dispersed, he went back to his quarters, overcome with a quiet melancholy. Life often had tricks up its sleeve, chance ruled, and fate often struck repeated blows. But this time it was different: his continuing disgrace was of little importance compared with an ambiguous destiny that offered him compensations which restored the balance. The discovery of Louis constituted the most important of these unexpected favours for which he had Providence to thank.


*Monday 3 October 1774*

Nicolas's first thought, after Mouchette had woken him as usual by breathing in his ear, was for his son, who was starting a new life that morning. He had explained to him why he would be absent when his coach left. He dreaded the emotion he would feel, which Antoinette's own emotional state would merely accentuate. He found it hard to think of La Satin as Antoinette, even though that was the name by which he had known her in the early days of their liaison. But, anxious for the past to be forgotten and to offer her son a mother worthy of the unexpected future opening up to him, she had certainly turned over a new leaf.

When he left Rue Montmartre, the pedestrians and the carriages were shrouded in autumnal fog. Where should he begin the errands he had planned? First of all, he had to purchase an oil for removing stains from clothes. He knew only too well how difficult it would be for a boarder like Louis to clean his clothes, since only underwear was washed by the establishment. This oil was designed to remove stains from any kind of material, however delicate, without in any way altering its colour or sheen. In addition, it possessed the useful ability to destroy bugs and their eggs, moths and other eaters of wool. It was in Rue de Conti in Versailles that he had discovered the inventor of this precious compound. The success of the formula had encouraged the man to start selling his product in Paris, at a haberdasher's shop in the Grande-Cour des Quinze-Vingts.[7] Nicolas knew that each bottle was wrapped in an explanatory note which would enlighten his son as to the best way to use this oil.

He also wanted to go to Madame Peloise's shop opposite the Comédie-Française, which stocked a large selection of imitation gemstones of various different colours. He would choose one, have his son's initials engraved on it, and have it mounted as a seal. The idea briefly crossed his mind of adding the Ranreuil arms, to link the grandson to the grandfather in a kind of continuation of the line. Some secret instinct made him hesitate, as if he feared that this initiative might cause inconveniences for young Le Floch. He stopped for a moment to wonder about his decision. Why had both he and his father found themselves in the situation of having illegitimate sons? A mere coincidence or a kind of fatal repetition, the reason for which escaped him? Last but not least, he thought he might take a stroll around the second-hand bookstalls, with a view to unearthing a few books to be added to the package he would soon be sending Louis at the school in Juilly.

He noted with satisfaction that all his shopping would take him to the same district, Rue Saint-Honoré and the environs of the Louvre. After a bracing walk, he began his rounds with Madame Peloise, who cleverly succeeded in making him spend much more than he had anticipated. An antique intaglio showing a Roman profile, mounted on a silver shaft, particularly attracted him and replaced his initial choice of a seal with initials. It was both more elegant and less banal, more discreet, too, and hard to imitate. From there, he proceeded to the shop selling the stain remover, where he was assured that the desired quantity of the product could be delivered to Juilly in the name of Louis Le Floch, which greatly simplified matters.

He left the maze of old streets around the Quinze-Vingts and walked to the galleries of the Louvre. He noted with regret that the former royal palace was increasingly disfigured by all kinds of excrescences. The colonnade had recently been cleared, and already a multitude of second-hand clothes dealers were insulting it with displays of rags and tatters. Nicolas also deplored the fact that the presence of the academies entailed lodging some of their members here, to the detriment of the surroundings. Everywhere, even within the precincts of the monument, frame houses had sprung up, adorned with shapeless staircases that detracted from the majesty of the complex. He recalled a conversation between Monsieur de La Borde and the Marquis de Marigny, the brother of Madame de Pompadour and super-intendent of buildings, about the noble plan to restore the palace to its former splendour. He had quoted Voltaire's complaint at seeing the Louvre, 'a monument to the greatness of Louis XIV, the zeal of Colbert and the genius of Perrault, hidden by buildings of the Goths and the Vandals'.

A multitude of stalls had taken root in the chinks of the vast edifice. Among them were those selling paintings and engravings. Fakes were more frequent here than genuine works, and the Lieutenancy General of Police was determined to settle a number of serious cases in which rich foreigners, victims of such swindles, had involved their embassies. In 1772, Nicolas had managed to unmask a group of forgers, which had been a salutary warning to the rest of the crooks.

He was well known to the merchants – both honest and dishonest – and his arrival always provoked a shudder of fear. Taking advantage of the presence of enlightened connoisseurs, some second-hand book dealers had chosen to join the sellers of prints and paintings, and offered customers a wide range, from the less good to, occasionally, the best. Nicolas recalled a few happy discoveries, like that of an original edition of François-Pierre de la Varenne's *Le Pâtissier Français*. He had presented this small red morocco-bound duodecimo volume, published in Amsterdam in 1655 by Louys and Daniel Elzevir, as a gift to Monsieur de Noblecourt, who had almost swooned at the sight of it. The dealers would visit the houses of the recently deceased, and buy whole libraries from the grieving families. Unfortunately, there was nothing now that was not known about, and rare books had gradually become impossible to find. The few there were would be immediately spotted by scouts who, in the know, no longer offered four sous for treasures which were worth a thousand times as much. Here and there, you also came across banned or condemned books, handled conspiratorially behind the stalls, in the hope of concealing them from the inquisitive glances of the police spies who frequented the place and were on the lookout for anyone bringing illicit brochures to sell or seeking out copies of such lampoons as had escaped the bonfire.

On one of the stalls, Nicolas discovered a Plautus, a Terence, the complete works of Racine and a Lesage, all of which ought to give great pleasure to a schoolboy. He found the sight of the other book lovers amusing, spellbound as they were by the range on offer. Much to the chagrin of the bookseller, who was always afraid that some work of value might be stolen, they would spend hours looking through the books and searching in the crates, often without buying anything in the end.

Absorbed in the account of a journey to the West Indies, Nicolas suddenly felt a hand tugging at one of his coat buttons. Turning, he recognised the humble, contrite face of one of the officers who worked for the Lieutenant General of Police in Rue Neuve-Saint-Augustin. The man was not alone: a second henchman, whom Nicolas did not recall having seen before, stood watching.

'Commissioner,' said the first man, 'you must follow us.'

'What do you mean?'

'We have orders to take you to Monsieur Lenoir immediately.'

Nicolas made an effort to conceal his astonishment. 'Let me at least pay for my purchases.'

Once that was done, Nicolas found himself in a cab with the two officers. With the windows raised and the curtains drawn, the unpleasant smell of unwashed bodies was overwhelming in such a confined space. He lowered the corner of his hat, withdrawing into himself to reflect on what appeared, for all the world, like an arrest. He was only too familiar with the procedures and customs of a system of which he had long been an agent. He had taken part in so many investigations and shared so many secrets that he could not help but wonder. Everything was possible, he knew. Would he be exiled to the provinces? Surely he was too small a figure for such a great honour. It was more likely that a *lettre de cachet* had been issued, and that he would be thrown into prison. But they would still have to find a reason to justify such treatment. Although . . . He laughed, making his two companions look at him in surprise. So many people had been arrested without knowing the reason. He wouldn't be the first and he wouldn't be the last! He might as well keep his composure: he would learn his fate soon enough.

Still watched by his two guards, he was left waiting in the antechamber, before the door opened and the friendly face of an elderly valet appeared. He motioned Nicolas to enter, then leaned over and whispered in his ear, 'He doesn't know anything himself!'

The old man was clearly talking about Lenoir. What was it he didn't know? Nicolas approached the desk. His chief was still writing, and had not even looked up.

'I am grateful to you, Commissioner,' he said at last, 'for responding so promptly to my summons.'

'How could I not, Monseigneur, when I was brought here by two officers? Quite an honour!'

'I think,' said Lenoir impassively, 'that they exceeded my instructions.'

'They found me, that's the main thing. As always, our police force has shown itself to be extremely efficient.'

Lenoir folded his hands. 'I am instructed to . . .' for a moment, he searched for the correct word, '. . . invite you to present yourself immediately at the Saint-Florentin mansion. The Duc de La Vrillière, Minister of the King's Household, has asked to see you.' He seemed surprised by his own words. 'I hope,' he resumed, 'that you've done nothing to offend him. You have not been assigned to any investigation for three months now. You wouldn't by any chance have become involved in some other case? I've already had occasion to deplore your independent behaviour during our first encounter.'

'Not at all, Monseigneur,' replied Nicolas. 'I have obeyed your orders completely and scrupulously. I have done nothing, I have enjoyed my leisure, and I have hunted. With His Majesty.'

His tone was so ironic that Lenoir sighed irritably. 'Go, and make sure you report back to me on anything that might be of interest to the King's service.'

'I shall not fail to do so,' said Nicolas. 'I shall take the cab which brought me here and go directly to the minister's mansion.'

With these words, Nicolas bowed and left the room. He descended the great staircase four steps at a time, watched with astonishment by the two officers, and jumped into the cab. We're back in business, he thought. His intuition told him that the Duc de La Vrillière needed him.

# II

# THE SAINT-FLORENTIN MANSION

It was neither tumult nor calm, but a silence like that
of a great fear and a great anger.

TACITUS

Like a rider facing a hurdle, Nicolas liked to give himself a lull
before launching into the thick of the action. He considered this
pause necessary to keep a clear head. He asked to be dropped at
Place Louis XV and, anxious to contemplate the Saint-Florentin
mansion, where he might well have a date with destiny, he sat
down on a bollard. Having kept him waiting for three months,
they could certainly wait a few more minutes. He admired the
classical trappings of the building, which extended the splendour
of the Garde-Meuble. For a moment, the past paraded before
him: images of that terrible night in 1770, the cries, the smoke,
the crushed bodies, and the statue of the King looking down
on the disaster of that failed firework display.[1] The facade
overlooked a small square with a fountain from which it was
possible to reach the Tuileries gardens. It had two large noble
floors and a roof crowned by a balustrade and decorated with
carved panoplies and two monumental urns. On Rue Saint-
Florentin was a splendid gate adorned with a stone coat of arms
held aloft by two deities. The coat of arms was divided into four
quarters, combining the blue of the Phélypeaux family, strewn

with gold cinquefoils and ermines, and the three red mallets of the Mailly family.

Nicolas had known Monsieur de Saint-Florentin, who was now the Duc de La Vrillière, since he had joined the police force. He pondered that remarkable career which had begun fifty years earlier in the King's councils and which had been built on a stubborn loyalty to the person of Louis XV. The man was not exactly popular, either at Court or in the city. Many envied his influence while condemning his weakness and timidity. He was also responsible for many arbitrary decisions and *lettres de cachet*. Madame Victoire thought him stupid, whereas others emphasised his gift for conciliation, his ability to appease dissenting parties without compromising the authority of the throne. On many occasions, he had demonstrated his trust in Nicolas, but a recent case in which his cousin the Duc d'Aiguillon had been involved seemed to have contributed to his current low opinion of the commissioner.

Nicolas again looked at the house, which had all the grandeur and nobility of a small palace and gave anything but a small idea of the fortune of the man who had built it. He recalled certain pieces of gossip concerning the minister's dubious morals. He lived a dissolute life in Paris, surrounded by women of ill repute, and neglected his wife in favour of a mistress, Marie-Madeleine de Cusacque, the Marquise de Langeac, whom he called 'the Beautiful Aglaé'. It was claimed at Court that this woman made use of her lover's influence and traded *lettres de cachet*, and there was good reason to believe that this was true. The duc had set up all the lady's children, despite their dubious lineage, but since the King's death he had had to conform to the new, stricter morality and give up seeing her. She had continued to appear, however, even provoking a gentleman to a duel and insulting a tribunal. Eventually, she had been ordered to remain fifty leagues from the Court and had withdrawn to an estate near Caen. As for her lover, his health had declined since this forced separation.

Nicolas finally decided to enter the mansion. A monumentally tall Swiss Guard, covered in silver braid, received him haughtily, softening only when he gave his name and occupation. He was led across the main courtyard and then up some steps into a vestibule where a valet greeted him. He was surprised by the lack of hustle and bustle in the house at this hour of the day. Several servants passed him without looking at him, with inscrutable expressions on their faces. On the great staircase, he noted a fine painting, an allegory of Prudence and Strength. On the first floor, a succession of antechambers led him to the minister's study. The valet tapped at the door. A familiar voice responded. The valet stood aside to let him in. The Duc de La Vrillière sat slumped beside the big marble fireplace, wearing a grey coat and no wig. He glanced at Nicolas expressionlessly. The man had certainly changed since their last encounter. Thin, stooped, hollow-jowled, he looked quite unlike the chubby little man Nicolas had known.

'Hmm, here's young Ranreuil,' he grunted. 'Quite cold, isn't it?'

He sighed, as if the name alone could summon up the ghost of the late King, his other passion in life. Things could have got off to a worse start, thought Nicolas.

'Monsieur,' said the minister, 'I have always held you in great esteem. I understand that you may have thought that you – how shall I put it? – did not have my trust. But that was a complete misunderstanding on your part.'

'I did indeed think so, Monseigneur,' replied Nicolas. 'In fact, I was quite convinced of it, even though I found it hard to explain. Others took it upon themselves to reinforce the impression.'

'Now who could that have been? Lenoir? Yes, that may well be what he thought. A word from me will disabuse him. It is no longer possible to do without your services. Monsieur de Sartine long ago convinced me of that. Today, I need you again.'

Nicolas had been right: he was indeed back in business. 'Monseigneur,' he said, 'I am at your service.'

The minister raised a hand clad in a grey silk glove and brought it down hard on the armrest of his chair. He sat up, and for a moment the image of the man he had been reappeared, an image of easy-going but real authority.

'Let's get straight to the point. Yesterday I was at Versailles. I came back early this morning to find my house turned upside down. The fact is, Monsieur, my major-domo has been killed.' He shook his head irritably. 'No, I'm wrong! One of my wife's maids has been killed, and my major-domo was found wounded and unconscious with a knife beside him. It would seem that, having killed the girl, he tried to punish himself by committing suicide.'

'What measures have so far been taken?' Nicolas enquired coldly, once again the professional who did not like other people to draw hasty conclusions for him.

'What? What? . . . Measures? Oh, yes, measures . . . I forbade anyone to touch the maid's body. The major-domo was taken to his room on the mezzanine, still unconscious. He is being watched by a doctor. As for the kitchens where the crime took place, I have forbidden access to them and the doors have been bolted while waiting for you to inspect the place.'

'Did you know the victim?'

The duc gave a kind of start. 'A chambermaid! One of the last to have entered my house. How could I? I don't even know her name.'

Nicolas thought to himself that servants were often regarded as furniture. Most of the time, their names were changed and their master was unaware of their real name, knowing nothing of them but the particular function for which they were paid.

'Monseigneur,' he said, 'may I be so bold as to demand full authority in this affair, which is all the more serious for having taken place in your house? No meddling, no interference, the possibility of questioning all the occupants of the house, and I mean all, and permanent permission to move around and to search.'

'All right, all right,' grumbled the duc, 'I suppose it's necessary. Sartine did tell me how inconvenient you can be.'

'The facts are more inconvenient than I. That's not all, Monseigneur. I should like to be assisted by Bourdeau. I trust you will consent.'

'The name sounds familiar. Isn't he one of our officers?'

'One of our inspectors, Monseigneur.'

'That's right,' said La Vrillière, striking his forehead, 'he's your loyal deputy. I like loyalty. Of course I consent.'

'What about Monsieur Lenoir?'

'Leave it to me. I'll reconcile the two of you. He'll be informed that this is my affair and you answer entirely to me. It's a private matter, and requires the greatest discretion. The Lieutenant General of Police will have to accede to your demands for any help or support that you may require. I hope that you will show the same zeal and efficiency in this affair as you have in others. A study has been set aside for you on the mezzanine, and orders will be given that you must be obeyed in all matters. My valet, Provence, will be your guide in this house. You can trust him, he's been with me for twenty years. Now do your work. Monsieur, I am at your disposal.'

The minister's tone was certainly in keeping with the circumstances. Nicolas had often noted in this unloved little man, lacking in personal prestige, a kind of unexpected grandeur which occasionally appeared, its roots constantly irrigated by the will and trust of the monarch. Thus, in a few short moments, the Duc de La Vrillière had been transfigured, animated by the concerns of State and the order it was his task to impose upon it. Everything vital having been said, Nicolas bowed and left the room. The valet was waiting at the door, and asked Nicolas to follow him. They took the same route by which they had come. Back on the ground floor, they came to a large hall that led to a succession of antechambers. In the third room on the right, the valet pointed out the entrance to a large study, which Nicolas judged to be situated more or less beneath that of the minister. The valet closed the door behind him. A fire was blazing in a white marble hearth, above which stood a bust of Louis XV. He stood for a moment contemplating it, suddenly overwhelmed with memories. Then he sat down at a small desk inlaid with bronze and lacquer and equipped with paper, quill pens, ink and lead pencils. He took out his little black notebook, an indispensable tool of his investigations. He was swept by a wave of excitement. It was the habitual thrill of the hunter setting off on the trail, the same ardour that sent him galloping off into the thickets of the forest of Compiègne. Already his mind was revolving around this case with which he had been presented, and his intelligence and intuition were on the alert.

Out of curiosity, he opened a door, which revealed to him a magnificently prepared bedroom. Behind this room were a fine bathroom and water closet in the English style, such as he had not seen since his return from London. He went back into the study and rang the bell. The valet appeared. The man was about fifty, with a crumpled, colourless face and faded eyes. He wore a grey wig, and his silver-trimmed blue livery hung loose on his slender frame. The only thing striking about him was how nondescript he was.

'What's your name, my friend?'

'Provence, Commissioner,' the man said, avoiding his gaze.

'What's your real name?'

'Charles Bibard.'

'Where were you born?'

'In Paris, in 1725 or 1726.'

Nicolas had been right about his age. 'Why Provence, then?'

'It was my predecessor's name. Monseigneur's father, by whom I was subsequently engaged, didn't like change.'

'Well, Provence, can you tell me what happened here this morning?'

'To be honest, I don't know much. Just before seven, I was busy making Monseigneur's apartments ready for his return from Versailles when I heard cries and screams.'

'Where were you?'

'In the bedroom. I went downstairs to the ground floor. The kitchen boy, the one who opens up in the morning, was screaming in terror and wringing his hands.'

'Was he alone?'

Nicolas noticed a slight hesitation.

'Everything was so chaotic . . . I think the Swiss Guard was there. Yes, I can see him now, just buttoning up his livery.'

'What happened then?'

'Jacques – Jacques Despiard, the kitchen boy – was kicking up such a fuss, it was impossible to understand what he was on about. He was stamping his feet like someone possessed. The caretaker arrived and helped us restrain him, then we left the caretaker to watch over him and went down into the servants' pantry.'

'So the door was open?'

'Yes. That was where Jacques had come from. The key was still in the door at the end of the passage.'

'And what did you find?'

Nicolas waited intently for the answer. Experience had taught him that a witness's first observations often turned out to be the most enlightening.

'It was still dark and the kitchen boy had dropped his candle. We went to look for another candle and lit it. There was nothing to see in the kitchen except some bloodstained footprints, but as soon as we got to the door of the roasting room we discovered Monsieur Missery lying face down on the floor in the middle of a pool of blood. We rushed to him, and I noticed there was a kitchen knife next to him.'

'What was the position of his head?'

'His right cheek was against the floor.'

'And where was the knife?'

'Also on his right. He was still breathing and, just as we were going to help him, the Swiss Guard turned and saw, slumped to her knees against the draining board, the body of a young woman. Her head looked as if it was detached from her trunk. The wound was terrible, Monsieur, she was like a pig that's been bled.'

'What happened then?'

'We carried Jean Missery to his room on the mezzanine.'

'The floor where we are now?'

'That's right, Commissioner, but on the other side of the courtyard, where you find the service rooms, the linen room, and accommodation for the Swiss Guard and the caretaker. The caretaker went to fetch a doctor from Rue Saint-Honoré. At that moment, Monseigneur arrived and took matters in hand. He immediately went down to the servants' pantry.'

'Alone?'

'Yes. Then he came back up and asked for the key I'd taken from the door and double-locked everything. Here it is – he gave it to me to give to you.'

Nicolas recognised the minister's way: his insecure character did not exclude a certain decisiveness and the greatest concern for detail. The valet handed him a thick envelope bearing the Saint-Florentin family seal.

'What did the doctor say?'

'That he'd recover. He bandaged the wound in his side, and told us to let him rest and to keep an eye on him.'

'We'll continue this conversation later. These initial facts are enough for the moment. Please show me to the kitchens.'

As they were leaving the room, Nicolas noticed that the valet's shoes, and their heels, were immaculate. He recalled a quip by Semacgus, although he did not immediately see its relevance to his observation. His friend liked to say that the doors of gilded salons were not closed to those whose minds were full of dirt, but that those same people would be turned away if there was dirt on their shoes. It was an interesting detail, which it would be worthwhile investigating further. The man led him down a smaller staircase, no doubt used by the servants. Nicolas, who had lowered his head in order not to miss the poorly lit steps, noticed some brownish prints still visible on the wood. His first reaction was to make an ironic remark on the poor maintenance of this area, so out of keeping with the gleaming splendour visible elsewhere in the mansion. On the ground floor, they walked across a small inner conservatory, then through some pantries, and found themselves in a passage which emerged into a larger one leading on the left-hand side towards the courtyard of the mansion and on the right to the door of the kitchens. Nicolas opened the envelope and took out a large key. He would have to check if there were any duplicates. His concern for details like that, which were often the most significant, was what made him a good policeman. He unlocked the door and entered the first room, where the light came in through large high windows.

'This is the kitchen itself,' said Provence, continuing towards another room. 'And this is the roasting room, this is where—'

Nicolas did not let him finish. 'Thank you,' he said with an amiable smile. 'I'd like to be alone now. Oh, there is one thing, though. Could you get a message to the duty office of the commissioners and inspectors at the Grand Châtelet?'

He tore a page from his notebook and, leaning against the wall, quickly wrote a note to Inspector Bourdeau, asking him to join him immediately at the Saint-Florentin mansion with a wagon, some officers and all the material necessary to transport a corpse. He knew that for the past few weeks his deputy had been spending every morning at the old prison in the always disappointed hope of a mission to be expedited. He searched in his pocket, found a piece of sealing wax, and used it to close his message. He wrote his signature across it with the lead pencil, in order to discourage inquisitiveness, and handed the whole thing to the valet, who seemed upset at being excluded from his exploration of the scene of the crime. This reaction seemed to him surprising. In his experience, witnesses connected with a violent crime usually preferred to avoid as far as possible the place where it had occurred. Once again he made a mental note of the fact. Perhaps, he thought, the man had been given the task by the minister of reporting back to him on Nicolas's first observations.

The floor of the roasting room was like that of a butcher's shop after an animal has been slaughtered. It was impossible to draw any conclusions from the prints still visible in the mire of blood on the black and white tiles. What did seem clear, though, was that a body had been dragged across the floor, presumably that of the major-domo, Jean Missery. On the floor, a kitchen knife with a wooden handle and a single rivet drew his attention: it was one of those common objects known as an *eustache*. It was of medium size and its blade measured a little more than a hand in length. The mustiness in the room reminded him of other situations dominated by the sickly-sweet, metallic smell of blood. Nicolas climbed on a stool to get an overall view.

The picture Provence had painted of the scene proved exact. First of all, the body of a young woman, slumped, as if kneeling, at the foot of a draining board. Her head was at a curious angle in relation to the rest of the body, and she had lost a lot of blood, which had spread, brown and glutinous, all around her. He noted an incongruous detail: her two feet, as white as ivory, as if spared by the outpouring of blood. A few steps away, another pool of blood, this one redder. You did not have to be very knowledgeable to realise that the two pools were of different origins: one from each of the two victims. Time, perhaps a long time – he would have to determine how long – had passed between the two effusions. He tried again to seek answers in the complex pattern of footprints, but was unable to discern anything other than a wild trampling. He went back to an examination of the body.

The young woman was wearing a skirt, a loose blouse, and an apron knotted at the waist and above all – the distinguishing mark of a chambermaid – at the bib. The hair was held up in a bun, revealing a narrow neck, almost a child's. The lace cap had slipped to the floor and lay in the blood. Nicolas was struck by the sight of two slippers lying a few paces from the body. These were not objects commonly associated with a young servant girl, but luxurious, even expensive items quite out of place here. He got off the stool and walked up to the body, making an effort to control his mixed feelings: apprehension at contact with a corpse and pity for a murdered human being. It was up to him to observe the state of the body and estimate the time of death. He realised that he had left his watch in Rue Montmartre. He had always been a stickler for accurate timekeeping, but, having had little to hurry him these past few months, he had become absent-minded. In his head, he tried to calculate how much time had gone by. He had left Noblecourt's house at nine, his shopping expedition had taken two hours, after which he had strolled idly among the second-hand bookstalls and had even indulged in a little reading. It must have been about midday that the officers had intercepted him. The carriage having been delayed by traffic on the way to Rue Neuve-Saint-Augustin, he must have entered Monsieur Lenoir's office at about half past twelve. Interview, cab, a conversation with the Duc de La Vrillière, another with Provence. It must now be about two o'clock in the afternoon.

He knew that rigor mortis only set in gradually. The longer it took to appear, the longer it lasted. You had to take the conditions and temperature of the place into account. Kitchens were usually cold at night, when all the lights were out and there was adequate ventilation. It was October now, and starting to feel distinctly cold. The duration of rigor mortis was supposedly shorter in damp, warm air than in dry, cold air. In addition, it was a constant feature that rigor mortis took a long time to appear when death was sudden, as seemed to be the case here. Touching the body, he noticed that there was still some residual stiffness. He estimated that the murder must have taken place between ten and midnight.

He leaned over to examine the terrible wound at the base of the neck. If a piece of wood had been driven in just below the right ear, the flesh could not have been any more bruised and shattered than it was. It was still possible to see, deep inside the wound, a piece of lace from the blouse. Life had fled from the poor girl's body in an endless haemorrhage. Her eyes stared unseeing, the corneas already obscured by a slimy membrane. He shuddered at the sight of that face, contorted in death: the forehead was lined, the nose was pinched, the lips hung over an open jaw, and the skin, dry and livid, gave the whole face a twisted appearance, as if frozen in a cruel, dazed stupor. He searched in the pockets of the apron and the skirt, and found nothing except a handkerchief and a cross on a small, broken metal chain, which had slipped into a fold in the fabric.

There was nothing else to do while waiting for the arrival of the stretcher which would take away these remains to the operating table in the Basse-Geôle. Whatever observations were made there could well open up new paths for the investigation. He still had to undertake a delicate experiment. As there was nothing to be learnt from the bloody mire on the floor, he would have to examine the surroundings. There, doubtless, there would be fewer traces and he would be able to read them more precisely. The kitchen and the roasting room were full of footprints: that was quite normal, given the servants who had come to take the wounded major-domo to his room on the mezzanine. In the kitchen, he found a whole series of knives identical to the one he had found on the floor. Was this latter a utensil that belonged to the mansion, or had it been brought in from outside? This was a good house, and the gleaming state of the whole area showed that it was well maintained. Perhaps an inventory . . . With one thought leading to another, he realised a startling fact: the broad, deep, prodigious wound to the young woman's neck could not have been caused by the *eustache*. He would have to examine Jean Missery's wound to see if the same knife had been used on him as on the maid. The result of this examination might point in a different direction.

He came back to the problem of prints. He was still obsessed by those found on the staircase between the mezzanine and the ground floor. He walked on tiptoe, trying to avoid the soiled areas, but still managed to add a few of his own prints to those already existing. A brownish trail took him to the passage leading to the courtyard. He took off his shoes to cross a section that was apparently untouched. He saw nothing in the wash house, in the small adjoining courtyard, or on the steps down to the cellars. He decided to go back along the route he had taken with Provence as far as the staircase. Nicolas carefully cleaned the soles of his shoes with water from a watering can he found in the small conservatory, then hesitated a moment. Should he continue to the first floor, where the minister's apartments were located? But where was the risk? Nobody would blame him, and besides the lead might turn out to be pointless. Provence, who had discovered the bodies, might have taken that staircase and, noticing that his shoes were dirty, immediately changed them. While he was thinking this through, a small inner voice whispered in his ear that he was right to persevere and to listen to his intuition, which, in all these years as a police officer, had stood him in good stead, on an equal level with his reason.

The trail continued, becoming increasingly indistinct. But Nicolas knew that blood, being thick and viscous, took a long time to vanish completely. He reached an empty room furnished with two old red velvet benches, with a stock of logs piled up against the panelling. He immediately realised that this was not the way to the Duc de La Vrillière's apartments, but rather a kind of halfway stage before you got to the upper parts of the mansion, given over, in this kind of dwelling, to the servants' rooms or to storerooms. He immediately began examining the state of the staircase, this time with a piece of candle he found lying in a corner. He lit it, and the flame illumined the steps. He looked as hard as he could, bent down, even lay down, his nose almost against the oak, but could not find any traces of blood. On the other hand, he did find some on the floor of the room, a trail leading to the French window at the corner of the building. As he approached, a cold draught made him shiver.

Why was it open? He saw that the catch was up. He opened the window, and immediately a keen wind lashed his face. The window led out onto a balcony with a balustrade, facing Rue Saint-Florentin. His heart beat faster: there were clear traces of blood on the stone. Bloody footprints led to the corner of the building, in the direction of the gate in the main courtyard. He followed them and leant over. Here, another surprise awaited him: he observed that there were also spots of blood on the narrow cornice of the wall, which was supported by columns. He decided to go and see at close quarters where that might lead. Luckily, unlike his friend Semacgus, he did not suffer from vertigo. During all his travels on the King's vessels, Semacgus had never been able to climb the top mast. Admittedly, he would say with a laugh, his functions as a surgeon rarely required this kind of exercise from him. Nicolas dreaded confinement and enclosed spaces, but, faced with a drop, he was as agile as a cat. Pressing his back up against the wall, he slid to the cornice above the gate. As he placed his feet on the projecting edge, he was struck by a stronger gust of wind and almost lost his balance: throwing his head back steadied him. He obtained a foothold on the cornice, holding on to the top of the upper parapet with his hands. There, the traces petered out. He sat down with his legs dangling, then lay on the edge to examine the underneath. He immediately realised that by putting his legs around the top of the column, he could easily get down as far as the spikes of the iron gate – they were only a few feet below him – and from there slide to the ground. There was one point where it could be dangerous, but the rest was child's play. He decided, however, not to go all the way with his experiment, as the flagstones, being muddy, seemed unlikely to reveal any further clues.

So someone had left the scene of the crime, gone up to the first floor of the mansion, opened the French window, and had escaped by performing a feat of acrobatics. That suggested several things: that the unknown person had a precise knowledge of the layout of the house, that his escape had taken place in the middle of the night, when there was less risk of being surprised, and, above all, that the individual was young, capable of such a difficult exercise, in which you might either fall or be impaled on the spikes of the gate. That raised some interesting questions about the sequence of events, and seemed to contradict the initial hypothesis of a murder committed by the major-domo, followed by an attempted suicide.

Nicolas put his feet back down on the balcony, but, as he was about to enter the room, he realised that, during his brief absence, the French window had been closed from inside. Whether this had been caused by a gust of wind or a human hand, he was faced with the problem of getting back inside. He thought for a moment of taking the perilous route adopted by the mysterious acrobat. He soon gave up the idea: that was all he needed, to be crushed to death in the street! He could not take the risk. He took a few steps and glanced in through the next window. There, in a kind of boudoir, was the Duc de La Vrillière, motionless and lost in thought. Unless he broke a pane in the first French window, the only thing he could do was make his presence known as naturally as possible. It took him several attempts to attract the attention of the minister, who eventually opened to him.

'Monsieur, Monsieur,' exclaimed the duc, 'I'd heard that you went out through the door and came in through the window! Well, no need to explain. That's your business.'

He appeared to reflect for a moment, then turned with a sigh to a large portrait of Louis XV, the cartouche of which indicated that it was a gift from the King, presented to Monsieur de Saint-Florentin in 1756.

'What a good master he was,' he murmured, in a tragic tone. 'He loved us, he really did. What a career you would have had, Marquis, if . . .' He left the phrase hanging. 'What he especially appreciated about you,' he resumed after a moment, 'was your handsome face, your very rare gift of being able to distract him, and an even more unusual quality: the fact that you never asked him for anything. I shan't even mention the services you rendered, performing miracles in difficult, delicate circumstances, even at the risk of your own life. Not many have been as valiant and loyal as you . . .'

Nicolas tried to take advantage of the duc's current good disposition towards him. 'Monseigneur, allow me to ask you a question. What is your opinion of your major-domo, Jean Missery?'

'To say that he keeps a firm grip on my household would be an understatement,' replied the duc. 'He's been with me for fifteen years, having succeeded his father. Everything concerning the general expenses of the mansion is his responsibility. He chooses the kitchen staff and the other servants, and he has full authority over them, including dismissing them if need be. It is also his job to buy bread, wine, meat, vegetables and fruit from the suppliers. For example, he buys wine by the cask and hands it over to the wine waiter to distribute, and the latter will report back to him on the state in which he has received it. He also has to deal with a grocer for sugar, candles, torches, oils and Lord knows what else! Wood, crockery, oats, hay, straw: all that's his province. Last but not least – by no means least! – he has to lay out the service for the lunches, dinners and midnight suppers which I give.'

'Do you think he's honest?'

'I believe he is, but, even if he were not, I would not trouble myself to constantly check up on a servant, however corrupt he might be. When we depend on others, we sometimes have to know when to close our eyes if we want to be well served. Now leave me, I still have some work to do.'

Nicolas knew there was no point in insisting. He retraced his steps to the antechambers and the great staircase. Deciding to visit the wounded man, he stopped on the mezzanine. He thought he knew his way around the house quite well by now, but realised that it was not possible to go from one wing to the other except via the ground floor. There, he had no difficulty in finding, to the left of the grand staircase, a small staircase leading up to the mezzanine. After several minutes during which he wandered through dark corridors, he at last came to a room with its door open.

It was a large room, with *bergame* hangings and three windows that looked onto an inner courtyard. A good fire was blazing in the hearth. The marble mantelpiece was adorned with a small pier glass with three mirrors set in gilded wood. On a bed with red flowered damask curtains, his legs half covered with a counterpane of quilted calico, lay a corpulent man, his torso wrapped in bloodstained sheets. On the floor, to the left of the bed, were a coat the colour of dead leaves, a matching pair of breeches, a white shirt, and a yellow cravat. The rest of the furniture consisted of a large oak wardrobe, a marquetry table, two armchairs upholstered in yellow serge, a chest of drawers, and a small writing table covered with papers. The overall impression was one of comfort, and even luxury, enhanced even more by the presence on the parquet floor of a Turkish carpet. On a chair with a dust cover sat a man in a black coat and grey wig, apparently dozing. Nicolas realised that this was not the case, and that what he was in fact doing was taking Jean Missery's pulse. The man turned. A fine pastel face, thought Nicolas, about sixty, perhaps a little more.

'Monsieur, whom do I have the honour of addressing?'

'Commissioner Nicolas Le Floch. I am in charge of the investigation. And you are Monsieur . . .?'

'Dr de Gévigland. I was sent for this morning to attend to this disaster. There was nothing I could do for the young woman. As for this man, as luck would have it, the blade of the knife missed a rib and did not harm any vital organs. In my opinion, he will recover.'

'Has he regained consciousness?'

'No – which is the only thing that worries me. The wound in itself was not the kind to put him in such a state. I fear there may be something else. He may have hit something in his fall, or it may be an inflammation of the cerebral humours. I really don't know. When it comes to this kind of symptom, our knowledge is far from complete.'

Nicolas was pleased to hear these remarks. It was comforting to know that at least one doctor was devoid of the pedantic arrogance of many of his colleagues, made no attempt to spin yarns, and approached with simple modesty and praiseworthy level-headedness the unfathomable mysteries it was his job to diagnose and treat.

'May I see the wound?'

'There is no reason why not. You will observe that the blood loss is clearly defined and that the wound is clean. If you lift the bandage a little, you can see how clean it is.'

The commissioner bent over the supine body. There was a bevelled cut across the abdomen, between the lower ribs. No comparison, he thought, with the gaping hole in the maid's neck. The kitchen knife perfectly matched the appearance of the wound. To set his mind at rest, he asked the question. The doctor's answer did not surprise him.

'The kitchen knife, which is of the sharp kind, was certainly responsible for this. That's obvious.'

'And the young woman's wound?'

'It's up to you, my dear fellow, to find the stopper that would plug up that hole!'

'I have a specific question to ask, Doctor,' said Nicolas. 'Does your observation of your patient, Monsieur Missery's, wounds point to a suicide, as some witnesses suggest?'

The doctor made a face and shook his head. 'As always, people talk without knowing what they're talking about. I have only one comment to make, but it's an important one. Would a man who intends to commit suicide strike himself on the right-hand side and risk injuring his liver and dying in terrible pain? The choice of death by a knife implies that you strike the heart, in other words on the left. Please note that I don't have all the facts that would allow me to plump for one hypothesis over another. However, let's imagine that someone attacked him from behind and, holding his head in a vice-like grip, struck him with a weapon held in his right hand. In the heat of such an attack, he may well have missed and struck the wrong side. The wounded man, having certainly lost a lot of blood, fainted and his attacker may well have thought he had killed him. Even if he didn't, the desired aim might have been to stop him escaping, thus ensuring that suspicion would fall on him.'

'Monsieur, you have clearly thought this through carefully, and what you say is very enlightening.'

Dr de Gévigland had articulated what Nicolas had already been thinking. As he had spoken, the commissioner had seen in his mind's eye, like the images in a magic lantern on the boulevards, Marguerite Pindron on her knees at the foot of the draining board in the roasting room. Were she and the major-domo both victims of a single attacker, whose steps he had detected and followed as far as the monumental gate of the Saint-Florentin mansion? Could it be that the same person had struck twice in succession in the same place? But in that case, why were the two wounds so different and apparently caused by such dissimilar objects? And why had one of those weapons been found on the floor while the other, still of an unknown nature, appeared to be missing? Was someone trying to convince them of a different theory? Nicolas's mind was racing. Someone had worked hard to create a situation so clear-cut that it would be accepted completely: a man kills a woman and then commits suicide. The two pools of blood in the roasting room, so different in appearance, flashed through his mind. He pulled himself together. An autopsy on the chambermaid's body was essential, and he expected a great deal from its conclusions. Then the refining fire of reason would clarify the various hypotheses.

'I would be grateful, Monsieur,' said Nicolas, 'if you could inform me as soon as your patient has regained consciousness. An officer will soon be here to keep an eye on him and make sure that he has no contact with anyone. For the moment, he remains our only suspect.'

'I only hope, Commissioner, that this won't take too much time. I'm needed back at my practice. If he regains consciousness, the wound itself will be a mere detail. A little rest, a good dressing, and everything will heal up nicely.'

Nicolas was back in the great vestibule on the ground floor when several carriages entered the courtyard. From one of them, Bourdeau emerged, rubbing his hands with glee. He was followed by a number of officers with a stretcher. Nicolas walked down some steps to greet his deputy.

'Good Lord,' said the inspector, 'this really is the high life! The Saint-Florentin mansion! Our minister's house! It seems we haven't been dismissed after all.'

'What you say is right, my dear Pierre,' replied Nicolas with a laugh. 'They can't do without our services, and I assure you that the case we are dealing with is not a trivial matter.'

'And our friend Lenoir in all of this?'

'I fear he has been overtaken by events. But we'll be good chaps and keep him informed. We must never insult the future.'

'You're very indulgent today!'

'It's the joy of having something to get my teeth into.'

He ordered the officers to wait, and led Bourdeau towards the stables. There, surrounded by the odour of horses, he related the facts of the case in detail. The inspector's first reaction was that the drama would turn out to be a trivial one, in which case recourse to such experienced authorities as themselves was like using a ton of gunpowder to open the door. Nicolas pointed out the ambiguous clues, the prints and other incongruous and suspicious details which had caught his attention. The inspector agreed that there was plenty to think about and added that it could turn out to be a distinctly tricky affair, given the place where the tragedy had occurred. He concluded with a laugh that, devil take the difficulties, here was a way to re-establish themselves in favour as long as luck was with them as they made their way through the thickets of this new investigation. Nicolas was delighted to see him looking so cheerful again and told him, embroidering the truth somewhat, that it was the Duc de La Vrillière himself who had wanted him to assist in the case. Bourdeau made no response to this, but the air of pride he immediately assumed spoke for itself. The commissioner loved him all the more for being so forthright and simple in his emotions.

With the officers, they proceeded to the kitchens. Before the body was taken away, Nicolas asked Bourdeau to examine the scene of the crime, in the hope that a fresh pair of eyes might spot some details that had escaped him. Like him, the inspector was struck by the very unusual nature of the wound to the young woman's neck. He also observed that she was wearing two small garnet earrings. Their presence might be of some significance, for a chambermaid on duty would never wear such ostentatious jewellery. This suggested that Marguerite Pindron had been more conscious of her appearance that evening than usual. Which in turn suggested that she might have had a rendezvous with a suitor . . . The quality of the slippers also intrigued Bourdeau. They would have to find out the provenance of these luxury items. As for the rest, his observations tallied with those of the commissioner. He searched the place meticulously, anxious to find the object that could have caused such a terrible wound. But to no avail. As he was coming to the end of his search, he stopped and looked at the corner of one of the draining boards. He bent down and delicately picked up between two fingers a small piece of metallic thread, which he held out to Nicolas.

'Looks like silver thread to me,' said Nicolas. 'What do you think?'

'I agree. Someone knocked against this wooden corner. Look at it, it's a nest of splinters. The embroidered garment they were wearing got caught and this came off. It must have been a sudden knock, and in his haste the person who was wearing the coat didn't notice.'

Who, could Nicolas remember often wearing a coat with silver embroidery? The late King, of course! But who else? He racked his brains. The figure of the Duc de La Vrillière emerged. He often copied his master's manner of dress. The commissioner had talked to the minister twice since arriving. The man had indeed been wearing a grey coat, but Nicolas could not recall the nature of the embroidery. Even if it had been silver, that would prove nothing: the duc had visited his kitchens, and in all the excitement of discovering the crime his coat might have caught on the draining board. But he would have to make sure. One thing was certain: the thread had not come from the major-domo's coat, for that was a quite different colour. He carefully slipped the little piece of silver between the pages of his black notebook, then gave the signal to take the maid's body away. Nicolas decided to go back up to the mezzanine and install himself with Bourdeau in the study that had been set aside there for him. They would carry out their interrogations there. In the antechambers, they came across Provence, who was pacing up and down in the shadow of the walls.

'Monsieur Bibard,' said Nicolas 'what was your master wearing when he got back from Versailles this morning?'

The man assumed an indefinable expression which might have escaped someone less accustomed than the commissioner to examining faces. 'A black cloak over a black silk coat, Monsieur. We are observing Court mourning to the letter.'

'But this morning? It seems to me . . .'

'This morning, as soon as he returned, Monseigneur changed into a grey coat.'

'Was this coat embroidered?'

'Yes, with silver flowers.'

'Of course! You see, Bourdeau, I wasn't wrong. The late King had one exactly the same. The minister's loyalty is really touching. Thank you, Provence.'

The man bowed, apparently relieved.

'One more thing,' said Nicolas. 'Would you please have the Swiss Guard, the caretaker and Monseigneur's coachman come to my study, to start with. I should like to question them in the company of Inspector Bourdeau.'

They reached the study, whose splendours Bourdeau examined half admiringly, half sardonically. The commissioner waited for one of those acerbic remarks Bourdeau was in the habit of making, but none came: the pleasure of being plunged back into action, he thought, had certainly had a most beneficial effect on his deputy's character.

'By the way, Nicolas . . .' Bourdeau said, reverting to the commissioner's first name as soon as they were alone. 'Did you notice our chambermaid's curious underwear? Please don't see anything licentious in the question.'

'God forbid, I know you too well!' said Nicolas, somewhat surprised. 'But what exactly do you mean?'

'Well, look. We live in strange times, and you know better than I that the honesty of women takes on some quite curious aspects these days. If an elegant woman, getting out of her carriage to enter a theatre or go for a stroll, lets curious idlers see the whole of her legs, she is in no way considered indecent. Showing one's calves is regarded as something so natural that, far from precautions being taken to prevent the sight, it is made all the easier. So, when she dresses, any woman of quality would fix a long ribbon to her belt to hold up her chemise from behind so that the legs are uncovered all the way up to the back of the knee.'

'I follow you,' said Nicolas with a smile, 'but I'm not sure how far you will climb.'

'Oh, I'm stopping there! I'm simply trying to say that our

chambermaid wears drawers, a sure sign of dubious or dissolute morals. Add to that the presence of those unusual slippers, and I think you'll see where these observations are leading me.'

'I suspect our investigation will reveal a great deal about the poor girl. This house is a closed world. I already know what's going to happen. They'll all be on their guard, resisting the temptation to gossip. Silence and mistrust will be our lot. But in the end, the hurdles will fall and everyone will have something to say, for good or ill, about everyone else. You know how servants are. The world of service is, like others, filled with hatreds, jealousies, resentments and love affairs. We're entering a fertile field, and we just have to harvest it. Everything will come together, all we have to do is wait and not frighten anyone off.'

'I'm sure of that,' said Bourdeau.

'In the meantime, Pierre, get a message to our friends Semacgus and Sanson. I hope the victim's body can be opened up as soon as possible: I need to have their opinion on that strange wound. I'd also like you to send an officer to keep an eye on the room where the suspect is.'

The inspector was away for a short time. No sooner was he back than the door leading to the suite of apartments burst open, and a fairly elderly woman entered at an angle, hampered by the wide pannier of her old-fashioned dress. She was in Court mourning. She wore a jade necklace round her already emaciated neck, her face was blotchy, without rouge or ceruse, and her expression was one of barely contained indignation. A black silk fan, which she was shaking violently, accentuated the impression produced by this dramatic entrance.

'Madame,' said Nicolas with a little bow.

'Monsieur, I am told that you are a commissioner at the Châtelet, and that you have been given the task of investigating the horrible death of that unfortunate creature. My God, how is it possible? What was I saying? Oh, yes, you are investigating, Monsieur. Your name is not unknown to me. Were you presented to the late Queen? Or to Mesdames?'

'I had the good fortune to serve Madame Adélaïde, who often honoured me by inviting me to her hunts.'

'That's it! You're young Ranreuil, who was so appreciated by the King. How fortunate we are, Monsieur, to be dealing with someone so well born, even though . . . Monsieur, you must hear me.' She threw a fierce glance at Bourdeau. 'Who is this gentleman?'

'My deputy, Inspector Bourdeau. Fully the equal of myself.'

'If you say so! Monsieur, this is all so terrible, but it was bound to happen. I had been dreading it for a long time. One cannot live like this without running the risk of such a tragedy one day.'

'Madame, may I ask you to tell me whom I have the honour of addressing?'

'What, Monsieur? I am the Duchesse de La Vrillière and this is my house.'

# III

## KNOT OF VIPERS

There is no true friendship among those
who serve in the same house
LOPE DE VEGA

This majestic announcement only half surprised Nicolas, who had already realised who the lady was. He had glimpsed her on several occasions at Versailles. She was reputed to be sanctimonious and sour-tempered, but he knew how unreliable Court rumours were, how often unjust and biased. Reacting to her with studied indifference had seemed to him the best way to take the sting out of this excessive display of wounded pride. It was, he thought with a smile, a kind of moral purging.

'Madame,' he said, 'I am your obedient servant . . .' Without letting her catch her breath, he continued, 'I've been given to understand that Marguerite Pindron was part of your entourage, as a chambermaid.'

'That's going a little far, Monsieur. Entourage is a big and noble word. We're talking about my domestic servants, that's all – indeed, one of the most subordinate. I don't know how she came to be working here, it happened quite recently, and, I should add, without my consent.'

Nicolas knew that with this kind of witness, it was necessary to adopt one of two strategies: either attempt to restrain and channel their natural outpourings, or let them have their say and hope that within the flood of their words there would be some interesting flotsam.

'It's true,' resumed the duchesse, 'that I have never had a word to say in this house, and that most of those who serve me were chosen for reasons which have nothing to do with me and which I prefer not to know. Oh, Monsieur, the misfortune of having to be served . . .'

On this point, Nicolas observed, the duchesse's sentiment hardly differed from her husband's.

'Servants, Monsieur,' she continued, 'are detestable. Even their zeal is offensive and they're always so clumsy. They complain, but have no idea of the trouble they cause you. After all, they are only in such a position because God has seen fit to reduce them to a situation of servitude in this world in order to aid our infirmity while we remedy their poverty. To be honest, we earn a place in heaven for them by heaping humiliation on their heads, just as we earn it for ourselves by the care we take of them.'

'In a way, Madame,' said Bourdeau, 'they are privileged people who owe their salvation to you.'

She looked at him as if seeing him for the first time. 'This gentleman is right, it is one of the most favoured states. Here are wretches who find themselves living in opulent houses, where they benefit greatly from all that is essential to life. They get good meat and good wine every day, wear nice clothes, are well washed, well bedded, well heated, are given easy jobs to perform, and have too much leisure time. Why should they not be satisfied? I ask you. And when they fail us or make mistakes, should we speak to them with a gracious air, neither too quickly nor too loudly, as my father confessor suggests?'

She collapsed onto a *bergère* – her dress made a great sighing noise as it was squeezed into the chair – and again began beating the air irritably with her fan.

Nicolas took advantage of the pause to get a word in. 'May I ask, Madame, how the events of last night in your house were brought to your notice?'

'Why, by all the noise and commotion my people were making below my windows just before six o'clock. I should point out that I am a light sleeper. Alas, who, in my situation, would be able to rest peacefully?' She raised her eyes to heaven and her hands shook around the ebony handle of her fan. 'On the advice of my doctor, I'm accustomed to taking some drops of Hoffman's solution with syrup of marshmallow and orange flower. If they prove to be ineffective, I use something more efficient, a mixture of ether and alcohol. I often fall into a deep sleep in the early hours of the morning. So there would have to be a lot of noise to wake me, as was the case this morning.'

'Are you quite sure of the time, Madame?'

'Monsieur, I am able to tell the time by the clock in my room.'

'Was it dark?'

'Completely.'

'What happened then?'

'My head chambermaid came into the room in great agitation and told me that something terrible had happened in the servants' pantry.'

'Do you remember the exact words she used?'

'Monsieur, my memory is as good as my sight. When I questioned her about the noise, she said breathlessly that it was bound to happen, and that the Pindron girl had been found murdered in the roasting room.'

'Was that all she said?'

'Monsieur!'

'Forgive my insistence, Madame. I need to know exactly what happened. Did she mention the major-domo?'

'What do you mean? Why would she have done that?'

'Because, Madame, the major-domo was found lying, wounded and unconscious, beside Marguerite Pindron's body, and he is suspected of having murdered her then turned his weapon on himself.'

The Duchesse de La Vrillière seemed so astonished by this that, unless she was an exceptional actress, it was impossible to doubt her good faith.

Nicolas looked at the clock on the mantelpiece. 'Have you seen your chambermaid again since then?'

'She's been no good for anything all day,' replied the duchesse, 'and I told her to go and rest. These people have no self-control! Another of my maids has the little room next to my bedroom. I went back to bed and heard the duc coming back from Versailles. His coach and horses are so noisy! I woke up at midday and this other girl dressed me.'

'What's her name?'

'Jeannette.'

'And her surname?'

'Are you mocking me, Monsieur? Do you imagine I clutter my mind with the surnames of servants?'

'It seems to me, Madame, that you knew Marguerite Pindron's surname.'

'That's possible, Monsieur. My chief maid called her by that name.'

'And what is the name of your chief maid?'

'Eugénie.'

'Did Jeannette talk to you about what happened last night?'

'How could she, she didn't know anything! She hadn't left my apartments and hadn't seen anybody.'

'Madame, may I ask what you meant when you said, at the beginning of our interview, that "it was bound to happen"?'

The duchesse rose and with an abrupt gesture snapped her fan shut. Her face seemed suddenly to have hardened. 'Of course, Monsieur. I was simply repeating what Eugénie said. I didn't mean any harm by it.'

'I'm sorry, Madame,' insisted Nicolas, 'but you added that you'd been dreading the news for a long time.'

'Monsieur, please do not persist. The hand of God always strikes houses where his commandments are ignored.'

'That is a very general statement, and may apply in many cases. Do you think, Madame, that such an assertion would be enough to convince a magistrate, by which I mean a judge or procurator dealing with a murder case?'

'Are you threatening me? Under my own roof? Do you know to whom you are talking, Monsieur?'

'I was merely advising caution.'

'That's enough. I know what I still have to do.' With both hands, she gathered her pannier and strode out of the room in a great silky shiver of fabric.

Nicolas sighed. The higher one climbed the ladder of society, the less natural respect was shown for law and order.

'What a tough nut to crack!' muttered Bourdeau.

'Let's be lenient,' countered Nicolas. 'Think of the life she has to lead. The duc is no paragon and she has had a lot to bear. But by her very reticence, the good lady implies many things. Is she suggesting, for example, that the underlying cause of this tragedy lies in the state of her household?'

'We still have to establish,' said Bourdeau, 'if it has something to do with her husband's dissolute life or some kind of intrigue or rivalry among the many servants. I'm not convinced that this grand lady takes too much notice of what her people do. At most, she lends a distracted ear to her maids' gossip when they're dressing her in the morning.'

'We shall see. Go and fetch the two chambermaids. Provence will help you to find them. He can't be far away, he's always roaming the antechambers. At my disposal, admittedly!'

Nicolas walked to the hearth, which was blazing away. He felt cold. These big fires made your throat dry without warming you, except to roast your thighs when you got close to them. What a strange business! Despite the horror of what had happened, it appeared at first sight mundane and unremarkable. Everything seemed to point to an affair of the heart between a man of a certain age and a young girl. Yet there were many details that did not tally with the generally convergent observations and testimonies so far gathered. The picture which presented itself to Nicolas, the one everybody seemed to be trying to make him accept, made him rather suspect that, beneath its plain varnish, there had been a certain amount of retouching. And what of the mysterious fugitive prowling in the shadows of the Saint-Florentin mansion and disappearing after a last bloody embrace with one of the columns of the gate?

He was drawn from his reverie by Bourdeau's return, accompanied by a woman in an apron and cap. His first reaction was to wonder why she was trying to appear older and uglier than she was. No doubt it was to avoid any comparison with the duchesse. Her hair was drawn back under her cap, making her face more angular, but her features were regular and her complexion splendidly milky. She seemed to be deliberately sucking in her lips, which made her cheeks taut and gave the impression of a strong will. He asked her to sit down, but she shook her head and remained standing, leaning on the back of an armchair. It was late afternoon by now, and the light was gradually fading. The reflection of the flames played over her face, alternately lighting it and plunging it into wavering shadow. Nicolas waited, saying nothing, aware of the effect this silence usually had on witnesses. But no emotion showed on this woman's face, if indeed she felt any. Only the whiteness of her fingers on the upholstery of the armchair attested to the tension in her hands.

'Are you Eugénie, head chambermaid of the Duchesse de La Vrillière?'

'Yes, Commissioner. Eugénie Gouet.'

'How old are you? Are you married?'

'I was thirty last Saint Michel's day. I'm single.'

'How long have you worked here?'

'In the service of Madame, since 1762. The mansion hadn't even been built then. I was still a child . . .'

'Are you one of the oldest servants?'

'Of course. With Provence, Monseigneur's valet.'

'Tell me what happened this morning.'

'I was getting ready in my room on the second floor, when I heard cries. I rushed out to find the kitchen boy, Provence, the caretaker and the Swiss Guard. They all went to the servants' pantry. Jacques, the boy, had discovered two bodies, that of Marguerite, who was apparently dead, and that of Monsieur Missery, who was still breathing. Thinking that all this noise had woken Madame, I went up to inform her.'

'Where are your mistress's apartments?'

'On the first floor, in the left wing of the mansion. Monseigneur lodges in the right wing.'

'Good. Let's take everything in order. What time was it when you went down?'

'About seven,' she said, without any hesitation.

'Was it dark?'

'Completely.'

That was a point on which everyone agreed, thought Nicolas.

'Of course,' he said, 'Provence had a dark lantern with him.'

It was a crude trap, and he wasn't sure she would fall into it. It was obvious the blow had struck home, but she recovered immediately.

'I don't know . . . I think . . . The sight of blood bothered me. It was all lit up. How? I couldn't say.'

Nicolas did not insist: that would have revealed that he was trying to trick her. The mention of the blood intrigued him. Did she mean the blood at the scene of the crime or the blood on Missery's body?

'Was your mistress asleep?'

'No, she was standing in the space between her bed and the wall, very angry, waiting to find out the reason for all the chaos – that was her word.'

'Hadn't she taken her sleeping draught the previous evening?'

She stared at him again with her grey eyes. There was something beautiful in her mixture of sadness and severity.

'Sometimes she takes it, sometimes she doesn't,' she said, slightly too curtly. 'Sometimes she remembers, sometimes she forgets, sometimes she takes more than she should.'

'But if she did take the medication, as she herself states, the noise should not have awoken her. And besides, you're the one who prepares it for her. Did you give it to her last night?'

He had thrown out this assertion at random, and had no evidence to back it up, but he had clearly hit the target, to judge by her agitation.

'No . . . Yes . . . At least what there was of it.'

'What does that mean?'

'The bottles had got broken and I was only able to collect a few drops. I was planning to get some more today from the apothecary.'

'A few drops of the potion?'

'No, of the ether and alcohol.'

'Can you show me what's left of those bottles?'

The question was a specific one, and there was no way of evading it. Nicolas was pressing home his advantage, convinced that he had put his finger on something – something that might be unconnected to the case but certainly seemed to be disturbing the duchesse's head chambermaid.

'I threw them into the cesspool, for fear that someone might get hurt,' she replied. 'If Madame had found them, it would have disturbed her peace of mind, for which I am responsible.'

These skilful excuses did not need any further commentary. She was a strong sparring partner, thought Nicolas, used to living by her wits and even able to use her own unease as a strength, presenting herself as an honest person who has been thrown into a state of shock.

He changed the subject. 'What can you tell us about Jean Missery?' he asked.

Eugénie's face turned slightly red. 'I am a chambermaid,' she replied, 'and he is a major-domo. Our tasks are different and keep us apart. It's Madame who deals with the women. However, he does sometimes reprimand us . . .'

'What about?'

'I don't know. Something about candles. It's one thing for our masters to exert their authority over us, but to obey those to whom they delegate part of their power, to be the servant of a servant, now that's something I can't stand!'

It was such a vehement assertion that Bourdeau, who was standing behind Eugénie, underlined it with an eloquent wink.

'I see,' said Nicolas. 'I suppose that kind of acrimony is perfectly common in large houses. What about the victim? What was your opinion of her? Like you, she worked for Madame, you knew her well. She must have been a friend of yours, with similar interests.'

This time, Eugénie made a contemptuous grimace. 'You can think that if you like! How could I have anything in common with that creature from the gutter, whose work consisted of emptying the buckets and cleaning the floors? She was introduced here by poor Missery. God knows where he'd met her! Everything about her suggested a dissolute origin. She led him by the nose, believe me. Her engagement here was a trap, and our major-domo fell into it. He lost his head and took advantage of Monseigneur's trust to impose a girl like that on Madame. If she'd at least been honest with him! But just think, Commissioner, she used to receive a suitor – a young one this time – here, in this very house. She would go out at night, even though Madame demands that we lead a good, regular life. She didn't suspect a thing! Just think, she'd got her claws into a widower, such a fine man, a major-domo to boot! She didn't respect him, even though he was so good, and so trusting.'

'In a word, you're saying that Marguerite Pindron was Jean Missery's mistress?'

'That's very definitely what I'm saying. Ask anyone. He'd become the laughing stock of the household. He didn't deserve it, he could have . . .'

She had been on the point of blurting something out.

'Could have what?'

'I know what I mean.'

'Do you think him capable of punishing himself?'

'He has a fiery temper. He gets angry quickly, and sometimes can't control himself. Everything about him is excessive.'

'One last thing,' said Nicolas. 'What did you mean when you told your mistress that it was bound to happen?'

She looked up, and there was a hint of provocation in her expression. 'That loose morals have fatal consequences. God teaches us that.'

'I see that we are in a very religious house,' said Nicolas with a smile. 'Thank you.'

She withdrew, bumping into Bourdeau as she did so, without a word of excuse. The two police officers looked at each other, each one sifting through his impressions for himself.

'She certainly has character!' said Nicolas. 'A somewhat enigmatic charm and a superb complexion. A bit thin, though.'

'You're not exactly sticking your neck out in saying that,' replied Bourdeau. 'As for myself, I'm less compassionate. She's trying to make us believe that butter wouldn't melt in her mouth, but I'd sum her up in this way: self-control, hatred and admiration. Self-control in the skilful way she makes innuendos, hatred towards the victim, even now, and admiration for Missery. But watch out! From admiration to love is but a step . . . And that step may have been taken.'

'I noticed that, too, as well as other contradictions,' Nicolas agreed. 'Here is a man whose authority is resented, but whose kindness, trust and good nature are praised. All these remarks are important, and I would wager that others will enlighten us on the relationship between the chambermaid and the major-domo. I don't exclude the possibility that there's something there. Bring in Jeannette. I assume she's in the antechamber. I hope Eugénie hasn't instructed her in what to say.'

As soon as the girl came in, he realised that someone had upset her. Her careworn expression, her tear-stained face, the way she was twisting a handkerchief in her hands: all these things revealed a terror that was in no way justified by the prospect of an interrogation. He felt sorry for her: she was little more than a child.

'My dear,' he began, in a fatherly tone, 'we need your help. What's your name and how old are you?'

'Jeannette,' she murmured in a faint voice, 'Jeannette Le Bas. I was born in Yvetot, in Normandy, and I'm seventeen.'

'How long have you been in service?'

'Two years, Monsieur. Since Saint Jean's day.'

'Sit down. Don't be afraid. Tell me what happened.'

She looked about her like an animal caught in a trap. 'I have nothing to say . . . Have pity, Monsieur . . . They can hear us.'

'Come now,' said Bourdeau, 'enough of this childishness!' He strode in turn to each of the doors and opened them. 'As you see,' he resumed, 'there's no one eavesdropping. What are you afraid of?'

She looked up and, as if taking a plunge into deep water, began speaking. 'Nobody. It's just that I'm not used to it. This morning, I heard a noise in Madame's bedroom, and so—'

'Wait, slow down. Where do you sleep?'

'On a bunk in the garderobe.'

'Does the room have an opening?'

'Yes, Monsieur, a window looking out on the main courtyard.'

'And you say it was your mistress who woke you?'

She blushed with embarrassment. 'Because she was using her commode.'

'Roughly what time was that?'

'I don't know, it was still dark. Then Eugénie arrived, yelling so much it was hard to understand what she was saying.'

'But you understood some of it?'

'Just that something terrible had happened. She mentioned blood, and a knife. I was so scared I put my fingers in my ears.'

'What happened then?'

'Madame went back to bed. I stayed where I was, waiting for her to call me. Which she did at midday.'

'I'd like to be clear about one thing,' said Nicolas, gravely. 'Was your mistress awake when Eugénie arrived?'

'Wide awake, I'd just seen her in the garderobe. What have I said? Is there something wrong? Oh God, protect me! I don't want to lose my job.'

'You won't lose anything at all if you tell us the truth. I promise you that. Did you know Marguerite?'

'Of course,' she replied, sniffling. 'She was very sweet and kind to me. She even wanted to teach me to read and write. I really liked her, though I shouldn't say it.'

'Why not?'

'Madame and Eugénie thought she was a bad girl.'

'And what was your opinion?'

'I think she'd had a lot of bad things happen to her, but despite all that, she had a good heart. For the rest, I don't judge.'

'Did she confide in you?'

'She told me she was very tired.'

'Tired of her work?'

'That, too. But especially the things her suitor made her do.'

'Jean Missery?'

The girl opened her eyes wide in surprise and began trembling. 'No, not him! The young man who called on her some nights.'

'Do you know his name?'

'No, she called him Aide.'

'Aide? That's unusual. Are you sure that was his name?'

'Yes.'

'What about the major-domo?'

'Oh, him! . . . He was always after her, and even . . .' Suddenly, she began shaking uncontrollably, she threw her head back, and her limbs tensed. Nicolas's first thought was that he was again confronted with a phenomenon he had once before observed in a young servant girl. Helped by Bourdeau, he laid her out on a bench. Gradually, the attack receded, and she regained consciousness, surprised to see the two men bending over her.

'My dear,' said Nicolas, 'you must calm down, nothing is going to happen to you. I've promised to look after you and I'm going to keep my word. Pierre, be so kind as to walk back with her.'

Once alone, Nicolas reflected. Of course, he was making progress with his investigation, but he had a growing feeling that the case was proving to be more complex than he had thought at first. The paths that might lead to the truth kept dividing, meeting again, merging, with so many abrupt and unexpected turns that you ended up losing your way in frustration. Why had the young servant girl had a sudden seizure just as she was talking about the major-domo? He vowed to mention it to Dr Semacgus. He recalled past conversations about strange cases of girls prone to that kind of attack. Clearly, none of the women or girls in the Saint-Florentin mansion were indifferent to Jean Missery. Bourdeau reappeared, followed by a young man with a waddling gait. Tow-coloured hair framed a regular, pimply face. His forehead was covered in sweat, and he was pulling on the lapels of his linen jacket as if trying to draw it tighter around himself.

Nicolas launched into the interrogation without further ado. 'Are you Jacques Despiard, the kitchen boy? How old are you?'

'That's me, Monsieur. I'm twenty-five.'

'How did you come to discover the bodies?'

'Every morning, I open the kitchens and light the stoves and the hearths in the roasting room. It takes a while to get things heated up properly, especially to get rid of the smoke. I always begin with the roasting room, because that's where the fire takes longest to get going. This morning, no sooner had I entered than I saw all that blood and the two bodies.'

He had started stammering, and passed his hand over his face as if to dismiss the vision. Nicolas took advantage of this pause.

'So it was light in the roasting room?'

The young man grew agitated, looking wildly from one of the two impassive police officers to the other, as if searching for help or inspiration.

'Do you understand my question?' asked Nicolas. 'At what time did you open the kitchen?'

'At six, I think.'

'I see. So it was dark?'

'If you say so.'

'The commissioner isn't saying anything,' Bourdeau cut in, irritably. 'This is about you, and we'd be grateful to you if you could remember what happened.'

'The inspector's right,' said Nicolas gently. 'How could you see the bodies in a dark basement room at six in the morning, at this time of year?'

'Did you have a candle?' asked Bourdeau.

'I can't remember . . . I don't know. You're confusing me. All that blood . . . Leave me alone!'

'Calm down. We'll come back to that when you've recovered. In the meantime, tell me about the victim.'

The young man's eyes shone through his tears. 'She was so beautiful! She always had a kind word. What a monster!'

'Who are you talking about?'

'The major-domo, Missery, of course. He killed her, he wanted all of them. But they said . . .'

'They said what?'

'Nothing.'

'You need to understand that, if you withhold the truth, you could well end up in a dungeon in the Châtelet prison, where other means will be used to make you talk. What can you tell us about Missery?'

The young man hesitated. 'A nasty piece of work,' he said at last. 'He takes it out on everyone. He sets traps for us to fall into, so he can throw us out on the street. To replace us with his pets, I suppose. He even threatened Monsieur Charles.'

'The valet?'

'Yes, Commissioner. Charles Bibard. Missery was planning to report him to Monseigneur for reselling pieces of candle from the house.'

'Perhaps Missery is just an honest man who can't tolerate certain excesses?'

The witness's face was red with indignation. 'Him, honest! He's trading illicitly with all the suppliers, taking a commission on every delivery and building up a nice little nest egg for himself. As if his wife's fortune wasn't enough for him. And he may have wept for her, but he's certainly had plenty of consolation since.'

'What do you know about that inheritance?'

'Only what everyone said. In her will, his wife left him all her fortune, but it would revert to her family if he died – unless, of course, he'd remarried and had children.'

'Thank you for your information. Try to clarify your whereabouts at the time of the murder, and we'll speak again.'


The young man fled as if he had a hundred devils at his heels. Provence appeared and announced formally, 'Commissioner, the doctor says that Monsieur Missery has regained consciousness.'

Nicolas and Bourdeau followed him to the other wing of the Saint-Florentin mansion. The inspector noted with curiosity the route they were taking through the maze-like building. On their arrival, and having dismissed the valet, they saw the major-domo sitting up in bed, propped up by pillows, his chest bandaged with pieces of his torn shirt. His eyes were closed and his head drooped over his chest. Monsieur de Gévigland was taking his pulse and passing a bottle of salts under his nose with the other hand.

'I thought,' said Nicolas, 'that your patient had regained consciousness?'

'So did I,' replied the doctor. 'But no sooner was he conscious than he fell into a swoon. It's only a slight relapse. He's finding it hard to extricate himself from the mists of sleep.'

At that moment, the man sneezed and his eyes opened then closed again, dazzled by the light. He was shaken by a coughing fit. Moaning, he put his hand on his side, where his wound was. Gradually, his breathing became easier and more sonorous. Meanwhile, Bourdeau was examining every nook and cranny of the room. While the doctor had his back to him, he took, with a wink to the commissioner, several objects from a drawer in the chest. Truly, his deputy was incomparable and never missed an opportunity. He continued his investigations discreetly. Now Missery was staring in surprise at the faces peering down at him.

'I don't feel well,' he said in a thick voice.

Nicolas noticed a strange smell emanating from his mouth.

'What are you doing in my room?' asked the major-domo. 'What's happened?'

Although his features were drawn, his face was still virile. His sparse grey hair, however, made him look older, forming a kind of crown around the baldness that had already pushed his hairline back off his forehead. His eyes went from one face to another like those of a frightened animal. He was biting his lip, giving the impression that his mind, still wandering in the mists of unconsciousness, was engaged in intense reflection.

'My dear fellow,' said the doctor, 'it is for you to enlighten us. We found you—'

Nicolas seized him by the arm to stop him saying any more. 'Asleep and wounded,' he said. 'I am a police commissioner at the Châtelet. Could you tell us what happened to you?'

'I have no idea what's going on,' replied the major-domo. 'I went to bed very late, and now I wake up and find you here! Did someone attack me while I was asleep?'

'Come on,' said Nicolas. 'Make an effort to collect your thoughts. We need to know your exact whereabouts last night.'

'Monseigneur was away. He was at Versailles with the King. Madame, indisposed as she so often is, did not dine. At about eleven o'clock, I had a last look around the house and then came up to bed.'

'Did you go down to the kitchens?'

The man showed no particular emotion. 'I had no reason to do so, the fires had been out since Saturday. So I came back to my room.'

'Did you have a candle?'

'Yes, you can see the candlestick there, on the desk.'

'And then?'

'I undressed, blew out the candle, and fell asleep.'

'The candle in that candlestick?'

'Of course.'

'Where was it?'

'Here.' And he pointed to a small marquetry bedside table on his left, half hidden by the bed curtains.

'Why is it on the desk now?' asked Nicolas. 'Was it you who moved it?'

Missery shook his head.

'You, then, Doctor?'

'Certainly not.'

'Go on,' said Nicolas.

'I fell asleep.'

'Did you have any visitors?'

He sensed a kind of imperceptible hesitation in the way the major-domo replied, 'No, nobody.'

'Doctor,' said Nicolas, 'may I have a word with you for a moment in private?'

He drew him into the corridor, leaving Bourdeau to watch over the wounded man.

'In your opinion, could that wound, which you described as benign, have led to a significant loss of blood?'

'It's strange that you should ask me that question,' replied the doctor. 'Just now, when I was replacing the bandage, I had another look at the cut. No vein or major vessel was damaged. There was no haemorrhage. And there are hardly any bloodstains on the man's breeches!'

'That tallies with my own observation. So what do you make of his loss of consciousness?'

'Oh, you shouldn't let that go to your head: some sensitive people faint at the slightest nick. There's no accounting for it! Anyway, our man doesn't appear to be aware of the gravity of the situation, and certainly isn't reacting like someone who has just tried to kill himself.'

They went back into the room.

'How is it, Monsieur,' Nicolas resumed, 'that you are not in your nightshirt?'

The man touched himself, and seemed only now to become aware of what he was wearing. 'I have no idea. I put on a freshly ironed nightshirt last night.'

'It's nowhere to be found,' said Bourdeau.

Missery seemed both appalled and frightened by this observation.

'Monsieur,' said Nicolas, 'what was your relationship with the Duchesse de La Vrillière's chambermaid, Marguerite Pindron?'

For the first time since the beginning of the interrogation, Missery looked up with a kind of contained fury. 'She's my mistress. Everyone will tell you that and it's true, and I defy anyone to . . .' He broke off.

'To what?' asked Nicolas.

'I don't know.'

'Jean Missery, you have to face certain facts. You are accused and suspected of having murdered your mistress, Marguerite Pindron, and of having tried to kill yourself in order to escape the just punishment for such a crime. As of now, you are in the hands of the law. On my orders, your condition permitting, you will be taken to the royal prison of the Châtelet to await the decision of the Criminal Lieutenant and an investigation of the case. This arrest does not imply a final judgement on your actions, but forms part of the necessary precautionary measures when there has been a murder. I can assure you that everything will be done to either invalidate or confirm the facts and presumptions for which you may well feel the full weight of the law.'

As he listened to Nicolas's solemn words, the major-domo collapsed on his bed, weeping, gasping and wringing his hands. He was soon nothing but a shapeless heap.

'Bourdeau,' said Nicolas, 'call the officers and have this man conducted to his destination. Make sure he's bound and guarded.'

Nicolas was still haunted by the memory of a sad case in which a suspect had killed himself in his cell. He felt that a surfeit of precautions and the observation of simple rules was necessary to avoid any recurrence of such a tragedy. Monsieur de Gévigland and Bourdeau helped Missery to his feet. He was made to put on his coat, which the commissioner took hold of for a moment and examined attentively. Bourdeau picked up the shoes and had a good look at them before helping the major-domo to put them on. The officer at the door of the room called his colleagues, and the suspect was taken away, closely guarded by the men from the Châtelet.

Nicolas turned to the doctor. 'Monsieur,' he said, 'I thank you for your valuable assistance and your very helpful comments. We will doubtless have need of your testimony.'

'I am at your disposal, Commissioner. Rest assured of my continued assistance. In addition, I would be honoured and delighted if one day, at your convenience, you would come to lunch or dinner. I live in Rue Saint-Honoré, opposite the Capuchin monastery. My wife and I would be happy to count you among the regular visitors to our dwelling.'

He wrapped himself in his cloak, adjusted his cocked hat, bowed to the two police officers and went out. Nicolas had been struck by the benevolence emanating from the doctor, and the elegant simplicity of his attire, embellished with a ribbon tying up his natural, unpowdered salt-and-pepper hair. Once the doctor had gone out, Bourdeau gave a slight bow.

'Everyone kowtows to the marquis,' he said. 'No sooner do they know him than they guess his rank, even if he calls himself Le Floch. Monsieur de Gévigland made no mistake! He fell into your snare.'

Nicolas did not reply to this gibe, which his friend had not been able to refrain from coming out with. To him, Bourdeau was all of a piece, with his faults and his qualities, the latter far outweighing the former in his judgement. The inspector was truly devoted to him, had twice saved his life, and had not hesitated to risk his career for his sake. Having fallen from favour together, they were now coming back into the light of day, more united than ever. What accumulated resentment, what brooded-over bitterness nourished these attacks of acrimony which Bourdeau seemed unable to control? The merest trifle could revive an unknown wound. The tragic death of his father, torn to pieces by a boar during a royal hunt, did not explain everything. The cruel game of respect and contempt which underlay a society based on the privileges of birth was something he found hard to accept. There was also a touch of possessive jealousy towards those who yielded to the commissioner's innate seductive charms. Their attentions disgusted the inspector, who always dreamed of an exclusive friendship. Fortunately, Noblecourt, La Borde and Semacgus escaped this devouring jealousy. They did not in any way threaten long-established habits, and their own feelings for the inspector were a bastion and an anchor in his life. Yes, the sensible thing was not to respond to his remarks. Nicolas dreaded that the regular recurrence of these ideas might one day lead his friend to take up extreme positions, the consequences of which he would be unable to control. It was an abscess that needed to be lanced, and perhaps he would make up his mind to speak to him about it. But the hour had not yet come for that discussion.

'Did you see the shoes?' Bourdeau went on. 'Not a trace of blood. Nothing. Clean and polished.'

'Perhaps he cleaned them, we'll have to ask him.'

Nicolas wrote something in his little black notebook, then asked Bourdeau what time it was.

'That's what I thought, it's getting late. But it's vital that we hear all the testimonies today. Let's divide up the task. I'll question the Swiss Guard and you have a word with the caretaker. Then we'll meet again and see what we've come up with.'

*

They again found the valet waiting for them in the shadows of the corridor. Once more, the thought crossed Nicolas's mind that the valet had not left them for a single second. Was he simply being diligent, to the point of obsequiousness, or had someone told him to keep an eye on everything they did? He led them into a new maze of corridors. They went past the linen room and came to some adjoining quarters. Provence pointed out to Bourdeau the entrance to the caretaker's lodge, then, taking another staircase, he led the commissioner to the Swiss Guard's sentry box on the ground floor below, at the corner of the left facade, near the gate. The man, who was tall and stooped, had taken off his wig, and his cranium gleamed in the candlelight. He immediately put his wig back on. He was truly monumental. Nicolas recalled that the largest houses in the city specifically sought out such giants to fill this kind of office. This one was so tall that the commissioner had to look up at him.

'You know who I am, you welcomed me earlier. What is your name and how old are you?'

'Pierre Miquete, about forty.' He did not wait for the questions. 'This is what I can tell you. There was a loud cry from the courtyard. I should tell you that the window of my bedroom looks out on the gate. I was eating my morning soup. I should tell you that I put in leftover dry bread, which the kitchen boy passes to me. It's better in soup. So, yes, the cry . . . I went running. There was Jacques, doing the same. Yes, I should tell you his name is Jacques, like the caretaker. Everyone was crying, "Murder! Murder!"'

'Everyone?'

'Provence, Eugénie, the caretaker and Jacques.'

'Was it light?'

'I don't remember. The emotion, you know. Seems to me . . .'

'Did you see the bodies?'

'Certainly not! The slightest drop of blood makes me faint.'

Nicolas risked something that sometimes worked. 'Were you in love with her?'

The response was rapid, but not what he had expected. 'With that girl? Of course not. I should tell you, Commissioner, that I've accumulated a certain amount since I've been in Monseigneur's service. I need something a bit more substantial than a little streetwalker. But the other one doesn't want me. And they all warmed his bed, her like all the rest. I could weep, I'm that besotted, but she doesn't want to know anything about me.'

'Who are you talking about?'

'I'm talking about Eugénie burning the midnight oil with Missery, but now that he's abandoned her, she still won't look at me.'

*Good Lord!* thought Nicolas. But he asked only, 'And where were you last night?'

'In my room.'

Nicolas went back to his study on the mezzanine. He wondered if he should respond immediately to the minister's wish to be informed of the initial results of the investigation. Nothing that he could tell him seemed likely to arouse his interest. Should he bother him with a host of bizarre details and vague, contradictory testimonies? Unlike Monsieur de Sartine, the Duc de La Vrillière had little taste for the nitty-gritty of police work: he needed something to get his teeth into. It would be better to hold off for the moment.

Nicolas sat staring at the fire. His mind flew back to the limbo of his childhood, and he saw himself at Guérande, watching rapt as the logs collapsed in a cloud of sparks. Night was falling by the time he returned to reality. This mansion oozed dissimulation and hatred: it was an impression that gripped him like a feeling of suffocation. All the elements had been in place for a tragedy. All the witnesses might have had reasons to hate the victim, but all of them were equally falling over each other to disparage the major-domo. It still remained to be established that the solution did indeed lie within the walls of the Saint-Florentin mansion. What was the role of that mysterious stranger whose bloody footprints had guided him as far as the balcony? Of course, that could have been an attempt to divert suspicion from the inhabitants of the house and to lead the investigators along a false path. He reflected for a long time. When Bourdeau entered the room, now dimly lit by the last gleams of the dying fire, he found him with his chin in his hand and his eyes staring into space.

'Good hunting, Pierre?'

'The caretaker, Jacques Blain, twenty-eight years old, well built, a bit of a lady killer, was mad about the chambermaid,' declared Bourdeau. 'Didn't see a thing. Just went to fetch the doctor from Rue Saint-Honoré. He hates Missery, in fact he hates the whole household. This mansion is a real cesspool of wickedness!'

'What else?'

'What else? A stew made with three rabbits, for one man. I saw the skins hanging in his window. He did me the honour of letting me try it.'

'Did you like the seasoning?'

'The sauce was a little thin. It didn't even cover the meat.'

'And what conclusion do you draw from that?'

'Where I come from, we mix the blood with vinegar to thicken the stew at the last moment and give the sauce more taste. The fact remains, three rabbits are a lot for one man. He even wanted to give me a second helping.'

'Does the mansion have a rabbit hutch?'

'Yes, in the inner courtyard.'

'We'll have a look. Any other discoveries?'

'You saw me taking some objects from the major-domo's chest of drawers. Here they are.'

The inspector had placed two boxes on a pedestal table. Nicolas leaned over them.

'Well, well! Some Sultana's Aphrodisiac and some pastilles of cantharides. Does Monsieur Missery have a few problems performing?'

'And that's not all,' said Bourdeau. 'In Marguerite's room, I found, hidden at the back of a cupboard, whole sacks full of pieces of candle. There has indeed been trafficking, but she was the culprit!'

'Three rabbits for a single man, a Don Juan who needs chemical help, and as much wax as you could wish! The plot thickens, and so does our investigation.'

# IV

## CONFUSION

*Ab hoc cadavere quidquam mihi opis expetebam?*
From this corpse left without burial, what resources could I draw?
CICERO

Sitting at a small pedestal table in Monsieur de Noblecourt's bedroom, Nicolas was just making a start on his third slice of Mainz ham. He poured himself another glass of light red wine. On his return, late in the evening, Catherine had put together this robust midnight supper and brought everything up to the bedroom. The master of the house, who had been about to go to bed and was alerted by his dog, Cyrus, of Nicolas's arrival, had rung down to make sure the commissioner was informed that he wished to speak to him. At his age you didn't need much sleep, either because your aches and pains kept you awake or because your happy or bitter memories of a long life led you into a half-dozing state of reverie. He took particular pleasure in these evening meetings in the course of which Nicolas would confide in him, taking careful note of his ever-sensible remarks. The magistrate's existence was now confined to his house, apart from a few ceremonial visits, his daily walk as prescribed by Tronchin, his doctor from Geneva, and the few special evenings when the splendours of his table were lavished on those close to him. Having devoured the ham, Nicolas next tackled a dish of orange and almond pastries all shiny with icing sugar. Two lustful pairs of eyes converged on this marvel: one belonged to the host, his mouth greedily half open, and the other to Mouchette, the cat sitting on his lap. From her difficult early days, the poor animal had retained an insatiable appetite which nothing could discourage and which extended to dishes not usually much appreciated by the feline species. Cyrus, ever the teacher, would watch over his young friend, always ready to instruct her, firmly but gently, in good manners. The old dog was indebted to her: his new responsibilities as the elder partner, wise in the ways of the house, had rejuvenated him. Monsieur de Noblecourt shook himself and adjusted his nightcap, as if wanting to break the spell the food and wine had cast on him. He delicately served himself a drop of amber-coloured herb tea from a small but thick Chinese porcelain teapot filled with hot water and maintained at the ideal temperature.

'Alas,' he sighed, tasting the beverage, 'here I am, reduced to the great King's diet! A compote of prunes and a sage tea. Fagon himself would not object.'[1]

'I assume your lunch and dinner are more abundant,' remarked Nicolas.

'Of course, but farewell the wonderful excesses I once enjoyed! One day, you'll see what it costs to restrain oneself.'

'Go on, complain! The world passes over you, leaving few traces. If you don't yield to temptations, you'll remain a young man.'

'That's enough, you flatterer. You'd do better to tell me about your day. But before that, let me tell you the latest news. A friend of mine, who came to lunch . . .'

'So you lunched in style?'

'I nibbled,' said Noblecourt with a laugh, 'and so did he. This friend of mine, as I was saying, who is well informed about the gossip at Versailles, not to mention what is said in the ministries of foreign courts, thinks – and this will interest you – that the Queen was not very happy that Monsieur de Sartine was chosen as Minister for the Navy. She's protecting him out of consideration for Choiseul, whose friend he was. She would have preferred him to succeed the Duc de La Vrillière as Minister of the King's Household. She was sorry to see that they had placed the former Lieutenant General of Police in a department so unsuited to his talents.'

'The Duc de La Vrillière does not appear to have fallen out of favour,' observed Nicolas. 'They say that the King is not on speaking terms with him because of his very existence, but Maurepas is his brother-in-law. And as for Sartine, his talents suit him for any kind of position, however distant from those fields he particularly favours.'

'Of course!' Monsieur de Noblecourt agreed. '*Secundo*, the mood of Mesdames, and especially of Madame Adélaïde, has become increasingly bitter as their influence has lessened. The Queen is said to have developed a certain bias against them, from which she will not depart. If they behave themselves, fine, but she won't tolerate any excessive pretensions, and the kind of conceit they're occasionally prone to will be repressed.'

'Mesdames have aged badly,' remarked Nicolas.

He remembered with nostalgia the radiant horsewoman in her hunting costume . . . Fourteen years had gone by since his first encounter with Madame Adélaïde in the course of a lively jaunt.

'*Tertio*,' Monsieur de Noblecourt went on, 'there's every indication that the Queen will act in the same way towards her brothers-in-law. Monsieur – reserved, cautious, even secretive – takes a certain amount of care over his conduct, but the Comte d'Artois has none and constantly falls into a familiarity he believes is permitted because it has been tolerated so far. As for the King, despite his austere life, everyone thinks he's soft and weak. He won't do anything to control his brother's activities. Only the Queen could put him in his place, if she wanted to. This situation's going to cause a lot of trouble.'

'Well, Mercury of the latest news, what of the *quarto*?'

'You can laugh, but this is much more serious. A pamphlet! No one is sure of its author, but Monsieur de Beaumarchais is suspected. Choiseul is the principal target along with the Queen, whose entourage is denounced as being in the pay of the former minister.'

He lowered his voice so much that the cat began miaowing anxiously.

'Be quiet, Mouchette!' Noblecourt growled. 'The pamphlet goes so far as to claim that the State is doomed if the King does nothing to curb his wife's ambition and coquetry. The gist of it – listen to this – is that Louis XVI cannot have children and that the princes, his brothers, should be on their guard against some new, loathsome intrigue which the young Queen may decide to go along with.'

'Yet one more example of the prevailing infection of the century!' said Nicolas, getting carried away. 'One more slander to add to all the others that have appeared over the years, against which we endlessly raise ever-illusory barricades!'

'I fear that the deplorable aberrations attributed to the late King opened the way to all kinds of knaves and rascals,' observed Noblecourt. 'We saw a succession of disturbances, scandals, injustices and upheavals. Morals and principles went by the board, and everything was left to chance. Now only the wicked remain on the scene to face a spineless government, and among them there is a spirit of intrigue and conspiracy of an intensity without precedent in this kingdom. The most sacred duties are forgotten and nothing is respected, nothing is safe from the blackest horrors.'

'Your friend seems to me quite well informed,' said Nicolas, choking on a pastry. 'And quite bitter, too.'

There was a silence. 'I won't conceal it from you any longer,' Monsieur de Noblecourt said at last. 'It was the Maréchal de Richelieu who honoured me with his visit. He stayed nearly two hours.'

It seemed to Nicolas that the maréchal, 'old Court' if anyone was, played almost no part in affairs of State now, even though, as First Gentleman of the Bedchamber, he still appeared at Versailles. Rebuffs and disdain had no effect on him: he continued to impose his presence on the new King, who looked at him without seeing him and paid him no heed. In these conditions, it was not surprising that he remembered his old friends, and Monsieur de Noblecourt, always susceptible to the attentions of the great lord, offered him the opportunity to harbour still the illusion of his own importance.

'Now I understand,' said Nicolas. 'The maréchal is champing at the bit, ever hoping for what will never come again. As I'm sure you know, his trial is dragging on in the *parlement* and is causing a scandal.'

'Not surprisingly,' said Noblecourt, again lowering his voice. 'He's accused by the opposing party, Madame de Saint-Ginest, of forgery and of bribing witnesses. They say the proceedings are alarming and the depositions unimaginably long!'

The candle in one of the candlesticks sputtered and went out, plunging the room into semi-darkness.

'That's all too true. Does he at least still seem all right?'

'The bile of the whole thing has affected his mind and he, who was always so carefree, has become embittered and endlessly repeats the same wicked barbs with which you are familiar. The things he comes out with!' Noblecourt raised a sententious finger. 'A bad word sometimes tells us more than ten beautiful sentences. He has dreamed all his life of joining the council. *Aut causa, aut nihil.*'

'No doubt,' said Nicolas. 'But what infirmity of mind makes him think he still has a future at his age? Why doesn't he prefer history, to which he contributed so much? Why doesn't he talk about his victories and the glory that went with them?'

'Alas, he lacks two essential qualities! Virtue and perspective. Concerned as he is with the impression he makes, he ought to stop complaining about the faults of the time. Serenity resides only in the soul of an honest man, and the maréchal is anything but that. But what about you? Tell me about your day.'

The former procurator sank into his armchair, his eyes half closed. Mouchette, having found nothing substantial to satisfy her appetite, began cleaning herself meticulously. Nicolas launched into a precise account, taking care not to omit any detail. He had sometimes noted Monsieur de Noblecourt's curious ability to absorb the facts of a case. His reflections often led to observations that seemed strange at first, but frequently proved to be wise and far-sighted. Nicolas's account was punctuated with exclamations of satisfaction and surprise, and when he had finished Noblecourt was silent for some time, while Nicolas, made thirsty by his speech and the salt in the ham, finished off the bottle of red wine from Champagne, more tawny-coloured than red in fact, and invigoratingly light.

'First, I must congratulate you,' Noblecourt said at last. 'Out of favour in the spring, back in favour by autumn! That's a disgrace to be envied! Here you are, back in the saddle, and I'm sure Monsieur Lenoir, in whose good faith I continue to believe, will reconsider his prejudices. I pray to heaven that the affair into which you have been drawn is not a trap intended to destroy the greatest expectations! You shake your head? Think about it. The Duc de La Vrillière has gone over the head of his Lieutenant General of Police. He's not doing you a good deed. He's involving you in an affair that concerns his own house and his own domestic staff. He himself is not so well thought of at Court, every week his exile is announced as being imminent, and only his kinship with the First Minister protects him. On the one hand, he places you in a situation in which you might annoy your own chief, and on the other, he drags you down with him in his fall, if such is the outcome. So follow my advice: tell Monsieur Lenoir everything. He will be grateful to you, and your combined interests will withstand the storms. Continue to appear at Court and try to keep the King informed. What happens privately in great kingdoms cannot leave him indifferent. In this way, you will protect your rear and be prepared for any eventuality.'

'That sounds like sensible advice to me,' said Nicolas, 'and I shall certainly follow it.'

'As for the case itself, it couldn't be more delicate. Cases involving domestics always are. It is a world in which treachery reigns. Take your chambermaids: a woman who serves another needs much more skill and flexibility than a man in the same situation. There is no middle way: a chambermaid is either in a position of the most gratifying intimacy or in one of the most humiliating dependence. A servant, if he wants to maintain his position, must always have a ready answer, anticipate his master's whim, remedy his bad mood, flatter his self-esteem, and, last but not least, feign sincerity. All this implies falsehood and deception. A noble house is a state in miniature, with its plots, its alliances, its dissimulation and, sometimes, its humble devotion.'

Noblecourt reflected for a moment before continuing.

'Add to all that one vital question. Why did the Duc de La Vrillière send for you? You are not, I wager, fooled by the compliments and vain protestations of goodwill he has lavished on you. He knows you're on the sidelines at the moment and sends for you. All right. But why? Is it because he thinks that anyone can be bought, and that a man on the sidelines, investigating a crime committed in a minister's mansion, might turn a blind eye to certain things?'

'Do you think him capable of that?'

Monsieur de Noblecourt sat up in his chair and struck the armrests with his hands. 'I am surprised, Monsieur,' he exclaimed, 'that, after so many years at the highest level of the police force, you still have that bedrock of innocence which is a tribute to your good heart but reduces your perceptiveness. But what can I do? Your old friend owes it to himself to be the devil's advocate, the worst is always a possibility and certainly shouldn't be ruled out *a priori.* I remember how hurt you were when, being yourself personally implicated in a crime, I was forced to investigate you. It was not that I believed you guilty, but the possibility had to be considered before it could be ruled out.[2] To tell the true from the false with full knowledge of the facts, one must first abandon the idea that one possesses the truth.'

Monsieur de Noblecourt always surprised Nicolas. This affable man had a strength and an authority which rarely manifested themselves but which, for that very reason, were all the more striking.

'To return to your victim,' Noblecourt went on, 'look into her origins. That's a procurator speaking. As you know, there are rules governing the servant classes, rules it's not advisable to contravene. A domestic cannot enter into service without declaring his or her name or nickname, his place of birth and where he has served. He must present a notice from his previous master, without concealing anything. He cannot leave him without his consent and a certificate. Unmarried servants of both sexes cannot have private rented rooms without the written permission of their masters. They are forbidden to give or lend their lodgings to tramps or other suspicious characters. A good police force should also be concerned with routine laws. When regulations and conventions are circumvented, we enter a shifting, uncertain terrain, which often conceals strange phenomena. The rule itself is seldom meaningful, but its lack sometimes is.'

A long silence ensued. Monsieur de Noblecourt sighed, pleased with his turn of phrase. His eyes wandered over the shadowy areas of the room, as if making an inventory of its details.

'Oh, what merit your profession possesses!' he resumed. 'The first is that of diversion. Monsieur Tronchin, my doctor, told me one day that, unable to purge certain catarrhs, he diverted them to another less dangerous part of the body . . . Dying should appear to us a natural, impartial accident. I am a happy man, in spite of everything. As a magistrate, I may have been cast aside, but I live through your investigations by proxy. Dying is a small thing, the most difficult part is to detach oneself from the affections and objects that surround one. My father often told me about the last days of Cardinal Mazarin, when he summoned up the strength to bid farewell to his collections. Alas, my books, my study, who will cast on you the loving gaze to which I have accustomed you?'

'Oh,' said Nicolas, 'I don't like you when you're in one of these strange moods. They're usually a sign that a bad attack's on the way.'

Noblecourt smiled. 'It's nothing but the melancholy of autumn.

> *But how could I confound*
> *That destiny whose round*
> *Gives each man his due . . .*
> *For I say goodbye to myself*
> *When I say farewell to you*[3]

My friends, my books, my cabinet of curiosities . . .'

'What a memory you have, like a young man's!' cried Nicolas, applauding.

'Insolent boy!' said Noblecourt, choking with laughter. 'In making that comment, you make things worse for yourself, since the second part of your sentence goes without saying.'

Reassured about his friend's condition, Nicolas took his leave and went up to his apartments. Mouchette followed him. The old tiled floor served her as a sleeping place next to the commissioner's bed.

*Tuesday 4 October 1774*

Nicolas awoke well before the daylight began turning the wallpaper in his room white. Every morning, Mouchette, sated with sleep but hungry and playful, would jump on her master's bed and tread all over it. Her purring would finally draw the sleeper from his slumbers, and he would go and open the door for her. She would run, her tail lifted in the air, to the delights left for her by Catherine, the first person up, who would be noisily lighting the stoves.

The commissioner had not given up washing in the courtyard. It was a reminder of his youth, a quick shock that restored vigour. He would then come back upstairs to shave and do his hair. Mostly he wore his natural hair, tied with a ribbon, except on solemn occasions or when he had to go to Versailles.

That morning, drawn by the hustle and bustle, the variety of sights offered to the pedestrian, he decided to go for a long walk on the banks of the river. Mentally, he ran through his schedule. Bourdeau was to inform him of the time set for the autopsy. Before that, he intended to report to Monsieur Lenoir: he would both meet the wish his chief had expressed and protect himself from the reprimand that might come from the man's irritation at a mission whose only instigator was the minister. He would have to find the most neutral, but also the most skilful way to present his report, and he always found walking a good way to clear his mind.

A bright autumn sun made everything look beautiful, bathing the scene in an already brilliant golden light. As he walked, Nicolas looked at faces. The animated crowd paraded around him, in rhythm with his steps, a plethora of brief encounters. This game fascinated him: the glances exchanged and missed, offered, retained or rejected, hinting at all kinds of possibilities. He tried – not always successfully – to bring a conclusive moral judgement to bear on each face, based on his experience as a collector of souls. He would arrange them in a corner of his mind, like the insects in the collections of the Jardin du Roi. He knew, however, how futile this approach was. If it always held true, how easy it would be to track down criminals! His own past experience had taught him that an angelic appearance could well conceal other appetites. The pace of the world and society was such that appearances often proved to be nothing but deception and illusion.

At the entrance to Pont-Neuf, he turned for a moment to look at the familiar peremptory figure of the bronze horseman, a helmsman steering the city towards the open sea.[4] He walked along Quai du Louvre, then Quai des Tuileries. He was heading towards the garden and the Terrasse des Feuillants when a crowd attracted his attention. This small chattering throng was bustling around a form lying on the edge of the embankment. He approached. An individual whom he recognised as a spy who patrolled the gardens eavesdropping on conversations immediately came up to him and informed him what was happening. A boatman had spotted a strange shape floating just below the surface as he was crossing the river on his boat. With his boat hook, he had retrieved what turned out to be a dead body. A porter turned the inert mass over with his foot, and the disfigured face of an old man was revealed. The crowd recoiled in horror. The drowned man's right eye had been gouged out, and the arch of the eyebrows was broken and gaping. Nicolas shook his head. He was accustomed to sights like this. Boatmen, for the most part, could not swim and they were sure to drown if they fell in the water. Whenever they had to rescue a drowning man, they would haul the body out of the water with a hook, latching on to an eye or wherever else the implement landed – which might well kill the person they were trying to save. In this way, even when the victim had survived the cold, the fear, the backwash from the boats, or hitting the pillars of the bridges, his rescuer's hook might well finish him off.

The watch took things in hand. Nicolas crossed the Tuileries Gardens and came to Place Louis-le-Grand[5] and Rue Neuve-Saint-Augustin, the location of police headquarters. He was greeted there by the footman as an old acquaintance and immediately led into the Lieutenant General's study. The fact that he was received so quickly and with such good manners was a favourable sign. Indeed, the reception was more courteous than usual. But there was also a hint of anxiety in it. Monsieur Lenoir could not have been expecting Nicolas to perform this requested duty so early in the case.

'I came as soon as I could,' said the commissioner with a bow, his tricorn in his hand, 'to answer your wishes, Monseigneur, and report to you, as is only proper, such news as is likely to retain your attention.'

'Rest assured, my dear Commissioner, that your zeal and promptness are much appreciated. I assume they are connected to the affair for which the minister summoned you, thanks to my intervention.'

He emphasised the word 'intervention', like an actor in the old Hôtel de Bourgogne. It seemed unnecessary to Nicolas, but his chief needed something to cling to if he wished to recover a prestige somewhat tarnished by the Duc de La Vrillière's lack of consideration towards his Lieutenant General of Police. The commissioner then embarked on an exercise at which he excelled, one which had once earned him the favour of Louis XV: telling a story without tiring, making suggestive or enlightening observations while bringing out the crucial elements. He kept strictly to the facts, careful not to mention the various hypotheses which he and Bourdeau had already formed. Lenoir listened with a forced little smile, constantly stroking his left cheek with the tip of the quill pen which he had been using when Nicolas had arrived. At the end, he did not ask any questions, and for a long while rummaged through the heap of papers on his desk. Nicolas thought nostalgically of the desk as it was in Sartine's day: never more than one paper, along with the current edition of the *Almanach royal*, or else wigs lined up as if on parade. The Lieutenant General seemed to be absorbed in his reading. At last, he looked up.

'Monsieur Le Floch, apart from the events in Rue Saint-Florentin, I would appreciate it if you could apply your usual discernment to a number of urgent matters which, given their importance, not only put me in an awkward position, but compel me not to entrust them to just anybody.'

'I await your orders, Monseigneur,' replied Nicolas soberly.

Lenoir cleared his throat. 'For example,' he resumed, 'Monsieur de Vergennes has just passed me a dispatch from our minister in Brussels. He draws our attention to the disappearance of two young girls of good family. They fled their mother's house a few days ago. One is twenty and the other seventeen. The first bears a few marks of smallpox . . .'

He plunged back into the document while Nicolas opened his notebook and began writing.

'That's a good idea, note down these details . . . What were we saying? Yes, smallpox, with a neat waist, blue eyes and black eyebrows. The younger girl also has blue eyes and black eyebrows: she is pretty and a little taller than her sister. They speak French, and also Flemish quite badly. The elder girl speaks English, better than the younger one who only knows a few words. They have a lot of good-quality clothes with them. I have a list here: two linen undershirts, camisoles embroidered in muslin, two yellow silk undershirts, one blue and grey striped satin undershirt, a blue-green dress on a white background with red flowers, a dress with a brown and yellow check pattern, a yellow damask dress, a taffeta dress with gauze embroidery, two white cotton dresses, two cotton undershirts with blue stripes, black and white English-style hats and some pink and blue satin muffs. But it's possible they've disguised themselves as men. They were seen taking the mail coach for France, and there is every reason to suppose they were planning to come to Paris. Since then, there's been no trace of them. I hardly dare imagine the dangers such innocent young girls may run in our capital . . . Look into it, and report back to me.'

'If I find them,' observed Nicolas, 'they'll have to be arrested.'

'Of course. They'll be put out of harm's way in a convent while their family makes arrangements to have them brought back home. If that happens, we'll immediately inform our people in Brussels.'

Nicolas was about to take his leave. His chief made a gesture to detain him.

'One more thing. If I am to believe what Sartine has told me about you, for a long time you were responsible for the safety of the King and the royal family.'

'Damiens's attempt on the late King's life revealed some glaring shortcomings,' replied Nicolas evasively.

'It so happens that the Queen has complained to His Majesty about the presence of mysterious strangers in her gardens at Trianon . . .' He consulted a paper. 'On 10 August, Claude Richard, the head gardener, and his son Antoine came across two women wearing dresses and hats they thought rather strange. The women looked them up and down. A relative of the Queen's had a similar encounter. The King told me about it yesterday after Mass.'

Nicolas gave a grimace of discontent. 'Why have we been informed of this so late in the day? In this kind of affair, speed is a guarantee of success.'

'I have no idea!' said Lenoir, shaking the quill he was still holding. 'The first time the Queen mentioned it to the King, he shrugged it off. She tried again after her servants started getting worried. Look into it and set her mind at rest. Last but not least . . .'

Nicolas could not believe his ears. Was there a shortage of police officers, that everything should be placed on his shoulders at the same time? He did, however, note that the instructions he had just been given implied that he should address the Queen directly.

'Last but not least,' said Lenoir solemnly, 'I am sending you on a mission of State to the cattle farmers in Faubourg Saint-Antoine. I want you to go outside the walls immediately, see the principal representatives and make sure each man takes the appropriate measures. Mutual interest calls for discreet and immediate action. The worst thing would be for the rumour to spread. The panic that would ensue if such disturbing news became known would ruin their business. I repeat, do your best and do it quickly. The King has been informed of the situation and is following the matter personally.'

He punctuated this exhortation with a blow with the flat of his hand. Nicolas, who understood nothing of this final affair, thought it all quite exaggerated. If only he had been able to grasp the nature of this new mission his chief wished to entrust to him!

'Monseigneur, I am your obedient servant, and at the King's command. But may I ask you to clarify—'

'Ah,' said Lenoir, bursting into laughter and making a small gracious bow, 'how absent-minded I am! I was talking to you as if to myself. The thing of it is, our southern provinces are infected by a putrid, pestilent disease which attacks cattle, one that has been making sporadic appearances since 1714.'

'The disease known as anthrax?'

Lenoir looked at him with a touch of surprise. 'Apparently. Not only does this plague affect animals, but the Faculty has established that it could also infect the human population. Where does it come from? you will ask. How has it reached our southern provinces? It actually began ten leagues from Bayonne, in the village of Villefranque, which only survives, it must be said, thanks to its tanneries.'

'So the problem originates with the hides?'

For the second time, Lenoir looked at Nicolas with interest. 'You think quickly, and you think well. These hides are usually unloaded at the port of Bayonne, some of them coming from Holland, but most from Guadeloupe. Be that as it may, the contagion has been rife for years among the Batavians and has destroyed most of the horned animals on our island. Whenever it has shown itself, they have tried burying the carcasses, but we have to take into account the fact that some may be tempted to disinter them in order to get at the leather. And what of the carnivores, like wolves, which try to eat them? These contaminated hides are a danger to those who work with them. For example, a letter from the priest at Salces, in the diocese of Mende in Gévaudan, notifies us that two skinners died within a few days of anthrax on the face, with monstrous swellings on the head, neck and chest.'

'Is there any known cure?' asked Nicolas.

'They keep trying to find one, they keep experimenting. The directors of the Royal Veterinary Schools have set out a presentation of the symptoms which has striking similarities to the description given by the ancients, so striking it's as if it were drawn directly from it. From which these learned men have concluded that we are no more advanced on this matter now than we were in the time of Lucretius, Virgil and Ovid, and that it is vital to bring the spirit of research and enlightenment of our present-day physicians to bear on this important subject. The doctors claim to have cured a patient with a potion composed of red wine from Bordeaux, *Theriaca Andromachi*, extract of cinchona, *contra-herva*, serpentine from Virginia, oil of amber, sweetened spirit of nitre, volatile spirit of eau-de-Luce ammonia, and God knows what else. A real alchemists' stew.'

'But surely, Monseigneur, there is no need to hurry, if the disease is confined to the south?'

'On the contrary! It has been reported that at Ploërmel in Brittany, several peasants have recently died of similar symptoms, after skinning animals who had died of putrid disease.'

'Is there no way to prevent the spread of the contagion?'

The Lieutenant General of Police smoothed his fine lace cravat with an ecclesiastical hand. 'We've certainly tried, as you can well imagine. The only weapons against this contagion are killing and separation. It is necessary to exterminate everything which is infected. That is the only way to save the entire State from this destructive scourge. The government will grant an indemnity to the owners whose cattle are sacrificed. This painful but necessary sacrifice should become easier to swallow if there is a benefit to be had from it! Failing to take such precautions would be fatal, and would make us complicit in the blindness of a rabble who threaten both their own future and the public good.'

'That implies that we must act on a large scale,' objected Nicolas.

'Indeed,' said Lenoir, 'we must not only stop animals moving from one province to another, using cordons of troops, but in villages where the scourge has struck, the cattle must be impounded and isolated. The experience of neighbouring countries proves that the slaughter of sick animals makes it possible to save the healthy ones. We need to convince the peasants of that, or their masters. The problem is when the promised indemnity is late. These delays lead some not to report the plague, in the hope, always a vain one, that their livestock might escape it. Severe measures are and will be taken by the intendants, aided by troops and by brigades of mounted constables. Everything will depend once again on good administration, on the vigilance, exactitude and efficiency of those who are given the task of applying these measures. It is also essential to permit neither the transport nor the sale of animals with the disease. Secret transactions and nocturnal transfers of animals must be suppressed ruthlessly. The worst kind of smuggling in the kingdom would be that of a single sick animal evading the cordons, bringing about the ruin of a whole province and threatening general prosperity!'

'What do you expect of me?' asked Nicolas.

'I want you to make contact with the leading lights of the guild. The regulation of supplies to Paris falls within my jurisdiction. It is absolutely vital to make them realise, although as discreetly as possible, that their salvation and the common interest require them to observe, as if they were gospel, the instructions His Majesty has issued in the southern provinces. They need to be made aware of these instructions and persuaded of their rightness. If they don't understand the reasoning behind these precepts, don't hesitate to raise your voice and remind them in no uncertain manner of their responsibilities. Paint for them a vision of their dead animals, their empty stalls, their reversed fortunes. Paint a picture of Paris hungry or, worse still, decimated by this plague which they themselves will not escape. Make it clear to them how much resentment, indeed anger, there would be towards them on the part of the common people. And if all that is not enough, threaten them with *lettres de cachet* and the Bastille, where I shan't hesitate to throw them if they disobey. But I know you are tactful and persuasive, skilful at brandishing the axe without bringing it down.'

Having no way of defending himself, Nicolas sighed inwardly. Where would he find the time to pursue his investigation at the Saint-Florentin mansion if he had to accede immediately to the Lieutenant General's three requests? Although he had no proof, he suspected Lenoir of deliberately wishing him to answer back, perhaps even to react impatiently or rebelliously, which, in the circumstances, would amount to a refusal to obey. He said nothing, bowed and withdrew without a word. With his hand on the doorknob, he heard Lenoir murmur a last request.

'I almost forgot, Monsieur. While you are conveying my orders to the cattle farmers, make sure you question them about your Marguerite Pindron. You'll find she's quite well known in those circles in Faubourg Saint-Antoine. Oh, one more thing! I have to entertain a person of quality. I am told that you have incomparable taste when it comes to food and drink. May I have your opinion? I have had brought from Strasbourg at great expense a *pâté de foie gras* prepared according to the recipe of the Maréchal de Contades. What should I serve with it?'

'A Hungarian Tokay would be ideal, Monseigneur, but if you want to stay French, I would recommend some quarter-bottles of Chaume, a wine found in Anjou which was a favourite of Madame Catherine, the widow of Henri II.'

'Thank you, Monsieur Le Floch. I am much obliged.'

*

Nicolas did not bat an eyelid, but clenched his teeth. Was he being mocked? As a connoisseur, he had to appreciate his chief's final remarks. Had he hoped to impress a subordinate with a piece of information that was easy enough to gather for someone who had at his disposal the immense army of informers of a police force admired by all the courts of Europe? Nevertheless the conversation had been devoid of aggressiveness or arrogance, and the last question had perhaps been meant as a kind of teasing from a powerful man rather than a gratuitously unpleasant gesture. Lenoir might have been trying to demonstrate that, like his predecessor, he was maintaining standards with authority and perspicacity.

As he was crossing the courtyard of the Gramont mansion, Nicolas felt himself being pulled by the skirts of his coat. Surprised, he turned to discover the jovial face of the young boy from the Grand Châtelet who, over the past few years, had so often taken the reins of his horses as he passed or delivered his letters for him. He had grown, but his cheap brown jacket had not followed suit, leaving his forearms largely uncovered.

'Monsieur Nicolas,' he said, 'the Lieutenant General wishes to see you.'

'I've just come from there!' replied Nicolas with a laugh.

'I meant Monsieur de Sartine,' said the boy contritely.

Nicolas strove to follow the boy, who was bounding along like a goat. He led him through a door in the orchard wall into the grounds of the adjacent mansion. It was here that Sartine had moved as soon as he had been appointed. He loved this new, spacious quarter, which was both well preserved and close to the vibrant centre of the city. Nicolas glimpsed an elegant building beyond the trees. On its steps, he was placed into the hands of an elderly valet who made no attempt to conceal his jubilation at seeing him again. He led him up the stairs to the first floor and admitted him to a sumptuous study of light oak with a barrel-vault ceiling bearing a painting of the Judgement of Paris. Sartine, standing behind a marquetry desk, noticed the visitor's admiring gaze.

'What do you think, Nicolas? The Judgement of Paris for the former Lieutenant General of the Paris police, isn't that appropriate? They must have been trying to flatter me . . .' He smiled. 'Don't worry, it was already here when I arrived.'

Nicolas recognised the jovial Sartine of old: entrance into the King's councils seemed to have done him good. He had given up his black coat, and now he, too, wore, whether by chance or out of loyalty, a silky pearl-grey coat.

'I owe my latest pleasure to you,' Sartine continued. 'What do you think of this wonder?'

He lifted from beneath his desk a sumptuous mass of white curls that tumbled softly over his arms like a cascade of white horsehair.

'Did I have something to do with that?' asked Nicolas.

'Have you forgotten? Not so long ago you told me about that incomparable English shop. Our ambassador went there and found this example. Apparently, it's identical to the one worn by the Lord Mayor of the City of London during ceremonies.'

He put down the wig, whirled round, and gave a little leap which brought him directly face to face with a stunned Nicolas. He took him by the shoulders and led him towards one of the walls of the study. Against it stood a cabinet of richly veined wood with bronze adornments. The most surprising feature was the dozens of ebony buttons, each marked with a number in ivory. The cabinet seemed to be some kind of extraordinary mechanism. Nicolas was immediately reminded of an organ case. With a childlike air of triumph that made him seem younger, Sartine pressed one of the buttons. There was a kind of hiss, as if air were escaping. Nicolas saw himself as a child beside a rock at Le Croisic that siphoned the great equinoctial tides. A series of clicks followed, a slow rattling noise, then jolly music. Again there was a hiss. A panel came sliding out softly, revealing, as if on a tray, a dummy's head wearing a russet wig.

'It's the Würtemberger,' said Sartine radiantly. 'What do you say to my new library of wigs? I can't find any other word for it. I shall have to question the academicians. Can you conceive of such a wonder? They're arranged in an unchanging order, like police files, protected from dust and light, and always ready to spring up on demand.'

'But who, Monseigneur, had the skill to imagine and build such a marvel?'

'And music! Music! I'm sure you recognised the tune of the pagodas from Rameau's *Paladins*. And that's not all. The man who made this has other strings to his bow. This master of the arts, who is attached to Monseigneur the Comte d'Artois and honoured with his protection, is also the inventor of various methods for writing codes. The main one, entitled *Unum toti uni totum*, was shown, in 1769, to the Duc de Choiseul, who granted its maker a bonus of six hundred *livres*. As the father of four children, he now finds it difficult to make ends meet and, despite the commission he received from me for my dear wigs, is looking for employment.'

'What kind of employment?'

'The kind that particularly interests us. He wishes to build a steganographical arcanum. It would be a desk six feet high and three feet wide, with a decagonal cylinder inside it, worked by a stirrup of ten pedals. On different frames, and without using his hands, he claims to be able to write coded messages as rapidly and simply as on a single board, with more than sixty thousand variations – all without any other frames than the ones attached to the cylinder. You see what I'm getting at.'

Nicolas did not see anything at all, but had no desire to disrupt Sartine's good mood. 'Of course, Monseigneur.'

'We know through the Abbé Georgel, secretary to Cardinal de Rohan, our ambassador in Vienna, that our encoding methods have been discovered. He learnt from an informer that Maria Theresa has been intercepting our messages for many months, uncovering our schemes and reading them like an open book. We can hardly be surprised, then, at her ostentatious hostility towards our ambassador – who, incidentally, hasn't made things any easier with his escapades! In short, I am interested in this machine, and I need several things from you. Make enquiries about this inventor, whose name is Bourdier. The last thing we need is to be dealing with someone who is in the pay of a foreign power, someone who makes us a machine and then hands its secrets over to our enemies. I understand your misgivings, but this is a service I require of you. And that's not the most delicate thing I expect of you. You know both the Court and the city, and you know what the situation is. I am opening my heart to you . . .'

Nicolas shuddered at these words.

'His Majesty, alas, has ideas and judgement, but he is limited by an apathy of mind and body. He seems still unformed. Of course, there is no lack of common sense, although hampered by his paralysing laziness of conception and his awkward behaviour. The smallest trifle disconcerts him, as if he were revolted by objections and difficulties. Above all, he is completely lacking in firmness of character and will, the cardinal virtues of a monarch. Anyone who approaches him is soon convinced of that. Of course he knows a certain amount about particular fields . . .'

'He speaks of many things intelligently and with wide knowledge, as I myself can testify,' said Nicolas.

'That's true, but where is the determination to put things into practice? His brother Provence puts it well: "Berry is like those oiled ivory balls which cannot be kept together." He is crucially lacking in egoism and toughness. He is a prince of idylls and moral tales. That is not what the French expect . . .'

Completely horrified by Sartine's words, Nicolas realised that the death of Louis XV had changed many things. This implacable judgement certainly bore the mark of Sartine's cynicism, and such remarks, coming from his former chief, would not have surprised him on any other subject, but they were about their young monarch. That was something to raise alarm bells.

Sartine continued to hold forth as if he were alone. He was now walking up and down the room. 'Since his accession,' he went on, 'the King has proclaimed that he was taught nothing but that he has read a little history and believes that the misfortune of this State was the King's wives and mistresses. Let us pray that he applies this precept to himself! I like the Queen, who protects me.

Nevertheless, I fear the consequences of her inexperience, both for her and for us. The future is getting darker, and I do not believe she has any of the qualities necessary to see the dynasty through possible unrest or to restore it amid all these troubles.'

'And what lessons do you draw from all this, Monseigneur?' asked Nicolas softly.

'My dear Nicolas, two names are currently in the spotlight. One is that of d'Aiguillon whose dubious intrigues you yourself have suffered.[6] The other is Choiseul, my protector, to whom I have, since his fall from favour, remained secretly loyal. He has superior talent and intelligence and the dazzling memory of a long and glorious ministry.'

Nicolas sighed, thinking of his Micmac friend, Naganda, and all those orphaned by the abandonment of New France. What was so glorious about the loss of Canada and the Indies?

'In addition,' Sartine went on, 'he has the support of the *parlements*, whom we always have to go along with, the better to control them. The philosophers' party constantly praises him to the skies. Only the King is against him, having been led to believe that he poisoned his father. Gossip picked up along the way by his nurse, Madame de Marsan, and taken up by his aunts. That's all Mesdames ever talk about, the birdbrains!'

'What about Maurepas?' said Nicolas.

'He carries no weight in this matter, and it will blow up in his face in the end. Maurepas is a puppet, an automaton from the past. Ingratiating and fickle, a subject for amusing anecdotes. He's just for show! He'll fizzle out, he has the same faults as the King. We will have to choose. The Queen will make all the difference, she hates d'Aiguillon.'

He sank gracefully into his armchair and immediately plunged his hands into the wig spread out in front of him, as if trying frantically to untangle its curls.

'Many ministers of the late King are still in place,' he went on. 'They are obstacles that will have to be put aside.' He struck the flat of his desk with his hand. 'The Duc de La Vrillière first of all. I gather he's given you the task of investigating a death that took place in his mansion? Your fall from favour has been brief, you have bounced back even higher than before.'

'Yes, Monseigneur.'

'Yes for the investigation, or for the bouncing back?'

The tone was inquisitorial: this, Nicolas thought, was the Lieutenant General of old.

'You should know,' said Sartine, 'that, contrary to what you think, the master was not at Versailles last night, but in Paris for a romantic assignation – if my information is correct, and it usually is, as you know better than anyone.'

'I will take note of it, Monseigneur,' answered Nicolas prudently.

'It is not enough to take note of it, Monsieur Le Floch. You must also get down to work and, if you believe me, put me in a position to help you.'

'I am your humble servant.'

'This affair is bound up with our interests. Anything that helps to bring down La Vrillière will hasten Choiseul's return. The salvation of the State is at stake. And should you feel any misgivings, think of the unworthy manner in which that depraved individual treated you at the time of the King's death.'

Nicolas, who had not lost his independence of judgement,

recalled that Louis XV had shamelessly chosen him as the instrument of a final intrigue. All that La Vrillière had been doing was following his master's example. But, although long initiated into the ins and outs of the secret world, he was left speechless by Sartine's proposition. Sartine himself walked towards the hearth, seized the poker and again began stirring nonexistent embers. Nicolas saw in this gesture a sense of unease perhaps equal to his own. The minister knew his loyalty and rectitude. He could therefore imagine the revulsion his suggestion must have provoked, and might well be regretting having exposed himself to such a degree.

Nicolas was torn between a number of feelings. Of course, he could take all this quite simply as a mark of the renewed confidence placed in him by Monsieur de Sartine. However, he recalled some unfortunate previous examples of the man's love and inclination for manipulating things behind the scenes. Beneath the veneer of the courtier, beneath the punctilious courtesy of the gentleman, there sometimes reappeared the coldness and inflexibility of someone dealing in hidden things that crouched in the darkness like nocturnal animals. Nicolas, despite his affection and gratitude, suspected him of finding a strange pleasure in such things, a pleasure nourished by a deeply felt contempt for human beings that was born of long years of familiarity with crime and human baseness. In so doing, was he not trying to exert an obsessive control over Nicolas, like the trainer of an animal that has finally been tamed tugging the end of its lead to make sure it is truly submissive? Or perhaps he just wanted to feel that his trust was still considered a favour and thus convince himself that all was not lost in this sad world. As for Nicolas, whatever answer he gave would place him in an ambiguous position. Whether he agreed or refused to yield to Sartine's injunctions, the reasons ascribed to him would not be the correct ones, and the most plausible would appear the least convincing. Bowing to his former chief's request would certainly make him lose his own self-esteem. He was a police officer, not an informer. He decided to be himself and to trust in fate, which had got him out of difficult situations so many times before.

The silence which had fallen was broken by Sartine. 'I asked you a question.'

'There is no doubt, Monseigneur, that you are best placed to make allowances.'

'What do you mean?'

'You have just demonstrated once again that you are the first to be informed of all things. However quick I am, reporting to you would be pointless. In addition, I cannot suppose that the Lieutenant General of Police, who knows everything, will not hasten to respond in detail to any demand you see fit to make of him. Why should I, a poor subordinate, interfere between two such powers?'

Sartine's face turned pale and tense. He began muttering, and Nicolas thought he made out the words 'disciple of Loyala' and 'emulator of the Jesuits of Vannes'. But then he calmed down, and looked at the commissioner with a kind of indulgent commiseration.

'You will never change! Fourteen years in the highest echelons of the police, and here you are, just as you were before, filled with honour and scruples and . . . mental limitations. But not devoid of skill, oh no! Yes, the marquis would be proud of you. The head of a Ranreuil and the skull of a Breton. Stubborn, but still a little innocent – apparently . . .'

'That's the second time in two days.'

'What do you mean?'

'That I've been called innocent. Last night, Monsieur de Noblecourt . . .'

'He's absolutely right. Well, be that as it may. At least promise me you'll let me know if anything in this case is likely to tarnish the throne. You certainly can't refuse that request.'

'I'll do my best, Monseigneur.'

'Now go on, get out of here, you rascal. I suppose you're rushing off to meet up with your usual accomplices and cut up some bloody body or other in order to stimulate that famous intuition of yours.'

Nicolas laughed. 'It's impossible to hide anything from you. Even the future.'

Sartine, half smiling, half angry, wagged a threatening finger at him and sighed.

Nicolas was walking towards the river, his face aflame. Although the interview had ended pleasantly enough, it had left him with a bitter taste in his mouth. He was torn between his joy at having seen his former chief again and a sense of anguish. How difficult life was! In a flash, he saw his father, the Marquis de Ranreuil, striding about the lower hall in the family chateau. While Nicolas, then a little boy, crouched beneath the chimney hood and looked on, the marquis, usually so ready to embrace change, cursed the mediocrity of the times. He missed the heroic days when history was made with great sweeps of the sword and the only skill lay in knowing how to die. He condemned that degenerate nobility 'of parquet floors and wood panelling, cut off from its roots, whose only world is one of ridicule and disputes over etiquette in the drawing rooms of Versailles'. Once again, Nicolas had the feeling of emptiness that had come over him so often since the death of Louis XV. Everyone was acting as if his successor was of no significance. Even Sartine gave the impression that he had broken the sacred bond connecting him with the new monarch. He was no longer the same man, and he seemed interested in nobody but Choiseul, dazzled by a star which Nicolas, colder or less committed, had long judged to be on a declining orbit. He would not have wagered a farthing on the possibility of the hermit of Chanteloup returning to affairs. Everyone knew the distaste, even the revulsion, which the former minister inspired in the monarch. In this situation, who was the real innocent? Sartine no doubt had ambitions to occupy the position of Minister of the King's Household, which had previously escaped his grasp. He still hoped to achieve it with the help of the Queen and Choiseul. The gods always blinded those they sought to bring down. As for himself, if he could prevent yet another disappointment for his protector, he would do so without hesitation.

The foamy ochre Seine was carrying all kinds of doubtful flotsam on its autumn tides. He spotted the carcass of an animal swirling round and round in an eddy, and recalled his conversation with Lenoir. Could that pestilential disease really spread to the whole of the kingdom and infect both animals and people? He continued thinking about this until he reached the gates of the old Châtelet. He sighed, feeling a kind of weariness at the thought of what was about to take place in the secrecy of the cellars of the Basse-Geôle. As he passed, he glanced mechanically at the grim slab where the latest bodies lay, washed and salted. He noted that the watch had been diligent and that the poor wretch fished out of the waters near the Quai des Tuileries was already resting beside his companions in misfortune. He heard the sounds of conversation, and was delighted to recognise the voices of his friends.

'Here is our Nicolas!' exclaimed Dr Semacgus in his bass voice.

He was carefully removing his doublet. Ever since he had abandoned himself to the tender tyranny of a relationship with his maid, the surgeon was always extremely well dressed and took as much care of his appearance as a young man. Beside him, Bourdeau sat on a stool, calmly smoking an old pipe. Nicolas took his snuff box from his pocket. The sight of it brought a pang to his heart: it was a present from Madame du Barry, and the lid bore the face of a young, smiling Louis XV. He shook Sanson's hand and offered him a pinch of snuff. There followed a pleasant session of sneezing.

'In this damp, cold weather,' said Sanson sententiously, 'tobacco protects against congestion and catarrh. Nicolas, Madame Sanson has asked me to tell you that our doors are always open to you and that she would deem it a great honour if you came at your convenience for lunch or dinner.' He blushed and hesitated. 'I should add that the children would be pleased to see their father's friend again.'

'A thousand thanks to your wife,' replied Nicolas. 'I would be glad to come, once this case has been cleared up.'

'Come, gentlemen,' said Semacgus solemnly, 'this is not a drawing room. Let's raise the curtain on the autopsy.'

With a grand gesture, he pulled the jute cloth off the victim's body. Bourdeau had risen, and they all leaned over the table where Marguerite Pindron lay. The torchlight cast their elongated, dancing shadows on the dark walls. Nicolas explained the circumstances under which the crime had been discovered, and also indicated his own estimate of the approximate time of death.

'A fine-looking girl,' said Semacgus. 'What's the temperature in the kitchens of the Saint-Florentin mansion?'

'It was as cold as outside,' said Bourdeau. 'No food had been served the previous night, Sunday, and the furnaces, chimneys and stoves had all been out since Saturday night.'

The two practitioners kneaded the body. Semacgus looked at his watch, said a few words in a low voice to Sanson, and seemed to be thinking hard.

Sanson cleared his throat. 'We believe death occurred sometime between ten and twelve o'clock.'

Nicolas could not conceal his surprise. 'I'm pleased to see that your expertise confirms my own impressions so closely. However, to truly enlighten me, would it not be possible for you to be more precise? Please understand that the peace of mind of the innocent depends on your observations.'

'The young rascal's trying to teach us our job,' grumbled Semacgus, 'even after we let him witness the birth of criminal surgery.'

They all started laughing. An overjoyed Bourdeau took several enthusiastic puffs at his pipe and Nicolas let out a long and very satisfying series of sneezes. He was not mistaken: proximity with the most tangible and terrifying forms of violent death often brought about these bursts of artificial and somewhat forced relaxation. Each man took advantage of them to conceal his emotions – sometimes, his horror.

'Alas,' said Sanson, 'your question contains its own answer. The coldness of the place no doubt slowed down certain natural phenomena. This context complicates our ability to judge and makes it difficult for us to deliver a more exact verdict.'

'As for the rest . . .' resumed Semacgus, who had just taken several shiny instruments from a small varnished wooden case and had noticed Nicolas's curious glance at this fine object. 'You're admiring my casket. You've never seen this one. I acquired it in the Dutch Indies. It's the only one of its kind. Cut to measure from a single stump of rot-proof ironwood.'

'Perfect, I imagine,' continued Nicolas, completing his friend's description, 'for avoiding erosion by dampness and salt while crossing the seas and oceans.'

'Precisely, the essential thing being to preserve my instruments from rust. As for the rest, as I was saying, in other words, the cause of death, it's perfectly obvious. What do you think, my dear colleague?'

Sanson smiled contentedly at this appellation. They leaned over the body. As always at an autopsy, Nicolas could not help comparing them to two crows he had seen as a child on a path on the edge of Vilaine, busy with the carcass of a dead animal. For a while, the usual ceremonial went through its obligatory phases. Constantly coming back to the neck wound, they proceeded with all the necessary examinations.

'Come closer, Nicolas,' said Semacgus, 'and you, too, Pierre. What do we observe? The wound in the hollow beneath the shoulder is deep, funnel-shaped and, by its very nature, fatal. Look how lacerated the inner walls of the wound are and how crushed and compressed the skin is. What do you deduce from that?'

'That we can rule out the use of a sharp instrument,' said Nicolas.

'That the object used was such a strange shape,' said Bourdeau, 'that it created a kind of pear-shaped hole!'

'That's a perfect description.'

Sanson whispered something in the doctor's ear. 'I agree,' he said, 'though I doubt that our friends will savour the experience!'

'As the good apprentices and scholars that we are,' proclaimed Nicolas, 'we accept anything that leads to the truth.'

'Of course, Bourdeau's tobacco and the cooking salt which I suspect is in the commissioner's pocket will help the two of you to bear it.'

Semacgus was alluding to something Fine, Nicolas's nurse in Guérande, always used to ward off the evil spells of the devil. This remark once again set them laughing. Once that was over, Semacgus clenched his fist and resolutely plunged his hand into the neck wound. It fitted almost exactly. The two police officers watched with shock and astonishment.

Bourdeau was the first to break the silence. 'Do you mean to say that someone killed this poor creature with their bare hands?'

Sanson shook his head. 'It isn't our intention to put that forward as a theory. A hand, even one of exceptional strength, would not be able to go through flesh and produce the cuts and compressions we've observed.'

Nicolas was thinking. 'So, if I understand correctly, the murder appears to have been perpetrated using an object shaped like a hand and sufficiently solid to penetrate flesh?'

'Penetration is not essential,' said Semacgus. 'Let's not forget the lacerations and compressions. Note, gentlemen, that the wound is in the right shoulder. From that I conclude either that the victim was attacked from the front, which does not tally with the description of the scene of the crime, or that she was attacked from behind, which would imply . . .'

He placed himself behind Sanson, pressed him against his chest with his left arm, and mimed striking a blow with his right hand.

'. . . that the attacker was armed with an unknown object. But if, unusually, that was the case, a hand would not have been able to twist and still keep its shape and strength.'

'Couldn't the wound,' said Bourdeau doubtfully, 'have been caused by repeated blows with a knife?'

'The cuts would have looked quite different.'

'I'm reminded of the wooden pegs they use for sealing barrels where I come from.'

'There speaks the man from Touraine!'

Semacgus let go of Sanson, who readjusted his plum-coloured coat where it had been displaced by the surgeon's extremely firm grip.

'I think our two practitioners should come to a conclusion,' said Nicolas, who was becoming impatient.

'The young woman died of a fatal blow to the base of her neck. This fatal wound opened the subclavian vessels of the large branches of the axillary artery. This was likely to cause immediate death through loss of blood.'

'As we observed,' said Nicolas.

'But most of it would have been internal,' said Sanson. 'The loss of blood compressed the lungs and suffocation followed.'

'In other words,' concluded Semacgus, 'it was quite unlikely that the victim could have survived.'

'Anything else?' asked Nicolas.

'Ah, yes! The girl had been leading a life of pleasure, and quite recently, too. Some of our observations indicate that clearly.'

'On the evening of the murder?'

'No, the previous day or days. I shan't go into the detail of our observations. They are similar to those noted in prostitutes of the lower class who sell themselves to one man after another.'

'So she indulged in debauchery?'

'Of the most dissolute kind, there's no doubt of it. We found significant erosion, as well as traces of an astringent lotion, the kind that makes it possible to remove all traces of excessive and repeated male penetration.'

'It's an unguent taken from the root of a rosaceous plant, the *pied-de-lion*,' Sanson remarked learnedly. 'The whores use it to repair all kinds of damage.'

'Last but not least,' said Semacgus, handing the two police officers something small and brown at the end of a small pair of pincers, 'this is what we discovered in the "window in the middle". It's an intimate preventive sponge, which proves at least one thing – that the girl was expecting to meet a suitor!'

A long silence fell over the gathering, soon broken by Nicolas's resolute voice. 'Pierre,' he said, 'when we've found the murder weapon, we'll be close to finding the murderer.'

# V

## BETWEEN CITY AND *FAUBOURGS*

His tongue is as a devouring fire.
ISAIAH XXX, 27

Bourdeau and Nicolas were both back in the duty office, the former filling his pipe, the latter preparing his battle plan. Nobody, Nicolas thought, was going to force him to do anything that he had not decided to do himself. Overwhelmed with requests from both the minister and the Lieutenant General of Police, he would take the path dictated by his own free will, certain that whichever he decided upon would be more innocent than any of the others, because it would be in pursuit of the truth. In the order of priorities, one choice appeared to be the imperative one. He would have to keep to it and discard anything superfluous in order to devote himself to what mattered most. He talked about this with the inspector after briefly relating his conversation with Lenoir. As for Sartine's strange request, he preferred to keep silent about it, at least for the moment. However, he did not conceal the question mark hanging over the Duc de La Vrillière's presence at Versailles on the night of the murder.

'Whatever the tasks imposed upon us, my dear Pierre, you know how important it is to solve a crime quickly. We must at all costs find the murder weapon, although I do not harbour any illusions on the subject. The sewer and the river were both quite close. I also need to question the family of the wounded major-domo. There may well be something to be gleaned there.'

'I have the names and addresses of his in-laws, the family of his late wife,' said Bourdeau, taking a paper from his pocket. 'It consists of three people: first of all, his sister-in-law, a nun at the convent of the Daughters of Saint Michel at Notre-Dame de la Charité, in Rue des Postes—'

'Of what order? There are so many in Paris.'

'The establishment was opened by the founder of the Eudists, with female boarders who wish to repent their past sins.'

'The nuns?'

'No, the boarders!'

'What is this person's name?'

'Hélène Duchamplan. Her religious name is Louise of the Annunciation. Then we have the first brother-in-law, Gilles Duchamplan, and his wife, Nicole. Finally, Eudes, the second brother-in-law, the younger of the two, who lives with them in Rue Christine.'

'Try to find out more about these people, and don't slacken with the servants in the Saint-Florentin mansion. One of them is bound to end up saying more than they intended. Let's meet in Rue Montmartre at dinner time. I'd be most surprised if Catherine and Marion couldn't find something for us to eat.'

'Aren't you afraid of disturbing Monsieur de Noblecourt?'

'Of course not. He doesn't have anything in the evenings except a few prunes and a herbal tea. I'm sure he'll be delighted to drink in our company. In fact, it will be an opportunity for him to come out with a few of those finely polished maxims which always seem to be miraculously applicable to the matter in hand.'

As he was leaving Bourdeau, Nicolas consulted his watch: it was midday. Walking out through the main entrance, he stepped aside to let a prisoner's funeral procession pass. He thought with a shudder of that coffin of chipped black wood which, it was said, had been used at the Châtelet for a century for the funerals of dead prisoners, and to which the gaolers gave the humorous nickname 'the pork pie': it had a panel in it which opened to let the body slide out into the common grave. The corpses of drowned people benefited from a different procedure: after being displayed on the stone in the Basse-Geôle, they were transported on a stretcher to the Hospitallers of Sainte Catherine, nuns whose constitutions committed them to washing these mortal remains, wrapping them in shrouds, and burying them in the cemetery of Saints-Innocents.

Amid the hustle and bustle of the street stalls, he hailed a cab. He wanted to get back to Rue Neuve-Saint-Augustin as soon as possible. Confined in the worn velvet of the narrow interior, he sank into a kind of dreamy somnolence which could have been more comfortable. His head half raised, he made out the tops of houses, the balconies, the barred windows, the corbels, and the pompous or grimacing figures decorating the facades of the buildings. When he walked, he mainly observed faces, but, ever since his arrival in Paris, he had realised the danger of admiring the tops of houses: anyone who indulged in this perilous distraction might find himself in trouble when, in a thunderous din, a carriage, cab or wagon suddenly loomed up, leaving him no chance of salvation other than to flatten himself against the wall, his face turned sideways, or to leap through the doorway of a shop.

When he got to police headquarters, he went straight to the offices. Through pursed lips, the first clerk he approached explained that it was necessary to distinguish between living animals and slaughtered meat and that, in consequence, the trade and control of livestock should not be confused with the business of butchery. In short, the person he was looking for did not work with Monsieur Lenoir, due to shortage of space, and he would have to ask for him elsewhere. After much equivocation, he was informed that he would have to go and see Monsieur Poisson in Rue Saint-Marc. Nicolas decided that he would get a horse from the stables of the Lieutenant General of Police, as he had been doing regularly for fourteen years. A groom who was new to the place arrogantly refused him one, and Nicolas, patient as he was and as little inclined to play the marquis, had to restrain himself from shaking the fellow. Champing at the bit, he was forced to go to another employee and request a signed paper. This man detained him for a long time, asking him a thousand trifling questions before agreeing to his demand. Once in the saddle, he regretted that he had not kept the cab. The horse, which was not of his choice, turned out to be restive and rattled several times, either by abruptly pulling up short and then kicking in all directions, or by going as close to the wall as possible at the risk of crushing its rider's leg.

In Rue Saint-Marc, a new discovery awaited him: Monsieur Poisson dealt with wine, fruit and vegetables, while butchery and livestock were the province of Monsieur Imbert, who could be found in Rue Richelieu. That was not far, and he proceeded there immediately. Unfortunately, it appeared that this Monsieur Imbert was indeed involved with meat, and also cattle, but only those that had passed through the city gates and were already the property of the butchers. Therefore he would have to glean the information he sought by addressing himself to Monsieur Collart du Tilleul in Rue de la Soudière, near the market of Saints-Innocents. Nicolas sped to his new destination, tempting his mount with a heap of cabbage.

He had to force open the door of his new interlocutor, who had claimed not to be available. Nicolas entered angrily, regretting that he did not have a riding crop with which to lash his boots. The panic-stricken clerk took shelter behind an unstable pile of official paperwork over the top of which only his trembling black skullcap appeared. His master assured Nicolas that Monsieur Longères, on Place Popincourt, both because of his age and the esteem and trust of his colleagues, appeared to be the primary authority among the cattle farmers in the viscounty and generality of Paris, and the man best able to answer questions from the authorities. Nicolas thanked Monsieur Collart du Tilleul curtly and ordered him to have the restive horse taken back to police headquarters. Exasperated by his mount's capriciousness, he had decided to continue his journey outside Paris by other means. He had to go all the way back to Rue Saint-Honoré before he found a cab cruising for fares. The interior was so dirty and the upholstery so repulsive, with dubious-looking stains, that he had to sit sideways on the very edge of the seat. His policeman's eye spotted a large number of bloodstains, which someone had tried to remove without success. What on earth had this vehicle been carrying? Some wounded person, no doubt, picked up from the gutter and carried home after a drinking session. He lowered the window to get a little air.

The cab advanced by fits and starts, steering a path through the hurrying, distracted crowd. It had to stop in front of a small gathering of laughing girls and boys dancing hand in hand in the middle of Rue du Faubourg-Saint-Antoine to the harsh, merry music of a hurdy-gurdy. The musician wore the costume of his remote province, and was turning the handle with one hand and playing the melody with the other, all the while tapping his clogs in time to the music. Nicolas contemplated this sight with a somewhat nostalgic benevolence. What remained to him of his youth? He remembered running off to the marshes with boys of his age. Then came his interminable studies, gloomy and stifling. He recalled the anguish of school, where, despite his successes, he was despised as a poor orphan by companions who came from the best families in Brittany, and his ambiguous position at the notary's office in Rennes, where his aristocratic connections had made him both envied and despised by the other pupils. Solitude had been his companion throughout these years, illumined however by the tutelary figures of Canon Le Floch and the Marquis of Ranreuil, his father, and by the even more moving figure, now distant and almost faded, of his sister Isabelle. He prayed that his son, Louis, would be spared such vicissitudes.

As they drove through Faubourg Saint-Antoine, in the shadow of the Bastille, he was struck once again by the diversity of the sights on offer. The various strata of the population all came together here: tranquil bourgeois strolling with their families, factory workers out for a good time, rich peasants from the *faubourg* whose costumes looked out of place, brazen women of the streets, and last but not least the armies of beggars and cripples, real or simulated, who poured into the capital of the kingdom from the provinces. Every day, poor wretches arrived by road, attracted by the prestige and illusion of Paris, and hoping to find a solution to their misfortunes and an end to their poverty. Statute labourers, pushed to the point of despair by the unimaginable drudgery of their work and the meagreness of their subsistence wages, would decide to take refuge in the cities, where they swelled the ranks of the destitute. As Nicolas had been observing for years, many of these people became petty thieves, pickpockets, and even murderers, and would end up in gaol, or in chains in the King's galleys, or worse still as pitiful figures on the gallows.

He ordered the driver to turn off towards Popincourt. As soon as they left the main road, the hustle and bustle gave way to a more provincial atmosphere, like that of a large country village. The main open space was shared by workshops, the shops of cabinet makers and artisans, and furniture factories, separated from one another by gardens and farms. The warm, heavy odour of manure imbued the air, chasing away the foul smells of the city. Nicolas noticed a sad troop of cows, their sides covered in mud and slurry, being led towards the city gates, from where they would proceed to the slaughterhouse.

By the side of the road, furniture had been laid out to attract customers. Nicolas remembered with some bitterness having one day bought a small writing desk from one of these workshops.

Monsieur de Noblecourt had been curious enough to climb the stairs to see it. His reaction had disappointed Nicolas: what was the meaning of that stifled laugh? He had been so happy with what he had thought was a genuine bargain that he had been really surprised when, a few weeks later, the desk had simply fallen to pieces. There were many crooks and fakers operating here, and they harmed the reputation of the genuine craftsmen, who were a credit to their guild and true artists in furniture. The dregs of the trade would continue to fabricate phantom constructions which, after a mere couple of weeks, would turn out to be rickety, obsolete and worm-eaten.

In a small dead-end street planted with lime trees, he finally came to a collection of rustic buildings surrounded by cowsheds, gardens and orchards. A woman sitting on a milestone looked at him curiously and confirmed that he was indeed outside the house of old Longères. He got out of the cab and paid the driver, who obstinately kept his hat pulled down over his face. Nicolas observed that the carriage had the number 34, followed by an N and the regulation two capital Ps on a white background. He laughed at the coincidence: the initial of his Christian name, and his own age. He was unsure whether or not to notify the transport office about the filthy state of the cab. In the end, he decided to drop it, given that favourable registration number. It was a weakness of his to believe in signs: although he claimed to be a good Parisian, his Celtic soul often came to the surface.

Cautiously, he entered the farm, anxious not to provoke a nasty-looking yellow dog which was barking and pulling on a rope. A stooped elderly man emerged from a lean-to. His face was lined and weather-beaten, and a crown of sparse white hair framed a skull covered in brown blotches. He was wearing a brown jacket with horn buttons, grey breeches, rough woollen stockings and sturdy hobnailed clogs. Leaning with both hands on a gnarled stick, he looked at the intruder without saying a word.

'Monsieur,' Nicolas said, feigning a detached, casual air, 'would you be able to tell me where I could find Monsieur Longères?'

The man turned aside and spat. 'Do you want the young one or the old one? If it's the old one, here I am.' He angrily kicked the beaten earth. 'Not the same bloody story again, damn it! We've already told you everything's been settled. I'd have thought the commissioner was satisfied. It's not going to look good for us. To tell you the truth, I'm the one who has to see to all that, and it doesn't make me popular in spite of my white hair . . .' He threw a stone at the dog, which was howling. 'Shut up, Sartine!' He gave Nicolas a sideways glance. 'No offence. He's a good guard dog.' He laughed and slapped his thigh with his hand.

Nicolas was smiling to himself. He had previously come across a parrot bearing the name of the former Lieutenant General of Police. He pretended to understand the meaning of the farmer's speech, convinced that the truth sometimes emerged from the most incoherent statements.

'I can well imagine,' he said solemnly, 'that your task has not been easy in these circumstances. And how did you first become aware of them?'

'No one told me anything. But everyone was talking about it, and then the police arrived. Otherwise, we keep our own house in order, if you know what I mean. Anyone who doesn't play fair, we obviously try to find out what's happening, confound the culprit and drive him away without any kind of trial, even if he doesn't want to go.'

'Let's be clear about this, Monsieur. If I understand correctly, when you discover a criminal in your ranks, your first reaction is to dispense justice, whatever his resistance?'

'That's right! My God, you're quick on the uptake!'

'Why, what did you imagine?'

'That you were from the police, and that you were investigating the traffic in spent grain.'

'Spent grain?'

'That's right, spent grain! You get it from the breweries, which are only too happy to get rid of it. Take the ripe crushed barley they've put to ferment. Well, some of us, the crooks among us, grab the residue at a low price and feed the cattle with that rubbish. And when I say some . . .'

'Well?'

'Well? Don't try and mollycoddle me. The animal swells up, the meat is spoiled, and the buyer has been had. Even the weight is faked: everyone's a loser, except the crook!' He stamped his foot in indignation. 'Me, I love my animals, Monsieur. I feed them like they're my own children. Well, that's all in the past. Why are you here? What do you want?'

'Don't worry, Monsieur Longères, my presence has nothing to do with the fraudulent use of spent grain. The Lieutenant General of Police, Monsieur Lenoir, has given me the task of informing your honourable guild of the dangers of an epidemic of anthrax which is spreading to several provinces of the kingdom.'

Nicolas was trying desperately to find a way to introduce the case of Marguerite Pindron. He explained, with a wealth of details, the reason for his coming to Popincourt, the scale of the epidemic, its consequences, and the risks incurred, while insisting on the government's desire to take precautionary measures. He sprinkled his words with so many veiled threats and admonishments that old Longères, horrified by what he heard, hunched over his stick, abandoning his own propensity to chatter.

'So,' continued Nicolas, 'what you need to do, immediately – but at the same time without raising the alarm because, as I'm sure you realise, any panic would be seen as your fault – is inform your colleagues of the present danger and the risks they are running, and insist on the importance of taking the necessary precautions.'

At this point, he respectfully touched on the King's kindly concern for his people, as well as that of his ministers and the Lieutenant General of Police, not to mention the *parlement*, in an affair so heavy with consequences for the life and smooth running of the kingdom. He punctuated his words with sweeping gestures, deliberately looking insistently at different parts of the cowsheds, as if trying to make an inventory of the contents and detect some anomaly. He strode towards one of the buildings and then immediately changed direction before again veering off, followed by the farmer, who had become extremely alarmed by this inquisition and the flood of words that accompanied it.

'Gather your colleagues, explain the situation,' Nicolas resumed, forcefully. 'The information needs to be passed to everyone in your guild, from Popincourt to Ivry, where there are so many dairies, and from Vincennnes to Chaillot. By the way . . .' he had decided to try a direct shot, '. . . how is old Pindron?'

The man stopped, as if taken aback by something incongruous. 'Old Pindron? The poor man died last year. A sad story, Monsieur, a really sad story. A good man. Yes. Not much of a laugh. No, certainly not much of a laugh, always stubbornly refused a drink. But a fine man, an honest man, who knew his job. Alas, his daughter killed him, or as good as. I assume you know the story?'

'Not all the details.' Nicolas was pleased with his ruse. He had hit the target at the first shot.

'A little madam who brought misfortune to two families. I have no hesitation in saying that. Yes, she killed the old man and launched a poor boy on a career of misfortune.'

'I'd like to hear all about it – if you have time, that is.'

'Certainly, Monsieur. Monsieur . . .?'

'Nicolas Le Floch, commissioner of police at the Châtelet.'

'By God, I knew it! Accept my hospitality and have a drink. Talking makes you thirsty, and so does listening. To tell you the truth, with age, my legs grow heavy. If I stand too long, I'm likely to take root.'

Old Longères led him to the elongated one-storey main building. They walked down a few steps into a vast room with a floor of beaten earth and whitewashed walls. A dresser, a long, worn oak table with two parallel benches, a resplendent copper drinking fountain and a fireplace with a trammel were the only furnishings. Old Longères clapped his hands. Immediately, an elderly maidservant limped in to take her master's orders. She went back out through a door in the corner of the room and down to the cellar, and came up again with a pitcher and two thick glasses. They sat down at the table, and the host poured a little raspberry-coloured wine.

'It's Suresnes, fresh from the cask.'

He pushed a bowl of walnuts towards Nicolas, and himself grabbed two and cracked them in his fist. The crumbs fell on his brown jacket.

'You can imagine the kind of things people said in the *faubourg*,' he began. 'That a beautiful girl from a good home should refuse the hand of a worthy suitor, a gardener like his father before him, was a real scandal. How could she reject the union of the garden and the farm? The fortunes of the Pindrons and the Vitrys would have been linked and everyone would have been satisfied. Why did she have to give it all up? It's as if, begging your pardon, she had a fire between her legs! Oh, I know what they said, that her suitor was a bit of a simpleton, that he wasn't able to charm her and drive out her crazy ideas. But isn't that what happens when people get married? They have to realise that self-interest is more important than excitement. That's what it's like in the *faubourg*: the only things that matter are the animals and the plants! What girls really want doesn't count. But believe me, marriages are no worse for that.'

'So it had a tragic end?'

'More than tragic! It killed old Pindron. We have a sense of honour round here. Madame Pindron sold everything to buy an annuity, and disowned her only daughter. She retired to her native province, far away from the scandal.'

'What happened to the daughter?'

'She vanished! No one's had any news of her. Oh, there've been rumours, every now and again. Some say she's in La Force prison, others say they saw her dancing with a bear at a fair on the boulevards, and some claim she's walking the streets around

Quai Pelletier and even that she's trawling for men in the wooden pyramids on the banks of the river, where you get all kinds of dissolute characters. Lord knows if there's any truth in these tales.'

'And what about the suitor?'

'Young Vitry? Anselme? He abandoned the garden and the vegetables he loved so much, not to mention his parents. They say he was seen in the Faubourg Saint-Marceau, rolling in the gutter. I heard that he caught a foul disease and did so many mad things that he was locked up in Bicêtre, either with the patients suffering from venereal disease or with the lunatics. That's quite some misfortune! The Vitrys don't want to have anything more to do with him.'

Nicolas had heard enough. To allay suspicion, he made another pointless speech about the epidemic, drank a few glasses of wine, ate some walnuts, then took leave of his host. Longères, delighted by his visit, made him promise firmly to return. He vowed that everyone – God bless the young King – would do their duty and strive to preserve the city from the anticipated calamity. If anyone grumbled, he himself would plunge his pitchfork into their backside. All the same, he had to point out, without wishing anyone any harm, that the butchers shouldn't be forgotten, and that the police should check that they really had certificates and receipts from those who sold them their animals. Not to mention their obligation to slaughter within twenty-four hours after purchase.

Nicolas promised everything that was asked for.

Once in the street, he regretted having paid his fare and dismissed the cab. He found himself forced to go back to Rue du

Faubourg-Saint-Antoine to find transport. Paris awaited him, and a projected visit to the major-domo's family. But before that, he planned to question Jean Missery's sister-in-law. Once past the Bastille, he would take Rue Saint-Antoine, then Rue Saint-Honoré as far as the junction with Rue Saint-Jacques, then turn right into Rue Planche Mitray, a true source of pestilence where you had to hold your nose, cross Pont Notre-Dame and the Petit Pont, carry on as far as Rue de l'Estrapade until, behind the Sainte-Geneviève Abbey, and not far from Place de la Vieille Estrapade, he reached Rue des Postes, where the house of the Daughters of Saint Michel was located.

He hailed a spruce-looking, freshly polished two-wheel carriage. He called out his destination to the coachman, then lost himself in his reflections, his eyes half closed. His little trip to Popincourt had proved highly instructive. Not only had he fulfilled to the letter his mission regarding the preservation of the cattle of Paris – or had that been only a pretext to send him in search of information about Marguerite Pindron? – but he had also learnt a great deal. When you thought about it, it was obvious that, as far as the anthrax was concerned, anyone else could have done the job as well as he had. Did that mean that Lenoir knew more than he had revealed? Was there, in spite of appearances, some kind of collusion between the minister and the head of police? Was the Duc de La Vrillière trying to control the progress of the commissioner's investigation? And yet, if Sartine was to be believed . . . But was he telling the truth or did he have some cards up his sleeve which changed the whole game? He shouldn't get carried away, thought Nicolas, shouldn't let his imagination run away with him. Take the bare facts as they came, sift through them, compare them, follow the new leads that were opened up. The Pindron girl had left her family home to escape an arranged marriage. Everything suggested that, having fallen into debauchery, she had wandered the streets of Paris before becoming, after who knew what encounters and what rebuffs, a chambermaid to the Duchesse de La Vrillière. The contradictions, heightened by the fog of hatred among this group of servants, a veritable battlefield of rivalries and jealousies, were endlessly intriguing. Nicolas vowed to take a closer look at the tangle of relationships among the occupants of the Saint-Florentin mansion. He even envisaged drawing up, in the form of a written document, a detailed picture of the testimonies they had so far gathered. He would also have to dispatch an officer to question the Vitry family, apparently market gardeners in Faubourg Saint-Antoine. The smallest piece of information would help to reconstruct the whole mosaic. He himself would go to Bicêtre, which he did not yet know, despite Monsieur de Sartine's recommendations to him to visit it. He recalled the grave air he had adopted whenever he happened to mention this establishment, which, he said, was comparable in horror to the hell described by Dante.

The coachman's cries of encouragement to his horse drew Nicolas from his meditations. The slope leading up to Place de la Vieille Estrapade, the highest point in the city, was steep. The services of the Lieutenancy of Police had recently examined a project for a hydraulic system to bring river water from the Port à l'Anglais with a view to building a public drinking fountain. Owing to the problems of transportation, the price of water was constantly increasing, and was a burden on the poorest inhabitants. Admittedly, in the past few decades, especially under the late King, this type of construction had proliferated in the city. The carriage set off again with difficulty, just in front of the sparkling sign of the monumental mason Caignard, who, it was said, could supply all kinds of tombs and epitaphs. At the entrance to Rue des Postes, he spotted the office where those Parisians who ventured out at night could hire children to carry lanterns for them. These lanterns were duly numbered, and their carriers registered by the police, who issued them with a stamped licence. Naturally, these young people also served as spies, and their daily reports were part of the gigantic spider's web whose threads all led back to the Lieutenant General of Police. Nicolas saw a group of austere buildings in the middle of which there rose a grim openwork steeple. His cab stopped, and the coachman pointed out the house of the Daughters of Saint Michel.

This time, Nicolas made sure he asked the driver to wait. Knowing what these men were like, he promised him a princely tip if he found him waiting faithfully at his post. In the corner of a massive door, he saw a handle which he supposed set off a distant bell, and was surprised, when he pulled the mechanism, to hear a metallic clanging from somewhere nearby. Some time passed before the wicket was opened. He introduced himself and stated that he wished to see Sister Louise of the Annunciation. The wicket closed again with a snap and his wait began. The door opened at last. The figure of a tall nun appeared, silhouetted against the light. She admitted him, then carefully closed the door behind him with a suspicious glance at the outside world. She glided rather than walked along the waxed tile floor of a long dark corridor, lit only at its end by a high stained-glass window depicting Saint Michel slaying the dragon. He was introduced into a kind of parlour on the left, where the only furniture consisted of two armchairs with old-fashioned upholstery.

'I am listening, Commissioner. I am Sister Louise of the Annunciation.'

The high-pitched voice took him by surprise. Behind him, a little slip of a woman had entered without a sound, so short that he had to lower his eyes to see her. She was as tall as she was wide, almost a dwarf, like one he had seen dancing with a macaque in aristocratic dress at the Saint-Germain fair. She had a puffy, blotchy oval face, and her half-closed eyes were deep-set, as if sunk into the skin. She had full lips, and was smiling vaguely. In her hands, she was twisting a rosary with black beads. With a movement of her head, she motioned him to sit down.

'Sister,' said Nicolas, 'I think that you know of the events which justify my presence and oblige me to disturb your holy work?'

'The world, Monsieur, is beyond these walls. Nothing can disturb the peace of this place. Are we to suppose that your arrival has some connection with one of our boarders? These sinners sometimes feel the tug of the devil long after they have come here.'

'Don't worry, that's not what this is about. Have you had any news of your brother-in-law, Jean Missery, major-domo to the Duc de La Vrillière?'

The nun's slit-like eyes narrowed even more, like those of a cat pretending to sleep. 'I have hardly seen him since the death of my sister, except at masses marking the anniversary. And even before that . . .'

She left the sentence unfinished. Nicolas said nothing: he was good at waiting.

'I always deplored that marriage,' she resumed. 'My sister wouldn't listen to me. Alas, it killed her.'

He could not let such a statement pass unchallenged. 'What do you mean by that?'

'That the Lord did not bless it and that its still-born fruit killed my sister.'

She opened her hands and the rosary fell, but she did not take any notice. Nicolas picked it up and handed it to her. She resumed speaking.

'But do you think he was stricken with remorse and contrition? Of course not. I doubt that he deserved such grace. At first, he feigned grief, and those who did not know him may have believed he was sincere. However, in the heat of charity, apparent zeal is only a passing mood, and not a movement of that same grace. It is only too true that the Lord knows our powerlessness . . . Perdition to him through whom scandal arrives! And as for us, we complain in secret that we are not permitted to condemn out loud, for one does not work for one's own salvation by neglecting that of one's brothers . . .'

What on earth, thought Nicolas, did this obscure speech mean? What was the point of such a pompous declaration? What dark resentment led her to these words full of bitterness and innuendo? He would have to bring her down to earth.

'Sister, Jean Missery was stabbed last night.'

'He's dead, then,' she said immediately.

He did not reply. The sentence was ambiguous. Was it a question, a statement, a kind of challenge, or was she trying to confirm something she already knew, something she had long wished for?

'I shall accuse myself in public confession of the joy that I feel,' she resumed. 'May God have mercy on him: "He puts no trust in His holy ones, and the heavens are not pure in His sight."'

He still could not determine whether or not she knew anything about what had happened. He would not have sworn to it.

'Don't you find your resentment quite surprising, Sister, you who wear that robe of pity and compassion?'

Her little eyes glittered with a cold light, and her voice turned very shrill. 'Pity? Compassion? Did he ever have any towards my sister? Did he ever show the least respect for her memory? He preferred to wallow in the mud, and let the beast immediately awaken in him . . .' She was wringing her hands. 'I say this quite bluntly: even if he had asked God to free him from the evil passions that possessed him, do you think that deep down he wished that prayer to be granted? What he wanted, he only half wanted. And to only half want something, means, as far as the result is concerned, not to want it at all.'

'I understand your emotion, Sister, but what exactly are you referring to?'

'I'm referring to the various criminal attachments in which my brother-in-law indulged after my sister's death. His heart was constantly occupied by the perverse concerns of his base being. He put all his senses at the service of his animal desires, adding the scandal of his dissolute conduct in public. Even the walls of this house were shaken by it.'

'And for these very human sins, did he deserve to lose his life? Could he not have made amends?'

She was looking at him suspiciously. 'There are a great many minds, my brother, with which there is no other stand to take but that of silence and disapproval. Whatever you say or do, you will never change them: "If your eye offends you, pluck it out, if your hand offends you, cut it off."'

'What I don't understand,' said Nicolas, 'is this hatred for a man who no longer had any connection with you.'

'My sister's marriage verged on misalliance. Consider that. To marry a man who was nothing but a servant!' The little woman rose to her full height.

'Would it not have shown humility to consent to a union sanctified by a sincere mutual affection?' asked Nicolas.

'You speak of it very lightly. Not content with getting his hands on a large dowry, he inherited from my sister a substantial fortune which would return to its legitimate source if he died.'

'Its legitimate source?'

'Us, the Duchamplans.'

Nicolas paused, then said, 'Sister, at this juncture I must ask you to clarify a certain number of points.'

She sat down, put her rosary back inside her sleeve, and her face reflected a kind of benign placidity.

'The words of the Gospel,' Nicolas went on, 'edifying as they may be, are not enough to illuminate more material facts. How were you kept informed of the dissolute life your brother-in-law had been leading since he became a widower?'

She shook her head in disgust, as if to say that these debauches had started even before her sister's death, perhaps when they were first married. 'My family kept me informed, as was only right: I am the eldest . . .'

'I must insist. You appear very familiar with everyday life at the Saint-Florentin mansion.'

She looked at him in silence, with a contemptuous expression on her face, as if he were talking nonsense.

'Madame,' Nicolas went on, 'I remind you that you must answer the questions of a magistrate engaged in a criminal investigation. I have the power to arrest you if I consider that you are not being as honest as I would have hoped. Do you understand that?'

'Do not threaten me, Monsieur. Do I, a poor Daughter of Saint Michel, need to remind you that your authority ceases where that of the Church begins?'

'What does that mean?'

'That, as a nun of this house, I am dependent on the abbot of Sainte-Geneviève, who has rights of lower, medium and high justice in the jurisdiction of his bailiwick. And please don't tell me that these rights were suppressed by Louis the Great in 1674. Later edicts have restored them to their legitimate holder.'

'I see, Sister, that you are very clever, argumentative, and a stickler for the rules, with a degree of knowledge hardly in keeping with the habit that you wear!'

'My late father, Commissioner, was a sealer of verdicts at the Châtelet.'

'That's as may be, but why argue in such an acerbic tone? You are not incriminated, as far as I know. I haven't forgotten my lessons, and I know that the monarchy prevails over all other authorities, although there is little danger that we will reach that point. There remain, nevertheless, some flaws in your reasoning. You're forgetting a vital detail, for example: the restoration of the rights of justice of which you speak is clearly defined in the texts as referring only to enclosures, courtyards and cloisters. Now, as far as I know, your house is located in Rue des Postes and not within the limits of the abbey. Therefore you are within my legitimate power.'

She immediately bristled, purple with rage. 'I shall appeal to the ecclesiastical authorities, I shall appeal to the Archbishop.'

'I know Monseigneur de Beaumont very well. In his position, he can hardly be expected to listen to an insignificant nun who rejects the justice of her King.'

She grew even more purple with outrage. 'I shall not yield.'

'Well, persist in this obstruction and I shall go to a magistrate and request a monitory, compelling you to reveal to your superiors everything you know about this case. After three monitories without response, you will be excommunicated.'

'All right, what do you want to know?'

'Who kept you informed of Jean Missery's conduct in the Saint-Florentin mansion?'

'It is painful for me to have to mention a highly placed lady, the Duchesse de La Vrillière, who, as you seem to be unaware . . .' here, her voice became ingratiating, even mocking, '. . . is a benefactress of this house. Without her charitable support, how could we hope to care for our unfortunate boarders?'

'So it was she who kept you informed?'

'She told me that for months he had been completely besotted with a little hussy, a girl of the streets who had entered her service. The duchesse had rejected her at first, but her husband had insisted. It made her weep with humiliation, and in her pain she came to our altar to pray for the duc's soul. I would pray with her.'

'So the duc, too . . .'

Sister Louise of the Annunciation closed her eyes with a sorrowful air.

'Didn't your brothers try to persuade the widower to behave in a more decent fashion?' Nicolas asked.

'The older one is spineless and the younger one lives a carefree life. As for my sister-in-law, she just keeps complaining instead of giving me nephews.'

'One last thing,' said the commissioner. 'What were you doing on the night of Sunday to Monday, let's say from seven o'clock in the evening to seven o'clock in the morning?'

'I was sleeping in my cell, until prime. Everyone here will confirm that.'

'I shall leave you now, Sister, but I would ask you to think carefully and see if you can recall anything that might be of interest to me.'

He took his leave of her. At the door, he turned and saw her standing a few paces behind him, on the alert. He could not resist a parting shot. 'I almost forgot. Your brother-in-law is not dead. His wound was only superficial. His mistress, on the other hand, was indeed murdered.'

She swivelled round like a top and disappeared through another exit, while the extern sister who had accompanied him came running to open the door.

'Why should Sister Louise run away like that?' he asked. 'I thought she was more concerned with decorum.' He thought he heard a little laugh in response. 'Sister,' he continued, 'when was the last time the Duchesse de La Vrillière visited your establishment?'

'Madame de Saint-Florentin? It's strange you should mention her. She was here just this morning and had a long talk with Sister Louise . . .' She burst out laughing. 'She's going to get up on her high horse again because of that, and . . . we'll be the ones to pay.'

'At what hour does the community retire?'

'At eight o'clock.'

'Sister Louise, too?'

'Oh, no, *she* has privileges. Her family has given so much money to this house that she sometimes dines in town.'

'On what days?'

'On Sunday evenings. With her brother, they say.'

'What about last Sunday?'

'Yes, she was out that night.'

He thanked her and left. In Rue des Postes, he found his coachman waiting impatiently. Night was already falling: he had to join Bourdeau. He was still reeling from what he had just learnt. So Louise of the Annunciation knew everything! She had tried to deceive him. What a dissembler! With that air of hers that would have made the most resolute slink away, she had hidden behind legal technicalities and taken him where she had wanted him to go. She had led him up the garden path, making him look a fool, much to her own amusement.

That mixture of anger, genuine confidences and clever omissions made him confused and uneasy. It was not easy to tell the difference between a truthful presentation of facts and a subtle attempt to divert suspicion. After all, she herself had revealed to him the interest the Duchamplans might have in Jean Missery's death. That reinforced the idea that they had been alarmed at the widower's passionate attachment to a young girl like Marguerite Pindron, especially if, since her escape from the *faubourgs*, she had acquired a certain experience. Whether that man, grief-stricken and tormented by desire, had managed to win her heart or she herself had discovered where her interest lay, a marriage could only be harmful to the expectations of the Duchamplan family. Marguerite had become a threat and an obstacle.

But her death did not resolve the matter. If the widower became infatuated with someone else, then the fortune he had inherited from his wife would melt like snow in the sun. Examples abounded, both at Court and in the city, of men of his age so ruled by their senses that they yielded to the most extravagant demands of greedy young girls, who in their turn hastened to transfer the goldmine to some good-looking and hot-blooded secret lover. In this way, a fortune could vanish in the blink of an eye. It would therefore seem much more sensible to get rid of the widower rather than his mistress, the latter being merely a stopgap solution. Admittedly, thought Nicolas, the Duchamplans were one lead among many others. He recalled Sister Louise's reaction to his announcement that her brother-in-law had been wounded. What had she known at that point? What had the Duchesse de La Vrillière told her during their long interview that morning? Nicolas recalled having told the duchesse at the Saint-Florentin mansion the previous evening that the major-domo was wounded and that it seemed likely he had turned on himself the weapon with which he was believed to have cut his mistress's throat.

The nun's reaction seemed false if that was what she had been told. Had she assumed that the facts were known, or did she have some hidden reason not to believe in the suicide theory?

It was already dark when Nicolas's carriage dropped him in Rue Montmartre. His sudden appearance interrupted the baker's boys from the shop on the ground floor as they were mercilessly teasing the bell ringer of the dead. This old man, dressed in a dalmatic adorned with an embroidered silver skull and crossbones, was shaking his bell with one hand and holding a lantern in the other, and calling out in a pitiful tone his lugubrious refrain:

> *'Wake up, wake up, all you who sleep,*
> *Pray for the dead who lie so deep!'*

He thanked Nicolas, who slipped him an *écu* before reprimanding the baker's boys with a smile. As soon as he entered the servants' pantry, he sensed that something dramatic had occurred. Marion sat slumped on a bench, her head in her hands, while Poitevin was polishing with fanatical care a pewter ewer which did not require so much attention. Only the sight of Bourdeau in an apron and of Catherine beside him, the two of them bent over the bread oven, reassured him somewhat. They did not seem to be part of the atmosphere of anxiety that weighed on the house.

'What's going on?' asked Nicolas.

'Oh, Monsieur Nicolas,' moaned Marion, 'our master was taken ill when he came back from Saint-Eustache. As you know, he's a churchwarden of his parish. This evening there was a meeting of the council. He came back completely red in the face, with the veins sticking out on his forehead! He collapsed in the doorway.'

'I went to fetch the doctor,' said Poitevin, 'the same one who tended Monsieur when he was attacked.[1] God be praised, Dr Dienert was at home in Rue Montorgueil, and came running immediately. At first, he suspected an apoplexy. We laid Monsieur down – he had already regained consciousness. We made him take some drops of *alcali fluor* diluted in water, as well as a decoction of tamarind, and we also made him tighten his garters to slow down the rush of blood to his head. He's much better now. He asked us not to bother you with his condition, he says he'll receive you with Monsieur Bourdeau as soon as you've finished eating. That's bound to cheer him up.'

Despite this advice, Nicolas was already rushing upstairs. Catherine stopped him with an emphatic look.

'Don't move, he'd only think he's worse than he is. He's quite all right. I should know. He's just too edgy. Something got on his nerves. Bourdeau was there, he'll tell you.'

Nicolas sighed, telling himself that Catherine, a former canteen-keeper in the King's armies and something of a witch, possessed the skill and the means to treat many illnesses, and that he himself had often benefited from her care.

'I gave him some liquid to counter it, the kind that you know,' she whispered in his ear.

He went upstairs to change after this day of constant errands, following Mouchette up the concealed staircase that led to his quarters. As usual, she kept putting her head between the bars and giving provocative little cries as she slouched up the steps. Every time he made a move to grab hold of her, she leapt out of his reach. Feeling fresher, he went back to the servants' pantry and discovered an unusual spectacle.

Bourdeau was hopping on the spot and moaning as he placed some steaming puffed-up rolls, which gave off an appetising odour, on the large table in the pantry. Once he had divested himself of his burden, he blew on his burning fingers and rubbed them on the vast apron that enveloped his paunch. Meanwhile, Catherine was bustling at the stove. Nicolas's nose quivered: the aroma of roast poultry reminded him how hungry he was.

'Oh, oh!' moaned the inspector. 'It's hotter than hot.'

'Your little creatures seem done,' said Catherine. 'I'll take out the pot.'

'Please don't lift the lid – the taste would escape with the steam. You should leave them to cool in their own juice.'

'Jesus, Mary and Joseph!' cried Nicolas. 'What feast is being prepared here? Is this some gluttonous annexe of Ramponneau's?[2] Have we been transported to Gargantua's pantry or to his "painted cellar" of Chinon?'

'He doesn't know how right he is!' cried Bourdeau, delighted.

Marion put a finger to her lips. 'My God, how noisy you all are. You're going to wake Monsieur.'

'A cousin of mine from Chinon is visiting my house,' explained the inspector. 'As a feast was expected and I didn't want to take Marion and Catherine by surprise, I plundered Madame Bourdeau's preparations and brought what we needed. Catherine lent me a hand baking the *pâtons*.'

'The *pâtons*?'

'Yes, here they are, all hot. Where I come from, they're called *fouées.*'

Bourdeau brought out a vast wicker basket from under the table. From it, he extracted an earthenware pot covered with an oiled paper tied with straw, and three bottles of wine.

'A *fouée*,' he went on, 'is like bread but much better. Ground flour, leaven, salt and water. Knead it well then let it rest. After that, you just have to shape the *pâtons* by hand, then into the oven with them. They pretend to ignore the heat, they move, shake, rise, swell, form bubbles, climb, collapse, rise again, relax, and finally turn golden brown, and you take them out and burn your fingers. That's the whole story!'

He grabbed one of these little treats, cut it with a knife, and opened the earthenware pot to reveal an immaculately white layer of fat. This he removed, then took out some crushed *rillettes* with which he stuffed the roll. Nicolas's mouth was watering at the mere sight of this operation. He only took a mouthful: it melted in the mouth, so well did the whole thing combine the crusty and the soft. The heat loosened the meat, which in turn moistened the bread with its juices.

'The secret of good *rillettes*,' said Bourdeau with his eyes lowered, 'lies in matching the pieces of pork used. These are of my own invention. I put in shoulder, loin, tenderloin, and belly, and add plenty of salt, pepper, herbs and spices. Plus my secret, which I shall reveal to you: a spoonful of honey and a splash of white wine! Add water until everything is covered and leave for six hours. When the whole thing has cooled down, I knead it and mix the meat and the fat.'

'You're a saint, my dear Pierre . . .'

Bourdeau continued stuffing the *pâtons*.

'And still the *fouées* keep coming!'

'Indeed,' a sepulchral voice suddenly proclaimed, 'it's not a fairy tale but a *fouée* tale!'

Monsieur de Noblecourt had appeared, draped in an indoor robe of wine-coloured calico, his head wrapped in a knotted madras.

Everyone laughed and cried out. A chair was brought forward and the newcomer dropped majestically onto it. Marion began complaining loudly about his foolhardiness, but Catherine, delighted by the turn that the evening had taken, calmed the old nurse.

'I'm starving,' said Noblecourt. 'My bedroom was gradually filling with sweet aromas that tickled my nose. Cyrus's nose, too, I think!'

The dog, who was lying under the armchair, barked happily at his master's voice. Bourdeau and Nicolas sat down in their turn. More *fouées* were prepared, which the magistrate gobbled up. He demanded wine.

'Where is this nectar from?'

'From a small, well-exposed vineyard, covered with flint gravel. Small peach trees grow between the vines. Their fruit with its pink and white flesh bursts with a thick, delicious juice . . .'

'Talking about fruit,' continued Noblecourt, 'no prunes and sage tea for me tonight. I'm eating and drinking. Does that good Dr Dienert think I don't know he suspected apoplexy? Why should I be living on light and not very nourishing food, and depriving myself of strong liquor, spicy and tasty food? From now on, I am going to stuff my face, and seek out violent passions, excessive heat and excessive cold!'

He looked around provocatively at his audience.

Catherine clapped her hands. 'Where there is appetite, there is no danger!'

'In truth,' said the procurator, 'the joy of finding myself surrounded by my friends tempers my irritation.'

'Tell us what happened,' said Nicolas. 'Nothing is likelier to calm the temperament and dispel an anxiety than to talk about it freely.'

'How right you are. You all know that I am a churchwarden of my parish, Saint-Eustache, and that I'm the oldest on the council. At six o'clock, I was there, dealing with council matters, when a man named Bouin suddenly appeared and demanded to be heard immediately. He was kicking up such a fuss that in the end we agreed to see him. All puffed up with arrogance, he introduced himself as a former timpanist of the company of the King's gendarmes.'

'There's that one,' said Nicolas, 'plus four companies of bodyguards: Charost, Noailles, Villeroi and d'Harcourt.'

'He continued in a shrill tone and told us quite bluntly that the King having granted, through the edict of 1756, the right of commensality to the timpanist of his gendarmes, after twenty years of service, of which this Bouin fellow felt justly proud, he should therefore enjoy the honours, prerogatives, privileges, franchises, freedoms, pledges, rights, fruits, profits, revenues and emoluments befitting his status. He peppered his speech with words which aroused the ire of the assembly, words so brazen I prefer to pass over them in silence.'

'Today's a day for petty quibbling,' sighed Nicolas.

'And toads who want to inflate themselves,' replied Noblecourt, his hearing as sharp as ever. 'Without getting off his high horse, and without drawing breath, he commanded us, the company of wardens of Saint-Eustache church, to make sure that he enjoyed full honours, was given precedence in assemblies immediately after the King's magistrates, and had the privilege of being brought in by the above-mentioned churchwardens . . . by us, would you believe it . . .'

He was choking with anger, and beating his chest with his clenched fists, startling Mouchette, who called him to order with a determined blow of her paw, her final warning before she retaliated by scratching him.

'Calm down, my darling, I'm not angry with you! Being brought in, as I was saying, by the churchwardens and presented with the consecrated bread immediately after the choir and the nobility, and before everyone else. Not content with this demand, he added the obligations of his rank in parish assemblies and processions, citing in support of this claim a royal decree of 1686. In short, I thought I was hearing again the bitter recriminations of my friend the Duc de Saint-Simon, fulminating against the disputes over precedence at the Court of the great King. But he was an eagle!'

He emptied his glass in large gulps and peered into the pot, which was still emitting little hissing noises.

'How could such an insignificant individual ever imagine that all this was possible? Did he really intend to appear with the characteristic insignia of his former state? Why not with his timpani? Does the scoundrel not know that the consecrated bread is always distributed indiscriminately, without any fuss, depending simply on the place occupied by each person in the church? Did

Our Lord, when he distributed the bread, establish a list of privileged people? Did he not say, "The first shall be last"? What nonsense to maintain, as this Bouin does, that in such an assembly, such a great throng of people, one should oblige each person to state his name and status, and assign him a chair to sit on, somehow describing oblique and circumflex lines, offering each parishioner a particular oblation according to his claims, while trying not to humiliate some nor arouse the jealousy of others.'[3]

'Who on earth put such an idea in his head?' asked Bourdeau.

'Do you need to ask? An outstanding casuist in the *parlement*: Président de Saujac, to name but one. Just when we needed it, his proverbial bad faith has blossomed into a cause without rhyme or reason. Although he versifies pleasantly enough, so I've been told. But he's taking poor Bouin for a ride, because for him the prose verdicts of that herald are gospel truth!'

'And, just like a young man, you're falling into the trap of this provocation! Your blood has been stirred and there's sweat on your brow!'

'That's how I've managed to stay so young,' said Noblecourt with majestic pomposity. 'Everyone thinks so, and you yourself just confirmed it.'

A new burst of laughter punctuated his words.

'But,' he continued, stirring in his armchair, 'isn't there something else to get my teeth into? This moaning, steaming pot is afraid, I think, of being neglected.'

'Oh,' said Bourdeau, 'that's my masterpiece. You will consider it as such after you've tasted it. Here are a couple of hens from my province. My cousins raised them lovingly. Last night, Madame Bourdeau poached them in a thick, well-conditioned poultry stock. Today, I braised them in the oven in a good-sized pot with the lid firmly closed. This method has the double advantage of not drying out the meat while at the same time giving it a crispy skin.'

'And I,' said Catherine, 'in order not to leave these poor beasts alone, have made some noodles from *my* province, some *spaetzle* gently fried in butter, with a touch of Muscat.'

Bourdeau took out the fowl with a delicacy unusual in this big, fiery man. He carved them with a silver knife handed to him by Poitevin. With each incision of the blade, little jets of juice and grease spurted out, like so many fragrant fountains. The three guests threw themselves on their plates. A great appreciative silence fell over the room, broken only by the snapping of bones, Cyrus's moans and Mouchette's imploring cries: both animals were trembling with envy and demanding their share of the feast.

'See how reasonable I am,' said Noblecourt, who had contented himself with a wing. 'I shall be the first to speak. Let us give thanks to Bourdeau for this delight. Assure your wife of our ravenous gratitude. I am your humble servant. That said, my children, where are we with our investigation?'

Bourdeau smote his head. 'I should have told you, Nicolas . . .'

'Is there some news? You're forgiven in advance. The hens plead in your favour.'

But Bourdeau's expression was sufficient indication that the joking was over.

'This morning in Rue Glatigny, at the bottom of the steps leading to the river, at the corner of the priory of Saint-Denis-de-la-Chartre, the watch discovered the body of a young girl.'

'Alas,' said Nicolas. 'Every day . . .'

'Except that this one had had her throat cut. I saw her in the Basse-Geôle. Exactly the same wound as the Pindron girl! A curious funnel shape and a great loss of blood . . .'

# VI

## DIVERSIONS OF THE HEART

If the grass had borne her, a flower would not
have received the imprint of her steps.
LA FONTAINE

Everything had frozen in the room, where, a moment earlier, the greatest merriment had reigned. It was Nicolas who broke the silence.

'Many crimes are committed in this city,' he said in an unsteady voice. 'It could always be a coincidence.'

'Highly unlikely. I went to the Basse-Geôle, where the body had, of course, been taken. I was able to proceed with the usual observations and Sanson, back from a session using the boot, was quite happy to help me. After much reflection, he went out and came back soon afterwards with a quarter-pound of plaster. He quickly prepared a paste and turned his attention to the body from the Saint-Florentin mansion.'

Marion gave a cry of horror.

'Catherine,' said Noblecourt, 'I think it's time for Marion to rest. She's been exerting herself far too much today . . . These evenings aren't good for her at her age; they're only for young men like me. Go, and may the night be kind to you.'

'The things I've seen on the field of battle without whining,' muttered Catherine, who was dying to hear the rest of Bourdeau's story.

But she obeyed and led Marion to her quarters. She was soon back.

'Why was Sanson so interested in the body of Marguerite Pindron?' asked Nicolas. 'What did he want with it?'

'With his plaster, he took a cast of the wound to the neck. The way they do with death masks.'

'Aren't they usually cast in yellow wax?'

'You're both right,' Noblecourt said, smiling wickedly. 'Before they bought themselves into the nobility of the robe, my ancestors were master wax moulders . . .'

There was a general cry of surprise.

'Now I understand why you're so interested in those theatres of corruption in your cabinet of curiosities,'[1] said Nicolas.

'An ancestor of mine helped to take the death mask of King Henry II in 1559, after he was mortally wounded by Montgomery's spear. It made a big impression on him, as the mask, cast only a few moments after death, cruelly revealed all the suffering that had preceded it. To go back to what I was saying, to make this kind of mask, you need to use thick strips of cloth, which surround and pull together the oval of the face, from the skull to the chin. You pour in the plaster paste, which, once solidified, gives a cast of the features, from which you can make a copy in wax.'

'What do they do with these masks?'

'Are you unaware, gentlemen, that the bodies of our kings are put on display except for the last one because of the risk of contagion from smallpox? Actually, they're just models wearing wax masks and the royal insignia, and the people troop past them to pay tribute. The impressions are preserved at Saint-Denis, where you can admire the collection.[2] But we're getting off the point.'

'There's always something to learn, Monsieur, from your wide experience.'

Noblecourt nodded, at the same time grabbing from the plate which Catherine had placed on the table a few quince pastries freshly removed from their moulds and put onto small lozenges of unleavened bread.

'It's a good thing Marion isn't here!' muttered Catherine.

'Let's get back to our corpses,' said Bourdeau. 'Sanson took the impression he'd made from Marguerite's body, and placed it on the wound of the unknown girl from Rue Glatigny. There was no room for doubt. Remember, Nicolas, that horrible funnel? The impression matched it almost exactly, with identical tears and compressions of the skin, looking for all the world like a shapeless hand.'

'Anything else?' asked Nicolas.

'Yes. The victim bears a strong resemblance to Marguerite Pindron. I mean, she's the same type of young woman, even though the two may differ in certain details.'

'An interesting comment. Do we have any idea of the time of death? It's vital to determine that. We already have many suspects for the murder in the Saint-Florentin mansion. Now we have another murder using the same method, with the added curiosity that the victims resemble one another. We need to find out if any of the possible suspects for the first crime could also have been the perpetrator of the second. If we know when death occurred, we can then check each of the suspects' whereabouts at the time.'

'It'll be no easy matter, Nicolas,' replied Bourdeau. 'The body is in very poor condition. It's not so much that it's been submerged in water at times, but rather that dogs, rats and crows have been at work on it. All things considered, Sanson estimates that death could not have occurred more than twenty-four hours earlier. We examined the corpse at one o'clock this afternoon.'

'Could it have been thrown in the river and then washed up?' asked Noblecourt.

'I don't think so. I went to the place. There are traces in the mud, tracks rather, suggesting that the body had been brought from the Cité, and before that from town. That bank of the island, opposite Quai Pelletier, is almost deserted at night.'

'All right,' said Nicolas. 'But nothing that would tell us more? Footprints, the marks of shoes?'

'Yes, lots, because people had started to gather before the watch arrived. I had a good look around. The mud is thick, and the backwash from passing boats and barges doesn't help. However . . .' He searched in his coat skirts. 'I did find this on the steps leading down to the river.'

He handed Nicolas a small stone that shimmered in the candlelight. The commissioner lifted it to his face.

'The button from a garment. It could be a gemstone, or—'

'An imitation gemstone,' Bourdeau hastened to say. 'I had it checked by a jeweller. Nothing but coloured glass.'

'It may have nothing to do with our case.'

'That's possible. We'll see.'

Nicolas slipped the button into his pocket.

'In the meantime,' resumed Bourdeau, 'I investigated a little more. There wasn't a body on the steps by the river between eleven o'clock on Monday night and about six o'clock this

Tuesday morning, when it was discovered. As the murder was not committed on the spot—'

'How do you know that?'

'By the fact that there's hardly any blood around. That gives us, let's see . . . one in the afternoon, take away twenty-four hours . . . Yes, a period on Monday between two in the afternoon and eleven o'clock in the evening, when there was still nothing on the bank.'

'Who told you that?'

'A man who lives in the area and walks his dog there every evening. Someone above suspicion, I checked.'

'And the victim?'

'Not many clues. A handkerchief, a key, a comb made of bone. A girl of lower class. However, I did find twenty-five *livres* and six sous in her pocket.'

'Good Lord, that's quite a lot for a girl of lower class. Was she wearing shoes?'

'No, we looked. Of course, so many people had been hanging around the corpse that they may well have been stolen.'

'Who found the body?'

'The old gardener from the priory of Saint-Denis-de-la-Chartre. He'd gone there to fetch water.'

'Doesn't the garden have a well?'

'It recently caved in.'

'Was the victim pretty?'

'Judging by what remained of her face, probably.'

'A prostitute?'

'The victim was dressed modestly but smartly.'

'Put your spies on the case,' ordered Nicolas. 'Speak to

Tirepot. He's getting older, and doesn't get around as much as he used to, but his network of informers is still unequalled. I need everything on this girl, and fast. For the rest, my dear Pierre, I rely on your discernment. I'll leave you the chore of checking our suspects' alibis for the time period you've mentioned. For my part, I have to go to Versailles tomorrow.'

'Are you seeing His Majesty?' asked Noblecourt.

'The King if I can, the Queen if I must, and two gardeners. I'll also pay my respects to Monsieur de Maurepas.'

'All the powers of the day united,' Bourdeau said, gently sardonic. 'You're young Court now!'

'Don't mock,' said Noblecourt. 'It's wise to conduct oneself well. Remember me to Monsieur de Maurepas. I knew him when I was young. In the thirties, he and I, along with the Chevalier d'Orléans, the legitimate son of the Regent and the Comtesse d'Argentan, d'Argenson, the minister of war and Caylus, would go, disguised in frock coats and round hats, to watch the parades at the Saint-Germain fair . . .'

He poured himself a full glass of wine and swallowed it in one go. 'Especially,' he went on, dreamily, 'when the strolling players took scenes from plays and parodied them. They were hilarious, with their bawdy ways and their strange pronunciation. God, how we laughed. With our mouths wide open and our breeches unbuttoned . . .'

But Nicolas was in a hurry to get back to the new case. 'Anything else, Pierre?'

'I thought I'd draw up a detailed chart of the activities of the various suspects on the night of the murder.' He moved his apron away from his coat skirts and took out a bulky document, the sheets of which were tied together by pieces of sealing wax. Seeing this, Nicolas stood up and, taking Bourdeau in his arms, kissed him on both cheeks, much to the amazement of the company. The inspector blushed with pleasure at this rare and unexpected demonstration of esteem from his chief.

'I tell you this,' proclaimed Nicolas, 'when it comes to *rillettes*, hens and investigations, he's irreplaceable. Now he even anticipates what I'm about to ask him to do!'

'Fourteen years of working together will do that,' said Noblecourt, clearly moved.

'Here in the first column,' resumed Bourdeau, 'you will find the names of the victim and the witnesses, including' – he lowered his voice – 'the Duc and Duchesse de La Vrillière.'

'Good for you,' remarked Nicolas. 'I have it on good authority that the duc was not at Versailles on Sunday evening as he claimed. And that he spent the night in Paris.'

'With the Beautiful Aglaé?'

'That would be surprising, given that she's in exile.'

Bourdeau nodded with a knowing air. 'The second column indicates the whereabouts of each person from ten o'clock to midnight on Sunday evening. The third shows their various activities the following morning. The fourth has each person's observations, the fifth my own observations, the sixth the clues found at the scene of the crime, the seventh the various opinions of the victim, and the eighth and last column the doctor's diagnosis of Jean Missery and his wound.'

Nicolas spent a while looking through the document. 'This is a very striking picture you paint. What are the first conclusions you draw from it?'

'Nothing really fits, neither the times, nor the testimonies. How to distinguish in all this what is the truth and what is a careful concealment of the truth? It all seems to me like one big conjuring trick.'

'I'd say the same,' said Nicolas, 'about the major-domo's sister-in-law, the nun. It's impossible to believe a word she says. She appears to tell the truth the better to lie, spends the night away from her convent but conceals the fact, and, note this, had a long conversation this very morning with the Duchesse de La Vrillière. What does it all add up to?'

'Is she a Carmelite?' asked Noblecourt.

'No, a Daughter of Saint Michel, a Eudist. Why do you ask?'

'The great King said one day to Monsieur, his brother, that he was well aware that the Carmelites might be deceivers, intriguers and weavers of yarns, but that he did not think they were poisoners. Admittedly, they had almost killed his niece with one of their medicines!'

Nicolas then recounted his day and his discoveries at Popincourt.

'Heaven,' said Noblecourt, 'has chosen you to untangle the most complex but also the most dangerous cases. Listen to a man who, although a recluse, lives with men …'

'And may on occasion be imbued with their prejudices, as Rousseau says,' Bourdeau cut in.

For the second time that evening, the inspector went red in the face as his two friends turned their appreciative gaze to him.

'So you read and esteem Jean-Jacques?' exclaimed Noblecourt.

'I admit I am quite infatuated with his work. Believe me, his ideas will change our world. There is a fervour in him, the fervour of the citizen. "The great man becomes small, the rich man becomes poor, and the monarch becomes a subject. We are approaching a state of crisis and a century of revolutions.'"[3]

'That may be so,' said Noblecourt: 'Our philosopher Bourdeau should, however, beware for, if the passionate man reasons badly and contrary to the laws of logic, the fool finds reason in the same source, for his passion is cold. My children, I am grateful to you for this evening, but I am feeling sleepy now.'

He stood up and walked to the staircase, escorted by Cyrus and Mouchette. On the top step, he turned.

'In this case of yours, remember that you have to look for the least likely solution, even if it seems to you highly unusual. Goodnight, gentlemen, goodnight . . .'

As soon as the familiar figure had disappeared, Bourdeau turned to Nicolas with a touch of anxiety in his voice. 'Didn't he strike you as strange this evening? That parting shot . . . the things he was saying . . .'

'Don't look so worried,' replied Nicolas with a laugh. 'You don't know him as well as I do. He has a surprising ability, of which I have often been the fortunate beneficiary, of seeing through to the kernel of a case even before we have all the facts. He cannot even explain it himself. It manifests itself, as it did a moment ago, in sententious phrases whose primary meaning escapes us, but which always conceal a truth that has somehow been revealed to him. In addition, thanks to your Chinon wine, he drank more than usual this evening. That's why he was so cheerful and so talkative.'

They conversed a little more, constructing hypotheses each of which fell short because of some detail they had neglected. No sooner were they formulated than they collapsed like so many houses of cards. Beside the stove, on a straw chair that looked more like a prie-dieu than any other piece of furniture, Catherine sat darning, her head drooping from time to time with tiredness. Old pains were reawakened, memories of long bivouacs in the icy rain on the battlefields of Europe. Her hearing, however, was still sharp, and, without appearing to, she was listening out to make sure that the stock she had prepared for next day's meals from three meats and some roots was boiling away nicely. Bourdeau took his leave, and Nicolas walked with him along Rue Montmartre. He was laden not only with the basket containing the pot and the bottles, but also with a lantern. The commissioner had insisted in spite of Bourdeau's refusals: at this hour, the spaces between the street lamps were wide enough to attract prowlers who were only held at bay by the watch and by a light, however feeble.

Nicolas went back up to his room, which had been deserted by Mouchette: the strumpet shared her favours, and sometimes preferred to nestle in Cyrus's fur, where she soon began to purr with the regularity of an automaton. That reminded Nicolas of the promise he had made Monsieur de Sartine to investigate Bourdier, the eminent creator of the library of wigs and the inventor of a new encoding machine. With this thought, he undressed and went to bed.

*Wednesday 5 October 1774*

Monsieur de Sartine grimaced as he manipulated the ivory and ebony keys of his library. The mechanism was no longer playing the joyful music of Rameau, but a grim chant, a kind of *Dies Irae*.

The drawer sprang out with a snap. Sartine clutched Nicolas, who was horrified to see, instead of the expected wig, the bloodstained body of a young woman. He turned. The minister had disappeared, and cut flowers were strewn on the ground. In a panic, he saw a man striking the trunk of a great oak with an axe. He seemed to be moved by strings, like the puppets sold on Pont-Neuf. Nicolas recognised Bourdeau's impassive face. He saw the flash of the blade as it struck his chest, but felt nothing except a light tap. He opened his eyes. Mouchette was treading on him, and affectionately pressing her nose to his chin.

As he dressed, he felt weighed down by this nightmare, whose meaning eluded him. He prepared his trunk, checked the rifles Louis XV had given him, then brushed his spare coats, his ceremonial dress, and his hunting costumes. Since Monsieur de La Borde no longer had an apartment in the palace, Nicolas was putting up at the Hôtel de la Belle Image in Versailles. His arms and his clothes now had to follow him wherever he went, an inconvenience which was a source of silent irritation. He did not wake the household, where even Catherine was still sleeping. A baker's boy from the shop on the ground floor ran to find him a carriage. Day had not yet risen, and it looked as if rain was on the way. It began to fall as soon as he had passed the Porte de la Conférence and did not stop, accompanied by a squally wind.

Nicolas, haunted by dark thoughts and sombre presentiments, remembered Monsieur de Noblecourt's fainting fit. He thought of how much he owed the former procurator and how fond of him he was. He felt a sense of anguish at the fleeting nature of life. Of all those who had mattered to him, many had already gone. His guardian, Canon Le Floch, to whose affection and kindness he owed his moral conscience. His father, the Marquis de Ranreuil, a model of intelligence and courage. Sartine, who had taught him so much. Even Commissioner Lardin,[4] whose death he had avenged without underestimating his faults, and whose cold, grim face often came back to him. Without showing Nicolas any real friendship, he had been an efficient, demanding and conscientious master.

The carriage drove along the Champs-Élysées, which looked wild and sinister in the pale light of this early morning storm. The late King, with his benevolence, had reinforced the innate devotion Nicolas had felt as a child seeing his finely chiselled face on the *louis d'or*. In their different ways, Sartine, Bourdeau and Semacgus had also made him the man he had become, and of course Noblecourt had had a very special place in those years when his character had been moulded. He realised with a kind of almost sacred terror that, in their concern for him and their generosity, they had been like a succession of fathers to him. All of them had prepared him for life and its threats, had armed him from head to foot. Yes, he really did owe them a lot. This thought chased away his feelings of gloom, and encouraged him to face his destiny with renewed strength, in the service of the King – God and Saint Anne willing.


Just before Versailles, as the carriage was crawling through the Fausses Reposes woods, the storm increased in intensity. It was one of those heavy, blustery autumn downpours that lashed the ground and laid waste to everything. Nicolas was gazing out, spellbound, at this upheaval when something strange attracted his attention. At first, it was a blur, like something seen through the lens of a badly focused telescope. An indistinct shape had collapsed on the ground not far from him. He knocked on the partition to stop the carriage. The vehicle swerved and slid, and finally came to a halt in a chorus of cries and neighing. He rushed outside. A woman was lying unconscious on the ground. He bent down and took her in his arms to raise her. She was so light that he quickly got her into the carriage. She had a thin, pale face framed by unruly brown curls that tumbled down over her bodice. There rose from her warm, wet body an imperceptible scent of verbena, along with wilder autumn aromas, the smell of wet earth and dead leaves. He took his handkerchief and wiped her hands, which were covered in scratches from the gravel. She stirred, moaned, and stretched her body against his. Her mouth brushed his chin. He thought of Mouchette, so fragile . . . She regained consciousness completely, and colour came back into her face. Her eyes opened inquisitively; grey, he noted, with dark-blue flecks. She folded her spotted lace fichu over her chest and sat up.

'Monsieur, I am quite confused. What happened to me?'

Nicolas loosened his embrace and gently sat her on the seat. Having had a chance to get a closer look at her, he judged that she might be just over twenty.

'I saw you fall, Madame, and stopped my carriage to come to your aid.'

She smiled. He noticed that she had perfect dazzlingly white teeth.

'You have saved me, Monsieur. Whom shall I thank?'

'Nicolas Le Floch, commissioner at the Châtelet.'

There was no reason for him to keep silent about an honourable position. Experience had taught him that doing so inevitably led to further complications.

'Ah,' she remarked, looking interested. 'Young Ranreuil.'

Nicolas's eyes immediately clouded over. This was encroaching on personal territory, and he felt it as an intrusion. It was his precious link with the royal family. The late King, the current King, Mesdames and, in the old days, the royal mistresses had all used the name to do him honour. She glanced at him out of the corner of her eye. Had she sensed his irritation? She rolled one of her curls and, with the other hand, squeezed the water from it before wiping it on her bodice.

'We have a mutual friend, Monsieur de La Borde,' she explained. 'His wife is a close friend of mine. He never stops singing your praises. I think he'd like to set them to music!'

She half raised herself as if trying to curtsey. 'Aimée d'Arranet, your humble servant.'

He relaxed. His irritation suddenly gave way to an astonishing sense of well-being. The young woman huddled into a corner of the carriage. The silence between them lengthened. Filled with wonder, he was becoming aware of the grace and sweetness she exuded. He felt like a young man again.

'And what were you looking for in this storm?'

'You're being indiscreet, Monsieur. Nevertheless, it would be bad taste of me not to satisfy your curiosity . . .' She opened a cloth pouch hanging from her belt. 'I was gathering chestnuts, if you must know, when I was caught in the rain.'

'So early in the morning?'

She gave an irritable little pout. 'He persists! I was walking at dawn, and to answer your question, Commissioner, the original aim of my stroll was to gather mushrooms. Did you not know that the best mushrooms open at dawn, when there is dew on the ground?'

The conversation risked coming to an abrupt end if it kept along that track, and he hastened to abandon the subject. Commentaries on autumn fruits were leading nowhere. Was she younger than he had supposed? Her self-assurance was misleading, her self-control, her charm, her lack of affected gestures, her casualness . . . He rebuked himself: where was this sudden elation leading him? He had not felt anything like this in a very long time, since a certain concert at Balbastre's house.[5] The memory of Julie de Lastérieux came back to him, bitter and sweet at the same time.

'Monsieur, you are suddenly very silent,' said the young woman. 'Oh, look, because of me, you're completely soaked!'

Before he could stop her, she had taken a lace handkerchief from her sleeve and was wiping his forehead. It was like a caress. He had to restrain himself from taking her hand.

'Mademoiselle, you're too kind . . . Where can I take you? The rain is getting heavier.'

She smiled again. 'My company is a burden to you, I think, and I have made you late. Come now, don't blush. That's how I am, impertinent by nature, always teasing. The house of my father, the Comte d'Arranet, is not far from here, in Avenue de Paris. But before that, could I ask you to fetch my shoes? The poor things must be floating, unless they've already sunk!'

He hurried outside and ran to collect the shoes, which looked quite pathetic. They were filled with water, and he emptied them before bringing them back.

'Oh, well, never mind,' she said. 'Perhaps you could drop me at the foot of the front steps. I'll jump up them in my stockings.'

She giggled. Nicolas ordered the coachman to drive on. The carriage swayed from side to side under the impact of the wind. A silence fell, while the young woman strove to rearrange her clothes. On the great avenue leading to the palace, Mademoiselle d'Arranet shouted some instructions to the coachman. The carriage turned right into a drive lined with old lime trees, towards an elegant two-storey dressed-stone house. Nicolas saw a swarm of footmen emerge to open the door and help his companion to descend. The house seemed as if it were raised up on a great foot.

'Monsieur, many thanks,' Aimée d'Arranet said, turning to him. 'But that doesn't mean you are free. I'll run and get changed. Tribord will show you to the library. My father absolutely must make the acquaintance of my saviour.'

'Oh, it was nothing, 'said Nicolas. 'I wouldn't like to exaggerate.'

'Come now, Monsieur, be quiet and obey with good grace.'

She put a finger on his mouth, and he fell silent. He got out of the carriage and meekly followed the footman in his red and grey livery who answered to this strange name. The man's face was covered in scars. Noticing Nicolas's curious gaze, he smiled although the smile was more like a grimace.

'Monsieur should not be surprised: I served with Mademoiselle's father.'

Once they had climbed the steps, they went in through the carved bronze double door and found themselves in a bright vestibule with black and white marble flagstones. From here, Nicolas was led into a library with grey and gold moulding on the ceiling, and walls completely covered in bookshelves apart from the fireplace and two windows. Above the mantelpiece, where a pier glass would normally have been, was a full-length portrait of a general officer. At first sight, he looked like a sailor, and Nicolas noticed a naval scene in the background of the painting. The room clearly functioned as a drawing room. Armchairs, pedestal tables and gaming tables were arranged harmoniously. His attention was drawn to an unusual piece of furniture occupying the centre of the room – a low table bearing a coloured plaster reconstruction of a battle at sea. He bent over it to take a closer look at the details of this curious assemblage. Six vessels with English colours seemed to be laying siege to two others, almost completely wrecked, flying a white flag. Everything was rendered meticulously. Each ship, a fragile construction the size of a hand, had its sails, tufts of oakum represented the smoke of cannon-fire, and little balls of lead the cannonballs strewn over the decks. Nicolas even noticed piles of corpses and an officer standing on a poop deck with a telescope under one arm and a raised sword in the other.

'Ah, Monsieur, there you are, leaning over the ship's rail. I can see you're intrigued by the spectacle.'

The voice, which was somewhat coarse, came from behind Nicolas. He turned and saw a tall, well-built man looking at him affably with merry grey eyes. He recognised the original of the painting above the mantelpiece. The man was wearing a dark blue coat of military cut with brass buttons and a sash of Saint Louis. His powdered wig did not in any way detract from the virile energy of a deeply lined, weather-beaten face. He was leaning on a walking stick. He held out his hand to the commissioner, in the English style.

'Thank you for having rescued my scatterbrained daughter who, ignoring my advice that the wind was getting stronger, took it into her head to go wandering in the woods at the crack of dawn.'

Nicolas bowed. 'Anyone would have done the same.'

'My daughter seemed pleased that it was you . . . I am extremely grateful to you. So you're a friend of La Borde's? A charming couple. His wife was at convent school with my daughter. I knew your father well, both at Court and in the field . . . You look like him. A brave man, and what a wit!'

Beneath his rough exterior, the man was not lacking in the social graces. Everything was said in such a way that it could not wound.

'I am the Comte d'Arranet, Lieutenant General of the Naval Forces. Unemployed. For the moment only, I hope.'

'Might I ask you, Monsieur, to be so kind as to enlighten me about this tableau, which has, I admit, aroused my interest and my curiosity? I hope I'm not being indiscreet . . .'

His request seemed to delight his host. 'Please take a seat, Monsieur. Your request pleases and honours me.'

He himself pulled up a *bergère* and sat down, making the chair groan under his weight. Nicolas noticed a slight limp, presumably the result of an old wound.

'This relief map depicts the battle of Cape Finisterre. In 1747, my then chief, François des Herbiers, the Marquis de l'Étenduère, had to escort a convoy of boats laden with provisions for the West Indies. What a sight! Imagine a long procession of two hundred and sixty merchant ships escorted by eight vessels, each with seventy or seventy-four cannon . . . My God, it gives me the shivers even now! Once we had left the harbour at Brest, Rear Admiral Hawke's English fleet, which was waiting off the cape, tried to cut us off.'

'Did they outnumber you?'

'By almost two to one, alas! They had fourteen large vessels lined up. The marquis, who was an excellent sailor, quickly formed his eight vessels into a line to resist the English attack. We managed to hold our own long enough to allow the convoy to get away, with the wind behind them.'

'And the enemy let you do so?'

'Oh, hardly! Hawke realised that he was risking the failure of his mission, and he dispatched the *Lion* and the *Princess Louisa* to chase the convoy. It was a risky move, given the progress of the battle and the state of the sea. Despite all that, they tried to pass in front of our line. As if we were ready to let them make headway! We fired linked cannonballs at them, making it difficult for them to continue their pursuit. Damn, this account is making me thirsty! While the filly's still rubbing herself down, let's take advantage. God has my late wife in His holy safekeeping, but looking after her daughter is easily the worst calamity that could befall a man of my character. The strumpet is in charge here!'

They walked towards a row of books. Inside a false binding were a crystal carafe and two glasses. He poured a fine amber liquid into them and held one out to Nicolas.

'An old rum from Île Bourbon. Do you like rum?'

'Indeed I do. A friend of mine, a naval surgeon, introduced me to it.'

'What's his name?'

'Guillaume Semacgus.'

Monsieur d'Arranet slapped his thigh. 'Guillaume! Good Lord, I owe him a leg! It was he who pulled out a piece of a sharp spar that had gone through my calf and broken a bone. I would be most happy, Monsieur, to see him again. Please be my ambassador.'

They drank. The rum had a strong but delicious taste.

'Getting back to my story, Hawke, who was furious, set out to destroy us. He threw his whole squadron at us. The defence was worthy of the attack. He overtook the rear of our line. Several of our vessels were forced to strike their flags after a terrible fight lasting eight hours. By the time the *Tonnant* surrendered, there was nothing left of it but a burning wreck filled with the dead and the dying. A guard named Monsieur de Suffren, who was twenty years old, wept with rage and absolutely forbade anyone to touch the halyard of the flag on the poop deck.'

He offered Nicolas another glass of rum, but the commissioner refused. He poured one for himself.

'As you wish! By the time the sun went down, the French squadron was not entirely reduced. There remained the *Tonnant*, where the admiral had his quarters, and the *Intrépide*, commanded by Vaudreuil, although, without its masts, the *Tonnant* was nothing but a piece of flotsam.'

'And where were you, Monsieur?'

'I was Vaudreuil's first mate. He attempted a desperate manoeuvre. He tacked under enemy fire, even though his shrouds and stays had been cut to shreds by the grapeshot, and lowered a small boat to carry two cables to the *Tonnant*. All within pistol range of the English. The *Intrépide* towed the *Tonnant* behind it, each vessel having its flag pinned to the small mast in its stern. Six days later, the commander of the squadron returned to Brest, but, more importantly, the convoy reached the West Indies and relieved the food shortage there.'

A merry voice rang out. 'Father, you'll never change! There you are holding forth, drinking your infernal liquor, and tiring our guest with your exploits!'

The comte assumed a contrite air. His daughter flung her arms round his neck and kissed him.

'What you haven't heard,' she went on, turning to Nicolas, 'is that the boat that saved the day was under his command. I see you have become acquainted.'

The comte winked at Nicolas. 'Look at how a girl brought up in a convent treats her old father! Did you know, Aimée, that our friend knows Guillaume Semacgus, whom I've told you so much about, you know, the man to whom I owe the fact that I'm still on my two legs? What a coincidence, eh? For that, I forgive you your foolishness.'

'He's a very dear friend, who means a lot to me,' said Nicolas. 'And where does the old pirate live now?'

'In Vaugirard, near the Croix-Nivert.'

'Monsieur, I've just remembered. I'm giving a dinner tomorrow in honour of Monsieur de Sartine, Secretary of State for the Navy. Would you like to come?' With a knowing air, he went on, 'I'm hoping for a command. Perhaps the evening will help me get one. He was, they say, your protector with the late King. Your name was enough . . . and the exploits people attribute to you . . . No doubt the former Lieutenant General of Police will be pleased to see you again.'

'Monsieur, I don't know if I can——'

'Come now, I shan't accept any refusal. It's an order. At best, a plea.'

'With which I associate myself,' said Aimée d'Arranet.

Her smile made his mind up for him.

'In that case,' said Nicolas, 'I accept.'

When he found himself back in his carriage after taking his leave, all he could think about was the young woman's face as she made a slightly mocking half-curtsey. Back on the avenue, he observed that destiny had sent him to the same place twice – for very near the d'Arranet mansion was the house where the solution to the mystery of the man with the lead stomach had gradually been revealed.

The wind was reaching its maximum intensity as the sun rose. As soon as the carriage turned in front of the large stables to reach the square, recently renamed Dauphine, Nicolas was gripped by the spectacle of nature in a state of crisis. The proud buildings were lit up as if by invisible barrages of gunfire. Like a tall, dark stem, the chapel stood out against a slate-grey sky that matched the colour of the palace roofs. The lightning accentuated the red hue of the bricks on the facade of the marble courtyard, while the ministers' wing emerged from the clouds haloed in liquid gold. Gradually, the rays of the sun shifted, striking each of the great windows in turn, causing the frames and panes to gleam. The light rippled, creating a semblance of life in the heart of the palace. Thick, high clouds pushed small purple and pink clouds before them; some escaped and ran towards the nearby forests, while others, tumbling, joined the darkest mass as if drawn to it by a magnet and soon melted into its blackness. There was a resplendent rainbow, which immediately faded. Everything was extinguished in an instant. There was a kind of lull, a moment of silence and calm, before the sky once again caught fire in a cascade of lightning flashes followed soon afterwards by the muted bass notes of thunder. The rain came down even harder, covering the glorious vision of the palace with a hazy curtain of liquid, blotting out the decorations and reliefs, reducing the whole thing to an unstable mass that seemed on the verge of dissolving. The smell of earth and saltpetre filled Nicolas's chest. His frightened team of horses gave a few kicks and set off again at a full gallop.

He reached the Hôtel de la Belle Image. Nicolas was familiar with this type of accommodation. The rooms, although cramped, were always clean and well maintained, and there were far fewer cockroaches in the bed linen than elsewhere. Nicolas's first concern was to find an emissary who could convey the Comte d'Arranet's invitation to Semacgus. He scribbled a few words of explanation on a page of his black notebook and sealed it with sealing wax. It did not take him long to discover a wine merchant who was returning to Paris, having completed his business, and who was due to pass through Vaugirard, where he had customers. He was very pleased to take on the errand. Nicolas, whose insides had been warmed by the morning's rum, offered him a light meal of eggs and bacon, which made the man his friend for life. He then went up to his room to sort out the contents of his trunks. He had plenty of time since there was no chance that he could participate in that morning's hunt. True, if he hurried up, he would be in time to join the royal cortege, but, in this domain, hurrying was contrary to good manners. The most important thing was to be well informed. You did not venture into the treacherous swamps of the Court without knowing what kind of game was being hunted. Although, for simple shooting parties, elaborate costumes had been tolerated by the late King, this was not the case when it came to hunting roe deer, stags or boar. The new monarch was reputed to be more punctilious than his grandfather in this regard. The usual hunting costume – rich blue with gold braid – was de rigueur and the arrangement of the braid indicated the kind of animal one was going to hunt. How strange it all was! thought Nicolas. Nevertheless, these apparently insignificant details were meaningful: what they meant, above all, was that one had a name and the right to enter the King's coaches, which was the equivalent, for a man, of being presented at Court for a woman. This privilege was something of which Nicolas could not help feeling proud. Of course, he owed it to his birth, even though it was illegitimate, but, more importantly, it was because of the word of Louis XV that it had been granted to him for ever. He saw himself again on that fateful day when he had found a father, acquired what others took centuries to obtain, and gained the right to serve his King.

He was annoyed to see some stains on the patina of one of his rifles. Nothing ought to tarnish the splendour of the royal gift. He did his best to wipe them off. His mind flew from object to object. When would such trifles be regarded with indifference? Once, coming back from a choral concert with his friend Pigneau de Behaine, now bishop of the mission in Cochinchina, he had heard him describe the religion of the Buddhist monks, which taught its followers to renounce all things, to become detached from all ties, in order to attain supreme indifference and the peace of the soul. He had rebelled against that idea, considering it an inaccessible dream, a kind of moral suicide in a universe in which nothing any longer had a price or a meaning. Pigneau had gently observed that this renunciation was not so different from the communion of the mystics and the saints with the power of the Lord, and that Christ, too, had called for asceticism in old age . . . I'm becoming quite a philosopher, he thought. In a corner of his mind, the laughing eyes of Aimée d'Arranet were staring at him with a touch of mockery. In the end he decided to go to the ceremony of the removal of the King's boots. He would glean the latest news, would enquire about the kind of hunting due to take place the next day, and would also have a chance to investigate the strange story of the Trianon garden. However well-organised and far-sighted he was, he was not unaware that at Court any plan was subject to whims and chance.

Nicolas dressed in half-mourning, intending to get to the palace on foot. At the sight of the potholes in the roadway, he immediately realised that he had made a mistake and that his costume would not withstand the mud. He resigned himself to hiring a sedan chair, a means of transport he hated above all others, its swaying making him nauseous and the use of his fellow men seeming to him an insult not only to their dignity but also to his.

He passed through all the cordons like a peer of the realm and came to the foot of the ambassadors' staircase. He proceeded to the room where the removal of the boots took place, where, on questioning the guards, he realised that he had a little time to spare before everyone got back from the hunt. This would be an opportunity to stroll through the palace. He went down to the ground floor, where large stone galleries filled with a buzzing crowd welcomed those whom the rain had chased from the gardens. Idle courtiers were conversing in small groups, peering at the bourgeois ladies and their maids who had come to gawp at the surroundings. Nicolas remembered how surprised foreign visitors always were to discover that the place was a kind of permanent fair. The setting up of shops and stalls had long been tolerated. They had gradually spread, and now filled the vestibules, corridors and even the landings of the great staircase, and, although they were eyesores, everyone was so used to them, they had stopped seeing them. The Queen, while still the Dauphine, had often lingered over these stalls, much to the horror of Madame Victoire and Madame Adélaïde. The two aunts did manage to get a perfume seller who had colonised the vestibule of the marble staircase to leave – with the support of the royal princes and the maréchals of France, who were the only people who had the right to bring their coaches up to the steps of the palace.

Nicolas suddenly sensed that someone was staring at him. He turned and saw a potbellied little man wearing a curious white wig. The individual, realising that he was being observed, immediately lowered his tinted glasses over his eyes, did an about-turn, and vanished into the crowd. Nicolas was about to set off after him to find out the reason for such strange behaviour when an arm held him back. By the time he had turned again, the man was out of sight and out of reach. Angrily, Nicolas was about to rebuke the busybody who had stopped him when he recognised the gentle face of La Satin looking at him with an expression of sweet adoration.

'Antoinette? You here, in Versailles? You made me . . . No, it doesn't matter.'

'The thing is,' she said, 'an opportunity presented itself to increase my little business.' She was talking very quickly as if out of breath. 'I've done a deal with Marie Mercier, a widow who owns a perfume shop with her sister in Rue de Satory in Versailles.'

'How did you meet them?' he said, immediately regretting his inquisitorial tone.

'They often go to Paris to replenish their stocks. They liked what I sell. We talked and the idea of forming a partnership gradually grew. After each season, it's the custom for well-dressed ladies and the Queen's entourage to sell off their dresses and lace finery once they've been worn. We've obtained the exclusive right to buy and sell them.'

'Of course,' he said, 'that must make everybody happy.'

She lowered her head like a child caught doing something wrong.

'And what about your shop in Rue du Bac?'

'I'm only at Versailles for two days. I've hired an assistant. The rest of the week, she looks after the house and does the shopping.'

He found it hard to disentangle his confused feelings. Of course, he was pleased to see La Satin so committed to her new life, but, on the other hand, her presence at Versailles could not help but disturb him. It was pointless trying to hide it: seeing his worlds come together like this disturbed him greatly. His annoyance increased the guiltier La Satin looked. They talked about Louis and the start of his school career. Both were waiting impatiently for his first letters. But even that did not bring them closer together. A wall had gradually risen between them. He blamed himself, but was unable to dismiss his unease. They bade each other farewell like strangers. He suddenly remembered the unknown man in the wig. What was Lord Ashbury, a member of the British secret service,[6] doing in Versailles, and why had he fled at his approach?

# VII

## THIS COUNTRY

Maurepas has returned in glory
No power, but that's another story
The King gives him a hug and says
You and I are birds of a feather
It's better that we stay together
ANON., 1774

Nicolas was striding through the gallery, having not even noticed the desolate look in Antoinette's eyes. Feeling faint, as if suffocating, but unwilling to look into the reasons why, he tried to distract himself by observing the curious manners of the Court. Husbands would meet their wives and greet them with an indifference appropriate to strangers. It was true, he thought, that these days men were busy increasing the number of their conquests and women publicly displaying their lovers. Couples living together hardly met, and never took the same carriage, nor did they ever find themselves in the same house, except in the palace. Possession for men, seduction for women: they were the only motives for attack or surrender. Loving without pleasure, surrendering without a fight, leaving one another without regrets, calling duty weakness, honour prejudice, delicacy dullness, such were the manners which Nicolas attentively observed: seduction had its code and immorality its principles.

The time had come for the removal of the King's boots. As he entered the room where the small company was beginning to gather, buzzing with the murmur of courtiers, guards, grooms and those who were only there because their position required it, an acrid, sickly-sweet smell, a mixture of musk, scent and powder seized him by the nostrils, and a claw-like hand gripped his shoulder. From the aroma, he recognised the Maréchal de Richelieu. Thirteen years earlier, he had been in this same room when Monsieur de Sartine had brought him to see Louis XV for the first time.

'Young Ranreuil, returning like a ghost!' exclaimed the old man. 'How nice to see you again. How is Noblecourt?'

The question did not require an answer, but Nicolas made the mistake of forgetting that. 'Very well, Monseigneur, like his contemporaries.'

'I thank you, Monsieur,' squealed the maréchal, with a horrible grimace. 'I am younger than him, by a long way! What work brings you to this country?'

'Hunting. I hope the First Gentleman of His Majesty's Bedchamber will permit me to question him about tomorrow's hunt.'

This respect for the proprieties seemed to delight the maréchal, who proudly lifted a face coated with ceruse and rouge. His grinning mouth revealed teeth that were well on the road to ruin.

'Well, Marquis, today they were tracking a monstrous boar, a creature of the devil usually confined to the great park. Damnation, the beast ran all the way to the gardens, frightening our people with his bloodthirsty eyes. The King, who is not a

Bourbon for nothing, gave orders for the animal to be hunted down. The big footprint it left this morning did the rest. By this time, they should be paying it their last respects.'

'And what about tomorrow?'

'Tomorrow, for His Majesty's pleasure, they'll be hunting both animals and birds in the plain of Grenelle.'

He rose up on tiptoe and clutched Nicolas's arm to whisper something in his ear, but his voice was still so high-pitched that Nicolas doubted his words escaped anyone.

'I'm going to tell you the latest piece of bad taste. The Prince-Abbé de Salms was crossing the bull's-eye antechamber yesterday with a few friends. Some young dandies who were warming themselves there started, if you can believe it, to mock him so loudly that he heard them. "There's Aesop and his court!" You know how deformed the man is! Well, he was not in the least disconcerted, and paid them back for their effrontery. "Gentlemen," he replied, "the comparison is quite flattering to me, for Aesop made the animals speak."'

'Alas,' said Nicolas, 'it seems there are countries where ridicule and flattery are so closely intertwined that it is impossible to practise one without producing more of the other!'

'You are very censorious today,' observed the maréchal. 'An unhappy love affair, perhaps? In this world, it is not enough to know that in order to succeed one must be ridiculous, one must also study carefully the circle in which our rank has placed us, the ridiculous ways which most concern our state, those, in a word, which are in credit, and this demands more delicacy and care than one may imagine.'[1]

Nicolas was surprised by the maréchal's tone. It was true that the wind had changed and that he was still determinedly trying to assert himself in a Court where everyone was turning away from him, including the young royal couple. This glorious relic had known the great King as a page, Madame de Maintenon, the young Duchesse de Bourgogne . . . He had seen the whole century. Nicolas could not help feeling a touch of compassion for this old man determined to perpetuate an immutable order.

'Tell me, tell me,' the maréchal continued, 'does your presence at Court have anything to do with the tragedy everyone is talking about?'

Surprised by these words, Nicolas remained silent.

'Madame de Maurepas's angora cat has been murdered! Since then, there has been nothing but wailing and gnashing of teeth, and the culprit's head demanded on a platter. No, I see it's something else.'

He breathed in. He had underestimated the Duc de Richelieu, as people so often did.

'Yes, I sense rather that you are here because of a somewhat unfortunate affair concerning Monsieur de La Vrillière. Are you going to tell me . . .?'

Nicolas did not bat an eyelid.

'Oh, don't worry, I can read you like a book. You say nothing, but your sealed lips are all the more eloquent. Could you at least—'

The cries of the ushers and the dull thud of the halberds striking the floor, announcing the return of the King's procession from the hunt, saved Nicolas, who ignored Richelieu's insistence and bowed deferentially. The room was a sea of bent backs. The King, his face flushed and his coat dripping water, looked around the gathering. He was so tall that he dominated it, and his hunting boots made him even taller, but, as he did not rise to his full height, the effect was not as majestic as it might have been. He seemed to look at everyone surreptitiously, screwing up his eyes without, however, appearing to recognise anyone. He made a few hesitant advances and retreats, his arms dangling. Nicolas noticed that his profile recalled that of the late King, but was less firm. His already bloated neck sank between his shoulders. His blue eyes were inscrutable, lacking the dark velvetiness of his predecessor's. On his lips there hovered an inexpressive, almost innocent smile. He passed Nicolas, approached him, bent down and focused his gaze on him.

'Ranreuil, follow me when I go back to my private rooms.'

These few words created a stir. All eyes turned to the beneficiary of the King's attention. Everyone knew how short-sighted the monarch was and how hard he found it to recognise his servants. The Maréchal de Richelieu saw fit to intervene at this point. 'Sire,' he said, 'please allow the First Gentleman—'

The King turned his back on him, without giving any indication that he had even heard him. Nicolas knew that the royal couple had been behaving particularly badly to Richelieu lately, hoping in this way to force him to give up his position and stop bothering them with a presence that reminded the Queen all too sharply of the hated Madame du Barry. But it was no good, he just kept on, pretending not to understand the many eloquent signs of his fall from favour and ignoring the many jokes of which he was the butt.

After the King had wiped himself down with towels, some of his servants changed his clothes. Or at least, with the twenty-year-old monarch behaving more like an adolescent, they tried to. With a laugh, he dodged the shirt he was handed, lowering his neck at the crucial moment. The grooms were accustomed to these jokes and played the game with good grace. The King choked with laughter and stamped now one foot, now the other. The arrival of a newcomer brought the joking to an end. Nicolas recognised Monsieur de Maurepas. He ceremoniously greeted Louis XVI, gave Richelieu a knowing smile, and looked at Nicolas inquisitively.

Tall and thin, with a noble bearing, lean legs, a high forehead, wide blue eyes and a pale face, Maurepas smiled without opening his small mouth. His image, nonchalant, self-assured, reassuring, was that of an old, still handsome man with a good-natured, easy-going air. Richelieu pulled Nicolas back and, again clinging to his arm to raise himself a little, whispered in his ear, 'Did you know that his reputation for impotence is extremely well founded? He has all the faults of a eunuch, loving and tormenting women without satisfying them . . .' He laughed. 'He hates nothing more than to have his back against the wall. Or should I say, against the bed?'

Nicolas was sweating blood for fear that the maréchal's shrill voice would be overheard. But the King was talking about the hunt and the solitary old boar, which he himself had dispatched with a well-aimed blow of his dagger. A murmur of approval followed this announcement. The minister began talking to the monarch in a low voice. The commissioner looked at this curious combination of the past and future. He knew what people said: that on the vessel of State, Monsieur de Maurepas was more of a passenger than a pilot, that there were two men inside him, the one who saw and the one who navigated. Alas, continued the rumour, the former was perceptive and enlightened, the latter fickle and irresolute. The King liked him, because his own qualities and flaws were similar to the old man's. It was as if he were seeing himself in a mirror.

With the ease of half a century's expertise, the minister, having begun speaking, would not stop. He talked interminably, for in him everything began and ended with words. He had the reputation of rarely listening to anyone else, and of always speaking before thinking. Nicolas watched the scene, and the attentive gathering around it, without really seeing them. What was he, the man for special investigations, doing here? What role was he playing? Of course, he was perfectly familiar with the circumlocution, the etiquette, the true and false faces, the traps of all kinds. A traveller accustomed to the tempests of this country, he nevertheless felt like an outsider. It was as if he were watching himself playing a game, a game in which he participated without becoming involved, a game in which he knew all the required words and gestures by heart but could only hold his own by remaining cold, analytical and devoid of passion. In this society where the only things that mattered were subtle distinctions and the precise hierarchy of rank and privilege, he was dancing on shifting sands to a music whose scales he had learnt a long time ago – to tell the truth, ever since his father's salons in the chateau at Ranreuil. Skilful at avoiding the dangers, never uttering a word for which he might have been reprimanded, a courtier by obligation, a servant by necessity, a man of the King by profession, loyal by inclination, he had mastered the customs of this world and these people without embarrassment or pleasure, but was separated from them by an invisible wall, and had no wish to know who had decided to build it.

Whether this wall was a means of attack or defence, even he himself was not sure. Free within his armour, nothing could touch him; no word, however deadly in these times of ridicule, could reach him. The only words that could have an effect on him were those that might come, whether through misfortune or by some strange chance, from the mouth of the King. He felt a kind of wave of happiness and pride at being, basically, so free and so detached. Yes, he thought, fate had thrust him into a setting from which he could always escape, just as in his childhood dreams, whatever the circumstances. That was how he was able to maintain his rightful place within a rigid system where the slightest false step could break a reputation, tarnish a name and compromise a career. This thicket of traps, the home to so many false reputations, was negotiated by Commissioner Nicolas Le Floch with polite indifference and the confidence of experience.

Maurepas continued to hold forth while the King listened in open-eyed wonder and his servants attended to him. Nicolas compared the minister to Noblecourt. More or less the same age, they had once attended the festivities of Regency Paris together. One seemed to have endured without learning anything, while the other belonged to 'that small, select number of excellent men who, having been endowed with a fine and particular natural strength, have carefully honed it, through study and by skill, and have brought it to the highest point of wisdom it can reach'. Montaigne's words had come spontaneously to his mind, a vestige of his adolescent reading in the library of the chateau at Ranreuil. His basic feelings about d'Aiguillon's successor echoed the public's judgement: Maurepas, well shaven, well powdered, well rejuvenated, gave the impression of thinking deeply about nothing.

The noise of the arms carried by the guards, announcing the departure of the King, brought him back to reality. He hastened to follow, along the same route he had taken during his first visit to Versailles. Reaching his apartments, the King turned and signalled to Nicolas to come with him to another, even more private domain. From the little gallery overlooking the Cour des Cerfs, there was a dark, narrow spiral staircase. This led them to a wide door, which opened into a large attic room dominated, from the first, by a strong smell of filings, leather and rope. From there, it was possible to reach a small belvedere with a view over the roofs of the palace, the gardens and the park. At a glance, Nicolas saw model ships, navigational instruments, clocks either intact or dismantled, locks and various mechanisms. Books and maps were scattered everywhere, along with other objects which all pointed to their owner's curiosity. Clearly this was a personal hideaway, a place for the King to relax. Of course, he had known his visitor for a long time.

'Will you be with us at tomorrow's shoot?' asked Louis XVI.

'Yes, Sire. I have brought the rifles you know to Versailles with me.'

'We like the fact that these memories of our grandfather are still in the hands of his most loyal servants. What's the latest about the investigation in the house of the Duc de La Vrillière?'

So he already knew. How could it have been otherwise?

'The elements are falling into place.'

'You're clever, you'll get there.'

He seemed embarrassed suddenly, like a child caught doing something wrong. He motioned to Nicolas to sit down. The commissioner bowed but did not move. He felt that he ought to help the King to express himself.

'Your Majesty knows my loyalty. What can I do to serve you?'

His interlocutor appeared to take the plunge. 'Monsieur, you must get me out of trouble . . . From time to time, from the belvedere, I fire at the cats that swarm on the roofs. They disturb us at night . . .'

A strange pastime, thought Nicolas, remembering dear Mouchette.

'Alas,' continued the King, 'I shot one that must have been Madame de Maurepas's angora cat. What do you advise me to do?'

'Sire, I fear that the only acceptable thing to do is to tell the truth. Your ancestor once dismissed a page who had tormented his cat. However . . .'

'However?' said the King.

'However,' said Nicolas, 'if Your Majesty will allow me to speak on his behalf, I will be his ambassador to Madame de Maurepas. I will go to the trenches to withstand the first attack. Of course, she will have to listen to reason and realise that what happened was an accident. The King was simply shooting at pigeons, and a cat got in the way . . .'

'That's it,' said Louis XVI approvingly, 'that's it exactly.'

He pushed the hand of a clock, and listened with delight as it rang. He rubbed his hands, filled with a satisfaction that he could not conceal. He changed the subject and began speaking with surprising fluency.

'Are you aware, Ranreuil, of the disputes over the northern passage? I am turning to my advantage the works that scholars send me. One of my correspondents, a native of the Swiss cantons, has called me "a delight of the human race".' He laughed. 'He stresses my principles of fairness, justice and humanity. Which Roman emperor was called that?'

'Titus, Sire.'

'That's it. I'd really like to send these newspapers and extracts from this friend's letters to Monsieur La Harpe,[2] who denounced the work of my predecessors in *Le Mercure*.'

The King was becoming increasingly heated, and his face turning redder and redder.

'The man has no respect for anything. Anyway, attacking the government of kings is small beer for him, it's religion this philosopher really attacks! If the people are constantly subjected to a flood of writings and ungodly lampoons, he'll end up destroying their ancient beliefs and their loyalty to both divine and royal majesty.'

Calmer now, he tapped a little morocco-bound book.

'My Swiss friend assures me that Monsieur de Bougainville, with whom he is in correspondence, is trying to find the best way to get to the pole and that this work partly deals with it.'

The King approached a window. He again appeared ill at ease and embarrassed. He walked towards a small forge, which had gone out, and worked the bellows.

'Have you asked to see the Queen?'

'Not yet, Sire. I was about to. My presence at Versailles . . .' He did not finish the sentence.

'Settle this Trianon business as quickly as you can, it's been going on for far too long. I don't want anything to trouble my wife's peace of mind. We have to put paid to these rumours.'

Nicolas found the tone too bourgeois by far. The King continued walking up and down, looking at various objects without lingering over any of them.

'I've not had any news from our Micmac,'[3] he resumed, again changing the subject. 'He's been going around the tribes, and I hope . . . But what I have had is a report from one of our naval officers which includes some information about your friend Pigneau.'

Nicolas gave a start. How did the King know that he was acquainted with the missionary? Sartine had to be somewhere behind it.

'His consecration,' Louis XVI went on, 'was deferred for a long time because of the bishop's absence in Pondicherry. You'll be pleased to hear that it finally took place in São Tomé, near Madras, last February. My God, how long news takes to reach us, and always by unusual routes!'

'Unusual routes? Well, that's better than usual routine, which is an inevitable evil!'

The King laughed, suddenly a young man again. 'That's a play on words I'll repeat. I was merely talking about unusual and roundabout ways.'

'May Your Majesty forgive me,' said Nicolas, also laughing.

'Not at all, I am grateful to you for this distraction. I understand it was one of the reasons my grandfather appreciated you. Your friend was preparing to go back to Cochinchina, after trying to assert his authority over the Franciscans. We wish him good luck with those people, they want it all for themselves. Is he a man of character at least?'

'Of very sturdy character, Sire, with a sharp, well-stocked mind.'

'Monsieur,' said the King, slightly hesitantly, 'I appreciate your judgement and your knowledge of men. Promise me you will always tell us the truth. I need honest men about me. You must help me . . .'

With his frank, sensitive nature, Nicolas was touched by this simply expressed appeal. He threw himself at the King's feet. Moved, the King raised him and led him, with disarming naturalness, back to the small staircase. In his embarrassment, Nicolas tried without success to withdraw backwards as etiquette demanded. He descended the stairs as if in a dream and walked through a maze of corridors until he found himself outside in the gardens. Moving as it was, the monarch's simplicity did raise a few questions. It elevated the private man in Nicolas's estimation, but what of the supreme symbol of the State? Could one feel as much respect for a person one knew too well? The love of royalty demanded a boundless respect for the conventions. But there was nothing servile about total obedience and humble submission when they were given to one who, as the representative of God on earth, would very soon be crowned at Reims.


He was now walking towards Trianon, dreading to return to a place where, a few months earlier, the late King, leaning on his arm, had climbed into his carriage for his last journey back to the palace. The park was suffused with the melancholy of autumn, and the pervasive smell of boxwood rose from the ordered clumps of trees. Coming to the vast steps of the chateau, Nicolas stopped to get his bearings. On his left was a short avenue which ended in a staircase leading to the door of the chapel. There, a man was busy gathering fallen leaves. Nicolas asked him where his chief was, and the man pointed to the greenhouse opposite the chapel. Nicolas walked along the facade of the chateau to the greenhouse, where Louis XV had striven to grow exotic species. Struck as soon as he entered by the damp, suffocating heat of this mass of enclosed vegetation, he saw two men in brown coats leaning over a workbench. Approaching, he recognised the older of the men as Claude Richard, the head gardener, whom he had often seen in the past. The other man must be his son. One thing, though, intrigued him: their attire. He was accustomed to seeing Richard in the red, white and blue livery of the King. As the young Queen now had the Petit Trianon at her disposal, they should have been wearing her livery, which was red and silver. He realised all at once that these two veteran servants were wearing mourning for their master after their fashion. The gardener looked up, annoyed at being disturbed. His son, intent on planting some kind of cutting, ignored the newcomer. Claude Richard looked hard at Nicolas. He had faded grey eyes and a weather-beaten face.

'Monsieur,' he said, 'I think I recognise you. I have seen you several times with the King, I mean, our late master . . .'

Nicolas was moved by this simple loyalty.

'He used to call you "young Ranreuil",' Richard continued with a smile.

'You have a good memory. Forgive me for distracting you from your task. Are you in the middle of some remarkable acclimatisation?'

'I was collecting root sprouts from this plant.'

He pointed to a shrub. Nicolas gave him a questioning look.

'Root sprouts are suckers that are detached from the mother plant and then replanted.'

'And this shrub?'

'It's a kind of acacia, a locust tree, which produces bunches of highly scented white flowers and fruit in the form of pods. But to what do I owe the honour of your visit, Marquis?'

Nicolas waved his hand as if chasing away an importunate fly. 'It is not the marquis who needs your help, but the police commissioner. His Majesty has told the Lieutenant General of Police how worried he is regarding a strange incident about which the Queen informed him. Those visitors in the gardens whom you also saw and whose presence you reported. Can you tell me what happened, in as much detail as possible?'

Richard seized a long stick to support himself and led his guest towards a wooden bench, onto which he collapsed heavily.

'Autumn revives my aches and pains, especially when I keep still,' he began. 'Now let's see. Last 10 August, my son and I were crossing the gardens, towards the avenue, when we came across two women. Even if they had not hailed us, we would have been surprised to see them.'

'Why is that?'

'Their dress, Marquis, their dress! We may not be up to date with the latest fashions here, but by God, we do see the Queen and her women, and we don't keep our eyes in our pockets. I had never seen such a costume. Shapeless dresses, quite plain, without bodices, blouses with sleeves swollen like goat's skins, square hats covered with muslin . . . Spectacles . . . And that accent . . .'

'So they spoke to you?'

'Yes, in an accent that reminded me of the English visitors who've been coming here in such numbers since the peace treaty.'

'Can you draw, Monsieur Richard?'

'In my job, you have to.'

'Could you make a sketch of these strange women?'

'Of course.'

The gardener took a folded sheet of paper and a piece of charcoal from his pocket, and struggled away with them for a few minutes. Nicolas looked in puzzlement at the drawn shapes, which were extremely vivid but resembled nothing in human knowledge. He had certainly not seen anyone dressed like that during his recent stay in London.

'What did they ask you?'

'The way to the palace.'

'Was that all?'

'Yes, and then they disappeared.'

'Disappeared? You mean they withdrew, walked away . . .'

'Oh no, I mean disappeared. The common people, as you know, have access to the gardens. I am worried sometimes for my flowers and the Queen's peace of mind. So I wanted to know where the visitors were really going. But when I turned into the avenue . . . Well, my son can confirm this. Right, Antoine?'

The young man nodded firmly. 'My father's right, Marquis. They just weren't where they'd been before.'

'In addition,' the father continued, 'one of my assistants who was coming in the opposite direction didn't pass them.'

'Was it hot?'

Nicolas was thinking of some stories that Semacgus had told

him about the phenomenon of mirages in hot dry weather in deserts. But mirages did not speak, and certainly did not ask the way.

'It happened at four o'clock in the afternoon. The sun was still high in the sky.'

'Have you ever seen them again?' Nicolas asked, after further reflection.

'No, not so far.'

'If anything should happen, please send for me immediately. Thank you for your help. I'll take your sketch with me.'[4]

Nicolas was puzzled. He considered Richard a man of experience and common sense. His testimony was unimpeachable, even if reason could not account for it. Deep down, Nicolas could not help linking this business to the presence of Lord Ashbury in Versailles. Why? He did not know. Of course, there had been peace between the two nations for years, but it was an armed peace, beset with mutual caution and suspicion. The English suspected the French of harbouring thoughts of revenge. This obsession was exacerbated by every new episode in the rebellion of the American colonies. He, of all people, was in a position to know that there was some foundation for this and that Naganda was not constantly travelling the length and breadth of the Indian Territories just to find new places to hunt caribou and beaver.

The questions were piling up. If these two women had harboured evil intentions towards the Queen, why would they have made themselves so conspicuous by their dress and way of speaking? And how to account for something which made the whole thing even more puzzling, that sudden disappearance, which brought back some very bad memories? He felt again the terror he had once before experienced in the face of the inexplicable and the nagging irritation of having failed to find a rational explanation for such phenomena.

It was well into the afternoon by now. Nicolas was wandering in the hall of mirrors, undecided whether to visit the Queen or to do what he had to do with Madame de Maurepas. Lost in thought, he bumped into someone, who held him back in a friendly way.

'Come now, Monsieur Le Floch,' said the newcomer, with a jovial expression, 'where are you going with such a puzzled air?'

He recognised Monsieur de Ville d'Avray, the First Groom of the King's Bedchamber. He had had the good fortune to meet him when he had taken up his post in succession to Monsieur de La Borde.[5]

'Walk with me,' he said, taking Nicolas's arm, 'and you can tell me your troubles. I'm just off to deliver a note to Monsieur de Maurepas.'

'Gladly. Your kind offer resolves my indecision. I was torn between the Queen and the minister, and now you've made up my mind for me!'

'Perfect timing! I'm going to see the Queen next. His Majesty has arranged a surprise for her and has asked me to take care of it. You can accompany me there once you've seen to your business with Monsieur de Maurepas. You see, everything works out without any effort. You just have to meet the right person.'

'Monsieur, I am your humble servant.'

'And I yours. I found the King very calm after he had seen you. Since yesterday, I had been finding him quite dejected. Something about a cat . . .'

Nicolas nodded. 'That's my business, as it happens. I have to convince Madame de Maurepas that he was shooting at a pigeon and missed.'

'A pigeon? I understand your anxiety. It won't be easy to get the good lady to swallow that. Do you know her?'

'She hasn't been at Versailles long, and I haven't been here very often lately . . .'

'Come on, you're here now, and very much in favour! The important thing is not to be put off by her repulsive exterior. In fact, she's quite open-handed. She acts high and mighty and likes nothing better than to grumble about the ills of her house – all material ones, don't worry – the failings of the time and the misfortune of being at Versailles. To do so, she persists in using the old language of the Regency period, with a vulgarity that has become second nature to her.'

'I fear the worst,' said Nicolas, with a smile.

'She has a natural wit which gives her the upper hand over those devoid of it, and, although you might find that she rattles on, she'll like you. She has a sixth sense about when people are being honest with her.'

That wasn't what Nicolas needed to hear. Was his pigeon idea the right one after all? They reached the apartments which the King had given the minister and which were close to his. They were admitted to a drawing room dominated by the harsh voice of an elderly woman of rare ugliness, sitting in a *bergère*, surrounded by a number of attentive ladies. Leaning on the mantelpiece, Monsieur de Maurepas was conversing with Richelieu. It seemed, however, that the lady's words were addressed to him.

'You run away from me because I get on your nerves, so you say, and I'm always grumbling. What else do you want? I got into the habit of doing it at Pontchartrain[6] for forty years through *lettres de cachet* and kicking up as much fuss as I could, so why shouldn't I do it at Versailles? All that time spent paying off your debts, and those of Monsieur de Pontchartrain, who acts like Solomon, and those of Monsieur de La Vrillière, may God confound him! And then those of the Archbishop of Bourges, who builds castles for his stupid brother and even the Marquis of Phélypeaux, who also ended up with debts . . .'

'She'll mention the whole family,' Ville d'Avray whispered in Nicolas's ear.

'The fact is, I paid millions, while being forced to skimp and save. All the same, I had a hundred and thirteen servants.'

'My darling . . .' said Maurepas.

'I know what I'm talking about. A hundred and thirteen servants to pay, and a hundred and ten people to see every day that God creates. So don't go throwing stones at me. That's right, laugh! You have no heart, no liver, no lungs, no spleen! You drag me to Versailles, and they kill my cat! My God, I must have had a jinx on me to fall for someone like you, who's always giving me a rough time!'

She looked long and hard at the new arrivals.

'Here's the hero of the day!' said Richelieu, addressing Nicolas. 'I was recounting your adventures to Maurepas, who was kind enough to enquire about you.'

What was irritating about the maréchal, thought Nicolas, was that smugness that shone through in everything he said, however well meant. He bowed to the minister.

'Monsieur,' said Maurepas, 'what the maréchal has revealed makes me anxious to know you better. My separation from the Court has not given me a chance to . . . Tell me, do you ever seize lampoons, songs or other seditious material?'

'That is indeed a frequent occurrence.'

'Good, good! Think of me sometimes. One example will suffice for me. I've been collecting material of this kind for many years. It's a mania of mine. Clairambault, the genealogist of the King's Orders, has already offered me a copy of his song book. If you can help me to enrich it, my collection will constitute the true history of the century.'

'I'll see what I can do, Comte.'

'There he goes, claiming an exclusive right to my visitors!' cried the duchesse. 'Approach, young man.'

This appellation delighted Nicolas, less and less accustomed to being addressed in this way.

'So, Monsieur, to what do we owe your presence?'

'Madame, His Majesty . . .'

'That's enough, Monsieur. Not another word.'

Had she understood? Did she know all about it? She rose, leaned on Nicolas's arm, waved the other ladies out of her way with an imperious gesture and, walking with a stoop, drew him into a cramped boudoir, where she collapsed into a love seat with a painful sigh. She gave him a stern look and urged him to speak.

'Madame, I shan't beat about the bush. The King is so unhappy about the loss of your angora cat that he does not dare speak to you himself. He genuinely wants you to know the truth: I admit to my great shame that it was I who suggested to him the excuse that he had been shooting at pigeons.'

A long silence ensued.

'Monsieur, tell the King that I am much aggrieved at having lost an old companion who guzzled and slept in my lap. But listen to this. I would far rather lose my cat than find out the King had lied. He does not need my forgiveness, I am his servant. He's a good boy, and so are you. Keep an eye on Monsieur de Maurepas.'

She held out her hand for him to kiss. Nicolas went back to the other room, and everyone turned to look at him, intrigued. For the second time that day, 'young Ranreuil' was creating a stir.

'No outbursts, no yelling,' said Ville d'Avray. 'I think I've been quite clairvoyant in this matter. He has cast a spell on the lady.'

'I'm an expert at exorcisms,' said Nicolas wryly. 'I followed your advice and have done well by it. May I ask you to tell His Majesty that the affair has been settled, truthfully . . . And without the pigeon. And that Madame de Maurepas is his servant.'

Ville d'Avray bowed. 'Thank you for making me the herald of such good news. I hope your mission to the Queen is less delicate.'

'It's only some information I must pass on to her at the King's request.'

They reached the room of the Queen's guards.

'Don't hesitate,' said Ville d'Avray, hurrying on, 'to call on my services. Your friend La Borde used to lodge you when you stayed at Versailles. Rest assured that there will always be a bed for you. The King has divided the rooms on the mezzanine once occupied by the Comtesse du Barry. He's given some to Monsieur de Maurepas and the rest, which are above his head, to myself. I've been loyal to him since his earliest childhood and he's always very good to me.'

'I'm grateful to you for your proposal.'

Nicolas reserved the right to decide later whether this offer had been made because he was now someone to be reckoned with or out of simple kindness.

'As you will have noticed,' resumed Ville d'Avray, 'everyone is alike in Madame de Maurepas's salon. That's the true Court, the ideal place to talk about politics. All those who matter – especially the ministers – frequent that highly convenient meeting place, and the kingdom is fashioned anew every evening.'

From the first-floor landing of the marble staircase, he entered the room of the Queen's guards. A spruce little old man, dressed all in black, was sitting waiting on a window seat, his chin resting on the pommel of his cane. Next to him, two grooms were carrying shapes wrapped in crimson velvet. Nicolas recognised Monsieur de Vaucanson, of the Royal Academy of Sciences, a renowned engineer and a maker of remarkable automata. Sartine, who made it his job to know everything, and at the urging of Madame de Pompadour, had once dispatched Nicolas to see the scientist under some pretext or other to try to discover the secret of his magic dolls. A few *louis* appropriately distributed to his servants had given him a clearer view of the matter.

Ville d'Avray told him that the King had sent for this visitor in order for him to show his masterworks to the Queen. It was therefore a kind of procession that entered the Grand Couvert antechamber where the presentation was to take place. The grooms carefully arranged the prodigious mechanisms on the table set up for that purpose. A large armchair awaited the Queen who, announced by the usher, entered surrounded by her women.

Her incomparable gait aroused Nicolas's admiration. She seemed to glide across the floor, her whole body swaying gently. This impression was strengthened by the haughty way she held her head. He was reminded of a swan. Since their first encounter, four years earlier, he had only seen her from a distance. She seemed to have broadened out a little; she was no longer a child, not yet a woman. Not very tall, with a dazzling complexion, she dominated the room, turning her slightly heavy but expressive blue eyes on each of her visitors. Her high, domed forehead recalled the portraits of her father, Emperor Franz. The gentleness of her smile countered the disdainful set of her mouth. She was wearing a taffeta dress adorned with flecked gauze, with trimmings of the same fabric and an English-style bonnet. Responding to her guests' bows, she gracefully inclined her head. Monsieur de Ville d'Avray introduced Monsieur de Vaucanson. At that moment, a woman with a stiff bearing and a severe expression whispered a few words in the Queen's ear. Her Majesty looked at Nicolas.

'Madame de Noailles[7] is intrigued by you, Monsieur,' she said. 'She is unaware that we are old friends from the forest of Compiègne.[8] Marquis, welcome.'

'Madame,' resumed Ville d'Avray, 'His Majesty has deemed it a pleasant idea to have Monsieur de Vaucanson show you two of his automata, which are famous throughout Europe.'

'The King has anticipated my desires. No one was more anxious than I to meet the father of these animated creatures, of which my mother so often spoke in Vienna.'

'Madame, this is too much honour for an old man,' said

Vaucanson, bowing. 'Allow me to present my children.'

He struck the floor with his cane. The grooms uncovered the first machine.

'Your Majesty, I have called this first automaton the Flute Player. It is a wooden statue, copied from *The Faun* by Coysevox, playing the transverse flute. He can play twelve different tunes with extreme precision. The fingers make the required movements. The automaton can modify the wind entering the instrument by increasing or decreasing the speed, following the different tones, varying the disposition of the lips to do so. The lips work a valve similar to a tongue which makes it possible to imitate everything a man is obliged to do.'

He approached the automaton and pressed a little button at the base of the mechanism. The musician suddenly came to life; his eyes moved, and he lifted the flute to his lips, while his nimble fingers ran up and down the body of the instrument. The thumb was in exactly the right place to produce the octave, and the raised and slightly tilted head seemed animated by the feeling of the music that now rose.

The assembly watched and listened, spellbound, to the small living form, born of the genius of its maker, which mimed the appearance of life to such perfection. The tune came to an end, and the flautist winked and resumed his initial position. Her head tilted and resting on her hand, the Queen seemed moved. She clapped, imitated by her women, apart from Madame de Noailles, who was muttering to herself, clearly appalled by this spectacle.

'Monsieur,' said the Queen, her German accent more noticeable because of her emotion, 'I thank you for this wonderful moment and for the sensitivity which made you choose an air by

Gluck, the Kappellmeister of the Empress in Vienna.'

Nicolas had also recognised the tune; it was from *Iphigenia in Aulis*, which Gluck had put on in Paris in April, a performance strongly supported by the Queen. Monsieur de Vaucanson was an experienced courtier. He bowed and again struck the floor. The grooms covered the flautist and unveiled a second mechanism. This object was smaller, and a murmur of surprise rose at the sight of a duck sitting motionless in a porcelain basin, into which the contents of a large flask of water were poured. The animal seemed more real than nature.

'May Her Majesty consider this second example,' said Vaucanson. 'This duck, motionless for the moment, will, at my command, rise up on its legs and move about like a farmyard fowl.'

He set off the mechanism. The duck rose, shook itself, moved its neck right then left, then quacked and splashed about, as if startled at finding itself in such noble company. All the poses of nature were exactly reproduced. Vaucanson took a small packet of grain from his pocket and approached the Queen.

'Would Her Majesty like to feed the bird?'

The Queen rose with all the enthusiasm of a child delighted with a new toy. Madame de Noailles tried to stop her, and was dismissed with a gesture.

'How should I proceed, Monsieur?'

'I'm going to empty the grain into Your Majesty's hand, and she will present it to the bird's beak. I assure you, there is no danger.'

She approached and held out her hand to the duck, which stretched its neck, seized the offered grain with a little shake and gobbled it up. Delighted, the Queen burst out laughing like a mischievous child. She went back to her seat. Vaucanson waited a few moments, then picked up the duck and placed it on a silver platter. The fowl froze and gave up its perfectly digested meal through the natural channels. Madame de Noailles appeared to be about to faint, but the rest of the gathering was swept by gales of laughter.

'Monsieur,' said the Queen, trying hard to keep a straight face, 'I shall never forget this session, and I will tell the King how much it interested and amused me. I am completely astonished by this latest expression of your genius. What is the secret of that perfect digestion?'

'May Your Majesty forgive me, but it's the secret of life!'

'I see. So you're a bit of a sorcerer, Monsieur!' She held out her hand to him, and he kissed it with devotion then withdrew. Ville d'Avray and Nicolas, who was uncertain what to do next, were about to follow him when the Queen made a sign.

'I wish to speak with the Marquis de Ranreuil. Leave us.'

Madame de Noailles took a step forward, apparently outraged by this decision. With an imperious look, Marie Antoinette silenced her.

'The Queen wishes it, the Queen demands it.'

The duenna withdrew, subdued. Nicolas approached.

'I believe you have some things to tell me, Monsieur.'

Nicolas informed her that, at the request of Monsieur Lenoir, he had made enquiries at Trianon and seen the Richards. That such incidents would not recur. That it might perhaps be a good idea to limit the common people's access to the gardens, and that in any case he would post informers to keep an eye on the area and report to him any suspicious intrusion or disturbing episode occurring on the Queen's estate.

'Thank you for dealing with this matter,' the Queen said. 'I don't wish access to the gardens to be forbidden. The people have a right to approach their monarchs, and I don't want to be confined, hiding my amusements behind bars like an animal in a menagerie. Continue, and keep me informed. I don't want the King to be upset with all this.' She smiled at him. 'You know everything. How does that duck of Monsieur de Vaucanson's digest the grain it is served? It's beyond me, and I shan't rest until I know the secret.'

'The Queen may hear a confession,' said Nicolas with a laugh, 'but she also knows that she cannot divulge its contents.'

'That may be so, Monsieur. Your conditions are quite tough . . .'

'Monsieur de Sartine, once questioned about this famous duck by Madame de Pompadour, gave me the task of investigating it and finding an answer. How indeed to explain this reconstruction of the natural functions: swallowing, dissolving, and expelling? In fact, the grain given to the automaton falls into a box placed beneath its belly, a kind of drawer which is emptied every three or four sessions. The material to be evacuated is prepared in advance, a kind of gruel composed of breadcrumbs coloured green. This is forced out by a pump to look as if it has really gone through a digestive process. The rest is a matter of mechanics; of cogs and springs and keys to be wound, a perfect piece of clockwork.'

'Then we shall share a secret . . . I understand why the King is so interested. Monsieur, have you been at Court for a long time?'

'My duties mainly keep me in Paris. However, Madame, I have often been here since 1762. As well as dealing with special investigations, I had the task of providing security for the King and the royal family.'

'As henchman to the marquise and the comtesse?'

It was a direct hit, and it seemed pointless to prevaricate. 'Madame, I was obeying the late King's orders.'

'Don't worry, I have been informed of his judgement on your loyalty. Did you know that the Duc de La Vrillière does not like me at all?'

It was rather the reverse: she could not forgive him for his support for Madame du Barry. It was clear to Nicolas that the Queen of France had not forgotten the offence caused to her as Dauphine.

'I am not in his confidence.'

'May I count on you, Monsieur?'

'I am your servant and the King's. I hope Your Majesty is convinced of that.'

Calmer now, she held out her hand. How could he refuse her anything?

Nicolas was unable to find Monsieur de Ville d'Avray, doubtless on his way to announce to the King that a peace treaty had been signed with Madame de Maurepas. Nicolas felt both pleased and anxious. Pleased that his appearance at Court had been marked by a dazzling return to favour which strengthened his position with both the Duc de La Vrillière and the Lieutenant General of Police, but anxious at the thought that the same favour might earn him many adversaries, the most dangerous not being the most visible. Everyone was turning to him to ensure his loyalty and demand his support and his services. Could he satisfy them all? The King must be served first; that was his motto and his yardstick, as always. After that, he would just have to see how things worked out.

Lost in thought, he returned to his hotel. The wind, which had continued blowing, had dried up the waters from that dawn's storm. Angry little gusts sent the dead leaves whirling madly. At the noisy table for guests, where he discouraged his neighbours with his silence, he dined on spit-roasted chicken and a blancmange soaked in cider. He went to bed early and dreamed of Mademoiselle d'Arranet.

*Thursday 6 October 1774*

Nicolas returned at the appointed time to the area between the palace and the park where the King's carriages were assembled for the day's hunt. Accustomed for years to the unchanging ceremonial of the hunt, he observed with indulgent curiosity the timidity and awkwardness of those newly presented. It had always seemed to him strange that hunting was chosen to mark this event, and that being presented, for a man, consisted simply of being able to climb into one of the King's carriages on a day marked down for hunting. It cost ten *louis* to the first groom who presented the horse and ten *louis* to the driver of the coach. He dozed as far as the plain of Grenelle, where his position was next to the King's. Radiant with happiness, the monarch gave him a little wave, which showed that he could see better at a distance than at close quarters. He was surrounded by pages from the large stable who had abandoned their blue costumes covered with crimson and white silk braid for blue twill jackets and gaiters of hide. They would stand behind the King, each with a rifle, and, once the monarch had fired, would provide him with another weapon while the first would be passed from hand to hand until it reached the arquebusier, who would reload it. Meanwhile, the first page would make sure the game was collected, keeping an exact account of it on little slates. The King, a great hunter like his forefathers, killed several hundred animals and birds at every shooting party.

Suddenly, Nicolas heard, somewhere to his left, a louder explosion than the usual shots. Cries rang out. He saw coachmen running, then returning carrying a body covered in blood. When he got back into his coach after the hunt, his neighbour explained to him what had happened. One of the newcomers being presented that day, a young gentleman from Berry, had brought an old family weapon for the occasion. Long unused, it had exploded, taking away his hand.

'All he can do now is ask for the address of the silversmith who made the silver hand.'

'The silver hand?'

'Yes, Monsieur de Saint-Florentin, or rather the Duc de La Vrillière, had the same thing happen to him a few years ago. The late King presented him with a substitute hand.'

Nicolas sat huddled and silent in a corner of the coach. So that gaping hole in the throats of the two victims, shaped like a stiff hand, could be . . . The idea seemed so monstrous, he bit his lips until they bled.

# VIII

## NAVIGATION

What is a naval battle? You fire cannon, you separate,
and the sea is just as salty as it was before!
MAUREPAS

Nicolas returned to the palace, frozen with fear. How could he
have forgotten that characteristic of the Minister of the King's
Household? So many years spent close to him, and yet . . . It was
precisely that proximity, a matter of habit and routine, which
played games with your memory and blunted your powers of
reasoning. He had long wondered about the nature of the late
King's fondness for that colourless little man who led a life of
debauchery and was so hated within the royal family . . . Madame
Adélaïde and Madame Victoire endlessly belittled him, and never
lost an opportunity to humiliate him in public. Had not the
Queen, as she had herself just reminded Nicolas, once told the
duc that she could not forget that he had taken sides against her at
the end of the former reign? For Nicolas, however, there
remained the minister's loyalty to Louis XV, not to mention the
vital support he had given his commissioner on a number of
critical occasions.

The new King had retained him against all the odds, although
he had exiled his mistress, the Beautiful Aglaé, and was keeping
him somewhat at arm's length. For what reason? Did his office

put him in a position to know too many State secrets? Was it too risky to even conceive of the idea of removing him? Or did the fact that he was a cousin of the First Minister demand a certain indulgence, at least for the time being? Sartine, who had long been his follower, had gradually distanced himself from him, having become aware that La Vrillière had benefited greatly from the successes of his service but had done nothing to support him when things had become unpleasant for him.

When it came down to it, Nicolas did not really care about all these intrigues, and followed their ins and outs only from a very great distance. What mattered was that he now found himself in possession of a clue, perhaps even a piece of evidence, the importance of which was still to be assessed. He could not dismiss the possibility that it was a coincidence, and it was vital that he be extremely cautious. Could somebody else have got hold of an object the Duc de La Vrillière obviously had to take off from time to time – to sleep, for example? Was it possible that someone had made a copy of the artificial hand with a view to compromising the minister? On the other hand, the initial stages of the investigation had revealed a number of contradictions in those testimonies which could have provided the master of the house with an alibi. Nor could Nicolas forget that even the duchesse had lied about Monsieur de La Vrillière being at Versailles on the night of the murder.

The minister's private life, which certainly could be called dissolute, was an open secret. So why, in this particular case, strive to conceal what he had been doing that night, unless in an attempt to cover up the unspeakable? Nicolas recalled his uncertainty about the real purpose of his mission: did they have such a low opinion of him as to imagine that, finding himself out of favour and removed from affairs, he would agree to be a malleable instrument and carry out the semblance of an investigation the conclusion of which was inevitable? He was thinking so fast that the blood was beating in his temples. There was no point tormenting himself with speculations, he just had to get a move on. Only a return to action would allow him to throw some light on an affair which was becoming increasingly obscured by new facts and in which sham and pretence were everywhere.

The most important thing was to determine if the Duc de La Vrillière still wore the silver hand given to him by the late King. How to proceed? Should he simply ask the minister, and never mind his possible reaction? As Nicolas prepared his strategy, he became aware of the enormity of the implications: whether he liked it or not, he was now considering the duc to be the prime suspect in a murder committed in his own house. His sense of embarrassment increased when a new thought occurred to him: a second victim had been discovered, bearing on her neck the same characteristic wound. The two murders seemed to have been committed using an identical weapon, which meant that the person responsible for the first could also have been responsible for the second. He would definitely have to verify the duc's whereabouts at those times. Nicolas rebuked himself for wasting too much time in hypothesising. Yes, it really was essential to get down to action and stop himself getting needlessly carried away.

The Minister of the King's Household must surely be back in Versailles, where the affairs of his office required him. He was a man of habit, and usually lunched at about one in the afternoon. Nicolas judged that this was a good time to be received. He would not change, as his hunting costume denoted his privileged rank at Court . . . He had a perfect excuse: to give an up-to-date report on his inquiry into the murder at the Saint-Florentin mansion.

In the ministers' wing, he was greeted like a regular visitor by the elderly groom, who, after tapping at the door, admitted him to the Duc de La Vrillière's study. As predicted, he was in the middle of lunch, sitting at a pedestal table near the window. A fire was blazing in the hearth.

'What, have the animals got into the palace?' he said, looking up. 'How long have you been at Versailles?'

Nicolas realised that the opening remark referred to his hunting costume. 'Since yesterday morning, Monseigneur. On the instructions of Monsieur Lenoir.'

'And you've only just deigned to come and pay me a visit!'

'His Majesty wanted to see me, then Monsieur de Maurepas, and, last but not least, the Queen. In addition, the King requested my presence at this morning's shoot.'

'Ah, that's how they poach our people . . .' The duc seemed tense, even anxious. 'I'm listening,' he said.

'Monseigneur,' began Nicolas, 'I should like to give you a brief report of my investigation. Most of your servants have been misrepresenting the truth, and sometimes openly lying. Your major-domo's attempted suicide was nothing but a minor cut. He doesn't remember a thing.'

'What?' said the duc, agitated. 'And will that be enough to exonerate him in your opinion?'

'I'm not saying that. I'm merely observing that there is nothing to support the charges against him, no significant corroborating evidence . . .'

'Come now, it must be him! Who else could it be? You need to speed things up, Monsieur.'

'Justice, Monseigneur, walks hand in hand with truth, which by definition is slow and cautious.'

The duc stiffened on his chair. 'I hope you're not trying to teach me a lesson, Commissioner.'

'God forbid,' replied Nicolas. 'It was merely an aside. There are many others who think the same way as you and are urging me to bring matters to a conclusion.'

The minister was eating *oublies*, dipping them into a cup of chocolate. A little pot contained the rest of the drink. The pedestal table was unsteady, and the pot badly balanced. The duc's gloved right hand was flat on the table, motionless. Only his left hand was moving. If he became any more irritable, thought Nicolas, the whole thing would come crashing to the floor. With a little luck . . .

'What?' yelled the duc. 'Who are these others? Why is an affair which should have remained secret being openly discussed? Who have you been talking to about it? Can't you hold your tongue after all these years? Sartine, of course! He doesn't matter any more, don't you understand? He doesn't matter at all!'

The little man was pallid with rage.

'Monseigneur is mistaken,' Nicolas replied, in his most placatory tone. 'It may well be that Monsieur de Sartine knows, he's always well informed about everything. Imagining the contrary would be an illusion. I was thinking of the Duc de Richelieu, who runs everywhere spreading news from group to group. Naturally he questioned me, and I pretended to know nothing. As for the King, he was of the opinion that I would succeed in the end.'

Purple blotches appeared on the minister's face. 'Richelieu! He's always fussing around, thinking he's indispensable. Why doesn't he just retire, after more than sixty years at Court? Damn the fellow! And as for the King . . .'

He raised his gloved hand and brought it down heavily on the pedestal table. The table swayed, the cup tinkled in its saucer, as if taking fright, and the pot overturned, covering the silk glove with dark liquid. Furious, the duc rose and took it off. Nicolas saw what he had wanted to see: the artificial hand was made, not of silver, but of wood.

The chaos which followed this incident gave Nicolas time to reflect on the measures to be taken. Monsieur de La Vrillière had rushed to take another glove from his desk drawer, while the groom repaired the damage and took away the soiled pedestal table. Now Nicolas would have to pull out all the stops, while pretending to continue with his report.

'There is still one strange fact of which I must inform you, Monseigneur . . .'

'Well, hurry up about it.'

'The examinations our people carried out at the Basse-Geôle allowed them to take a plaster cast of the weapon used to cut the throats of the two victims.'

'What two victims? As far as I know, my major-domo didn't die, you just told me he was barely scratched. Are you inventing new victims for your own pleasure?'

'Alas, no! Another young girl was discovered in Impasse

Glatigny on Tuesday morning, with her throat cut in an identical way. There can be no possible doubt: the same weapon was used on both occasions.'

He had the impression that the blow had struck home.

'So you found it and took a cast?' the minister said, in a cold, measured tone.

'We took a cast from the shape of the wound. Just as one can get back to the original seal by taking a cast from the seal on a letter.'

'And what's so strange about it?'

'Its strangeness justifies the question you will forgive me asking, Monseigneur. The cast is in the shape of a hand. Now, no living hand could produce the wounds we found. I note that you are wearing a wooden hand. Where is the silver hand given you by our late lamented King and master?'

La Vrillière did not bat an eyelid. He looked Nicolas in the eye, as if trying to grasp his precise motive in daring to ask such a question. 'Monsieur Le Floch,' he said, 'I wear what I feel comfortable with. The hand given me by our late master I reserve for special occasions.'

'Nevertheless, Monseigneur, you always wear a glove . . . I'm sure you will permit me to examine the precious original more closely. The fact that it is sometimes out of your sight gives rise, if it were necessary, to the suspicion . . . What if someone borrowed it, or worse still . . .'

The minister appeared to have lost patience. 'Of course, of course . . . I've never claimed that it was still in my possession. To tell the truth . . . to tell the truth, I've lost it. I may have left it somewhere.'

'Monseigneur must recall where this loss took place?'

'Yes, yes, of course,' he said, and appeared to hesitate. 'At Madame de Cusacque's house in Normandy.'

'Is it conceivable that this object, which is precious for more than one reason, could have been stolen?'

The minister appeared increasingly perturbed. 'How should I know? Anything's possible.'

'Monseigneur, one last detail. Who actually made that silver hand? Some details on the nature of the object would be useful to me.'

'Monsieur de Villedeuil. In 1765, he was an engineer in Place Royale. Dead now, I think. Le Floch, does the King know about this affair?'

'Yes, Monseigneur. His Majesty mentioned the matter briefly to me, as I have already said.'

The minister took up his quill, dipped it in the inkwell, and began writing. Nicolas understood that the interview was over.


The Court carriage took him back to the Hôtel de la Belle Image, where this triumphant arrival added greatly to his prestige. He immediately went up to his room, shut himself in, and, while once again cleaning his rifles with fanatical care, reflected on what he had just heard, trying to hone his impressions of the encounter with the Duc de La Vrillière. His first observation, a vital one, concerned the lack of openness and honesty in the interview. The second concerned the major element of the artificial hand.

The minister's assertion that he wore a wooden model for everyday use was plausible. Perhaps the original really had disappeared, and its owner really did not know the exact circumstances. His answers about the place where it had been stolen or lost were exceedingly vague. Had it happened in Caen, where his mistress Madame de Cusacque, the Beautiful Aglaé, lived in exile? If so, that would certainly not help them get at the truth. The minister was in a position to know that no inquiry would be carried out in the immediate future so far from Paris and that his word would suffice to put an end to the question.

The duc's anger on learning that the news of the tragedy in his Parisian mansion had spread to Versailles, as well as his acrimony towards Sartine, also gave the commissioner food for thought. Should it lead him to respond favourably to the former Lieutenant General of Police's demand to be kept informed of everything concerning the Minister of the King's Household? He did not really like such a role. But could he refuse Sartine, to whom he owed everything and whose actions had always been dictated by an overriding concern for the interests of the throne? A final thought helped him to make up his mind: if the pot of chocolate had not been overturned, would he have discovered that Monsieur de La Vrillière's silver hand had disappeared? Deep down, he thought himself quite a casuist; if Sartine had been there, he would again have called him a disciple of Loyola . . .

Nicolas knew he was becoming over-excited, and to calm down he decided to write to his son. He could not help being slightly anxious about the beginning of Louis's life as a schoolboy. How would a boy like that, his character already well formed, a boy in whom Nicolas was delighted to find traces and memories of his own father, the Marquis de Ranreuil, react to school? However extraordinary his situation might seem to him,

Louis appeared to rise above it with a praiseworthy straight-forwardness and sense of proportion. Nevertheless, Nicolas could not quite shake off the unease caused by the circumstances of his early youth. On the one hand, he was the spoilt child of a brothel, and on the other, the brilliant, refined schoolboy who had delighted everyone in the Noblecourt household. Nicolas had to give due recognition to La Satin for having, in such conditions, been able to avoid the worst. Louis was now proud of the glorious family of which he was the descendant, but was quite lacking in arrogance. Did he fully realise, though, the ambiguity of his position in the world? The steep path of truth had been chosen for him, and it might lead him down many treacherous side roads. Nicolas dreaded the suffering it might bring him, while hoping that, if such strains did indeed make themselves felt in such a young soul, he would gain from them, like a burning blade made supple and hard by being dipped in water. It was therefore a tender letter full of the most judicious advice – the very same advice he had received twenty years earlier from the Marquis de Ranreuil – which he addressed to his son. He corrected it carefully, copied it out neatly, and sealed it. Then he set about getting ready for his dinner at the Comte d'Arranet's house.

He shaved with a dexterity he had inherited from his father. When he had reached the age when he needed to start shaving, much to the consternation of Canon Le Floch, for whom all care of the body was the work of the devil, the marquis had taught him the rudiments and given him a little treatise, which contained instructions on how to shave without danger to oneself, which stones to use for sharpening blades, and how to prepare leather for a strop. He chose a dark-grey coat; the colour was known as

London chimney soot, and it was a recent model from the workshop of his tailor, Master Vachon, the discreet elegance of whose clothes were ideally suited for the end of the period of mourning. He took from his portmanteau some fine Mechlin lace cuffs and a cravat and shirt that were both dazzlingly white, the result of the combined care of Catherine and Marion: the old servant had taught her protégée the use of a charcoal iron, which had not been a feature of her life in military camps. He brushed his hair, straightened his wig, powdered it, arranged the strands of hair that peeped out with a little agate handle, and checked his flattering reflection in the mottled mirror on the dressing table. Last but not least, he fastened the old sword which, two years earlier, a messenger from Brittany had left in Rue Montmartre, wrapped in a blanket, without a word of explanation. Nicolas had recognised the Marquis de Ranreuil's ceremonial sword and had assumed that it was his half-sister Isabelle who had sent it to him, just as, not long after the death of her father, she had given him the signet ring bearing the family arms, which he would one day pass on to Louis. Nostalgia overcame him for a moment. He closed his eyes and saw again the wild shore of the ocean, almost heard the cries of the seabirds above his head . . .

Having dismissed the Court carriage, he asked for a cab to take him to the d'Arranet mansion. Night had fallen. Nature was calm again, the wind having dropped at sunset. The hotel-keeper bustled around him obsequiously, suddenly convinced that he was dealing with some important person travelling incognito. Since Peter the Great, northern princes had taken to moving about under false identities. It was true that Nicolas, with his grave, silent demeanour, looked the part.

Having reached his destination, he was greeted by the formidable footman and former sailor, who gave him a friendly wink.

'The admiral's in the library, Monsieur, with that damned butcher who's suddenly turned up again. He was the one who sewed up my throat after a bloody Biscayan had cut it. He did it in the blink of an eye, while I was biting into a piece of leather soaked with rum. The bastard was good, I'll give him that. By God, it's really good to see him again!'

'Tribord, I like you,' said Nicolas, slipping a double *louis* into his hand. 'Dr Semacgus is my friend, too.'

He was happy to discover some unknown aspects of the naval surgeon. The footman opened the door to the library. There was a mixture of odours: the warm smell of candles and the exotic scent of rum. The Comte d'Arranet was at one of the open windows, talking to Semacgus. Their words were punctuated by gales of laughter. Nicolas was struck by the majestic presence of the former general officer, who had put on his uniform for the occasion. Flame-red breeches, a matching doublet braided and embroidered in gold, a blue coat, the sash of the order of Saint Louis threaded through the epaulette on the right shoulder; everything contributed to the splendour of his appearance. The uniform gleamed in the lights, its martial elegance accentuating the energy in d'Arranet's face. Semacgus, in his black coat and powdered wig, made a distinguished foil for his former chief and companion at arms.

'Ah, here's Ranreuil,' said the admiral, turning. 'You are both on familiar territory.'

Before it could even get under way, the conversation was interrupted by the sound of a number of carriages stopping at the front steps. The host put down his glass and hurried, one hand supporting his wounded leg, to greet the newcomers. Monsieur de Sartine and La Borde appeared in a symphony of grey, which reinforced Nicolas in his choice of coat. Monsieur d'Arranet introduced Semacgus to the minister, who recalled, with some humour, that he had had the pleasure of finding the naval surgeon innocent in a criminal case during which he had been wrongly imprisoned fourteen years earlier.[1] All of this was recounted with that air of self-satisfaction that always made Nicolas angry, even though he was accustomed to the former Lieutenant General of Police taking credit for his men's successes. But he was wrong about the object of his annoyance; its target was not Monsieur de Sartine, or only by default. He had in fact just realised that this was a dinner for men only and that Mademoiselle d'Arranet would not be making an appearance. He was surprised at how displeased he felt. Drinks were served and the company grew lively. La Borde immediately drew Nicolas into the garden. He wanted to get something off his chest. His young wife's health had hardly improved, despite the rigorous treatment to which she was being subjected. Her nervous irritation persisted, accompanied by convulsions and by a melancholy that nothing appeared able to dispel. It was difficult to break through her apathy. Nicolas was upset to see his friend so concerned, and he also sensed that he was still just as affected by the loss of the King. He had not realised, a few days earlier at Noblecourt's house, how false his good mood had been and how tactfully he had striven not to cast a shadow over the party given in honour of

Louis. He assured him of his loyalty and his wish to be introduced to Madame de La Borde at a more propitious time. Tribord announced that the dinner for the minister was served, and they moved to the dining room.

Nicolas suspected Aimée's hand in the arrangement and discreet elegance of the table. There was a dazzlingly white table runner on which stood emblazoned items of silverware interspersed with pieces of white coral containing mixed flowers. Monsieur de Sartine presided at the head of the table, with his host on his left, and Monsieur de La Borde on his right. Tribord supervised the five servants who stood behind the guests and served them food and drink. The first course consisted of mussels in an egg and lemon juice sauce, turbot coated in breadcrumbs, and a huge trout frozen in jelly and accompanied by *pannequets* of prawns and carved vegetables. Wine from Champagne and Burgundy waited in silver-gilt cooling pitchers.

'Admiral,' said Sartine, 'you honour me with a most uncommon creature of the depths. I haven't come across one of this size since those which occasionally appeared at the late King's little dinners, and which were brought from Switzerland at top speed by relays of couriers. How much does it weigh? Twelve, fifteen pounds?'

'More than that!' said d'Arranet, beaming. 'It's twenty pounds at least and yesterday morning was still swimming in Lake Geneva. I love fresh fish, although some claim that you should leave it for a few days to enhance the taste. I'm not one of them.'

'It's true of skate,' said Semacgus, 'which is inedible on the first day. But you have to be careful. A little too long and the animal gets too much ammonia and starts to smell.'

'Is fishing practised on our vessels?'

'During longer crossings, it can be a pleasant diversion, and a definite improvement on the routine fare on board. I can still see Semacgus, abeam off Taranto, catching some fifteen tuna in a row! The crew thought they were eating fresh meat. That was on the frigate *Cassiopée*.'

'Otherwise, it's always beef and salted pork, I suppose?'

'Always,' said the comte, 'and it's often old and rotten. Now there's a reform you could make: supplies.'

'You never take live cattle or poultry on board?'

'Yes, of course! On departure and at every port of call. But they don't last long, and if there's a battle, it's a disaster. All it takes is one cannonball hitting a scuttle, and it's farewell to the livestock.'

'I observe,' said Sartine pensively, 'that supplying the navy is not a simple business. Well, I've come here wanting to learn. I've never sailed.'

'Nor I,' said La Borde.

'I crossed the English Channel on a steamship,' said Nicolas.

'Comte,' Sartine went on, 'you're an old sailor, I mean an experienced sailor, not one of those officers who are all show but never put to sea, you know what I mean . . . What advice would you give me?'

'God forbid that I should presume to give advice to one of my master's ministers! However, I can make a few fairly obvious suggestions. The first is that you must restore hope to the navy. Monsieur de Choiseul may have meant well, in his day, but this century has been disastrous for a force so vital to the greatness of France.'

'It is a false accusation that people make against the late King,' Sartine replied curtly. 'Not you, Admiral, but others. The truth is that it was all a matter of savings and economy. Louis XV used to complain bitterly about it, but his ministers did nothing to raise his hopes. To tell the truth, we were living with political choices conceived under the Regency and pursued by Cardinal Fleury.'

'And on what principles were these choices based?' asked La Borde.

They broke off while the second course was laid on the table: pigs' trotters with truffles, a hare pie and a salad of young rabbit. A Madeira brought back from the Indies, which they immediately sampled, met with unanimous approval.

'To answer your question,' resumed Sartine, 'it is necessary to understand that our policy consisted of not making the other maritime powers jealous, especially England. It was believed that the surest way to maintain peace was to reduce the navy in order not to offend that nation.'

'But, Monseigneur,' cried d'Arranet passionately, 'it is contrary to the honour and interests of the kingdom to have left our navy in the same state of weakness and decay for so long!'

'Alas! As I said, the incompetence of the people involved, the financial crisis, the constant problem of debt, and the permanent opposition of the *parlements*, all these factors conspired to compromise everything. For more than twenty years, when Monsieur de Maurepas was in charge of the navy, he hoped to obtain a ratio of one to three in relation to the English fleet, but couldn't manage it. Will I? I'm certainly going to try my best, especially now that events in the English colonies in America have made it vital for us to stay on the alert. Have I answered your question, Admiral?'

'Yes, indeed! But my second suggestion is a bolder one. I fear that we need to reflect on the way we fight. Let me explain. We French fight in a line and try essentially to knock down the enemy's masts and cripple him. Applied mechanically, this tactic encourages routine and makes it impossible for us to adapt to circumstances. The English method is quite different; they fire directly into the hull. You should see the damage when a well-aimed shot has sliced through a ship, the splinters of wood like so many daggers . . . And what about when a vessel is behind you and tearing your stern to pieces with general fire that goes the whole length of the ship? The loss of life is appalling. Not to mention the fact that it takes a long time to replace the most experienced men.'

'So what do you suggest?' asked Sartine.

'That we need to think about it! A career at sea requires courage, endurance, competence, but also reflection and a spirit of decisiveness in the most varied circumstances. I don't think one should become too attached to a single tactic, but that each should be applied as and when the situation calls for it, sometimes both in succession. I know the English are very well trained. They really learn how to fire, how to board an enemy ship in heavy weather, and everything's always precisely timed. While we, on the other hand, train very little and always with the thought of making savings. Faced with the enemy's formidable efficiency, we've paid a high price for our lack of training!'

'I tend to agree with you,' Semacgus cut in. 'When the time

comes for battle, the amount of time spent at sea counts more than the size of the cannon!'

'Talking of cannon, Monseigneur,' d'Arranet went on, 'I hope your offices have sent you the announcement of the invention by an English engineer of a new type of cannon: the caronade, which is already being used by the Royal Navy.'

'I've heard of it,' replied Sartine, 'though I haven't quite grasped how it works.'

'It's shorter, doesn't have wheels, and its gun carriage consists of two wooden boards that can be slid one on top of the other. Its great interest, apart from that, is that it has a line of sight and a lever with a threaded shaft that make it possible to give the weapon the desired angle of fire. With a double load or filled with grapeshot, the caronade can cause havoc . . .'

Sartine was thinking. He glanced around him. The servants had cleared away the second course, and no one could overhear.

'I have a plan, my friends, to create a service whose job will be to gather information on the English fleet and what those gentlemen in the Admiralty have in store for us. It's all still a bit vague in my mind, but the salvation of the State depends on being well informed. We'll have to do some recruiting to find suitable men for this great project.'

He threw Nicolas a long, eloquent look. The servants were coming back, and the comte created a diversion.

'The frigate is the queen of battleships,' he declared. 'Quick, and easy to handle. The seventy-four has good firing strength and can still manoeuvre. Apart from that, they're ungovernable monsters whose losses are proportionate to their mass. Just think: nearly nine hundred men on board! It's not a good idea to put all one's eggs in one basket . . . Finally, Monsieur, one last thing: I believe it's necessary to develop infantry on our vessels. At sea, our crews are not armed. They're handed out rifles and pikes. I think it would be advisable to strengthen a corps to provide heavy fire during close combat or boarding.'

'A well-aimed shot that kills the commander can change the outcome of a battle,' said Semacgus. 'That's happened before.'

The third course was ready: bacon pies, ramekins of Italian cheese, puréed partridge, duck à l'espagnole, tendrons of veal with Bengal curry, cardoons with grated cheese, and fried celery.

The minister adjusted his wig with both hands, a gesture which always indicated that he was highly satisfied. 'We haven't really looked into the question yet,' he said, 'but your observations have enlightened me in no uncertain manner. I'm planning to carry out some on-the-spot investigations. I shall start with a study journey to Brittany, concentrating on the administration of our ports and arsenals. I plan to dig new dry docks and increase the capacity for building vessels of the line. What would you say, Admiral, to helping me prepare for this visit and coming with me? I really need the opinion of a man who has sailed, fought and commanded! Later, once a plan of action has been drawn up, we'll be joined by another officer of great merit, the Chevalier de Fleurieu, who at the moment is trying to improve the navy's precision clocks to make the calculation of longitude easier. The King will like the man, he's very fond of that kind of research.'

'Monseigneur, I am at the minister's service,' said a delighted d'Arranet, half rising in his chair.

'That's settled then! Present yourself at my offices as soon as you can. My clerks will have orders to settle you in immediately.

We shall work in concert. Nicolas, tell us a little of the news of the city; I miss it. That'll cheer us up after this grim conversation.'

'Most of the rumours,' replied Nicolas, 'are about the opera and the theatre, as usual! It's said that in Vienna, the Emperor has become very fond of Chevalier Gluck and doesn't want him to leave his Court any more. In order to make sure of this, he's just granted him a pension of two thousand crowns. Out of consideration for his sister, our Queen, and in order not to deprive him of the advantages he has in France, the Emperor has given him permission to come here every year to put on some of his works.'

'Her Majesty won't appreciate the way her brother treats her favourite musician.'

'She was very grateful to Monsieur de Vaucanson for his choice of music yesterday, after the flute player played some tunes by Gluck.'

'It should be said,' remarked La Borde, 'that Ranreuil has caused quite a stir at Court. The whole of Versailles is buzzing with his return to favour. A private audience with the King, an intimate interview with Madame de Maurepas, a conversation with the First Minister, and, to crown it all, an interview with the Queen away from the prying eyes of Madame de Noailles. Last but not least, they say he amiably resolved a domestic drama . . .'

'For a newly-wed who's withdrawn from the world,' said Nicolas, 'I find you're extremely well informed. You are violating my discretion. Let us talk rather of the exploits of our actresses. The second rumour concerns the quarrel between Mademoiselle Arnoux and Mademoiselle Raucoux, which has degenerated into open war. It's said that Mademoiselle Arnoux's lover, Monsieur

Bellenger, the draughtsman of the Menus,[2] has taken up the cudgels on her behalf against the Marquis de La Villette, Mademoiselle Raucoux's knight errant. Words were exchanged – more than words, threats, and in the presence of many witnesses. Fearing the marquis's wrath, Bellenger brought a criminal complaint. However, others have mediated and the two rivals have come to the rather absurd arrangement that they will meet one another with their swords in their hands and that then they will immediately be separated. This ludicrous reconciliation has given rise to a story in the Persian manner condemning the marquis's cowardice.'

'Where is the honour in all that?' cried the Comte d'Arranet. 'It's a farce, and a fine example of the madness that affects such people over totally trivial matters!'

'May the former Lieutenant General of Police remind you, gentlemen,' said Sartine with a laugh, 'that duelling is forbidden and that the King has vowed never to pardon the slightest disobedience regarding this.'

Sweets now appeared on the table, then the host rose and led his guests into the library. Sartine drew Nicolas into a corner of the room.

'The navy is not the police,' he began, in the tone of someone talking to himself. 'I am alone there, under observation and without support. Age has increased Maurepas's egoism, and I fear that the one aim of his ministry is to avoid any upheaval, to abstain from any great measure that might disturb his peace and quiet. All he wants is to keep his position and live the rest of his life with no problems! But how are you getting on with your case?'

The question was abrupt, but it had the merit of getting straight to the point.

'Quite well, as far as the murder weapon is concerned,' replied Nicolas. 'There is no doubt that it was an artificial hand, made of silver, similar to the one once given by the late King to Monsieur de Saint-Florentin after a hunting accident. The fact remains that—'

'A silver hand . . .' murmured Sartine, pensively. 'Imagine that!'

'When I asked the Duc de La Vrillière to explain this coincidence, his answers were vague and prevaricating. Apparently he uses a wooden replica, and claims not to know the whereabouts of the original. He's not even sure if it was stolen or lost. He suggests it may have happened at Madame de Cusacque's house in Normandy.'

'Ah, the Beautiful Aglaé! Well, well! Now that's something new; I congratulate you. And you think—'

'I try not to think, Monseigneur. I merely observe that the duc is now a suspect, especially as he refuses to give an account of his whereabouts that night.'

He told the minister about the discovery of a second victim.

'Did the King talk to you about this case?' Sartine asked, with a thin-lipped smile.

'He did in fact enquire about it.'

'Please keep me informed of any new developments, Nicolas.'

He was about to rejoin the company when Nicolas detained him.

'Is there something else?'

'Yes, Monseigneur. An unexpected encounter which I'd like

to bring to your attention. Yesterday, in the lower gallery of the palace, I met a man who appeared to be wearing makeup and had spectacles with tinted lenses. He fled when he saw me approach.'

'Did you recognise him? Who was he?'

'Lord Ashbury, with whom I had dealings in London. That mission with which you are familiar . . .'

Sartine reflected for a moment. 'The head of British intelligence in Paris! That's as strange as it's disturbing. I don't like it. Inform Lenoir. Find out what foreigners entered our ports and Paris. We need to know what false name he's using. Nicolas, we've never stopped working together, and the future . . . But don't forget to check up on Bourdier. The navy is waiting for its system of codemaking.'

Nicolas was pleased that Sartine had not reiterated his obsession with the return of Choiseul. He was under no illusions about the sincerity of a man whose capacity for secrecy and devious intrigues he had often observed. Working beside him every day for many years had convinced him that Sartine tended to conceal the true reasons behind his actions. He kept his secrets close to his chest and, like all good politicians, always had several irons in the fire. In addition, one area of his activities was still a closed book to the commissioner: his membership of the Freemasons. Did his work in the lodge lead him to embrace the theories of the philosophers' party? In doing so, was he conforming to the spirit of the times, or had he compromised with this hidden influence the better to control it?

In truth, what bound Nicolas to Sartine, apart from a grateful loyalty reinforced by the vicissitudes of the investigations and tribulations they had been through together, was the certainty that this Frenchman from Barcelona, who did not belong to the high nobility – less even than the commissioner himself – constantly demonstrated at every moment a devotion, a passion, a love of the public good in the person of the King. It was not for nothing that the ermine that adorned his magistrate's gown, a symbolic part of the mantle of ceremony, represented the authority and exercise of a justice delegated to him by the monarch.

As for Nicolas, he felt himself to be above all these political choices. The religious debate which had scarred the century only preoccupied him as a cause of public unrest. What made him indignant was the mingling of opposites, the unnatural collusion between the pious, the Jansenists and the *parlements*. The constant aggressive opposition from the *parlements*, briefly brought down by the imperious will of Maupeou with the support of the late King, made him fear the future, especially as Louis XVI's youth and inexperience made it unusually hard to predict. But he would do his duty, trying to remain an honest man amid the compromises required by his position.

Midnight was approaching when the Comte d'Arranet walked the minister to his carriage. The scene was illumined by the torches of the servants, who stood in a semicircle. Semacgus offered Nicolas a lift back to the Hôtel de la Belle Image in his carriage. La Borde was returning to Paris, where his young wife was waiting for him. As he was leaving the house, Nicolas thought he caught a glimpse of a face at the top of the staircase, a face that could only be Aimée's. Sartine's proposal had filled the admiral with excitement. Clearly, the prospect of leaving this period of inactivity behind delighted a man who, like so many general officers of his age and seniority, feared he would no longer be able to serve. They all promised to see each other soon, and Nicolas was asked to regard this house as his own.

Semacgus's carriage slowly turned into the drive which led to the Avenue de Paris. As it was about to go through the gate, it suddenly came to a halt.

### Friday 7 October 1774

Distant voices echoed in his head. They faded then came back again, sounding more distinct. There was some kind of pressure on his left temple. Where was he? In what kind of dream? He could not open his eyelids, they were too heavy . . . He had an overwhelming desire to let go, to spiral slowly down into a bottomless pit. To sink, to sink for ever . . .

'Damnation! He's fainting again. Pass me the vinegar, Mademoiselle.'

'It's a good thing he has a hard head,' said d'Arranet. 'And that the shot went wide. And that you're here, my dear Semacgus.'

'It's my coachman you should thank. His reflexes were good; without him we'd be holding a wake!'

'Trying to kill my guests at my door, in Versailles! Could the real target have been the minister?'

'Anything's possible,' said Semacgus. 'This isn't the first time they've tried to kill him. It's been a bad year for him, this is the third time. Ah, now he's getting a bit of colour back.'

Nicolas opened his eyes. He was lying on a bed in a richly decorated room. Semacgus was looking at him anxiously, the Comte d'Arranet standing beside him. Aimée was sitting on the bed, holding his hand. He tried to sit up, and the pain went to his head. But it was no worse, he thought, than when he'd been hit while playing with his schoolmates in Guérande.

'Don't move,' said Semacgus. 'A bullet grazed your temple. With that kind of wound, you lose a lot of blood and you faint. But you've been through worse. I'm going to put a bandage on. Mademoiselle will now tear your beautiful shirt to shreds.'

To his embarrassment, Nicolas realised that he was bare-chested.

'And you will sleep here, Monsieur,' said d'Arranet. 'That's an order. The idea of someone trying to kill people on my property! I feel responsible for your condition . . .'

Nicolas tried to protest.

'Not a word. I'm going to check the surrounding area. Tonight, everyone will take turns on watch. Tribord will see to that. Semacgus, you will sleep here, and don't argue.'

'Why did they miss me?'

'Heavens!' said the surgeon with a laugh. 'I fear the wound has made him stupid. Instead of congratulating yourself! My coachman, caught by surprise when that long face appeared, hesitated for a moment and then struck the individual with his whip. The lash was red with blood. Watch out for people with scars from now on. That deflected the shot from its intended trajectory and saved you.'

'Didn't you catch him?'

'There's gratitude for you!' retorted Semacgus, showing him his blood-spattered grey doublet. 'You fell into my arms. For all I knew, you were dying. Was I supposed to leave you there?'

'I'm sorry, Guillaume. I'm not quite myself yet.'

Could it be that this attempt had some connection with the

progress of his investigation into the murder at the Saint-Florentin mansion? Semacgus cauterised the wound with rum, as if he were back on board ship and tending the wounded during a sea battle. He made his patient take a large swig of the liquor, lightly bandaged his head, told him he ought to get some sleep, and snuffed out the candles. He would look in on him again tomorrow. There was a certain amount of bustling about as a room was got ready for the doctor. For some time after that, Nicolas could hear the master of the house giving orders to his servants. Aimée took a last glance at the wounded man and went back to her room. The d'Arranet mansion went to sleep, protected by the comte's men, who were posted about the grounds with lanterns.

Nicolas woke with a start. The parquet floor was creaking so much that it was impossible to mistake the source of the sound: someone had entered the room. His heart began to pound. He forced himself to remain still and tried to control his breathing. Perhaps because of the emotion, the pain in his temple, he realised, had receded. Someone had very carefully turned the key in the lock and was now approaching the bed. He was surprised to find that he did not feel afraid. He breathed in a smell of verbena, and another aroma, that of a warm body. A moist finger touched his mouth and a hand slid over his chest. He sensed rather than heard a garment being impatiently removed and falling to the floor. His mind was a mixture of confusion and expectation. Suddenly, he was submerged in a stream of hair. He put out his hands, touched a naked body, and at the contact that body collapsed on him. His mouth found another mouth, lips that opened. The satiny softness of a shoulder devastated him. Slowly, he turned over. Between the kisses sighs replaced words. More tender, more complex, more ardent, they responded to the sensations, marked their stages, and the last sigh of all, which hung suspended for a time, told Nicolas that he should render thanks to love.

A deep voice was muttering something close to him. He sat up with a start.

'Well, well!' cried Semacgus. 'You've been fighting windmills! Your bed is ravaged. You must have had a fever . . . You've even lost your breeches.'

Embarrassed, Nicolas pulled up the sheet. Semacgus lifted the bandage and examined the wound. His big nose was quivering and his eyes smiling in a manner that was extremely ironic.

'It's looking good. The wound has already closed and a scab is forming. One more scar to your name. You bear your service record on your body. It enhances your innate charm.'

Nicolas was wondering about what had happened that night. Had it been a dream? But there were so many details he remembered . . . Wasn't he completely unpregnated with a light scent and the smell of another body? It was obvious that the wily Semacgus had noticed, which explained that air of smugness. He mocked himself. Was it only when someone tried to kill him that he found himself in such a flattering position? The same thing had happened with La Satin . . . He felt sufficiently recovered to get back to Paris. The naval surgeon had no objection.

After putting on one of the admiral's shirts, his own having been torn to shreds, Nicolas again donned his fine grey coat, now stained, and went down to take his leave. He was greeted warmly by the Comte d'Arranet, who again invited him to consider this house as his own. There was no sign of Aimée; admittedly, it was early. His departure went off without incident. The coast was clear: the servants had been up all night to make sure that no new danger threatened him. Tribord gave him an enthusiastic wave. Semacgus remarked that he had made a friend, a friend who could be useful.

Nicolas did not reply, still trying to catch any allusion on the part of the surgeon to the events of the previous night. From time to time, he wondered if it had all been a dream. And yet, the memories and traces of Mademoiselle d'Arranet's nocturnal visit remained so vivid, so tangible that he found that hard to believe. He strove not to think, putting off until later the task of contemplating a situation the consequences of which were hard to untangle in the heat of the moment. Too many different feelings were at work in him. Above all, he preferred for now to dismiss his qualms at having betrayed the Comte d'Arranet's trust and violated the laws of hospitality.

So it was that they rode back to the Hôtel de la Belle Image in silence. There, he changed and paid his bill. On the road to Paris, Semacgus abandoned him to his thoughts. Nicolas pretended to sleep. In the end, he shook himself like a horse confronted with a hurdle and, once past the Porte de la Conférence, asked to be taken to the Châtelet. There was no more time to lose; the investigation had to resume. It was almost midday and he was hoping to find Bourdeau.

Looking grave, the inspector greeted them at the door of the duty office with the news that a third victim of the killer with the hand had just been discovered in the early hours of the morning, on the banks of Île des Cygnes.

# IX

## APPROACHES

The justice of the combat will challenge fervour
PETRARCH

As Semacgus wanted to take part in the expedition, he put his carriage at their disposal. Without omitting any detail, Nicolas informed them of the events that had taken place at Versailles and the state of his investigations. What he had discovered about the Duc de La Vrillière's artificial hand astounded them. The inspector admitted that it was an extremely important clue, which could take the investigation into some very murky areas. He spontaneously posed the question that Nicolas had already been asking himself: why had he, supposedly loyal to Sartine, been chosen to conduct the investigation?

Semacgus suggested two possible answers: either the minister was hoping in this way to keep a close watch on the investigation by using a colleague who was well known to him, or he considered the case so serious that only Nicolas appeared to him capable of solving it. To this, Nicolas himself objected that, if that were so, the minister should have been perfectly open with him, which had not been the case. A long silence followed, in which the three friends continued to pursue their thoughts. The carriage had crossed the Seine and was driving along the *quais* on the left bank, through the neighbourhoods of Beau Grenelle and

Gros Caillou, to get to the *faubourg* downstream of the city.

Nicolas forced himself out of his reverie. 'How did you learn of the discovery of the third body?' he asked.

'There was a general instruction to all the commissioners and inspectors, as well as the men of the watch, to report any discovery of this nature to the duty office,' replied Bourdeau.

'Do we know anything so far?'

An unformulated thought crossed his mind like a sacrilege: he would have to include the Duc de La Vrillière among the suspects and check his whereabouts at the time of the murder.

Bourdeau appeared embarrassed. 'What we know so far is fairly gruesome. You know the nature of the place where the victim was discovered. The hundred thousand oxen brought into Paris to be slaughtered for meat leave behind four hundred thousand feet, not to mention horns and intestines. All these remains are collected together, put on wagons, taken to that infernal island and thrown into vast incinerators, which work round the clock, to be turned into oil for lamps, night lights, frying, and to grease the cogs of machines. That's Île des Cygnes!'

'A pretty name for such an unpleasant place!' said Semacgus. 'It would appear that we're getting close to it, judging by the stench. It's worse than the bilges on a three-decker!'

The carriage turned right towards the little arched bridge over the canal separating the island from the bank. A number of rudimentary smoke-shrouded buildings rose amid dismal vegetation strewn with a few poplars. They saw horses, a stretcher, an empty wagon and a group of men who seemed to be waiting for them.

Nicolas recognised Rabouine, no doubt dispatched by Bourdeau to keep an eye on things, and an officer of the watch named

Baroliot, whom he had met several times in the course of his investigations. A large red-faced man was talking to them excitedly and wiping his brow with a kind of rage.

Baroliot approached and greeted them. 'Nasty business, Commissioner.'

He led them to the far end of a small yard, where a wagon was parked, with a grey nag harnessed to it. The contents were piled high, and covered with a tarpaulin; the stench that escaped from it left no doubt as to their nature. Behind the wagon was a tall openwork door half concealing the top of a huge incinerator from which thick black smoke emerged.

'The tripe shop of Île des Cygnes,' said Rabouine.

Helped by Baroliot, he removed the tarpaulin. The smell became even more overpowering. Bourdeau took out a pipe and hastened to light it. Nicolas took out his snuff box, hurriedly took a pinch, and abandoned himself with delight to a prolonged bout of sneezing.

At first sight, the wagon contained a heap of feet, horns and guts. The last flies of the season covered it like a thick black cloak, making it difficult to get a good look at the contents. It was only when they moved closer that they were able to make out a body amid this horror, although all that could really be seen was a pale, almost yellow face with its eyes open, the young, almost childlike features frozen in an expression of terrified surprise. Nicolas ordered the corpse to be taken down. Some workers were called. Armed with huge wooden shovels, they carefully dug out the body and placed it on a stretcher. Semacgus waved a branch which he had just torn off a shrub to disperse the persistent swarm of insects. He leant over the body.

'A young girl or woman of about, hmmm . . . eighteen or twenty . . . Marks of smallpox. Eyes blue, as far as it's still possible to judge. Gaping wound on the neck. Appears to be almost naked. An undershirt, striped.'

'Time of death?' asked Nicolas.

'Hard to say. We should find out more from the autopsy.'

'Who found her?' asked Bourdeau.

The fat man hurried forward. 'The morning shift, as they emptied the wagon.' He pointed to the tall door. 'There's a slope up there. The guts are slid straight into the incinerator. The men are so used to it, they don't really think about it any more.'

'Could the body have escaped their attention?'

'Yes, of course. According to them, they carry out their work quite mechanically.'

'So something unusual alerted them?'

The man opened his hand and gave Nicolas a small round object. 'The rays of the rising sun hit this; that was how they saw the girl. Actually, apart from that, the wagon seemed less full than usual.'

'A sweet box,' said Nicolas. He turned it, making it shimmer. It was golden, and bore a garland of green stones and, on the lid, a coloured enamel miniature representing four Cupids freeing birds from a cage, with the words 'Cupid the engraver' and four lines of verse:

> *In childhood love dreams*
> *That when the birds are freed*
> *To our hearts it seems*
> *That pleasure is what we need*

He asked Semacgus for his spectacles. The doctor handed them to him, annoyed at having to put on public display a resource that had become indispensable to him. Nicolas folded them to use as a magnifying glass. He turned the sweet box, now this way, now that. At last, with a sigh of pleasure, he made out a hallmark depicting the head of a pointer. He opened the box.

'My friends,' he said, 'this is, in fact, a pill box . . .' When he saw the contents, he exclaimed in surprise, 'Cantharides! What are these stimulants doing on the body of a young girl?'

'Or a prostitute,' said Semacgus. 'The less robust of them use it as an aid. It also helps to release a reproductive frenzy in the most barren of women.'

In this field, thought Nicolas, Semacgus's experience was unequalled, although he was never sure if it was his experience as a doctor or as a former libertine. The other thing that occurred to him was that this was the second time this particular aphrodisiac had made an appearance in the investigation.

Pursuing his thoughts, Nicolas turned to Rabouine. 'Do you have any idea how these workers managed to see this object? In any case, I think we should thank them for their honesty.'

'It must have slipped out of the pocket of her undershirt . . . There's a gusset.'

Nicolas was musing over these various pieces of information, trying to pull them all together. There was one element missing.

'I need to know the exact route followed by this wagon, as well as its timetable, if that's possible. Bring me the driver.'

The fat man with the bulging eyes stepped forward. 'You need to understand, Commissioner, that this transport goes on without interruption throughout the day. The last wagon arrives here at about three in the morning, and the driver comes and picks it up, empty, at about seven. Today he never turned up . . .'

'That's an interesting point, and it limits the period of time during which the murder may have been committed. If Semacgus can narrow it down even more, we won't be far from the truth.'

'Quite right, Pierre,' said Nicolas. 'Let's draw up a plan of campaign. The body needs to be taken to the Basse-Geôle, where Monsieur Semacgus will give it a closer examination. If he agrees.'

The surgeon nodded his consent.

'Pierre and Rabouine, I have two missions for you,' the commissioner went on. 'Find me the driver of this wagon. I want to question him. As for this sweet box or pill box, try to find an expert who can determine its origin. It's an expensive item and I have no doubt we will find its maker. And when we do . . .' He consulted his watch. 'Let's meet again at the Grand Châtelet on the stroke of six to see where we've got to. Bourdeau, anything new on the second victim?' His mind was racing. 'Unfortunately, we only have the doctor's carriage at our disposal.'

'No,' said Bourdeau, 'I arranged for another one to follow us in case we needed it. As for the second victim, fate has smiled on me. My spies have been concentrating on the world of prostitutes. It's a world where everyone knows everyone else and the slightest absence, however short, or a change in habits, gets noticed.'

He tapped out his pipe, put it away, took out his glasses and a piece of paper, and started reading.

'Mademoiselle Julie Jeanne Marot, born in Suzonnecourt, Champagne, aged nineteen. Lost both her father and mother, vineyard owners of that locality, and came to Paris a year ago to enter service. Was picked up by Madame Larue, a midwife of Rue Bourg-l'Abbé, well known as a brothel-keeper. She immediately procured her to a young man of her acquaintance, an old customer, who, despite the girl's screams, deflowered her. Later, the girl, realising that the old woman was prostituting her without paying her anything, left her and went and joined La Hilaire, in Cul-de-sac Saint-Fiacre. Her new mistress thought she was the perfect addition to her stable and took better care of her. She renamed her L'Étoile and introduced her to everyone as the new star. Now completely adapted to the life, she participated in parties and dinners of extreme debauchery.'

'Congratulations! We must go further into this. Who was keeping her? Were there several men? Apart from servicing casual customers, these girls usually combine business and pleasure and latch on to some good-looking beau. What were her haunts? Make the usual enquiries. You know what to do, and you do it much better than I could.'

The corpse was placed on a wagon belonging to the watch and covered with a tarpaulin. The cortege set off towards Paris. Nicolas, looking out through the lowered window, noticed a street at right angles to the one they were on.

'Let's not forget the Invalides slaughterhouse, it's quite close to here. We mustn't forget to check if the wagon from Île des Cygnes stops there.'

He was thinking aloud, and Semacgus, who was listening, did not think he had to answer.

'It's vitally important that we determine when and where the body was dumped on the wagon. Either to be discovered, or to disappear without a trace in the incinerator on Île des Cygnes.'

'And the sweet box?' said Semacgus. 'Valuable items like that often bear the name either of the donor or of the person who receives it.'

'There's the rub! Nothing, silence. Just the hallmark. Why abandon such a treasure? Was it simply forgotten? I don't think so, the girl was half naked. I suspect that it was put there on purpose, to arouse our curiosity.'

'That answers your previous questions. In that case, the body was meant to be found.'

'It seems like it. Let's sum up. The murderer dumps the body on the wagon. For some reason, the sweet box is with it. It's assumed, even hoped, that it will be discovered.'

'Perhaps. But there's no name on the box.'

'Precisely, precisely!' He gave a disconcerted Semacgus a friendly tap on the shoulder. 'Isn't it the subtlest thing to pretend to fall into traps which are set for us?'

'I don't quite know what you mean.'

'Could we be dealing with someone really clever? This sweet box is urging us to wager on our own intelligence.'

Semacgus was starting to be worried. Was this some kind of attack, a result of last night's wound? Nicolas certainly appeared feverish.

'I'm finding it increasingly hard to follow you.'

'Just think! If this sweet box, being such an obvious clue, led us directly to its owner or to the person who received it and made him or her a suspect, we would be within our rights to doubt the genuineness of the clue and we would be led to assume that someone was trying to force our hand.'

'Instead of which . . .'

'Without direct clues, we're faced with a difficult task, which may present us with more genuine discoveries. Let me remind you that the Duc de La Vrillière remains the prime suspect, because of the very nature of the murder weapon. That this weapon has disappeared without his being able to account for that disappearance. That his whereabouts at the time of the first murder do not appear to give him an alibi. That we need to determine his whereabouts for the two other murders, once we've narrowed down the exact time of the latest one.'

'If I understand correctly, you fear there will be no alibi for any of the three crimes?'

'I do indeed fear so, for, if our hypothesis is correct, we are dealing with a tough adversary.'

A long silence fell. Semacgus did not like to see Nicolas looking so feverish. He also knew how stupid it would be to try to calm him down. Like a hunting dog, when he was on the trail he would not give up.

'Are you feeling all right?' he asked, to set his mind at rest.

Nicolas did not reply. There was a fleeting thought at the back of his mind, something he could not at the moment pin down, but something he was convinced was important. He was still searching for it when they were in the main hall of the Basse-Geôle. Pressed for time, he had given up the idea of sending for Sanson. He needed a rapid result to give the investigation a new impetus. Semacgus had had to borrow some instruments from the local doctor at the Châtelet, who had only agreed on the express orders of the commissioner. A few days earlier, thought Nicolas, there was no doubt that he would have been refused, considered by that mediocre little world as being on the sidelines, discredited, in virtual exile. The news of his return to favour had spread like wildfire, and everything had returned to normal.

Nicolas looked closely at the undershirt the surgeon had just taken off the corpse. Something was nagging at him. He cursed his own forgetfulness. It drove out any good ideas he had and, in his job, that was tantamount to a sin. He felt in the bottom of his pocket for his little black notebook, pulled it out, and looked through it with a kind of rage. Why hadn't he thought of this earlier? When Lenoir had burdened him with all those assignments to such a point that it had even occurred to him that it was a deliberate attempt to thwart his investigation, one of them had been to track down two young girls who had run away from Brussels. He looked at the page where he had noted their descriptions. 'The first . . . smallpox . . . blue eyes, black eyebrows.' And further on – and this was what had unconsciously stirred his memory – 'Undershirt . . . blue and grey striped satin.' He glanced at the soiled, bloodstained garment. It exactly matched the description he had written down.

'Guillaume,' he said, 'do you see any marks of smallpox on the face?'

'Of course,' replied Semacgus. 'I told you that back on the island. Blue eyes, black eyebrows and marks of smallpox. For the rest . . .' He poured water over his arms and hands from an earthenware jug. 'The poor girl wasn't a courtesan. She hadn't even been a woman for long . . . I mean she'd recently been deflowered, and probably raped several times, from the front and the rear. A sad business!'

'Are you sure?'

'I'd swear it before a judge, without any qualms.'

'Time of death?'

'That's harder to establish. Taking a number of factors into account – the night temperature, the heat given off by a heap of decomposing animal flesh – I estimate the probable time of death at about two in the morning. Let's say between one and two.'

'We know that the wagon arrived on Île des Cygnes at about three . . . We need to know where it was about two, or even a little earlier.'

He was thinking hard, but Semacgus, with an expression of barely suppressed jubilation on his broad, ruddy face, interrupted this exercise.

'That's not all, Nicolas. There's another observation I've made, I don't know how important it is, but I'm sure you'll find it intriguing. Before she died, the victim was immersed in a soapy solution, which dried as it evaporated. You just have to wet the skin to notice it. You can still smell the scent a bit.'

'You'll need to be a little clearer than that, Guillaume. Don't forget you're talking to someone who's had a bit of a shock and spent last night . . .'

He broke off, noticing Semacgus's mocking look. He felt his face go red.

'The girl took a bath,' said the surgeon. 'A scented bath, to boot!'

'I'll refrain from drawing any conclusion from that for the time being. I'll just remark that, at every stage in this case, water is never very far away. The Saint-Florentin mansion, close to the Seine. Rue de Glatigny, on the banks of the Cité. And, finally, Île des Cygnes. We're never far from the river!'

'Which makes it all the more interesting to find out where the wagon gained its deadly load.'

'Any other observations?'

'One last one. I found a fragment of nail with some skin attached. The attacker must have grabbed hold of the victim's garment during the struggle. Here it is, for what it's worth. I don't suppose it'll help you find the person it belongs to, but who knows? It's just possible it may be of use to you . . .'

Nicolas put the item inside a folded sheet of his black notebook. 'You haven't mentioned this,' he said, 'but I assume that the murder weapon—'

'Is indeed the artificial hand. At least, the plaster cast fits the wound. There's no doubt about it. What are you going to do now?'

'I've put off meeting the major-domo's in-laws for too long. After that, I'm going to Bicêtre to see what I can find out about the rejected suitor of the first victim, Marguerite Pindron.'

Deep in thought, they went back up to the duty office, where they were greeted by Old Marie, the usher, who, having followed Nicolas's career from the beginning, was delighted that things were getting back to normal for him. He handed him a small folded note on which he immediately recognised the three sardines of Monsieur de Sartine's coat of arms. The message was a brief one: 'Monsieur Bourdier, the man I spoke to you about, is living with his family in a furnished room in Rue Galante.'

Nicolas, who always kept spare clothes and clean linen in a cubbyhole, changed and asked Old Marie to take his fine grey coat to the cleaner.

'Marie,' he said, 'I'm a bit short of men. Could you do me a service? I know you're perfectly capable.'

'By God, I'd jump out of the window for you! Problem is, with my damned aches and pains, I'd find it hard to climb up onto the sill!'

'I'm not asking that much,' said Nicolas with a laugh. 'I'll send you a box of camphorated beaver fat that Monsieur de Noblecourt swears by. Aren't you bored in your cage?'

'Of course, Monsieur Nicolas! At least I have my pipe and my cordial. Apart from that, I'm bored stiff.'

'All right, then. What would you say to searching in the register of foreigners for a middle-aged Englishman, of medium height and with a definite paunch? He's wearing tinted folding glasses and speaks quite good French. I'd also quite like to have a list of foreigners staying in furnished hotels in Paris and Versailles.'

'It would be very careless of him to always frequent such conspicuous establishments,' said Semacgus.

'Lodging with the locals would be even more so. It's possible he's staying with the British ambassador. Lord Ashbury is a clever man. We'll see . . . So, Marie, is that all right with you?'

'I'll go and look at the registers straight away.'

Nicolas handed him a few *louis*.

'That's far too much,' said the usher, stunned.

'It's to pay the cleaner. Keep the change for tobacco and cordial.'

He set off at top speed.

'You're good, I'll give you that,' said Semacgus. 'Always a promise of scraps from the table.'

'I don't have to try too hard. He's a good man, and a Breton, to boot. *Evit ur baoninqenn, kant modigenn!* "For a little pain, a hundred pleasures," as they say where we come from. I'm going to visit the Duchamplans in Rue Christine. Will you come with me? I don't have much time, so we'll have to skip lunch. We can dine together this evening, we'll have plenty of time then . . .'

Semacgus was grimacing at the thought of this sacrifice.

'Would you dare to abandon a patient?' joked Nicolas. 'Imagine if I failed in my duty—'

'You're beating down my defences. All right then, I'll fast in your honour. This evening, you'll all be my guests.'

The surgeon's carriage was waiting for them at the entrance. Nicolas suddenly remembered to thank the coachman, who, by his presence of mind, had probably saved his life. The man in question, blushing with emotion, told them that he had taken advantage of their absence to buy, from one of those stalls which cluttered the square all the way to the Apport-Paris, a basket of little hot pies from Champagne and two bottles of simple wine. He had guessed that the gentlemen, too absorbed in their affairs, were going to have to tighten their belts. Both congratulated him on his initiative, and Nicolas again got rid of a few extra *écus*.

Assuaging their raging hunger, they crossed the Seine and soon reached Rue Christine, which was situated between Rue des Grands-Augustins and Rue Dauphine. This tranquil street was full of large bourgeois houses. The Duchamplan house was not out of place here, with its austere facade devoid of excessive decoration, apart from a mascaron depicting the face of a chubby Triton. Six floors including the attic, noted Nicolas. The three upper floors appeared, from certain aspects, to be given over to furnished rooms. They went through the carriage entrance. The caretaker was sitting on a stool with the straw removed, shelling beans. He told them that Monsieur Duchamplan the elder lived on the first and second floors, and Monsieur Duchamplan the younger on the mezzanine. But the latter was not in at the moment; in fact, he had not been in for several days. There was nothing to explain this absence, which appeared to worry his brother greatly. To the left of the courtyard was an impressive flight of stairs, the state of which indicated that it was for the exclusive use of the owner, while everyone else used a more modest staircase, as did the servants, the suppliers, the carriers of water and wood . . .

Nicolas remarked to Semacgus that chance remained the most constant element in investigations, and that you often discovered things when you were least expecting to. It would be useful to speak a bit more to such a talkative character as that caretaker. Having rung the bell-pull, they waited until a middle-aged manservant opened the door. Nicolas asked to see the master of the house. A few minutes later, the man himself appeared.

From the first, Nicolas found it hard to define his appearance. He was neither tall nor short, neither fat nor thin, and wore a black, rather old-fashioned coat. He was pale, with washed-out eyes, and resembled his sister the nun, although his face was puffier. His hands, hidden beneath wide cuffs, were clasped together, as if he were trying to overcome a degree of nervousness.

'Nicolas Le Floch, commissioner at the Châtelet. Dr Guillaume Semacgus.'

He stopped there. It was the best way to force the witness to make the next move.

'Please come in, gentlemen.'

He admitted them into a large, richly furnished drawing room. The curtains at the windows looking out on the street were half drawn, plunging the room into relative darkness. He motioned them to take their seats in large high-backed armchairs from the previous century.

'I'm listening, Monsieur,' said Nicolas.

'You've rather caught me on the hop, Commissioner. I've just learnt about the tragedy that happened at the minister's house and my brother-in-law Missery's wound.'

This was not getting them very far.

'Could you tell me who informed you of these events?'

'My sister, Hélène, who's a nun with the Daughters of Saint Michel. But you know that, since you've already met her.'

This was said with a kind of bitter irony.

'So you're aware of the serious accusations made against your brother-in-law?' said Nicolas.

'I find it hard to believe that he could be capable of something so terrible. He can be violent, yes, touchy, difficult, not always very honest, much given to debauchery, but a murderer, no, I don't really think so.'

As a connoisseur, Nicolas appreciated the man's skill at appearing to be contemptuous of the major-domo while avoiding directly accusing him. The overall picture, though, was certainly a black one.

'Has your relationship with him remained close?'

'We rarely see each other.'

'When did you see him last?'

'At the Mass for the anniversary of my sister's death.'

'Do you have any joint interests? I should point out to you, before anything else, that I know all about your family affairs. Missery is in possession of your sister's fortune – correct me if I'm wrong – and it will revert to your family if he should die.'

'Whether he has remarried or not, Monsieur. That is quite important.'

'I assume you're referring to the danger represented by his passionate relationship with a chambermaid in the Saint-Florentin household?'

'Precisely. Let's be clear about this: if you're trying to insinuate that my brother-in-law was nearly murdered on account of the coincidence of our interests, you're making a big mistake. Didn't you tell my sister that he was merely grazed?'

He was still expressing himself in a restrained, level-headed manner, staring straight ahead, never looking at the commissioner.

'That's all well and good, Monsieur,' said Nicolas. 'I've heard your answers on your joint interests with your brother-in-law, and we've talked about your sister's fortune. Are you yourself involved in some occupation?'

'I manage my money. I have a private income, and I also earn revenue from my interests in a number of companies of which I am the administrator.'

'What companies?'

'Aren't you going beyond your prerogatives? I am known and protected by the Prince de Condé.'

'Do you have a position in his household?' asked Nicolas with a touch of sarcasm.

'The prince and I,' retorted Duchamplan proudly, 'are in

partnership on a project to supply the city with water.'

'I only know of one such project: that of the Perier brothers, supported by the Duc d'Orléans.'

The man seemed surprised by Nicolas's knowledge. 'You are badly informed, there are others.'

'And are you involved in other enterprises?'

'A transport company.'

'And what else?'

'I am an administrator of the royal hospital of Bicêtre.'

'I see,' said Nicolas. 'I assume that covers everything. Where were you on the night of Sunday to Monday?'

'Here, with my wife and my sister.'

'Did you go out?'

'Not at all. We went to bed about eleven.'

Nicolas noted that the time could be approximate. The contradiction with the sister's declaration that she had gone to bed at ten was only a small one. Of course, she had 'forgotten' to mention that she had visited her family.

'When you say "we", are you including your brother, Eudes?'

'My brother is a young man who has his own amusements, and we don't interfere with them. He lives on the mezzanine, and has his own entrance.'

'And did he come home the following day?'

'I have no idea. He comes and goes. He's a will-o'-the-wisp . . . whom I support come what may.' His mouth tensed in a grimace that was meant to be a smile.

'I'd like to speak to your wife,' said Nicolas.

'She's gone out to pay a visit.'

The words had come out very quickly. It was better to

stop there for the moment. Nicolas was just standing up when Semacgus raised his hand.

'With your permission, Commissioner. Monsieur Duchamplan mentioned a transport company. What kind of company?'

'We have a fleet of cabs.'

'One company has the monopoly on cabs in Paris. Is it that one?'

Duchamplan gave Nicolas a look of commiseration. 'As I'm sure you know, that monopoly has long since been superseded. There are more than a thousand cabs and more than seven hundred hired coaches in Paris now, and joint-stock companies have proliferated. The vehicles just have to be numbered and registered.'

'I see. I would be grateful if you could inform me as soon as your brother reappears.'

'I shall certainly do so, although he is often away a long time.'

In the courtyard, the shelling of beans was still going on. Nicolas offered the caretaker a pinch of snuff, which was gratefully accepted. There followed a vigorous series of sneezes.

'You're softening up the customer,' said Semacgus in Nicolas's ear.

The commissioner winked, then asked the caretaker a straight question. 'What time did Madame Duchamplan go out?'

'Go out? That poor pale thing, who's always coughing? I'd like to see her go out! You must be joking, Monsieur. She's been confined to her room for several days now.'

'Since when?'

'Monday, I think,' said the man, sneezing.

'And what about Monsieur Duchamplan's sister?'

'Oh, that one . . . For a nun, she certainly has a lot of pride. Never a greeting, never a smile. The last time I saw her come here for dinner was Sunday.'

'What time did she leave?'

'About ten. I had to run out in the cold to hail a carriage, at my age!'

'Thank you very much.'

'At your service. This snuff is good! Not like the sawdust you sometimes find. Count on me whenever you want. The name's Taqueminet.'

As they were leaving Rue Christine, Nicolas, who was looking in the direction of Rue des Grands-Augustins, suddenly cried out and set off at a run, much to the surprise of Semacgus. He seemed to be trying to catch up with a carriage which was speeding away and which soon disappeared round the corner. Breathless and furious, the commissioner came walking back. He had to catch his breath before explaining what had just happened. He took off his tricorn and wiped his forehead, which was half covered with a bandage. Semacgus noticed blood spreading over the linen and gently reprimanded him.

'How could you think of getting in such a state? You've reopened your wound. We'll have to find an apothecary and get it seen to. Good Lord, you ran off like the fire of a fuse trying to reach Saint Barbara!'

Nicolas laughed. 'I'm sorry, I'm not twenty years old any more! Perhaps I was dreaming, and yet I'm sure the person I saw get into that carriage is the very same person who ran away the day before yesterday in the lower gallery of the palace at my approach. I told you about him. Lord Ashbury. I just saw him coming out of a house . . . The head, or one of the heads, of the British secret service. Is that fever or reality?'

Semacgus grabbed his wrist and took out his watch, then felt his forehead. 'It's not fever. Your pulse is fine now that you've caught your breath, and your forehead is cool.'

Nicolas tugged at his arm. 'Let's take a look at that house, I want to set my mind at rest. How stupid I am! We should have got in our carriage . . .'

'There's no point regretting that, it would have had to make a U turn!'

They walked back up Rue Christine as far as a fine-looking double-fronted building, which, according to the inscription on its pediment, was the Hôtel de Russie. A well-dressed lady greeted them.

'Welcome, gentlemen. No doubt you wish to take lodgings in our establishment, which is so well known that the *Almanach Parisien* draws the attention of foreigners and visitors to it . . .'

She spoke so quickly it was impossible for Nicolas to interrupt her.

'We only lodge persons of the first rank, who have carriages. We have richly furnished apartments, bedrooms, wardrobes, reception rooms with damask hangings and other appropriate adornments. There are véry clean water closets on every floor. You can use the sheds and stables for your carriage. We don't provide food, but we allow you to have what you need brought in from the best caterers in the neighbourhood, and we have information on the best inns in the city. I am at your disposal.'

She gave a deep curtsey which would have made a duchess envious.

'Madame,' said Nicolas, 'you misconstrue the reasons for our visit. We simply wish to have some information about a customer of yours who left barely five minutes ago and got into a carriage.'

These words immediately cast a cloud over her welcoming face, and she assumed an inscrutable, almost duplicitous air. 'Who are you talking about? No one went out as far as I know.'

'Madame,' said Nicolas firmly, 'I would have preferred not to have to remind you of your duties. I am a commissioner of police at the Châtelet. I seem to remember that the owners of hotels and furnished rooms must inform us in good time of all foreigners staying with them. Whenever a foreigner arrives, within twenty-four hours the Lieutenant General of Police needs to know his name, where he comes from, the reason for his visit, where he is staying, with whom he is in correspondence, and whom he receives. That supposes that the said owners are devoted to His Majesty's interests. Have I made myself quite clear? Do you realise how much at fault you've been? I fear you may have to follow us to a less pleasant location to be checked and interrogated.'

This speech seemed to have hit home; the lady burst into tears, and made no further attempt to brazen it out. Nicolas confirmed his resolution by remaining sternly impassive.

'Alas, alas, Commissioner, do you want to ruin me – me, a poor widow, with a family to support, working myself to death to run this establishment? I am, it is true, guilty of having neglected my duties, but only because of my good heart. The foreign gentleman, an Englishman I think, forbade me to report his presence. The reason he's in France is because he wants to track down a child he once had with a French lady who's now married. Think how discreet he needs to be about something like that!'

'Madame, I fear that is simply a tall tale which you, in your innocence, swallowed whole. Under what name did this gentleman present himself?'

'He said his name was Francis Sefton – though he asked me in a threatening tone never to mention it – and that he bought and sold racehorses.'

'A clever story, horse racing is becoming fashionable. When did he arrive?'

'On 20 September.'

'Did he have any luggage with him?'

'Some portmanteaus. The servant girl told me that he had a lot of coats, all very different from each other, with some wigs and even some ladies' dresses. No doubt to sell them when he returned to his island.'

'Has he received anyone?'

'No, nobody.'

'Did he have a carriage?'

'A cab came to fetch him.'

'Has he been regular in his habits?'

'Definitely not! He often comes back early in the morning and sometimes stays out all night. He's been paying his weeks regularly. He left in a hurry this morning, after being away for two days, and obligingly paid for an extra week even though the week isn't yet over. He asked me again not to say anything about his being here, because his old friend's husband has been informed of his presence in Paris.'

'All right, Madame. If he comes back, tell the local commissioner immediately to inform Commissioner Le Floch at the Châtelet. For your guidance, I must tell you that you risk the closure of this hotel as well as legal action if you contravene these instructions. Now show me Monsieur Sefton's apartment.'

She led them to a cosy apartment on the first floor, comprising a bedroom, a bathroom and a small drawing room. The bed had not been slept in. Nicolas noted a bottle of port and two glasses on a pedestal table. He sniffed, then went to the fireplace: a large number of papers had been burnt. In the heap of ashes he discovered part of a sheet that had escaped the destruction. On it were only a few printed letters: '*elles ne*'. A newspaper, an official document, an advertisement? They would have to see.

'Has he had a visitor?' Nicolas asked the hostess, pointing to the two glasses.

'No.'

He sniffed the glasses. 'Last night, I'd say . . . No, he wasn't here . . .This morning, then. Are you telling me that you're behind your desk for twenty-four hours a day?'

'Of course not, but . . . To tell the truth, I really don't know what to think any more, it may have happened.'

Once again she burst into tears. Nicolas shrugged, depressed by so much thoughtlessness. Semacgus pointed out the rim of one of the two glasses. There were traces of rouge.

'Who knows?' said Nicolas. 'These days men sometimes make themselves up more heavily than women. They all smear rouge and ceruse on their faces. For the moment, let's just make a note of it.'

*

As soon as they had got back in the carriage – the hotel-keeper had followed them out, lamenting volubly – Nicolas tried to draw a few conclusions from their visit to Rue Christine.

'Using a false identity, Lord Ashbury has been in Paris for two weeks. That woman's stupidity and our own people's shortcomings – I fear that since Sartine's departure there has been some laxity – explain the fact that he has managed to evade all police supervision of foreigners. He comes and goes quite freely, meets whoever he likes, and even goes to Versailles for God knows what intrigue. There, he almost comes face to face with me, runs away, but finds the time and the means to have me followed and, I believe, orders me to be killed. An attempt is made outside the Comte d'Arranet's house, and fails. What's the reason? He assumes that I'm pursuing him. He hurries back to Paris, says he has business, receives an associate, and then escapes into the big city! But where?'

'He may simply have set off for Calais,' said Semacgus.

'I don't think so. His mission isn't over. Somehow, I've got in his way. What are his intentions? I'll tell you this: there's no such thing as coincidence . . .' Nicolas was beating the plush seat with his fist, raising small clouds of dust. 'No one's going to make me believe that Lord Ashbury, alias Francis Sefton, has been staying at a hotel a few doors from the Duchamplan house by mere chance. I don't know why he has, but I'm going to find out!'

'It is indeed vital to discover why he came to France,' said Semacgus, 'especially as it's a clandestine visit. And there are also these Duchamplans, who seem to me very much involved in all these mysteries.'

'I didn't want to take things too far by going back up to see the wife. We must give them the false impression that they're safe. It won't hurt them to wait. As for the younger brother, I get the feeling he won't be back very soon. I find it hard to believe that the motive for the murder in the Saint-Florentin mansion is financial gain. These people are very well off. What is it then?'

'You must calm down, or the fever will come back.'

'I fear I'm going to have to start all over again. Lenoir has assigned me to so many different cases they've made me lose the thread of the main one. We must question Missery again. Where did he find Marguerite Pindron? I'll also need to have a conversation with the Duchesse de La Vrillière. The rumour of her good relations with Madame de Maurepas may help me . . . Last but not least, I need to find the Pindron girl's young man. He's the real mystery. The duchesse's young Norman maid told me his name is Aide.'

'Did she have a Norman accent?' Semacgus suddenly asked, slyly.

'Indeed she did, a very strong one.'

'Then we've found the lover. Your Aide is quite simply Eudes, the first name of the younger Duchamplan. Missery, if he's telling the truth, ought to confirm that, and it would explain many things.'

'Thank you, my dear Guillaume. That's the second time today you've been a great help. And your coachman saved my life. However, even though it opens up some interesting avenues, it doesn't solve everything. There are elements in this case that are being deliberately hidden from us.'

Semacgus called to the coachman to take them to Rue de la Joaillerie, to the shop of Monsieur Nicaise, the apothecary.

# X

## BICÊTRE

I was not aware that Bicêtre had been built to
engender disease and give birth to crime.
MIRABEAU

Nicolas recognised the apothecary: Monsieur Nicaise had
bandaged him up once before, during his investigation into
the disappearance of Commissioner Lardin. Semacgus and he
conferred for a short time after examining the wound. They
rejected the use of spirits, tinctures and balms: the wound was not
serious enough to warrant it. In addition, such remedies, far from
speeding up the healing process, delayed it, often turning a simple
wound into an ulcer. They stopped the blood from flowing but
made the injured parts callous. The two men settled for a common
agglutinative plaster to close the wound. As the bullet had burnt
and ripped the skin, they cleaned it with calcined alum and placed
over it a plaster of breadcrumbs and milk mixed with olive oil, to
be changed three times a day. Listening to them, Nicolas thought
they were discussing him as if he were a chicken they were getting
ready to cook.

Night was falling by the time the carriage dropped them at the
entrance to the Grand Châtelet. Bourdeau and Rabouine were
waiting for them in the duty office. The inspector was very
concerned about the consequences of Nicolas's wound. He still

felt mortified, blaming himself for not having been with his friend at such a dangerous moment.

'Bourdeau likes people to try and kill you just so that he can save you,' said Semacgus, provoking general laughter.

'Well, now, my bloodhounds,' said Nicolas, 'any news?'

'First,' said Bourdeau, 'about the sweet box, because that's what it in fact is. We went to the Johac mansion in Rue Saint-Merri, where there's a large shop selling all kinds of precious boxes, including snuff boxes, in vast quantities, all different from one another and all in the latest fashions. I would never have thought there were so many, in gold, silver, enamel, pasteboard, shell, ivory, Irish leather, shagreen and God knows what else!'

'I see you were dazzled.'

'Shocked, rather, by this display of pointless luxury. What it all cost could have fed a great many starving mouths.'

'Ah,' said Semacgus sardonically, 'here comes Rousseau again!'

'You may mock, but the day will come . . . Well, now's not the time. Anyway, we showed them the box. Although they weren't absolutely sure, they all thought it was the work of a master. One of the assistants, the oldest of them, suggested that although there was no signature, it might be from the hand of Robert-Joseph Auguste, a highly regarded maker, who lives in Rue de la Monnaie. We found him and questioned him. He's a silversmith who supplies the leading courts of Europe. He formally identified his work from his hallmark, the pointer's head.'

'But who was the buyer?'

'I'm coming to that,' said Bourdeau, amused by Nicolas's impatience. 'This is going to surprise you. The box turns out to have been ordered by the Comte de Saint-Florentin, Duc de La Vrillière, the current Minister of the King's Household.'

'Let's take things one at a time. Was he sure it was him?'

'No, because he didn't come in person. He sent a messenger. But Auguste, who appears to know the Court, recognised this messenger as a person of quality. In addition, he paid the full amount in one go.'

'Which is not always characteristic of a gentleman these days,' remarked Nicolas with a smile. 'Did he provide you with a description?'

'Medium height, a haughty expression, bulging eyes, expensive clothes. Powdered wig.'

'That won't get us very far! But good work all the same!'

'I have something even more curious, if possible,' said Rabouine, straightening his thin body. 'That particular wagon only covers the left bank of the river. It leaves from Pont des Tournelles. We found the driver. Where? At the police station in the Port aux Tuiles. He told us a really unbelievable story . . .'

'Yet another one!'

'This morning, about one or one thirty, he got down to pass water near the Fort des Tournelles. He had already begun his shift outside the walls. He exchanged a few words with a man who wanted a light for his pipe. To thank him, this individual offered to buy him a drink in a low tavern. Our driver claims to have drunk too much and can't remember anything else after that. He came to on the river bank, stripped of his clothes and money, surrounded by boys and outraged women shouting, "What a mess!" He was taken to the police station, but couldn't give any other details.'

'To cut a long story short,' said Bourdeau, 'he can't throw any light on what happened to his load. The fact remains that an unknown person, having got the driver drunk, stripped him and presumably put on his clothes to deceive the night watchman on Île des Cygnes. What about the next stops on the itinerary? you will ask. The wagon didn't stop to pick up anything between Quai Saint-Bernard and the Gros Caillou, much to everyone's surprise.'

'But how in heaven's name,' said Semacgus, 'could the guard at the incinerator on Île des Cygnes not notice anything?'

'He's half asleep by the time he opens the gate. It was pitch dark. There was a new moon.'

Nicolas consulted the calendar in the *Almanach royal* for 1774, which as usual was lying on the table. 'That's correct, new moon on 5 October, the feast day of Sainte Aure, the abbess. Well, gentlemen, I'm very pleased with your work. Let's sum up. The body was dumped on the wagon between one and one thirty, two at the latest, by an unknown person who got rid of the driver. Bearing in mind the estimate of the time given by Dr Semacgus here, I think we can state without too much fear of contradiction that the murder was committed somewhere quite close to Quai des Tournelles.'

'Unless,' said Bourdeau, 'it was taken there to put us off the scent.'

Semacgus seemed puzzled. 'I wonder about this elaborate staging. They could have just hidden the body, if they wanted to be sure it would go into the incinerator.'

'That's precisely what the criminal didn't want,' replied Nicolas. 'If he had let the wagon do its usual round, the body of the unfortunate victim would have been well hidden and would never have attracted attention and been discovered. Of course, there was still a risk it might not have been, but the gamble paid off and the body was found. It's also obvious that whoever did this knew that the round existed. All of which brings us back to the idea that the solution to this mystery can be found in the area of Pont des Tournelles.'

'Water,' Semacgus went on, 'and consequently the river, are ever present in this case. What our friends here don't know is that the body of the victim, who was raped, was covered with evaporated soapy water. What do you make of that?'

At this point, Old Marie appeared, bearing Nicolas's beautiful grey coat, now perfectly cleaned. Nicolas checked that the bloodstains had left no trace that might have condemned Master Vachon's masterpiece to the attentions of the second-hand clothes dealers. The art of the cleaners was more than a match for the dangers of a dirty city. But Marie was shaking his head sadly.

'I didn't find anything about your foreigner, Monsieur Nicolas, although I looked in all the registers. He must have slipped through the net.'

'Don't worry,' said Nicolas. 'His name is Francis Sefton, and he arrived in Paris on about 20 September. He's passing himself off as a racehorse merchant. And for good measure, let me tell you that the lover of Marguerite Pindron is very likely to have been young Duchamplan, first name Eudes.'

'Good Lord!' said Bourdeau. 'Where did you find that out?'

'It was all thanks to Dr Semacgus's knowledge of the Norman accent.'

*

The doctor invited the company to dinner at an inn in Rue Montorgueil chosen as much for its reputation for good food as for its proximity to Noblecourt's house. He did not want to tire Nicolas out, knowing how trying his night and day had been. At first, the conversation of the four guests continued to turn around the case that had brought them together. A hamper of oysters gave Nicolas the opportunity to assert that he loved this mollusc when it was white and fat, which scandalised the rest of the table, except for Semacgus, who did not give an opinion, but merely stated that he could not imagine any other joy for the oyster than health, which pleased everyone. A macaroni pie followed. The final course was a dish of sheep's tongues in parcels, which they enjoyed so much that the host was treated to a drink and asked to conform to tradition and detail all the stages of the making of this delight. What you had to do, he said, was cut the tongues in half and fry them in a little oil with parsley, chopped shallots, diced chives and mushrooms, salt, pepper and nutmeg. When they had cooled, you had to place them, one by one, between thick slices of bacon then wrap them in paper. Once they were wrapped, you grilled them and served them when they were simmering. As a final touch, before serving you sprinkled a little veal juice over them. Wild applause greeted this poem, before a dish of late vineyard peaches appeared to refresh both mouths and heads. Semacgus accompanied Nicolas back to Rue Montmartre, where only Catherine was still up, dozing by the fireplace in the servants' pantry. He did not wake her, but was unable to escape the vigilance of Mouchette, who spat at him, doubtless angered by an absence she found unacceptable. But she was not one to bear a grudge; no sooner had Nicolas got into bed than he heard her purr and felt her weight on his chest and her little cold nose come to rest against his cheek. He fell asleep immediately.

*Saturday 8 October 1774*

Nicolas rose refreshed by a dreamless sleep. Catherine, who was shocked by nothing after the horrors of war, changed his plaster and bombarded him with questions. Given the hour, Monsieur de Noblecourt had not yet rung, so Nicolas wrote him a little note to reassure him and to give him a brief summary of the progress of his investigation. As he was planning to visit Bicêtre, he would have to appear in a manner befitting the solemnity of his office. He put on his black magistrate's gown. The width and length of the sleeves allowed him to conceal two loaded pistols. He gave up the idea of wearing a wig, which would compress his wound and stop it healing. He took his ivory rod, the symbol of his authority.

Before he left, it occurred to him that the presence of Lord Ashbury demanded a degree of caution. In spite of his cumbersome attire, he would have to leave Noblecourt's house by an unusual route. With Poitevin's help, he placed a ladder against the wall between Noblecourt's garden and that of the neighbouring house. Thanks to this ploy, he was able to leave through a carriage entrance leading to Rue du Jour, opposite the convent of the Daughters of Sainte Agnès.

From there, he got to Rue Coquillière, where he hired a cab for the day. He left Paris through Faubourg Saint-Marceau, which was just waking up. He was struck once again by the hustle and bustle of the countless taverns serving adulterated brandy, cheap wine and cider to a sinister-looking collection of characters – and sometimes even to children.

Barely a league separated Bicêtre from the centre of Paris. Nicolas, leaning out of the window, suddenly saw on the horizon a huge building on the top of a hill to the right of the road to Fontainebleau. From that distance, the hospital looked like a palace, its bright mass towering over the surrounding countryside with its vineyards, windmills, and, in the distance, the Seine. It seemed to Nicolas that this ideal location must be of great benefit to the sick. The air there must be pure, not to be compared with the miasma enveloping hospitals in the city. But he changed his mind when he began gradually to smell a stench that reminded him of the great knacker's yard at Montfaucon and the incinerator on Île des Cygnes.

His carriage arrived at the main entrance just as an elegant coupé was coming to a halt ahead of it. A man dressed all in black got out and gave him a friendly wave. As Nicolas approached, he recognised Dr de Gévigland, who had treated Jean Missery at the Saint-Florentin mansion. He took off his tricorn and returned the doctor's greeting.

'I didn't think I'd see you again so soon,' he said. 'I'm more delighted than I can say. Have you come to see a patient?'

The doctor smiled but appeared embarrassed. 'Believe it or not,' he murmured, 'I've come to buy a few corpses.'

Nicolas, hardened by his experience of the Basse-Geôle, did not bat an eyelid. 'For anatomical purposes, I assume?'

Gévigland's black eyes grew even more sombre, as if drowning in sadness. 'Alas, I wish that were the case, but it so happens that for a long time now I've been studying the bodies of those suffering from venereal diseases or, more precisely, I've been performing autopsies in order to assess the side-effects of the remedies inflicted on them, from which, most of the time, they die. Sometimes, the cure is deadlier than the disease.'

'What methods do they use here?'

'Rubbing with mercury ointment, sulphur baths and a prolonged diet. Patients are immersed four at a time for several hours in the same bathtub, because there aren't enough of them. Nor is there enough access to water. One single very deep well, inadequate channels, and thousands of inmates! Is this your first visit here?'

'My duties have never brought me here before. All I know is that Bicêtre is both a prison and a hospital.'

'A prison for the most repulsive dregs of humanity, a hospital for the most terrible of diseases, and a tomb for the incurably insane. May I suggest you visit the place in my company, unless you're here on urgent business . . .?'

'I'm here in connection with my investigation into the case with which you are familiar. I am looking for a man who's suffering from venereal disease, the victim's former fiancé. Is he still here? I have no idea. In the meantime, I'll gladly follow you.'

'Leave it to me, I know everyone here. The house is run by a mother superior who has officiating nuns and an army of assistants at her command. Admittedly, the population of this place fluctuates during the year. In winter, it can reach four thousand five hundred.'

With a pang in his heart, Nicolas followed his guide, who explained to him in measured tones the terrible scenes that appeared before them. The hospital, which they visited first, housed individuals infected with venereal disease. The wards were filled with rows of beds that seemed to stretch to infinity. He noted that each bed often contained five or six unfortunates stagnating in their own excrement. The atmosphere was so stifling that he was almost overcome with nausea. Hideously cankered creatures crawled across the floor towards the visitors and held out their hands.

'They prefer the hard floor,' said Gévigland, 'to the infection and filth of the beds.'

'Are they forced to take refuge in this hell?' asked Nicolas, appalled.

'The police pick them up in places of ill repute. Others come of their own accord. Some reserve their places a long time in advance, when they're still only suffering light symptoms. By the time they finally get here, the disease has often reached its deadliest stage.'

'Do any of them ever recover?'

'Yes, sometimes. But I should point out that it's the rule in this hospital that recovery must occur within a given time. Unfortunately, the disease itself doesn't play by the rules. The result is that the patient, after being tormented with useless remedies, leaves without being cured. You can imagine the consequences!'

They entered a series of long, echoing galleries. Through the windows, the great well in the central courtyard could be seen. They climbed some steps, descended others, and finally reached the area for the insane and the common prisoners. Gévigland gave his name, and the gate to the insane enclosure was opened.

'Here begins the final circle of hell,' he said. 'Everything you've seen so far was nothing. This isn't a hospital, it's a freak show. The worst part of it is that the sane prisoners are mixed with the mad. This means that men who are in any case despised for their conduct, have to bear, in addition to their sentence, the aggression and insults of the insane. As a result, a stay in this house of detention often becomes a slow descent into madness.'

'What do the doctors do?'

'You must be joking! They've never had any doctors. Worse still, the place has become a kind of theatre for fashionable society. From time to time, for a little money to the guards, people who like that kind of thing come to feast their eyes on these degrading visions. Being treated as objects of curiosity causes slight signs of madness to degenerate into paroxysms of frenzy. They start out mad and end up rabid. Some of these visitors treat them as if they were wild beasts in cages, teasing them and provoking their fury. You have to see it to believe it.'

'To think that I, a commissioner at the Châtelet, knew nothing of these horrors!' said Nicolas, his blood running cold with revulsion.

Their presence unleashed a pandemonium of cries and obscene gestures.

'That doesn't surprise me,' replied the doctor. 'For many Parisians, especially among those of the highest rank and the most enlightened, the cruelties committed at the very gates of the city are as foreign as those of the savage populations in the New World.'

'What about the Church?' asked Nicolas.

'The opinion of the Church is that the patients should be grateful for the charity shown them and that the prisoners must expiate their sins. You have to understand that everyone follows the logic of his own viewpoint. The philosophers obviously protest at prisoners and madmen being put together. But in their sensitive humanity, they're interested – with justification – in what happens to the prisoners, but they ignore how badly the insane are treated, with the horrors of prison added to the terrible burden of their condition. Everyone agrees they should be hidden away and prevented from harming others, but it might be more sensible to understand them and treat them.'

They proceeded to a building reserved for young children. Gévigland explained to Nicolas that only those aged under twelve were kept there.

'You mean, I suppose,' said Nicolas, 'that this is part of the hospital, and that these are orphans who've been brought here through public charity.'

'Not a bit of it. They're actually prisoners, and the parents of these wretches are still alive.'

'I'm astonished that creatures of that age can become the victims of laws of which they know nothing and which they wouldn't understand even if they'd known of them. If they've committed punishable acts, they should be sent back to their parents to be chastised by them.'

'But these children haven't broken the laws of the kingdom in any way. They're only guilty of small domestic misdemeanours. It's their parents who've placed them here.'

'And I assume this terrible treatment doesn't reform them?'

'You assume correctly. They usually leave prison worse than when they came in. A hundred times worse. Even separated into cells, they can at least hear each other, corrupt each other with their words, urge each other to vice. In this way, blind parents themselves become the instruments of their own children's depravity and inflict on them the most refined as well as the most terrible of all punishments.'

The worst still remained to be seen. The doctor led Nicolas to the centre of the hospital courtyard. The commissioner shuddered at the sight of the barred windows that overlooked it, behind which pale, hideous figures screamed insults.

Gévigland stamped his foot on the cobbled ground.

'Just imagine, Monsieur, twenty feet underground, directly below where we are now, there are different kinds of dungeons, veritable tombs. Can you see these narrow slits here and there? They're skylights, which let in a feeble semblance of light, not into the dungeons, which have to be kept in total darkness, but into the passage that leads from one to the other. But if I were ever, by some misfortune, to find myself in such a deplorable situation, I think I'd prefer the tomb-like solitude of these cells rather than the communal room in the prison.'

'Why is that?'

'The foulest excesses are committed on the prisoners' very bodies. All kinds of vices are practised as a matter of course, and even in public. Simple decency forbids me to go into detail. I'm told that many prisoners are "*simillimi faeminis moeres, stuprati e constupratores*", lost to all modesty.'

'But who are the unfortunates who've been plunged into this hell?'

'Do you need to ask?' said the doctor, with bitter irony. 'Minor offenders, guilty of street brawls, drunkenness, indecency, debauchery, and God knows what else. None is here after being convicted of the worst crimes in a regular court. They're all here for what are called offences of disorder.' He smiled. 'Please don't think that observation is directed at you. I can see how indignant these things make you feel, and I appreciate that.'

'But it should be directed at me,' replied Nicolas. 'At the beginning of my career I recall reading a report addressed to Monsieur de Sartine, who was then Lieutenant General of Police, which said that the prisoners at Bicêtre were there because of arrests made by the military police, courts martial, the Criminal Lieutenant, and local justices, especially for poaching. You can rest assured that I shall inform Monsieur Lenoir of the situation here.'

'Nobody so far has ever taken the slightest steps to remedy such terrible conditions.'

For a long time they were silent, while their presence continued to provoke a cacophony of cries and insults.

'I think your gown has a lot to do with this welcome,' observed Gévigland. 'They recognise that you're a commissioner . . . But I've taken up too much of your time. I'll take you to the mother superior and she will point you in the direction of the gaolers who keep the registers.'


An elegant staircase led them to the first floor of the central building. A nun hurried forward, making the flagstones resonate. Nicolas asked her to announce him to the mother superior, and took his leave of Monsieur de Gévigland. He was admitted into a small cell in which the only furniture consisted of a deal table and two stools. A short woman shrouded in black veils was looking at him, her hands in her sleeves.

'Many commissioners pass through this house,' she said in a

high-pitched voice, 'but few have asked to see me. Is this another inspection, like the one in 1770? Isn't the charity dispensed by this establishment enough to justify its existence? Are you trying to pick a quarrel with us?'

She made a gesture with her hand, as if swatting flies.

'Don't worry, Reverend Mother,' replied Nicolas, 'I haven't come to Bicêtre for an inspection. In connection with a case I'm investigating, I need to find someone I believe is currently in this house.'

'A madman or a patient?' she asked curtly.

'A patient, according to our sources. Admitted in the last six or eight months. His name is Anselme Vitry, he was a gardener in Popincourt, and he's between twenty and thirty years of age.'

'Did he come here of his own free will, or was he brought here by the military police? That's an important point.'

'Without being absolutely sure, I would incline to the second hypothesis.'

She clapped her hands. The nun who had ushered Nicolas in immediately appeared and received instructions from her superior.

'Do you know the Duchamplan family, Reverend Mother?' asked Nicolas.

She seemed to relax as soon as she heard this name. 'Of course! Monsieur Duchamplan the elder is an administrator of Bicêtre, and we can always count on his benevolence. As for his sister, Louise of the Annunciation, of the Daughters of Saint Michel, we sometimes write to one another. Occasionally, she sends us unfortunate creatures to treat, and sometimes, in her great compassion, she takes in patients of ours who've been cured.'

'You must surely also have met her younger brother?'

She laughed. 'Such a charming boy! He sometimes comes to visit our patients. He talks to them and brings them treats.'

'Isn't that a somewhat unusual activity for a young man of his age?'

'Charity has no age,' she said, testily.

The nun came back into the cell. 'The commissioner must come with me to the clerk's office.'

'I shall not detain you, Monsieur,' said the mother superior.

He bowed to her and left the room.

The clerk, an unassuming man, eventually found Anselme Vitry in the registers. Some marginal annotations beside his name cast light on his situation. Arrested during a raid on a brothel in the company of an infected girl, he had been brought to Bicêtre. There, it had been found that he was not suffering from the disease. As they were not sure what to do with him, he had been freed after a short stay in the house of detention.

'I remember him well, Commissioner,' said the clerk. 'He would tell his story to anyone who'd listen. That he'd been betrayed by his fiancée, that he'd felt so desperate he'd left his house, his parents and his beloved garden. But he was lucky, the rascal.'

'In what way, my friend, did this luck manifest itself?'

'A gentleman who often visits us took an interest in his fate. And as this gentleman was looking for a coachman and Anselme knew how to handle horses, he ended up hiring him.'

'Can you tell me the name of this unexpected saviour?'

The man again consulted his register. 'His name is Monsieur Duchamplan.'

Nicolas rewarded the clerk and left Bicêtre. For a long time, he had the feeling that the foul stench of the place was following him about. So, as he had foreseen, a new suspect had emerged in the case of the murder of Marguerite Pindron. However, this discovery, far from simplifying his conducting of the investigation, was leading him down some disquieting paths. A definite connection had been established between the victim's former fiancé and the major-domo's family. It was now all the more vital to question Eudes Duchamplan, and also to track down young Vitry. Nicolas ordered his coachman to return to the Grand Châtelet. On his arrival, Old Marie told him in a low voice that a strange visitor was waiting for him in the duty office. There, he was greeted as soon as he entered by a man with a sickly face, wearing a beaver hat, whom he knew well, having benefited from his help on a previous case.

'Good day to you, Monsieur Restif,' he said, removing his black gown. 'Has "the owl" trapped some prey he would like to offer the police as a tribute?'

'There's no need to mock me, Monsieur Le Floch. Fate has pursued me since our last encounter. The roof of my lodging at the Presles mansion collapsed. I am now living in Rue du Fouarre. I am pursued by creditors demanding I pay off the debts of my last wife, who abandoned me, and reduce my publisher's bankruptcy. In addition, I'm suffering the consequences of a nasty bout of the clap. As you know, I'm never in a brothel without a purpose. For years, I've been seriously engaged in a rational organisation of vice in Paris: in a word, bringing order to disorder.'

Nicolas knew that, if he did not intervene, he was in for a long sermon. 'Yes,' he cut in, 'we know you're determined that order and morality should reign in our streets, and we appreciate it, believe me. But have you something particular to confide in me?'

Restif de la Bretonne lowered his head and looked down at his dog-eared shoes. His demeanour was a surprise to Nicolas, who was accustomed to the fellow being boastful.

At last, Restif made up his mind to speak. 'As you know, I'm in the habit of roaming the streets of this vast capital in the middle of the night. I try to do good, and sometimes manage to save a poor girl from perdition. A week ago, on the corner of Rue Pavée and Rue de Savoie, I saw a man running after a girl of about twenty. You can imagine the kind of thing he was saying to her. She seemed more curious than lost. I approached and introduced myself as usual. I told the man he was committing a terrible act, he'd even gone so far as to suggest . . . I spoke to the girl about honour and modesty and implored her not to yield to the corrupter. The man went off to other base acts, and the girl cursed me, told me to leave her alone, and ran away . . . Imagine my surprise, on the night of Sunday to Monday, as I was looking at the river at the end of Impasse Glatigny, to discover on the steps leading down to the water the body of that same girl, with her throat cut.'

'Why didn't you call the watch immediately?'

'Nothing could have brought her back to life, and where she was she was sure to be discovered as soon as the sun rose. But . . . you know my little ways . . . I couldn't resist . . . they were so delightful . . .'

From his brown woollen frock coat, he took a pair of dancing shoes similar to those worn by Marguerite Pindron, and of the same elegant workmanship.

'The interest of what you've brought me somewhat tempers my anger at the fact that you concealed information and clues from the King's police force,' said Nicolas. 'Are you aware how great a sin that is?'

'I dare to hope, Commissioner,' replied Restif, hypocritically, 'that the interest of my words, and what I still have to tell you, will appease your legitimate annoyance.'

'I'm listening.'

'Not only did I recognise the girl, but I have a description of the man who was talking to her.'

'As far as the girl's concerned,' replied Nicolas, impassively, 'you're not off the hook yet. You'll have to come with me to the Basse-Geôle to identify the body, and take a look at another.'

'Will I be able to see the feet?'

Nicolas shrugged in exasperation. 'That's enough, Monsieur! Just carry on, I'm listening.'

'The corrupter in Rue Pavée,' he said, rubbing his hands, 'was not unknown to me. This wasn't the first time I'd caught him at these vile activities.'

'Do you know his name?'

'Oh, no. Nor can I describe him, for he habitually wears a cloak with the collar turned up and his hat pulled right down. On the other hand, I've twice managed to follow him. He uses a cab and, would you believe, drives it himself.'

'Would you by any chance have noticed the number?'

'Indeed I did,' said Restif triumphantly. 'It's 34 NPP.'

Nicolas gave a start. Could it really be that, by some incredible coincidence, the cab he had taken to go to Popincourt, the number of which echoed his own age, had been driven by someone involved in this grim affair? Sometimes, a detective's luck depended on coincidence.

'Do you think he picks up women for himself?'

'Hardly! My instinct tells me he's part of a group. In fact, I'm convinced of it. The brothel-keepers probably know more about this than I do. They're the ones you should ask.'

There was a knock at the door of the duty office. It opened and the merry faces of Sanson and Semacgus appeared. Restif turned pale when he recognised the executioner, and had to sit down as if he were about to faint. Nicolas drew his friends into the gallery and asked Old Marie to give the visitor a shot of his herbal remedy.

'My dear friends, you both look very cheerful. And you seem in a hurry to tell me something.'

'Very definitely,' said Sanson. 'The doctor and I have continued our examination of the two victims, and we've been able to make an observation which we're sure will surprise you.'

'An observation,' said Semacgus, 'that would have been surprising in only one victim, but in two . . .'

'Gentlemen, tell me what you have to say, I'm undergoing tortures just listening to you.'

'In the stomachs of the two victims, we found traces of their last meals.'

'Is that all?' said Nicolas, stamping his feet with impatience.

'Without Monsieur Semacgus, who has been around the world, and whose knowledge of botany is considerable, I wouldn't have known what it was. But undigested fibre is not all that common.'

'To cut a long story short,' said Semacgus, 'they had both been gorging themselves on pineapples. Now in this part of the world, even cultivated in a greenhouse, this *bromelia* doesn't always ripen well, which can make it hard to digest. Whether we may conclude from this that they were both in the same place, I leave to a certain highly able commissioner at the Châtelet to determine.'

Nicolas was silent for a moment. 'What would I do without the two of you? Semacgus, where can one find greenhouse pineapples in Paris?'

'At the Jardin du Roi, certainly. In some aristocratic mansions and, outside the walls, in certain private houses.'

Now Bourdeau appeared, followed by Rabouine. Nicolas suddenly remembered that Restif was waiting. They went to fetch him, and a long procession wound through the bowels of the old feudal castle. It did not take Restif long to identify the girl from Impasse Glatigny. To be even more certain, Nicolas had the shoes tried on the corpse. They were also found to match the ones discovered in the roasting room of the Saint-Florentin mansion. Restif had recovered his spirits and was watching these experiments with an expression of ecstasy. He was unable to identify the other body. He was ceremoniously conducted to the entrance of the Grand Châtelet, where he immediately melted into the crowd. The conference resumed in the duty office. Nicolas informed those who had not been present what he had just learnt from 'the owl'.

'In order to restrict the search,' he said, 'I suggest we rule out the aristocratic mansions and the Jardin du Roi. We can always go back to them if our search proves fruitless. Given that the corpses have been discovered in Paris, the solution lies in the city or in the *faubourgs*.'

'What are your immediate intentions?' asked Bourdeau. 'Any instructions?'

'Following Restif's advice, I'm going to pay a little visit to the Dauphin Couronné. I want to find out a little more about these Parisian parties and the people who organise them. I'm sure La Présidente will be able to tell me something on the subject. As for you, Pierre, I'd like you to investigate Monsieur Bourdier, the engineer who lives at the corner of Rue des Canettes. He's needed for some top-secret work. Monsieur de Sartine wants to know if he can count on the man's loyalty.' He looked at his watch; it was two thirty. 'Let's meet here again at seven.'

Nicolas got back to his carriage. He noted that a new young messenger boy had replaced the old one, who had shot up and now served the Secretary of State for the Navy. In passing, he also observed that Rue Royale was being cleared, and that the stones and trenches which had caused the terrible disaster of 1770 had completely disappeared. The door of the Dauphin Couronné brought back memories of his early years in Paris. The little black girl who used to open the door to him was now a tall young woman who greeted him joyfully and threw her arms around his neck.

'Madame will be pleased to see Monsieur!'

Her words surprised him somewhat, for his relations with La Présidente had always been quite distant – although he was grateful to her, of course, for her indiscretion in London, without which he would never have discovered that he was a father.

He thought he had gone back ten years into the past. There, on an upholstered chaise longue, lay La Paulet, the former mistress of the place, enveloped in a satin chenille with a flowery pattern, apparently asleep. Her slack face revealed her ravaged, distended flesh, in whose folds, as always, the top layers of cream and rouge had cracked. Her dressing gown had slipped, revealing monstrously swollen legs, wrapped in bands of pink fabric. He felt as if he were in front of a flower stall in the market from which a pair of swollen feet stuck out incongruously, spilling over the sides of her soft leather slippers. He coughed, to announce himself. The mass shook itself, and all at once he saw those familiar inquisitive little eyes. An ambiguous smile lit up her face. She lifted her wig and scratched her ivory-white cranium. He remembered that in the old days she would take great care of what remained of her hair, massaging it every day with ointment of beef extract and orange flower water. The years had passed . . .

She guessed what he was thinking. 'You're peering at . . . my poor head,' she said with her customary familiarity. 'There were only a few tufts left. Now I just sponge it. No more vermin, no more scabs. Everything is clear. Damn it, don't just stand there gawping! I know you're surprised to see me. Yes, I'm back on duty and plan to make a few new appointments.'

'But what about La Présidente?'

'Oh, don't talk to me about her! No sooner was she in the saddle than she started playing the grand lady, looking down her nose at everyone as if she was born in the chapter of Notre-Dame!' She crossed herself. 'Instead of running the business as I asked her, she lorded it over everyone, got drunk, spent her money on trifles. The way it was going, everything that had taken years of hard labour on my part to build up would soon have been frittered away.'

'So what happened?'

'You know me. I don't bear a grudge, but things had gone too far, and the bailiffs would have been at the door before long. I left my retreat and my poor people to save the house. Otherwise, ruin! You can't imagine how hard it was to restore order. La Présidente had lost control, and everyone was taking advantage of her, to the detriment of the house's reputation. Once Madame Disaster had been booted out, I got down to work despite my infirmities.' She sighed. 'Oh, how I miss La Satin!'

'But you seem to be in rude health,' said Nicolas. 'You've put on a little weight perhaps, but your complexion is just as rosy.'

'That's very bold of you to make fun of me! All this is your fault. Did you have to make La Satin desert me? I was too good-hearted. And why did you thrust me into the arms of your smooth-talking master, that Monsieur de Noblecourt I didn't know from Adam? He really hoodwinked me, that one! Madame Paulet here, Madame Paulet there. I should have stuck to my path, which is to believe only what I find out for myself and not listen to yarns. He played on old Paulet, staking everything on my goodness: my affection for the boy, my concern to please an old friend like you. And to what end? Here I am, plunged back into business and putting my immortal soul at risk.'

She began to weep, but Nicolas noticed that no tears fell.

'Come now,' he said, 'you've made La Satin and my son very happy. That should weigh heavily in the eyes of the Lord.'

'Don't talk to me about La Satin!' she retorted through pursed lips. 'You've made her really unhappy. I visited her yesterday in Rue du Bac. You wanted to put her in a shop, as if white lace could wipe out the past . . . Well, why don't you let her do as she sees fit? You seem to forget that your son was born in the aristocracy of the lower depths and that, whether you like it or not, he will graze where he has crawled! Oh yes, Marquis . . .'

Nicolas bit his lips in order not to reply. Nothing good would come of quarrelling. He knew there was a kernel of truth in the old woman's criticisms. Better to avoid saying anything he could not retract; that would only make her more stubborn.

'That's a private matter,' he said. 'We can talk about it again when we've both cooled down. For the moment, my friend Paulet should not forget that her house enjoys a special leniency from the police and that if she does not want things to change . . .'

She gave a forced smile. 'I knew that was coming . . . So, if I understand correctly, you have something to ask old Paulet?'

'My dear Paulet, you always understand men who know the right way to speak to you. In the old days, you used to organise parties in certain well-equipped houses, little performances in which you couldn't tell where fantasy ended and reality began. What about now?'

'They still go on,' she said, obstinately. 'But times have changed, and the devotees handle it all themselves.'

'What do you mean?'

Her little eyes twinkled, as if hit by a strong light. 'A young man came here several times and asked me to supply him with young girls for his seraglio and some well-built stallions, as he put it, who could provide . . . La Paulet doesn't stoop to things like that.'

'Can you describe him?'

'Young, the usual buck.'

'If he shows up again let me know.'

'I don't dip my toes in those waters, my boy. I have my morality. I've already told you too much. Alas, everything's going from bad to worse, girls are flooding in from all over, driving the taste for novelty. The days when we were like a family — that's all over! This is the age of matchmakers and pimps!'

'As always, La Paulet remains true to her principles,' concluded Nicolas with a smile. 'A well-kept house, no gambling, regular girls and the best possible relationship with the police. I bid you farewell.'

'Go on, make fun of your poor friend,' she grunted. 'You've always brought me trouble.' She collapsed onto her chaise longue which creaked beneath her weight.

'This is the first time you haven't offered me any ratafia.'

As he went out, he heard a curse and the sound of a piece of porcelain smashing against a wall.


At seven o'clock, Bourdeau and Rabouine joined Nicolas at the Grand Châtelet. They had had the idea of consulting a botanist from the Jardin du Roi to try and establish who had made enquiries about purchasing pineapple seeds. In this way, they had drawn up a list of some fifteen residences, which would all have to be checked the following day. Then they had proceeded to Rue des Canettes. It was here that the man who had made Monsieur de Sartine's organ of wigs had his workshop. The family were in desperate straits. Driven into a corner, Bourdier had revealed that he was under pressure from an Englishman who was offering him a fantastic fee to go to England and use his skills in a cotton mill, where he would make technical improvements for the benefit of the East India Company. The description of his English contact matched that of Lord Ashbury, alias Francis Sefton. Nicolas reflected for a moment.

'This man is under threat, and so are our interests,' he said. 'He will end up yielding to these blandishments from across the Channel. Take the carriages you need and bring him here with his family. I'll go and see Sartine, he'll deal with it.'

Bourdeau sat down and began filling his pipe. 'It's already been done,' he said sardonically. 'The Bourdier family are waiting for you downstairs.'

# XI

## MANOEUVRES

And the liberty that follows our places
stops the mouths of all find-faults.
SHAKESPEARE

A cohort of three carriages set off, with Nicolas in the first. In the middle carriage, the panic-stricken engineer hugged his wife and four children to him. When they got to Rue Neuve-Saint-Augustin, they found that the minister had not yet returned from Versailles. But his return was imminent, as the royal family were getting ready to move to their hunting quarters in Fontainebleau. Nicolas thought of going to Monsieur Lenoir's house, which was nearby, but just as he was about to make up his mind to do so, a carriage arrived, and Sartine got out. He took him into his study and immediately began mechanically playing his organ of wigs; a magnificent specimen, full of curls and knots, appeared in all its dazzling blondness.

'It comes from Vienna, from the person who supplies Prince Kaunitz, who's a great connoisseur like me!' He was lovingly stroking the wig. 'The Abbé Georgel, Prince Louis's secretary, sent it to me. But tell me what's going on in my courtyard. *Quid novi* in your investigation? As always, corpses have been piling up, and your usual acolytes are getting ready to poke about inside them. Or am I mistaken?'

'Have you ever been mistaken, Monseigneur? First of all, your organ maker seems to me a very honest man although, reduced as he is to poverty, he has almost been persuaded with false pretexts and tempting offers to go to England.'

The minister dropped his wig, which spread over the desk like a sea creature stretching its tentacles. 'Don't tell me the British secret services have had their hands on him!'

'Indeed they have. And again it's the work of Lord Ashbury, alias Francis Sefton. To avoid such a thing happening, I've made the first move – or, rather, Bourdeau has – by immediately moving our man and his family. I've promised Bourdier that we'll make sure nothing happens to him and that he will be taken to a residence of the State where his work will be protected.'

'Excellent. So that was the screaming, moaning cohort that greeted me in my courtyard, was it? Let them stay here tonight. I'll give the necessary instructions for them to be taken somewhere safe tomorrow. And what of your investigation?'

'Everything seems to point to the Duc de La Vrillière, but I've yet to be convinced that he's guilty. There are still elements I can't explain, but I have the feeling I'm slowly getting closer to the truth. By the way, there are now three corpses, and I haven't given up hope—'

'Of finding even more?' Sartine said, his cold face lighting up in a smile. 'I wish my successor luck . . . How are you getting on with him?'

'Our last audience went well, with no acrimony.'

After reassuring the Bourdiers about their fate and receiving their thanks and blessings, he went back to Rue Montmartre, where Catherine changed his dressing and served him some soup.

He dipped croutons into it and washed it down with wine, then climbed on a stool to cut several thick slices from a ham on the mantelpiece, which he devoured greedily. Fresh nuts and apples rounded off this rustic snack. Later, as he was about to fall asleep, exhausted, three faces came into his mind, that of his son, that of La Satin, and finally that of Aimée d'Arranet.

*Sunday 9 October 1774*

Nicolas was woken by the distant trilling of a flute. Monsieur de Noblecourt was practising, which suggested that he was feeling fit and was in a good mood. Immediately Nicolas had dressed and had his breakfast, he joined him. The sight that greeted him would have delighted a painter skilled at capturing intimate domestic interiors. The morning light enveloped the old magistrate in a golden halo as, marking time with his foot, he played a countrydance tune with his usual mastery. Cyrus and Mouchette sat shoulder to shoulder, watching him attentively. Nicolas, motionless, was carried away by the tranquillity of the moment and waited for the piece to end before he showed himself.

'What a pleasure it is to see you recovered,' he said.

Noblecourt sank into his favourite armchair. 'You, on the other hand, seem to have been collecting wounds and bumps.'

'Oh,' said Nicolas, 'I'm used to being under fire. When I was ten, a guest of my father's nearly killed me after mistaking me for a hare! Bullets are in the habit of grazing me.'

'Don't try to laugh it off, your friends live on their nerves when you're far from them. But tell me about your latest adventures. It'll cheer me up and give me a rest from all this trilling. You can't imagine how difficult it is, when there are two trills in succession, to avoid playing them both in the same way!'

Nicolas launched himself into the details of his stay at Versailles and the progress of his investigation. His old friend became quite troubled and pensive.

'Have you thought carefully about the implications of this attempt on your life? If we disregard the fact that it is similar to those to which you were subjected at the beginning of this year – since those responsible have already been banished – we must conclude that your attacker, or rather your would-be assassin, is determined to prevent you from pursuing your investigations. Who are you threatening? What interests are jeopardised by your actions? Wisdom and logic would suggest that this mysterious Englishman is lurking in the shadows, as is common for people of his ilk, not showing himself in public . . .'

'All the same . . .'

'I foresee your objection: you recognised him in the great gallery despite his disguise. If he is determined to thwart you, it must be because your actions have touched on a sensitive area where your interests conflict. Since you are investigating a series of murders in which suspicion seems gradually to be pointing to one of the King's ministers, that means, if you follow my reasoning, that the Englishman in question could well be in league with the killers. Your skills as a detective are threatening his mission, which seems to me, infirm of mind and body as I am, to be targeting a great man. Consider this: Monsieur de Saint-Florentin would hardly have called you in to investigate a murder committed by himself – did I say murder? I mean murders – and then try to get rid of you! It doesn't make any sense. There is something else behind this inexplicable sequence of events.'

He sank further into a kind of trance-like meditation.

'You attract double-dealing, my dear Nicolas. In the fourteen years you've dealt with special investigations, you have been waging an endless struggle against shadows. Self-interest, revenge, ambition, lust and hatred have, like ghosts, dragged you into the forest of crime, and the dead seem to you like the two-faced god of ancient times.'

'Good heavens,' said Nicolas, 'you remind me of a certain Micmac who used to question the spirits by playing on his drum! With you, it's the flute. You are the Delphic oracle of Rue Montmartre!'

'You may mock! At my age, I have a licence to indulge certain whims, and if I choose to be erratic . . .'

'No one would ever dream of denying you that right.'

'I'd like to see him try! For now, the oracle is hungry. Let them bring me my soup and almond biscuits.'

Their attention was suddenly attracted by a song about the Duc de La Vrillière being bawled by a singer in the street, which rose to them through the open window.

> *Minister with no talent that anyone can see,*
> *Man more debased than a minister can be,*
> *We want you to go, we want you to fall,*
> *Out the window with you for the good of all.*

'The rhyme is poor but the content is poisonous,' said Noblecourt. 'The man is not liked – as if a minister could ever be liked. Will you come with me to High Mass at Saint-Eustache?'

'With pleasure, if the music and the food have dispelled the warden's annoyance with those who claim to usurp the privileges of the consecrated bread. And if you don't fear the presence beside you of a man who for some time has been a target for evildoers!'

'I would be dying in noble company, Marquis . . .'


To go the short distance from the house to the church, Nicolas would have preferred to use the cul-de-sac, which led to a side entrance, but Noblecourt wished to make a grander entrance through the front door. There, a large number of parishioners rushed forward to assure the former procurator of their friendship. He doffed his hat to the plaque bearing the epitaph of General Chevert, which had recently been placed there, and proceeded to the pews reserved for the churchwardens, surrounded by a flattering, respectful murmur. Nicolas took his seat a few paces back, near a pillar on which hung a notice from the priest of Saint-Eustache informing his flock of the parish's funeral charges. He noted the size of the sums demanded, doubtless a reflection of the fact that this was a wealthy district. Prices were listed for everything: the digging of the grave, the decoration of the master altar, the choir, the confessor, the white gloves, and the coffin which had to be bought from the parish workshop and not from an outside carpenter. There was a disparity here in the way death was dealt with that gave Nicolas food for thought.

The service was beginning, and Nicolas let himself be carried away by the litany, following it with simple devotion. He looked up into the upper reaches of the building. From where he was, he could see Colbert's black marble tomb behind the choir. The officiating priest mounted the pulpit for his sermon, which today was on the theme of charity. '"Who does not know that all property originally belonged to all men in common, that nature itself knew nothing of property or division and that it first left each of us in possession of the whole universe?"'[1] Nicolas thought of Bourdeau, who would no doubt have approved this introduction. He could not make up his mind whether the inspector's increasingly frequent outbursts were part of his very nature, a consequence of his personal history, or whether, with the passing of the years, it was developing into a more active desire to overthrow the traditions of society and of a power structure which he nevertheless continued to serve without demur.

He had just decided to abandon these reflections, which were leading nowhere, when he heard sounds of creaking and shaking. The door of the central porch suddenly opened with a strident creak, and an angry ox ran into the nave and began overturning everything it found in its path, its bellowing joining the chanting of the service. Chairs and worshippers were thrown to the ground, barricades were raised as protection from the creature's horns. For a good half-hour, Nicolas strove to organise a response. It turned out that the beast had not been properly killed and had escaped from a butcher's stall. The butcher's colleagues in the guild were sent for and eventually got the animal under control. The injured were evacuated and the service resumed.[2] It was not, however, destined to pass without further incident. A man in black clothes and boots came walking down the aisle, clearly looking for someone. Some of the worshippers cursed this noisy intrusion. The Swiss Guard raised his halberd and brought it down on the flagstones. Nicolas recognised the tall, raw-boned figure as Rabouine. Getting to his feet, he made a sign for the spy to follow him.

'What was the meaning of that catastrophic entrance?'

'I had no choice. Bourdeau sent me to fetch you from Rue Montmartre, where Poitevin told me you were here. The thing is, they've found an abandoned cab near the summer pleasure gardens. In it is the body of a young man, and all the indications are that it might be Jean Missery's brother-in-law.'

'The elder Duchamplan?'

'No, the younger one, Eudes. Everything's been taken to the Châtelet, where the inspector is waiting for you. I came in a carriage to take you there. It's waiting in the cul-de-sac.'

Nicolas went to tell Monsieur de Noblecourt. He explained the situation, and advised him not to wait for him to come back.


Outside the entrance to the Grand Châtelet, a noisy, restless crowd were trying to break through the cordon of French Guards and men of the watch surrounding the cab. The little messenger boy was trying without much success to control the horse, which was neighing in panic, startled by the movements of the crowd. Nicolas jumped down, followed by Rabouine, and approached. From the outside of the cab, nothing was visible; a dark film seemed to cover the windows, which were broken in places.

'Curious,' said Nicolas.

'Open, and you'll understand,' said Rabouine, with a fixed expression on his face.

He followed his spy's suggestion. More than most people, he had had to confront some unspeakable scenes in his time, but few as horrifying as this. The whole of the inside of the cab was covered in dried blood. On the seat, arms outstretched, was the body of a man with his face completely shot away. The floor was covered in a blackish liquid, and a large-bore cavalry pistol lay at the man's feet.

Rabouine, seeing what his chief was looking at, nodded and said, 'Suicide, at first sight.'

Nicolas slowly closed the door again. The horse was still neighing softly, stamping the ground with its forelegs, shivers rippling through its coat like waves, eyes wide with fright. He approached it and whispered in its ear, then boldly massaged its gums. The animal moved its head slowly up and down and gradually calmed down.

'You're good with horses,' said Rabouine admiringly.

Nicolas was thinking hard. 'We have to get all this out of the public gaze as soon as possible, or we'll be in trouble. I want the courtyard of the prison cleared so that we can take the cab in there. We'll unharness the horse, and the body can be taken into the Basse-Geôle. It'll have to be cleaned.'

Bourdeau had joined them. 'Today, a Sunday? We'd have to get hold of the guards, and even then . . . No, we'll have to do it ourselves.'

'Then we will. We've been through worse things in the past. Get Old Marie to find some of those leather aprons in the torture chamber, the kind Sanson's assistants sometimes use. Don't forget to retrieve the weapon and examine the bodywork of the cab. The autopsy will be done tomorrow. We'll have to inform

Sanson in Rue d'Enfer as soon as possible. A member of the watch can do that.'

What followed would remain one of Nicolas's worst memories, and he already had quite a few of those. Once the corpse had been taken away on a stretcher to the Basse-Geôle, he examined the bodywork of the cab in the minutest detail. This examination went on for so long that Bourdeau, who knew his chief, assumed he must have discovered a clue. As so often, the commissioner preferred to keep silent until he had had the chance to confirm his findings with other observations. The inspector noticed that he gave equal attention to the wheels, the insides and outsides of the doors, and the frame. Nicolas took out a small pocket knife, scraped some mud or earth from the axles, wrapped it in paper and placed it carefully in his pocket. Then they both descended into the bowels of the Châtelet. In the autopsy room, they put on leather aprons and carefully cleaned the bloodstained body. Bourdeau moved a torch closer and pointed to the coat pocket. In it was the letter which had made it possible to identify the dead man. It was unsigned, an invitation to a rendezvous in Versailles: *'Join us in the place you know.'* Nicolas noted that it had been sent on the very day he himself had arrived at Court.

'Is this why Rabouine said it was the younger Duchamplan?'

'That's the name on the address. The letter must have been delivered by hand, there's no postmark.'

They continued to wash the body, although without undressing it. The water fell from the table in a purple stream, and there was a sickening metallic odour. No conclusions could be drawn from the mangled face. For a long time, Nicolas looked at the hands. Then he took off the shoes and stockings, and gave the feet the same kind of examination. They would have to wait for Sanson's conclusions the following day before they could speculate any further. They went back up to the courtyard of the Châtelet. It was then that Nicolas, looking mechanically at the cab, was struck by the number: 34 NPP. Could it be the same vehicle that had driven him to Popincourt, where he had conveyed Lenoir's instructions to the dairy farmers, and the conversation had turned to the misadventures of Marguerite Pindron's fiancé? Closing his eyes, he tried to recall the driver's face, but found it impossible. All he remembered was a seat stained with what could well have been blood.

'Bourdeau,' he said, 'what would you say to a little visit to Boulevard Saint-Martin and then to the Duchamplan house in Rue Christine?'

'I'd say that my orphans won't see their father today, and that Madame Bourdeau . . .'

'. . . will curse Commissioner Le Floch and the Châtelet, as one might expect!'

In Boulevard Saint-Martin, the inspector showed Nicolas the place where the watch had found the cab. Nicolas sniffed about, his nose to the ground, entered the vast area of the pleasure gardens, and picked something up from the muddy ground. Again, Bourdeau preferred not to ask any questions, even though the action seemed incomprehensible at first sight. They got back into their carriage and drove across Paris. Nicolas, his chin on the door and his eyes half closed, was thinking, whistling an opera aria and beating time with his foot.

'We really mustn't procrastinate,' he said to Bourdeau as they were crossing Pont-Royal. 'This has gone on far too long.'

The inspector made no attempt to find out what he was referring to.

'Let's go straight to our target. That mezzanine apartment in Rue Christine. I need to know what it contains right now. I'd be very surprised if it didn't tell us something about its occupant. Do you have your picklocks?'

Bourdeau struck the pocket of his coat, making a metallic sound.

'Good,' said Nicolas. 'We'll open the door. Forget about due process and authorisation.'

'Do you have an idea in mind?'

'Not one, but several. Don't be offended by my silence, Pierre. It's only a reflection of the fact that I'm torn between various hypotheses. To reveal one would be to throw out the others. They need to remain together until the mind is able to take one last look at all of them and come down in favour of the most likely.'

'You haven't been talking to Monsieur de Noblecourt this morning, have you?' said Bourdeau with a smile. 'Your style bears his imprint.'

'It's impossible to conceal anything from you. As he is wont to say, the most obvious answer is often that which is the least hidden.'

'Which means, I assume,' said Bourdeau, laughing, 'that the solution is near.'

'Much more so than if you had actually thought it within reach.'

When they reached Rue Christine, they found the courtyard of the Duchamplan house deserted. A domestic quarrel could be heard from the upper floors, but there was no sign of the caretaker. They ran to the staircase. Once on the mezzanine, Bourdeau did not take long to pick the lock, and the door opened onto a small, dark antechamber. No sooner had they cautiously entered the apartment than they heard creaking, followed by hurried footsteps. They rushed forward, trying to find their way in the darkness. They pulled open a door, discovered a wardrobe, retraced their steps and chose another door, which this time led to a foul-smelling water closet. The third was the right one. They found themselves in an untidy drawing room where the remains of meals and empty bottles lay strewn over the furniture. At the far end of the room, where the light came in through windows looking out on the courtyard, there was another door. Bourdeau grabbed hold of the handle, but it resisted. He was about to step back and rush at it with his shoulder when Nicolas stopped him, moved him aside and pointed to a small chest of drawers. They slid it across the floor and slammed it into the door, which shattered. Immediately, there was a deafening explosion, and pieces of marquetry and marble were projected into the middle of the drawing room. Bourdeau's wig was blown off, and fell to the floor like a ball of wool, covered in splinters.

'I think,' he said, pale and out of breath, 'that I owe you my life.'

'It's merely a first instalment,' said Nicolas with a bow. 'I'm still in debt to you.'

'But how did you know?'

'Intuition. I had a feeling there was someone armed waiting behind the door.'

Entering the room, which was quite small, they discovered an ingenious mechanism, consisting of a rifle fixed at an angle to the wall, its trigger being connected to the door by a horsehair thread wound around a pulley. Anyone entering would have been unable to escape its effects.

'Where is he?' asked Nicolas, regaining his composure. 'There's no other door, and the window's closed. He can't just have disappeared. Look at the fireplace, it may be similar to Richelieu's.'[3]

Bourdeau took out a folding knife, opened it, and began to probe the surround of the fireplace, without finding anything. Nicolas looked under the bed, then opened a cubbyhole which led into a narrow corridor ending, after a few steps, with another door. They opened it cautiously, revealing a stone spiral staircase.

'It's like Sartine's secret exit at the Châtelet,' said Bourdeau.

The staircase took them down into a cellar, from which an openwork door led out to a little orchard. The bird had well and truly flown. They went back up to the mezzanine. Nicolas continued searching. As he walked, he trod on something. He bent down and picked up a broken pair of glasses with tinted lenses.

'No need to look any further,' he said. 'Lord Ashbury must have taken refuge here after we flushed him out of the Hôtel de Russie.' He struck his head with his fist. 'Noblecourt was right! Isn't it obvious that the safest hiding place was a stone's throw from the hotel, a place where no one would ever think of looking for him? He's played us, well and truly played us. Who took him in?' he went on feverishly. 'Clearly, his accomplice, Eudes Duchamplan, who I assume is one of his agents! The body may be his. Did he kill him, and if so, why? Did he get rid of him before he went to earth in here? What really angers me is the thought that he may already be a long way away.'

'Who brought him food?' asked Bourdeau.

'He's a master of disguise. We know now that there's a way out. It wouldn't have been difficult for him to come and go.'

Nicolas went back to the wardrobe at the entrance. It contained cloaks, hats and shoes. He picked up a pair of shoes and handed them to Bourdeau.

'Keep hold of these, they may prove useful.'

Bourdeau nodded, not quite sure he understood what his chief was alluding to. The commissioner was walking in and out with long strides, as if measuring something.

'You see,' said Nicolas, 'however thick the wall between this wardrobe and the drawing room, it can't be as thick as all that, it's impossible.'

They walked into the wardrobe and moved aside the clothes. The wooden wall at the back was panelled. The commissioner discovered that one of the panels had been cut along the edge: it must surely be movable. He carefully manipulated it until it came out at a right angle, releasing a mechanism which revealed the wall as a hidden door. Once through the door, they discovered, by the light of a candle, what looked like the lair of a second-hand clothes dealer, filled with female clothes – dresses, undershirts, camisoles, petticoats, shawls, lace, bodices, mantles – and a collection of wigs that would have turned Monsieur de Sartine green with envy. These wigs were hanging on nails; some were women's, others men's, and they were of extraordinary variety and elaboration.

'It reminds me of our own collection of disguises,' said Bourdeau, delighted.

There were also some women's shoes. Nicolas compared them with the pair he had already found; they were identical in size.

Bourdeau laughed. 'My God, you anticipated that as well!'

'Not exactly,' said Nicolas, who really had not imagined anything like this.

In a corner lay a man's shirt, rolled into a ball and covered in blood. Nicolas was pondering the fact that, ever since the beginning of this investigation, they had amassed a large number of significant but contradictory clues, but had not yet found a thread to connect them. He was reflecting on this when two people entered the apartment. They turned to see the horrified faces of the elder of the Duchamplan brothers and a woman of indeterminate age, pale and red-eyed, wearing a grey dress and matching mantilla.

'May I ask, Commissioner, what you are doing in my brother's apartment? We heard a terrible explosion.'

Nicolas stood in front of the door to the wardrobe, concealing its contents. 'Have you seen your brother again since my last visit?'

'No. What's happened here?'

He was trying to push Nicolas aside to see inside the wardrobe, but Bourdeau had blown out the candle.

'Someone has been living here,' declared Nicolas sternly. 'Did you know that?'

'Certainly not.'

Nicolas made a signal to Bourdeau, who stood aside and relit the candle.

'Well, then, what can you tell me about this bazaar? Don't you have any useful comment to make about a closet of old clothes worthy of the Temple?'

Duchamplan looked around, more aghast than surprised. The

woman, who had moved closer, was clinging to her husband's arm. She had started trembling.

'You must tell him,' she moaned. 'You can't keep quiet. You've delayed too long.'

'Tell me what?' growled Nicolas, threateningly. 'What are these women's clothes?'

'Old oddments from my wife's trousseau.'

'Indeed?' said Nicolas. 'I congratulate you, Madame, on having such elaborate wigs to wear, and on being able to get rid of such adornments when they are still almost new. I can quite understand that you cast them off! The shoes, too, I assume?'

'Certainly, Monsieur.'

'In that case, let's see, Madame. Would you please try these on?' He handed her some dancing slippers covered with white lace.

'But, Commissioner, what is the point of that?'

'I advise you, Madame, to do as I say.'

She hesitated, wrung her hands, and looked at her husband. Finally, she burst into sobs.

'Monsieur,' she said, 'I have no wish to deceive the law. These shoes are not mine, nor are the clothes.'

'Thank you, Madame, I wanted to hear you say it. It was perfectly obvious to me that they weren't your size. So whose are they? Does your younger brother, Monsieur – your brother-in-law, Madame – sometimes wear women's clothing?'

'That may occasionally happen,' said Duchamplan, embarrassed. 'I assume it's just a game, some harmless amusement, a carnival joke, the stuff of masked balls and—'

'How often?' asked Nicolas.

'Several times a week,' said the woman, with a kind of spite.

'Alas,' said Duchamplan, 'I fear my younger brother is perversity itself. He has become accustomed to dressing up like this for parties. I have no idea what he does at these parties . . . but I'm always terrified to see the state he's in when he returns.'

'Did your elder sister know about these practices?'

'She surprised Eudes some time ago. He made up some vague story about helping the Duc de La Vrillière to seduce some girls, the go-between being none other than our brother-in-law Missery, the minister's major-domo.'

'So your sister knew . . .'

For a moment, he envisaged a new scenario – Sister Louise of the Annunciation informs the Duchesse de La Vrillière, and the duchesse confronts the minister – but it did not get him very far.

'I ought to have both of you incarcerated until this affair has been settled,' said Nicolas. 'But I will trust in your good faith. You will remain confined to your home. Rest assured that you will be watched day and night by my men. Please withdraw.'

Once the couple had gone out, he picked up the bloodstained shirt and wrote something down in his little black notebook.

'Wouldn't those two be better off at the Châtelet?' asked Bourdeau.

'It's possible they're being watched by someone other than ourselves, and I don't want to raise the alarm. In any case, as I've discovered here, I'm not the only one to take precautions and leave by the back way!' He told Bourdeau about his departure from Rue Montmartre. 'Is the British embassy under surveillance?'

'Permanently, since the peace treaty. Of course, routine may have set in.'

'Lord Ashbury may try to find refuge there, so we need to tighten the surveillance. What have we found out so far about the growing of pineapples?'

'Rabouine is going through the list at the Châtelet and has flooded Paris and the suburbs with spies. He may have found what you're looking for by now.'

'I fear for your Sunday, Pierre. Your family will curse me.'

'They're used to it after a quarter of a century!'

They closed up the secret passage, barricaded it to prevent anyone coming in from outside, and placed seals on the front door. It did not take them long to get back to the Grand Châtelet, where Rabouine was waiting for them, looking very excited.

'I would guess your search went well,' said Nicolas, 'judging by that air of smugness.' He placed the bloodstained shirt on the table.

'Judge for yourself,' said Rabouine, waving a paper. 'Of all the residences on the list, only one attracted my attention, for two reasons.'

'Tell us what they were.'

'The first is that the person who lives there is in our records. He appears in Marin's daily reports, once intended for Monsieur de Sartine and now for Monsieur Lenoir, on the information gathered by our inspectors and spies. He comes into the category dealing with prostitution and licentious behaviour, and inhabits the borderline between vice and crime.'

'He's got us hooked!' said Bourdeau, sitting with his elbows on the table and his head on his folded hands.

'Anyway, to cut a long story short, it appears that the man in question is very well known in the world of vice. Why?'

'Yes, why?' said Nicolas impatiently. 'Come on, Rabouine, get to the point! We don't have much time, and you're keeping us waiting.'

'All right. He's the grand master of a libertine society known as the Order of Happiness. His followers vow to make each other happy. They're an androgynous group, who like men to become women, women to become men, and all points in between . . .'

'And where do they meet?'

'Sometimes at the grand master's mansion in Montparnasse, which is where he has his greenhouse of exotic plants. Sometimes in the quarries at Vaugirard, sometimes in other places we have yet to discover.'

'This is indeed most strange! And the second of your reasons?'

'This lover of young flesh, whose influence within the society seems to increase with every passing day, is none other than the Marquis de Chambonas, who married Mademoiselle de Lespinasse-Langeac, the illegitimate daughter of the Duc de La Vrillière and the Beautiful Aglaé.'

'Good Lord!' said Bourdeau.

'And that's not all,' Rabouine went on. 'The only motivation for the marriage was to shore up Chambonas's failing fortune. But when things didn't live up to his expectations, he unearthed a nasty secret he's been using to blackmail the minister: the Beautiful Aglaé is said to have once married a certain Comte Sabatini, who was wrongfully deported to the West Indies on the minister's orders.'

'Let's not waste any time,' said Nicolas. 'I want the Marquis de Chambonas's mansion to be put under surveillance immediately. What Rabouine has just told us matches the information we had from Restif, the things La Paulet hinted at to me, and what we found in Rue Christine. Bourdeau, take this shirt and go straight to the Saint-Florentin mansion. Find the minister's valet and spare no effort to discover if the shirt belongs to his master. Last but not least, and I don't care how we get it, I must have, as soon as possible, a detailed report on the Duc de La Vrillière's movements over the past week so that we can check his alibis.'

'There's no need, Monsieur Nicolas,' said Rabouine. 'I'm already on drinking terms with the minister's coachman, who likes a tipple whenever he has a moment to spare. With a little bit extra thrown in, solid this time rather than liquid – I'll put in my expenses claim as usual – I've managed to get the necessary information from him.'

'Rabouine, you will have your reward, plus a bonus.'

'There are always bonuses for immorality,' said Bourdeau wryly.

'It sometimes happens, Inspector,' said Nicolas, 'that men whom we believe to be without principles are strongly imbued with the religion of efficiency. We're listening, Rabouine.'

'Well, his magnificence the Duc de La Vrillière has not been sleeping at home for several months . . .'

'There's nothing new about that. There was the Beautiful Aglaé, and plenty of other loose women before her.'

'That's as may be,' continued Rabouine, 'but at night, he asks to be driven to different places, then dismisses his coachman and disappears. His servants are very intrigued and have tried to follow him without success. Anyway, what that means is that the minister has no alibi for any of the three murders we've been investigating.'

'My God!' cried Bourdeau in alarm. 'We know that these crimes are linked. Who knows the horrors that may have been committed before our attention was called to the Saint-Florentin mansion?'

'Which makes your mission all the more important, my dear Pierre,' said Nicolas. 'We must find out if this shirt is indeed the minister's.'

Nicolas remained alone in the duty office. He needed this interlude to see how things stood with the investigation. He took out his little black notebook. As he read through it, he noted particular points on a separate sheet, making a list which, he hoped, would lead him to discern a clear, logical path to the truth. He had reached a point where any advance in his understanding of the case could only be brought about by a stark, deliberate demonstration of authority. The more he reread his notes, the more he realised that the testimonies he had gathered at the time of Marguerite Pindron's murder had clouded his vision, confused his mind, and sent him off on false trails. Yes, he would have to go back to the beginning and drive the dubious witnesses into a corner. But he did not have time for persuasion. However distasteful he found the means of coercion available to the law, means that Sanson and his assistants could apply, he believed that the threat of torture should be enough in itself to convince the most stubborn. Only one thing held him back from resorting to it: being inclined to think that torture had the effect of making people confess even when they were innocent, he feared that its threat would do the same. Eventually, though, he made up his mind to play that trick, and he began reflecting on the best and most convincing way to put it into effect. He would have to choose the witnesses to be subjected to this test. It was useless to try it on all of them. After all, he could hardly put the Duchesse de La Vrillière in a torture chamber. He just had to pick the right targets. If a false picture had been built up about what had happened and when it happened, all it needed was one element to yield, and the whole thing would come crashing down. It seemed to him that Eugénie Gouet, the duchesse's head chambermaid, was the ideal element in this strategy. She would be more than a match for him. Next, a proper interrogation of Jacques Blain, the caretaker who had been in love with Marguerite, was sure to be of interest. He recalled something Bourdeau had said: why make a stew of three rabbits without adding blood to the sauce? Finally, a friendly conversation with young Jeannette Le Bas might well shed some light on the life of Marguerite Pindron. What Nicolas was hoping for from all this was to speed things up, to find the one thread which, pulled out of the warp and weft of the crime, would cause the whole thing to unravel.

He resolved to give himself a brief respite, unable for the moment to make a crucial decision. Wisdom dictated that he should wait for the results of the missions he had given his men. It was late afternoon by now, and he was starting to feel hungry. Leaving the old prison, he was caught up in the feverish activity of the surroundings. The smell emanating from an open-air pot of capons cooked in coarse salt tempted him, and he greedily devoured a bowlful of this stew. The grains of salt cracked beneath his teeth, and he closed his eyes and saw again the dazzling salt marsh at Guérande and himself as a little boy, licking his fingers as he collected marine crystals . . . He crossed the Seine on foot, the physical effort helping him to clear his mind of the clutter of contradictory thoughts and establish a clean slate on which he would then be able to map out a logical argument.

A longer walk took him beyond the boulevard, towards the Observatory. He knew there was an entrance here to the quarries which abounded in that area. It was late, and the porter was reluctant to guide another visitor, but Nicolas's position and the promise of a substantial reward soon overcame his reluctance. They plunged into a complex, shadowy labyrinth. It was easy to lose your way here, and the porter had to warn him frequently. The thing that Nicolas, who hated confinement, most dreaded was that their torches would go out, plunging them into darkness. He discovered to his astonishment a vast underground city, filled with weirdly shaped streets and crossroads and squares. Most of the galleries were of uneven height, and they were sometimes forced to stoop. There were stalactites in places, and the porter claimed, boastfully, that the river was just above their heads. Nicolas, who was well aware of the distance they had come, strongly doubted this.

For years, he had heard people talking about the danger these quarries posed for the city up above; it had been supported by them for many centuries, retrieving in the light of day what it borrowed from the earth. He noticed pillars half crushed beneath the weight bearing down on them and apparently on the verge of collapse,[4] and quarries on two levels where the pillars of the upper level were precariously balanced.

Engaging his guide in conversation, he learnt that some of the poorest families in the city took refuge in this place, especially in the dead of winter. Others used it as a hiding place, only coming out at night to gather provisions or commit crimes. These people included escaped convicts, deserters, and a whole collection of rogues and vagabonds, a true court of miracles. Lowering his voice, the porter said that there were also rumours of strange meetings held here, of groups indulging in reprobate practices. Nicolas tried to get him to say more, but to no avail.

This visit gave him an opportunity both to assess the dangers of this maze of galleries piled one on top of the other, and to get some idea of the uses that were made of it. The safety of Paris depended on the dimensions of this underground complex being duly noted by the King's engineers, a detailed plan being drawn up, structural weaknesses being identified, and stricter controls being put in place concerning the disquieting collection of individuals who haunted it. As far as his present investigation was concerned, the visit confirmed the plausibility of the rumours reported by Bourdeau about the very special use that some people made of the seclusion and intricacy of these hidden depths.


He found Monsieur de Noblecourt reading Montluc. Mouchette climbed on him and settled in her favourite place on his shoulders.

'I've just returned from the underworld,' he said simply.

'Monsieur de Sartine is right,' Noblecourt said with a smile, 'you create havoc. The whole of Rue Montmartre is talking about the High Mass this morning and the untimely appearance of the devil in the appetising form of a dazed and angry fatted ox. I think it deserves an inscription in marble, in gold letters, a fine lapidary formula we can ask Louis to translate for us, something like, *Here Nicolas Le Floch slew the minotaur, adding this exploit to his many others!*'

'You may well mock, I saw you leaping onto your pew like a young man! As for me, having already confronted the minotaur, I've now had to suffer the torments of the labyrinth and the terrors of confinement!'

He told Noblecourt of his descent into the quarries.

'They were always places,' said Noblecourt, 'conducive to strange practices, even satanic meetings. The Regent, the Duc d'Orléans, once tried to summon the devil there. It's beyond me how, in the century in which we live, people can still believe in such nonsense! It's been too long that people have been tearing each other to pieces, with the tongue and the pen, over the contents of a papal bull or a *billet de confession*, and that the *parlement* has been defying the authority of the monarch to the renewed cries of agitators foaming at the mouth over the tomb of an obscurantist deacon. Is this really the triumph of reason and philosophy? There is a balance to be struck. Look at the regent, a rational man apparently, a chemist, an engineer, a fine musician and a statesman. How could he become involved in such things? Now everyone's trying to go beyond the bounds of knowledge, striving to explore the treacherous regions of the garden of evil. I tell you this: we will see far worse things before the end of this century!'

He had raised his voice so much that Cyrus began howling lugubriously.

'You see, you've awakened the dog Cerberus!'

The evening continued with a light supper and a long discussion of the practice of tremolo in playing music, while from the servants' pantry there rose the delicious smell of quince jelly.

# XII

## CONFRONTATIONS

Assist me and stay by my side,
because I am about to attack them.
Montluc

*Monday 10 October 1774*

Sanson was operating while Nicolas watched attentively, sickened by this morning autopsy. Was it the sight of the executioner's clothes brushing against that mutilated face, or the feeling that he was getting close to the end of his investigation? He was restless with exhaustion and impatience.

'A man of about twenty-five,' announced Sanson. 'Well built. The face has been torn to pieces by a discharge of small shot. In my opinion, it's quite impossible for such a terrible wound to have been caused by the pistol you found beside the corpse.'

'As it happens,' said Nicolas, 'my examination of the inside of the cab did puzzle me: the shot had been scattered far too widely, and the windows had been broken. From which I conclude—'

'That it can't have been a suicide.'

'In which case, what weapon could have been used?'

'A hunting rifle seems a likely hypothesis, but I'm not happy with it. It would have had to be fired from quite a distance in order to produce such scattering.'

'So the mystery remains impenetrable.'

'Oh, no! There are weapons that could produce such a result, such as a blunderbuss.'

Nicolas began thinking aloud, while Sanson, who had broken off his work, looked on curiously. 'Now that's strange. When I was faced with that scene of carnage, two things struck me. I couldn't help thinking that someone had tried to arrange things in such a way as to deceive a superficial examination. It seemed to me that all the elements were too neatly in place, and all led to the same observation: the body was that of a man who had killed himself, and the weapon he had used lay at his feet. And yet . . . several details had already attracted my attention: the shot scattered around the interior, but also the body itself. My friend . . .'

The word moved Sanson, whose amiable face lit up.

'. . . could you examine the hands and feet of this corpse and tell me the results of your observations?'

Sanson proceeded with a meticulous investigation of the parts concerned, then looked up with a puzzled expression. 'I'm not sure what I'm looking for. The only thing I can say for certain is that, despite the rich garments he's wearing, this was a young man of lower class. A worker rather than a bourgeois. I would even say a peasant. The hands are callous, the nails black and soiled with earth, and scratched by thorns. The feet are wide and also possess particular characteristics. Frequently walking barefoot hardens the heels. Not very well cared for generally. Does that satisfy you?'

'It confirms my suspicions. And when we know what this corpse was supposed to represent, or rather what it had the task of making people believe, there is, I think you'll agree, good reason to wonder about the fairy tale they were trying to dish up! Added to which, apart from a letter obligingly telling us the identity of the corpse, we discovered nothing in the pockets of his coat, none of those trinkets that everyone carries with them. Nothing!'

'Not even a little black notebook?' said Sanson with a smile.

'Nothing at all. All of which means that this was an attempt to lead us astray. However, it appears to me so obvious – so obvious in its very falsity – that I've even started to wonder if we were meant to notice the attempt.'

There was a thought lurking at the back of his mind, a thought he did not want to formulate too hastily. He had not yet seen everything, and other elements might emerge to confirm the possibility. Perhaps . . . No, it was too soon. There was not much more to be learnt from this corpse. Everything pointed to the fact that it could not possibly be the younger Duchamplan, but was actually Vitry, the young gardener rescued from Bicêtre to become a coachman, engaged for God knows what dubious errands. It was he who, by pure coincidence, had driven Nicolas to Popincourt: the number of the cab proved that.

He thanked Sanson and prepared with him the interrogation he was planning of some of the servants from the Saint-Florentin mansion. The instructions he gave were specific: what they had to do was inspire fear merely by displaying the instruments of torture. He hoped that the terror this display would instil in witnesses who were little accustomed to the ways of the law would dissuade them from lying. His method consisted of paralysing the will to resist, but without, however, going as far as to exert direct pressure, which would take away any likelihood of honest answers.

At that moment, Bourdeau appeared, with a package in his hand. He greeted Sanson in a friendly manner.

'So, Pierre, anything to report?'

'I put all the servants at the minister's house through hell, and finally, having wooed the linen maid in the wash house, I obtained what we were looking for.'

He untied the package and took out two shirts, one bloodstained, both freshly ironed, both identical in style and size.

'That's very good,' said Nicolas. 'I hope the linen maid was comely.'

The three friends laughed, then Nicolas summarised the results of the autopsy for Bourdeau.

'You're losing me,' said the inspector.

'I'm not surprised,' said Nicolas. 'But let's look at it logically. Either we're wrong in our observations, and this body is that of Eudes Duchamplan. In that case, which is highly unlikely, for the reasons that I've stated, in whose interest was it to kill him? Or else the body we see here is that of the cab driver, Anselme Vitry, the gardener from Popincourt and Marguerite Pindron's former fiancé, and if we take into account a few doubtless deliberate blunders, it seems as though someone wanted us to assume, thanks to that bloodstained shirt, that the Duc de La Vrillière had been involved in another murder. Having been implicated in this latest one, that would confirm him as a suspect for the others.'

'How could anyone have foreseen that we would search the apartment in Rue Christine?' asked Bourdeau.

'It was an easy assumption to make! Whether we took the body at the pleasure gardens for Duchamplan or someone else, the note found on the body was bound to take us to Rue Christine. What they hadn't counted on was how quick we'd be. We arrived so early that we surprised Lord Ashbury.'

'And what if all this was the work of the minister? What a brilliant idea, to implicate himself in such a way as to give us good reasons to exonerate him! He may be in league with Eudes Duchamplan, having probably frequented the same places of ill repute, with his major-domo as the go-between. That would tally with what the elder brother told us.'

'Let's not go too far,' said Nicolas, 'but stick as closely as possible to the facts. We have a corpse which someone tried to pass off as that of a suicide. We find a bloodstained shirt in the lodgings of the supposed victim. Whom does it implicate? The Duc de La Vrillière.'

Nicolas was pacing up and down.

'It may be that we came in on the first part of something that had not been completely thought through,' he resumed. 'The linstock hasn't yet reached the fuse. Imagine this shirt linked with the corpse at the pleasure gardens; the staging increased the horror of the crime and pointed to the supposed perpetrator.'

'What are you planning to do now?'

'I've given instructions to our friend Sanson here.'

'I'm going to prepare everything in total earnest,' said Sanson, 'just as you asked.'

'Are you going down that route, Nicolas?' said Bourdeau, with a disapproving look on his face.

'I have to, but it'll only be a piece of play-acting.'

'You do realise that, in such cases, a confession is merely a way of avoiding pain.'

'I'm not necessarily after confessions, but information which has been concealed from the eyes of the law. I know I'm disregarding all the rules, since those I am summoning have not been accused.

It's just a question of flushing each one out from his position, using the elements of surprise and threat. Some of them, I fear, are concealing a great many secrets.'

'We need to arrest them, then,' said Bourdeau.

'You will summon them to follow you to the Châtelet without further ado for an interview with Commissioner Le Floch.'

Nicolas tore a sheet of paper from his black notebook, scribbled a few lines on it, and handed it to Bourdeau, who nodded and left without a word. Sanson remained in his lair, lighting his fires like Vulcan in his forge. Nicolas went back up to the duty office and again went through his notes, his lead pencil in his hand.

An hour later, Bourdeau reappeared, his face quite flushed.

'You seem upset,' said Nicolas.

'I've had to confront a female dragon, whom the social graces demand I call the Duchesse de La Vrillière. She fought tooth and nail to stop me from proceeding with the arrests. Like all women, the last card she played was a fit of the vapours. I took advantage of that to leave her in helping hands.'

'Good,' said Nicolas. 'She'll get over it. We're going to play several acts one after the other. Have these people taken into the corridor. We'll leave the door open, and talk about it so that they think they're in for a little interview designed to soften them up.'

Everything went as planned. Bourdeau returned and asked, 'What are your intentions, Commissioner?'

'Keep the witnesses ready to appear – I say witnesses, I ought to say suspects — in the torture chamber. I believe the torturer and his assistants are ready to get down to the job?'

'Indeed they are.'

'Then let's proceed with the preliminary session.'

'An extraordinary one?'

'Oh, no. Ordinary. I think that'll suffice.'

'Yes, of course. Five or six tin cauldrons. Tying the suspect to a plank and drowning him usually loosens his tongue.'

They both laughed.

'Anything else?'

'The boot, of course. We need to make sure the legs are held tight in the frames. Separate the kneecaps and ankles with two thick planks and put wedges between them. Wood for the women and iron for the man. And don't forget to hit hard with the mallet. I think we should take the number of wedges all the way up to the authorised figure of twelve. That's all. Take them down, I'll join you in a moment.'

Nicolas soon followed Bourdeau and joined the group of witnesses, who were sitting, surrounded by members of the watch, on a stone bench in the dark gallery leading to the torture chamber. Strange noises were coming from the chamber, a particularly frightening din for anyone who had just heard Nicolas's words. He decided to begin with Madame de La Vrillière's head chambermaid, Eugénie Gouet, hoping to confound her with this atmosphere of menace. But she entered with her head held high and no apparent emotion. She was no longer as fresh and white as she had been before; her complexion now was grey, with red blotches. She gave him a look of defiance. In the gothic chamber, the assistants bustled about to the orders of a man in a green coat.

Bourdeau was standing behind a lectern, pen in hand, ready to take down a verbatim record of the interrogation.

'You are here,' said Nicolas in a monotonous voice, 'as a witness and suspect of the murder committed at the Saint-Florentin mansion on 2 October 1774. The apparatus of justice you see around you should encourage you to answer my questions with complete honesty, the only response that will satisfy me as a magistrate and save you from the worst consequences.'

This speech did not seem to have any effect on the woman, but she was convulsively clenching her left fist, something Nicolas had already observed during her first interrogation and noted in his little black notebook.

'Master Sanson, ask your assistants to be silent.'

The assistants froze. Only the crackle of the coals in the brazier continued to awaken echoes in the depths of the chamber.

'Let's begin,' said Nicolas. 'Were you the mistress of Jean Missery, at least until he developed a passion for the victim?'

She did not reply, her eyes fixed on the floor.

'Am I to take your silence as assent?'

She raised her head. 'I prefer to tell you the truth. Yes, Jean had been my lover. He'd even promised to marry me.'

'That, in fact, is what the Duchesse de La Vrillière told a friend of hers, who passed the information on to me,' said Nicolas, lying with an impassiveness that astonished Bourdeau.

The chambermaid's reaction was one of despair, and she looked from right to left like an animal caught in a trap.

'You agree, then. We know also that this domestic Don Juan had some difficulty in satisfying his new young friend, and wasn't always in a state to—'

'He wasn't like that with me!' she said angrily.

'I believe you unreservedly. He wasn't like that with you. But let's imagine that someone gives the poor man some relaxing potion, something that would – not to mince words – make him impotent? Couldn't the sleeping draught used and abused by Madame de La Vrillière have the ability, much appreciated by a neglected and jealous lover, to calm and even extinguish the ardour this man feels for another?'

She said nothing.

'And if we imagine that the poor man, to overcome this new infirmity, starts using other more efficient additives, wouldn't it then be advisable to double the dose of the potion in order to stop him joining his young mistress in ecstasy? I order you to speak, or I shall immediately hand you over to the torturer, who will extract the truth as he sees fit, I promise you that. I accuse you of having known that Marguerite Pindron would be in the kitchen that evening. Who was she meeting?'

Again she moved her head from side to side. Suddenly there came the sound of hurried footsteps. The door of the torture chamber was flung open and Monsieur Lenoir appeared, red-faced and out of breath, his double chin held tightly in his cravat.

'Monsieur, I order you to cease this unjustified interrogation. It is contrary to all the rules established under my authority, which cannot be contravened. Free this unfortunate woman immediately, as well as the other witnesses currently awaiting your pleasure.'

Nicolas made a sign to Bourdeau, who conducted the Gouet woman, Sanson and the assistants out of the room.

'So, Commissioner,' said the Lieutenant General of Police

sternly, 'I find you engaged in an unauthorised interrogation, without having requested permission of the Criminal Lieutenant, without even – I hardly dare utter these words – without even informing me! Of course, Monsieur Testard du Lys has already had to suffer on account of your illicit procedures! How am I to describe such an attitude which violates all principles and is an insult to the majesty of the law? Well? Aren't you going to say anything?'

Nicolas felt annoyance rise within him like a desire for violence, but he restrained himself. Monsieur Lenoir's prompt arrival proved that not everyone here was his friend and that envy was still rife. Or else – although he found this hard to believe – that the Duchesse de La Vrillière had been quick to act. Or the duc . . . Not that it really mattered.

'Monseigneur,' he said, 'I am here on the orders of the minister, who expressly gave me the responsibility for this affair. When your untimely arrival interrupted the interrogation, I'm sure I was on the point of obtaining vital information that would have helped me to understand a case whose ramifications you are unaware of and in which the greatest haste is called for.'

'I can't believe your insolence! It's beyond me. What on earth are you saying? If I'm badly informed, whose fault is that?'

'It's the fault of those who attack the Crown and its servants. How much time have I had, would you say, to devote to an investigation which at present involves four corpses, including three young women, one almost a child, affairs of State, secret societies, the moral failings of men in high places and the interests of a powerful enemy? It is quite unwise to give instructions from a distance to a subordinate and then leave him alone to confront the difficulties. Since he has been entrusted with a mission, one should rely on him and not hamper him with other assignments which the constantly changing circumstances make it impossible to carry out.'

'Monsieur!'

But Nicolas was launched. 'An investigation in which I myself was the object of an attack which I narrowly escaped,' he went on. 'How else would you like me to describe such a sequence of events, and how, knowing nothing of the way things have developed, can you accuse me of violating laws which I have been serving for fourteen years under the authority of the late King and your predecessor, Monsieur de Sartine?'

'I beg you to lower your voice and forget the absent and the dead,' replied Lenoir curtly. 'You're letting your mind wander! How could you possibly think that, under an easy-going King and my authority, you would be justified in flouting the law and using means which are well known for providing confessions but no proof?'

'Why don't you ask me, instead of demanding but not listening? The only reason I set this solemn and terrifying apparatus in motion was precisely in order not to have to use it. I was hoping that merely displaying it would dissuade these false witnesses from lying. My intention was to dig deep into these frightened souls, to draw out the past and the future, the involuntary word, the barely concealed admission, the detail long held back. That said, Monsieur, allow me to tell you that your words hardly surprise me, coming from a man who, from the beginning, has shown me nothing but rejection and disdain, and made light of a devotion developed over long years.'

He knew, in saying this, that he was exaggerating, but that it was necessary to lance the wound. Otherwise, it would be impossible ever to establish trust between them, and he himself would lose his self-esteem.

'You are forgetting yourself, Monsieur,' said Lenoir, his broad face turning red.

'I describe things as I see them. If you wish to remove me from this case, do so. If you wish me to leave the police force, demand it. If you are determined to conceal the truth and leave this case unsolved, then continue to hamper the work of your investigators. To someone whose loyalty has been called into question, it really doesn't matter any more. I shall see His Majesty, who hoped that I would see this through to the end, and when he questions me on the progress of the case, I shall admit to him immediately that, on the orders of the Lieutenant General of Police, he can no longer count on his commissioner for special investigations. Exit Monsieur Le Floch. The Marquis de Ranreuil is off to hunt stags at Fontainebleau. I bid you farewell. Your humble servant!'

Nicolas was striding towards the door when Monsieur Lenoir ran to cut him off before he reached the gallery. 'Monsieur, why didn't you tell me all this earlier?'

Tense and inscrutable, Nicolas did not reply.

'I'm sorry if I gave you the impression that I did not trust you,' continued Lenoir. 'The cases in which you have been involved over the years were of such a nature as to give rise to an unreasonable feeling of suspicion in me. I fear I was mistaken, and that I have offended you so seriously that I feel angry at myself. But put yourself in my shoes. I was bewildered by the very small amount of information coming back to me, and angry when I learnt that you were using torture. I was deceived by false information. I am sorry about that. You are an honest man, for who else would dare to talk to me as you have done? With such arrogance . . . Did you ever attempt that with my predecessor?'

'As a matter of fact, I did,' said Nicolas, whose anger had immediately abated. 'I once presented my resignation to Monsieur de Sartine. It was at the beginning of my career, and he had seen fit to use me as a plaything in an intrigue of his. I told him a few home truths.'

'And how did he take it?'

'Lieutenants General of Police come and go, and are all pretty much the same. Like you, he made honourable amends, to which I responded as I respond to you: I am touched by your words and I am all yours. However, Monseigneur, we don't have much time. Sit by this brazier. One can catch one's death of cold in these underground chambers. Let me enlighten you.'

Nicolas spoke for a long time, in the dancing blue light of the coals. From time to time, Monsieur Lenoir would look up in surprise. He asked a few questions, reflected for a while, then stood up.

'Monsieur, I fear I may have spoilt your skilful performance. You can't catch birds twice in the same trap. This case may have repercussions we can barely begin to imagine. Did you know that Monsieur de Chambonas, to whom my attention has already been drawn, has some very highly placed friends? The Duc de Villars, the Duc de Bouillon, the Comte de Noailles and others of his kind are working on his behalf . . . Take care, the man has cutthroats at his disposal, who would be only too happy to silence anyone who talks too much. If your suppositions prove correct and you remain the target of the English enemy . . .' He paused for a moment. 'I am pleased that the misunderstanding between us has been dispelled. It was quite unjustified, except perhaps by my constant concern for the King's service. We must be grateful for this outburst, which has allowed us to put aside the false impressions under which we were both labouring. Rest assured that, from this point on, the Lieutenant General of Police grants you his full and total confidence and that he asks you to consider him as you considered Monsieur de Sartine.'

Nicolas smiled and bowed. 'I would be very ungrateful not to defer to your wishes, for that, Monseigneur, is how I always understood my place with you. My position is an unusual one, forged year after year by my presence beside the late King, by my birth, and by the very unusual cases in which I have been involved. The only thing to which I aspire is truly to become once again the instrument in your hands of the King's service, the only concern that drives me and gives me satisfaction.'

'What are you planning to do?'

'Continue with the surveillance, see what it brings us, and finally confound the guilty parties.'

'Do you think that the Duc de La Vrillière is implicated in this series of crimes?'

'I don't think so, Monseigneur. But I understand your legitimate anxiety regarding the minister. Nothing will be done by me to implicate a person so close to the throne; you would be duly informed and the decision would no doubt revert to the King. In such a case, it would be sensible to avoid any kind of public reckoning. That would be contrary to the dignity of the State, and other measures would have to be envisaged.'

'Commissioner, I am completely satisfied. You mentioned His Majesty . . .'

'The King has been kept informed of this affair and is hoping for the imminent success of the investigation. So is the Secretary of State for the Navy; the presence of an English spy and the attack upon myself which seemed at one point to have been targeting the minister, all these things—'

'Yes, yes, I understand, there's no need to go back over all that. Until we meet again, my dear Commissioner.'

Lenoir withdrew, his old affable self. Nicolas took a deep breath. It was as if a weight had been lifted from his chest. The great confrontation had taken place; it had been necessary, and it had been complete. Its intensity had thrown light into the dark corners of a hierarchical relationship which could only be exercised happily when trust was given and accepted. The rest had been nothing but empty promises. He could now hope that on that front at least, he would be protected and have freedom of movement. Nevertheless, the Lieutenant General's sudden appearance in the torture chamber remained fraught with consequences. Now, the slyest of witnesses – and the Gouet woman clearly belonged to that category – would clam up like oysters. He called Bourdeau. His deputy's eyes expressed both amusement and anxiety.

'Monsieur Lenoir just passed me, looking red in the face but surprisingly serene. What fly bit you and transformed you into that ranting and raving monster?'

'Please don't exaggerate,' replied Nicolas. 'We exchanged a few words. I only raised my voice a little.'

'Yes . . . like the trumpet on the Day of Judgement.'

'Nothing that went beyond the rules a subordinate of a certain rank sets himself with regard to a magistrate of a higher rank.'

'So what happened?'

'What I said was very well received, and I have reason to believe that it will facilitate our work. It's just a question of knowing when to appear sincere . . . You know how things are, Pierre. There is always a risk in confronting someone when you are of unequal weight: it's the earthenware pot against the iron pot. Nobody can escape it in the course of a life in which the mark of subordination is uncertainty. The fact remains that if, at that decisive moment, your moral strength abandons you, you will never regain it, nor will you ever again be in a position to convince others. We had reached that crossroads. From now on, the clouds are dispelled, except that it spoilt our little piece of play-acting.'

'The Gouet woman hastened to decamp, along with the caretaker,' said Bourdeau. 'I made no objection, not wishing to irritate Monsieur Lenoir more than was necessary. Only little Jeannette, who was shaking and sobbing, didn't dare move an inch.'

'Send her in. Who knows? Perhaps she can help us.'

A red crumpled face soon appeared. The girl was trembling and looking wildly about her. Nicolas took her gently by the arm and sat her down on a stool.

'So, Jeannette, you're not like the others, are you? You're a good girl, and we have no wish to harm you, you can rest assured of that. I just need you to clarify certain details, do you understand?'

She was breathing in convulsive little spasms. The sweat had plastered her curly hair to her forehead, and in a flash Nicolas saw the Fausses Reposes woods, and Aimée d'Arranet's face in the pouring rain. He shook himself, took out his handkerchief and blew her nose as if she were a child. This simple gesture appeared to relax her, and she gave a little half-smile.

'There we are, that's better. Now listen carefully to what I'm going to ask you. You don't know anything, you were asleep, you didn't see anyone, you didn't hear anything. That's fine, I believe you. But you were Marguerite's friend, and the other day, before you were taken ill, you were about to tell me something.'

She lowered her head, and again assumed a stubborn, distant air.

'Your friend was supposed to be meeting somebody that night. A young man, I assume. You were her confidante, did she tell you about him?'

She shook her head from side to side, blank-eyed. Nicolas clapped his hands and she stopped immediately, and went back to normal.

'Just calm down. Admit it: Marguerite told you she was meeting someone.'

She looked at him for a long time before making up her mind. 'Yes, she did, and she also told me she didn't like it but couldn't get out of it.'

'Good! Was it her young man? The one you call Aide?'

'No! It was the old man, the major-domo.' She was expressing herself more firmly now.

'Are you sure? Did you hear her arrange to meet him?'

'No, of course not. I saw the note. She was supposed to be in the kitchen that evening.'

'Did you read the note?'

'No, I can't read. But I saw it.'

'Can you describe the handwriting?'

'It was in big letters, that was all I could recognise. It was on an old piece of paper used for wrapping candles.'

'And did Marguerite keep this piece of paper?'

'She was so fed up with the whole thing that she tore it up into little pieces and threw it out of the window.'

'I'm grateful to you. Is there anything else you have to tell me?'

'No, Monsieur.'

'You can go. Would you like a carriage to take you back?'

'No, I'd be ashamed. I'll go down Rue Saint-Honoré.'

'As you wish. Don't tell anyone what we talked about, your safety depends on it. Please don't forget that.'

She left the room, glancing behind her in panic as if fearing that she would be recalled.

'I'm starting to think we're making progress.'

'A fine haul, indeed,' said Bourdeau. 'A young girl, and the Lieutenant General of Police. By the way, I didn't know you were now claiming your title of marquis.'

Nicolas smiled. 'It was intended *ad usum Delphini*, a little oratorical fig leaf. I think Monsieur Lenoir is sensitive to the prestige of rank. To return to our case, let's sum up. The corpse in the cab is almost certainly not Eudes Duchamplan. He didn't kill himself. We may assume it's the gardener, Vitry, the Pindron girl's former fiancé.'

'That's good to know, but doesn't get us very far.'

'I agree, but it does narrow our search. What about the Duc de

La Vrillière's mysterious midnight flits? Where does he go? And what about the surveillance of the Marquis de Chambonas's mansion? That's where we'll pick up the threads again. And where is the second young girl from Brussels?'

Bourdeau looked at him, puzzled.

'I fear I haven't mentioned that to you,' Nicolas went on, having noticed the inspector's expression. 'The clothes and appearance of the corpse on Île des Cygnes reminded me of something Monsieur Lenoir requested me to look into: the case of two young girls who fled Brussels for Paris. The victim is one of them, and I assume we can fear the worst for her sister. But there's still a chance we may save her, if she's fallen into the same hands. It's a question of time. From my conversation with Monsieur Lenoir, I gather that the Marquis de Chambonas is protected, which means we won't be able to take a close look at his mansion. It's likely that he's being cautious at the moment and that his Roman orgies are now taking place in more secluded spots.'

'I agree with you. So we're dependent on our spies, surveillance, and all the usual methods of a well-regulated police force.'

'We have to wait for something to start. Then we'll pursue the hydra, faithful Iolaos.'[1]

'The many-headed hydra.'

'Indeed. In the meantime, I'm going to pay the minister a visit. I want to set my mind at rest.'

'Is that wise?'

'I'm not risking anything. I'm sure he knows all about my suspicions. My questions at Versailles regarding his silver hand

353

can have left him in no doubt about that. He's aware of what we know and what we suspect. Either he's guilty, and my words, which I hope will be blunt and to the point, can only lead to an extreme reaction, or he's innocent, in which case he must help us and allow us to establish that he has nothing to do with these murders.'

Nicolas left the Châtelet. He was breathing more easily now. Something that had been weighing on his mind since the death of Louis XV had vanished: a nagging sense of shame and grief which had led him to feel guilty of a sin he had not committed, hurt as he was to the depths of his being by a sense of betrayed loyalty and despised trust. The force that had driven his replies to Monsieur Lenoir derived from this legitimate resentment. It seemed that the Lieutenant General of Police had understood his suffering. The reaction to statements which he himself had known were excessive redeemed in his eyes a man who, until now, had been sparing in his respect. He hoped he was not wrong in his observation; what he wanted more than anything was to get back to the former situation of devotion and loyalty.

His steps led him to the banks of the river, and he decided to let his unconscious choices guide him. With a calm mind and a sharp eye, he contemplated the spectacle of his beloved city. On Quai de la Mégisserie, he thought of Naganda on seeing a group of crimps eyeing up some likely-looking young customers. Whores, gambling, alcohol and food would be the traps laid for them. The Micmac had almost been enlisted, and only the vigilance of the police had saved him. Where was he now, that distant friend? No doubt tirelessly pursuing the mission he had set himself:

continuing to serve the King of an ungrateful country. A little further on, an old woman was stoking an oven, enveloping passers-by in smoke. The smell that assailed his nostrils as he passed told him that, instead of using decent oil or lard to fry her doughnuts, she was using pork grease, which she probably stole from the drivers who used it on the wheels of their coaches. A stocky dark-haired, bow-legged workman was devouring one of these hot, sticky delicacies straight from the oven. Coming to the arcades of the Louvre, he had a look at the second-hand clothes market. A penniless crowd frequented this place, where old clothes suspended on string were buffeted in the wind like hanged and shrivelled bodies. The police sometimes dispersed the crowd, for it was quite common for the clothes of those who had died of consumption or pneumonia to be sold here instead of being burnt. The infected clothes passed from the bodies of the dead to those of the living, and the diseases were passed on with them.

Nicolas announced his name at the entrance to the Saint-Florentin mansion. On the grand staircase, he passed the Duchesse de La Vrillière, who responded to his greeting with a look of terror. She seemed to have been weeping and was now getting ready to go out. She was dressed in a large grey coat with a black lining, her head covered with a grey hood. He was still climbing the steps when he heard a murmur behind him. Turning, he saw that the duchesse had stopped, and was looking at him imploringly.

'Marquis . . .'

Another one! They all thought they could get round him by giving him his title, but hadn't he himself used it when dealing with Monsieur Lenoir?

'My cousin Madame de Maurepas holds you in high esteem,' the duchesse said. 'May I present you with a plea?'

'Madame, I am your servant.'

'Help the duc. He won't listen to me. In fact, he's never listened to me.'

'Madame, you can help him by helping me. I am convinced that you know more about this affair than you have been willing to tell me thus far.'

She was twisting one of the ribbons in her wig. 'I can't tell you anything. There was nothing else we could do . . .'

'What do you mean? Madame, I beseech you.'

'Save him, Monsieur.'

She turned abruptly and flew rather than walked to the front steps.

Here, thought Nicolas, was something that amply justified his decision to talk to the minister at all costs. The valet did not conceal his surprise when he appeared and began by refusing to inform his master, who had told him that he did not want to be disturbed. The commissioner firmly pushed the servant aside and went on. He reached the gallery, and then the study where this whole adventure had begun. He tapped at the door and, without waiting for a reply, entered resolutely. Monsieur de La Vrillière was sitting slumped in an armchair by the fireplace. He was in shirt and breeches, with his cravat untied, and wore over his shoulders a thick brightly coloured cloth, the ends of which he had pulled tight over his chest. He had taken off his wig, and his bald cranium gleamed in the firelight. It was a pitiful sight. He looked like a sick, crushed old man. Nicolas felt compassion for someone whose manner had always been more commanding.

'What is it?' said the duc. 'Why am I being disturbed, and who gave you permission?'

He had not recognised Nicolas.

The commissioner leaned towards him. 'This is urgent, Monseigneur. What I have to say to you cannot be postponed.'

'I'm tired.'

Nicolas dismissed the objection and gave a complete account of his investigation, omitting none of the details, not even those – and there were many of them – that incriminated the duc. He presented and commented on the various hypotheses, but the few questions he asked went unanswered. The only thing he omitted to mention, out of caution, was the practical measures he and his men had taken to discover the motivation behind this affair. He insisted on the fact that four people had paid with their lives for the sake of some obscure plot that everyone was striving to make even more obscure. In conclusion, he recalled the new King's desire to see light cast on the various aspects of this tragedy. Last but not least, he talked of the security of the State – this to a man who had long believed himself the embodiment of it – and underlined how disturbing it was that the secret representative of a foreign power should be involved in a criminal case in which so many illustrious names were implicated.

The minister seemed increasingly overwhelmed by all this, unable to stop his head collapsing on his chest. At last, though, he pulled himself together.

'Alas!' he sighed. 'I can't tell you anything, nor do I wish to. The late King loved you and put all his trust in you. If I were to tell anyone a secret, it would be you, having known and respected you for years. But you yourself, who have served me, how can you believe these vile slanderers and walk into the trap set by their bloodthirsty machinations? I don't claim to be a saint, but how could I have committed these terrible murders? There is nothing, I swear to you, to link me with these horrors. Will you believe me, Nicolas Le Floch, you whom the King considered the purest of his servants? Truly, truly . . .'

'Monseigneur, you only have to tell me one thing. Where were you at the times that these crimes were being committed? It's a simple question, and requires a simple answer from you.'

The minister looked straight at him, and Nicolas was surprised to see tears running down his face.

'I won't tell you, even if I have to pay the price for my silence a hundredfold! Monsieur de Chambonas . . . Nothing will oblige me to reveal what I wish to keep to myself.' He sighed again. 'It is the one and only part of myself which I hold dear, along with my loyalty to the late King . . . Please go now.'

Nicolas withdrew, lost in thought.


A sedan chair took him back to the Châtelet, where a long wait began. He once again brought his notes up to date, trying to omit none of the elements that had continued to pile up. There were so many of them that the sheer volume made it hard for him to see his way through. On the stroke of one, Old Marie silently and considerately let him share his lunch. This turned out to be an appetising stew of cow's udders, a dish of which the common people were fond due to its cheapness. This meal was washed down with a cheap wine, which, remarkably, was not too vinegary. Nicolas finally dozed off with his head between his arms on the table, the accumulated fatigue of an emotionally and physically draining week crashing down all at once on his shoulders.

At five o'clock, Bourdeau and Rabouine appeared and woke him from a strange dream. In it, an unknown man had been working an automaton, like those of Vaucanson, its right arm, equipped with a silver hand, cutting the throat of another doll whose face, he was horrified to discover, was the Queen's. He struggled and tried to intervene, but an unknown force held him still, as if paralysed.

'We have news,' announced Bourdeau, 'important news! And on all fronts!'

'It's about time,' said Nicolas, now completely awake. 'I was beginning to despair!'

'Well, you won't be disappointed. We've gleaned two pieces of information which, I believe, should give us something to keep us occupied for a while and help us make progress.'

'Don't keep me on tenterhooks. My wait and Old Marie's wine made me doze off, otherwise I would have been dying of impatience. I'm listening.'

'It's your head wound, it's healing up but it's also getting you heated. Right, listen to this. Rabouine here, who's quite a good-looking fellow beneath his gangling exterior, sometimes combines business with pleasure. Mademoiselle Josse, better known under her *nom de guerre* of La Roussillon, a vivacious brunette with a pretty face, has a soft spot for our spy. She's constantly teasing him and, if he consented, would make him her beau.'

Rabouine, whose face had turned red, lowered his head.

'In short,' continued Bourdeau, 'one thing leading to another, she tells him all her gossip. She's really a terrible gossip, and can never keep anything to herself. Anyway, she tells our man here that she's been feeling increasingly guilty about the kind of things that go on at parties organised by . . . can you guess who?'

'The Marquis de Chambonas?'

'No. A suitor whose description she gave to Rabouine. He can take over from here.'

'The description matches Anselme Vitry, but in the light of what you've discovered it's much more likely to be Eudes Duchamplan.'

'And why does this girl complain about such parties? They should be part of her usual activity.'

'She's a good girl, and she's had enough of the vile acts she's seen committed. In addition, one of her prostitute friends caught a terrible disease from these parties, the kind you don't catch in a convent or when you're celibate. She doesn't want to have anything more to do with that kind of debauchery. She was invited to another party this evening, and refused.'

'This is all well and good,' said Nicolas, 'but I need something more concrete if we're going to be able to do anything about it. Where, when, how?'

'I should say, Monsieur Nicolas,' said Rabouine, 'that her gossip isn't just idle chatter. She's let me in on a number of secrets in case anything unfortunate should happen to her. It was a kind of guarantee for her.'

'I understand. Carry on.'

'A cab is supposed to be coming to fetch her from the corner of Rue des Vieilles Tuileries and Passage du Manège at ten o'clock this evening. She doesn't know where the party will be held. The previous times, they took place in private houses or in underground quarries. She's also noticed that she wasn't necessarily invited on every occasion.'

'How is it that she has finally agreed this time?'

'I persuaded her.'

'In return for what?' asked Bourdeau.

'Our protection and support. She's been very sensible and has put together a little nest egg. As a native of Bordeaux, she wants to move back there and take up an honest profession.'

'Well,' said Nicolas pensively, 'that should be possible. Anything else that might be of use to us?'

'Yes! The guests at this party have to wear masks and show a card, the ace of hearts, half torn in the middle. Which means that one of our men could certainly get in.'

Nicolas took a piece of paper and started writing, speaking as he did so.

'Gather all our men together, including the spies. Inform the French Guards and the watch. We'll need men around the quarries near the Observatory and spies to track any unusual movement of carriages. I doubt that the surveillance will be easy. It's quite likely that these people don't use the official entrance, and I know that many private houses have special access via the cellars – that's our misfortune! Remember, Pierre, the cellar of the Lardin house in Rue des Blancs-Manteaux. Apart from that, we're going to need people at Montparnasse . . .'

'There's already permanent surveillance there,' said Bourdeau.

'We also need surveillance around the Saint-Florentin mansion. We really can't afford to lose sight of the minister if he goes out and abandons his carriage. I want to know the destination of these nocturnal adventures he stubbornly refuses to explain. Some spare carriages at the Châtelet, and a good mount for me. Not a nervous animal that stamps all the time, a quiet, good-natured horse. It's vital that I'm not noticed.'

'I hope you're not planning to go in person,' said Bourdeau anxiously.

'I certainly am.'

'That's madness! At least let me go with you.'

'Oh, no, my dear Pierre. You'll remain at the Châtelet and be the guiding light of the operation. Knowing you're here will be a comfort to me and a guarantee that everything will go according to plan.'

'So if I understand correctly, you want to follow La Roussillon and enter the location of the party in secret? You're too well known, you'll be recognised immediately. Think of the consequences . . .'

'That's not a convincing argument. I'll be wearing a mask, and I'll be armed. Someone find me an ace of hearts and a large black cape with a detachable collar. It'll all be show. I'll pretend to be a greybeard who's acting younger, with a blond wig, a cerused face and a lot of rouge.'

'All right. I still think you're being reckless, but I'll go now and start getting things ready. Where will you be stationed?'

'In Rue des Vieilles Tuileries, obviously, where La Roussillon has her rendezvous. Otherwise, we'd lose too much time, having someone come to inform me . . . So, a horse for me, and a second rider to follow me at a distance and take my mount when I reach the destination. A third rider in reserve ready to take messages or to lend a hand. He'll be the one who'll have the task of—'

'The second rider,' interrupted Bourdeau in a resolute tone, 'will be me, whether you like it or not.'

'Out of the question!'

'On the contrary, it's vital. Look at it logically. Think of the time it will take to inform me where you are, think of all the coming and going that would involve.'

Nicolas looked at the inspector. 'All right, I give in. It's true we'll need at least three-quarters of an hour to surround the scene of the operation. Well, as my father, who was at Fontenoy, used to say, it's up to us to support the King's house.'

He had continued writing while he was talking, crossing out a word from time to time, as if he were keeping the minutes of this conversation. He folded the paper without sealing it, handed it to Rabouine, and asked him to take it straight to the Lieutenant General of Police in Rue Neuve-Saint-Augustin.


The end of the day was spent preparing and going over the various scenarios which might occur. Monsieur Lenoir had hastened to reply to Nicolas, granting him a free hand and full powers to decide what to do depending on how the evening developed. The commissioner was pleased to see that the note concluded with an expression of concern that Nicolas should not lay himself too open to danger in this risky undertaking. By eight o'clock, all the arrangements were in place and Nicolas made an appearance, much to the astonishment of Bourdeau and Rabouine, as an old rake, stooped and made up like Richelieu, beneath a curly blood-red wig. He was brandishing a torn ace of hearts.

The next stage went as planned. He waited on his horse just inside a carriage entrance set somewhat back from the meeting place. The street was deserted and poorly lit, especially as street lighting was not allowed when the moon was full, and the moon tonight was veiled by clouds. Just before ten, a figure who could only be La Roussillon appeared. She might have been a soldier, pacing up and down as if on parade, her tall hat surmounted by a plume. She wore a mask, and her Polish-style dress emphasised the curve of her waist. A few minutes after ten, an ordinary cab appeared and came to a halt. La Roussillon approached it and negotiated for a few moments, then gathered her petticoats and hoisted herself inside. The vehicle set off at a jog trot. Nicolas waited for a moment and only gave his horse its head once the cab was almost at Rue du Cherche-Midi. Nicolas could hear, far behind him, Bourdeau and the third rider. What kind of apocalypse were they heading towards?

# XIII

## TRAPS

Be quiet! Can one say such things?
RIVAROL

The route took them along Rue du Four as far as Place Saint-André-des-Arts, then Rue de la Huchette and the Port aux Tuiles. The carriage crossed the Tournelles. Nicolas noted with a shudder that they had returned to one of the places that had already figured in the investigation. The cab slowed down and suddenly turned towards the river. It came to a halt not far from the bank. Nicolas saw La Roussillon extricate herself and walk towards the river, stepping hesitantly in the mud. The rising fog seemed to swallow her up. Where could she be going? There was a gap in the clouds for a moment, revealing a long barge, clearly a floating bathhouse. The establishment resembled two houses with an entrance in the middle, indicated by a lighted lantern. The girl vanished inside. Hidden behind a pile of wood, Nicolas struck a light and looked at his watch. It was after ten thirty. He heard Bourdeau, and soon saw him approaching on foot, his horse's bridle over his arm.

'Good, here's the place!' he whispered.

'Outside the walls, therefore outside police supervision . . .' said Nicolas.

'Let's apply our plan.'

'Go back to our courier, and tell him to head straight back to the Châtelet and give Rabouine the go-ahead. Action stations. In three-quarters of an hour, at exactly . . .' he again looked at his watch, – '. . . twenty past eleven, everything must be in place. Make sure the boats are silent once they get past Île Saint-Louis. There are still some moored at Quai d'Orléans. We must keep an eye open for trouble on the side facing the river. The trap needs to be closed completely. Now go, Pierre, then come back and join me here. I suspect the other guests will be arriving soon.'

Having checked that the coast was clear, Bourdeau withdrew. He soon returned and the anxious wait began, punctuated by the guests gradually arriving for the party. Nicolas could not conceal his impatience. He had stopped looking at his watch, fearing that striking a light might reveal their presence. Eventually, they saw Rabouine appear. The plan had been applied down to its smallest detail and some sixty men were now surrounding the barge. It was possible to go in but certainly not to come out. On the river, three boats were patrolling in the fog, and they would be able to approach the floating establishment if necessary. The moment had come for Nicolas to go in.

He adjusted his tricorn, feeling as he did so for the pocket pistol concealed in one of the wings of the hat. This gift from Inspector Bourdeau had got him out of more than one tight corner. He also checked that his sword was in place. He shook the inspector's hand, then Rabouine's, and walked with a firm step towards the landing stage. He crossed the gangway and was greeted at a kind of counter by a footman who, without saying a word, checked his torn ace of hearts. Still silent, the man pointed to his hat, cape and sword. He hesitated for a brief moment, but managed, as he took off his tricorn and unfastened his cape, to slip the pocket pistol into his coat. He was glad he had not chosen the Marquis de Ranreuil's sword, which was reserved for nobler expeditions. The entrance hall led to two symmetrical staircases which descended towards a much larger central room, from which he could hear the sounds of a party drifting up. He walked down and discovered a crowd of masked people, all drinking. The wooden walls of the room were hidden behind hangings of pink taffeta set off with silver braid. Candles gave a bright sheen to the guests' make-up. Nicolas was attracted to a little scene being played out in a corner, and went closer with some difficulty because of all the people already gathered around.

Two young people, a girl and a boy, were uttering a string of obscenities. Each phrase was echoed by double entendres and vulgar jokes from the audience, accompanied by gestures that revealed a deep corruption. Gradually, the atmosphere of the place was changing. Eyes gleamed behind the masks, words and gestures became more provocative. Couples were forming, and sometimes groups, who headed towards the bathing cabins. Nicolas thought he ought to do something to allay suspicion. He had spotted La Roussillon, recognising her from her plume and her arched back. She seemed nervous, could not stay in one place, and rejected all advances. With some difficulty, he went up to her and whispered in her ear that he had been sent by Rabouine and had to talk to her. To get away from prying eyes and ears, he proposed they take refuge in one of the cabins. That way, everyone would think they had got down to business. She immediately drew him into the central gangway, on either side of which were the cabins. After trying several doors and provoking cries of protest, which indicated to Nicolas that the rooms were not provided with locks, they managed to find a free one. In it was a copper bathtub, a bench, a pedestal table on which a bottle waited in a cooling pitcher, a toilet bowl and a chaise longue. He also noticed a curious contraption he had once seen in an actress's house. It was a kind of tin basin mounted on a wooden base, with a leather border, a sponge and two glasses of water. He remembered that it was known as a bidet – Semacgus, with his love of the risqué, had once called it an ornamental pond for the thighs.

No sooner had they entered than a valet dressed in blue twill, whose expression was anything but servile, brought them towels, bergamot-scented soap and two pairs of slippers. He came in and went out several times, pouring pitchers of hot water into the tub. This task over, he asked Nicolas, with a winning air, if the young lady and he wished to take advantage of his services. He did not conceal his disappointment at being dismissed with the usual tip.

'That's one of the stallions who cater for the vices of some and the impotence and exhaustion of the others,' explained La Roussillon.

'Rest assured, Mademoiselle,' said Nicolas, 'that we shall not forget your help. If we were to do so, Rabouine would certainly hasten to remind us. I'm not going to stay in this cabin. My aim, as I'm sure you realise, is to prevent the person who organises these parties from doing any more harm. He's holding a young girl whose sister has been murdered. We must find him. You're a good girl and I'm sure you're going to help me. Where do you think he is?'

'I'll do as you ask, Monsieur. But you must agree to protect me, as I'm running a great risk doing this. As you've observed, we're in the corridor on the left-hand side. On the right the bathrooms are reserved for the organiser's associates. I have every reason to believe that it's there they do mysterious things that are forbidden to anyone who hasn't been specifically invited.'

Nicolas closed his eyes, trying to come up with a feasible plan. 'We're going to pretend we're doing what they expect us to be doing . . .'

'With you, Monsieur,' she said, giving a little curtsey, 'it would have been a pleasure.'

He laughed. 'I like Rabouine too much to do that to him! We'll block the door with the bench in case they come to check the veracity of our lovemaking, then I'm going to go out of the window and try to get to the other side of the boat. How many rooms on each side?'

'Five or six. Not all of them have baths. Some of them are steam rooms.'

'I assume there's a handrail all round the deck?'

'It's very narrow, and the whole thing moves. The river's high because of the autumn rains.'

'All right. While I'm trying to get to the other end, make all the noises you need to, to convince anyone spying on us that we really are making love.'

She smiled; the prospect seemed to amuse her. He opened the window, and a damp draught blew in, making the candle flames flicker. The wooden frame was wet, and he almost slipped and fell. No sooner had La Roussillon closed the window than he heard muffled sounds of water and moans. He was sure she was someone who always tried to amuse her customers. He tried not to think about the black waves beating on the hull of the barge not far below him, and felt reassured at the thought of the boats moving around, ready, if necessary, to come to his rescue. He reached the middle of the barge. An unpleasant surprise was waiting for him there: an iron gate with spikes barred the way. Strips of cast iron, sharpened at the ends, protected the gate on both sides. Nicolas made such an effort trying to push it that he was suddenly bathed in sweat despite the cold of the night. Going back was tantamount to giving up the whole operation. Calling one of the boats floating invisibly on the river risked attracting the attention of those on the barge. In the course of his career, similar situations had often presented themselves, and he had always found a way out of the difficulty. His fertile mind was toying with various solutions, each more fanciful than the other when, having approached the gate, his coat got caught on one of the strips of iron. It was not easy to get free, but the incident made him think, and a light went on in his mind. He would take off his coat and use it as a kind of rope to get over the gate, avoiding all danger of contact with the strips and spikes. He immediately set about applying his idea. He took off his coat after emptying the contents of the pockets into a kind of broad gusset sewn into the inside of his breeches, which usually provided a safe hiding place for documents or rolls of *louis*. He managed to get everything into it, including his pocket pistol. For a moment, the thought crossed his mind that he could have used his unrolled cravat, but he feared that the fine muslin would not withstand either his weight or the sharpness of the metal.

He hooked the collar of his coat onto the top of the gate, raised himself up on tiptoe, as far as he could go, hoping that the stitching – the work of Master Vachon's apprentices – would stand the strain. He gave a sharp tug, and nothing tore. He now had to judge his jump. Any error would be fatal: he would fall back with all his weight and would inevitably impale himself on the cast iron. Stepping back, he retreated to the handrail, stretched the line of fabric, pressed hard with his right foot on the side of the boat and jumped. It all happened very quickly: a leap, a rustling sound, and a violent landing on the other side. He hit the side of the barge head first. The impact left him stunned. He staggered back, his feet sliding on the damp wood. He slipped and fell, but grabbed the handrail with both hands and finally managed to steady himself. He sat down with his legs dangling, out of breath. He felt a hot liquid spreading over his stomach. The dim lights on the barge did not provide enough illumination, but the pain that went through his body took his breath away and made him realise that he was injured. He put his hand on his stomach then raised it to his mouth: blood. One of the strips of metal had sliced through his shirt and cut him on the abdomen. It was a painful but superficial wound. He was glad he had kept his cravat. He wrapped it tightly around his stomach, using it as a bandage to stem the flow of blood. He waited for his breathing to settle and his heart to slow to its usual rhythm.

Now he had to get down to the serious work. Was the mysterious organiser of these parties behind one of these windows? He shuddered, thinking that he could just as easily be in a bathrooom situated on the shore side, facing the Port au Bois. Nevertheless, it seemed to him that, out of caution, the man was likely to have chosen the side facing the river, which was more hidden. He walked forward. His stomach hurt. The first room, a steam room, was empty. In the second, two couples in indecent positions were paying homage to Venus. With horror, Nicolas recognised one of the participants as one of the great names of France. The third was some kind of storeroom. Approaching the fourth, he heard muffled cries. He looked in through the window and saw a heavily made-up woman take a blackish substance from a little box and dissolve it in a glass of water. He was about to proceed to the fifth window when more distinct moans reached his ears. He could not see the part of the fourth room from which they seemed to come. He hesitated. Was this another of those scenes of which he had already had a taste, or was it . . . The woman was brandishing a riding crop and striking someone. The other person screamed now, and the scream was like a child's. There was an unusual amount of venom in the woman's actions. To set his mind at rest, Nicolas went and looked in the last room; it was empty. He retraced his steps. The woman was still half bent over her victim, viciously beating her. It was then that he noticed it: beneath the frills and flounces of the dress was a pair of men's riding boots. So the woman was a man, which threw a new light on things. He still had to decide what to do. Go back? He'd have to get over the gate again, which was risky. Hail the police boats? Although the men on the shore would stop the guests escaping, it would put paid to any idea of catching any of these people *in flagrante*. The culprits could well get lost in the panic following a police raid. Everything depended on him, as usual. It was he, the King's commissioner, who had to act appropriately. But how?

Could he force open the window and jump into the room? It might be possible to take a leap from the top of the handrail. He tried the window with his hand, in the unlikely event that it was not locked. It was. Manifesting his presence by knocking on the window might force the man to open up, but in doing so he would lose the advantage of surprise. The idea crossed his mind that he could shoot the unknown man through the window, but he rejected it immediately; he was too honourable to fire at a suspect without a specific reason. Nevertheless he had to rescue the young girl, who might well be one of the two fugitives from Brussels.

A variation of the previous option occurred to him. He would fire his pistol at the window handle to get inside the room. He would place himself to the left of the window for a better aim and to avoid hitting anyone in the room, then climb inside, his smoking pistol in his hand. He looked in one last time, and the sight of the tortures the victim was suffering convinced him to act without further delay.

He fired. The fragile frame shattered. He threw himself inside, fell on his shoulder and rolled on the ground, losing his pistol as he did so. Everything happened in a flash. He saw the girl tied to the bed, lying on her stomach, with bleeding stripes across her back. The creature had immediately turned and leapt for his sword, and was now walking towards Nicolas, who was still on the ground. He rolled on his side, still stunned by his fall, and grabbed a stool as a weapon. He made an initial parry. The sword thrusts came thick and fast, ever closer to his chest. But then the sword became stuck in the soft wood of the stool. Nicolas pressed so hard with the stool that the weapon first bent, then broke with a snap. The creature threw the broken sword at him, then came towards him with his hands out. He grabbed him by the neck and tried to strangle him. They struggled for a while, with neither man yielding, until, having gone round and round the restricted space of the cabin, they found themselves by the shattered window. The broken pane rattled each time their feet hit the floor. The man redoubled his efforts to strangle him. Nicolas felt his strength waning and his stomach wound opening and bleeding profusely. He tried to thrust his attacker off him. What was left of the window frame shattered and collapsed. Tightly bound together, the two men fell into the river.

Entering the black icy water was a ghastly moment for Nicolas, who hated darkness. He felt as though he were sinking into a tomb. The vice was tightening round his neck. He was swallowing the muddy water. He could not breathe. Red and yellow flames danced in front of his eyes. He felt himself yielding, and lost consciousness.

'He's moving! He's moving!'

A familiar voice was grunting somewhere in the distance. 'To lose consciousness twice in a few days! These Bretons do just what they like! I told him to be careful, but he didn't listen to me. He's always so foolhardy . . .'

'A man of strong character does not worry about threats,' said another voice, in measured tones. 'I was worried too, knowing his reputation.'

Nicolas could feel the heat of a blazing furnace somewhere nearby. There was whispering round him, but he could not understand a word that was being said.

'It's all thanks to my cordial! He's already had some.'

Suddenly, he opened his eyes and yelled, 'My notebook! Give me my little black notebook!'

'Well, now,' said the first voice, 'he hasn't lost his common sense. The first thing he thinks of is the one thing he needs.'

A familiar face bent over him: the friendly face of Bourdeau. 'Bless the inside pocket of your breeches,' he said. 'It didn't let the water in. The notebook is intact. Your sword and even your pistol have been recovered.'

Another face entered his field of vision.

'Monsieur, I am very pleased to see you out of danger. What would we do without you?'

He recognised Monsieur Lenoir, and was moved by his concern. 'Monseigneur, I'm—'

'Don't speak! You must stay calm and rest.'

'But I'm curious to know what happened after I thought I was drowning, strangled by that creature.'

'The inspector will tell you everything.'

'You fell in the river while struggling with your attacker,' said Bourdeau. 'The noise of your fall alerted one of our boats and you were both fished out with hooks. You lost consciousness. You were brought back to the Châtelet, undressed, dried, warmed up, and Old Marie did the rest.'

Nicolas made a gesture. 'What about . . . the other man?'

'Don't worry, he's under guard, chained up in his cell.'

'Well guarded?'

He remembered the livid face of an old soldier found hanged in his cell. Thanks to a lack of precautions . . .

'Very well guarded. I know what you're thinking about . . . Alarmed by the turn events had taken, I immediately launched our offensive. Our men surrounded the establishment, and the sister of a previous victim was found and taken to the Hôtel-Dieu to be tended and comforted. The poor girl had suffered incredible tortures. Unfortunately some of the guests—'

'Who shall remain nameless,' Monsieur Lenoir cut in.

'Some guests were able to withdraw without being bothered,' continued Bourdeau in an acrimonious tone. 'Including Lord Ashbury, who was also caught in the net.'

'He, too!'

'We couldn't keep him,' said Lenoir. 'An hour, no longer than that . . . The English ambassador appeared in Rue Neuve-Saint-Augustin as if by magic and ordered me to hand the fellow over, as a plenipotentiary enjoying the King's immunity. Ashbury gave us a look of total contempt and arrogance and said that although Commissioner Le Floch's life had been spared in England, he was still an enemy of the English King and needed to constantly beware.'

Nicolas sat up in a rage. He realised that he was in the Lieutenant General's study, lying wrapped in a blanket on the large Savonnerie rug by the hearth, in which a fire blazed.

'On the other hand,' continued Lenoir, 'trailing the Duc de La Vrillière has brought results. We now know where he goes at night. To a little apartment on the second floor of a house in Rue des Tournelles . . .'

'What? Rue des Tournelles!'

'Yes, opposite the monastery of the Minimes, almost on the corner of Rue Neuve-Saint-Gilles.'

'Quai des Tournelles, Rue des Tournelles. Why does that name keep cropping up? Do you remember that piece of paper we found in the younger Duchamplan's apartment? Could it be he knew the minister's secret? Which would mean Ashbury also knew it!'

'The house is being watched,' said Bourdeau. 'We'll let him come out without showing ourselves, and only then will we investigate the nature of these nocturnal visits.'

'I'm going there right now.'

'You're hardly in a fit state.'

Lenoir intervened, somewhat briskly. 'I do in fact think that it's the commissioner's place, and that, if his condition allows him, it would be preferable and more appropriate . . .'

Nicolas looked at Bourdeau's stubborn face. 'You can come with me, Pierre.'

Bourdeau relaxed. Nicolas understood his chief's concern. What would he discover in that apartment? The fewer witnesses there were, the better it would be for the honour of the King's councils. Not that the Lieutenant General mistrusted Bourdeau, but he knew that Nicolas was more accustomed to these State secrets, which he was always able to bury deep in his consciousness.

*Tuesday 11 October 1774*

He thanked Old Marie for his care, went back to the duty office to change, and then he and Bourdeau rushed to their carriage.

'How has Eudes Duchamplan been behaving himself?' asked Nicolas. 'I'm sure it was him on the barge. I hope he didn't have the effrontery to deny his identity?'

'He was very indignant, though he didn't conceal his name. I noted, once he had taken off his make-up, that he was bleeding, and we saw that he had a wound on the left side of his face. I found that interesting.'

'What do you deduce from that?'

'That it was a scar from a recently closed wound that had just been reopened, perhaps deliberately. I thought of your account of the attack on you at Versailles, when Semacgus's coachman struck the would-be assassin with his whip. That was on the left cheek, wasn't it?'

'Everything in fact tallies with what you're telling me. So it was he who shot at me . . . How did he take it?'

'I was careful not to let him know. Curiously, he claimed, of his own accord, that the wound was the result of his fight with you. He said he'd had no idea why you burst in like that, threatening him, and he'd taken fright.'

'What about the girl? Had he been whispering sweet nothings in her ear?'

'He claimed she was only there for the usual amusements common in that kind of party, and that he'd never met her before!'

'In other words, he's a gentle soul, who denies everything. He must be confident someone's going to come to his rescue.'

'As if those who ran off into the darkness with their hands over their faces, looking for their carriages, are going to intercede on his behalf! He has a curiously naive idea of the compassion of men in high places!'

'As soon as possible,' resumed Nicolas, 'we'll have to set up a hearing before Lenoir and the Criminal Lieutenant. There always comes a moment when Monsieur Testard du Lys needs to be, let's say, "accommodated". And I'll wager the Lieutenant General of Police won't spoil the party. I have an idea of how we can stage it for maximum effect. I'll have to talk to you about it.'

'This expedition worries me on account of your health . . .'

'I'm perfectly fine, don't worry. My head's a little empty, my stomach's like cardboard, but my curiosity's aroused! Old Marie's cordial would waken a dead man!'

'Rue des Tournelles begins at the Bastille, doesn't it?' said Bourdeau.

'Of course! And stretches almost as far as Place Royale, being joined to it by Rue du Pas-de-la-Merle.'

'Your knowledge of the city amazes me! The Bastille and Place Royale! Amusing, even significant. The two Tournelles are connected.'

'That remark is typical of you!'

'I wanted to thank you,' said Bourdeau. 'I wasn't fooled earlier. I know Monsieur Lenoir was trying to keep me away.'

'Quiet, now. There are times when it's best not to know too much.'

Bourdeau smiled and said nothing. Both men felt moved; this exchange had spoken volumes. They continued crossing the nocturnal city. They passed a few late walkers, a few whores standing beside bollards, some dubious-looking men who jumped into the shadows as the carriage passed, watch patrols and a priest carrying the holy sacraments to a dying man. They soon reached Rue des Tournelles.

'The duc,' said Bourdeau, 'abandoned his coach in Place Royale. After that, he looked around cautiously before hurrying to his destination.'

'Did he notice anything?'

'Nothing at all! We wouldn't be here otherwise. Our men stayed with him in relays of three, always one behind the minister, another preceding him, and the last one as relief. He couldn't have escaped.'

They positioned themselves in Rue Saint-Gilles, standing a little way back, but with a good view of a tall narrow house in Rue des Tournelles. On the second floor, a weak light could be seen in one window. Shadows were moving behind a curtain.

'He's still there,' whispered Bourdeau. 'And our spies too, I can see them.'

'You have good eyes!'

'They're the colour of walls,' said the inspector with a laugh.

Nicolas looked at his watch. It was nearly two. Bourdeau squeezed his arm. 'We've arrived just in time.'

A man wrapped in a black cloak, his tricorn pulled down over his eyes, was leaving the house. He hesitated a moment, peering right and left into the darkness, then took up a position under the lantern at the corner of the two streets. He glanced suspiciously at the stationary cab. The stillness of the driver, who was pretending to sleep, seemed to reassure him that the coast was clear. With hurried steps, he turned into Rue des Tournelles.

'There is no doubt he's going back to Place Royale,' said Bourdeau. 'His carriage must be coming to pick him up.'

'I assume we're going to make sure he returns to the fold?'

'That's the plan. For the moment, I don't think you have any other choice than to go in. In the meantime, I'll watch out for trouble outside the house. Let's not forget the English threats.'

The commissioner appreciated his deputy's sensitivity. It showed that, having implicitly understood Lenoir's anxiety, Bourdeau was determined to act accordingly and in such a way that his friend should not be constantly aware of it or, if he was aware of it, did not need to talk about it. More than anything, this kind of understanding revealed their complicity, a complicity which had been strengthened over the years by all the many trials they had been through together and had never once faltered.

Once he had entered the house, Nicolas had to strike a light to find his way. On the second floor, he knocked at the one door lacking a knocker. An anxious voice immediately asked, 'Is that you, Charles?'

'I am a commissioner of police.'

The door slowly opened. Lit by the candle she was carrying, a young blonde woman stood there, looking him up and down in alarm. She was bare-headed, and wore a lilac chenille undershirt.

'Oh, my God, something must have happened to Charles. I'm always telling him not to go out at night. Is that it, Monsieur? Don't try to hide it from me.'

He entered, and looked around at the apartment. It was small, but furnished in exquisite taste and far more luxurious than might have been expected from the exterior.

'Calm down, Madame. It's nothing serious, I assure you. I simply need some information about the man who has just left this building.'

'Why, what has he done? Why are you concerned with him?'

She could not have been much more than twenty, he estimated.

'His movements at such a late hour have attracted our attention.'

'The poor man! Such a good friend, so generous!'

'What does he do and what's his name?'

'Charles Gobelet. He's a bailiff at the Châtelet.'

Nicolas could not help smiling at the profession chosen by the Duc de La Vrillière. 'And may I ask what he is to you, Madame?'

She blushed, lowered her head, and murmured in a confidential tone, 'He's my friend and the father of my child.'

Taking him by the sleeve, she drew him into a small white room in the centre of which was a wicker cradle covered in muslin. She pulled aside the fabric and he saw a pretty infant, fast asleep. Without a sound, they went back to the other room.

'How did you meet him?'

'My name is Marie Meunier. I was born in Meaux. A year ago, I lost my mother, who had long been a widow. Having nothing to live on, I came to Paris to ask for charity. Someone must have noticed me, for, soon after my arrival, a very polite man brought me here, and then Charles arrived. He said he wanted to help me. I believed him. Thanks to him, I have found a home and sustenance.'

'And what of the child?'

She blushed again. 'Charles convinced me of the sincerity of his affection. I owed him everything. That's our child, and its father showers us with such care and love you yourself would be moved by it.'

'Madame, I am satisfied with these explanations. There will be no need to bother Monsieur Gobelet. Please don't mention my visit to him.'

'I shall do as you say, Monsieur. Charles's peace of mind matters to me more than anything. He seems so worried sometimes.'

'One last question. Why does he keep your house and his visits so secret?'

'Alas, Commissioner, it's because he has children from a first marriage! They wouldn't be very happy to find out—'

'I understand. Thank you for that explanation.'

She walked him to the door. 'Protect him, Monsieur. He takes so many precautions that sometimes I imagine he must feel threatened.'

He remembered the Duchesse de La Vrillière's last plea. All of the duc's women wanted to protect him.

'We'll be sure to,' he said.


Nicolas rejoined Bourdeau, who was waiting for him downstairs. They walked back to their carriage. After a long silence, which the inspector respected, he recounted his visit, but as if talking to himself.

'So that was it!' he said in conclusion. 'The pure side of an impure man.'

'Heavens!' said Bourdeau. 'Please stop "Noblecourting", and put it in plain words.'

'The minister has a secret family: a charming young lady, and a child about a year old. It's clearly a side of his existence he wants to preserve at all costs. Hence these nocturnal escapes and this desire to keep his double life a complete secret.'

'What a man!' exclaimed Bourdeau. 'Who would believe it to look at him? The Beautiful Aglaé, countless other women, responsibilities of State, and what else?'

'As for me,' replied Nicolas gravely, 'I have no idea where the truth of the man lies. In his licentiousness or in this garden of innocence preserved as it was before the Fall?'

'Anyone listening to you would think that the more like a devil a man is, the more he aspires to get back to the Garden of Eden.'

Nicolas laughed and grimaced at the same time. 'Don't make me laugh, it pulls on my wound. I'll only be able to smile for the next few days, although the circumstances hardly lend themselves to much smiling. I'm going to get a few hours' rest and then we'll meet again at dawn, at the Châtelet.'

'What are your instructions?'

'Send some men to Rue Christine to collect the contents of the younger Duchamplan's wardrobe and bring them to me. We'll also have to get the body of the unfortunate Vitry identified, or at least what's left of him. It won't be easy, but I don't have much doubt it's him. I'll go and see Lenoir and Testard du Lys. Not forgetting Sartine, if he's in Paris. I'll put together my case, and the day after tomorrow we'll summon the suspect.'

'Who for now is only charged with acts of debauchery on a minor.'

'Not forgetting kidnapping, which, if all goes well, will earn him the whip, the brand, the iron collar and life imprisonment in a house of detention.'

'That's true, although I fear we can expect a lot of argument and a lot of outside interference from those trying to thwart our procedure.'

'That's why I think it's vital that we expedite things as quickly as possible. Like you, I expect the worst.'

'What about Chambonas?'

'I fear he's untouchable. The Lieutenant General has had proof of his secret activities for a long time now. To implicate him would be the equivalent of untangling a thread that would lead us too close to the throne.'

'Will the time ever come when the law applies to everyone?'

'When the Bourdeaus are in power,' said Nicolas affectionately.

Nicolas gave his last instructions concerning the interrogation of the younger Duchamplan and, if need be, other protagonists in the case, as well as some special instructions which he had now had time to think about. He was a little angry with himself at not opening up more to Bourdeau, but he did not like to reveal a plan of campaign which depended to a large extent on his intuition – even though there was a degree of material evidence to corroborate it. It was a kind of superstition in him to keep quiet about his intentions. A detective was like an artist: he did not like to reveal too much all at once.

In Rue Montmartre, the whole household was asleep; only Mouchette was waiting for her master. She gave some questioning little cries and disapprovingly sniffed the smell of muddy water that he gave off. He decided to remedy this, unable to imagine slipping into his bed in such a filthy state. Hot water was cooling in the kettle on the stove. He undressed, and as he did so, weariness overcame him, and all his pains revived. Catherine, wakened by the noise, found him as naked as the day he was born, trying unsuccessfully to wash himself. She gave a cry when she saw the bloodstained bandage around the middle of his body. She took matters in hand. He was washed, soaped, combed, and rubbed down, and his bandage gently but firmly changed. After sipping a schnapps eggnog flavoured with cinnamon, he went upstairs, exhausted but already feeling his old self, and slipped into his bed for a few hours' rest.

The day was a long one. Nicolas, although feeling as tired as he had after his hurried return from England a few months earlier, nevertheless gave his utmost. He went to see Monsieur Lenoir, who approved his plan. Next, he had to confront the long pale face of the Criminal Lieutenant. Overtaken by events as usual,

Monsieur Testard du Lys at first balked at the commissioner's plans, denouncing practices which were alien to him. Nicolas had to remind him that he had never had reason in the past to complain about initiatives which might not have conformed to the routine way of doing things but which had always led to the confounding of the guilty and to the King's having an even higher opinion of a justice system of which the Criminal Lieutenant was the most eminent representative. Of course, Monsieur Testard du Lys did not have the wit to realise that these solved cases did not bring anyone any reflected glory, since they were all special investigations, mostly relating to the private justice of the monarch. Defeated, he washed his hands like a new Pilate and irritably dismissed Nicolas. As a final argument, the name of Sartine had been bandied about; he still filled the Criminal Lieutenant with fear.

The contents of the wardrobe in Rue Christine were carefully recorded and examined item by item. Nicolas also received Sanson. He next went to the Hôtel-Dieu, where he questioned the girl discovered in the bathing establishment. She confirmed everything they had assumed. She and her sister, starving, lost in Paris, had been picked up by Duchamplan who, under false pretences, had taken them to an unknown house, and then delivered them, in a number of different places, to the lust of his accomplices.

Nicolas then had himself driven to Quai des Tournelles, where the spies who were protecting him from a distance, on Bourdeau's orders, saw him indulging in some strange exercises, with his nose to the ground. A final meeting at the Châtelet reunited him with the inspector. It was followed by an inspection of the hall of the Basse-Geôle, which had been laid out for the following day's secret hearing. Finally, he signed a safe conduct for La Roussillon, whose help and cool head had been vital to the success of the operation.

Again, he went to bed quite late. Catherine had waited up for him, concocting one of her special dishes for him. It consisted of steaming cabbage cut into slices and those roots she stubbornly cultivated in the kitchen garden behind the house, much to the despair of Poitevin: those potatoes which people were starting to talk about at Court and in the city. She would roughly crush the two vegetables, making sure that the flesh of the cabbage remained somewhat crunchy. She would then throw the mixture into a cast-iron dish in which some diced smoked bacon had been cooked in salt, pepper, nutmeg, garlic and juniper berries. You had to make sure to keep turning it all over with a spoon, so that everything benefited from the heat, until it had turned a nice golden colour. This dish revealed to him how sweet the new root could be when treated in this way, set off as it was by the crunchiness of the cabbage and the softness of the bacon, the whole thing covered in a grated cheese crust during the baking. This robust snack, washed down with a bottle of Burgundy from Irancy, which Noblecourt always called the great King's wine, led him to a peaceful, restorative sleep.

# EPILOGUE

So you will perhaps have powerful objections to make to the principles I have just established. Convey them to me and I will receive them gratefully, because I am looking for the truth in very good faith.

LAMOIGNON DE MALESHERBES

*Wednesday 12 October 1774*

Everything had been meticulously prepared. In a hall close to the Basse-Geôle, a kind of courtroom had been installed: a long table and two armchairs with flaps, one for Nicolas and one for Bourdeau, who would keep a record of the hearing. The various items of evidence lay on the lid of a chest in the centre of the room, in front of the defendant's seat. Opposite the long table, two trestles supported a half-open coffin, revealing the bloodless, livid face of the corpse found on Île des Cygnes. Two candlesticks framed it. Always thoughtful, Old Marie had seen fit to install a kind of brazier on which incense burnt. Torches fixed into rings on the wall threw their dancing light over the scene.

The Lieutenant General of Police and the Criminal Lieutenant entered in magistrates' gowns and sat down, after throwing alarmed glances at the coffin. Nicolas walked towards them and began to speak.

'Gentlemen, we are gathered here today in a hall of the Grand

Châtelet, in an extraordinary and secret commission, to try to bring to an end a case which has cost the lives of four people. I shall attempt to untie the threads of a mystery which inextricably combines the passions of human perversity and the deleterious actions of agents of a foreign power . . .'

'Allow me to express surprise,' exclaimed Monsieur Testard du Lys, 'at the unfortunate revival of such an outrageous procedure of common law! I had dared to hope that under a new reign, which has already led to certain changes, we might have avoided recourse to such regrettable arrangements.'

'It is by order of the King, on my instructions and with my support,' said Lenoir, 'that Commissioner Le Floch has been forced, given the circumstances, to adopt such unconventional measures.'

'But did he have to subject us to such an unfortunate confrontation?' muttered the Criminal Lieutenant, lifting a fine cambric handkerchief to his nostrils.

Nicolas pretended to ignore this exchange. 'Allow me, gentlemen,' he went on, 'to remind you of the circumstances under which I was assigned this investigation. The Duc de La Vrillière, Minister of the King's Household, summoned me, through the intermediary of Monsieur Lenoir, to his mansion near Place Louis XV, to inform me that Marguerite Pindron, the duchesse's chambermaid, had been discovered early that morning in the kitchens with her throat cut. Near her body, the major-domo, Jean Missery, had been found unconscious and wounded. My first observations turned up a number of clues. There was no weapon matching the victim's terrible wound. The major-domo's wound was of quite another nature. Everything led one to suppose that, after having murdered his young mistress, and struck with the horror of his action, he had tried to take his own life. The kitchen knife found near him appeared derisory in comparison with the victim's horrible wound. The cellar floor had been much trodden over. A trail of bloody footprints led me to the second floor and onto a balcony overlooking the gate of the mansion. Clearly someone had escaped by that route. In the kitchen, I found some silver thread and observed that Marguerite Pindron's slippers resembled, in their luxury, those worn at balls. The first testimonies revealed panic and a certain amount of confusion as to how exactly things had happened. Some said it was pitch dark when the bodies were discovered, others that the day had already risen. One thing that surprised me was that everyone was keen to tell me how bad their relations with the major-domo were. Some admitted that they had not been indifferent to Marguerite Pindron.'

'But this major-domo wasn't dead, was he?' the Criminal Lieutenant cut in. 'Did you question him?'

'He couldn't remember anything, only that he had fallen asleep. In addition, his wound was a light one, hardly a scratch, which didn't exactly explain the amount of blood there was around him.'

'How do you know,' said Lenoir, 'that this blood did not come from the body of the young woman?'

'The two pools of blood were quite distinct in nature. For the rest, I found, as is common in a great house, the usual conflicts among the domestic staff.'

'But surely this was a simple affair,' said Testard du Lys. 'You had a culprit, in the person of the major-domo. The nature of his wound was of little importance. Why go searching all over the city?'

'Alas, Monseigneur, the reality is much more complex, and a number of discoveries led me to rule out such a simple solution. Inspector Bourdeau was invited by Jacques Blain, the caretaker of the mansion, to try some rabbit stew.'

The Criminal Lieutenant sat up in his chair, very red in the face. 'Here again is one of these whims so frequent in Monsieur Le Floch's repertoire. What are you trying to prove now?'

'I'm simply trying to point out, Monseigneur, that you can't make a good stew without mixing some of the animal's blood in with the sauce, along with a trickle of vinegar.'

'What of it? I don't follow you at all.'

'What of it? That sauce didn't have any blood. Is it normal for someone to go and get three rabbits from their hutch in the middle of the night, kill them and cook them? This caretaker fellow seems not only to suffer from insomnia, but also to have a formidable appetite!'

'And what do you conclude from that?' asked Lenoir.

'Let me tell you a story. Poor Marguerite Pindron, about whom I made enquiries in Faubourg Saint-Antoine, left her family after breaking off her engagement with young Vitry, a gardener, and wandered the streets of Paris for a long time. I don't know how, but somehow she ended up as a chambermaid to the Duchesse de La Vrillière. Who introduced her into that noble house? Thanks to my investigation, I can state that it was Eudes Duchamplan, the brother-in-law of the major-domo, Jean Missery. The latter, a widower, believes it's his right to press his attentions on the female staff of the house. He falls madly in love with Marguerite. Why would he have wanted to kill her? Did he suspect the relationship between Marguerite and Eudes? Was he angered by the other male servants' interest in her? I don't believe any of that. Marguerite Pindron was killed by someone from outside the house. The autopsy performed on the victim allowed us to determine the nature of the murder weapon. A cast was made from the wound. Its shape was that of a hand, and was an attempt to implicate the Duc de La Vrillière who, after a hunting accident, was given an artificial silver hand by the late King.'

'Another tall tale!'

Nicolas ignored this interruption from the Criminal Lieutenant. 'The fact is,' he continued, 'Marguerite Pindron had to die. Many reasons can be adduced. She may have witnessed something she should not have seen and been blackmailing the person or persons involved, or she may have constituted a financial threat to the Duchamplan family if Jean Missery had taken her as his second wife. Eudes Duchamplan has, I believe, access to the Saint-Florentin mansion. He also has in his possession the Duc de La Vrillière's silver hand, no doubt stolen. That Sunday, he gets into the house. He's made an appointment with Marguerite, who is to be in the kitchens to meet her older suitor.'

'How do you know that?' asked the Criminal Lieutenant.

'The testimony of Jeanne Le Bas, known as Jeannette, another chambermaid, who saw the note in question, anonymous and written in large letters. Marguerite was sure it came from Jean Missery. She therefore makes her way to the kitchens. There, her throat is cut.'

'But if the intention was to implicate the Duc de La Vrillière,' objected Lenoir, 'why wasn't the murder weapon left at the scene?'

'It couldn't be left at the scene. If the duc is guilty, can one imagine him incriminating himself by leaving his silver hand in such a conspicuous position? What is done is much more subtle. If the murder weapon disappears, it is because it has to reappear. However, other clues have to be left which implicate the master of the house. So it is that I find a silver thread which can reasonably be supposed to have come from the minister's coat, being in conformity with the end of the period of mourning. But something else will complicate this fiendish plan: the actions of a jealous woman.'

'We seem to be in a novel by Crébillon!'

'The truth is always stranger than fiction, Monseigneur,' said Nicolas with a smile. 'Eugénie Gouet, the head chambermaid, used to be the major-domo's mistress, and seems to have nurtured the hope that she would one day marry him. The awareness that she is getting older and has been abandoned sharpens the resentment she feels towards her younger rival. The conversation between Marguerite and Jeannette about that evening's rendezvous is overheard by this angry woman. It gives her the means to take her revenge. Oh, we're not talking about a crime, but about a very wicked act. She takes the duchesse's sleeping draught – she will claim later that the bottle was broken – and drugs her former lover with it.'

'But how?' asked Lenoir. 'That's not so easy to do. There needs to be a pretext.'

'Which she finds, Monseigneur. Eugénie Gouet knows all about Missery. She knows that, although his desire is insatiable, he's sometimes unable to perform. Having pretended to remain his friend, she advises him on this matter and persuades him to take this potion in place of the usual aphrodisiacs that he uses – we found pastilles of cantharides in his room. As a result, he sinks into a deep sleep. Eugénie obviously wants to savour Marguerite's disappointment, or at least to scold her for being there at such an uncommon hour. As she gets to the kitchens through the service passage, she sees a man in a grey coat running away along the corridor to the staircase leading to the upper floors. Taken by surprise, she's convinced it was Monsieur de La Vrillière she saw. She carries on to the roasting room, hears no noise, lights a candle, and discovers Marguerite lying there with her throat cut.'

'Let's stop for a moment,' said Monsieur Lenoir. 'If this unknown killer was able to get into the house, why did he have to escape through the upper floors?'

Nicolas approached the long table and handed the two magistrates some documents. 'These are the plans, cross-sections and elevations of the Saint-Florentin mansion, as drawn up by its architect, Monsieur Chalgrin. You will observe on the plan of the ground floor that the staircase is the only exit for someone who's trying to leave the kitchens and can't take the service passage leading to the courtyard. To Eugénie Gouet, there's no doubt. She's been serving the Saint-Florentin family since she was very young, and is totally devoted to it. No one is either black or white, people are mixed. The best and the worst cohabit. What's going on in her mind? We can try to imagine. She believes she has to do everything she can to save her master – we can't rule out the possibility that she may once have been his mistress. She probably waits for a while, until she's sure the duc has managed to get out of the house, then runs to tell the Duchesse de La Vrillière. The duchesse immediately takes matters in hand. Something will have to be done. They confer. Eugénie Gouet admits her plot against Jean Missery. The fact that he's still unconscious constitutes their last hope. They decide to take him down into the kitchens. But the man is too heavy for the two women, and they're forced to tell some of the other servants. They give him a superficial cut and, to make it more convincing, they spread the blood of three freshly killed rabbits all around his body. The duc returns early in the morning; it's impossible to be sure of the exact time as the testimonies are so confused. He finds the house in a state of agitation, but no one dares tell him about the events of the night. The duchesse visits Jean Missery's sister-in-law, Sister Louise of the Annunciation, and opens her heart to her.'

'Didn't it take you a long time to rule out the possibility that the duc might be guilty?'

'With good reason! He claimed to have returned from Versailles. But we gradually discovered that he was in Paris and in fact, for the three murders that followed, it was quite impossible to verify his alibis. Questioned by me after I had noticed that he wore a wooden replica of his hand under his glove, he was unable to indicate to me where the original was, or if it had been stolen or lost.'

'And the supposed murderer?' asked the Criminal Lieutenant in a more affable tone. 'How did he escape? Had he remained in the house?'

'I just had to follow the bloody footprints which I mentioned at the beginning of my presentation. He escaped through the gate, from the first-floor balcony. It should be mentioned, incidentally, that this was a difficult thing to do, only possible for an agile young man, since it involved descending a stone column to reach a side gate.'

'One last point,' said Testard du Lys. 'Why did the major-domo only have a slight wound? If one wanted to pin the blame on him, killing him would have been more appropriate.'

'Monseigneur, think of the horror of that terrible night, of those two distraught women, who are trying to find a way to exonerate the duc. They make the decision together. They won't go any further than a small cut. They are not criminals.'

Monsieur Lenoir raised his hand. 'At the point we have reached in your account, Commissioner, the motives and consequences you describe seem plausible. The fact remains that this whole edifice rests on nothing but your discursive intelligence and your intuition, not to mention your imagination. Of course, there are many clues, and they seem to corroborate your theories, but we need evidence, some confirmation so obvious that it will convince us that the presumed killer, Eudes Duchamplan, not only committed the murder in the Saint-Florentin mansion but also the other three murders. For the next two, that of the prostitute whose body was found beside the river, and that of the young fugitive from Brussels, the killer's methods were identical. One may therefore presume that we are dealing with the same perpetrator. For the fourth, that of Anselme Vitry, a firearm was used. Commissioner, we are listening.'

'For the Marot girl, known as L'Étoile,' replied Nicolas, 'we have a piece of corroborating evidence. The owl . . .'

'What's an owl got to do with it?'

'The Criminal Lieutenant may be unaware,' said Lenoir, with a touch of irony, 'that this is the *nom de guerre* of one of our most distinguished journalists, Monsieur Restif de la Bretonne. His dissolute life sometimes allows him to show some welcome consideration towards the police.'

'Are you implying that you turn a blind eye to some of his aberrations?'

'Certainly, if that allows us to pursue criminals who disturb public order.'

'To cut a long story short,' Nicolas went on, 'the owl stole the slippers from this girl's feet, and they turned out to be identical to those found next to Margerite Pindron.'

'The fact that one pair of slippers resembles another pair of slippers,' said Testard du Lys impatiently, 'does not convince me.'

'See for yourself,' said Nicolas, pointing to the two pairs on the chest. 'I understand the Criminal Lieutenant's reticence. Fortunately, I have another piece of evidence.'

He walked towards the chest and unfolded a jade-green coat adorned with imitation gemstones.

'Look at this coat, gentlemen. It was seized, in the proper fashion, from the wardrobe of the younger Duchamplan. Note, beside this buttonhole, a series of imitation gemstones, bluish white in colour, of which one is missing.'

He took from his pocket a small piece of paper, folded in four, which he placed on the long table and unfolded.

'Here it is. It was found on the river bank, next to the body of the Marot girl.'

A long silence followed Nicolas's demonstration.

'Fortunately, heaven sometimes aids the law,' resumed Nicolas. 'It allows us to discover the silver thread deliberately abandoned by a killer and then helps us find a stone accidentally lost by the same killer. Heaven also favours the investigator, helped, admittedly, by the skill of doctors able to see what others cannot in the secret depths of the human body. Thanks to an examination of their entrails, it was discovered that both the Marot girl and the young girl found on Île des Cygnes had ingested, not long before their deaths, large quantities of the fruit of the pineapple, an exotic plant from the West Indies which a number of noble houses have been trying, with some difficulty, to acclimatise. I once saw some fine ones in the late King's hothouse at Trianon.'

'Apart from these loathsome details, you are not claiming, are you,' said Testard du Lys indignantly, his pale face growing longer at the thought of the prospects this opened up, 'that these victims frequented royal houses?'

'Certainly not! On the contrary, I carefully avoided sending my investigators there. Our search was confined to civil residences, not too distant from those places beside the river where the corpses were found. Imagine our surprise on discovering that this fruit was cultivated in the Montparnasse house of the Marquis de Chambonas, a person to whom our attention had been drawn by a brothel-keeper well connected with circles in which certain nocturnal parties are held. The bathing establishment where Duchamplan was arrested gave us some idea of the nature of these parties.'

'It should be pointed out,' Monsieur Lenoir said to the Criminal Lieutenant, 'that this person is well known to our inspectors for his extravagant behaviour. He is the grand master of a libertine society created by his father. He has many debts and a highly dubious reputation. He married one of the Duc de La Vrillière's illegitimate children, the daughter of the Marquise de Langeac, the

Beautiful Aglaé. It is said that the couple are very ill-matched and that the marquise is beaten repeatedly. Her husband, having seen in this marriage the possibility of both financial gain and social cachet, bears a grudge against the minister for his mother-in-law's fall from favour and the consequent dishonour of such a misalliance.'

'I understand what you're saying,' said Testard du Lys. 'But all this jumble of information makes me even more confused. What connection can there be between all these crimes?'

'Monseigneur,' replied Nicolas, 'I am firmly convinced that someone wanted to implicate Monsieur de La Vrillière in a series of murders. The first, that of Marguerite Pindron, met a number of needs. Drawn by her young lover into attending parties which revolted her with their criminal excesses, I imagine that she became a danger, in that she might either speak out or resort to blackmail. Add to that the advantage for a Duchamplan of getting rid of someone Jean Missery might be thinking of marrying, thus avoiding any squandering of the fortune from which the major-domo had benefited since his wife's death. Subsequently, since the first attempt seemed to have failed, there needed to be further opportunities to compromise the minister. I fear that the reality of the matter is that Eudes Duchamplan is a monster who used the plot in which he had become involved to satisfy his own perversions. I saw him, with my own eyes, torture a young girl, with a terrifying expression of morbid delight on his face. The madmen at Bicêtre look more human in their frenzy.'

'"I imagine, I think, I believe . . ."' The Criminal Lieutenant was hopping on his chair like a doll worked by a spring.

Nicolas bowed. 'I must now bring in a new element which

directly concerns the interests of the kingdom. This plot is not simply a family affair, the work of a madman, but the culmination of a conspiracy woven in secret by the representatives of a foreign power. Lord Ashbury, a member of the British secret service, whom I know well from having met him in London, was recognised by me in the lower gallery of the palace of Versailles. He fled when I approached. Our investigations led to us seeing him again at the Hôtel de Russie in Rue Christine, near the Duchamplan house. Sought by all the police forces of the kingdom, it is in that house that he goes to earth, doubtless convinced that it is the last place anyone would think of looking for him. When I search it, I discover a fragment of paper mentioning the Tournelles. Eventually, he is arrested in our raid on the bathing establishment in that very place.'

'Why should this plot have targeted the Duc de La Vrillière?' asked Lenoir, who had been taking notes as he listened to Nicolas's demonstration and had made him an imperceptible sign of caution when he had mentioned the Tournelles.

'We are at peace with England,' said the commissioner, 'but the English fear that we are actively supporting the growing unrest in their American colonies. They suspect us of wanting, in this way, to take our revenge for the treaty of Paris and the loss of New France. The reason Lord Ashbury, alias Francis Sefton, is in Paris is to take personal charge of setting up a plot whose aim is to weaken the kingdom. The Duc de La Vrillière is an ideal prey, because of his private conduct and also because of his family connection with the Comte de Maurepas. Compromising him would eventually bring about the fall of the government and a scandal which would tarnish the circles around the throne.'

'But surely, Nicolas,' said Lenoir, 'if that were the case it might also bring about the return of the Duc de Choiseul, who is well known to be hostile to their interests and concerned to wipe out the memory of past setbacks.'

'That's an eventuality they didn't take into account, because they're convinced that the King would never accept Choiseul's return, given his animosity – despite the Queen's insinuations – towards a man who gravely offended his father the Dauphin. They are counting on the confusion that would follow the success of their actions. So much for that objection. The English services have done their work well and know the lives of our great men in detail. Lord Ashbury makes contact with the Marquis de Chambonas, and doubtless teams up with the younger Duchamplan. Do you need proof of that? The day after I recognise Ashbury, someone tries to kill me at Versailles. The guilty party? The younger Duchamplan, whose left cheek still bears the trace of the whiplash inflicted by Dr Semacgus's coachman. Yes, truly, there is a foreign plot, concealed beneath the terrifying disguise of a web of private vengeance and corruption.'

'There remains the last murder,' said the Criminal Lieutenant, who seemed nonplussed by all this. 'How do you explain that?'

'It is without doubt the most difficult of these murderous acts to get to the bottom of. Duchamplan recruited young Anselme Vitry, the rejected fiancé of Marguerite Pindron, from among the venereal disease sufferers at Bicêtre, a hospital of which his brother is an administrator, and which he often visits out of an unhealthy fascination with states of madness. He hires him as a driver in his brother's cab company and uses him at every opportunity. Was it he who drove Duchamplan to the Saint-Florentin mansion on the

*401*

night of the murder? Be that as it may, it was certainly he who, by an extraordinary coincidence, drove me to Popincourt where I was making enquiries about his fiancée. I was struck by the stains in the interior of the cab, which could only have been blood. The driver seemed to be hiding his face. That is understandable if it was indeed Vitry, who did not want to be recognised in an area where he had lived. The body found in the cab near the pleasure gardens was unquestionably his. The mud on the cab is identical to that on the bank near the Tournelles bathing establishment. What did Vitry's killer hope to achieve? You have to bear in mind, gentlemen, that he was counting on two possible scenarios. In one, the watch, or ourselves, would take the fake suicide at face value. Then Duchamplan, dead in the eyes of the world, could disappear without encountering any opposition. It is likely, in that case, that the shirt stolen from the Saint-Florentin mansion would have reappeared, implicating Monsieur de La Vrillière in another murder. The most extraordinary thing in this affair is that Duchamplan had also foreseen that we might not be convinced after all, and in that case, too, the shirt would have been used, with the same results. I sense a question coming from the Criminal Lieutenant. Why did Duchamplan kill Vitry? One could say out of pure cruelty and because he needed a young man's corpse. I fear – but here again I must imagine – that he simply wanted to get rid of an inconvenient witness, or else that he had no wish to describe Marguerite Pindron's hideous death to the poor boy, thereby provoking an angry reaction that might prove deadly. With that terrible observation, gentlemen, my demonstration is over. I am firmly of the belief that Duchamplan is not only an accomplice in a plot against the State, but is also guilty of four dreadful murders.'

A great silence fell over the hall. Old Marie entered to stoke the brazier and throw in more pieces of incense. For a long while, the two magistrates did not move, apparently lost in thought. At last, Monsieur Testard du Lys spoke up.

'Commissioner, I have listened to you with great interest. My interventions, untimely as they may have seemed to you, were only intended to gain a better grasp of the truth. But however much I have gone over your words and put your arguments side by side in an attempt to make sense of a story whose elements are scattered like the pieces of a playing card that has been cut up, I remain unconvinced by all this. I need to ask you two vital questions before I make a judgement. If Monsieur de La Vrillière, to whom everything points, is innocent, where are his alibis? And secondly, you have amassed observations, clues, assumptions, suppositions and a whole hotchpotch of details, as if trying to convince us by sheer volume. Give me one piece of evidence, regarding one of these murders, that proves that Eudes Duchamplan is guilty, and I will accept all the accusations you have made as true and legitimate.'

'Monsieur,' intervened Lenoir, 'before Commissioner Le Floch defers to your request, I'm going to answer your first question. You have my word, Monsieur, that the Duc de La Vrillière has unimpeachable alibis for the times when the four murders were committed. However, I am unable, on the orders of the King, to communicate them to you. I leave the floor to Monsieur Le Floch.'

'Bring in Eudes Duchamplan,' said Nicolas simply.

A young man in chains entered the hall, surrounded by men of the watch. He was wearing a shirt and maroon breeches. Nicolas was struck by his resemblance, in shape and height, to young Vitry. Only his long, thin hands did not belong to a gardener. On his left cheek was a gummed taffeta bandage. He threw the two magistrates a defiant look.

'I protest, gentlemen!' he cried. 'I am being held here against my will.' He indicated Nicolas with his chin. 'I have been a victim of this gentleman, who tried to drown me during a private party.'

'We shan't go into those details,' replied Lenoir curtly. 'You are accused of a conspiracy against the State and of the murders of Marguerite Pindron, the Marot girl, a young girl who had fled the Low Countries, and the gardener Anselme Vitry. In addition, you are charged with the kidnapping of minors and the attempted murder of a magistrate of the King. Commissioner Le Floch, please continue.'

The man looked Nicolas in the eye. The commissioner suddenly saw again Brière's snake-like gaze, the green eyes of Mauval and his brother. He shuddered and made an effort to pull himself together. Evil was still abroad in the land.

'Monsieur Duchamplan,' he said at last, 'it would be customary for me to list in detail all the accusations which have been brought against you. That would be tiring for us, and for you, so I am going to present to the magistrates just one piece of evidence concerning one of these murders. If this proof is conclusive, it will mean that not only are you guilty of this one, but also of all the others.'

Nicolas stood up and walked slowly towards Duchamplan. The dancing light of the torches projected his huge shadow onto the wall. He seized the young man by his shirt collar, lifted him from his seat and, with a great clanking of chains, dragged him towards the coffin. With a blow of his fist, he threw the lid down on the flagstoned floor and forced Duchamplan to lower his head so that it almost touched the head of the corpse.

'Look at your work, that mutilated face, those hollow eyes! Contemplate one of your victims and dare now to claim that you did not kill her!'

He let go of him, leaving him moaning beside the coffin, and walked quickly back to the long table.

'Gentlemen,' he continued, 'I ask you to look at that man. During the discovery of the victim on Île des Cygnes, I found in the young girl's undershirt, in the presence of Inspector Bourdeau, a human fragment. A nail which had got caught on the cloth and been torn off, taking a piece of skin with it. Here it is.' Nicolas took out his little black notebook and carefully unfolded a piece of silk paper containing a fragment of nail and dried skin.

'Eudes Duchamplan, approach.'

Bourdeau had to go and get him.

'Remove his chains.'

As if filled suddenly with an absurd hope, the man rose to his full height, once again as arrogant as ever; he had not even heard what Nicolas had said.

'Show us your hands,' said Lenoir.

'What reason would I have to show you my hands?'

'Don't argue.'

The two magistrates leaned forward. Duchamplan had rather long nails. But the nail on the middle finger of the right hand was broken, and there was a still visible cut on one of its edges. Nicolas approached, and grasped the hand firmly. The fragment in his possession exactly fitted the wound on the finger.

'What's the meaning of this?' stammered Duchamplan.

'The meaning, Monsieur,' said the Criminal Lieutenant, 'is that the evidence gathered by Commissioner Le Floch confirms the accusations made against you. Take him away.'

*December 1774*

'So, Nicolas,' said Noblecourt, carefully putting down the fine porcelain cup, 'the year has finished better than it started! What a terrible, unbelievable series of events!'

It was two months since Nicolas had confounded Duchamplan at the Grand Châtelet. He lifted his head with a sigh.

'Alas, they're not over yet. I've just learnt some surprising news.'

'Tell me.'

'Duchamplan, secretly tried by an ad hoc commission, has escaped the death penalty. The galleys for life, that's not much to pay.'

'I already knew that. Secrets are never well kept . . . I was told that your brilliant demonstration and the weight of the evidence presented didn't completely convince the learned assembly. What else did they need? It was only a pretext, I fear, to spare someone who knew too much about certain people.'

'What you don't yet know is that Duchamplan was discovered to have choked to death on the road to Toulon. His companions on the chain hadn't noticed a thing. The dust from the straw in the prison at Clamecy is believed to have asphyxiated him!'

'Was there an autopsy?'

'Of course not! He was immediately buried in a common grave.'

'Are we certain it was really him?'

'I dare to hope so. With Mauval and Camusot still at large, not to mention my English friends, that now makes a lot of people after me. I really need to be careful.'

'You've been through some difficult times: 1774 will remain for you the year of mourning and slander . . . both against you and against La Vrillière. Did the duc at least show his gratitude for having got him out of trouble?'

'I was hardly expecting him to do so. There's a kind of embarrassment between us now. I know too much about him. And he still doesn't know the main thing. He's still a minister, but it's been noticed at Court that the King is more distant towards him than before. The duchesse sent me a gracious message through Madame de Maurepas, who is still very besotted with "young Ranreuil".'

'Now you really are "new Court"! At the home of Philemon and Baucis . . . In a way, the wife of the gravedigger.'

Nicolas did not understand the allusion. 'The gravedigger?'

'Alas, my friend, close as I may be to the *parlement* and its little schemes, I've always supported the rights and prerogatives of the Crown against the encroachments and ravings of a body which has led us, among other things, to chase out the Jesuit fathers, with the consequences I once pointed out to you. Now, on 12 November, the well-chosen day of Saint-René . . .'

'The first name of the Comte de Maurepas.'

'Precisely! That day, the King presided over a bed of justice ratifying the recall of the *parlement* and sounding the death knell of the Maupeou reforms.'

'It's a mistake, when you really look at it.'

'A mistake, yes. A sin, certainly. It will remain vaguely in people's minds that the *parlement* is a power that cannot be broken since we are forced to reinstate it. The whole of Paris is repeating the comment of Chancellor Maupeou: "Thanks to me, the King won a trial which had gone on for a hundred and fifty years. If he wants to lose it again, he is the master!"'

'Now I understand what the English ambassador meant,' remarked Nicolas. 'Monsieur Lenoir, whose complete trust I now enjoy, asked me to translate for him an extract from a dispatch intercepted from Lord Stormont.'

'What did it say?'

'Basically, that the young King thought that his authority had been sufficiently established by this act of recalling the parliament. He concluded with this terrible phrase: "Clearly he will be disappointed by the end of his reign."'[1]

'May heaven grant that I do not see it! The late King would never have yielded, I'm sure of that.'

'To get back to our case,' said Nicolas, 'the young girl from Brussels has returned home, her mother having immediately come to fetch her. They left in tears, taking back the remains of their sister and daughter. You know the role that corpse played.'

'Yes, all that was well arranged. What about Chambonas?'

'The marquis seems to be recruiting again.'

'And those mysterious creatures whose strange appearance at Trianon you told me about?'

'They have been seen on two occasions, still dressed in those extraordinary garments. No one has yet been able to explain their presence. The last time, the alarm having been raised, the gardens of the Trianon were surrounded by guards and servants. It was nothing more nor less than a hunt, an attempt to lure the unknown women into a trap. Nothing! No one! In this particular case, my foresight has been called into question. The Queen has gently mocked me. What can I do?'

They were silent for a moment. A log collapsed in ashes in the fireplace.

'And how is your son?' asked Noblecourt.

'Oh, he's a Breton, which means he adapts well to difficult circumstances. He's been accepted and has avoided the roughest ragging, although I suspect he's received and distributed a few blows along the way.'

'He seems to have his father's powers of seduction.'

'And his grandfather's! In his last letter, he asked me to thank you again for the *friponnes* from Cotignac that you gave him. They contribute very pleasantly to the transition between day and night and make a welcome change from the dreary repetition of the college routine. Hard bread, stringy beef, beans in rancid oil, lentils with stones, rice mixed with weevils, sour vegetables and dessert noticeable by its absence. I quote him.'

'It seems,' said Noblecourt, barely containing his gaiety, 'nothing has changed in our schools, whether they are Jesuit or Oratory! Your son describes it very well. I predict he'll be a skilful wielder of the pen. His father knew how to tell a story, the son will know how to write. Like father like son, as our late lamented monarch liked to say. I was sometimes unfair towards him. Despite his many faults, he was a king!'

Darkness was falling. It was a moment of peace, a moment to daydream. Cyrus and Mouchette lay asleep on the floor near the chimney screen. Poitevin entered the room carrying two letters, which he handed to Nicolas. A porter had delivered the first, and the second had been handed in from a well-appointed coach.

Asking Noblecourt to excuse him, the commissioner began reading. The old magistrate, who had been dozing off, opened his eyes when he heard a sigh from Nicolas.

'Bad news?'

'Some bad, some good.'

'Then they cancel each other out.'

'One won't make up for the other.'

Silence fell again.

Nicolas, as if reluctantly, began speaking. 'I've had a letter from Antoinette, informing me that she's leaving Paris. She's sold the business in Rue du Bac and is moving to London to open a lace shop there. She left the city two days ago after paying a visit to Louis in Juilly . . .'

He stopped, a lump in his throat. So many images and memories had suddenly risen up from the past.

'She preferred not to see me. She entrusts Louis to me.'

With a grave air, Noblecourt sat up in his armchair. 'What happened to explain this unexpected gesture?'

'I think I know, and I alone am responsible. In October, when I was at Versailles for my investigation, I met La Satin in the lower gallery of the palace. She was there on business, selling trinkets from a stall a few days a week. Her presence there upset me, and I wasn't quite able to conceal my reaction. In addition, at that moment, I recognised Lord Ashbury and set off after him . . . An unfortunate combination of circumstances.'

'I understand what was at the bottom of your mind, Nicolas. It wasn't that her presence was inconvenient to you, am I right?'

'Of course not! I was thinking of Louis, the last of the Ranreuils. I don't know if my half-sister Isabelle is married, or if she will ever have any offspring . . . I suddenly imagined, somewhat frivolously I admit, Louis as a page to the King, or as a bodyguard, to which his name entitles him . . . And his mother selling things in the gallery.'

Noblecourt was thinking, his head nodding gently. 'My friend, without absolving you of your reaction, which you were unfortunate enough to reveal, I think you should consider the possibility that La Satin understood the situation perfectly. It would have been better for her to think before she acted and avoid placing you in such a delicate situation. The wrong having been done, she decided to sacrifice her love as a woman and a mother for the future of her son. Understanding you without a word being spoken, she has elevated herself to a kind of heroism, and you should be grateful to her. There's no point now in feeling remorse. The only thing she can expect of you is to respond to her silent appeal by guiding Louis towards a destiny worthy of the glorious name he will no doubt bear one day. She made the right decision. Remember she's still young, and so are you. Your life is still ahead of you, and she is entitled to a second chance. It can't have been easy for her to remain in your shadow, you to whom she owed both love and loyalty.'

'But what of Louis? What will he think? He'll be angry with me.'

'I'm certain La Satin didn't tell him about your encounter. The reasons she will have put forward won't set the son against the father. Louis is mature enough to have already understood that your relationship had ended. At his age, he needs you. Reassure him and reassure yourself. And what of the good news?'

'Oh, a trifle. Admiral d'Arranet has invited me to dinner in Versailles in three days.'

'That's very good. You're young, you should take advantage of such things. They say he has a lovely daughter.'

Noblecourt knew nothing, but always suspected everything. Nicolas sighed. Happiness was never unalloyed. You always had to pay for it, and dearly. This terrible, painful year was coming to an end. Time was slipping away like sand in an ever-open hand, and at the same time strengthening his soul. He closed his eyes and took a deep breath. The shores of his childhood reappeared, swept by wind and sea spray. He saw the horizon receding in the distance, and a new headland emerging. He was going to have to reach it before discovering the next one. The way appeared clear and free, but he knew now that he would have to allow for the opposing currents of life. Realising that fact nourished his anguish and his hope.

*La Marsa, la Bretesche, Glane, Ivry*
*August 2002–November 2003*

# NOTES

## CHAPTER I

1. See *The Nicolas Le Floch Affair*.
2. The author would like to thank Professor Daniel Teyssère of the University of Caen for these details about La Borde.
3. A kind of tunic worn over armour in the Middle Ages.
4. See *The Phantom of Rue Royale*.
5. Saint Greluchon was prayed to in cases of infertility.
6. Boileau, *Art Poétique*, chant III.
7. The hospice of the Grand-Cour des Quinze-Vingts was founded by Saint Louis in aid of a brotherhood of crusaders blinded by the Saracens. It stretched from the present-day Place du Théâtre-Français to a third of the way down the Cour du Carrousel. In 1779 it was transferred to Rue de Charenton.

## CHAPTER II

1. See *The Phantom of Rue Royale*.

## CHAPTER IV

1. Fagon (1638–1718), Louis XIV's doctor.
2. See *The Nicolas Le Floch Affair*.
3. François de Malherbe, 'Dure contrainte'.
4. Statue of Henri IV.
5. Place Louis-le-Grand is now Place Vendôme.
6. See *The Nicolas Le Floch Affair*.

## CHAPTER V

1. See *The Phantom of Rue Royale*.
2. Ramponneau was a famous innkeeper in La Courtille.
3. This debate is taken from contemporary archives, as quoted at length by the historian A. Franklin.

CHAPTER VI

1. See *The Châtelet Apprentice*.

2. These masks were destroyed in 1793 during the violation of the royal tombs.

3. Rousseau's *Émile*.

4. See *The Châtelet Apprentice*.

5. See *The Nicolas Le Floch Affair*.

6. Lord Ashbury: a character in *The Nicolas Le Floch Affair*.

CHAPTER VII

1. This subtle analysis is borrowed from Crébillon.

2. La Harpe (1739–1803) was a critic.

3. See *The Phantom of Rue Royale*.

4. In August 1901, two Englishwomen, Miss Moberly and Miss Jourdain, were transported to the eighteenth century while walking at Trianon and met people in period dress. This journey through time remains a mystery to this day. I thought it might be amusing to tell the story the other way round.

5. See *The Nicolas Le Floch Affair*.

6. The Maurepas had been exiled to Pontchartrain by Louis XV.

7. Madame de Noailles was a lady-in-waiting known as Madame l'Étiquette.

8. See *The Phantom of Rue Royale*.

CHAPTER VIII

1. See *The Châtelet Apprentice*.

2. The Menus-Plaisirs was the establishment that made sets and costumes for Court celebrations and ceremonies.

CHAPTER XI

1. Jean-Baptiste Massillon (1663–1742), French Catholic preacher.

2. This incident actually happened.

3. A reference to a revolving fireplace used by the Maréchal de Richelieu during an amorous adventure.

4. Many houses collapsed at the time.

CHAPTER XII

1. Iolaos was Hercules' companion in his struggle with the hydra.

EPILOGUE

1. A genuine quotation from Lord Stormont after the recall of the Parlement in 1774.

# ACKNOWLEDGEMENTS

First, I wish to express my gratitude to Isabelle Tujague for devoting such care, and so much of her free time, to preparing the final version of the text. I am also grateful to Monique Constant, Conservateur Général du Patrimoine, for her encouragement over a long period; to Maurice Roisse, for his tireless checking of my manuscripts; and to my publisher and his colleagues for their friendship and support.

# Five Nights at Freddy's

# THE TWISTED ONES

# Five Nights at Freddy's

## THE TWISTED ONES

by
**SCOTT CAWTHON**
**KIRA BREED-WRISLEY**

Scholastic Inc.

ISBN 978-1-74276-257-9

17 18 19 20 21 / 1

Printed in Australia by Griffin Press

First printing 2017

Book design by Rick DeMonico

# CHAPTER ONE

**D**on't trust your eyes."

Dr. Treadwell walked back and forth across the platform at the front of the auditorium. Her steps were slow and even, almost hypnotic.

"Your eyes deceive you every day, filling in the blanks for you in a world of sensory overload." An image of dizzying geometric detail lit up the canvas screen behind her. "When I say 'sensory overload' I mean that quite literally. At every moment, your senses are receiving far more information than they can process all at once, and your mind is forced to choose which signals to pay attention to. It does that based on your experiences, and your expectation of what is normal. The things we are familiar with are the things we can—for the most part—ignore. We see this most easily with olfactory fatigue: your nose ceases to perceive a smell when you've been around it for a while. You may be quite thankful for this phenomenon, depending on the habits of your roommate."

The class tittered dutifully, then became quiet as the image of another multicolored design flashed onto the screen.

The professor gave a hint of a smile and continued.

"Your mind creates motion when there is none. It fills in colors and trajectories based on what you've seen before, and calculates what you *should* be seeing now." Another image flashed onto the overhead screen. "If your mind didn't do this, then simply walking outside and seeing a tree would consume all your mental energy, leaving no resources to do anything else. In order for you to function in the world, your mind fills in the spaces of that tree with its own leaves and branches." A hundred pencils scribbled all at once, filling the lecture hall with a sound like scurrying mice.

"It's why when you enter a house for the first time you experience a moment of dizziness. Your mind is taking in more than usual. It's drawing a floor plan, creating a palette of colors, and saving an inventory of images to draw on later, so you don't have to go through that exhausting intake every single time. The next time you enter that same house, you'll already know where you are."

*"Charlie!"* An urgent voice whispered her name, inches from her ear. Charlie kept writing. She was staring straight

ahead at the display at the front of the lecture hall. As Dr. Treadwell went on, she paced faster, occasionally flinging an arm toward the screen to illustrate her point. Her words seemed to be falling behind as her mind raced on ahead; Charlie had realized by the second day of classes that her professor sometimes broke off in the middle of one sentence, only to finish an entirely different one. It was like she skimmed the text in her head, reading out a few words here and there. Most of the students in her robotics class found it maddening, but Charlie liked it. It made the lesson kind of like doing a puzzle.

The screen flashed again, displaying an assortment of mechanical parts and a diagram of an eye. "This is what you must re-create." Dr. Treadwell stepped back from the image, turning to look at it with the class. "Basic artificial intelligence is all about sensory control. You won't be dealing with a mind that can filter these things out for itself. You must design programs that recognize basic shapes, while discarding unimportant information. You must do for your robot what your own mind does for you: create a simplified and organized assembly of information based on what's relevant. Let's start by looking at some examples of basic shape recognition."

"*Charlie,*" hissed the voice again, and she waved her pencil impatiently at the figure peering over her shoulder—her friend Arty—trying to shoo him away. The gesture cost her a moment, put her half a step behind the professor. She hurried to catch up, anxious not to miss a single line.

The paper in front of her was covered in formulas, notes in the margins, sketches, and diagrams. She wanted to get everything down all at once: not just the math, but all the things it made her think of. If she could tie the new facts to things she already knew, she'd retain it much more easily. She felt hungry for it, alert, watching for new tidbits of information like a dog under the dinner table.

A boy near the front raised his hand to ask a question, and Charlie felt a brief flare of impatience. Now the whole class would have to stop while Treadwell went back to explain a simple concept. Charlie let her mind wander, sketching absently in the margins of her notebook.

John would be here in—she glanced restlessly at her watch—an hour. *I told him maybe someday we'll see each other again. I guess it's someday.* He had called out of the blue: "I'm just going to be passing through," he said, and Charlie hadn't bothered to ask how he knew where she was. *Of course he would know.* There was no reason not to meet him, and she found herself alternately excited and filled with dread. Now, as she absently sketched rectangular forms along the bottom of her note paper, her stomach jumped, a little spasm of nerves. It felt like a lifetime since she last saw him. Sometimes, it felt like she'd seen him yesterday, as if the last year hadn't passed. But of course it had, and everything had changed for Charlie once again.

That May, the night of her eighteenth birthday, the dreams had begun. Charlie was long accustomed to nightmares, the worst moments of her past forced up like bile, into twisted versions of memories already too terrible to recall. She shoved these dreams into the back of her mind in the morning and sealed them away, knowing they would only breach it when night fell again.

These dreams were different. When she woke, she was physically exhausted: not just drained but sore, her muscles weak. Her hands were stiff and aching, like they'd been clenched into fists for hours. These new dreams didn't come every night, but when they did, they interrupted her regular nightmares and took them over. It didn't matter if she was running and screaming for her life, or wandering aimlessly through a dull mishmash of the various places she'd been all week. Suddenly, from nowhere, she would sense him: Sammy, her lost twin brother, was near.

She knew he was present the same way she knew that *she* was present, and whatever the dream was, it dropped away— people, places, light, and sound. Now she was searching for him in the darkness, calling his name. He never answered. She would drop to her hands and knees, feeling her way through the dark, letting his presence guide her until she came to a barrier. It was smooth and cold, metal. She couldn't see it, but she hit it hard with one fist and it echoed. "Sammy?" she would call, hitting harder. She stood, reaching up to see if she could scale the slick surface, but it stretched up far above her head. She beat her fists against the barricade until they hurt. She screamed her brother's name until her throat was raw, until she fell to the floor and leaned on the solid metal, pressing her cheek to its cool surface and hoping for a whisper from the other side. He was there; she knew it as surely as if he were a part of herself.

She knew in those dreams that he was present. Worse, when she was awake, she knew he was not there.

In August, Charlie and Aunt Jen had their first fight. They'd always been too distant to really argue. Charlie never felt the need to rebel, because Jen provided no real authority. And Jen never took anything Charlie did personally, never tried to stop her from doing anything, as long as she was safe. The day Charlie moved in with her at the age of seven, Aunt Jen had told her plainly that she was not a replacement for Charlie's parents. By now, Charlie was old enough to understand that Jen had meant it as a gesture of respect, a way to reassure Charlie that her father wouldn't be forgotten, that she would always be his child. But at the time it had seemed like an admonishment. *Don't expect parenting. Don't expect love.* And so Charlie hadn't. Jen had never failed to care for Charlie. Charlie had never wanted for food or clothing, and

Jen had taught her to cook, to take care of the house, to manage her money, and to fix her own car. *You have to be independent, Charlie. You have to know how to take care of yourself. You have to be stronger than*—she'd cut herself off, but Charlie knew how the sentence ended. *Than your father.*

Charlie shook her head, trying to jerk herself free of her own thoughts.

"What's wrong?" Arty said next to her.

"Nothing," she whispered. She ran her pencil again and again over the same lines: up, over, down, over, the graphite wearing thicker and thicker.

Charlie had told Jen that she was going back to Hurricane, and Jen's face turned stony, her skin paling.

"Why would you want to do that?" she asked with a dangerous calm in her voice. Charlie's heart beat faster. *Because that's where I lost him. Because I need him more than I need you.* The thought of returning had been nagging at her for months, growing stronger with each passing week. One morning she awoke and the choice was made, final, sitting in her mind with a solid weight.

"Jessica's going to college at St. George," she told her aunt. "She's starting the summer semester so I can stay with her while I'm there. I want to see the house again. There's still so much I don't understand; it just feels . . . important," she finished weakly, faltering as Jen's eyes—dark blue, like marble—fixed on her.

Jen didn't answer for a long moment then she said simply, "No."

*Why not?* Charlie might once have said. *You let me go before.* But after what happened last year, when she and Jessica and the others went back to Freddy's and discovered the horrifying truth behind the murders at her father's old pizzeria, things had changed between them. Charlie had changed. Now she met Jen's gaze, determined. "I'm going," she said, trying to keep her own voice steady.

Then everything exploded.

Charlie didn't know which of them started shouting first, but she screamed until her throat was fiery and sore, hurling at her aunt every pain she'd ever inflicted, every hurt she had failed to prevent. Jen shouted back that she only ever meant to care for Charlie, that she had always done her best, flinging reassuring words that somehow dripped with poison.

*"I'm leaving!"* Charlie screamed with finality. She started for the door, but Jen grabbed her arm, yanking her violently back. Charlie stumbled, almost falling before she caught herself on the kitchen table, and Jen let her hand drop with a shocked expression. There was silence, and then Charlie left.

She packed a bag, feeling as if she had somehow diverged from reality, into an impossible parallel world. Then she got in her car and drove away. She didn't tell anyone she was going. Her friends here were not close friends; there was no one she owed an explanation.

When Charlie got to Hurricane, she'd intended to go straight to her father's house, to stay there for the next few days until Jessica arrived on campus. But as she reached the city limits, something stopped her. *I can't*, she thought. *I can't ever go back.* She turned the car around, drove straight to St. George, and slept in her car for a week.

It was only after Charlie knocked, and Jessica opened the door with a startled expression that Charlie realized that she'd never actually mentioned her plans to Jessica, on whom they all depended. She told her everything, and Jessica, hesitantly, offered to let her stay. Charlie had slept on the floor the rest of the summer, and as the fall semester approached, Jessica didn't ask her to leave.

"It's nice to have someone who knows me here," she had said, and uncharacteristically, Charlie hugged her.

Charlie had never cared about high school. She never paid much attention in her classes, but As and Bs came easily for her. She had never really thought about liking or disliking her subjects, though sometimes one teacher or another would make her feel a spark of interest for a year.

Charlie hadn't thought much beyond the end of the summer, but as she idly flipped through Jessica's course catalog and saw advanced courses in robotics, something clicked into place. St. George was among the colleges she'd been accepted into earlier that year, though she hadn't really intended to go to any of them. Now, however, she went to the administrative office and pleaded her case until she was allowed to enroll, despite having missed the deadline by months. *There's still so much I don't understand.* Charlie wanted to learn, and the things she wanted to learn were very specific.

Of course there were things she had to learn before a robotics course would make any sense at all. Math had always been straightforward, functional, sort of like a game to Charlie; you did the thing you were supposed to do and got the answer. But it had never been a very interesting game. It was fun to learn something new, but then you had to keep doing it for weeks or months, bored out of your skull. That was high school. But in her first calculus class, something had happened. It was as if she'd been laying bricks for years, forced to work slowly, seeing nothing but her mortar and her trowel. Then suddenly someone pulled her back a few steps and said, "Here, look, you've been building this castle. Go play inside!"

"And that's all for today," Professor Treadwell said at last. Charlie looked down at her paper, realizing she'd never stopped moving her pencil. She had worn dark lines right through the page, and drawn on the desk. She rubbed the marks halfheartedly with her sleeve, then opened her binder to put away her notes. Arty poked his head over her shoulder, and she closed it hastily, but he had already gotten a good look.

"What is that, a secret code? Abstract art?"

"It's just math," Charlie said a little curtly, and put the notebook in her bag. Arty was cute in a goofy way. He had a pleasant face, dark eyes, and curly brown hair that seemed to have a life of its own. He was in three of her four classes and had been following her around since the beginning of the semester like a stray duckling. To her surprise, Charlie found that she didn't mind it.

As Charlie left the auditorium, Arty took up his now-accustomed place at her side.

"So, did you decide about the project?" he asked.

"Project?" Charlie vaguely remembered something about a project he wanted to do together. He gave a little nod, waiting for her to catch up.

"Remember? We have to design an experiment for chem? I thought we could work together. You know, with your brains and my looks . . ." He trailed off, grinning.

"Yeah, that sounds—I have to go meet someone," she interrupted herself.

"You never meet anyone," he said, surprised, blushing bright red as soon as the words were out of his mouth. "I didn't mean it that way. Not that it's any of my business, but, who is it?" He gave a broad smile.

"John," Charlie said without elaboration. Arty looked crestfallen for a moment but recovered quickly.

"Of course, yeah. John. Great guy," he said teasingly. He

raised his eyebrows, prompting for details, but she gave none. "I didn't know you were—that you had a—that's cool." Arty's face took on a look of careful neutrality. Charlie looked at him oddly. She hadn't meant to imply that she and John were a couple but she didn't know how to correct him. She couldn't explain who John was to her without telling Arty far more than she wanted him to know.

They walked in silence for a minute across the main quad, a small, grassy square surrounded by brick and concrete buildings.

"So, is John from your hometown?" Arty asked at last.

"My hometown is thirty minutes away. This place is basically just an extension of it," Charlie said. "But yeah, he's from Hurricane." Arty hesitated, then leaned in closer to her, glancing around as if someone might be listening.

"I always meant to ask you," he said.

Charlie looked at him wearily. *Don't ask about it.*

"I'm sure people ask you about it all the time, but come on—you can't blame me for being curious. That stuff about the murders, it's like an urban legend around here. I mean, not just around here. Everywhere. Freddy Fazbear's Pizza—"

"Stop." Charlie's face was suddenly immobile. She felt as if moving it, making any expression at all, would require an arcane skill she no longer possessed. Arty's face had changed, too. His easy smile drained away. He looked almost frightened. Charlie bit the inside of her lip, willing her mouth to move.

"I was just a kid when all that happened," she said quietly. Arty nodded, quick and skittish. Charlie made her face move into a smile. "I have to go meet Jessica," she lied. *I have to get away from you.* Arty nodded his head again like a bobblehead doll. She turned and walked away toward the dorm, not looking back.

Charlie blinked into the sunlight. Flashes of what happened last year at Freddy's were batting at her, snatches of memory plucking at her clothing with cold, iron fingers. *The hook above, poised to strike—no escape. A figure looming behind the stage; red matted fur barely concealing the metal bones of the murderous creature. Kneeling in pitch-dark on the cold tile floor of the bathroom, and then—that giant, hard plastic eye glaring through the crack, the hot miasma of lifeless breath on her face.* And the other, older memory: *the thought that made her ache in ways for which she had no words, sorrow filling her as if it had been wrought into her very bones. She and Sammy, her other self, her twin brother, were playing their quiet games in the familiar warmth of the costume closet. Then the figure appeared in the doorway, looking down on them. Then Sammy was gone, and the world ended for the first time.*

Charlie was standing outside her own dorm room, almost without knowing how she'd gotten there. Slowly, she pulled her keys from her pocket and let herself into the room. The lights were off; Jessica was still in class. Charlie shut the door behind her, checking the lock twice, and leaned back against it. She took a deep breath. *It's over now.* She straightened decisively and snapped on the overhead light, filling the room with a harsh illumination. The clock beside the bed told Charlie that she still had a little under an hour before John arrived—time to work on her project.

Charlie and Jessica had divided the room with a piece of masking tape after their first week living together. Jessica suggested it jokingly, said she'd seen it in a movie, but Charlie had grinned and helped her measure the room. She knew Jessica was desperate to keep Charlie's mess off her side. The result was a bedroom that looked like a "before and after" picture advertising either a cleaning service or a nuclear weapon, depending on whose side you looked at first.

On Charlie's desk there was a pillowcase, draped over two indistinct shapes. She went to her desk and removed it, folding it carefully and placing it on her chair. She looked at her project.

"Hello," she said softly.

Two mechanical faces were held upright on metal structures and attached to a length of board. Their features were indistinct, like old statues worn away by rain, or new clay not yet fully sculpted. They were made of a malleable plastic, and where the backs of their heads ought to be there were instead networks of casings, microchips, and wires.

Charlie bent down toward them, looking over every millimeter of her design, making sure everything was as she'd left it. She flipped a small black switch and little lights blinked; tiny cooling fans began to whir.

They didn't move right away, but there was a change. The vague features took on a sense of purpose. Their blind eyes didn't turn to Charlie: they looked only at each other.

"You," said the first. Its lips moved to shape the syllable, but never parted. They weren't made to open.

"I," the second replied, making the same soft, constrained movement.

"You are," said the first.

"Am I?" said the second.

Charlie watched, her hand pressed over her mouth. She held her breath, afraid of disturbing them. She waited, but they had apparently finished, and were now simply looking at each other. *They can't see*, Charlie reminded herself. She turned them off and pulled the board around so that she could peer into their backs. She reached inside and adjusted a wire.

A key slid into the lock of the door, and Charlie startled at the sound. She snatched the pillowcase and threw it over the faces as Jessica entered the room. Jessica paused in the doorway with a grin.

"What was that?" she asked.

"What?" Charlie said innocently.

"Come on, I know you were working on that thing you never let me see." She dropped her backpack on the floor, then flopped dramatically back on the bed. "Anyways, I'm exhausted!" she announced. Charlie laughed, and Jessica sat up. "Come talk to me," she said. "What's up with you and John?"

Charlie sat down on her own bed, across from Jessica. Despite their different lifestyles, she liked living with the other girl. Jessica was warm and bright, and while her ease as she went about the world still intimidated Charlie a little, now she felt like a part of it. Maybe being Jessica's friend meant absorbing some of her confidence.

"I haven't seen him yet. I have to leave in . . ." She peered over Jessica's shoulder at the clock. "Fifteen minutes."

"Are you excited?" Jessica asked.

Charlie shrugged. "I think so," she said.

Jessica laughed. "You're not sure?"

"I'm excited," Charlie admitted. "It's just been a long time."

"Not that long," Jessica pointed out. Then she looked thoughtful. "I guess it sort of has been, though. Everything is so different since the last time we saw him."

Charlie cleared her throat. "So you really want to see my project?" she asked, surprising herself.

"Yes!" Jessica declared, springing up from the bed. She followed Charlie to her desk. Charlie switched on the power then flung off the pillowcase like a magician. Jessica gasped and took an involuntary step back. "What is it?" she asked, her voice cautious. But before Charlie could answer, the first face spoke.

"Me," it said.

"You," the other replied, and they both fell silent again. Charlie looked at Jessica. Her friend had a pinched expression, like she was holding something tightly inside.

"I," the second face said.

Charlie hurried to switch them off. "Why do you have that look on your face?" she said.

Jessica took a deep breath and smiled at her. "I just haven't had lunch yet," she said, but something lingered in her eyes.

Jessica watched as Charlie replaced the pillowcase lovingly over the faces, as if she were tucking a child into bed. She looked uncomfortably around the room. Charlie's half was a disaster: clothes and books were strewn everywhere, but there were also the wires and computer parts, tools, screws, and pieces of plastic and metal Jessica didn't recognize, all jumbled up together. It wasn't just a mess; it was a chaotic tangle where you could lose anything. Or hide anything, she realized, with a pang of guilt at the thought. Jessica turned her attention back to Charlie.

"What are you programming them to do?" she asked, and Charlie smiled proudly.

"I'm not exactly programming them to do anything. I'm helping them learn on their own."

"Right, of course. Obviously," Jessica said slowly. As she did, something caught her eye: a pair of shiny plastic eyes and long floppy ears were peering out from a pile of dirty laundry.

"Hey, I never noticed you brought Theodore, your little robo-rabbit!" she exclaimed, pleased to have remembered the name of Charlie's childhood toy. Before Charlie could respond, she picked the stuffed animal up by his ears—and came away with only his head.

Jessica let out a shriek and dropped it, clapping a hand over her mouth.

"I'm sorry!" Charlie said, hastily grabbing the rabbit's head off the floor. "I took him apart to study; I'm using some of his parts in my project." She gestured at the thing on her desk.

"Oh," Jessica said, trying to hide her dismay. She glanced around the room and suddenly realized that the rabbit's parts were everywhere. His cotton-ball tail was on Charlie's pillow, and a leg hung off the lamp above her desk. His torso lay in the corner, almost out of sight, ripped open savagely. Jessica looked at her friend's round, cheerful face, and frizzy shoulder-length brown hair. Jessica closed her eyes for a long moment.

*Oh, Charlie, what's wrong with you?*

"Jessica?" Charlie said. The girl's eyes were closed, her expression pained. "Jessica?" This time she opened her eyes and gave Charlie a sudden, bright smile, turning on cheer like a faucet. It was disconcerting, but Charlie had gotten used to it.

Jessica blinked hard, like she was resetting her brain. "So, are you nervous about seeing John?" she asked. Charlie thought for a moment.

"No. I mean, why should I be? It's just John, right?" Charlie tried to laugh, but gave up. "Jessica, I don't know what to talk about!" she burst out suddenly.

"What do you mean?"

"I don't know what to talk about *with him!*" Charlie said. "If we don't have something to talk about, then we'll start talking about . . . what happened last year. And I just can't."

"Right." Jessica looked thoughtful. "Maybe he won't bring it up," she offered.

Charlie sighed, glancing back at her covered experiment with longing. "Of course he will. It's all we have in common." She sat down heavily on her bed and slumped over.

"Charlie, you don't have to talk about anything you don't want to talk about," Jessica said gently. "You can always just cancel on him. But I don't think John's going to put you on the spot. He cares about you. I doubt what happened in Hurricane is what's on his mind."

"What does *that* mean?"

"I just mean . . ." Jessica gingerly pushed aside a pile of laundry and sat next to Charlie, placing a hand on her knee.

"I just mean that maybe it's time that you *both* move past that. And I think John is trying to."

Charlie looked away and stared fixedly at Theodore's head, facedown on the floor. *You mean, get over it? How do I even begin?*

Jessica's voice softened. "This can't be your whole life anymore."

"I know." Charlie sighed. She decided to change the subject. "How was your class, anyway?" Charlie wiped her eyes, hoping Jessica would take the hint.

"Awesome." Jessica stood and stretched, bending over to touch her toes and incidentally giving Charlie a chance to compose herself. When Jessica stood again, she was smiling brilliantly, back in character. "Did you know that corpses can be preserved in peat bogs like mummies?"

Charlie wrinkled her nose. "I do now. So is that what you're gonna do when you graduate? Crawl around in peat bogs looking for bodies?"

Jessica shrugged. "Maybe."

"I'll get you a hazmat suit for your graduation gift," Charlie joked. She looked at her watch. "Time to go! Wish me luck." She brushed her hair back with her hands, peering into the mirror that hung on the back of the door. "I feel like a mess."

"You look great." Jessica gave her an encouraging nod.

"I've been doing sit-ups," Charlie said awkwardly.

"Huh?"

"Forget it." Charlie grabbed her backpack and headed for the door.

"Go knock his socks off!" Jessica called as Charlie left.

"I don't know what that means!" Charlie replied, letting the door swing closed before she'd finished speaking.

Charlie spotted him as she approached the main entrance to the campus. John was leaning on the wall, reading a book. His brown hair was as messy as ever, and he was wearing a blue T-shirt and jeans, dressed more casually than the last time she'd seen him.

"John!" she called, her reluctance falling away as soon as she saw him. He put away his book, grinning widely, and hurried to her.

"Hey, Charlie," he said. They stood there awkwardly, then Charlie extended her arms to hug him. He held her tightly for a moment then abruptly released her.

"You got taller," she said accusingly, and he laughed.

"I did," he admitted. He gave her a searching look. "You look exactly the same, though," he said with a puzzled smile.

"I cut my hair!" Charlie said in mock-outrage. She ran her fingers through it, demonstrating.

"Oh yeah!" he said. "I like it. I just mean, you're the same girl I remember."

"I've been doing sit-ups," Charlie said with a rising panic.

"Huh?" John gave her a confused look.

"Never mind. Are you hungry?" Charlie asked. "I have about an hour before my next class. We could get a burger. There's a dining hall not far from here."

"Yeah, that would be great," John said. Charlie pointed across the quad.

"That way, come on."

"So what are you doing here?" Charlie asked as they sat down with their trays. "Sorry," she added. "Did that sound rude?"

"Not rude at all, although I would have also accepted, 'John, to what circumstance do I owe the pleasure of this delightful reunion?'"

"Yeah, that sounds like me," Charlie said drily. "But seriously, what are you doing here?"

"Got a job."

"In St. George?" she asked. "Why?"

"In Hurricane, actually," he said, his voice self-consciously casual.

"Aren't you in school somewhere?" Charlie asked.

John blushed, looking down at his plate for a moment. "I was going to, but . . . it's a lot of money to read books when a library card is free, you know? My cousin got me a job in construction, and I'm working on my writing when I can. I figured even if I'm gonna be an artist, I don't have to be a starving one." He took an illustrative bite of his hamburger, and Charlie grinned.

"So why here?" she insisted, and he held up a finger as he finished chewing.

"The storm," he said. Charlie nodded. The storm had hit Hurricane before Charlie came to St. George, and people talked about it in capital letters: The Storm. It wasn't the worst the area had ever seen, but it was close. A tornado had risen up from nowhere and ripped through whole towns, razing one house to the ground with sinister precision, while leaving the one next to it untouched. There hadn't been much damage in St. George, but Hurricane had seen real destruction.

"How bad is it?" Charlie asked, keeping her tone light.

"You haven't been?" John said incredulously, and it was Charlie's turn to look awkwardly away. She shook her head. "It's bad in places," he said. "Mostly on the outskirts of town. Charlie . . . I assumed you'd been." He bit his lip.

"What?" Something about his expression was worrying her.

"Your dad's house, it was one of the ones that got hit," he said.

"Oh." Something leaden was growing in Charlie's chest. "I didn't know."

"You really didn't even go back to check?"

"I didn't think of it," Charlie said. *That's not true.* She'd thought a thousand times of going back to her father's house. But it had never occurred to her that the house might have been hit in the storm. In her mind, it was impregnable, unchanging. It would always be there, just as her father had left it. She closed her eyes and pictured it. The front steps sagged in disrepair, but the house itself stood like a fortress, protecting what was inside. "Is it—gone?" Charlie asked, the words faint.

"No," John said quickly. "No, it's still there, just damaged. I don't know how much; I just drove by. I didn't think I should go there without you."

Charlie nodded, only half listening. She felt far away. She could see John, hear him, but there was a layer of something between them, between her and everything else, everything but the house itself.

"I would have thought—didn't your aunt tell you what happened?" John asked.

"I have to get to class," Charlie said. "It's that way." She gestured vaguely.

"Charlie, have *you* been okay?" She didn't look at him, and he placed his hand over hers. She still couldn't look up. She didn't want him to see her face.

"Okay," she repeated, then slipped her hand out from under his and shrugged her shoulders up and down, like she was trying to get something off her back. "I had my birthday," she offered, and she finally leveled her gaze to meet his.

"I'm sorry I missed it," John said.

"No, no, that's not . . ." She tipped her head from side to side, as if she could level out her thoughts, too. "Do you remember how I had a twin?"

"What?" John sounded puzzled. "Of course I do. I'm sorry, Charlie, is that what you meant about your birthday?" She nodded, making tiny motions. John held out his hand again, and she took it. She could feel his pulse through his thumb.

"Ever since we left Hurricane . . . You know how twins are supposed to be connected, have some kind of special bond?"

"Sure," he said.

"Ever since we left—ever since I found out he was real—I've felt like he was there with me. I know he's not. He's dead, but for that whole year, I didn't feel alone anymore."

"Charlie." John's hand tightened on hers. "You know you're not alone."

"No, I mean *really* not alone. Like I have another self: someone who's a part of me and is always with me. I've had these feelings before, but they came and went, and I didn't pay much attention to them. I didn't know they meant something. Then when I learned the truth, and those memories started coming back to me—John, I felt *whole* in a way I don't even know how to describe." Her eyes began to fill with tears and she pulled her hand back to brush them away.

"Hey," he said softly. "It's okay. That's great, Charlie. I'm glad you have that."

"No. No, that's the thing. I don't!" She met his eyes, desperate for him to understand what she was so awkwardly trying to say. "He's disappeared. That sense of completeness is gone."

"What?"

"It happened on my birthday. I woke up and I just felt—" She sighed, searching. There wasn't a word for it.

"Alone?" John said.

"Incomplete." She took a deep breath, pulling herself back together. "But the thing is, it's not just loss. It's—it's like he's trapped somewhere. I have these dreams where I can *feel* him on the other side of something, like he's so close to me, but he's stuck somewhere. Like he's in a box, or I'm in a box. I can't tell."

John stared at her, momentarily speechless. Before he could figure out what to say, Charlie stood abruptly. "I need to leave."

"Are you sure? You haven't even eaten," he said.

"I'm sorry—" She broke off. "John, it's so good to see you." She hesitated then turned to walk away, possibly for good. She knew she'd disappointed him.

"Charlie, would you like to go out with me tonight?" John's voice sounded stiff, but his eyes were warm.

"Sure, that would be great," she said, giving a half smile. "Don't you have to get back to work tomorrow, though?"

"It's only half an hour away," John said. He cleared his throat. "But I meant, do you want to *go out* with me?"

"I just said yeah," Charlie repeated, slightly irritated.

John sighed. "I mean on a date, Charlie."

"Oh." Charlie stared at him for a moment. "Right." *You don't have to do anything you don't want to do.* Jessica's voice echoed in her head. And yet . . . she realized she was smiling.

"Um, yes. Yes, a date. Okay, yeah. There's a movie theater in town?" she hazarded, vaguely recalling that movies were something people did on dates.

John nodded vigorously, apparently as lost at sea as she was, now that the question had been asked. "Can we have dinner first? There's that Thai place down the street. I can meet you there around eight?"

"Yeah, sounds good. 'Bye!" Charlie grabbed her backpack and hurried out the dining room door, realizing as she stepped into the sunshine that she'd left him to clean up their table alone. *Sorry.*

As Charlie headed across the quad to her next class, her step grew more purposeful. This was a basic computer science class. Writing code wasn't as exciting as what Dr. Treadwell taught, but Charlie still liked it. It was absorbing, detailed work. A single error could ruin everything. *Everything?* She thought of her impending date. The idea that a single error could ruin everything suddenly carried an awful weight.

Charlie hurried up the steps to the building and stopped short as a man blocked her path.

It was Clay Burke.

"Hey, Charlie." He smiled, but his eyes were grave. Charlie hadn't seen Hurricane's chief of police—her friend Carlton's father—since the night they'd escaped Freddy's together. Looking now at his weathered face, she felt a rush of fear.

"Mr. Burke, er, Clay. What are you doing here?"

"Charlie, do you have a second?" he asked. Her heart sped up.

"Is Carlton okay?" she asked urgently.

"Yes, he's fine," Burke assured her. "Walk with me. Don't worry about being late. I'll give you a note for class. At least, I *think* an officer of the law has authority do that." He winked, but Charlie didn't smile. Something was wrong.

Charlie followed him back down the stairs. When they were a dozen feet from the building, Burke stopped and met her gaze, as if he were looking for something.

"Charlie, we've found a body," he said. "I want you to take a look at it."

"You want *me* to look at it?"

"I need you to see it."

*Me.* She said the only thing she could.

"Why? Does it have to do with Freddy's?"

"I don't want to tell you anything until you've seen it," Burke said. He started walking again, and Charlie hurried to keep up with his long stride. She followed him to the parking lot just outside the main gate, and got into his car without a word. Charlie settled into her seat, a strange dread stirring within her. Clay Burke glanced at her and she gave a sharp, quick nod. He pulled the car out onto the road, and they headed back to Hurricane.

# CHAPTER TWO

So, how are you enjoying your classes?" Clay Burke asked in a jovial tone.

Charlie gave him a sardonic look. "Well, this is the first murder of the semester. So things have been going fine."

Burke didn't answer, apparently aware that further attempts to lighten the mood would fail. Charlie looked out the window. She thought often of going back to her father's house, but each time the memory of the place rose up she slammed it back down with almost physical force, cramming it into the tiny corners of her mind to gather dust. Now something was stirring in the dusty corners, and she feared she might not be able to keep it away much longer.

"Chief Burke—Clay," Charlie said. "How's Carlton been?"

He smiled. "Carlton's doing great. I tried to convince him to stay close for college, but he and Betty were adamant. Now he's out east, studying acting."

"Acting?" Charlie laughed, surprising herself.

"Well, he was always a prankster," Clay said. "I figured acting was the next logical step."

Charlie smiled. "Did he ever . . ." She looked out the window again. "Did you and he ever talk about what happened?" she asked with her face turned away. She could see Clay's reflection faintly in the window, distorted by the glass.

"Carlton talks to his mother more than he talks to me," he said plainly. Charlie waited for him to go on, but he remained silent. Though she and Jessica lived together, from the beginning they had an unspoken pact never to talk about Freddy's, except in the barest terms. She didn't know if Jessica was sometimes consumed by the memories, as she was. Maybe Jessica had nightmares, too.

But Charlie and Clay had no such pact. She took in shallow, quick breaths, waiting to hear how far he would go.

"I think Carlton had dreams about it," Clay said finally. "Sometimes in the morning he would come downstairs looking like he hadn't slept in a week, but he never told me what was going on."

"What about you? Do you think about it?" She was overstepping but Clay didn't seem ruffled.

"I try not to," he said gravely. "You know, Charlie, when

31

terrible things happen you can do one of two things: you can leave them behind or you can let them consume you."

Charlie set her jaw. "I'm not my father," she said.

Clay looked immediately contrite. "I know, I didn't mean that," he said. "I just meant you have to look forward." He flashed a nervous grin. "Of course, my wife would say there's a third thing: you can process the terrible things and come to terms with them. She's probably right."

"Probably," Charlie said distractedly.

"And what about you? How are you doing, Charlie?" Clay asked. It was the question she had practically solicited, but she didn't know how to answer it.

"I have dreams about it, I guess," she muttered.

"You guess?" he asked in a careful tone. "What kind of dreams?"

Charlie looked out the window again. There was a weight pressing on her chest. *What kind of dreams?*

Nightmares, but not of Freddy's. *A shadow in the doorway of the costume closet where we play. Sammy doesn't see; he's playing with his truck. But I look up. The shadow has eyes. Then everything is moving—hangers rattle and costumes sway. A toy truck drops hard on the floor.*

*I'm left alone. The air is growing thin, I'm running out. It's getting hard to breathe and I'll die like this, alone, in the dark. I pound against the closet wall, calling for help. I know he's there. Sammy is on the other side, but he doesn't answer my cries as I begin to gasp, choking for air. It is too dark to see, but even so I know my vision is going black, and in my chest my heart is slowing, each pump swelling me with pain as I struggle to call his name one more time—*

"Charlie?" Clay had pulled over and stopped the car without her noticing. Now he was looking at her with his piercing detective's gaze. She looked at him for a moment before she could remember how to answer, and she made herself smile.

"I've mostly been focused on school," she said.

Clay smiled at her but it didn't touch his eyes. He looked worried. *He's wishing he hadn't brought me*, she thought.

He opened his door but didn't get out of the car. The sun had begun to set as they drove, and now it was verging on dark. The turn signal was still on, flashing yellow onto the dirt road. Charlie watched it for a moment, hypnotized. She felt as if she might never move again, just sit here watching the endless, measured blinking of the light. Clay switched the signal off, and Charlie blinked, as if a spell had been broken. She straightened her spine and unbuckled her seat belt.

"Charlie," Clay said, not looking directly at her. "I'm sorry to ask this of you, but you're the only person who can tell me if this is what I think it is."

"Okay," she replied, suddenly alert. Clay sighed and got out of the car. Charlie followed close behind him. There was a barbed wire fence all along the road, and there were cows in the field beyond it. They stood around, chewing and staring in the vacant way of cows. Clay lifted the top wire for

Charlie and she climbed gingerly through. *When's the last time I got a tetanus shot?* she wondered as a barb caught briefly on her T-shirt.

She didn't have to ask where the body was. There was a floodlight and a makeshift fence of caution tape strung between posts that jutted from the soil in a scattered formation. Charlie stood where she was as Burke climbed through the fence after her, and they both surveyed the area.

The field was flat, and the grass was short and patchy, worn down daily by dozens of hooves. A single tree stood some distance from where the crime scene was marked. Charlie thought it was an oak. Its branches were long and ancient, heavy with leaves. There was something wrong with the air; along with the smell of cow dung and mud wafted the sharp, metallic scent of blood.

For some reason, Charlie looked at the cows again. They weren't as calm as she'd assumed. They shifted back and forth on their feet, clustering in groups. None of them came anywhere near the floodlight. As if sensing her scrutiny, one of them lowed a mournful cry. Charlie heard Clay's sharp intake of breath.

"Maybe we should ask *them* what happened," Charlie said. In the stillness, her voice carried. Clay started toward the floodlight. Charlie followed closely, not wanting to fall too far behind. It wasn't just the cows; a weight of something *wrong* hung over the place. There was no sound, only the shocked quiet that follows a terrible violence.

Clay stopped beside the marked-out spot and ushered Charlie forward, still saying nothing. Charlie looked.

It was a man, stretched in a ghastly posture on his back, his limbs contorted impossibly. In the glaring, unnatural light, the scene looked staged; he might have been an enormous doll. His whole body was drenched red with blood. His clothes were torn, almost shredded, and through the holes Charlie thought she could see ripped-up skin, some bone, and other things she couldn't identify.

"What do you make of it?" Clay said softly, as if he were afraid of disturbing her.

"I need to get closer," she said. Clay climbed over the yellow tape, and Charlie followed. She knelt in the mud beside the man's head, the knees of her jeans soaking with mud. He was middle-aged, white, his hair short and gray. His eyes, thankfully, were closed. The rest of his face slack in a way that could almost have looked like sleep, but did not. She leaned forward to peer at the man's neck and blanched, but didn't look away.

"Charlie, are you all right?" Clay asked, and she held up a hand.

"I'm fine." She knew those wounds; she'd seen the scars they left. On each side of the dead man's neck was a deep, curved gash. This was what had killed him. It would have been instantaneous. *Or maybe not.* Suddenly she pictured Dave, the guard at Freddy's, the murderer. She had watched him die. She'd triggered the spring locks and seen his startled eyes as the locks drove into his neck. She'd watched his body jolt and seize as the costume he wore shot jagged metal through his vital organs. Charlie stared at this stranger's wounds. She reached down and ran her finger along the edge of the cut on the man's neck. *What were you doing?*

"Charlie!" Clay said in alarm, and Charlie drew back her hand.

"Sorry," she said self-consciously, wiping her bloody fingers on her jeans. "Clay, it was one of them. His neck, he died like . . ." She stopped talking. Clay had been there; his son had almost died the same way. But if this was happening again, he had to know what he was dealing with.

"You remember how Dave died, right?" she asked.

Clay nodded. "Hard thing to forget." He shook his head, patiently waiting for her to get to the point.

"These suits, like the rabbit suit that Dave was wearing, they can be worn like costumes. Or they can move around on their own, as fully functional robots."

"Sure, you just put the suit on a robot," Clay said.

"Not exactly . . . The robots are always inside the suits; they're made of interlocking parts that are held back against the inner lining of the costumes by spring locks. When you want an animatronic, you just trip the locks, and the robotic parts unfold inside, filling the suit."

"But if there's someone inside the suit when the locks are tripped . . . ," Clay said, catching on.

"Right. Thousands of sharp metal parts shoot through your whole body. Like, well—that," she finished, gesturing at the man on the ground.

"How hard is it to accidentally trigger the spring locks?" Clay asked.

"It depends on the costume. If it's well cared for, pretty hard. If it's old, or poorly designed—it could happen. And if it's not an accident . . ."

"Is that what happened here?"

Charlie hesitated. Dave's image came to her again, this time alive, when he bared his torso to show them the scars he bore. Dave had once survived being crushed like this, though the second time had killed him. Somehow he had survived the lethal unfolding of a costume, a thing that should have been impossible. But it had left its marks. She cleared her throat and started again. "I need to see his chest," she said. "Can you get his shirt off?"

Clay nodded and took a pair of plastic gloves from his pocket. He tossed them to Charlie but they fell to the ground unnoticed. "If I'd known you were going to stick your fingers in the corpse, I'd have given these to you earlier," he said drily. He put on a pair of his own and produced a knife from somewhere on his belt. The man was wearing a T-shirt. Clay dropped to his knees, took hold of the bottom, and began to saw through the cloth. The sound of wet, tearing fabric cut through the silent field like a cry of pain. At last he was done, and he pulled back the shirt. Dried blood clung to the fabric, and as Clay pulled it back the body pulled with it, giving a brief, false sense of life. Charlie bent over, picturing Dave's scars. She compared the pattern to the wounds she saw here. *This is what happened to Dave.* Each piercing of the man's flesh seemed like a killing blow; any one of them might have punctured something vital, or simply been deep enough to drain him of blood in minutes. What was left of him was grotesque.

"It was one of them," Charlie said, looking up at Clay for the first time since they reached the body. "He must have been wearing one of the costumes. It's the only way he could end up like this. But . . ." Charlie paused and scanned the field again. "Where's the suit?"

"What would someone be doing wearing one of those things out here?" Clay said.

"Maybe he wasn't wearing it willingly," Charlie answered.

Clay leaned forward and reached for the man's open shirt, pulling it closed as best he could. Together they got up and headed back to the car.

As Clay drove her back to campus, Charlie stared out the window into the darkness.

"Clay, what happened to Freddy's?" she asked. "I hear it was torn down." She scratched her fingernail on the car seat nervously. "Is that true?"

"Yes. Well, they started to," Clay said slowly. "We went through the whole place, clearing everything out. It was a funny thing; we couldn't find the body of that guard, Dave." He paused and looked directly at Charlie, as though expecting her to answer for something.

Charlie felt the warmth drain from her face. *He's dead. I saw him die.* She closed her eyes for a moment and forced herself to focus.

"That place was like a maze, though." Clay turned his eyes casually back to the road. "His body probably got stuffed into some crevice no one will find for years."

"Yeah, probably buried in the rubble." She looked down, trying to put the thought out of her head for the moment. "What about the costumes, the robots?" Clay hesitated. *You must have known I would ask*, Charlie thought with some annoyance.

"Everything we took out of Freddy's was thrown away or burned. Technically I should have treated it like what it was: a break in the missing kids case, over a decade old. Everything would have been bagged up and gone over. But no one would have believed what happened there, what we saw. So I took some liberties." He glanced at Charlie, the suspicious look gone from his face, and she nodded for him to continue. Clay took a deep breath. "I treated it only as the murder of my officer; you remember Officer Dunn. We recovered his body, closed the case, and I ordered the building to be demolished."

"What about . . ." Charlie paused, trying not to let her frustration show. "What about Freddy, and Bonnie, and Chica, and Foxy?" *What about the children, the children who were killed and hidden inside each one of them?*

"They were all there," Clay said gravely. "They were lifeless, Charlie. I don't know what else to tell you." Charlie didn't respond.

"As far as the demolition crew was concerned, all they'd found were old costumes, broken robots, and two dozen folding tables. And I didn't correct them," he said with hesitation in his voice. "You know how these things go. Whether building up or tearing down, it takes time. From what I hear, the storm hit and suddenly everyone was needed elsewhere; the demolition was put on hold."

"So it's all still standing there?" Charlie asked, and Clay gave her a warning look.

"Some parts are standing, but for all intents and purposes, it's gone. And don't even think about going back there. There's no reason to and you'll get yourself killed. Like I said, everything that mattered is gone anyway."

"I don't want to go back there," Charlie said softly.

When they reached the campus, Clay let her out where

he'd found her. She'd only taken a few steps from the car, however, when he called to her from the car window. "I feel like I need to tell you one more thing," he said. "We found blood at the scene, in the main dining room where Dave . . ." He looked around cautiously. There was something unseemly, talking about gruesome things on the sheltered grounds of the campus. "It wasn't real blood, Charlie."

"What are you talking about?" Charlie took a step back toward the car.

"It was, like, costume blood, or movie blood. It was pretty convincing, though. We didn't realize it was fake until the crime lab looked at it under a microscope."

"Why are you telling me this?" Charlie asked, although she knew the answer. The terrible possibility was pounding in her mind like a headache.

"He survived once," Clay said plainly.

"Well, he didn't survive the second time." Charlie turned to walk away.

"I'm sorry you have to be involved in this," Clay called.

Charlie didn't answer. She looked down at the pavement and clenched her teeth. Clay raised the window without another word and drove away.

# CHAPTER THREE

Charlie checked her watch: she was on time to meet John, even early. She passed under a streetlight and looked down at herself, checking her clothes. *Oh no.* The knees of her jeans were wet with mud, and there was a dark stain where she had wiped her fingers clean of the dead man's blood. *I can't show up covered in blood. He's seen me like this too many times already.* She sighed and turned around.

Thankfully, Jessica was gone when she got back to the room. Charlie didn't want to talk about what had just happened. Clay hadn't explicitly told her to keep it a secret, but she was fairly sure she shouldn't broadcast her private visit to a crime scene. Charlie cast a glance at the faces under their pillowcase cover, but didn't go to them. She wanted to show her project to John, but, like Jessica, he might not understand.

She opened a dresser drawer and stared down at the contents without registering them. In her mind, she saw the body again, its limbs splayed out as if it had been thrown down where it lay. She covered her face with her hands, taking deep breaths. She had seen the scars, but she'd never seen the wounds of the spring locks fresh. Now Dave's eyes came to her, the look of shock just before he fell. Charlie could feel the locks in her hands, feel them resist, then give way and snap. *That's what happened. That's what I did.* She swallowed, and slid her hands down to her throat.

Charlie shook her head like a dog shaking off a wet coat. She looked at the open drawer again, concentrating. *I need to change. What is all this?* The drawer was filled with brightly colored shirts, all unfamiliar. Charlie startled, a dim panic seizing her. *What is all this?* She picked up a T-shirt and dropped it again, then forced herself to take a deep breath. *Jessica. They're Jessica's.* She'd opened the wrong drawer.

*Get it together, Charlie,* she told herself sternly, and somehow it sounded like Aunt Jen's voice in her head. Despite everything that lay between her and her aunt, just imagining her cold, authoritative voice made Charlie a little calmer. She nodded to herself, then grabbed what she needed: a clean T-shirt and jeans. She dressed hurriedly, then left to meet

John, her stomach fluttering, half-excited, half-sick. *A date,* she thought. *What if it doesn't go well? Worse, what if it does?*

As she neared the Thai restaurant, she saw that John was already there. He was waiting outside, but he didn't look impatient. He didn't spot her right away, and Charlie slowed her pace for a moment, watching him. He seemed at ease, gazing into the middle distance with a vague, pleasant expression. He had an air of confidence he hadn't possessed a year ago. It wasn't that he'd been unsure of himself then, but now he looked . . . adult. Maybe it was because he'd gone straight to work after high school. *Maybe it was what happened last year at Freddy's,* Charlie thought with an unexpected sense of envy. Although she'd moved out on her own, to a new home and a new college, she felt as if the experience had left her more a child, not less. Not a cared-for or protected child, but one who was vulnerable and unmoored. A child who had looked under the bed and seen the monsters.

John noticed her and waved. Charlie waved back and smiled, the expression unforced. Date or not, it was good to see him.

"How was your last class?" he said by way of greeting, and Charlie shrugged.

"I don't know. It was class. How was the rest of work?"

He grinned. "It was work. Are you hungry?"

"Yes," Charlie said decisively. They headed inside and were motioned to a table.

"Have you been here before?" John asked, and Charlie shook her head.

"I don't get out much," she said. "I don't even come out to town that often. The college is sort of its own little world, you know?"

"I can imagine," John said cheerfully. Now that the secret was out that he wasn't in school, he'd apparently shed his earlier discomfort. "Isn't it a little bit . . . ?" he searched for words. "Doesn't it feel a little isolated?"

"Not really," Charlie said. "If it's a prison, it's not one of the worst."

"I didn't mean to compare it to a prison!" John said. "So, come on, what are you studying?"

Charlie hesitated. There was no reason not to tell John, but it seemed too soon, too risky to announce that she was eagerly following in her father's footsteps. She didn't want to tell him she was studying robotics until she had some idea of how he would respond. Just like with her project.

"Most colleges make you do a set of classes your first year: English, math, everything like that," she said, hoping it would sound like a response. Suddenly Charlie didn't want to talk about school; she wasn't sure she could keep up a conversation about *anything*, really. She looked at John, and for a moment imagined the spring-lock wounds in his neck. Her eyes widened and she bit the inside of her cheek, trying to ground herself.

"Tell me about your job," she said, and saw her own hesitation mirrored on his face.

"I mean, I like the work," he said. "More than I thought I would, actually. There's something about doing physical labor that kind of frees my mind. It's like meditation. It's hard, though, really hard. Construction workers always make it look so easy, but it turns out it takes a while to build up that kind of muscle." He stretched his arms comically over his head, and Charlie laughed, but couldn't help noticing that he was clearly well on his way to that kind of muscle. John leaned to his left and gave his armpit a quick sniff, then made a look of mock-embarrassment. Charlie looked down at her menu and giggled.

"Do you already know what you want?" she said. Then the waitress appeared out of nowhere, as if she'd been listening nearby.

John ordered, and Charlie froze. She'd said it just to say something, but she didn't know what to get. Suddenly she noticed all the prices. Everything on the menu was impossibly expensive. She hadn't even thought about money when she accepted John's invitation, but now her mind jumped to her wallet, and her nearly empty bank account.

Misreading her expression, John leaped in. "If you've never had Thai food, Pad Thai is good," he suggested. "I should have asked," he said awkwardly. "If I'm buying a lady dinner, I should make sure she likes the food!" He looked embarrassed, but Charlie was flooded with relief. *Buying a lady dinner.*

"No, I'm sure I'll like it," she said. "Pad Thai, thanks," she told the waitress, then gave John a mock-glare. "Who are you calling a lady?" she said playfully, and he laughed.

"What's wrong with that?"

"It just sounds weird, you calling me a lady," Charlie said. "So anyway, what do you all day besides meditate?"

"Well, the days are long, and like I said, I'm still writing, so there's that. It's strange being in Hurricane again, though. I didn't mean to put down roots."

"Put down roots?"

"Like, join a bowling team or something. Ties to the community, things like that."

Charlie nodded. She of all people understood the need to remain apart. "Why did you take the job here, then?" she asked. "I know they needed people because of the storm, but you didn't *have* to come, right? People are still building things in other places."

"That's true," he admitted. "To be honest, it was more about getting away from where I was."

"Sounds familiar," Charlie muttered, too softly for him to hear.

The waitress returned with their food. Charlie took a quick bite of rice noodles and immediately burned her mouth. She grabbed her water glass and drank. "Yikes, that's hot!" she said. "So what were you getting away from?" She asked the question casually, as if the answer would be simple. *Do you have nightmares, too?* She held back the words, waiting for him to speak.

John hesitated. "A . . . girl, actually," he said. He paused, searching for a reaction. Charlie stopped chewing; that wasn't at all the answer she'd been expecting. She swallowed, nodding with self-conscious enthusiasm. After an excruciating silence, John went on.

"We started dating the summer after . . . after Freddy's. I told her I wasn't looking for anything serious, she said she wasn't, either. Then suddenly it was six months later, and we were serious. I had just started working. I'd moved out on my own, and had this grown-up relationship. It was a shock, but a good one, I guess." He stopped, not sure whether he should continue. Charlie wasn't sure she wanted to give him permission.

"So, tell me about her," she said calmly, avoiding eye contact.

"She was—is, I mean. I'm not dating her, but it's not like she's dead. Her name is Rebecca. She's pretty, I guess. Smart. She's a year older than me, a college student studying English; has a dog. So yeah, she was all right."

"What happened?"

"I don't know," he said.

"Really," Charlie said drily, and he smiled.

"No. I felt . . . on guard around her. Like there were things I couldn't tell her, things she'd just *never* understand. It wasn't because of her. She was great. But she knew I was holding something back; she just didn't know what it was."

"I wonder what it could have been?" Charlie asked quietly. The question was rhetorical; they both knew the answer.

John smiled. "Well, anyway, she broke up with me, and I was devastated, blah, blah, blah. Actually, I don't think I was that devastated." John looked down, focusing on his food but not touching it.

"Have *you* ever tried to tell anyone about Freddy's?" John glanced back up and pointed his fork at Charlie. She shook her head. "It wasn't just what happened," he went on. "I can't imagine telling that story and having her believe me, but it wasn't only that. I wanted her to know the facts of it, but more, I wanted to tell her what it did to me. How it changed me."

"It changed all of us," Charlie said.

"Yeah, and not just last year. From the beginning. I didn't realize it until after we'd all gone back, how much that place had just . . . *followed* me." He glanced at Charlie. "Sorry, it must be even weirder for you."

Charlie shrugged uncomfortably. "Maybe. I think it's just different."

Her hand was resting on the table beside her water glass, and now John reached out to touch it. She stiffened, and he drew back.

"Sorry," he said. "I'm sorry."

"It's not you," Charlie said quickly. *His dead face, the dead skin of his throat.* She had barely noticed it at the time, overwhelmed by the whole experience, but now the feeling of the dead man's neck came back to her. It was as if she were touching him right now. She could feel his skin, slack and cold, and slick with blood; she could feel the blood on her fingers. She rubbed her hands together. They were clean— she knew they were clean—but still she could feel the blood. *You're being dramatic.*

"I'll be right back," she said, and got up before John could respond. She made her way around the tables to the bathrooms at the back of the restaurant. It was a three-stall bathroom; thankfully it was empty. Charlie went straight to the sink and turned the hot water on full-blast. She pumped soap onto her hands and scrubbed them for a long time. She closed her eyes and focused on the feeling of hot water and soap, and slowly the memory of blood faded. As she dried her hands she looked at herself in the mirror: her reflection looked wrong somehow, off, as if it wasn't herself she saw, but a copy. Someone else dressed as her. *Get it together, Charlie,* she thought, trying to hear the words in Aunt Jen's voice, as she had before. She closed her eyes. *Get it together.* When she opened them again she was back in the mirror. Her reflection was her own.

Charlie smoothed her hair, and went back out to the table, where John was waiting for her with a concerned expression.

"Is everything okay?" he asked nervously. "Did I do something?"

Charlie shook her head. "No, of course not. It's been a long day, that's all." *There's an understatement.* She glanced at her watch. "Do we still have time for a movie?" she asked. "It's almost eight thirty."

"Yeah, we should go," John said. "Are you done?"

"Yeah, it was really good, thank you." She smiled at him. "The 'lady' liked it." John smiled back, visibly relaxing. He went to the counter to pay, and Charlie went outside, waiting for him on the sidewalk. Dark had fallen, and there was a chill in the air. Charlie wished briefly that she'd thought to bring a sweatshirt. John joined her after a moment.

"Ready?"

"Yeah," Charlie said. "Where is it?"

He looked at her for a moment and shook his head. "The movie was your idea, remember?" He laughed.

"Like I said, I don't get out much." Charlie looked down at her feet.

"The theater's only a few blocks away."

They walked in silence for a while.

"I found out what happened to Freddy's," she said without thinking, and John looked at her, surprised.

"Really? What happened?"

"They were tearing it down, then the storm came and everyone got called away. Now it's just standing there, half collapsed. All the stuff is gone, though," she added, seeing the question in John's eyes. "I don't know what they did with . . . them." It was a lie; Charlie couldn't tell him what had really happened without telling him how she knew. All those questions led back to the same place: the dead man in the field. *Who were you?*

"What about your father's house?" John asked. "Did you ask your aunt Jen about it? What's she going to do with it?"

"I don't know," Charlie said. "I haven't talked to her since August." She fell silent, not looking at John as they walked.

They reached their destination, a shabby, one-screen movie theater named the Grand Palace. Its name was either ironic or wishful thinking. Emblazoned on the marquee was their current showing: *Zombies vs. Zombies!*

"I think it's about zombies," John joked as they went inside.

The movie had already started. Someone onscreen was screaming, as what were apparently zombies came at her from all sides. She was surrounded. The creatures crouched like wild dogs, ready to spring and devour her. They moved to attack—and a man grabbed her arm, pulling her to safety.

"Charlie." John touched her arm, whispering. "Over there." He gestured to the back row. The place was half-full, but the back row was empty, and they made their way furtively to the middle. They sat, and Charlie turned her attention to the screen. *Thank goodness*, she thought. *Maybe we can finally relax.*

She settled back in her seat, letting the images on the screen blur past her. Shrieks, gunfire, and thrumming music filled the silence between them. From the corner of her eye she saw John glance at her nervously. Charlie focused her attention on the movie. The main characters, a man and woman with the generic, angular good looks of the big screen, were shooting automatic weapons into a crowd of zombies. As the first ranks were killed—not killed, stopped; though severed in half by the guns, they still twitched on the ground—the ones behind climbed over their fallen cohorts. The camera switched back to the man and woman, who jumped a fence and took off running. Behind them the zombies kept coming, struggling forward, oblivious to the undead bodies they waded through. The music was urgent, the baseline pounding like an artificial heartbeat, and Charlie relaxed against the seat, letting herself be absorbed into it all.

*What was he doing there?* The image of the dead man returned to her. Something about the wounds bothered her, but she hadn't been able to put her finger on it. *I recognized* those wounds. *They all matched what I remembered, but* something *was different. What was it?*

She sensed movement next to her, and saw John trying to stretch an arm toward her. *Really?* she thought.

"Do you have enough room?" she asked him, and scooted away without waiting for a response. He looked embarrassed, but she glanced away, planting her elbow on the other armrest and staring fixedly at the screen.

*Enough room, that's it.* She closed her eyes, concentrating on the image in her head. *The wounds were slightly larger and more spaced out. The suit he was wearing was bigger than the suits from Freddy's. The man was probably five foot ten or five foot eleven, which means the suits must have been at least seven feet tall.*

Onscreen, there was quiet again, but it was short lived. Charlie watched, mesmerized, as the dirt spilled away of its own volition, moving like magic as the zombie rose. *It wouldn't be like that,* Charlie thought definitively. *It's not that easy to get out of a grave.* By now the zombie onscreen was halfway out, crawling to the surface and looking around with its glassy, mindless eyes. *You can't get out that fast.* Charlie blinked and shook her head, trying to stay focused.

*Zombies. Lifeless things. The closet was full of costumes, lifeless yet ever-watching, with plastic eyes and dead, hanging limbs. Somehow their corpselike stares had never bothered her, or Sammy. They liked to touch the fur, sometimes put it in their mouths and giggle at the funny way it felt. Some was old and matted; some new and soft. The closet was their place, just for the two of them. Sometimes they babbled together in words that had meaning only to them; sometimes they played side by side, lost in separate worlds of make-believe. But they were always together. Sammy was playing with a truck when the shadow came. He ran it back and forth on the floor, not noticing that their ribbon of light had been cut off. Charlie turned and saw the shadow, so still he could be an illusion, just another costume out of place. Then the sudden movement, the chaos of fabric and eyes. The truck clanked as it fell to the floor, and then: loneliness. A dark so complete that she began to believe she'd never seen at all. The memories of sight had only been a dream, a trick of the utter blackness. She tried to call his name—she could feel him nearby—but all around her were solid walls. "Can you hear me? Sammy? Let me out! Sammy!" But he was gone, and he was never there again.*

"Charlie, are you okay?"

"What?" Charlie looked at John. She realized she'd pulled her feet up on the chair and was hugging her knees to her chest. She sat back, setting her shoes back on the floor. John gave her a concerned look. "I'm fine," she whispered, and gestured to the screen.

John put a hand on her forearm. "Are you sure you're okay?" he asked.

Charlie stared straight ahead. Now there were people running, the zombies lurching after them. "This doesn't make sense," Charlie muttered, mostly to herself.

"What?" John leaned toward her.

Charlie didn't move, but she repeated herself. "It doesn't make sense. Zombies don't make sense; if they're dead, the central nervous system is shot, and they can't do any of this. If there's a functioning central nervous system, which has somehow decayed to the point that movement and thought are possible, but severely hindered, fine. If it makes them violent, fine. But why would they want to eat brains? It doesn't make sense."

*That man wouldn't have been able to walk on his own in a suit so oversized. He didn't walk into that field; the suit did. The animatronic was carrying him inside. It walked into that field of its own accord.*

"Maybe it's symbolic," John suggested, eager to engage, however odd the conversation. "You know, like the idea that you eat your enemy's heart to gain their power? Maybe the zombie eats its enemy's brain to gain its . . . central nervous system?" He glanced at Charlie, but she was only half listening.

"Okay," she said. She'd been irritated by the movie, now she was irritated by the conversation she herself had introduced. "I'll be right back," she told John, and got up without waiting for him to respond. She made her way out of the row, through the lobby, and out the door. On the sidewalk, she took a deep breath and felt an intense relief at the wash of fresh air. *Dreams about being trapped are common,* she reminded herself. She'd looked it up when they began. They were only slightly less common than dreams of showing up to class naked, plummeting from a great height, or having your teeth all suddenly fall out. *But this didn't feel like a dream.*

Charlie jostled her thoughts back to the present, where even the crime scene of a gruesome murder seemed like a safer place to keep them.

*There must be tracks. He didn't walk there himself. There must be some clue of what carried him into that field, and where it came from.*

Charlie shivered. She went back inside the building. *John's going to think I'm nuts.* She arrived at the swinging theater doors and stopped—she couldn't do it. She had to know. There was a young man at the concession stand, and she asked him if the place had a pay phone. He pointed silently to his right, and Charlie went, fishing in her pocket for a quarter, and for Chief Burke's card.

She dialed carefully, pausing between numbers to check the card again, as if the writing might have changed since she looked. Clay Burke answered on the third ring.

"Burke."

"Clay? It's Charlie."

"Charlie? What's wrong?" He was instantly alert; Charlie could picture him leaping to his feet, ready to run.

"Nothing, I'm fine," she assured him. "Everything is okay, I just wanted to see if you've found anything else."

"Not so far," he told her.

"Oh." Burke let the silence stretch between them, and Charlie finally broke it. "Is there anything else you can tell me? I know it's confidential, but you've brought me in this far. Please, if there's anything else you know. Anything else you found, anything you know about the man—the victim."

"No," Clay said slowly. "I mean, I'll let you know when we find something."

"Okay," Charlie said. "Thanks."

"I'll be in touch."

"Okay." Charlie hung up the phone before he could say good-bye. "I don't believe you," she said to the phone on the wall.

Back in the theater, her eyes took a moment to adjust as she inched along the back row toward her seat, careful not to make noise. John looked up at her with a smile as she sat down, but didn't say anything. Charlie smiled back with a grim determination, and settled back in her seat, then scooted over until her shoulder was pressed against his. From behind her head, she heard him make a surprised noise, then he shifted, putting his arm around her shoulders. He gripped her tightly for a moment, halfway to a hug, and Charlie leaned in a little, unsure how else to reciprocate.

*What if someone put him in the costume, like some kind of wind-up deathtrap? Stuck him inside that thing, then sent it walking until the spring locks went off. But who would know how to do that? Why would someone do that?*

"Did I miss anything?" Charlie asked, though she hadn't paid any attention to the first half of the movie anyway. It was daytime onscreen, and it looked like there were more people, holed up in some sort of bunker. Charlie couldn't remember which of them had been the original characters. She wriggled in her seat; John's arm around her had relaxed, but now the arm of the seat was digging into her side. He started to move away, but she settled herself again.

"No, it's okay," she whispered, and his arm circled her again. "Just get on with it," Charlie said, flustered. John startled.

"Sorry, I didn't want to be too aggressive."

"No, not you." Charlie gestured toward the screen. "They should just build a minefield around the bunker and wait for them to all blow up. The end."

"I think that's actually what they do in the sequel, but we'll have to wait to watch it for ourselves." He winked.

"There's another one?" She sighed.

When the credits started to roll, they gathered their things and headed to the exits with the rest of the small crowd, not speaking until they got outside. On the sidewalk, they stopped.

"This has been nice," John said, sounding—somehow—like he meant it, and Charlie laughed, then groaned, covering her face with both hands.

"This has been *awful*. This has been the worst date ever. I'm so sorry. Thanks for lying, though."

John gave an uncertain smile. "It was nice to see you," he said with cautious levity.

"It's just—can we go somewhere to talk?"

John nodded, and Charlie started back toward campus with him following behind.

The quad was usually empty late at night, or at least mostly empty. There was always someone walking across, some student finishing up late night work in a lab, some couple ensconced in a dark corner. Tonight was no different, and it was easy enough to find their own dark corner to talk. Charlie sat down under a tree, and John copied her, then waited for her to talk as she stared at the gap between two buildings, where you could almost see the woods.

Finally, he prompted her. "So what's up?"

"Right." She met his eyes. "Clay came to see me today." John's eyes widened, but he didn't say anything. "He took me to see a body," Charlie went on. "He had died inside one of the mascot costumes."

John was frowning; she could almost see his thoughts, working through what this meant, and why it involved Charlie.

"That's not all: Clay told me that they found blood in the main dining room at Freddy's. Fake blood."

John's head jerked up. "You think Dave's alive?"

Charlie shrugged. "Clay didn't come out and say it. But all those scars—he had survived the spring locks of a mascot costume before. He must have known how to escape the building."

"It didn't look to me like he escaped," John said doubtfully.

"He could have faked it; it would certainly explain the blood."

"So what then? Dave is alive and stuffing people into spring-lock suits and killing them?"

"If I could just go back to the restaurant one more time, to make sure that—" Charlie stopped, suddenly aware of growing anger in John's face.

"To make sure that *what*?" he asked sternly.

"Nothing. Clay has it under control. Everything is best left with the police." She clenched her jaw, gazing out over the horizon.

*Jessica will go with me.*

"Right," John said with a surprised look. "Right, you're right."

Charlie nodded with forced enthusiasm.

"Clay has men for this sort of thing," she continued with a furrowed brow. "I'm sure they're on top of it."

John took Charlie's shoulders lightly. "I'm sure it's not

what you think it is, anyway," he said in a hearty, reassuring tone. "There's a lot of crime in this world that doesn't involve self-imploding furry robot suits." He laughed and Charlie forced a smile.

"Come on." John extended a hand and Charlie took it. "I'll walk you to your dorm."

"I appreciate the gesture," she said. "But Jessica's there, and we'd have to go through the whole reunion, you know?"

John laughed. "Okay, I'll save you from Jessica and her relentless camaraderie."

Charlie grinned. "My hero. Where are you staying, anyway?"

"That little motel you stayed at last year, actually," John said. "I'll see you tomorrow maybe?"

Charlie nodded and watched him go, then started on her own way home. Excruciating though the date had been, the last half hour felt like a homecoming. It was her and John again; they were familiar again. "All we needed was a good old-fashioned murder," she said aloud, and a woman walking her dog gave Charlie an odd look as she passed in the opposite direction. "I was at a movie, *Zombies vs. Zombies!*" Charlie called halfheartedly after her retreating back. "You should go check it out! They don't put mines around the bunker; spoiler alert."

Charlie had half hoped Jessica would be asleep, but the

lights were on when she reached their room. She flung open the door before Charlie had her key out of her pocket, her face flushed.

"So?" Jessica demanded.

"So what?" Charlie asked, grinning in spite of herself. "Hey, before you start into this, I need to ask you something."

"So you know what!" Jessica cried, ignoring her question. "Tell me about John. How did it go?"

Charlie felt the corner of her mouth twitch. "Oh, you know," she said casually. "Listen, I need you to go somewhere with me in the morning."

"Charlieee! You have to tell me!" Jessica moaned exaggeratedly, and flopped back on her bed. Then she sprang back up into a sitting position. "Come here and tell me!" Charlie sat, drawing her legs up under her.

"It was weird," she admitted. "I didn't know what to say. Dates just seem so . . . uncomfortable. But about what I was saying—"

"But it's John. Shouldn't that outweigh the 'date' part?"

"Well, it didn't," Charlie said. She looked at the floor. She could tell her face was red, and suddenly she wished she hadn't told Jessica anything at all.

Jessica put her hands on Charlie's shoulders and looked at her seriously. "You are amazing, and if John isn't just falling all over himself for you, that's his problem."

Charlie giggled. "I think he kind of is. It's *part* of the problem. But there is something else if you would just listen for a second."

"Oh, there's more?" Jessica laughed. "Charlie! You need to save *something* for the second date, you know."

"What? No, no. *NO!* I need you to go somewhere with me in the morning."

"Charlie I have a lot going on right now; I have exams coming up, and . . ."

"I need you . . ." Charlie clenched her jaw for a moment. "I need you to help me pick out new clothes for my next date," she said carefully, then waited to see if Jessica would believe a word of it.

"Charlie are you kidding me? We'll go first thing in the morning!" She jumped up and gave Charlie a giant hug. "We'll have a girls' day out! It will be amazing!" Jessica flopped back to her bed. "Sleep for now, though."

"It won't bother you if I work on my project for a while, will it?"

"Not at all." Jessica waved limply, then went still.


Charlie turned on her work lamp: a single, bright beam that was focused enough to not illuminate the whole room. She uncovered the faces; they were at rest, their features smooth as if in sleep, but she didn't turn them on yet. The switches that made them move and talk were only one part of the whole. There was another component: the part that made them listen was always on. Everything that she and Jessica said, every word spoken in the room, outside the window, or even in the hall, they heard. Each new word went into their databases, not only as a single word, but in all its configurations as they emerged. Each new piece of information was stuck to the piece of information most like it; everything new was built on something old. They were always learning.

Charlie turned on the component that allowed them to speak. Their features rippled softly, as if they were stretching themselves.

*I know*, said the first, more quickly than usual.

*So what?* said the second.

*Know what?*

*You know so what?*

*Know what?*

*Now what?*

*What now?*

*Know how?*

*Why now?*

Charlie switched them off, staring as the fans slowed to a stop. *That didn't make sense.* She looked at her watch. It was about three hours too late for bed. She changed quickly and climbed under the sheets, leaving the faces uncovered. There was something unnerving about their exchange. It was faster than it had ever been, and it was nonsensical, but there was something about it that rang familiar—it struck her.

"Were you playing a game?" she asked. They couldn't answer, and just stared blankly into each other's eyes.

# CHAPTER FOUR

S he removed the pillowcase gently, taking care not to let it catch on anything. Beneath their shroud, the faces, blank and sightless, were placid; they looked like they could wait, ever listening, for eternity. Charlie switched them on, and bent over to watch as they began to move their plastic mouths without sound, practicing.

Where? *said the first.*

Here, *said the second.*

Where? *said the first again. Charlie drew back. Something was wrong with the voice; it sounded strained.*

Here, *repeated the second.*

Where? *said the first with a rising intonation, like it was growing upset.*

That's not supposed to happen! *Charlie thought, alarmed. They shouldn't be able to modulate their voices.*

Where? *the first wailed, and Charlie stepped back. She leaned down slowly to peer under the desk, as though she might find an entanglement of wires that would explain the strange behavior. As she stared, puzzled, a baby began to cry. She stood at once, knocking her head painfully on the edge of the desk. The two faces looked suddenly more human, and more childlike. One was crying, the other watching with an astonished look on its face. "It's okay," said the calmer face. "Don't leave me!" The other wailed as it turned to look at Charlie.*

*"I'm not going to leave you!" Charlie cried. "Everything will be okay!" The sound of crying swelled, higher and louder than human voices should be, and Charlie covered her ears, looking desperately around for someone to help. Her bedroom had darkened, and heavy things hung from the ceiling. Matted fur brushed her face, and her heart jolted:* the children are not safe. *She turned back, but an acre of fabric and fur had somehow fallen between her and the wailing babies.*

*"I'll find you!" She shoved her way through, tripping on limbs that dragged on the ground. The costumes swung wildly, like trees in a storm, and a little distance away, something fell to the floor with a hard clunk. At last, she reached her desk, but they were gone. The howling went on and on, so loud Charlie couldn't hear herself think, even as she realized that the screaming was her own.*

Charlie sat up with a loud, raw gasp, as if she had actually been screaming.

"Charlie?" It was John's voice. Charlie looked around with one bleary eye to see a head peering through the bedroom door.

"Give me a minute!" Charlie called as she sat up straight. "Get out!" she cried, and John's head shrank back; the door closed. She felt shaky, her muscles weak. She'd been holding them tense in her sleep. She changed quickly into clean clothes and tried to brush her slightly tangled hair into something more manageable, then opened the door.

John poked his head in again, taking a cautious look around.

"Okay, come in. It's not booby-trapped, though maybe it should be," Charlie joked. "How did you get in here?"

"Well, it was open, and I . . ." John trailed off as he took in the room around him, momentarily distracted by the mess. "I thought maybe we could go to breakfast? I have to work across town in about forty minutes, but I have some time."

"Oh, what a nice thought, but I . . . ," she said. "Sorry for the mess. It's my project, I sort of get wrapped up in it and forget to—clean." She glanced at her desk. The pillowcase was in place as it should be, the vague outlines of the faces just visible beneath it. *It was just a dream.*

John shrugged. "Yeah? What's the project?"

"Um, language. Sort of." She looked around the room curiously. Where had Jessica wandered off to? Charlie knew John would be suspicious of her sudden, unprecedented interest in clothes shopping, and was hoping to avoid explanations. "Natural language programming," she went on. "I'm taking . . . computer programming classes." At the last moment, something stopped her from saying the word *robotics*. John nodded. He was still eyeing the mess, and Charlie couldn't tell what had caught his attention. She plunged back into her explanation. "So, I'm working on teaching language—spoken language—to computers." She walked briskly to the door and peered out into the hall.

"Don't computers already know language?" John called.

"Well, yeah," Charlie said as she returned to the room. She looked at John. His face had changed, stripped down to something more adult. But she could still see him as he'd been the year before, captivated as he watched her old mechanical toys. *I can tell him.*

But then a look of alarm crossed John's face. He surged forward to her bed, stopping a few inches from it. He pointed.

"Is that Theodore's head?" he asked carefully.

"Yeah," Charlie said. She walked to the windows and peeped through the blinds, trying to spot Jessica's car.

"So you *have* been to the house?"

"No. Well, yeah. I went back once," she confessed. "To get him." She looked back at John guiltily.

He shook his head. "Charlie, you don't have to explain yourself," he said. "It's your house." He grabbed the chair from her desk and sat down. "Why did you take him apart?"

She studied his face worriedly, wondering if he was already asking himself the next, obvious question: *What if it runs in the family?*

"I wanted to see how he worked," Charlie said. She spoke carefully, feeling like she had to appear as rational as possible. "I would have taken Stanley and Ella, too, but, you know."

"They're bolted to the floor?"

"Pretty much, yeah. So I took Theodore; I'm actually using some of his components in my project." Charlie looked down at the disembodied bunny's head, into its blank glass eyes. *Took him apart. Using his component parts. That sounds rational.*

She had gotten Theodore from her father's house just before school began. Jessica hadn't been home. It was early evening, not quite dark, and Charlie had smuggled Theodore inside her backpack. She took him out, set him on the bed, and pressed the button to make him talk. As before, there was nothing but a strangled sound: "—ou—lie," the scrambled, decayed traces of her father's voice. Charlie had felt a pang of anger at herself for even trying.

"You sound pretty awful," she said harshly to Theodore, who just looked up at her blankly, immune to the reprimand. Charlie rifled through her bag of tools and parts, which hadn't yet taken over her side of the room. She found her utility knife, then went grimly to her bed where the bunny waited.

"I'll put you back together when I'm done." *Right.*

She looked up at John now, saw the doubt on his face. Or maybe it was concern, just like Jessica. "Sorry, I know everything's a mess," she said, hearing the edge in her own voice. "Maybe I'm a mess, too," she added quietly. She set the bunny's head down on her pillow, and the part of his leg beside it. "So, do you still want to see my project?" she asked.

"Yes." He smiled reassuringly and followed her to her desk. Charlie hesitated, looking down at the pillowcase. *Just a dream.*

"So," she said nervously. Charlie carefully switched everything on before unveiling the faces. Lights began to blink and fans began to whir. She glanced at John again, and took off the cloth.

The faces moved in little patterns, as if stretching out after waking, though there was little they could stretch. Charlie swallowed nervously.

*You, me,* said the first one, and Charlie heard John make a surprised sound behind her.

*Me,* said the second. Charlie held her breath, but they fell silent.

"Sorry, they usually say more," Charlie said. She grabbed a small object from the table and held it up: it was an oddly shaped piece of clear plastic with wiring inside. John frowned for a moment.

"Is that a hearing aid?" he asked, and Charlie nodded enthusiastically.

"It used to be. It's something I'm experimenting with: they listen all the time, they pick up everything that's said around them, but they're just collecting data, not interacting with it. They can only interact with each other." She paused, waiting for a sign that John understood. He nodded, and she went on. "I'm still working out the kinks, but this thing should make the person wearing it . . . visible to them. Not literally visible, I mean—they can't see—but they'll recognize the person wearing the device as one of them." She looked expectantly at John.

"Why . . . What does that mean?" he asked, seeming to search for words. Charlie closed her hand on the earpiece, frustrated. *He doesn't understand.*

"I made them. I want to interact with them," she said. His expression grew thoughtful, and she looked away, suddenly regretting having shown him the object. "Anyway, it's not really finished." She edged to the door and glanced out.

"It's really cool," John called after her. When Charlie returned from the hallway, he gave her an odd look. "Is everything okay?"

"Yes. You should go, though. You'll be late for work." Charlie approached the faces. She looked down thoughtfully at her creations, then sighed and reached for the pillowcase to cover them. As she did, the second face moved.

It jerked back on its stand and pivoted, locking its blind eyes on Charlie's. She stared back. It was like looking at a statue; the eyes were only raised bumps in the molded plastic. But Charlie swallowed hard, feeling herself rooted to the spot. She studied the blank gaze until John put a hand on her shoulder. She jumped, startling him as well, then looked down at the earpiece in her hand. "Oh, right," Charlie mumbled, and pressed the tiny power button on the side of it. She placed the earpiece carefully on top of the mess in her desk drawer, then closed the drawer. The face was still for a moment, then it slowly turned back to its place. It settled there, locked in a mirrored stare with its double, as if it had never moved at all. Charlie covered them and switched them off, leaving them with only enough power to listen.

At last she looked up at John. "Sorry!" she said.

"Does that mean *no* to breakfast?"

"I have plans this morning," Charlie said. "Me and Jessica. You know, girl stuff."

"Really?" John said quietly. "Girl stuff? You?"

"Yes! Girl stuff!" Jessica squealed as she entered the room excitedly. "Shopping; I finally convinced Charlie it's worth trying on her clothes before she buys them. We might even move past jeans and boots! Are you ready?"

"Ready!" Charlie smiled, and John squinted at her.

Jessica began escorting him gently out the door. "Right," John said. "I'll see you later then, Charlie?" Charlie didn't respond, but Jessica gave a bright smile as she closed the door behind him.

"So." Jessica clasped her hands. "Where do you want to start today?"

When they got to the parking lot of the abandoned mall, it was early afternoon.

"Charlie, this isn't what I had in mind," Jessica cried as they got out of the car. Charlie started for the entrance, but Jessica didn't follow. When Charlie turned, she was leaning against the car with her arms crossed.

"What are we doing here?" Jessica asked, her eyebrows raised.

"We have to look inside," Charlie said. "People's lives might depend on it. I just want to see if there is anything left of Freddy's, then we can go."

"Whose lives depend on it? And why now, suddenly?" Jessica asked.

Charlie looked at her shoes. "I just want to see," she said. She felt like a petulant child, but she couldn't bring herself to tell Jessica the whole story.

"Is this because John is here?" Jessica asked suddenly, and Charlie looked up, surprised.

"What? No."

Jessica sighed and uncrossed her arms. "It's okay, Charlie. I get it. You haven't seen him since all of this happened, and then he shows up again—of course it brings everything back."

Charlie nodded, gratefully latching on to this rationale. It was easier than hiding the truth from her. "I doubt there's much left, anyway," she said. "I just want to walk through and remind myself that—"

"That it's really over?" Jessica finished. She smiled, and Charlie's heart sank.

*It's really, really not over.* She forced a smile. "Something like that."

Charlie walked quickly through the mall, but Jessica lagged behind. The place felt entirely different. Sunlight poured in through massive gaps in the unfinished walls and ceiling. Shafts of light sifted between smaller cracks and splashed against stacks of concrete slabs. Charlie could see moths—maybe butterflies—hovering at the windows, and as they passed through the empty halls on their way to Freddy's, she could hear birds chirping. The deathly quiet she remembered, the overpowering sense of dread, was gone. Yet, Charlie thought as she glanced at the half-constructed storefronts, it still felt haunted, maybe even more than before. It was a different kind of haunting, not frightening. But Charlie had the sense that something was present, like stepping onto hallowed ground.

"Hello," Charlie said softly, not sure whom she was addressing.

"Do you hear something?" Jessica slowed her pace.

"No. It feels smaller." Charlie gestured at the open mouths

of the never-opened department stores, and the end of the hall ahead of them. "It seemed so intimidating last time."

"It actually seems kind of peaceful." Jessica spun in place, enjoying the air from outside, which was flowing freely through the empty spaces.

Jessica followed Charlie through the doorway and they stopped dead, blinded by bright sunlight. Freddy's had been torn apart. Some of the walls still stood—the far end looked almost intact—but in front of her was a field of debris. Old bricks and broken tiles were strewn in the dirt.

The two of them stood now on a slab of concrete that lay baking in the sun. The passage inward, along with the entire side wall of the restaurant, was gone. The walls and ceiling were just a line of rubble against the trees. The concrete walkway was still there, worn dark by years of dank and leaking pipes.

"So much for Freddy's," Jessica said in a hushed voice, and Charlie nodded.

They made their way through the debris. Charlie could make out where the main dining room had been, but everything was gone. The tables and chairs, the checkered cloths, and the party hats had all been removed. The merry-go-round had been ripped out, leaving nothing but a hole in the floor and some stray wires. The stage itself had been assaulted, though not removed. They must have been in the middle of that when the job was stopped. Boards were torn up across the main stage area, and the left-hand set of stairs was gone. What was left of the wall behind the stage broke off at the top, like jagged mountains along the sky.

"Are you okay?" Jessica looked to Charlie.

"Yeah. It's not what I expected, but I'm okay." She thought for a moment. "I want to see what's still here." Charlie gestured to the stage, and they crossed what was left of the dining area. The floorboards cracked, the linoleum torn. Jessica peered under a pile of rock where arcade machines had been. The consoles that had stood like dusty gravestones were gone, but they could see the outlines of each one. Square patches remained where they'd been torn from their posts. Stray wires huddled in small piles in the corners. Charlie turned her attention back to the main stage. She climbed up to where the animatronic animals had once performed.

"Careful!" Jessica cried. Charlie nodded an absent acknowledgment. She stood to one side, remembering the layout. *This is where Freddy stood.* The boards were torn up in front of her and in two more places—the destruction here was where they had taken out the pivoting plates that bolted the mascots to the stage. *Not that they stayed bolted very long,* Charlie thought wryly. She could see it now if she closed her eyes. *The animals were going through their programmed motions, faster and faster, until it was clear they were out of control. Moving wildly, as if they were afraid. They were rocking on their stands, and then the awful sound of cracking wood as Bonnie lifted his bolted foot and tore himself free of the stage.*

Charlie shook her head, trying to rid herself of the image. She made her way to the back of the stage. The lights were all gone, but a skeleton of exposed beams crisscrossed the open sky where the lights had been.

"Jessica!" she called. "Where are you?"

"Down here!"

She followed the sound of the girl's voice. Jessica was crouched in the place where the control room had been, peering into the gap under the stage.

"Nothing?" Charlie asked, not sure what answer she was hoping for.

"It's been gutted," Jessica said. "No monitors, nothing." Charlie climbed down beside her, and they peered in together.

"This is where we were trapped last time," Jessica said quietly. "Me and John; there was something at the door, and the lock caught. I thought we would be stuck in that little room and . . ." She looked at Charlie, who simply nodded. The horrors of that night were unique to each of them. The moments that beset them in their sleep, or assailed their thoughts without warning in the middle of the day, were private.

"Come on," Charlie said abruptly, heading again toward the mound of rubble where more games had been. Charlie crouched under a large slab that leaned to the side and acted as a doorway to what was left of the place.

"This seems dangerous." Jessica tiptoed over the loose rock.

The floor was still covered in carpet in most places, and Charlie could see the deep grooves where the arcade machine had been. *She hurled herself at the console, and somehow, it was enough. It wobbled on its base, then fell, knocking Foxy to the ground and pinning him there. She ran, but he was too quick: he caught her by the leg and ripped his hook right through her; she screamed, staring down at the snapping, twisted metal jaws, and the burning, silver eyes.* She heard a noise, almost a whimper, and realized it was her. She clapped her hands over her mouth.

"I thought we were all going to die," Jessica whispered.

"Me too," Charlie said. They looked at each other for a moment, an eerie stillness settling over the sunlit wreckage.

"Hey, this place is probably going to fall on us soon, so . . ." Jessica broke the silence, gesturing to the leaning slabs of concrete surrounding them. Charlie crawled back out the way they'd come and stood up. Her knees were crawling with pins and needles. She rubbed them, then stomped the ground.

"I want to check the costume room, see if anything is left," Charlie said without expression.

"You mean to see if any*body* is left?" Jessica shook her head.

"I have to know." Charlie gave her jeans a final brush and started off toward it.

The room stuck out of the rubble, alone and intact. It was the place where the costumes had been kept, and where Carlton had briefly been held prisoner. Charlie cautiously poked her head inside, studying the physical details around her: the chipped paint on the wall, the carpet that someone had begun to tear up but left unfinished. *Don't think about last time. Don't think about what happened here.* She let her eyes adjust a moment longer, then went inside.

The room was empty. They did a cursory search, but everything had been removed—there was nothing left but walls, floor, and ceiling.

"Clay did say they had gotten rid of everything," Charlie said.

Jessica gave her a sharp look. "Clay? When?"

"He said he was going to, I mean," Charlie said hastily, covering the slip. "Last year."

They took a final look around. As they were leaving, Charlie spotted a glint of light from something in the corner. It was the plastic eyeball of some unknown animatronic mascot. Charlie was about to go to it, but stopped herself. "There's nothing here," she said.

Not waiting for Jessica, she headed back through the debris, looking down at her feet as she stepped over bricks and stones and shattered glass.

"Hey, wait," Jessica called after her hastily. "Pirate's Cove. Charlie! Look!" Charlie stopped. She watched Jessica as she climbed over a steel beam and stepped carefully over the remains of a fallen wall. In front of her, a curtain lay strewn across what had appeared to be a pile of rubble. Charlie followed her, and when she caught up she could see that the curtain concealed a gap in the ruins. The tops of a few glittering chairs peeked out from the stones. A row of broken stage lights lay across the top of the curtain, as though holding it in place.

"It looks pretty good, compared to the rest of the place," Jessica said. Charlie didn't answer. There was a dirty poster lying flat on the ground, depicting a cartoonish Foxy delivering pizzas to happy children.

"Jessica, look." Charlie pointed to the ground.

"Those look like claw marks," Jessica said after a moment.

There were long scratches and scrapes running the length of the floor, and dark marks that looked like traces of blood. "It's like someone was being dragged." Jessica stood and followed the scratches. They led behind the curtain, away from the area where Pirate's Cove once stood.

"The stage," Jessica said.

When they moved the curtain aside, they found the stage had a small hatch at the back. "Storage," Charlie murmured. She pulled on it, but the hatch wouldn't open.

"There has to be a latch somewhere," Jessica said. She cleared away dirt and broken wood from the base of the stage, uncovering a deadbolt that went into the floor.

She pulled it up, releasing the door, which swung open like something was pushing against it.

A face lurched out of the darkness, two gaping eyes swinging forward. Jessica screamed and fell backward. Charlie recoiled. The masked face hung lifelessly from a rotted fur costume. An entire mascot suit was inside, crammed into a space much too small for it. Charlie stopped, her whole body numb with shock as she stared at the thing with a dread almost as old as she was. "The yellow rabbit," she whispered.

"It's Dave," Jessica gasped. Charlie took a deep breath, forcing herself back into the present.

"Come on, help me," she said She stepped forward and grabbed at the fabric, pulling on whatever she could reach.

"You're kidding. I'm not touching that thing."

"Jessica! Get over here!" Charlie commanded, and Jessica came reluctantly over.

"Ew, ew, ew." Jessica touched the suit, then recoiled. She gave Charlie a flat look and tried again, yanking her hands away as soon as she touched it. "Ew," she repeated quietly, then finally screwed her eyes shut and took hold of it.

Together they pulled, but nothing happened. "I think it's stuck," Jessica said. They shifted positions and finally heaved the mascot out of the cramped space. The fabric caught on stray nails and jagged wood, but Charlie kept pulling. At last the creature was out, splayed heavily on the ground.

"I definitely don't think Dave faked his own death," Charlie said.

"What if it's not him?" Jessica peered carefully into the face.

"It's him." Charlie looked at the dried blood soaked into the mascot's fingertips. "The spring locks might not have killed him right away, but this is where he died."

They could see Dave's body through the gaps in the costume, and the wide carved eyes of the mascot head showed through to his face. His skin was desiccated and shriveled. His eyes were wide open, his face expressionless and discolored. Charlie moved closer again. Her initial shock had passed, and now she was curious to see more of him. She probed carefully at first, in case some of the spring locks inside might still be waiting to snap, but it was clear that they'd already done their damage. The locks had been driven so deeply into his skin that the bases of each were flush against his neck; they looked like part of him.

Charlie studied the chest of the costume. There were large tears in the yellow fabric, which had gone green and pink with mold in patches. She grabbed hold of the sides and pulled the gap open as wide as she could. Jessica watched, fascinated, her hand over her mouth. Skewers of metal protruded through his entire body, dull and crusted with his blood. And there were more complex parts, twisted knots of gore with many layers of machinery that stuck out from his body. The suit's fabric was stiff with blood, too, yet the man didn't seem to have rotted, despite the year that had passed.

"It's like he's fused with the suit," Charlie said. She tugged at the mascot head, trying to pull it off, but gave up quickly. The gaping eyes stared up at her, behind which was the dead man's face. With the light directly on him, Dave's skin appeared sickly and discolored. Charlie felt a sudden rush of nausea. She pulled back from the corpse and looked up at Jessica.

"So now what?" Jessica said. "Did you want to give him a foot massage, too?" She abruptly turned her head away, gagging at her own joke.

"Listen, I have class in . . ." Charlie checked her watch. "About an hour. Did you still want to do some shopping?"

"Why can't I have normal friends?" Jessica groaned.

# CHAPTER FIVE

W e are learning all the time. Hopefully at least some of you are learning right here in this class." Dr. Treadwell's students laughed nervously, but she continued over them; it had apparently not been a joke. "When we learn, our minds must decide where we will store that information. Unconsciously we determine what group of things it is most relevant to and connect it to that group. This is, of course, only the most rudimentary explanation. When computers do this, we call it an information tree . . ."

Charlie was only half listening; she knew this already and was taking her notes on autopilot. Since their expedition to Freddy's the day before, she hadn't been able to get the image of Dave's body out of her head: his torso and the gruesome lace of scars that had covered it. When he was alive, he'd shown them off to her, boasting of his survival. While he never told her what had happened, it must have been an accident. *He used to wear those suits all the time.* She could see him now, before all the murders, dressed as a yellow bunny and dancing merrily with a yellow bear . . . she shook her head suddenly, trying to get rid of the image.

"Are you okay?" Arty whispered. She nodded, waving him off.

*But the dead man in the field—that wasn't an accident. Someone forced him inside. But why?* Charlie restlessly tapped her fingers on her desk.

"That will be all for today." Dr. Treadwell set down her chalk and stalked off the auditorium stage with a purposeful step. Her teaching assistant, a flustered graduate student, scurried forward to collect the homework.

"Hey, do you have any time to go over some of this?" Arty asked Charlie as they gathered up their things. "I'm in a little bit over my head in this class."

Charlie paused. She'd promised to make up her first date with John, but she wasn't meeting him for over an hour. Now that she'd been to Freddy's, Charlie almost felt like she was on familiar ground, even if it was soaked in blood.

"I have some time now," she told Arty, who lit up.

"Great! Thanks so much, we can go work over at the library."

Charlie nodded. "Sure." She followed him across the campus, only half engaged as he explained his difficulties with the material.

They found a table, and Charlie opened her notebook to the pages she'd taken down today, pushing them across so Arty could see them.

"Actually, do you mind if I sit next to you?" he asked. "It's easier if we're both looking at the same thing, right?"

"Oh, yeah." Charlie pulled her notes back over as he came around and sat next to her, scooting his metal folding chair next to hers, just a few inches closer than she would have preferred. "So, where did you get lost?" she asked him.

"I was telling you on the way over," he said, with a hint of reproach in his voice, then cleared his throat. "I guess I understood the beginning of the lecture, when she was reviewing last week's material."

Charlie laughed. "So, basically you want to review everything new from today."

Arty nodded sheepishly. Charlie started from the beginning, pointing at her notes as she went. As she flipped through the pages, she noticed her own scribbles in the margins. Charlie leaned in closer, where harsh outlines of rectangles lined the bottom of the page. They were all colored in, like slabs of granite. She stared at them with a sensation of déjà vu: they were important. *I don't remember drawing that*, she thought uneasily. Then, *It's just doodles. Everybody doodles.*

She turned the page to the next segment of the lecture, and a strange alertness rose at the base of her neck, as if someone might be watching her. There were more doodles in the margins of this page, too, and the next one. All of them were rectangles. Some were large and some were small, some scribbled and some outlined in so solidly that her pen had wet the paper through and torn it. All of them were vertical, taller than they were wide. Charlie stared, tilting her head to see from different angles, until something pinged inside her.

*Sammy*, she thought, then, *Is this you? Does this mean something I don't understand?* Charlie glanced at Arty; he was staring at the paper, too. As she watched, he turned the page again. The next pages were the same. They were filled with neat, clear notes, but little rectangles were squashed into every available spot on the page: stuffed into the space between bullet points, crammed into the margins, and tucked away where lines came up short. Quickly, Arty flipped the page back. He looked up at her and smiled, but his eyes were wary.

"Why don't you try the first problem here?" Charlie suggested.

Arty bent over his worksheet, and Charlie stared down at her notebook. Her mind kept returning to her father's house, and the shapes she'd drawn only made the impulse stronger.

*I have to go back.*

"Are you okay?" Arty leaned in cautiously. Charlie stared down at her notebook. Now that she'd noticed the rectangles, they seemed more prominent than the notes; she could focus on nothing else. *I have to go back.*

Charlie shut the notebook and blinked hard. She ignored Arty's question, shoving the notebook into her backpack.

"I have to go," she said as she stood up.

"But I'm still stuck on the first problem," Arty said.

"I'm sorry, I really am!" she called over her shoulder as she hurried away. She bumped into two people as she passed the circulation desk but was too flustered to mutter an apology.

When she got to the door, she stopped, her guts twisting. *There's something wrong.* She hesitated, her hand suspended in the air, as if something was blocking her path. She finally took hold of the knob, and instantly her hand felt fused to it, as if by an electrical current. She couldn't turn it, and she couldn't let go. Suddenly, the knob moved on its own; someone was turning it from the other side. Charlie yanked her hand away and stepped back as a boy with an enormous backpack brushed past her. Snapping back into the moment, she slipped out before the door could swing shut again.

Charlie sped toward Hurricane, trying to calm herself as she drove. The windows were cracked open and wind was rushing in. She thought back to Treadwell's lecture earlier in the week. *At every moment, your senses are receiving far more information than they can process all at once.* Maybe that was Arty's problem in class. Charlie gazed at the mountains ahead, the open fields on either side. Watching them go by, she began to feel like some restraint had been loosened. She'd been spending too much time in her room or in class, and not enough out in the world. It was making her jumpy, exaggerating her natural awkwardness.

She rolled her window down farther, letting in the air. Over the field to her right a few birds were circling—no. Charlie stopped the car. *Something is wrong.* She got out, feeling ridiculous, but the last few days had put her on a hair trigger. The birds were too large.

She realized they were turkey vultures, and some of them were already on the ground, cautiously approaching what looked like a prone figure. *Could be anything.* She leaned against the car. *Probably just a dead animal.* After another moment, she turned back toward her car in frustration, but didn't get in.

*It's not a dead animal.*

She clenched her teeth and started to the spot the vultures were circling. As she got closer, the birds on the ground flapped their wings at the sight of her and soared away. Charlie dropped to her knees.

It was a woman. Charlie's eyes went first to her clothing. It was ripped up, just like the dead man Clay Burke had shown her.

She leaned over to check the woman's neck, though she knew what she would find. There were deep, ugly gouges from the spring locks of an animatronic suit. But before she could examine them closely, Charlie stopped, horrified.

*She looks just like me.* The woman's face was bruised and scratched, which obscured her features. Charlie shook her head. It was easier to imagine more of a resemblance than there really was. But her hair was brown and cut like Charlie's, and her face was the same round shape, with the same complexion. Her features were different, but not *that* different. Charlie stood up and took a deliberate step back from the woman, suddenly aware of how exposed she was in the open field. *Clay. I need to call Clay.* She looked up at the sky, wishing for a way to keep the vultures at bay, to protect the body. "I'm sorry," she whispered to the dead woman. "I'll be back."

Charlie started off to her car, then broke into a run, faster and faster across the field until she ran like something was right behind her. She got in and slammed the door, locking it as soon as she was inside.

Panting heavily, Charlie thought for a second. She was about halfway between Hurricane and the school, but there was a gas station just down the road where she could call Clay. With a last glance at the spot where the body lay, Charlie pulled out onto the road.

The gas station seemed to be empty. As she arrived, Charlie realized that she had never actually seen anyone fueling up here. *Is this a working gas station?* The place was old and shabby, which she had noticed in passing, but she'd never stopped to look around. The pumps looked functional, though not new, and there was no shelter above them. They simply stood on concrete blocks in the middle of a gravel driveway, exposed to the weather.

The little building attached to the station might have been painted white once, but the paint had worn down to reveal gray boards underneath. It seemed to be tilting slightly, slipping on its foundation. There was a window, but it was filthy, almost the same color gray as the building's outside walls. Charlie hesitated, then went to the door and knocked. A young man answered, about Charlie's age, wearing a St. John's College T-shirt and jeans.

"Yeah?" he said, giving her a blank stare.

"Are you—open?"

"Yeah." He was chewing gum and wiped his hands on a grimy rag. Charlie took a deep breath.

"I really need to use your phone." The boy opened the door and let her in. There was more space inside than she'd thought. In addition to the counter, there was a convenience store, though most of the shelves were empty and the line of refrigerators at the back was dark. The young man was looking at Charlie expectantly.

"Can I use your phone?" she asked again.

"Phone's for customers only," he said.

"Okay." Charlie glanced back at her car. "I'll get gas on the way out."

"Pump's broken; maybe you want something out of the cooler," he said, nodding at a grimy freezer with a sliding glass top and a faded patch of red paint that must once have been a logo. "We've got Popsicles."

"I don't want—fine, I'll take a Popsicle," Charlie said.

"Pick out any one you want."

Charlie leaned into the cooler.

Pale, glassy eyes stared back at her. Beneath them was a furry red muzzle, its mouth open and poised to snap.

Charlie screamed and hurtled backward, banging into the shelf behind her. Several cans fell off the shelf and rolled across the floor. The sound echoed in the empty space.

"What is that?" Charlie yelled, but the boy was cackling so hard he was gasping for breath. Peering back inside, Charlie realized that someone had placed a taxidermic animal in the cooler, maybe a coyote.

"That was great!" he finally managed to say. Charlie drew herself up, shaking with rage.

"I would like to use your phone now," she said coldly.

The boy beckoned her to the counter, all smiles, and handed her a rotary phone. "No long distance, though," he warned. Charlie turned her back and dialed, walking toward the cooler as the phone rang. She peered in the top, studying the stuffed canine from the high angle.

"Clay Burke here."

"Clay, it's Charlie. Listen, I need you to meet me. It's another . . ." She glanced at the young man behind the counter, who was watching her intently, not trying to hide the fact that he was listening. "It's like that thing you showed me before, with the cows."

"What? Charlie, where are you?"

"I'm at a gas station a few miles from you. Looks like someone painted an outhouse."

"Hey!" The boy behind the counter straightened for a moment, taking offense.

"Right, I know where you're at. I'll be right there." There was a click from the other end.

"Thanks for the phone," Charlie said begrudgingly, and left without waiting for a reply.

Charlie crouched again where the woman's body lay. She looked anxiously up the road for Clay's car, but it didn't appear. At least the vultures hadn't returned.

*I could just stay in the car until he gets here*, she thought. But Charlie didn't move from her spot. This woman had died horribly and been abandoned in a field. Now, at least, she didn't have to be alone.

The more Charlie looked at her, the harder it was to dismiss the resemblance. Charlie shivered, even though the sun was warm on her back. She was filling with a cold, crawling dread.

"Charlie?"

Charlie spun around to see Clay Burke, then sighed and shook her head.

"Sorry, I got here as fast as I could," he said lightly.

She smiled. "It's okay. I'm just on edge today. I think that's the third time I've jumped in the air when someone said my name."

Clay wasn't listening. His eyes were fixed on the body. He knelt carefully beside it, scrutinizing it. Charlie could almost see him filing every detail away. She held her breath, not wanting to disturb him.

"Did you touch the body?" he asked sharply, not looking away from the corpse.

"Yes," she admitted. "I checked to see if she had the same injuries as the man."

"Did she?"

"Yes. I think—I know she was killed the same way."

Clay nodded. Charlie watched as he got up and circled the woman, dropping down to look more closely at her head, and again at her feet. Finally, he turned his attention to Charlie again.

"How did you find her?" he asked.

"I saw birds—vultures—circling above the field. I went to check."

"Why did you go to check?" His eyes were hard, and Charlie felt a trickle of fear. Surely Clay didn't suspect her.

*Why wouldn't he?* she thought. *Who else would know how to use the spring locks? I bet he could come up with a million theories about me. Twisted girl avenges father's death. Acts out psychodrama. Film at eleven.* She took a deep breath, meeting Clay's eyes.

"I checked because of the body you showed me. It was in a field—I thought it might be another one." She kept her voice as steady as she could. Clay nodded, the steely expression slipping from his face, replaced by worry.

"Charlie, this girl looks like you," he said bluntly.

"Not that much like me."

"She could be your twin," Clay said.

"No," Charlie said, more harshly than she intended. "She looks nothing like my twin." Clay gave her a puzzled look, then comprehension dawned.

"I'm sorry. You had a twin, didn't you? Your brother."

"I barely remember him," she said softly, then swallowed. *All I do is remember him.* "I know she looks like me," she added weakly.

"We're right near a college town," Clay said. "She's a young white female with brown hair—you're not a rare type, Charlie. No offense."

"Do you think it's a coincidence?"

Clay didn't look at her. "There was another body found this morning," he said.

"Another girl?" Charlie drew closer.

"Yes, as a matter of fact. Been dead for a couple of days, probably killed two nights ago." Charlie looked down at him in alarm.

"Does that mean this is going to keep happening?"

"Unless you think we can stop it," he said. Charlie nodded.

"I can help," she said. She looked again at the woman's face. *She's nothing like me.* "Let me go to her house," she added abruptly, seized by a sudden impulse to prove it, to gather evidence that she and the victim were not the same.

"What? *Her* house?" Clay said, giving her a dubious look

"You asked me to help," Charlie said. "Let me help."

Clay didn't answer; instead he reached into the woman's pockets one by one, searching for her wallet. He had to move the body to do it, and she jerked a little as he did, like a ghastly puppet. Charlie waited, and at last he came back with her wallet. He handed Charlie her driver's license.

"Tracy Horton," she read. "She doesn't look like a Tracy."

"You got the address?" Clay scanned the road for police cars. Charlie read it quickly and handed the license back. "I'm going to give you twenty minutes before I radio this in," he told her. "Use it."

Tracy Horton had lived in a small house off a back road. Her nearest neighbors' houses were visible, but Charlie couldn't imagine they would have heard her scream. If she'd managed to scream at all. There was a small blue car in the driveway, but if Tracy had been taken from her home—since presumably she hadn't just been wandering through that field—it could easily have been hers.

Charlie pulled in behind the car and went to the front door. She knocked, wondering what she was going to do if someone answered. *I really should have thought this through.* She couldn't be the one to inform a parent, spouse, or sibling of the young woman's death. *Why did I assume she lived alone?*

No one answered. Charlie tried again, and when there was still no response, she tried the door. It was unlocked.

Charlie walked quietly through the house, not really sure what she was looking for. She glanced at her watch—ten of the twenty minutes had passed just driving here, and she had to assume that the police would get here faster than she did. *Why did I follow the speed limit the whole way here?* The living room and kitchen were clean, but they conveyed no information to her. Charlie didn't know what peach-painted walls said about a person, or the fact that there were three dining room chairs instead of four. There were two bedrooms. One had the sterile air of a guest room that was slowly being taken over by storage; the bed was made and clean towels were folded on the chest of drawers, but cardboard boxes filled a quarter of the room.

The other bedroom looked lived-in. The walls were green, the bedspread pale blue, and there were piles of clothing on the floor. Charlie stood in the doorway for a moment, and found she could not go inside. *I don't even know what I'm looking for.* This woman's life would be sifted through to the last grain by trained investigators. Her diary would be read, if she had one; her secrets would be revealed, if she had any. Charlie didn't need to be a part of it. She turned and walked quickly but quietly back to the front of the house, almost running down the front steps. Standing by the car, she checked her watch again. Six minutes before Clay called in the body.

Charlie went to the little blue car and peered inside. Like

the house, it was neat. There was dry-cleaning hanging in the back window, and a half-empty soda in the cup holder. She walked all around it, looking for something—mud in the tires, scratches in the paint, but there was nothing unusual. *Five minutes.*

She walked briskly through the unkempt grass that bordered the sides of the house. When she reached the backyard, she stopped dead. Before her were three huge holes in the ground, longer than they were wide. They looked like graves, but at a second glance they were too messy, their outlines poorly defined.

Charlie walked around them in a circle. They were lined up next to one another, and they were shallow, but the dirt at the bottom was loose. Charlie grabbed a stick off the ground and poked it into the middle hole: it went in almost a foot before it was stopped by denser soil. The dirt dug out of them was strewn messily all around. Whoever dug the holes had carelessly tossed it everywhere, not bothering to pile it up.

*Two minutes.*

Charlie hesitated for another moment, then lowered herself into the middle hole. Her feet sunk into the loose dirt and she fought to steady herself, catching her balance. It wasn't too deep. The walls came up to her waist. She knelt and put her palm against the wall of the grave—*the hole*, she reminded herself. The dirt was loose here, too, and the wall was rough.

Something had been hidden there, under the ground. *The air is growing thin. I am running out of oxygen, and I will die like this, alone, in the dark.* Charlie's throat seized; she felt as if she couldn't breathe. She climbed out of the hole and up onto the grass of Tracy Horton's backyard. Charlie took a deep breath, focusing all her attention on pushing away the panic. When she was free of it, she checked her watch.

*Minus one minute. He's already called them.* But something kept her there, something familiar. *The loose dirt.* Charlie's mind raced. *Something climbed out of these.*

From a distance, a siren was wailing; it would be here in no time. Charlie hurried to her car and pulled out of the driveway, taking the first corner without caring where it would take her. The holes stayed in her mind, the image like a stain.

harlie slowed her car. With half the cops in Hurricane converging on the area, now was not the time to be stopped for speeding. She was grubby with dirt from the dead woman's backyard, and had a nagging feeling there was something she was forgetting about.

*John*, she realized. She was supposed to meet him—she checked the clock on the dashboard—almost two hours ago. Her heart sank. *He'll think I stood him up. No, he'll think I'm dead*, she amended. Given the perilous history of their relationship, he'd probably think the second was more likely.

When she got to the restaurant where they had planned to meet, a small Italian place across town, Charlie ran in from the parking lot at full speed. She skidded to a stop in front of the teenage hostess, who greeted her with a flustered look.

"Can I help you?" she asked Charlie, taking a step back.

Charlie caught a glimpse of herself in the mirror behind the hostess counter. There were streaks of dirt on her face and clothes; she hadn't thought to clean up first. She quickly wiped her cheeks with her hands before answering the girl.

"I'm supposed to be meeting someone. A tall guy, brown hair. It's kind of . . ." She gestured vaguely at the top of her head, attempting to indicate the habitual chaos of John's hair, but the hostess looked at her blankly. Charlie bit her lip in frustration. *He must have left. Of course he left. You're two hours late.*

"Charlie?" A voice rang out. *John.*

"You're still here?" she cried, too loud for the quiet restaurant, as he appeared behind the hostess, looking profoundly relieved.

"I figured I might as well eat while I'm here." He swallowed what was in his mouth and laughed. "Are you okay? I thought you might . . . not be coming."

"I'm fine. Where are you sitting? Or are you still sitting? Well, I mean, you're obviously not sitting. You're standing. But I mean before you were standing, where were you sitting?" Charlie ran her fingers into her hair and clenched her fists against her scalp, trying to reassemble her thoughts. She mumbled an apology to the room, not sure who it was for.

John glanced around nervously, then gestured toward a table near the kitchen. There was a mostly empty plate with a half-eaten breadstick resting on it, a cup of coffee, and a second place setting, untouched.

They sat down and he looked at her appraisingly. Then John leaned across the table and asked in a low voice, "Charlie, what happened?"

"You wouldn't believe me if I told you?" she said lightly.

His face remained concerned. "You're filthy. Did you fall down in the parking lot?"

"Yes," Charlie said. "I fell in the parking lot and rolled down a hill and into a Dumpster, then fell out of the Dumpster and tripped on the way in. Happy? Stop looking at me like that."

"Like what?"

"Like you have the right to disapprove of me." John pulled back in his chair, his eyes wide. He blinked hard, and Charlie sighed.

"John, I'm sorry. I'll tell you everything. I just need some time; some time to collect my thoughts and to clean up." She laughed, an exhausted, shaken sound, then buried her face in her hands.

John leaned back and signaled for the waitress to bring the check. Breathing heavily, Charlie looked around the restaurant. It was almost empty. The hostess and the only other waitress were talking together near the door, with no apparent interest in anything their customers were doing. There was a family of four by the front window, the children just barely out of toddlerhood. One kept sliding out of his chair and onto the floor every time his mother turned her attention away. The other, a girl, was happily drawing on the tablecloth with markers. No one seemed to care what was going on. But the emptiness made Charlie feel exposed.

"I'm going to go clean up," she said. "Bathroom?" John pointed.

Charlie got up and left the table just as the waitress arrived to deliver his ticket. There was a pay phone in the hallway, and Charlie stopped at it, wavering. She craned her neck to see if John was watching, but from where she stood, she could only see a tiny corner of their table. Quickly, she called Clay Burke's office.

To her surprise, he answered. "You saw her backyard," he said. It wasn't a question.

"Can you give me the other addresses?" Charlie asked. "There could be a pattern—something."

"There sure could," he said drily. "That's why I raced back to the station instead of sticking around to measure the holes. You have a pen?"

"Hang on." The hostess was briefly absent from her station, and Charlie dropped the phone, letting it swing on its metal cord as she hurried to the podium and snatched a pen and a take-out menu. She rushed back. "Clay? Go ahead." He recited names and addresses, and she scribbled them dutifully in the margins of the menu. "Thanks," she said when he was done, and hung up without waiting for him to respond. She folded the menu and slipped it into her back pocket.

In the bathroom, Charlie washed off as much of the dirt as she could. She couldn't clean her clothing, but at least her face was scrubbed, and her hair was rearranged a little more neatly.

As she moved to exit the bathroom, an image flashed unbidden through her thoughts. It was the face of the dead woman.

*She could be your twin*, she heard Clay say, in his low, authoritative voice.

Charlie shook her head. *It's a coincidence. He's right. How many brown-haired, college-aged women are there around here? The first victim was a man. It doesn't mean anything.* She grabbed the doorknob to leave, but froze. It was just like in the library. Charlie released the knob and it spun slowly back into position, releasing a horrible creak as it moved.

*The costumes had been disturbed, and the creaking noise was so faint and careful she scarcely even heard it. Charlie looked up from her game: there was a figure in the door.*

Charlie glanced wildly around the room, pulling herself back to the present. With a swell of panic, Charlie pulled on the bathroom door, but it had somehow sealed shut. She mouthed words, but no sound came out:

*I know you're there. I'm trying to get to you.*

"I have to get inside!" she screamed. The door burst open, and Charlie fell into John's arms.

"Charlie!"

She collapsed to her knees. Charlie looked up to see the scattered handful of customers all staring at her. John glanced into the bathroom behind her, then quickly turned his attention back to Charlie, helping her to her feet.

"I'm okay. I'm fine." She shook loose of his hands. "I'm fine. The door was stuck. I felt hot." Charlie fanned at her face, trying to make a sensible story of it. "Come on, let's get to the car." He tried to take her arm again but she shook free. "I'm fine!" She dug her keys out of her pocket and walked straight for the door, not waiting for him. An old woman was openly staring at Charlie, her fork suspended in the air. Charlie returned her stare. "Food poisoning," Charlie said plainly. The woman's face went pale, and Charlie walked out the door.

When they got out to her car, John sat down in the passenger's seat and looked at Charlie expectantly. "You're sure you're okay?"

"It's been a rough day, that's all. I'm sorry."

"What happened?"

*Tell him what happened*, Charlie thought.

"I want to go to my dad's—my old house," she said instead, surprising herself. *Be honest*, her inner voice said harshly. *You know what kind of creature is doing this, and you know who built it. Stay focused.*

"Right," he said, his voice softening. "You haven't seen it since the storm." She nodded. *He thinks I want to see the damage.* She'd forgotten about the storm until now, but the sudden kindness in John's voice made her nervous. *Is there anything left?* She imagined the house razed to the ground and felt a sudden *wrongness*, like a part of her had been ripped away. She'd never thought of the house as anything but a house, but now, as she drove toward what was left of it, she felt a painful knot in her stomach. It was where all her clearest memories of her father were kept: his rough hands building her toys, showing her his new creations in his workshop, and holding her close when she was afraid. They'd lived there together, just the two of them, and it was the place where he had finally died. Charlie felt as if the joy, the sorrow, the love, and the anguish of their two lifetimes had poured off into the very bones of the old house. The idea of it being wrecked by a storm was an utter violation.

She shook her head and gripped the wheel tighter, suddenly aware of how angry she was. Her love of the house, even of her father, could never be simple. They had both betrayed her. But now there was a new monster out there. She clenched her jaw, trying to fight the tears that welled up in her eyes. *Dad, what did you do?*

As soon as they were out of the town center, Charlie sped up. Clay would be tied up dealing with the newest victim for a while, but eventually he would think to come to her father's house as well. She could only hope that she'd connected the dots first. *You're on the same side.* Charlie put a hand to her head and rubbed her temple. The impulse to guard her father's reputation from what was coming was visceral, but it was also nonsensical.

Less than a mile from the house they passed a construction site. It was set back too far from the road for Charlie to see what it was, though it looked abandoned at the moment.

"I did a little work over there when I first got here," John said. "Some huge demolition project." He laughed. "You have some weird stuff out here; you wouldn't know by looking at it." He studied the countryside for a moment.

"Isn't that the truth," Charlie said, not sure if there was something else she was supposed to say. She was still trying to calm herself. Finally, they came to her driveway. She pulled in with her eyes on the gravel, the house only a dark smudge in her peripheral vision. The last time Charlie had been here she'd run in and out without pausing to look at anything. All she'd wanted was Theodore, and she had grabbed him and gone. Now she regretted her haste, wishing for some final mental image. *You're not here to say good-bye.* She turned the car off, steeled herself, and looked up.

The house was surrounded by trees, and at least three of them had fallen, striking the roof directly. One had landed squarely on the front corner, crushing the walls beneath its weight. Charlie could see through the broken beams and crumbled drywall, into the living room. Inside there was only debris.

The front door was intact, though the steps to it were splintered and split. They looked as if they'd give way as soon as they bore weight. Charlie got out of the car and headed toward them.

"What are you doing?" John's voice was alarmed. Charlie ignored him. She heard his door slam, and he caught her arm, wrenching her back.

"What?" she snapped.

"Charlie, look at this place. That house is going to fall over any day now."

"It's not going to fall," she said flatly, but she did gaze up again. The house seemed to be listing to the side, though it must have been an illusion; surely the foundation itself couldn't have sunk. "I'll be out before I get killed, I promise," she said more gently, and he nodded.

"Go slow," he said.

They carefully climbed the steps to the porch, staying close to the sides, but the wood was sturdier than it looked. They could have taken three steps to the right and walked through the open wall, but Charlie took out her key and unlocked the door as John waited patiently, letting her go through the unnecessary ritual.

Inside, she paused at the foot of the stairs to the second floor. The holes in the ceiling were beaming down shafts of thin sunlight, dimming as the sun began to wane. It made the place feel almost like some sort of shrine. Charlie tore her eyes away from the holes and started upstairs to her bedroom.

As with the outdoor steps, she kept to the side, holding on to the bannister. The water damage was visible everywhere. There were dark stains and soft spots in the wood. Charlie reached out to touch a place where the paint had bubbled out from the wall, leaving a pocket of air.

Suddenly a cracking sound came from behind her and she spun around. John grabbed the bannister, struggling to hold on as the stair gave way under him. Charlie reached out, but John braced himself unsteadily. He hissed and gritted his teeth.

"My foot's stuck," he said, nodding down. Charlie saw that his foot had gone clear through the wood, and now the jagged edges dug into his ankle.

"Okay, hold on," Charlie said. She crouched down until she could reach him on the step below her, though the awkward angle made it hard to maintain her balance. The wood was only rotting in some places, while in others it was still intact. She grabbed the smaller pieces and pulled them cautiously back from John's foot, her hands growing raw with the rough and splintered surface.

"I think I've got it," John said finally, flexing his ankle.

She looked up and grinned. "And you thought *I* was going to get myself killed."

John gave her a weak smile. "How about we both make it out alive?"

"Right."

They made their way up the rest of the stairs much more slowly, each of them testing their weight before they took the next step. "Careful," John warned as Charlie reached the top.

"We won't be here long," Charlie said. She was much more aware of the danger now. The house's instability grew more obvious with each step they took; the very foundation seemed to wobble from side to side as they moved.

Her old bedroom was on the undamaged side of the house—or the side not struck by trees, at least. Charlie stopped in the doorway, and John came up behind her. The floor was strewn with glass. One window had been broken by something, and the shattered glass had blown into the room.

She took a deep breath, and it was then that she saw Stanley. The animatronic unicorn had once run on a track around her bedroom. Now he was lying on his side. Charlie went to him and sat down, pulling his head into her lap and patting his rusty cheek. He looked as if he'd been torn violently from his track. His legs were twisted, his hooves missing chunks. When she looked around the room she saw the missing pieces, still attached to the grooves in the floor.

"Stanley has seen better days." John smiled ruefully.

"Yeah," Charlie said absently, as she set the toy's head back on the floor. "John, can you turn that wheel?" She pointed to a crank soldered together at the foot of her bed. He complied, crossing the floor agonizingly slowly. Charlie bit back her impatience. He turned the crank and she waited for the littlest closet door to open, but nothing happened. John looked at Charlie expectantly.

She stood and went to the wall where the three closets stood, closed and apparently untouched by the weather. Even the paint was bright and immaculate. Charlie hesitated, feeling as if she might be disturbing something that no longer belonged to her, then forced the smallest door open.

Ella was there, the doll who had been the same size as Charlie when she was much younger. She, like Stanley, had once run around on a track, and she seemed to still be attached to it. She was entirely undamaged. Her dress was clean, and the tray she held in front of her was firm in her motionless hands. Her wide eyes had been gazing into the darkness since the last time Charlie saw her.

"Hi, Ella," Charlie said softly. "I don't suppose you can

tell me what I'm looking for?" She scanned over the doll quickly and brushed at her dress. "You just want to stay in here from now on?" Charlie studied the tiny frame of the door. "I don't blame you." She closed the closet door again without saying good-bye.

"So," she said, turning back to John. He seemed lost in thought, staring at something in his hand.

"What is that?" Charlie asked.

"A photo of you, when you were no bigger than her." John smiled and gestured toward Ella's door, then handed the picture to Charlie.

It looked like a school photo. A short, chubby girl gave a toothy grin for the camera—minus one tooth. Charlie smiled back at her. "I don't remember this."

"That doll is a little creepy, standing in the closet," John said. "I'm a bit on edge, I won't lie."

"Waiting for a tea party," Charlie said acerbically. "How sinister." She started to leave the room, but as her hand touched the doorframe, she paused. *Doors.* She stepped back through into her bedroom, and looked for a long moment at each of the rectangular closet doors. "John," she whispered.

"What?" John looked up, trying to follow Charlie's gaze.

"Doors," Charlie whispered. She took several long steps back to study the whole wall at once. The scribbles all over her notebooks had been shaped like dozens—hundreds—of rectangles. She drew them without thinking, as if they were pushing up through her mind, trying to break out of her subconscious. Now they had. "They're doors," she repeated.

"Yes. Yes, I see." John tilted his head curiously. "Are you okay?"

"Yes, I'm fine. I mean, I'm not sure." She ran her eyes over the wall of closets again. *Doors. But not these doors.*

"Come on, let's go look at the workshop," John said. "Maybe we can find something else there."

"Right." She gave a pained smile. She looked back once more at the three closets that sat in silence.

John nodded, and they went cautiously back down the stairs, testing each step before they took it. Outside, they stopped by the car. The workshop was invisible from the driveway, hidden behind the house. The backyard had once been surrounded by trees, a small wood that acted as a fence.

"Don't go into the woods, Charlie," she said, then smiled at John. "That's what he always told me, like something out of a fairy tale." They walked a bit farther, twigs snapping under their feet. "But the woods were only ten feet deep," she said, still peering into the trees as though something might leap out. As a child these trees had seemed impenetrable, a forest she might be lost in forever, if she dared to wander in. She started toward what remained of them, then stopped dead when she saw where some of the fallen trees had landed.

Her father's workshop had been crushed. A massive trunk

had hit the workshop's roof dead center, and others had come with it on all sides. The wall closest to the house was still standing, but it was bowed beneath the sagging roof.

It had been a garage when they moved in, and then it had become her father's world: a place of light and shadow that smelled of hot metal and burnt plastic. Charlie peered down at the rotting wood and broken glass with careful attention, looking for something she might otherwise miss.

"We're definitely not going in there," John said.

But Charlie was already lifting a piece of sheet metal that had once belonged to the roof. She threw it violently to the side, and it hit the ground with a resounding clang. John startled and kept his distance as Charlie continued to throw things. "What are you—what are *we* looking for?"

Charlie wrestled a toy from under the debris and threw it carelessly to the ground behind her, continuing to lift sheets of metal and toss them aside. "Charlie," John whispered, picking up the delicate toy and cradling it. "He must have made this for you."

Charlie ignored him. "There's got to be something else in here." She fought her way deeper into the workshop, toppling a wooden beam out of her way. Her hand slipped on the wood, and she realized it was wet; her arm was bleeding. She wiped her hand on her jeans. From the corner of her eye, she saw John set the toy carefully on the ground and follow her in.

Amazingly, there were still shelves and tables standing upright, with tools and shreds of fabric where her father had last set them. Charlie glanced at them for a passing moment, then swept her arm across the table nearest her, knocking everything to the ground. She didn't pause to see what had fallen before moving to the shelves. She began picking things off the nearest shelf one item at a time, inspecting them and throwing them to the ground. When the shelf was empty, she grabbed the board itself with both hands, wrenching at it violently, trying to pull it from the wall. When it didn't come loose, she began pounding at it with her fists.

"Stop!" John ran to her and grabbed her hands, pinning them to her sides.

"There has to be something here!" she screamed. "I'm supposed to be *here*, but I don't know what it is that I'm supposed to find."

"What are you talking about? There's a lot left. Look at this stuff!" He held the toy up to her again.

"This isn't about the storm, John. It's not about happy memories, or closure, or whatever you think I need. This is about monsters. They're out there, and they're killing people. And you and I both know that there is only one place they could have come from: here."

"You don't know that," John began. Charlie looked at him with a stony rage, stopping him short.

"I'm surrounded by monsters, and murder, and death, and spirits." At the last word her fury ebbed, and she turned away from John, surveying the workshop. She wasn't sure now what damage the storm had done, and what had been her. "All I can think about is Sammy. I *feel* him. Right now, I can feel him in this place, but he's—cut off. It doesn't even make sense. He died before my father and I moved here. But I know I'm here for a reason. There's something that I'm supposed to find. It's all connected, but I don't know how. Maybe something to do with the doors . . . I don't know."

"Hey, okay. We'll find it together." John reached out for her. Charlie's strength gave way and she let him pull her close, pressing her face into his shirt. "I know it's hard to see everything torn apart like this," he said. Charlie's anger drained away, fading into exhaustion. She rested her head on John's shoulder, wishing she could stay like this just a little longer.

"Charlie," John said with alarm, and Charlie came back to attention. He was looking over her shoulder, in the direction of the house.

The entire back face of the house had been torn open, as if someone had taken a massive hammer to it; inside was only dark.

"That's right under your room, isn't it? We could have fallen through the floor," John said.

"That should be the living room," Charlie said, wiping her sleeve across her face.

"Yeah, but it's not." John looked at her expectantly.

"That's not even a part of the house," she said. A sudden spark of hope revived inside her. Something was out of place. That meant there was something to find.

Charlie approached the chasm, and John didn't try to stop her as she climbed up several large slabs of broken concrete. John stayed a step behind her, close enough to catch her if she slipped. Charlie turned to him before entering. "Thank you," she said. John nodded.

"I've never seen this room before," Charlie whispered as she crept into the hollow space. The walls were made of dark concrete, and the room was small and windowless, a box jammed into the house and sealed away between the rooms. There were no decorations, and nothing to indicate what was stored here. Just a dirt floor and three large holes, deep and oblong like graves.

"Those don't look like storm damage," John said.

"They're not." Charlie went up to the edge of the nearest hole, looking down.

"Were you . . . expecting to find these?"

These holes were deeper than the ones she'd found at Tracy Horton's house. Perhaps it was the shadowy room, but these looked like real graves. They were a foot or so deeper than the ones she'd found before and partially filled with loose dirt.

John was standing patiently behind her, waiting for her answer.

"I've seen them before," she admitted. "Behind the house of a dead woman."

"What are you talking about?"

Charlie sighed. "There was another body. I found her today, in a field. I called Clay, and then I went to her house while he waited for the rest of the cops to show up. There were holes like this in her backyard."

"That's what you wouldn't tell me? Another body?" John sounded hurt, but his wounded expression lasted only seconds before it cleared. He started scanning the room again, his eyes intent on the walls and floor.

*That, and the fact that she looked like me*, Charlie thought.

"So what do you think the holes are?" he asked finally.

Charlie barely heard him. Her gaze had fixed on the blank concrete wall on the far side of the room. It was empty, whitewashed then left to turn gray with dust and mildew. But something drew her to it. Leaving John alone by the open graves, Charlie walked slowly to it, drawn there by a sense of sudden recognition. It was like she'd just remembered a word that had been on the tip of her tongue for days.

She hesitated, holding her hands out flat, less than an inch from the wall, uncertain what was holding her back. She steeled herself and placed her palms against the wall. It was cold. She felt a slight shock of surprise, as though she'd expected to feel warmth from the other side. John was speaking, but to her it was only murmurs in the distance. She turned her head and delicately placed her ear against the surface, closing her eyes. *Movement?*

"Hey!" John's voice broke her focus, waking her as if from a trance. "Over here!"

She turned. John was bent over the mound of dirt next to the farthest grave. Charlie started toward him, but he put up a hand to stop her.

"No, come around the other way."

She carefully made her way around the perimeter of the little room until she was beside him. At first she couldn't tell what he was trying to show her. Something was almost visible, veiled in a thin layer of dirt, so that it blended into the ground as if deliberately camouflaged.

But eventually she saw it—rusted metal, and the glint of a staring, plastic eye. She glanced at John, who just looked back at her. This was her territory now. Carefully, Charlie poked the mostly buried head of the thing with the toe of her sneaker, then yanked her foot back. The thing didn't move.

"What the heck is this?" John asked, glancing around the room. "And why is it in here?"

"I've never seen this before," Charlie said. She knelt, curiosity overtaking her fear, then used her hand to scrape aside some of the dirt, clearing off a little more of the creature's face. Behind her, John drew a sharp breath. Charlie just stared down. The creature had no fur, and its face was smooth. It had a short muzzle and oval ears sticking out from the sides of the head. It had the general appearance of an animal's head, though much larger than the animatronic animals from Freddy's. Charlie couldn't guess what kind of animal it was supposed to be. Running down the center of its face was a long, straight split, exposing wires and a line of metal frame. A thick plastic material was stuck to the face in large patches. Maybe it had been encased in it at some point.

"Do you recognize it?" John asked quietly.

Charlie shook her head. "No," she managed to say after a moment. "Something's wrong with it." She brushed back more dirt and found it came away easily. The thing had only been partially buried beneath the floor; that, or it had almost escaped. She started digging her hands into the dirt, trying to pry it out of what remained of its grave.

"You've got to be kidding me." John groaned as he knelt to help, getting his hands around any part of it he could. In one concentrated effort, they heaved it upward, managing to pull most of the torso out of the dirt. They let it drop, then fell back on the ground to study it while they caught their breath.

Like the face, the body was smoother than the animatronics that Charlie was used to. It had no fur, and no tail or other animal appendages. It was too large for a human being to wear, probably eight feet tall when standing. Still, Charlie couldn't shake the feeling that she recognized this creature. *Foxy.*

There was something sick about the creature, a weirdness that gripped her at the most basic, primal level and cried, *This is wrong.* Charlie closed her eyes for a moment. Her skin felt strange, like something was crawling all over it. *It's just an oversized doll.* She took a deep, deliberate breath, opened her eyes, and inched forward to examine the thing.

As her hand touched the creature, a wave of nausea hit her, but it lasted only a split second. She continued. She turned the head to the side, its joints resisting. The left side of its skull had been crushed. Charlie could see that the insides were broken, half the wires torn out. Just behind the eye, on the side that had been completely buried, a piece of the casing was missing. She could see a mass of plastic with a tangle of wires running in and out of it. Something had melted one of the circuit boards. Moving slowly down the body, Charlie examined its joints: one arm seemed fine, but on the other both the shoulder and elbow joints had been bent out of shape. Charlie looked up at John, who was watching her with a worried expression.

"Anything familiar?"

"I don't recognize it. It's not something my dad ever showed me," Charlie said.

"Maybe we should put it back in the ground and get out of here. This feels like it was a mistake."

"But on the inside . . ." Charlie ignored him. "The hardware, the joints—it's older technology. Maybe he made them earlier? I don't know."

"How can you tell?"

"I recognize some of this as my dad's work." She frowned and pointed at the creature's head. "But then a lot of it is foreign to me. Someone else may have had a hand in it. I'm not sure if my dad made it or not, but I have a feeling he's the one who buried it."

"I can't imagine it was designed to be onstage. It's hideous." John was noticeably nervous, and now he placed his hand on Charlie's arm. "Let's get out of here. This place gives me the creeps."

"'Gives me the creeps,'" Charlie said lightly. "Who says that? I'm going to try and get it the rest of the way out. I just want to see . . ." She moved away from John's touch, leaning down to dig again by the creature's buried torso.

"Charlie!" John cried, just as a metal shriek rang out.

The animatronic's arms lifted, and its chest opened like an iron gate. Its metal pieces slid out of place to reveal a dark, gaping pit where sharp spikes and spring locks were just barely visible. It was a trap waiting to be triggered. Yet, disorientingly, something else about it had transformed at the same time. Its artificial skin took on a luminescence, and its movements were fluid and sure. Its casing suddenly appeared to have skin and fur, though they were blurry, flickering like a trick of the light.

Charlie jumped backward, but it was too late: the thing had her in its grip and lifted her high into the air. It was pulling her toward it. She beat against its bent and damaged arm, but the other arm steadily forced her closer to the chest cavity. John stumbled backward for a moment, bending forward with one hand over his mouth, as if struck by a wave of nausea.

Charlie struggled to break free, but her strength was no match for the creature. Out of the corner of her eye she could see John lunging toward the beast. He grabbed its head, wrenching at it, trying to force it sideways. Beneath Charlie, the animatronic began to spasm, a stuttering, uncontrolled movement. The creature's grip came loose and its arms swung around wildly. Charlie struggled to get to her feet, but her legs slid in the dirt. The creature seized her again, and its cold fingers drew her closer.

Charlie braced her shoe against the ground, trying to give herself leverage, but she was being pulled down by an overwhelming force. Suddenly she was face-to-face with the beast, her shoulder already inside its chest cavity. The thing pressed her closer, then suddenly it jerked and released her. She rolled away and heard the sound of snapping spring locks. The creature convulsed on the ground in front of her, headless. Charlie looked at John. He was holding the thing's head in his hands, his eyes wide with shock. He dropped it and kicked it across the floor.

"Are you okay?" John scrambled to her. Charlie nodded, staring at the broken animatronic head. It still seemed alive. Its fur bristled and skin moved, as if there were muscle and sinew underneath.

"What the heck just happened?"

John raised both hands in surrender.

Charlie carefully picked up the massive head and flipped it upside down, peering into it through the base where John had torn it off the neck.

"Ugh." John bent over, his hands on his knees. His face was pale. He stifled a retching sound.

Charlie started toward him, surprised. "What's wrong with you? You've seen worse than this."

"No, it's not that. I don't know what it is." He straightened, then stumbled toward the wall, bracing himself. "It's like there's some horrible smell in the air, but without the smell."

Charlie held her finger to her ear, listening. There was a tone in the air, so high-pitched and quiet it was almost imperceptible. "I think something is still . . . on," she said.

She set the giant head on the ground. John had a hand to his ear, listening, but when she looked at him he shook his head.

"I can't hear anything."

Charlie returned to the body of the creature and peered into its gaping chest cavity. "Are you okay?" she asked half-heartedly, not taking her eyes off the robot.

"Yeah, I feel better back here." He heaved and she turned. John's face was strained, and his arm was tight across his stomach. "I think it's passing," he said, then doubled over, barely getting out the last syllable.

"This thing." Charlie clenched her teeth and jerked her weight back and forth, trying to wrestle something loose from inside the chest cavity.

"Charlie get away from it!" John took a step toward her, then swayed back, as if he were tethered to the wall. "There is something *really* wrong with that thing."

"Now *this* I've seen before," Charlie said as she pulled the object out at last. It was a flat disc, about the size of a half-dollar coin. She held it up to her ear. "Wow, that's really high-pitched. I can barely hear it. The sound is why you feel sick."

Charlie wedged her fingernail into a small groove on the side of the object and flipped a thin switch. John took several deep breaths, then stood upright again slowly, testing himself. He looked at Charlie. "It stopped," she said.

"Charlie," John whispered, nodding toward the beast on the ground. Charlie looked, and a shock went through her.

The illusion of fur and flesh was gone. It was nothing more than a broken robot with unfinished features.

John picked up the head once again, turning it to face them. "That thing, it did something," John said, nodding toward the device in Charlie's hands. "Turn it back on." He lifted the creature's head a bit higher and stared into its lifeless round eyes.

*Are you sure that's a good idea?* she was about to say, but curiosity got the better of her. John could handle a little more nausea. She slipped her nail back into the groove and flipped the tiny switch. Before their eyes, the fractured and worn face became fluid and smooth, warping into something lifelike. John dropped the head and jumped backward.

"It's alive!"

"No, it's not," Charlie whispered, flipping the switch off again. She cradled the strange device in her hands, gazing down at it, mesmerized. "I want to know more about this. We have to get back to the dorm." She got to her feet. "I've seen something like this. When I came back here for Theodore, I grabbed a bunch of stuff and put it in a box to study later. I know I saw something like this."

For a long moment, John said nothing. Charlie felt a surge of shame. He was looking at her the way Jessica had, the way he had when he first saw her experiment. The little disc in Charlie's palm felt suddenly like the most vital thing in the world. She closed her hand on it.

"Okay, then," John said plainly. "Let's go." His tone was calm, and it caught Charlie off guard. John was being deliberately agreeable. She wasn't sure exactly why, but it was reassuring nonetheless.

"Okay." Charlie smiled.

# CHAPTER SEVEN

**W**hen they got back to the college, Charlie headed for the dorm.

"Hey, slow down!" John struggled to catch up.

"You have that disc?"

"Of course." He patted his pocket.

"I know I've seen something like this before," she said. "I'll show you." She glanced at John as she let him into the room she shared with Jessica, but his face remained impassive. He'd already seen the mess. But John didn't look in the direction of Charlie's desk and the covered faces.

"You can clear off the chair," Charlie said as she shoved a stack of books out of the way. She crawled under the bed and emerged a moment later with a large cardboard box. John was standing beside the chair, looking perplexed. "I said you can clear it off," she said.

He laughed. "Clear it off to where?"

"Right." The chair had a stack of books on the seat, and a stack of T-shirts draped over the back. Charlie grabbed the shirts and threw them onto the bed. She set the box on the bed and settled herself cross-legged behind it, so that John would be able to look through it, too.

"So what is all of this?" He leaned slowly over the box as Charlie rummaged through it, pulling parts out one by one and setting them in a straight line on the bed.

"Stuff from my dad's house: electronics, mechanical parts. Things from the animatronics, from his work." She glanced at him nervously. "I know I said that I just went back for Theodore, and I did. But I may have grabbed a few things on the way out. I wanted to learn, and these classes—John, you know some of the tech my father was working with was ancient. It's practically ridiculous now. But he was making it up as he went along; he thought of stuff that's still unique, that no one else has thought of yet. I wanted all of it. I wanted to understand it. So, I went back to get what I could."

"You stripped the house for parts, I get it." John laughed as he picked up Theodore's severed paw and considered it for a moment. "Even your favorite toy? Don't you think that's a little . . . heartless?"

"Is it?" Charlie picked up a piece from the box, a metal

joint, and weighed it in her hands. "I took Theodore apart because I wanted to understand him, John. Isn't that the most loving thing there is?"

"Maybe I should reconsider this whole dating thing," John said, wide-eyed.

"He was important to me because my father made him for me, not because he was stitched up to look like a rabbit." She discarded the joint, setting it next to her on the bed. She turned her attention to the box, picking up pieces one by one and setting them in a row. She was sure she'd recognize what she needed when she saw it.

Charlie looked at circuitry and wires, metal joints and plastic casings, examining each piece carefully. Something would cry out to her, just like the animatronic beast had done, with that raw sense of *wrongness*. But after a while her neck grew sore from bending over the box. Her eyes were beginning to glaze over. She discarded the piece of metal tubing in her hand, tossing it onto the growing pile on her bed. At the clanking sound, John looked up.

"Where do you even sleep?" he asked, gesturing not only to the growing pile of electronic and mechanical parts, but to the clothing and books, and the smaller piles of electronic and mechanical parts.

Charlie shrugged. "There's always room for me," she said mildly. "Even if just barely."

"Yeah, but what about when you're married?" John's face

flushed before he'd even finished the sentence. Charlie looked up at him, one eyebrow hinged slightly higher than the other. "Someday," John said hastily. "To someone. Else." His face grew grimmer. Charlie felt her eyebrow lift higher of its own volition. "So, what are we looking for again?" John furrowed his brow and scooted his chair closer to the bed, peering into the box.

"This." Spotting a glimmer in the pile, Charlie took hold of a small disc and carefully placed it in the palm of her hand. She held it out so John could see. It looked just like the metallic disc they'd found in the body of the animatronic, but one side of it had been damaged, revealing a curious metal framework inside. Several wires extended, connecting to a black keypad not much larger than the disc itself.

"Funny." Charlie chuckled to herself.

"What?"

"The last time I held this, I was more interested in the keypad." She smiled. "This part is a common diagnostic tool. Someone must have been testing it."

"Or trying to find out what it was," John added. "That thing doesn't look like anything else in the box; just like that monster we found doesn't look like anything your dad made. I mean, it *kind of* looked like Foxy, but not the one your dad made. This was some sort of twisted version of Foxy."

She pulled a heavy metal joint from the box. "This doesn't belong here, either."

"What's wrong with it?"

"It's meant to be an elbow, but look." She bent the joint all the way over, then all the way back the other way, then looked at John expectantly.

He looked blank. "So?"

"My father wouldn't have used this. He always put stops so that the joints couldn't do things humans can't do."

"Maybe it's not finished?"

"It's finished. It's not just that, though, it's . . . it's the way the metal is cut, the way it's put together. It's like—you write things, right? So, you read other people's work?" He nodded. "If I ripped up some books and gave you a big pile of pages, and asked you to pick out the ones by your favorite author, could you do that, just based on the style?"

"Yeah, of course. I mean, I might be wrong about a few, but yeah."

"Well, it's the same thing here." She held the heavy piece up again to make her point. "My dad didn't *write* this."

"Okay, but what does it mean?" John asked. He unplugged the broken disc from the diagnostic keypad and took the second disc from the monster out of his pocket. He fiddled with it briefly, then managed to unhinge one side of it. Frowning with concentration, he attached the wires from the keypad to the new disc. When he was finished, he hesitated. "I don't want to flip any of the switches," he said. "I don't think my stomach can take it."

"Yeah, don't touch anything yet. After what happened at the house, we shouldn't assume that we know what any of this does." Charlie set the box on the floor and started shuffling through the parts again, looking at the patterns, trying to see something in them. "There has to be something else in here that I'm missing."

"Charlie," John said. "Sorry to interrupt your conversation with yourself, but look." He passed her the broken disc he'd just unhooked. "Look on the back."

The back had once been smooth, but it was scratched a lot since it was first made. Charlie stared at it for a minute, then finally saw it: there was writing along one edge. She had to bring the piece of plastic close to her face to make the letters out. They were tiny, and written in an old-fashioned, flowing script. They read: *Afton Robotics, LLC.* Charlie dropped the disc immediately.

"Afton? William Afton? That's my father's old partner. That's—"

"That's Dave's real name," John finished. Charlie sat silently for a moment, feeling as if something very large and unwieldy had been shoved into her head.

"I thought he was just a business partner for Freddy's," she said slowly.

"I guess he did a bit more than that."

"He's dead, though. It's not like we can ask him questions. We have to figure out what's happening now." She grabbed the cardboard box and swept the extraneous pieces—the pieces that had been her father's—into it, then shoved it back under the bed. John ducked out of her way as she maneuvered around the small space.

"And how do you think we should do that?" he asked. "What *is* happening now? There have been two bodies so far, both killed by something like what we just found."

"Three bodies," Charlie said, flushing slightly. John covered his face with his hands for a moment and took a deep breath.

"Okay, three. Are you sure it's not four?"

"I didn't see the third one. Clay just told me about it, after she was found. It had been out for a few days—she was the first one, I think."

"So why them? Are these robots just going on a killing spree? Why would they do that? Charlie, is there anything else about this that you're not telling me?" Charlie bit her lip, hesitant. "I'm serious. I'm in this with you, but if I don't know what's happening, I can't help you."

Charlie nodded. "I don't know if it means anything. Clay said it was just a coincidence. But the woman I found in the field—John, she looked like me."

His expression went dark. "What do you mean, looked like you?"

"Not exactly like me. Brown hair, same size, sort of. I don't know, if you described me to someone and asked them to pick me out of a crowd, they might come back with her. There was just this awful moment when I looked down at her, and it was like looking at me."

"Clay said it didn't mean anything?"

"He said it's a college town; there are a lot of brown-haired girls around. One of the other two victims was a man, so . . ."

"Probably a coincidence then," John offered.

"Yeah," Charlie said. "I guess it was just . . . unsettling."

"There must be something else that's linking them together. Another person, a job, a location maybe." John looked toward the window. Charlie caught him smiling, and John's expression sobered, looking suddenly self-conscious.

"You're enjoying this," she said.

"No." He shrugged. "I wouldn't put it that way. I don't want any more bodies. But—it's a mystery, and it's an excuse to spend some time with you." He smiled, but quickly made his face serious again. "So what about the bodies? Where were they found?"

"Well." Charlie brushed the hair off her face, slightly distracted. "They were all found in fields, miles apart. The first one—the one they just found—was over on the far side of Hurricane, and the girl I found today was left by the side of the road between Hurricane and here."

"Where on the road? How far from here?"

"About halfway . . ." Suddenly her eyes widened. "Forget

the fields. Or don't forget them, but they're not the point, or at least not the whole point. The holes were behind the woman's house. They take them from their homes. That's where they're starting; it's where we should start, too." She headed for the door, and John followed.

"Wait, what? Where are we going?"

"My car. I want to look at a map."

When they got to the car, Charlie pulled a stack of papers out of the glove compartment and rifled through them, then pulled out a map and handed it to John.

"Give me a pen." She held out her hand, and John pulled two from his front pocket, handing her one. Charlie spread the map out on the hood of the car and they bent over it.

"The woman's house was here," she said, circling the spot. "Clay gave me the addresses of the others." She pulled the now slightly grubby menu from her pocket and handed it to John. "You look for that one," she said quietly.

Even though they both knew the area, tracing the streets for the victim's houses took longer than Charlie had expected.

"Found it," John announced.

"1158 Oak Street is right . . . there." She circled the point and stepped back.

"What's that?" John said, pointing to something scribbled in the margin. Charlie picked up the corner of the map and her heart skipped. It was another drawing of a rectangle. She didn't remember making it. *It's a door. But what door?* She stared down at it. It had no knobs or latches, nothing to indicate how she would get inside. Or where it was. *What good is it to know what I'm looking for, if I don't know why, or how to find it?*

"Just a doodle," she said sternly, to redirect his attention. "Come on, concentrate."

"Yeah," John said. At least the pattern was instantly clear; the houses made a crooked line from Hurricane toward St. George, truncated halfway between.

"They're all about the same distance apart," Charlie said, a swell of dread rising in her chest. John was nodding as if he understood. "What does it mean?" she asked urgently.

"They're moving in a specific direction, and traveling roughly the same distance between." He paused. "Killing."

"Who's killing who?" A voice rang out behind them.

Charlie gasped and whirled around, her heart pounding. Jessica was behind her, holding a stack of books to her chest. Her eyes were wide and a grin of excitement broke across her face.

"We were just talking about the movie we saw last night," John said with a casual smile.

"Oh yeah, okay." Jessica gave him a quick look of faux seriousness and glanced at Charlie. "So, Charlie, what's the map for?" she asked, gesturing at it elaborately. "Oh, does it have to do with Freddy's?" she said with excitement in her voice. John looked at Charlie suspiciously.

"Did she tell you?" Jessica looked to John, and John looked back at Charlie, eager to hear the rest.

"Jessica, now probably isn't the best time," Charlie said feebly.

"We went to Freddy's yesterday," Jessica said in a hushed tone, although no one else was around.

"Oh, really? Funny, Charlie didn't mention that. Was that before or after all that shopping?" John folded his arms.

"I was going to tell you," Charlie murmured.

"Charlie, sometimes I think you're just trying to get yourself killed." John put his hand over his face.

"So what's the map for?" Jessica repeated. "What are we looking for?"

"Monsters," Charlie said. "New . . . animatronics. They're murdering people, seemingly at random," she continued, not fully convinced of what she'd just said.

Jessica's face grew grave, but her eyes still held a twinkle of eagerness as she walked around the side of the car to dump her books on the backseat. "How? Where did they come from? Freddy's?"

"No, not Freddy's. They came from my dad's house, we think. But they weren't his, Jessica. He didn't build them. We think it was Dave . . . Afton . . . whatever his name is." The words had come tumbling out all at once, nonsensical, and John stepped in to translate.

"She means that—"

"No, I get it," Jessica cut in. "You don't have to talk to me like I'm uninitiated. I was at Freddy's last year, too, remember? I've seen some crazy things. So, what are we going to do?" She looked at Charlie, her game face on. She looked far more together than Charlie felt.

"We don't know what any of it means for sure," John said. "We're still figuring it out."

"Why didn't you tell me?" Jessica asked. Charlie looked up at her hesitantly.

"I just didn't want it to be like last time," she said. "There's no need to put everyone at risk."

"Yeah, just me." John smirked.

"I get that," Jessica said. "But after what happened last time . . . I mean, we're in this together."

John leaned back against the car, glancing around for anyone who might be listening.

"So . . ." Jessica stepped around her to look at the map. "What are we doing?"

Charlie leaned in and squinted at the distance key on the map. "There's about three miles between each location." She studied the map again for a moment, then drew another circle. "That's my house—my dad's house." She looked up at John. "Whatever is out there killing people came from there. They must have . . ." Her voice trailed off.

"When the storm broke the wall," John muttered.

"What?" Jessica asked.

"A section of the house was sealed until the storm broke through."

With firm strokes, Charlie drew a straight line from her father's house, through the three houses of the victims, and continued the line across the map. "That can't be right," Jessica said when she saw where the line finally ended. John peered over Charlie's shoulder.

"Isn't that your college?" he asked.

"Yeah, it's our dorm." The excitement had left Jessica's voice. "That doesn't make any sense."

Charlie couldn't take her eyes off the paper. It felt a little like she had drawn the path to her own death. "It wasn't a coincidence," she said.

"What are you talking about?"

"Don't you get it?" She let out a faint laugh, unable to stop herself. "It's me. They're coming for me. They're *looking* for me!"

"What? Who are *they*?" Jessica looked to John.

"There were three empty . . . graves at her dad's house. So, there must be three of them out there somewhere."

"They move at night," Charlie said. "I mean they can't walk around in the daylight. So they find a place to bury themselves until nightfall."

"Even if you're right, and they're coming for you," John

said, bending down and trying to catch her eye, "now we know they're coming. And going by this, we can at least guess where they might go next."

"So, what are you saying? What does that matter?" Charlie heard her own voice break.

"It matters because those things are out there, right now, buried in someone's yard. And when the sun goes down they're going to kill again, in the most horrible way possible." Charlie said nothing, her head bowed. "Look." John straightened out the map and pushed it into Charlie's lap, so she couldn't help but see it. "Somewhere in here." He pointed to the next circled area on the line. "We can stop them if we can find them first," John said with urgency.

"Okay." Charlie took a breath. "We don't have much time, though."

John grabbed the map, and they all got into the car.

"Just tell me where to go," Charlie said grimly.

John peered down at the map. "So this is where we need to be?" he confirmed, pointing to the fifth circle, and Charlie nodded. He turned the map and squinted. "Turn left out of the parking lot, then take the next right. I know this place. I've driven past it. It's an apartment complex. It's pretty run-down from what I remember."

Jessica leaned forward, poking her head between the front seats. "Those circles don't look too precise; it could be any-where in the area."

"Yeah, but I'm guessing it's going to be the place with the three fresh graves in the backyard," John said.

Charlie glanced at each of them for a second before fixing her eyes back on the road. There was safety in numbers. Last year when they were trapped at Freddy's together, Jessica was the one who had gotten them inside the restaurant in the first place. She was brave, even when she didn't want to be, and that meant more than whatever notion of romance John was entertaining.

"Charlie, turn right!" John exclaimed. She yanked the wheel, barely making the turn. *Focus. Imminent murder first, everything else later.*

Before them lay sprawling fields, lots marked out and prepared for construction and future development but never finished. Some had never even begun. Slabs of concrete were stacked here and there, almost completely obscured by overgrowth. A few lots away, steel beams had been erected to make a foundation that was never filled in. The place had decayed before it was completed.

In the farthest lot back was a cluster of what seemed to be finished apartment complexes. Grass and weeds grew rampant around them, however, climbing up their very walls; it looked like years of growth. It was hard to tell whether anyone lived inside. Years ago, the city had been diligently preparing for a population boom, one that never arrived.

"Are there even people out here?" Jessica was gazing out the window.

"There must be. There are parked cars." John craned his neck. "I think those are cars. I don't know where we're supposed to look, though."

"I think we just have to drive around." Charlie slowed the car as they traversed the road leading toward the buildings.

"Maybe not," John said. "I bet it's somewhere near the edge of the development. Most people would probably call the police if they saw eight-foot monsters digging holes in someone's backyard. There is a lot of visibility out here."

"Of course," Charlie said with dread in her voice. "They're buried, out of sight, and strategically placing themselves so as not to be found." She looked at John expectantly, but he just stared back. "They're intelligent," she explained. "I think I would have liked it better if they were just roaming the streets mindlessly. At least then someone could call the national guard or something." Charlie kept her eyes on the fields.

They drove around the outer edges of the development slowly, looking at the yards of each house. Some of the buildings looked abandoned, the windows boarded up or torn out completely, opening the apartments to the elements. The storm had done its damage, but little had been done to repair it. A tree had fallen across one cul-de-sac, blocking a building off completely. But it didn't look like anyone was trying to get in or out; the tree rotted where it lay. There was litter strewn in the abandoned streets, collecting in the gutters and bolstering the curbs. Maybe one apartment in five had curtains in the window.

Occasionally they passed a parked car or a toppled tricycle on the patchy grass. No one came outside, though Charlie thought she saw a curtain pull shut as they drove past. In two backyards there were aboveground pools filled by rainwater, and one had a large trampoline, its springs rusted and its canvas torn.

"Just a second." Charlie pulled to a stop, leaving the car running as she approached a tall wooden fence. It was too high to climb, but there was a single board that hung loose off its nail near the base. She squatted down and pried it away to peek inside.

Two round black eyes glared at her.

Charlie froze. The eyes belonged to a dog, a massive thing, which started to bark, its teeth gnashing and its chain clanking. Charlie slammed the board back in place and walked to the car. "Okay, let's keep going."

"Nothing?" Jessica asked dubiously, and Charlie shook her head. "Maybe they didn't make it this far."

"I think they did," Charlie said. "I think they're doing exactly what they mean to." She pulled the car over to the shoulder of the winding road and looked at the apartment buildings on either side. "This could have been a nice place to live," she said softly.

"Why are we stopping?" John looked confused.

Charlie leaned back in her seat and closed her eyes. *Locked in a box, a dark and cramped box, can't move, can't see, can't think. Let me out!* Her eyes flew open, and she grabbed the handle of the car door in a panic. She pulled against it hard.

"It's locked," John said. He leaned across her to pull up the button lock.

"I know that," she said angrily. She got out and closed the door. John moved to follow her, but Jessica placed her hand on his shoulder.

"Leave her alone for a minute," she said.

Charlie leaned over the trunk, propping her chin on her hands. *What am I missing, Dad?* She stood up straight and stretched her arms over her head, turning her whole body slowly to study her surroundings.

There was an empty lot beyond the development, not far from where they were. It was marked out with telephone poles, only one of which had wires. A breeze dragged the loose wires through the dirt, scattering gravel. It didn't look like it had ever been paved. There was a coil of barbed wire as tall as Charlie, sitting uselessly in a corner. Empty cans and fast-food wrappers littered the ground, the paper quivering and the cans rattling in the slight wind, like they sensed something awful. The wind rushed up behind Charlie and blew past her, straight toward the field, rustling the papers and cans and sending waves across the patches of brown grass. *Something wrong is planted there.*

Filled with a new energy, Charlie opened the car door just enough to lean inside.

"That lot. We have to go look."

"What do you see? It's kind of out of the way," John said.

Charlie nodded. "You said it yourself. If an eight-foot monster is digging up the neighbor's backyard, someone's going to notice. Besides, I just have . . . I have a feeling."

Jessica got out of the car and John followed at her heels. Charlie already had the trunk open. She pulled out a shovel, the big Maglite flashlight she always kept close by, and a crowbar.

"I've only got one shovel," she explained, making it clear she was keeping it for herself. Jessica took the flashlight and made a practice swing with it, as if hitting an invisible assailant.

"Why would you even have a shovel?" Jessica asked in a suspicious tone.

"Aunt Jen," John said by way of explanation.

Jessica laughed. "Well, you never know when you might have to dig up a robot."

"Come on," Charlie said, tossing John the crowbar and starting off. He caught it with ease and jogged beside her, leaning in so Jessica wouldn't hear.

"How come I don't get the shovel?"

"I figure you can swing a crowbar harder than I can," Charlie said.

He grinned. "Makes sense," he said confidently, gripping the crowbar with new purpose.

When they reached the edge of the lot, John and Jessica stopped, looking down at the ground before them, as though scared of what they might step on. Charlie went ahead across the loose dirt, gripping the shovel tightly. The field was mostly barren soil, studded with large mounds of gravel and dirt that had been left for so long that grass had begun growing on them.

"This must have been the dumping ground for when they were building," John said. He took a few steps into the lot, avoiding a broken glass bottle.

At the opposite edge was the tree line. Charlie studied it carefully, tracking its path back in the direction they'd come.

John knelt beside a pile of gravel and carefully poked at it with his crowbar, as though something might leap out. Jessica had wandered toward a cluster of bushes. She crouched to pick something up, then quickly dropped it and wiped her hands on her shirt. "Charlie, this place is disgusting!" she cried.

Charlie had reached the tree line and began walking alongside it, studying the ground.

"See anything?" John yelled from the other side of the lot.

Charlie ignored him. Deep grooves in the dirt extended from the trees, snaking around the bushes. The large rocks nearby were freshly marked with gashes and scrapes. "Not exactly footprints," Charlie whispered as she followed the grooves in the soil. Her foot touched soft ground, a sudden contrast to the hard-packed dirt of the rest of the lot. She stepped back. The dirt at her feet was discolored, familiar.

Charlie struck her shovel into the ground and started to dig, the metal rasping noisily on the gravel mixed in with the dirt. Jessica and John ran toward her.

"Careful," John warned as he approached. He hefted the crowbar in his hands like a baseball bat, ready to strike. Jessica hung back. Charlie saw that her knuckles were white on the flashlight's handle, but her face was calm and determined. The dirt was loose and came away easily. At last the blade of the shovel struck metal with a hollow *clunk*, and they all jumped. Charlie handed the shovel to John and knelt in the mess of scattered earth, brushing away the dirt with her hands.

"Careful!" Jessica said, her voice higher-pitched than usual, and John echoed her.

"This was a horrible idea," he murmured, scouting the area. "Where's a police car when you need one? Or any car?"

"It's still day for a little while longer," Charlie said absently, focused on the ground as her hands ran through it, prying away rocks and clods of dirt, digging to find what lay beneath.

"Yeah, it's day. It was also day when that twisted Foxy attacked you earlier, remember?" John said more urgently.

"Wait, WHAT?" Jessica exclaimed. "Charlie, get away from there! You didn't tell me that!" She turned on John accusingly.

"Look, a LOT has been going on, okay?" John raised his hands, palms out.

"Yeah, but if you're going to sign me up for this stuff, then you need to tell me about things like that! You were attacked?"

"Sign you up for this? You had one foot in the car at the first mention of murder! You practically invited yourself."

"Invited myself? You talk like I crashed your date, but you didn't exactly fall over yourself to refuse my help." Jessica planted her hands on her hips.

"Charlie," John sighed. "Can you please talk to—OH JEEZ." He jumped backward, and Jessica followed suit as soon as she looked down. Beneath them, gazing up from the loose dirt, was an enormous metal face, staring toward the sun. Charlie didn't say anything. She was still busy scooping away the soil from the edges, revealing two rounded ears on the sides of its head.

"Charlie. Is that . . . Freddy?" Jessica gasped.

"I don't know. I think it was supposed to be." Charlie heard the anxiety in her own voice as she stared down at the large, lifeless bear with its perpetual smile. The crude metal frame was covered with a layer of gelatinous plastic, giving it an organic appearance, almost embryonic.

"It's huge." John gasped. "And there's no fur . . ."

"Just like the other Foxy." Charlie's hands were getting sore. She cleared the hair from her face and stood up.

It was Freddy, but somehow not. The bear's eyes were open, glazed over with the inanimate look of lifelessness Charlie knew so well. This bear was dormant, for now.

"Charlie, we have to go," John said with a tone of warning. But he didn't move, still staring downward. He knelt beside the face and began to claw at the dirt above its forehead, clearing the earth away until he saw it: a filthy, battered black top hat. Charlie felt a smile tugging at her mouth, and she bit her lip.

"We should call Burke," Jessica said. "Now."

They all turned back toward the development as the wind rose again, rushing past them and making waves in the tall grass. The earth was still, and the sun was sinking lower behind the rolling hills in the distance.

# CHAPTER EIGHT

Charlie tossed her keys to John. "You go. There's a gas station a few miles back the way we came. You can call from there." He nodded, jangling the keys in his hand.

"I'll stay with you," Jessica said instantly.

"No," Charlie said, more forcefully than she intended. "Go with John." Jessica looked confused for a moment but finally nodded and headed off toward the car.

"Are you sure?" John asked. Charlie waved her hand at him dismissively.

"Someone needs to stay with it. I'll keep my distance. I promise. I won't disturb . . . it."

"Okay." Like Jessica, John hesitated for a moment. Then they left Charlie alone in the empty lot. After a minute, she heard the engine start, and the noise of the car faded as they drove off down the empty streets. She sat at the top of the mound where she had uncovered the misshapen bear and gazed down at it.

"What do you know?" she whispered. She stood and paced slowly over the other two plots of disturbed soil, wondering what lay beneath. The bear was frightening, misshapen, an imitation of Freddy created by someone else. It was a strange variation, into which her father had never breathed life. *But William Afton—Dave—did.* The man who designed these things was the same man who had stolen and murdered her brother.

A thought surfaced, a question that had visited her many times before: *Why did he take Sammy?* Charlie had asked herself, the wind, and her dreams that question endlessly. *Why did he take Sammy?* But she had always meant, *Why not me? Why was I the one who lived?* She stared down at the soil beneath her, envisioning the bear's strange, embryonic face. The children murdered at Freddy Fazbear's had lived on after death, their spirits lodged somehow inside the animatronic costumes that had killed them. Could Sammy's spirit be imprisoned somehow, behind a large, rectangular door?

Charlie shivered and stood up, suddenly wanting to put as much distance as possible between her and the twisted Freddy buried in the soil. The image of his face came to her again, and this time it made her skin crawl. Did the other two mounds hide similar creatures? Was there a malformed rabbit hidden in the dirt just there? A chicken clutching a cupcake to its grotesque chest? *But the thing that tried to kill me—tried to envelop me—it was designed to kill. There could be anything buried down there, waiting for nightfall.* She could look, dig up the other two mounds to see what lay slumbering beneath. But as soon as she thought it she could almost feel the lock of metal hands on her arms, forcing her inside that deathly, cavernous chest.

Charlie took a few deliberate steps back from the mounds, wishing just a little that she had allowed Jessica to stay.

"How has your visit with Charlie been?" Jessica asked in a conspiratorial tone as they made the final turn out of the development and onto the main road.

John didn't take his eyes off the road. "It's been fun to see her again. You, too," he added, and she laughed.

"Yes, you've always loved me. Don't worry, I know you're here to see her."

"I'm here for a job, actually."

"Right," Jessica said. She turned and looked out the window. "Do you think Charlie's changed?" she asked abruptly.

John was silent for a moment, picturing the bedroom Charlie had turned into a scrap heap and Theodore, ripped apart and strewn in pieces. He thought of her tendency to retreat into herself, losing whole minutes as if she were stepping briefly out of time. *Do I think she's changed?*

"No," he said finally.

"I don't think she has, either." Jessica sighed.

"What did you find at Freddy's?" John asked.

"Dave," Jessica said plainly, waiting for a moment before looking at John. "Right where we left him."

"And you're sure he was dead?" John looked down.

Jessica swallowed hard, suddenly seeing the body again. She pictured the discolored skin and the costume that had sunken into his rotting flesh, fusing the man to the mascot in a grotesque eternity.

"He was dead all right," she said hoarsely.

The gas station was just up ahead. John parked in the small lot and got out of the car without waiting for Jessica. She followed at his heels.

"What a dump." Jessica spun, marveling at the surroundings. "Surely there was a better place to . . ." Jessica stopped short, suddenly seeing the teenage boy behind the counter. He was staring into space, watching something just behind them and to the left.

"Excuse me," John said. "Do you have a public phone?" The boy shook his head.

"No, not public," he said, gesturing to it.

"Could we use it? Please?"

"Customers only."

"I'll pay for the call," John said. "Look, this is important." The boy looked at them, his eyes finally focusing, as if only just registering their presence. He nodded slowly.

"Okay, but you have to buy something while she makes the call." He shrugged, helpless against the rules of management.

"John, just give me the number," Jessica said. He dug it out of his pocket and handed it to her. As she went behind the counter, John scanned the shelves impatiently, looking for the cheapest item available.

"We have Popsicles," the kid said.

"No, thanks," John said.

"They're free." He pointed at the cooler.

"Well, how's that going to help me if they're free?"

"I'll let it count as a purchase." The boy winked.

John clenched his jaw and lifted the lid of the cooler, jerking slightly at the sight of the taxidermy coyote hidden inside.

"Brilliant. Did you stuff that yourself?" he asked loudly.

The boy laughed, a sudden, snorting sound. "Hey!" he yelled as John grabbed the carcass by the head and yanked it out of the cooler. "Hey! You can't do that!" John marched to the door, out into the parking lot, and hurled the dead thing into the road. "Hey!" The boy screamed again and ran out into the street, disappearing into a cloud of dust.

"John?" Jessica hurried out from around the counter. "Clay's on his way."

"Great." He followed her out to the car.

Charlie was still walking in circles, glancing up at the horizon every few seconds. She felt like a sentry, or the keeper of a vigil. She couldn't stop imagining the animatronics buried there, whatever they were. They weren't in boxes, not even shielded from the dirt; it would sink into their every pore and joint, it would fill them. They could open their mouths to scream, but the relentless dirt would just flow in, too fast for sound to escape.

Charlie shivered and rubbed her arms, looking up at the sky. It was turning orange, and shadows from the weeds began stretching out across the ground. Giving the mounds a sideways glance, she walked with deliberate steps to the other side of the lot where the only telephone pole with wires stood. They hung down from it like the branches of a weeping willow, dragging in the dirt. As Charlie got closer she saw small, dark shapes by its base. She approached slowly: they were rats, all lying stiff and dead. She stared down at them for a long moment, then whirled, startled, at the sounds of cars.

John and Jessica had returned, and Clay was just behind them. He must have already been in the area.

"Watch out for that pole," Charlie said by way of greeting. "I think the wires are live."

John laughed. "No one touch the wires. Glad you're okay."

Clay didn't speak; he was busy examining the patches of dirt. He walked around them as Charlie had, peering at them from every angle, then finally came to a stop when he'd made a full circle. "You dug one of these up?" he asked, and Charlie could hear the strain behind his level voice.

"No," John said hastily. "We just uncovered part of it, then covered it back up."

Clay looked down again. "I'm not sure if that makes it better or worse," he said, his eyes still on the mounds.

"It looked like Freddy," Charlie said urgently. "It looked like a strange, misshapen Freddy. There was something wrong with it."

"What was wrong?" Clay asked gently. He looked at her with serious eyes.

"I don't know," Charlie said helplessly. "But there's something wrong with all of them."

"Well, they're murdering people," Jessica offered. "I'd count that as something being wrong with them."

"Charlie," Clay said, still focused on her, "If you can tell me anything else about these things, then now's the time. We have to assume that, as Jessica told me over the phone, they're going to kill again tonight."

Charlie dropped to her knees in the place where they had dug up the twisted Freddy, and began digging again.

"What are you doing?" John protested.

"Clay needs to see it," she muttered.

"What in the . . ." Clay inched forward to study the face, then took a long step back to observe the disturbed plots of earth, measuring the size of the things buried at their feet.

"We have to evacuate these buildings," John said. "Otherwise, what are we going to do when these things get up? Ask them to go back to bed? There aren't that many apartments in this area that actually have people living in them. There's only one building in the whole block," he said, pointing, "maybe two, that looked occupied."

"Okay, I'm going to go check it out and see who's home. Keep watch over these things." Clay studied the row of buildings and made his way toward them.

"So we wait," John said.

Charlie continued watching the skyline. Dark clouds were rolling over the sun, making it appear as though night had fallen early.

"Do you hear that?" Jessica whispered.

Charlie knelt beside the metal face half-buried in the ground and turned her ear to it. "Charlie!" John startled. She lifted her head and stared at the face again. It had changed from one moment to the next. Its features had smoothed over, become less crude. She looked up at John, her eyes wide. "It's changing."

"Wait, what? What does that mean?" Jessica said, looking horrified.

"It means something is very wrong," he said. Jessica waited for him to explain.

"We're not at Freddy's anymore," was all he offered.

Clay returned from across the field.

"Everyone into the car," he said.

"My car?" Charlie asked.

Clay shook his head. "Mine." Charlie was about to protest, but Clay gave her a stern look. "Charlie, unless your car has a siren and you've had high-speed pursuit training, stand down." She nodded.

"What did you tell them?" Jessica asked suddenly.

"I told them there was a gas leak in the area," Clay said. "Scary enough to get them out, not so scary as to start a panic." Jessica nodded. She looked almost impressed, like she was taking mental notes.

They piled into Clay's car, Jessica quickly claiming the front seat, though Charlie suspected that she just wanted to leave her alone next to John. The cruiser sat at the edge of the lot, as far from the mounds as they could be without edging onto the road. As the sun sank below the horizon and the final streaks of light bled away into darkness, a single streetlight flickered on. It was old, the light almost orange, and it sputtered at intervals, as if it might fail at any moment. Charlie watched it for a while, empathizing.

John was busy staring out across the field, unblinking, but as the hour passed he began to slouch in his seat. He let out a yawn, then quickly brought himself back to alertness. An elbow poked him in the ribs and he turned to find Charlie with a mess of wires in her lap, studying something carefully. "What are you doing?" he asked, then turned his gaze back to the field.

"I'm trying to see what exactly this thing does." Charlie had the metal disc firmly in her hand. It was the one they'd wrestled from the monster that day. She was trying to connect it properly to the diagnostic tool's small keypad and display.

"Okay, John, don't puke on me." She smiled, her finger ready to flick the switch.

"I'll do my best," he grumbled and tried to concentrate on the dimly lit field.

"What is that?" Jessica whispered.

"We found it inside the animatronic that attacked us today," Charlie was eager to explain. Jessica leaned in closer to see. "It emits some kind of signal; we don't know what it is."

"It changes what those things look like." John turned his head from the window with a nauseated look.

"It changes our *perception* of what they look like," Charlie corrected.

"How?" Jessica seemed captivated.

"I'm not sure yet, but maybe we can find out." Charlie dug her nail into the groove and pulled the switch. "Ugh, I can hear it already."

John sighed. "And I can feel it."

"I can't . . ." Jessica tilted her head to listen. "Maybe I can. I don't know."

"It's very high-pitched." Charlie was busy turning small knobs on the handheld display, trying to get a readout from the device.

"It gets into your head." John rubbed his forehead. "This morning it almost made me sick."

"Of course," Charlie whispered. "It gets into your head."

"What?" Jessica turned toward her.

"These readings looked nonsensical at first. I thought something was wrong."

"And?" John said impatiently when Charlie suddenly went silent.

"In class we learned that when the brain is overstimulated, it fills in gaps for you. So, say you pass a red hexagonal sign on the road, and someone asks you what words were on it. You'd say 'STOP.' And you'd imagine that you saw it. You'd be able to picture that stop sign the way it should have been. That is, of course, if you were properly distracted and didn't notice an obviously blank sign. This thing distracts us. Somehow it makes our brains fill in blanks with previous experiences, the things we think we *should* be seeing."

"How does it do that? What's in the actual signal?" John glanced back again, only half listening.

"It's a pattern. Sort of." Charlie leaned back, letting her arms relax, the device cradled in her hands. "The disc emits five sound waves that continuously vary in frequency. First they match one another, then they don't; they go in and out of harmony, always on the edge of forming a predictable sequence, then branching away."

"I don't understand. So, it's *not* a pattern?" John said.

"It's not, but that's the whole point. It almost makes sense, but not quite." Charlie paused, thinking for a moment. "The tone fluctuations happen so fast that they're only detected by your subconscious. Your mind goes mad trying to make sense of it; it's immediately overwhelmed. It's like the opposite of white noise: you can't follow it, and you can't tune it out."

"So the animatronics aren't changing shape. We're just being distracted. What's the purpose of that, though?" John had turned away from the window, giving up the pretense of ignoring the conversation.

"To earn our trust. To look more friendly. To look more real." As the possibilities stacked up, a grim picture began to form in Charlie's mind.

John laughed. "To look more real, maybe. But they certainly don't strike me as friendly."

"To lure kids closer," Charlie continued. The car got quiet.

"Let's just focus on getting through the night, okay?" Clay said from the front seat. "I can't call this in as is. Right now it's just buried junk in a field. But if you're right, and something starts moving out there . . ." He didn't finish. John leaned against the car door, propping his head against the window so he could keep watching.

Charlie leaned her head back, letting her eyes close for just a few moments. Across the field, the orange bulb continued to flicker with a hypnotic pulse.


Minutes passed, and then almost another hour. Clay glanced at the teenagers. They had all fallen asleep. Charlie and John were awkwardly leaning on each other. Jessica had curled up with her feet on the seat beneath her and her head resting on the narrow window ledge. She looked like a cat, or a human who was going to wake up with neck problems. Clay shrugged his shoulders up and down, seized with the odd alertness he always felt when he was the only one awake. When Carlton had been a baby, he and Betty would take turns getting up with him. But while Betty had been exhausted by it, barely making it through the following day, Clay had found himself almost energized. There was something about walking through the world when no one else was stirring. It made him feel as if he could protect them all, as if he could make everything all right. *Oh, Betty.* He blinked, the orange streetlight suddenly shimmering as his eyes moistened. He took a deep breath, regaining control. *There was nothing I could say, was there?* Unbidden, the memory of their last conversation—their last fight—reared in his mind.

*"All hours of the night. It's not healthy. You're obsessed!"*

*"You're as consumed by your work as I am. It's something we have in common, remember? Something we love about each other."*

*"This is different, Clay. This worries me."*

*"You're being irrational."*

*She laughed, a sound like breaking glass. "If you think that, then we're not living in the same reality."*

*"Maybe we're not."*

*"Maybe not."*

The light changed. Clay glanced around, fully focused on the present again. The orange streetlight was fading, the flickering growing faster. As he watched, it gave a final heroic burst and went dark.

"Damn it," he said aloud. Jessica stirred in her sleep, making a small protesting noise. Quietly, but quickly, Clay exited the car, grabbing the flashlight from its place beside his seat. He closed the door and started toward the mounds, his frantic light shaking out across the field until it disappeared.

Charlie roused. Her heart was racing, but she couldn't tell if it was from the sudden awakening, or from the remnants of a dream she could no longer recall. She shook John.

"John, Jessica. Something's going on." Charlie was out of the car and running before they could answer, heading toward the mounds. "Clay!" she called. He jumped at the sound of her voice.

"They're gone." Charlie gasped, stumbling on the upturned earth. Clay was already running toward the apartment nearest him. "Go back to the car," he barked over his shoulder. Charlie ran after him, glancing back, trying to spot John and Jessica. Charlie's eyes weren't adjusted yet and Clay's flashlight seemed to sink into the darkness ahead of him. Charlie could only follow the sounds of his footsteps as he charged through the shallow grass.

She finally came to a brick wall and sprinted around it to the front of the apartment. Clay was at the door already. He banged against it and impatiently peered into the nearest window. No one answered; no one was inside.

A scream cut through the night, and Charlie froze. It was high-pitched and human, reverberating off the walls of the houses. It came again. Clay aimed his light in the direction of the sound.

"We missed someone!" he shouted. He darted around the side of the house, running blindly back across the field. The scream seemed to be in motion, making its way rapidly toward the black trees.

"Over here!" Charlie cried, breaking from behind Clay and running toward an indistinct movement in the dark.

"Charlie!" John's voice cut distantly through the night, but Charlie didn't wait for him. The sound of gravel under her feet was deafening. She came to an abrupt stop, realizing she'd lost her bearings. "Charlie!" someone yelled in the distance. The rest was lost in the rustle of the trees as a night wind swept through. She tried to keep her eyes open as grains of sand pelted her face. Then the wind finally calmed, and there was another rustle of branches nearby, this one unnatural. Charlie stumbled toward the sound, holding her arms in front of her until she could see again.

Then it was there. Just at the edge of the tree line, a misshapen figure stood hunched in the darkness. Charlie stopped short a few yards away, struck still, suddenly aware that she was alone. The thing lurched to the side, then stepped toward her, revealing a sleek snout. A wolf's mane ran over the top of its head and down its back. It was stooped over, one arm twisted downward while the other flailed up. Perhaps its control over its limbs was uncertain. It was looking at Charlie, and she met its eyes: they were piercing blue and self-illuminating. Yet while the eyes held a steady light, the rest of the creature was in flux, morphing in a disorienting fashion even as she watched. One moment it was a groomed and agile figure covered in silver hair, the next a tattered metal framework, partly coated in rubbery translucent skin. Its eyes were stark white bulbs. The creature flinched and convulsed, finally settling on its crude metal appearance. Charlie drew in a sharp breath, and the wolf broke its stare.

It spasmed alarmingly, doubling over. Its chest split open, folding outward like a horrid metal mouth. The parts made a grinding, abrasive sound. Charlie stifled a scream, rooted to the spot. It lurched again, and something fell from inside it, landing solidly on the ground. The wolf toppled forward beside it, shuddered, and went still.

"Oh no." Clay arrived from behind Charlie, staring at the human body that lay writhing in the grass.

Charlie remained motionless, captivated by the wolfish pinpoints of light that stared back at her. The thing tucked its head down, suddenly flowing again with a silver mane. It folded its long, silken ears, and slunk backward, disappearing into the woods. There was a rustling in the trees, and then it was gone.

No sooner had Jessica arrived than Clay was forcefully shoving the light into her hands. "Take it!" Clay knelt by the body doubled over in the grass and checked for a pulse. "She's alive," he said, but his voice was hard. He bent over her, looking for something else.

"Charlie!" It was John, tugging at her shoulder. "Charlie, come on, we have to get help!"

John took off running and Charlie followed more slowly, unable to take her eyes off the woman who seemed to be dying on the ground. Clay's voice faded into the darkness behind them.

"Miss, are you all right? Miss? Can you hear me?"

# CHAPTER NINE

Professor Treadwell seemed restless. Her face was calm as ever, but as the students worked, she paced back and forth across the auditorium stage, the heels of her shoes making a repetitive click. Arty poked Charlie, nodded toward the professor, and quickly mimed screaming. Charlie smiled and turned back to her own work. She didn't mind the sound. The professor's sharp, regular steps were like a metronome, marking the time.

She reread the first question: *Describe the difference between a conditional loop and an infinite loop.* Charlie sighed. She knew the answer; it just seemed pointless to write it down. *A conditional loop happens only when certain conditions* she started, then scratched it out and sighed again, staring out over the heads of the other students.

She could see the face of the wolf again, shimmering back and forth between its two faces: the illusion and the frame beneath it. Its eyes stared into her own, as if reading something deep inside her. *Who are you? Who were you supposed to be?* she thought. She had never seen it before, and it worried her. Freddy Fazbear's Pizza didn't *have* a wolf.

Charlie had a near-photographic memory, she'd realized last year. It was the reason she had such recall of even her early childhood. But she didn't remember the wolf. *That's silly*, she told herself. *There's plenty you don't remember.* And yet her memories of her father's workshop were so strong: the smell, the heat. Her father bent over his workbench, and the place in the corner where she didn't like to look. It was all so present within her, so immediate. Even the things she didn't remember without prompting, like the old Fredbear's Family Diner, had been instantly familiar as soon as she'd seen them. Yet these creatures had no foothold in her memory. She didn't know them, but they clearly knew her.

*Why were they entombed in the back of the house like that? Why not just destroyed?* Her father's deep attachment to his creations had never outweighed his pragmatism. If something didn't work, he dismantled it for parts. He had done the same with Charlie's own toys.

She blinked, suddenly recalling.

*He held it out to her, a little green frog with horn-rimmed glasses over its bulging eyes. Charlie looked at it skeptically.*

"No," she said.

"Don't you want to see what he does?" her father protested, and she crossed her arms and shook her head.

"No," she mumbled. "I don't like the big eyes." Despite her protests, her father set the frog on the ground in front of her and pressed a button hidden beneath the plastic at its neck. It rotated its head from side to side, then suddenly leaped in the air. Charlie screamed and jumped back, and her father rushed to pick her up.

"I'm sorry, sweetheart. It's okay," he whispered. "I didn't mean for it to startle you."

"I don't like the eyes," she sobbed against his neck, and he held her for a long moment. Then set her down and picked up the frog. He put it on his workbench, took a short knife from the shelf, and sliced its skin along its entire length. Charlie clapped a hand over her mouth and made a small, squeaking sound, watching wide-eyed as he carelessly peeled the green casing off the robot. The plastic split with a loud cracking noise in the quiet workshop. The frog's legs kicked helplessly.

"I didn't mean it," she said hoarsely. "I'm sorry, I didn't mean it! Daddy!" She was speaking aloud, but it was mostly air. Her voice was somehow constrained, like in dreams where she tried to scream, but nothing came out. Her father was intent on his work and didn't seem to hear her.

The stripped-down robot lay prone before him on the bench. He prodded it and it made a horrible twitch, its back legs kicking out uselessly, repeating the motion of its leap into the air. It tried again, more frantically, like it was in pain.

"Wait. Daddy, don't hurt him," Charlie mouthed, trying and failing to force out the sound. *Her father selected a tiny screwdriver and began to work at the frog's head, deftly unscrewing something on each side. He removed the back of the skull to reach inside. Its whole body convulsed.* Charlie ran to her father's side and grabbed his leg, tugging at the knee of his pants. "Please!" *she cried, her voice returning.*

*He disconnected something, and the skeleton went completely limp. Joints that had been stiff collapsed into a slump of parts. The eyes, which Charlie had not even noticed were lit, dimmed, flickered, and went dark. She let go of her father and moved back into the recess of the workshop, putting both hands over her mouth again so that he would not hear her cry as he began to methodically dismantle the frog.*

Charlie shook her head, pulling herself back to the present. The child's guilt still clung to her, like a weight in her chest. She gently pressed her hand there. *My father was pragmatic,* she thought. *Parts were expensive, and he didn't waste them on things that didn't work.* She forced her mind to the problem at hand.

*So why would he have buried them alive?*

"Buried who alive?" Arty hissed, and she turned, startled.

"Shouldn't you be busy doing something?" she said hastily, mortified to have spoken aloud.

The creatures had been buried in a chamber like a mausoleum, hidden in the walls of the house. Her father hadn't wanted to destroy them for some reason, and he had wanted them nearby. *Why? So he could keep an eye on them? Or did he even know they were there? Did Dave somehow hide them there without his knowledge?* She shook her head. It didn't matter. What mattered was what the creatures were going to do next.

She closed her eyes again, trying to envision the wolflike creature. She'd only seen it for that moment, as it disgorged the woman inside it and hovered between states, its illusion flickering like a faulty lightbulb. Charlie held on to the image, kept it frozen in her mind. She'd been fixated first on the victim, then on the wolf's eyes, but she had still seen the rest of it. Now she pictured the scene, ignoring the wolf's gaze, ignoring the panic that had seized her, the others shouting and running around her. She watched it happen again and again, picturing the chest sliding open one tooth-like rib at a time, then the woman falling out.

She realized she had a better picture of the same thing stored away: the creature in the tomb, just before it tried to swallow her. She visualized its chest opening, searching her mind to see what lay beyond the hideous mouth, inside the cavernous chest. Then she bent her head over her exam book and began to draw.

"Time," called one of the graduate students. The other three began to march up the aisles, collecting blue books one by one. Charlie only had half a sentence in answer to the first question, and it was crossed out—the rest of the book was a mess of mechanisms and monsters. Just before the teaching assistant reached her, she quietly tucked the book under her arm. She exited the row, blending in with the students who had already finished. She didn't speak to anyone on the way out, drifting more than walking, focused on her own thoughts as her body carried her aimlessly down the familiar hallway. She found a bench and sat. She looked around at the passing students, chatting to one another or lost in thoughts of their own. It was as if a wall had risen up, circling only her, completely isolating her from everything around her.

She opened her book again, to the page where she'd spent her test time scribbling. There, staring back at her, were the faces she understood: the faces of monsters and murderers, with blank eyes that pierced right through her, even from her own sketches. *What are you trying to tell me?* She stood, clenching her book, then took one last look at her surroundings.

It felt as though she were saying good-bye to a chapter of her life, another passage that would become nothing more than a haunting memory.

"Charlie," John's voice said from nearby. She glanced around, trying to find him through the thick flow of students exiting the building.

She finally spotted him off to the side of the stairs. "Oh, hey," she called and made her way over. "What are you doing here? Not that I'm not glad to see you, I just thought you had to work," she added hastily, trying to settle the whirling thoughts in her head.

"Clay called me. He tried your dorm, but you were here I guess. The woman we . . . from last night. She's going to be okay. He said he went to the next area, the next spot on the map, and drove around." John glanced at the crowd of students streaming past them and lowered his voice. "You know, the next place they're going to—"

"I know," Charlie said quickly, forestalling the explanation. "What did he find?"

"Well, it's a lot of empty space and fields mostly. One plot for future development, but it's vacant. He thinks we should focus on tomorrow instead. He has a plan." Charlie looked at him blankly.

"We're going to have to fight them," he said at last. "We both know that. But it won't be tonight."

Charlie nodded. "So what do we do tonight then?" she asked helplessly.

"Dinner?" John suggested.

"You can't be serious." Charlie's tone dropped.

"I know there's a lot going on, but we still need to eat, right?"

Charlie stared at the ground, collecting her thoughts. "Sure. Dinner." She smiled. "This is all pretty awful. It might be nice to get my mind off it, even if just for an evening."

"Okay," he said, and shifted awkwardly. "I'm going to run home and change then. I won't be long."

"John, none of this has to involve you," Charlie said softly. She gripped the straps of her backpack with both hands, as if they were tethering her to the ground.

"What are you talking about?" John looked at her, his self-consciousness gone.

"It doesn't have to involve anybody. It's me they're looking for."

"We don't know that for sure," he said, and put a hand on her shoulder. "You have to get that out of your head for a while. You'll drive yourself crazy." John smiled briefly, but he still looked worried. "Try to do something relaxing for a bit, take a nap or something. I'll see you for dinner, okay? Same restaurant at seven?"

"Okay," she echoed. He looked at her helplessly and gave a distressed smile, then turned and went.


Jessica was gone when Charlie got back to the dorm. She closed the door behind her with a sense of relief. She needed quiet. She needed to think, and she needed to move. She looked around, paralyzed for a moment. Her system of piling everything up as she used it was functional day-to-day, but when searching for something she hadn't touched in weeks, the system broke down.

"Where is it?" she muttered, scanning the room. Her eyes lit on Theodore's head, lying tumbled up against the leg of her bed. She picked it up and brushed off the dust, stroking his long ears until they were clean, if matted and patchy. "You used to be so soft," she told the rabbit's head. She set it on the bed, propped up on her pillow. "I guess I did, too," she added and sighed.

"Have you seen my duffel bag?" she asked the dismembered toy. "Maybe under the bed?" She got down on her knees to check. It was there, all the way at the far side, crushed by a pile of books and clothing that had fallen through the space between the bed and the wall. Charlie wriggled under the bed until she could snag the strap, then dragged it out and set it on top.

It was empty—she'd dumped out the contents as soon as she arrived, a harbinger of the messy habits to follow. She grabbed her toothbrush and toothpaste and zipped them into the bag's side pocket.

"I lied to John," she said. "No, that's not right. I let him lie to me. He has to know it's me they're coming for. We all do. And this isn't going to stop." She picked up clothing from what she thought was the clean pile, pulling out a T-shirt and jeans, socks and underwear, and shoving them emphatically into her bag as she spoke. "Why else would they be coming in this direction?" she asked the rabbit. "But . . . how would they even know?" She threw two textbooks into the bag and patted her pocket, reassuring herself that the disc and the diagnostic keyboard were there. She zipped up the bag and tilted her head, meeting Theodore's plastic eyes.

"It's not just that," she said. "This thing . . ." She measured the disc in her hand and studied it anew. "It made John sick. But it sings a song to me." She broke off, unsure of what that meant about her. "I don't know if I've ever known anything with quite such certainty," she said quietly. "But I have to do this. Afton made them. And Afton took Sammy. When I was with John, I could feel . . . something in the house. It had to be him; it was like the missing part of me was *there*, closer than it had ever been. I just couldn't quite reach it. And I think those monsters are the only things in the world that might have answers."

Theodore stared back at her, unmoved.

"It's me they want. No one else is going to die because of me." She sighed. "At least I have you to protect me, right?" She slung the bag over her back and turned to go, then paused. She grabbed Theodore's head by the ears and held him up to her own eye level. "I think today I need all the support I can get," she whispered. She shoved him into her bag, then hurried out of the dorm to her car.

The map was in the glove compartment. Charlie took it out and spread it in front of her, glancing at it momentarily then putting it away with confidence. She drove slowly out of the lot. Though she passed people and other cars on her way, she felt as though she was just part of the background, unseen to the world. By the time she and her car slipped out of sight, she'd already be forgotten.

The sky was cloudy; it gave the world a sense of waiting. It seemed like Charlie had the road to herself, and peacefulness overtook her. She'd been preoccupied with isolation today, but the speed and openness were comforting. She didn't feel alone. The tree line seemed to race across the field when she watched it from the window, an illusion made by the speeding car. She began to feel as though there were something in the woods matching her speed, darting through the blur of branches, a silent companion, someone coming to tell her everything that she ever wanted to know. *I'm coming*, she whispered.

The street dwindled from a highway to a country road, then to a gravel path. It rose up a long hill, and as Charlie slowly ascended, she could see clusters of houses and cars in distant, more populated areas. She turned a corner and left it all behind: there were no more houses, no more cars. The rows of trees had been replaced with lines of stumps and piles of brush, accompanied by the occasional blank billboard that, presumably, would someday announce what was to come. Slabs of concrete and half-paved driveways interrupted the countryside, and an abandoned bulldozer sat in the distance. Charlie took Theodore's head from her bag and set it on the passenger seat.

"Stay alert," she said.

Then she saw it: a single ranch-style house stood at the center of it all, surrounded by bulldozed land and the bare rib cages of half-built houses jutting from the ground. It was out of place: painted, fenced, and even planted with flowers in the garden. That's when it made sense. *A show house.*

The road stopped a few yards into the development, replaced by worn-down tracks in the dirt where the machinery came in and out. Charlie slowed the car to a stop. "Even you can't follow me this time," she said to the rabbit's head, then got out and closed the door, giving Theodore a smile through the window.

Charlie walked the trail slowly. The hulking, unfinished frames of the houses seemed to watch her reproachfully as she trespassed. The gravel crunched under her feet in the silence. There wasn't even a breeze; everything was still. She stopped when she reached higher ground and surveyed her surroundings for a moment. Everything was disturbed. Everything was upturned. She glanced above her as a single bird passed overhead, barely visible from its soaring height. Her eyes returned to the wasteland. "You're here somewhere, aren't you?"

At last she reached the lone finished house. It was set at the center of a neat square of perfectly trimmed grass, towering above its stooped, half-constructed neighbors. Charlie stared at the lawn for a moment before realizing that it must be fake, just like whatever furniture was inside.

She didn't try the door right away, instead going around to the backyard. It was laid out in a neat square of AstroTurf, just like the front, but here the illusion had been ruined. Ragged strips of grass had been torn up. The place radiated a sense of distress, now eerily familiar. Charlie just stared for a moment, certainty pulsing through her. She clenched her jaw, then went back around to the front door. It opened easily, without even a whisper of sound, and Charlie went inside.

It was dark in the house. She flipped a light switch experimentally, and it illuminated the whole place in an instant. A fully furnished living room greeted her, complete with leather chairs and a couch, and even candles on the fireplace mantle. She started to close the front door behind her, then hesitated, leaving it ajar. She walked farther into the living room, where there was an L-shaped couch and a wide-screen TV. *I'm surprised it hasn't been stolen*, she thought. But when she went closer she saw why—it wasn't real. There were no cords or cables coming from it. The whole place had a sur-real quality, almost of mockery.

She walked slowly into the dining room, her feet clapping against the polished hardwood floor. Inside was a beautiful, mahogany dining set. Charlie bent over to look at the underside of the table. "Balsa wood," she said, grinning to herself. It was a light, airy wood, made for model airplanes, not furniture; she could probably lift the table over her head if she wanted to. Down a short hallway from the dining room was a kitchen with gleaming new appliances, or at least imitations of them. There was also a back door in the kitchen. She unlocked it and pushed it open halfway, leaning outside and looking again at the expansive, tortured landscape. There were several stone steps here, leading down into a small garden. She stepped back inside, being sure to leave the door hanging slightly open.

There was a second long hall off the living room. This led to bedrooms and a small room fashioned into an office or den, complete with tall bookshelves, a desk, and an inbox tray full of empty file folders. Charlie sat down in the desk chair, finding herself enchanted by the utterly surface imitation of life. She spun the chair once, then stood again, not wanting to get distracted. There was a door to the outside here, too, though it was oddly placed beside the desk. Charlie opened it, fiddling with the latch until she was sure it would stay open. She continued on her way, walking through the house systematically, unlocking and opening each window she came to. Then she went down to the basement, where a storm cellar hung over a set of steep stone stairs. She opened that as well, leaving the doors gaping wide. Outside, dark had fallen.

There were several bedrooms, each furnished and made up with bright curtains and silk sheets, and a large bathroom with marble sinks. Charlie turned the faucet to see if there was water, but nothing happened, not even the grinding of pipes trying and failing. There was a master bedroom with an enormous bed, a guest room that somehow looked even less lived-in than the rest of the house, and a nursery with a life-size menagerie painted on the wall and a mobile hanging above a crib. Charlie glanced inside each, then went back into the master bedroom.

The bed was wide and covered in a light canopy of white mosquito netting. The covers were white as well, and the moon shone through the window to illuminate the pillows. It had an uncanny effect, as if whoever slept there would be on display. Charlie went to the window and leaned out, breathing in the soothing, cool night air. She looked up at the sky. It was still cloudy; there were only a few stars visible. She'd been moving with such grim, impulsive energy until now, but this part would be agonizing. Long hours might pass before anything happened, and all she could do was wait. A nervous fluttering had begun to fill her stomach. She wanted to pace, or even to run away, but she closed her eyes and clenched her jaw. *It's me they want.*

At last, Charlie pulled herself away from the window. She'd packed pajamas in the bag out in the car, but this sterile house full of props and imitations felt too strange for her to actually dress for bed. Instead she just took off her sneakers and considered her bedtime rituals complete. She laid down on the bed and tried to conjure her nightmares, gathering up those final moments with Sammy and holding them close to her like a talisman. *Hold on*, she thought. *I'm coming.*


John checked his watch. *She's just running late. But she was late last time, too.* The waitress caught his eye, and he shook his head. *Of course, last time she showed up covered in filth.* He'd already called her dorm room, but the phone just rang and rang. He'd seen what he'd thought was an answering machine when he was there, but realized only as he was waiting for it to pick up that it could have been one of Charlie's projects, or some piece of discarded junk. The waitress refilled his water glass, and he smiled at her.

She shook her head. "Same girl?" she asked gently.

John let out an involuntary laugh. "Yes, same girl," he said. "But it's okay. She's not standing me up, she's just . . . busy. College life, you know."

"Of course. Let me know if you want to order." She gave him another look of pity and went away. He shook his head.

Suddenly, he saw Charlie's hands on her backpack straps, holding on so tight that her knuckles had gone white. *They're coming for me*, she'd said. Charlie wasn't the type to wait around patiently for something to happen to her.

He got up and walked urgently to the pay phone at the back of the restaurant. Clay picked up on the first ring.

"Clay, it's John. Have you heard from Charlie?"

"No. What's wrong?"

"Nothing," John said reflexively. "I mean, I don't know. She was supposed to meet me, and she's—twenty-four minutes late. I know it's not a lot, but she said something earlier that's bothering me. I think she might do something stupid."

"Where are you?" John gave him the address. "I'll be right there," Clay said and hung up before John could reply.

# CHAPTER TEN

For the first few minutes, Charlie kept her eyes shut, feigning sleep, but after a little while they began to flutter of their own accord. She squeezed her eyes shut, trying to force them to stay closed, but it became unbearable. She opened them into the darkness and at once felt relief.

The house had grown cool with night. The open window let in fresh, clean air. She breathed deeply, trying with each exhalation to make herself calm. She wasn't anxious so much as impatient. *Hurry up*, she thought. *I know you're out there.*

But there was only silence, and stillness.

She took the disc out of her pocket and looked at it. It was too dark to see any details, not that there was anything on it she hadn't already memorized. A little light shone in from the moon outside, but the shadows in the corners were deep, like there was something hidden there eating up the light. She rubbed the side of the disc with her thumb, feeling the bumps of the letters. If she didn't know they were there, they'd be scarcely noticeable.

*Afton Robotics, LLC.* She'd seen pictures of William Afton, the man who Dave had been: pictures of him with her father, smiling and laughing. But she only remembered him as the man in the rabbit suit. *My father must have trusted him. He must not have suspected. He would never have built a second restaurant with the man who murdered one of his children. But those creatures—he had to have known they were buried beneath our house.* Charlie clenched her teeth, stifling a sudden delirious urge to smile. "Of course there was a secret robot graveyard under my bedroom," she murmured. "Of course that's where it would be." She covered her face in her hands. All the threads were tangling in her mind.

She pictured it unwillingly. *The creature in the doorway. At first he was a shadow, blocking the light, then he was a man in a rabbit suit, and even then it didn't occur to Charlie to be afraid. She knew this rabbit. Sammy hadn't even noticed him yet. He continued to play with his toy truck, running it back and forth hypnotically across the floor. Charlie stared up at the thing in the doorway, and a coldness began to gather in the pit of her stomach. This was not the rabbit she knew. Its eyes shifted back and forth subtly between the twins, taking its time: making its choice. When the eyes settled on Charlie, the cold feeling spread all through her, then he looked away again, at Sammy, who still hadn't turned around. Then a sudden movement, and the costumes on their hangers all leaped together, covering her so she couldn't see. She heard the toy truck hit the ground and spin in place for a moment, then everything was still.*

*She was alone, a vital part of her cut away.*  ·

Charlie sat up, shaking herself to try and set the memories loose. She'd grown accustomed to sharing a room with Jessica. It was a long time since she'd been completely alone with her thoughts in the dark.

"I forgot how hard it is to be quiet," she whispered, her voice as soft as breath. She glared down at the strange disc in her hand, as if it was bringing these visions on her. She tossed it across the room and into a dark corner, out of sight.

Then she heard it. Something was inside the house.

Whatever it was, it was being cautious. She heard creaks from somewhere distant, but they were slow and muted. Silence followed; whatever moved was hoping the sound would be forgotten. Charlie crept from the bed and approached the door carefully, pushing it farther open and leaning out agonizingly slowly, until she could see deep into the living room, and the dining room beyond that. A part of her kept returning to the thought that she was in someone else's house, that she was the intruder.

"Hello?" she called, almost hoping for an answer, even an

angry one demanding to know what she was doing there. Maybe John would answer, happy to have found her, and come running from the darkness.

Only silence returned her call, but Charlie knew she wasn't alone anymore.

Her eyes widened, her heartbeat drumming in her throat, making it hard to breathe. She took careful steps over the stone tiles, down the short hall to just outside the living room, where she stood to listen again. A clock chimed the hours in a different room. Charlie walked to the edge of the living room and stopped again. She could see most of the house from here, and she scanned the area for anything out of place. Doorways surrounded her like gaping mouths, breathing night air from the windows she'd opened.

There was a long hall leading from the farthest corner of the living room to a different bedroom. It was one of the few places she didn't have a clear line of sight into. She edged around the leather sofa in front of her and across the circular rug that filled the room. As she walked, she could see more of the hall slowly revealing itself. It stretched out, farther and farther.

Charlie stopped midstep. She could see into the far bedroom now. It was full of windows and blue moonlight, and there was something obstructing her view, something she hadn't noticed while she was moving. Now its silhouette was unmistakable. Charlie carefully looked around again, her eyes adjusting to her surroundings. To her right, another large door led down a single step and into the large den. Bookcases stretched up to the ceiling, and a putrid air emanated from inside. Beyond the bookcases was another shadow that didn't belong. Charlie bumped into a lamp and startled. She hadn't even realized she was moving backward.

The front door was open wide. Charlie nearly bolted toward it to escape, but she stopped herself. She took a breath and stepped softly back toward the bedroom, checking over her shoulder as she went. She went back to the bed, sliding her bare feet on the wood floor so her steps would make no sound, and eased herself slowly onto the mattress, cautious to keep the springs from creaking. Charlie lay back, closed her eyes, and waited.

Her eyes twitched, every instinct she had shouting the same thing: *Open your eyes! Run!* Charlie breathed steadily in and out, trying to make her body go limp, trying to look asleep. *Something is moving.* She counted the steps. *One, two, one, two—no.* They were slightly asynchronous: there was more than one of them. Two, maybe all three, were inside the house. One set of footsteps passed her door, and she let her eyes flutter open for an instant, just in time to see an indistinct shadow cross before the crack in the door.

Another set of footsteps sounded like they were in the side hallway, while a third . . .

She screwed her eyes shut tight. The steps fell still outside her door. Her breath was shuddering; she almost hiccupped as she inhaled and she bit her lips together. The door was gliding open. Her lungs tightened, pressing her for air, but she refused. She hung on to that single breath as if it were the last one she'd ever get. *I'll find you.* She clenched her fists, determined to remain still.

The footsteps were through the door now, crossing the floor with a heavy tread. She kept still. The air above her stirred, and through her closed eyelids, the darkness grew even darker. Charlie opened her eyes, and breathed in.

The space above her was empty; nothing was looking down at her.

She turned her head slowly, peering into the open hall to her left. The noises had all stopped.

Suddenly the blankets were yanked off her, pulled from the foot of the bed. Charlie shot up and finally saw what had come for her. An enormous head rested its chin at her feet. It looked like something from a carnival game, its eyes rolling from side to side, clicking each time they moved. A pitch-black top hat was perched on its head, cocked slightly to one side, and the giant cheeks and button nose gave him away immediately. *Freddy.*

It was no longer the sleek and featureless head she had unearthed in the abandoned lot. His head was lively and full of movement, covered in wavy brown fur and bouncy cheeks. Yet there was something disjointed about it all, as though every part of his face was moving independently.

Charlie fought to remain still, but her body was acting of its own accord, squirming and pulling to get away from the mouth opening up toward her. Freddy's face slid across the bed like a python. His head lost its shape as it folded outward, taking hold of her feet and beginning to swallow, moving slowly upward as she fought not to scream or fight. A giant arm reached up and clapped the side of the bed, shaking the room as it anchored itself and pulled the giant torso higher. Freddy's jaw made motions of chewing as the distorted face pulled Charlie's legs inside it. His cheeks and chin dislocating further. It no longer resembled a living thing.

Panic took hold and Charlie screamed. She clenched her fists, but there was no longer a face to strike. There was only a squeezing and spiraling vortex of fur, teeth, and wire. Before she could struggle further, her arms were pinned to her side, trapped inside the thing. Only her head remained free. She gasped for a last breath, then was violently scooped up, consumed by the creature.


Clay Burke stopped the car without slowing down. The brakes screeched as they fishtailed in the dirt. John was out of the car before Clay had gotten it under control, running up the hill toward the house.

"Around back," Clay said, catching up to John, his voice low and tight. They made their way around the house to the back door, which was gaping open. "Check that way." Clay gestured to his right as he ran left. John stuck close to the wall, peering into doorways as he passed them.

"Charlie!" he cried.

"Charlie!" Clay echoed, entering the master bedroom.

"CHARLIE!" John ran from room to room, moving faster. "CHARLIE!" He arrived at the front door. He swung it wide open and stepped outside, half expecting to catch someone fleeing the scene.

"Clay, did you find her?" he shouted as he raced back inside.

Clay walked briskly back into the living room, shaking his head. "No, but she was here. The bed was unmade and there was dirt all over the floor. And these . . ." He held up Charlie's sneakers. John nodded grimly, only now noticing the trails of dirt strewn through the house. He glanced again to the front door.

"She's gone," John said, his voice catching in his throat. He looked at the older man. "Now what?" he asked.

Clay just stared at the floor, and said nothing.

lay!" John repeated. His alarm grew as the older man stared down at the dirty floorboards, apparently lost in thought. John put a hand on his arm, and Clay startled. He looked as if just he'd realized he wasn't alone. "We have to find her," John said urgently.

Clay nodded, springing back to life. He broke into a run and John followed close at heel, barely making it into the passenger's seat before Clay started the engine and took off, speeding down the half-made road.

"Where are we going?" John shouted. He was still struggling to close the door against the wind. It flapped like a massive wing, pulling against him as Clay swerved down the hill. Finally John yanked it shut.

"I don't know," Clay said grimly. "But we know about

how far they can get." He drove wildly back down the hill and out to the main road, flipping on his police lights. They went less than a mile before he turned quickly onto a small, unpaved lane.

John's shoulder banged hard against the door. He gripped his seat belt as they barreled down the trail, high brush scraping the sides of the car and thumping the windshield.

"They have to come through here," Clay said. "This field is right in the middle of the path between that house and the next area on the map. We just have to wait for them." He stopped the car abruptly and John jerked forward.

Together they got out of the car. Clay had stopped at the edge of an open field. There were trees scattered here and there, and the grass was tall, but there were no crops, and no livestock grazed. John walked out into the open, watching the grass ripple like water in the wind.

"You really think they'll come by here?" John asked.

"If they keep moving the direction they've been going," Clay said. "They have to."

Long minutes passed. John paced back and forth in front of the car. Clay positioned himself closer to the middle of the field, ready to run in any direction at a moment's notice.

"They should have been here by now," John said. "Something's wrong." He glanced at Clay, who nodded.

The sound of a car engine rose from the distance, growing louder. They both froze. Whoever it was, they were coming fast; John could hear branches whipping against the car's body in an irregular percussion. After a few seconds the car shot out from the lane and screeched to a halt.

"Jessica." John walked toward the car.

"Where's Charlie?" Jessica asked, stepping out onto the grass.

"How did you find us?" Clay demanded.

"I called her," John put in quickly. "From the restaurant, right after I talked to you."

"I've been driving all over the place. I'm lucky I found you. Why are we stopped here?"

"Their route crosses through here," John explained, but she looked skeptical.

"What does that mean? How do you know?"

John glanced at Clay, neither of them looking confident.

"They have her already, right?" Jessica said. "So why would they keep going toward her dorm?" Clay closed his eyes, putting a hand to his temples.

"They wouldn't," he said. He looked up at the sky, the wind battering across his upturned face with a raw touch.

"So they could be going anywhere now," Jessica added.

"We can't predict what they're doing anymore," John said. "They got what they wanted."

"And she wanted this? She planned this?" Jessica said, her voice rising. "What's *wrong* with you, Charlie?" She turned back to John. "They might not have even wanted *her*. It could have been anyone! So why did she have to go up there, like some kind of—of—"

"Sacrifice," John said quietly.

"She can't be dead," Jessica muttered, her voice shaky even under her breath.

"We can't think like that," John said sternly.

"We'll form a perimeter," Clay said. "Jessica, you and John take your car and start driving that way." He pointed. "I'll loop back the other direction. We'll make circles and hope we catch them. I can't think of any other way." He looked at the teenagers helplessly. No one moved, despite Clay's new plan. John could feel it in the air; they had all surrendered. "I don't know what else to do." Clay's voice had lost its strength.

"I might," John said abruptly, the idea forming even as he spoke. "Maybe we can ask them."

"You want to ask them?" Jessica said sarcastically. "Let's call them and leave a message. 'Please call us back with your murderous plot at your earliest convenience!'"

"Exactly," John said. "Clay, the mascots from Freddy's: Are they *all* gone? When you say you threw them out, what does that mean? Can we get access to them?" He turned to Jessica. "They helped us before, or at least they tried to, once they stopped trying to kill us. They might know something, I don't know, even if they're on a scrap heap somewhere, there must be something left. Clay?"

Clay had turned his face up to the sky again. Jessica gave him a sharp look. "You know, don't you?" she said. "You know where they are."

Clay sighed. "Yeah, I know where they are." He hesitated. "I couldn't let them be dismantled," he went on. "Not knowing what they are, who they had been. And I didn't dare let them be casually tossed out, considering what they're capable of doing." Jessica opened her mouth, about to ask a question, then stopped herself. "I . . . I kept them," Clay said. There was a rare note of uncertainty in his voice.

"You what?" John stepped forward, suddenly on guard.

"I kept them. All of them. I don't know about asking them any questions, though. Ever since that night, they haven't moved an inch. They're broken, or at least they're doing a good impression of it. They've been sitting in my basement for over a year now. I've been careful to leave them alone. It just seemed like they shouldn't be disturbed."

"Well, we have to disturb them," Jessica said. "We have to try to find Charlie."

John scarcely heard her. He was staring searchingly at Clay.

"Come on," Clay said. He set off toward his car with a heavy look, as if something had just been taken from him.

John and Jessica exchanged a glance, then followed. Before they reached Jessica's car, Clay was already heading toward the main road. Jessica stepped on the gas, catching up just as Clay made a sharp right turn.

They didn't speak. Jessica was intent on the road, and John was slouched in his seat, thinking things through. Ahead of them, Clay had switched on his flashing lights, though he left off the siren.

John stared into the darkness as they drove. Maybe he'd spot Charlie just by chance. He kept his hand loose on the door handle, ready to jump out, to run and save her. But there were only endless trees, scattered with the orange windows of distant houses, which hung on the hills like Christmas lights.

"We're here," Jessica said, sooner than John had expected.

John pushed himself upright and peered out the window.

She made a left turn and slowed the car down, and as she did John recognized it. A few yards ahead was Carlton's house, surrounded by a cove of trees. Clay pulled into the driveway and they came in behind him. Jessica stopped the car inches from his bumper.

Clay jangled his keys nervously as they approached the house; he looked like an altered man, no longer the assured police chief in control of every situation. He unlocked the door, but John hung back. He wanted Clay to go in first.

Clay led them into the living room, and Jessica made a noise of surprise. Clay gave her a sheepish look. "Sorry for the mess," he said.

John glanced around. The room was mostly the same as he remembered, full of couches and chairs all fanned around a fireplace. But both couches were piled with open files and stacks of newspapers, and what looked like dirty laundry. Six coffee mugs sat crowded together on a single end table. John's heart sank as he noticed two bottles of whiskey lying on their sides between an armchair and the hearth. He cast his eyes around quickly, spotting two more. One had rolled under a couch; the other was still half-full, sitting beside a glass with a distinct yellow tinge. John snuck a look at Jessica, who bit her lip.

"What happened here?" she asked.

"Betty left," Clay said shortly.

"Oh."

"I'm sorry," John offered. Clay waved a hand at him, staving off further attempts at comfort. He cleared his throat.

"She was right, I guess. Or at least she did what was right for her." He forced a laugh and gestured at the mess that surrounded him. "We all do what we have to do." He sat down in a green armchair, the only seat completely free of paperwork and debris, and shook his head.

"Can I move these?" John asked, pointing to the papers that filled the couch opposite Clay. Clay didn't respond, so John stacked them up and put them to one side, careful not to let anything fall. He sat, and after a moment so did Jessica, though she eyed the couch as if she thought it might be carrying the plague.

"Clay—" John started, but the older man started talking again, as if he'd never stopped.

"After all of you left—after all of you were safe—I went back for them. Betty and I had decided it might be a good time for Carlton to get out of town for a while, so she took him to stay with her sister for a few weeks. To be honest, I don't remember if she suggested it, or if it was me who put the idea in her mind. But as soon as I saw them pull down the driveway and out of sight, I got to work.

"Freddy's was locked up. They'd taken away Officer Dunn's body and completed their search, under my careful guidance, of course. They took some samples, but nothing else had been removed from the premises, not yet. They were waiting on me to give the go-ahead. The place wasn't even under guard—after all, there was nothing dangerous inside, right? So, I waited for things to calm down. Then I drove to St. George and rented a U-Haul.

"It was raining when I picked up the truck, and by the time I got to Freddy's there was a full-on thunderstorm, even though the forecast had been clear. I had keys this time; all the locks were police-issue now, so I just walked right into the place. I knew where I would find them—or at least, I knew where I'd left them and prayed they were still here. They were all piled together in that room with the little stage."

"Pirate's Cove," Jessica said, her voice barely a whisper.

"I half expected them to be gone, but they were sitting patiently, like they'd been waiting for me. They're immense, you know. Hundreds of pounds of metal and whatever else was in there, so I had to drag them one by one. I loaded them all up eventually. I figured I would bring them down through the storm cellar, but when I got back home the lights were on and Betty's car was in the driveway. She'd come back from her trip early, it seemed."

"What did you do?" Jessica asked. She was hunched over, her chin in her palms. John shook his head, mildly amused. She was enjoying the story.

"I waited across the street. I watched the lights, staking out my own house. When the last light went out, I pulled into the driveway and started dragging those things again, lowering them down into the cellar one by one. I drove the truck back to St. George and came back home, all without anyone seeing me. It would have never worked if I hadn't had the cover of thunder and lightning to mask what I was doing. When I came in, I was soaking wet and my whole body ached. All I wanted was to go upstairs to bed, next to my wife . . ." He cleared his throat. "But I didn't dare. I took a blanket and I slept in front of the basement door, just in case something tried to come out."

"Did it?" Jessica asked. Clay shook his head slowly back and forth, like it had taken on extra weight.

"In the morning, they were exactly the way I'd left them. Every night after that, I went down there when Betty was asleep. I watched them, sometimes I even . . . talked to them, trying to provoke them somehow. I wanted to make sure they weren't going to kill us in our sleep. I went back over the case files, trying to figure out how we'd missed Afton. How had he managed to come back without anyone suspecting?

"Betty could tell something was wrong. A few weeks later, she woke up and came looking for me—she found me, and them." Burke closed his eyes. "I don't remember exactly how the conversation went, but the next morning she was gone again, and this time she didn't come back."

John shifted on the couch restlessly. "They haven't moved since then?"

"They're just sitting there like broken dolls. I don't even think about them anymore."

"Clay, Charlie's in danger," John said, standing. "We have to go see them."

Clay nodded. "Well, then let's go see them." He stood and gestured toward the kitchen.

The last time John had stood in the Burkes' kitchen was the morning after they'd all escaped from Freddy's. Clay had been making pancakes and kidding around. Betty, Carlton's mother, was sitting next to her son as if she were afraid to leave his side. They were all giddy with relief that the ordeal was over, but John could tell that each of them, in their own particular ways, was struggling with other emotions, too. Someone might stop talking in midsentence, forgetting the rest, or stare for several moments at the empty air in front of them. They we

had been bright.

smells of coffee and par

to reality.

Now, John was struck hard by

rank smell, and he could see immed

counters and table were strewn with dirty

with leftover meals. Most had scarcely been

were two more empty bottles in the kitchen sink.

Clay opened the door to what looked like a close

turned out to be the basement steps. He flipped a light switch

illuminating a dim bulb right above the stairs, and motioned

them in. Jessica started forward, but John put a hand lightly

on her arm, stopping her. Clay went first, leading their

descent, and John followed, guiding Jessica behind him.

The stairs were narrow and a little too steep. Each time

John stepped down he felt a slight lurch, his body unpre-

pared for the distance. Two steps down the air changed: it

was damp and moldy.

"Watch out for that one," Clay said. John looked down to

see that one of the boards was missing. He stepped over it

carefully and turned, offering Jessica a hand as she made the

awkward jump. "One of many things that's on my to-do

list," Clay said offhandedly.

The basement itself was unfinished. The floor and

walls were nothing but the unpainted inner surface of the

ler

. At
The
d his
wide,
rmous
bright
d look.
latching
y a little
d, he still
wide and

re all just barely recovering. But the kitchen
ght sparkled off the counters, and the
cakes were reassuring, a connection

the contrast. There was a
ately what it was: the
dishes, all crusted
eaten. There

but

his eyebrows ra... s about to
happen. His microphone was missing, a... ld his arms
out stiffly before him, grasping at nothing. Chica leaned
against Freddy, her head drooping to the side. The weight of
her yellow body—inexplicably covered in fur, not feathers—
seemed to rest entirely on him. Her long, orange chicken
legs were splayed out in front of her, and for the first time
John noticed the silver talons on her feet, inches long and
sharp as knives. The bib she always wore had been torn. It
had read: LET'S EAT!!!, but it was faded by time, along with the
damp and mildew of the basement.

John squinted at her. Something else was missing.

"The cupcake," Jessica said, echoing his thoughts.

Then he spotted it. "There on the floor," he said. It was sitting alone beside Chica, almost huddled, its evil grin maniacal and pathetic.

Set a little apart from the three was the yellow Freddy, the one that had saved all their lives. He looked like Freddy Fazbear, and yet he did not. There was something different about him besides the color, but if someone had asked John what it was, he knew he wouldn't be able to name it. Jessica and John looked at it for a long moment. John felt a sense of quiet awe as he studied the yellow bear. *I never got to thank you*, he wanted to say. But he found he was too scared to approach it.

"Where's—" Jessica started, then cut herself off. She pointed to the corner where Foxy was propped against the wall, clothed in shadows but still visible. John knew what he would see: a robotic skeleton covered with dark red fur, but only from the knees up. It had been tattered even when the restaurant was open. Foxy had his own stage in Pirate's Cove. As John peered at him now, he thought he could see more places where the fur covering was ripped, and the metal frame showed through. Foxy's eye patch was still fixed in place above his eye. While one hand drooped at his side, the arm with the large, sharpened hook was raised above his head, poised for a downward slash.

"Is this how you left them?" John asked.

"Yep. Exactly how I left them," Clay answered, but he sounded suspicious of his own words.

Jessica approached Bonnie cautiously and crouched down to make her eyes level with the enormous rabbit. "Are you in there?" she whispered. There was no response. Jessica reached out slowly to touch his face. John watched, tensing, but as Jessica petted the rabbit, not even dust stirred in the mildewed basement. Finally she straightened and took a step back, then looked helplessly at John. "There's nothing—"

"Shh," he interrupted. A noise caught his attention.

"What is it?"

John bent his head, craning closer to the sound, though he couldn't tell exactly where it was coming from. It was like a voice on the wind, words swept away before he could catch them, so that he couldn't be sure it was a voice at all. "Is anyone . . . here?" he murmured. He looked at Freddy Fazbear, but as he tried to focus his attention, the sound situated itself. He turned to the yellow Freddy suit.

"You're here, aren't you?" he asked the bear. He went to the animatronic and crouched in front of it, but he didn't try to touch it. John looked into its shining eyes, searching for any of the spark of life he had seen that night, when the golden bear entered the room and they all knew as irrefutable fact that Michael, their childhood friend, was inside. John couldn't remember precisely how that knowledge had come: there was nothing behind the plastic eyes, nothing different physically. It was just pure certainty. He closed his eyes, trying to call it back. Maybe by recalling that essence of *Michael*, he could conjure him again. But he couldn't catch it, couldn't sense the presence of his friend as he had that night.

John opened his eyes and looked at all the animatronics one by one, remembering them alive and mobile. Once, the children stolen by William Afton had watched him back from inside. Were they still inside now, dormant? It was horrible to think of them moldering down here, staring into the darkness.

Something flickered in the yellow bear's eye, almost imperceptibly, and John drew in a sharp breath. He glanced behind, checking for a light that might have glanced off the hard plastic surface, but there was no obvious source. *Come back*, he pled silently, hoping to see the spark again.

"John." Jessica's voice pulled him back to reality. "John, I'm not sure that this was a good idea." He turned toward her voice, then stood, his legs cramping. How long had he been there, staring into the blind eyes of the mascot?

"I think there's still someone in there," he said slowly.

"Maybe so, but this doesn't feel right." She looked down from John toward the suits again.

Their heads had moved; they tilted up unnaturally, facing John and Jessica.

Jessica screamed and John heard himself shout something unintelligible, leaping back as if he'd been stung. They were all looking directly at him. John took three experimental steps to the left, and they appeared to track him: their eyes stayed fixed on him, and him alone.

Clay had grabbed a shovel and was holding it like a baseball bat, ready to strike. "I think it's time to go." He stepped forward.

"Stop, it's okay!" John exclaimed. "They know that we aren't enemies. We're here because we need their help." John opened his palms toward the creatures.

Clay lowered the shovel, though he kept it in his hand. John looked at Jessica, who nodded rapidly.

John turned back to the mascots. "We're here because we need your help," he said again. They gazed back at him blankly. "Remember me?" he asked awkwardly. They continued to stare, as frozen in their new poses as they'd been before. "Please listen," he went on. "Charlie, you remember her, right? You must. She's been taken by . . . creatures like you, but not like you." He glanced at Jessica, but she was watching anxiously, trusting this to him.

"They were animatronic suits, buried under Charlie's house. We don't know why they were there." He took a deep breath. "We don't think they were built by Henry; we think they were built by William Afton."

As soon as John said the name, the robots all began to shudder, convulsing where they sat. It was as if their machinery was being jump-started by a current too powerful for their systems to absorb.

"John!" Jessica cried. Clay stepped forward and grabbed John by the shoulder.

"We have to get out of here," Jessica said urgently. The mascots were seizing wildly, their arms and legs jerking. Their heads banged against the back wall with painful clanks. John stood rooted to the spot, torn between the impulse to run *to* them, to try and help, and the urge to run away.

"Go, now!" Clay shouted over the noise, pulling John backward. They made their way back up the basement stairs, Clay followed behind with the shovel raised defensively. John watched the mascots convulsing on the ground until they were out of sight.

"We need your help to find Charlie!" he shouted one last time, as Clay slammed the basement door and snapped three shiny new deadbolts shut.

"Come on," Clay said. They followed him, chased by hideous clanking and banging noises, only slightly muffled by the floor beneath. He led them back through the living room to a small study branching off from it, where he shut the door and bolted it.

"They're coming up," John said, pacing and watching the ground beneath his feet. Metal ground against metal; something crashed like it was slammed against the wall. The echo reverberated through the floor.

"Block the door," Clay ordered, grabbing one side of the desk in the corner. John grabbed the other side as Jessica cleared a path for them, yanking two chairs and a lamp out of the way. They dropped it in front of the door as, beneath them, something scraped across the concrete like it was being dragged.

Heavy footsteps shook the foundation of the house. The high-pitched whine of malfunctioning electronics filled the air, almost too high to hear. Jessica rubbed her ears. "Are they coming for *us*?"

"No. I mean, I don't think so," John said. He looked to Clay for reassurance, but Clay's eyes were on the door. The whine intensified and Jessica clapped her hands over her ears. The footsteps grew louder. There was a noise like cracking wood.

"At the door," Clay whispered. There was a loud thud, and then another. John, Jessica, and Clay sank down behind the desk, as if it would better hide them. Another thud resounded, then a sound of splintering wood. The earth-shaking footsteps came closer. John tried to count them, to see if the creatures were all together, but there was too much overlap. They layered one over another, rattling his teeth and shaking through his chest. It felt like the sound alone might break him to pieces.

Then, quickly, the footsteps faded and were gone. For a long moment no one moved. John gasped to breathe, realizing only now that he'd been holding his breath. He looked at the others. Jessica's eyes were closed, and she gripped her hands together so tightly that her fingertips had gone white. John reached out and touched her shoulder and she jumped, her eyes flying open. Clay was already standing, tugging at the desk. "Come on, John," he said. "Help me get this out of the way."

"Right," he said unsteadily. Together they shoved it aside and hurried out into the hall. The front door stood wide open to the night. John rushed out to look.

The grass outside had been torn up where the mascots shuffled through it. The tracks were obvious and easy to follow, leading straight into the woods. John broke into a run, chasing after them, Clay and Jessica at his heels. When they reached the cover of trees they slowed. In the distance, John saw a blur of movement for only an instant, and he motioned the others to hold back. They would follow, but they didn't dare be seen by whatever was leading the way.

# CHAPTER TWELVE

The world thundered around Charlie, shaking her rhythmically back and forth, strange objects digging harder into her each time she was jostled. Charlie opened her eyes, and remembered where she was. Or rather, what she was inside. The awful image of the malformed Freddy sucking her into its mouth like some kind of snake hit her, and she closed her eyes again, biting her lips together so that she wouldn't scream. The thuds were footsteps, she realized: the animatronics were on the move.

Her head throbbed with each blow, making it hard to think straight. *I must have been knocked unconscious when it threw me in here*, she thought. The torso of the thing was connected to the head by a wide neck, which was almost level with her own, though its head stretched up another foot above her. It was like looking at the inside of a mask: the hollow of a protruding snout, the blank spheres that were the backs of the eyes. When she carefully tilted her head up, she could even see the bolt that attached the black top hat.

Charlie's legs were cramped and bent at odd angles, wedged between pieces of machinery. She must have been stuck this way for some time, but she had no way of knowing how long. Her arms were constrained, suspended away from her body into the arms of the suit. Her whole body was covered in small points of pain, bruises and cuts from tiny pieces of plastic and metal that deepened each time they banged against her. Charlie could feel blood trickling down her skin in half a dozen places. She itched to wipe it away but had no idea how much she could struggle without triggering the springs. Her mind flashed to the first murder victim, the lacerations that covered his body almost decoratively. She thought of Dave's screams as he died, and the bloated corpse beneath the stage at Pirate's Cove. *That can't be me. I can't die like that!*

Charlie had told Clay what she knew about the spring-lock suits. The animatronic parts were either recoiled, making room for a person inside to use it as a costume, or fully extended, so the mascot would work as a robot. But that was what Charlie knew from Fredbear's Family Diner—this creature was different. She was inside a cavity made for a human being, but the suit was moving with complete autonomy. Its insides were full of metal architecture and wires, all except for the space that Charlie occupied.

The animatronic lurched unexpectedly to the side, and Charlie was smacked against the jagged wall again with greater force. She cried out this time, unable to help herself, but there was no break in Freddy's stride. Either the creature hadn't heard, or it didn't care. She clenched her teeth, trying to quell the pounding in her head.

*Where are we going?* She craned her neck this way and that, looking through the holes in the animatronic's battered suit. There were only a few holes, small and on either side of the thing's torso. All she could make out was the forest: trees rushing by in the darkness as they hurried to their mysterious destination. Charlie sighed in frustration, tears welling up. *Where are you? Am I getting closer to you? Sammy, is it you?*

She gave up looking for hints outside and stared straight ahead at the inside of the suit. *Stay calm*, Aunt Jen's voice said in her head. *Always stay calm. It's the only way to keep your head clear.* She stared up into the mask, at the inside-out features of the twisted Freddy.

Suddenly, the blank spheres rolled back and the eyes flipped in, staring straight down at her with an impassive, plastic gaze. Charlie screamed and jerked back. Something behind her snapped, lashing a whiplike piece of metal into her side. She froze in terror. *No, please no.* Nothing else triggered, and after a moment she cautiously settled herself in place, trying not to meet the shiny blue eyes above her. Her side where the piece of metal had hit her shocked with pain each time she breathed. She wondered, alarmed, if a rib had broken. Before she could be sure, the animatronic lurched to the side again, and Charlie fell with it, hitting her head so hard that the blow reverberated through her body. Her vision darkened, closing to a tunnel, and as she faded into unconsciousness again, all she could see were Freddy's watching eyes.

John's lungs were beginning to burn, his legs turning rubbery as they ran on and on through the forest. They had been running for what felt like hours, though he knew it couldn't be. That was just his exhaustion playing tricks on his mind. The trail had faded. When they entered the forest, the trees had been their guide. They followed ripped, ragged bark and broken branches, and even torn roots where massive, careless feet had stepped.

But the signs had grown farther between, then stopped entirely. Now John ran on in the direction the creatures seemed to have been headed.

Truthfully, he might have been lost.

As he darted around trees, trekked up and down small hills, and stumbled on uneven ground, John began to lose his sense of direction entirely. Ahead of him, Jessica ran confidently onward. He followed, but for all he knew they could be running in an endless circle.

Behind him, Clay's steps were slowing, his breathing heavy. Jessica, a few paces ahead, doubled back, jogging in place as she waited for them to catch up.

"Come on, guys, we're almost there!" she said energetically.

"Almost where?" John asked, struggling to keep his tone even.

"I'm just trying to be encouraging," she said. "I was on my high school cross-country team for three years."

"Well, I was always more of a heavy-lifter, you know," John panted, suddenly defensive.

"Clay, come on, you can do it!" Jessica called. John glanced back. Clay had stopped running and was doubled over with his hands on his knees, taking gasping breaths. With relief, John slowed to a walk and turned back. Jessica let out a frustrated sound and followed him to Clay.

"Are you all right?" John asked.

The older man nodded, waving him back. "Fine," he said. "Go ahead, I'll catch up."

"There's nowhere to 'go ahead' to," John said. "We're running blind. When's the last time you saw tracks?"

"A while back," Clay said, "but they were heading this way, and it's all we have to go on."

"But it's nothing to go on!" John's voice rose in frustration. "There's no reason to think they went this way!"

"We're losing them," Jessica said urgently. She was still running in place, her ponytail bouncing like a little nervous animal behind her. Clay shook his head.

"No, we've already lost them."

Jessica stopped running, but she kept shifting from one foot to the other. "So now what?"

Something rustled in the trees ahead of them. Jessica grabbed John's arm, then released it quickly, looking embarrassed. The sound came again, and John started toward it, raising a hand to signal the others to stay. He made his way cautiously through the trees, glancing back once and noting that Jessica and Clay were close behind, despite his attempt to keep them back.

A few feet farther on, the trees broke into an open field; they had reached the far side of the woods. Jessica gasped, and a split second later John saw it. Halfway across the clearing a figure stood in the darkness. It was almost featureless and flat, scarcely distinct from the shadows. John squinted, trying to get hold of the image, to assure himself he was really seeing it. Heavy, black electrical wires stretched above the field like a canopy, but besides the wires, the field was clear. Though it was dark, there was no way for them to sneak closer to the figure without being seen.

So John straightened his shoulders and began to walk slowly and openly toward it.

The field was untended, and tall grass brushed John's knees as he walked. Behind him, Jessica and Clay made rustling sounds with every step. The wind whipped the grass against their legs, blowing more ferociously with each step they took. Almost halfway across the field, John stopped, puzzled. The figure was still there, but it seemed as far away from them as when they'd started. He glanced back at Jessica.

"Is it moving?" she whispered. He nodded and started walking again, not taking his eyes from the shadowy figure. "John, it looks like . . . Freddy?"

"I don't know what it is," John answered cautiously. "But I think it wants us to follow."

*I can't breathe.* Charlie coughed and gagged, coming suddenly awake. She lay on her back, dirt pouring down onto her. It filled her mouth, clogging her nose and covering her eyes. She spat, shaking her head and blinking rapidly. She tried to raise her hands but couldn't move them. She remembered suddenly that they were trapped inside the arms of the suit and would be mutilated if she struggled to free them.

*Buried alive! I'm being buried alive.* She opened her mouth to scream and more dirt fell in, hitting the back of her throat and making her gag again. Charlie could feel her pulse in her throat, choking her from the inside as surely as the dirt from outside. Her heart was beating too fast and she felt light-headed. She took faster breaths, trying in vain to fill her lungs, but she only stirred up the dirt and inhaled it. She spat, gargling at the back of her throat to catch it before she swallowed, and turned her head to the side, away from the soil that fell like rain. She took a shuddering breath that shook her chest, and then another. *You're hyperventilating*, she told herself sternly. *You have to stop. You have to calm down. You need your head clear.* The last thought came in Aunt Jen's voice. She stared at the now-familiar side of the suit and took deep breaths, ignoring the dirt settling in her ear and sliding down her neck, until her fluttering heart slowed, and she could breathe almost normally again.

Charlie closed her eyes. *You have to get your arms free.* She concentrated all her attention on her left arm. Her T-shirt left the skin of her arms bare against the suit, so she could feel everything that touched her. With her eyes still closed, Charlie began to draw a map. *There's something at the shoulder joints on either side, and a space just below. Spikes in a line all the way down to my elbow on the outside, and the inside has—what is that?* She rocked her arm slowly, gently, back and forth against the objects, trying to envision them. *They're not spring locks.* She froze, focusing again on the place where the arm joined the torso. *THOSE are spring locks. Okay, I'll get to it. Hands.* She flexed her fingers slightly: the sleeves were wide, and her hands—which reached roughly to the creature's elbows—were less constrained than anything else. She spat out dirt again, trying not to notice that it was still pouring in steadily, piling up all around her. *Breathe. While you still can.* She clenched her jaw, envisioning the sleeve that encased her arm, and slowly began to work her way out of it. She dipped down her shoulder, rotated forward, held her breath—and pulled her arm three inches out. Charlie let out a shuddering sigh. Her shoulder was free of the spring locks. *That was the hardest part. The rest of my arm won't touch them if I'm careful.* She kept going, avoiding the things she thought might snap or stab her. When she was halfway out, her elbow at the shoulder seam, she twisted her arm too quickly and heard a snap. She stared horrified at the suit's shoulder, but it wasn't the spring lock. Something smaller inside had triggered, and now she could feel the burn of a fresh cut. *Okay. It's okay.* She got back to work.

Minutes later, her arm was free. She flexed it back and forth in the small space, feeling a little like she had never had an arm before. *Now the other one.* She wiped her face with her hand, smearing away the dirt, closed her eyes, and began again with her right arm.

The second sleeve took less time to get out of, but fatigue and the growing mounds of dirt around her made Charlie careless. Twice she triggered small mechanisms that bruised her painfully, but didn't break her skin. She yanked herself free too fast, bumping the spring locks and only barely snatching her hand away before they cracked open. The arm jumped and jolted as the robotic skeleton inside it unfolded with a noise like firecrackers. Charlie clutched her hand to her chest, cradling it against her pounding heart as she watched. *That could have been . . . It wasn't. It wasn't me. Focus. Legs.*

Her legs weren't pinned in place as her arms had been. They'd simply been awkwardly positioned, wedged between metal rods that ran through the body of the mascot. Without the weight of her body resting on them, she was able to maneuver. Cautiously, Charlie lifted her right leg into the air, pulling it over the rod and into the center of the torso. Nothing triggered, and she did the same with her left.

Her limbs freed, Charlie looked down the length of the animatronic, at the door to the chest cavity. The latch was on the outside, but these creatures were old; their parts were rusted and weak. She reached out and put her hands against the metal, feeling for springs and other devices. She couldn't quite see from where her head was stuck, and she couldn't move down safely. *Unless.*

The dirt had piled up almost a foot on either side of her head, and it covered the lower half of her body. Charlie abandoned the door momentarily, and began to slowly move the dirt. She lifted her head slightly and brushed at the mound with her hands, pushing soil into the space she left. She rocked her body back and forth, using her hands to sweep dirt under her, until she lay on it like a thin bed. It wouldn't protect her from the suit if she triggered it, but it would give her an extra cushion, make it slightly harder for her to jostle something and be skewered alive. She glanced at the arm of the suit that had been triggered, now filled with metal spines and hard plastic parts. A shiver went down her back.

Now she inched down until she could see the chest plates, placed her hands in the center, and began to push upward with all her might. After a moment they came apart and a rush of dirt cascaded in. Charlie coughed and turned her head, but she kept pushing as the dirt rained down on her. She managed to get the plates a foot apart, then crouched beneath them and paused for a moment. *How deep am I?* she thought for the first time. If she'd been buried six feet down, she might be escaping only to suffocate in the home stretch. *What else am I going to do?* Charlie closed her eyes, took a deep breath, and held it. Then she pressed herself up to the doors and began to claw her way out of the grave.

The dirt wasn't packed tightly, but it still took effort: she scratched and scraped at it with her bare hands, wishing for a tool as her fingernails split and bled. As she hacked at the dirt, her lungs began to burn and clench, trying to get her to breathe. She scrunched her face up as hard as she could and scratched harder. *Are you out there? I'm coming, but help me, please, I have to get out of this. Please, I can't die here, buried ali—*

Her hand broke the surface, and she drew it back in shock. *Air.* She gasped gratefully until she no longer felt starved of oxygen. Then she closed her eyes and battered her fists at the tiny hole above her head, breaking the sides until it was large enough to wriggle through. Charlie stood up, her feet still planted in the chest cavity of the suit. There had been little more than a foot of dirt covering her. She braced her feet on the half-open doors and clambered out of the hole, hauling herself up. She collapsed beside it, shaking with exhaustion. *You're not safe yet,* she scolded herself. *You have to get up.* But she couldn't bring herself to move. She stared, horrified, at the hole she had escaped from, her face wet with tears.

Time passed, minutes or hours; she lost track completely. Finally mustering her strength, Charlie pushed herself up to a sitting position, wiping her face. She couldn't tell where she was, but the air was cool and still. She was indoors, and somewhere in the distance was the sound of rushing water. With the adrenaline gone, her head ached again, throbbing along with her heartbeat. It wasn't just her head—everything hurt. She was covered in bruises, her clothing was stained with blood, and now that she wasn't suffocating, she was aware again of the stabbing sensation in her rib cage every time she inhaled. Charlie prodded her ribs, trying to feel if anything seemed out of place. The bruises were already brightly colored, especially where parts of the suit had struck her, but nothing was broken.

Charlie stood up, the pain receding enough to at least move and get her bearings. As she looked around, her blood went cold.

It was Freddy Fazbear's Pizza.

*It can't be.* The wave of panic rose again. She glanced around wildly, backing up, away from the hole in the ground. *The tables, the carousel in the corner, the stage—the tablecloths are blue.* "The tablecloths at Freddy's weren't blue," she said, but her relief was quickly washed away by confusion. *Then what is this place?*

The dining room was larger than the one at Freddy's, though there were fewer tables. The floor was black and white tile, except for large patches where the tiles were missing, revealing plots of packed dirt. It was oddly incongruous with everything else, which looked finished and brand-new, if dusty. As she turned to the opposite wall, she saw that she was being watched. Large plastic eyes stared back from the dark, glaring down at Charlie, seeming to identify her as an intruder. Fur and beaks and eyes stood poised like a small army halfway up the wall.

For a long moment she stood stock-still, bracing herself. But the animatronics didn't move. Charlie took a small step to one side, then the other; the eyes did not track her. The creatures looked forward, unseeing, at their fixed points. Some of their faces were animals, and some seemed to be painted like clowns. Others appeared disturbingly human.

Charlie moved closer and saw what it was they were perched on. All along the wall, arcade games and carnival attractions were lined up, each with its guardian beast or a giant face mounted on top. Their mouths were wide open, as if they were all laughing and cheering some invisible spectacle. As Charlie peered through the darkness, she saw that the animals were unnaturally posed, their bodies twisted in ways no animal should be able to twist. She scanned the wide-mouthed faces again and shivered. With their bodies so torturously bent, they looked like they were screaming in pain.

Charlie took deep breaths. As she calmed herself she realized that there was music playing through the speakers overhead. It was quiet; familiar, but she couldn't name it.

She approached the nearest of the games. A massive, contorted birdlike creature with a wide, curved beak presided over a large cabinet with a fake pond. Rows of ducks sat still in paper water, waiting for rubber balls to knock them down. Charlie looked up again at the creature perched on top of the game. Its wings stretched wide, and its head was thrown upward in the midst of an elaborate dance. It cast a shadow in front of the game, right where the player would stand. Charlie turned, not stepping any closer. Besides the duck pond, there were three arcade consoles lined up next to one another, their screens dusty. Three large chimpanzees squatted atop them, the tips of their toes gripping the edges above the screen. Their arms were raised, frozen in motion, and their teeth were bared in mirth, rage, or fear. Charlie stared for a moment at the teeth; they were long and yellow.

Something about the arcade games nagged at her. She looked them up and down carefully, but nothing tripped her memory. None were turned on, and none of them were games she had ever seen before. She wiped the dust from the screen of the central console, revealing a glossy black screen. Her face, distorted in the curved glass, showed only a little bruising and a few visible cuts. Charlie self-consciously smoothed her hair.

*Wait.* At Freddy's Pizza, ghostly images had been burned into the arcade screens after years of play. She pressed a couple of buttons experimentally. They were stiff and shiny—untouched.

"That's why it feels so empty," she said to the chimp above her. "No one's ever been here, have they?" The great ape didn't respond. Charlie glanced around. There was a doorway to her left, the bluish glow of an unseen black light emanating from the room beyond. Charlie went toward the light, through the door, and into another room of games and attractions. Here, too, they were all guarded by mascots, some more identifiable than others. Charlie staggered for a moment and put her hand on her forehead. "Strange," she whispered, regaining her balance. She looked back the way she'd come. *It must be the light making me dizzy*, she thought.

"Hello?" someone called faintly in the distance. Charlie whirled around as if someone had shouted in her ear. She held her breath, waiting for it to come again. The voice had been high and scared, a child. The sudden impression of life in this place shook her, as if waking her from a dream.

"Hello!" she called back. "Hello, are you all right? I won't hurt you." She glanced around the room. The sound of rushing water was louder here, making it hard to judge how far away the voice had come from. She moved quickly through the room, ignoring the wide-eyed creatures and the strange and garish games. A simple, skirted table in the corner caught her attention, and she went to it swiftly. Charlie crouched down, careful to keep her balance, and lifted the cloth. Eyes stared back at her and she startled, then steadied herself.

"It's okay," she whispered, flipping the cloth up over the table. The glimmer of the eyes faded with the rush of light. There was no one there after all.

Charlie put her hands on her forehead and pressed hard for a moment, trying to ward off the growing pain in her temples.

She went through another door, now unsure which way she'd come from, and discovered the source of the running water. Springing from the center of the wall to her left was a waterfall. It cascaded down over a rock face protruding several feet out, and joined with a riverbed below. The water rushed from a wide pipe only partly concealed by the rock.

The stream below was maybe three feet wide. It crossed the room, splitting the floor in two, and disappeared into the open mouth of a cave.

Charlie watched it for a moment, mesmerized by the water. After a moment, she noticed a narrow gap in the rock face behind the waterfall, just big enough for a person to walk through. "Hello?" Charlie called again, but only half-heartedly; here the white noise of the water was louder than anywhere else. She realized after a second that it was a recording, overpowering the sound of the actual water.

She surveyed the rest of the room: except for the waterfall and the little river it was empty, but she noticed the floor had a gray border. *No, it's a path.* It was narrower than a sidewalk, paved with square gray cobblestones. It ran alongside the curved wall, tracing the way to the waterfall, and led through a narrow passage under the fall itself. Charlie crouched down to touch the stones: they felt like hard plastic given a rough finish. The path was likely there for a time when the place would be filled with other attractions; she could probably just walk straight across the room. *Probably.*

Charlie stepped onto the cobblestones carefully, expecting them to give way under her weight, but they held. The manufactured coarseness of the rocks' surface was sharp—it hurt a little to walk on it. Charlie dutifully followed the walkway, keeping close to the wall. She had a vague sense that stepping off onto the open floor might be dangerous.

When she reached the waterfall, she went to the gap and gingerly touched the rock surface. It was the same plastic as the cobblestones. Like the path, the cliff was hard plastic, solid, but because it looked like rocks it felt insubstantial when she touched it. Charlie took her hands away and wiped them on her jeans. She stepped carefully sideways, scooting through the hole behind the waterfall. The cavern was only a few feet long, but she stopped for a moment at the center. She felt trapped in the darkness, though she could see light on either side. *Trapped.* Her chest tightened, and she screwed her eyes shut. *Calm down. Focus on what's around you*, she thought. Charlie took a long, steadying breath and listened.

Standing beneath the waterfall, the tape recording was muffled. She thought she could hear the water itself, rushing over her head and spilling down in front of her, though she couldn't see it. There was something else as well, quiet but distinct. From above her, or maybe behind, Charlie could hear the cranking of gears. A machine was churning the water, keeping it flowing in a giant cycle, making the whole thing work. The sound of the machine at work calmed her; the rising panic subsided, and she opened her eyes.

She took another sideways step, moving closer to the light, and stubbed her toe on something hard. A shock of pain jolted her. The object tipped over, making a sloshing sound as it fell. Grinding her teeth, she waited a moment for her toe to stop hurting, then maneuvered herself into a crouch. It was a fuel can. *For the waterfall,* she realized as the machinery ground on overhead. There were several more, all neatly arranged along the wall, but this one had been in the middle of the path. If she had been going faster, she would have fallen over it. Charlie set it firmly beside the others, and stepped quickly into the other half of the room.

"Hello?" The voice again, this time a little louder. Charlie stood up straight, immediately on alert. It had come from ahead. She didn't respond this time but moved carefully toward it, staying on the path and keeping close to the wall.

The hallway opened out into another room. The lights were dimmer here. In the corner opposite Charlie was a small carousel, but there seemed to be little else. Charlie scanned the room, and then her breath caught. The child was there, motionless, almost hidden in the shadows in the far corner of the room.

Charlie approached slowly, apprehensive of what she might find. She blinked and shook her head hard, her dizziness resurging. The room seemed to spin around her. *Who are you? Are you all right?* she wanted to ask but kept silent. She stepped closer, and the figure came into focus. It was just another animatronic, or perhaps just a normal doll, made to look like a little boy selling balloons.

He was perhaps four feet tall, with a round head and a round body, his arms almost as long as his stout legs. He wore a red-and-blue striped shirt, and a matching propeller beanie on his head. He was made of plastic, but his shiny face had something old-fashioned about it. Its features mimicked fairy-tale dolls carved from wood. His nose was a triangle and his cheeks were made rosy with two raised circles of dusky pink. His blue eyes were enormous, wide, and staring, and his mouth was open in a grin that bared all his even white teeth. His hands were fingerless balls, each gripping an object. In one he held a red and yellow balloon nearly half his size on a stick. In the other he raised a wooden sign reading BALLOONS!

He was nothing like the creatures Charlie's father had made, nothing even like the animatronics that had kidnapped her. They were horrible, but she recognized them as twisted copies of her father's work. This boy was something new. She circled around him, tempted to poke and prod, but she held back. *Don't chance triggering anything.*

"You're not so bad," Charlie murmured, cautious not to take her eyes off him. He just kept grinning, wide-eyed, into the darkness. Turning her attention to the rest of the room, Charlie looked thoughtfully at the carousel, the only thing there besides the boy. She was too far away to make out the animals.

"Hello?" said the voice, right behind her. She spun back just in time to see the boy turn toward her with a single, swinging step. Charlie screamed and ran back the way she came from, but beneath her feet the dirt began to stir. It jolted, as if something were bumping upward. She scrambled backward as the dirt rose again, and something broke through the surface.

Charlie ran for the carousel, the only cover in the room. She ducked behind it, lying down on her stomach so her body would be hidden behind its base. She stared down at the ground and listened to muffled scratches and beating sounds as some creature climbed free of its grave. The spinning sensation took hold of her again. The black-and-white tiles swam beneath her. She tried to push herself up to peek over the carousel, but her head felt leaden. The weight of it held her down, threatening to pin her back to the ground. *There's something wrong with this room.* Charlie gritted her teeth and yanked her head up; she scrambled to her feet, steadying herself against the carousel, and ran back the way she came, not looking back.

The room with the games and the harsh black light was dizzying as well, and it sprawled out in all directions. Everything seemed farther apart than before, the walls miles away. Her mind was numb. She fumbled to remember where she was, unable to tell which way was which. She stumbled forward, and another mound of earth rose ahead of her. Something glimmered. Her eyes lit on the silhouettes of arcade machines, their reflective surfaces acting as beacons in the dark.

She staggered toward them, her head swaying, so heavy she could hardly stay upright. The walls were crawling with activity. Small things skittered disjointedly all over the ceiling, but she couldn't see what they were—they were wriggling *under* the paint. The surface undulated chaotically. There was a strange ringing in the air, and though she only now registered it, she realized it had been sounding all along. She stopped in her tracks and looked desperately for the source, but her vision was clouding and her thoughts were slow. She could barely name the things she saw. *Rectangle*, she thought fuzzily. *Circle. No. Sphere.* She looked from one indistinct shape to another, trying to remember what they were called. The effort distracted her from staying on her feet, and she fell to the ground again with a hard thud. Charlie was sitting upright, but her head dragged at her, threatening to pull her over.

*Hello?* A voice called again. She put her hands on her head, forcing it back, and looked up to see several children standing around her, all with plump little bodies and broad smiling faces. *Sammy?* She moved toward them instinctively. They were blurred, and she couldn't see their features. She blinked, but her vision didn't clear. *Don't trust your senses. Something is wrong.*

"Stay back!" Charlie screamed at them. She forced herself unsteadily to her feet and stumbled toward the shadows cast by the arcade towers. There, at least, she might be hidden from whatever worse things lurked in the room.

The children went with her, rushing in trails of color around her and sweeping in and out of view. They seemed more to float than walk. Charlie kept her eyes on the towers; the children were distracting, but she knew there was something worse nearby. She could hear the sickening grind of metal, and plastic twisting, and a rasping noise she recognized. Sharp feet scraped against the floor, digging grooves into the tile.

She crouched low, fixing her eyes on the nearest open door, and was struck with a certainty that this was the way she had come. She crawled desperately toward it, moving as fast as she could without fully standing. Finally, she collapsed under her own weight and lay flat on the tile again. *You have to get up, now!* Charlie let out a scream and clambered to her feet. She ran headlong into the next room, barely keeping her balance, and skidded to a stop. The room was full of dining tables and carnival games; it was where she'd started, but something had changed.

All the eyes were tracking her. The creatures were moving, their skin stretching organically, their mouths snapping. Charlie ran for the dining table in the center of the room, the largest one with a tablecloth that almost reached the floor on all sides. She slid to the ground and crawled under it, curling herself into a ball and pulling her legs tight against her. For a moment, there was only silence, and then the voices began again. *Hello?* a voice called from somewhere nearby. The tablecloth rustled.

Charlie held her breath. She looked at the thin gap between the tablecloth and the floor, but she could see only a sliver of the black-and-white tile. Something shot by, too fast to see, and she gasped and drew back, forgetting to be silent. The cloth rustled again, swinging gently inward. Someone outside was prodding it. Charlie maneuvered herself onto her hands and knees, feeling as if she had too many arms and legs. The cloth moved again, and this time a swirl of color appeared and vanished in the gap. *The children.* They had found her. The tablecloth swung again, but now it was moving on all sides, jouncing up and down as the children brushed against it. The strange, colorful trails of movement appeared and vanished all around the edges of her hiding place, surrounding her like a wall of living paper dolls.

*Hello? Hello? Hello?* More than one spoke at a time now, but not in a chorus. Their voices overlapped until the word became a meaningless layer of sound, blurred like the floating children themselves.

She turned her face to the side. One of the children stared back—it was under the cloth and gazing at her with a fixed grin and motionless eyes. Charlie jumped up, banging her head on the tabletop. She looked around wildly. She was surrounded: a smiling, blurry face was staring at her from every side. *One, two, three, four, four, four.* She turned in an awkward circle on her hands and knees. Two of the children feinted at her, making little jumps as if they were about to spring. She turned again, and the next one leaped at her, swimming under the cloth in a bright streak of blue and yellow. Charlie froze. *What do I do?* She scrabbled at her sluggish brain, trying desperately to revive it. Another sweep of color whooshed at her, all purple, and her brain awoke: *RUN.*

Charlie scrambled to the tablecloth on her hands and knees and grabbed it, yanking it off the table as she stood. She threw it down behind her and ran, not looking back as someone called again, *Hello?*

She raced toward a sign propped up in the middle of the room, knocking it over behind her as she ran past. Then a shadow near the stage caught her attention, and she swerved. She tripped over a chair and just barely managed to catch herself on another table. Her head was still too heavy. It jerked her forward, and she shoved the table aside, managing to stay upright. She arrived at the stage, and in the shadow there was a door.

Charlie fumbled with the knob, but it was spongy, too soft to turn. She grabbed it with both hands, putting the whole force of her body behind it, and it moved at last: the door opened. She hurried through and slammed it shut behind her, feeling for some kind of latch. She found one and snapped it shut, and as she did her hand brushed a light switch.

A bulb flickered for a moment, then came on dimly, a single glowing strand of orange illuminating the room. Charlie stared at it for a minute, waiting for the rest of the light. No more appeared.

She leaned back against a cabinet beside the door and slid down to sit, putting her hands on her temples and trying to shove her head back to a normal size. The relative darkness steadied her. She stared down at the floor, hoping whatever was happening to her was almost over. She looked up, and the room shifted nauseatingly. *It's not over.* Charlie closed her eyes, took a deep breath of the stale air, and opened them again.

*Fur. Claws. Eyes.* She clapped a hand over her mouth to stop herself from screaming. A jolt of adrenaline cut briefly through the fuzziness. The room was full of creatures, but she couldn't make sense of them. The dark fur of a simian arm lay on the floor, inches from her feet, but out of it spilled coils and bare wire. The rest of the ape was nowhere to be seen.

There was something large and gray right in front of her, a torso with arms and webbed, amphibious hands, but there was no head. Instead, someone had balanced a large cardboard box where the neck would have been. Past the torso were standing figures, a phalanx of shadows. As she stared at them, they resolved into something comprehensible. They were unfinished mascots, as distorted as the ones outside.

A rabbit stood at the back. Its head was brown like a jack-rabbit and its ears were swept back, but its eyes were just empty holes. The rabbit's body was hunched to the side, and its arms were short, held up as if in surrender. Two metal frames stood in front of it. One was headless, and the other topped with the head of a red-eyed, slavering black dog, whose fangs stuck out from its mouth. Charlie kept her eyes on it for a moment, but it didn't move. Beside it—

Charlie cringed and ducked her head, covering her face with her arms. Nothing happened. Cautiously, she lowered her hands and looked again.

It was Freddy—the misshapen Freddy that had been buried. Charlie glanced at the door, then back at Freddy. He stared straight ahead, his eyes blank and his hat askew. *It can't be him*, she told herself. *It's just another costume.* But she shrank back, trying to make herself smaller.

Something delicately stroked the top of her head. Charlie screamed and yanked herself away. She turned to see a disembodied human arm on the shelf above where she'd been sitting. Its hand stuck out at just the right height to brush her head. Other arms were stacked beside it and on top of it, some covered in fur and others not. Some had fingers, some simply ended, cut off at what would have been the wrist. The other shelves were stacked with similar things: one with pelts of fur, another with piles of detached feet. One just had dozens of extension cords tangled up in an ugly nest.

From outside the door Charlie heard the voice again. *Hello?* The doorknob rattled. She squeezed past the mutilated arcade games and chopped-off parts, gritting her teeth as she crawled over soft things that squelched beneath her weight. As she stepped back, her shoulder crashed into one of the standing metal frames, the headless one. It rocked on its ungrounded feet, threatening to topple. She tried to pull away, but the frame followed, swaying for a moment as she fought to free her hands. She yanked them back and ducked as more metal frames came crashing to the ground.

She squatted down beside one of the large arcade cabinets. The plastic casing was cracked so badly the words and pictures were entirely obscured. Right beside her, inches away, were Freddy's stocky legs. Charlie huddled down, pressing against the game as if she could blend in with it. *Don't turn around*, she thought, eyeing the motionless bear. The dim light seemed to be moving like a spotlight. It glinted off the dog's red eyes, then the gleaming tusk, then off something sharp-cornered at the back of the rabbit's hollow socket.

Just out of her line of sight, something moved. Charlie whipped her head around, but there was nothing there. From the corner of her eye, she saw the rabbit straighten its spine. She turned frantically back toward it but found it hunched in its same agonized posture as before. Slowly,

Charlie looked around her in a half circle, keeping her back pressed against the console.

*Hello?* The doorknob rattled again. She closed her eyes and pressed her fists to her temples. *No one's here, no one's here.* Something rustled in front of her, and Charlie's eyes snapped open. Scarcely breathing, she watched as Freddy came alive. A sickly twisting sound filled the room, and Freddy's torso began to turn. *Hello?* Her eyes shifted to the door for a split second, and when she looked back again Freddy was still. *I have to get out of here.*

She took a moment to measure the path, looking first to the door, then to Freddy in front of her, mapping a blurry route. At last she went, looking down at her hands and nothing else as she crawled steadily around the motionless legs of the standing animatronics, and past the half-bestial games. *Don't look up.* Something brushed against her leg as she passed it, and she pressed on, her head down. Then something grabbed her ankle.

Charlie screamed and flailed, trying to kick herself free, but the iron grip tightened. She looked frantically over her shoulder: Freddy was crouched behind her, the light glinting off his face and making him seem to smile. Charlie yanked her foot back with all her strength, and Freddy pulled even harder, dragging her closer. Charlie grabbed the leg of a pinball game and hoisted herself up to her knees. As Freddy tried again to drag her back, the game shook and rattled like it was about to fall. Clutching at it with all her might, Charlie jerked her body up and forward. Freddy's claws tore her skin as she wrenched herself free, and the pinball machine collapsed under her weight.

Freddy lurched forward. That horrible mouth unhinged again like an enormous snake. He crouched down, coming toward her in a sinuous motion. She scrambled over the broken game toward the door. Behind her, something rustled and scraped, but she didn't look back. Her hand on the doorknob, Charlie stopped as the room around her swayed. The noise behind her grew louder, closer, and she turned to see Freddy crawling toward her in a predatory crouch. His mouth was widening. Dirt poured out of it in a steady stream.

"Hello? Charlie?" came a voice from outside. But this voice was different; it wasn't the animatronic child. Charlie fumbled at the knob, the spinning sensation in her head worsening as Freddy came slowly, purposefully closer. The room swayed again, and her hand closed on the knob and turned it. She shoved the door open and stumbled into the light.

"Charlie!" someone cried, but she didn't look up. The sudden brightness was piercing, and she held up a hand to shield her eyes as she forced the door shut again. The ringing hadn't stopped while she was in the closet, but now it was louder. It filled her ears like a skewer, plunging into her swollen brain. She fell to her knees, wrapping her arms around her head, trying to protect it. "Charlie, are you okay?" Something touched her, and she shied away, her eyes screwed shut against the light. "Charlie, it's John," the voice said, cutting through the awful noise, and something in her went still.

"John?" she whispered, her voice raspy. The dust from the grave had settled in her throat.

"Yeah." She turned her head and peered up through the shield of her arms. Slowly, the blazing light calmed, and she saw a human face. *John.*

"Are you real?" she asked, uncertain what kind of answer would convince her. He touched her again, a hand on her arm, and she didn't pull away. She blinked, and her vision cleared a little. She looked up, feeling as if she were opening herself to attack. Her eyes lit on two more people, and her halting mind slowly named them. "Jessica . . . ? Clay?"

"Yeah," John said. She put her hand on his and tried to focus. She could see Jessica, who was doubled over, her hands over her own ears.

"The noise," Charlie said. "She hears the noise, too. Do you?" It grew louder, drowning out John's response, and Charlie grabbed his hand. *Real. This is real.* "The children!" she cried out suddenly, as a swath of undulating colors rose from underneath the tables. They flew, their feet not touching the ground, their bodies leaving comet-like trails of color behind them. "Do you see?" Charlie whispered to John.

"Jessica!" he shouted. "Look out!" Jessica straightened, dropping her hands, and yelled something indistinct. The children converged on her in a swarm, dancing around her, darting in close, then back out again, as if it were a game, or an ambush. Two rushed on Clay, who stared them down until they shriveled and swirled back to join the circle around Jessica.

"The lights!" Jessica cried, her voice rising above the painful ringing noise. "Clay, it's coming from the lights on the walls!" She pointed up, where Charlie could just make out a long row of decorative colored lights, evenly spaced.

A gunshot cut through the clamor, and Charlie gripped John's hand tighter. Jessica's hands were on her ears again. The children were still in motion, but it was a nervous, shimmering movement. They'd stopped in place. Clay stood with his back to them all, his gun pointed at the wall. Charlie watched, wide-eyed, as he took aim again, and shot out the bulb of the second light fixture. The room dimmed slightly, and he moved on to the third, then the next, then the next. As one shot rang out after another, Charlie's head began to equalize, like whatever stuff had filled her to the point of bursting was slowly being drained. The room darkened, one bulb at a time. *Bang.* She looked up at John, and his face was clear. "It's really you," she said, her voice still choked with dust. *Bang.*

"It's really me," he agreed.

*Bang.*

The children's shimmering slowed, giving glimpses of arms and legs and faces. Jessica took her hands from her ears.

*Bang.*

Clay shot the last light, and the children stopped shimmering. They wavered briefly on the edge of solidity, a sickening ripple of lights in a scattered harmony, and then they were still. The room was silent. It was still lit by the overhead lights, but all the others were dead. Jessica looked around her, bafflement and horror taking turns on her face. The children were no longer children. They were wind-up toys, plastic boys in striped shirts, wearing plastic smiles and propeller beanies, and offering balloons.

"Jessica, come here," Clay said in a low voice, holding out his hand. She stepped toward him, glancing warily at the balloon boys as she moved between them. He took her hand to help her through, as if he were pulling her out of a chasm. Charlie slowly let go of John's hand and put hers to her temples, checking to make sure everything was still there. Her head no longer ached; her vision was clear. Whatever had come over her was gone.

"Charlie," Jessica said. "Are you all right? What's going on in here? I feel . . . drugged."

"These things aren't real." Charlie steadied herself and slowly got to her feet. "I mean, they're real, but not how we're seeing them. This whole place is an illusion. It's twisted somehow. Those things . . ." She gestured toward the wall where Clay had shot out the lights. "Those things are like the disc we found. They emit some kind of signal that distorts how we see." Charlie shook her head. "We have to get out of here," she said. "There's something worse here than these."

She pushed over a balloon boy, and it toppled easily. Its head popped off as it hit the ground, and it rolled across the floor. *Hello?* it muttered, much quieter than before.

ohn prodded the plastic balloon boy's head with his toe. It rolled a little farther, but did not speak again.

"Charlie?" Jessica said shakily. "Where are they? The big ones."

"I don't know. My head is still spinning." Charlie glanced around quickly, then drew closer to the others as they surveyed the room. Everything had changed when Clay shattered the fixtures. The realistic beasts and vicious-looking creatures were gone, replaced with strange, hairless versions of themselves. They no longer had eyes, only smooth, raised bumps of blank plastic.

"They look like corpses," John said softly.

"Or some kind of mold," Clay said thoughtfully. "They don't look finished."

"It's the lights," Charlie said. "They were creating an illusion, like the chip."

"What are you talking about?" Jessica said. "What chip?"

"It's—it's some kind of transmitter, embedded in a disc," Charlie said. "It scrambles your brain, cluttering it with nonsense so that you see what you expect to see."

"Then why don't they look like that?" Clay pointed to posters on the walls depicting a very cheerful Freddy Fazbear with rosy cheeks and a warm smile.

"Or that." John had found another, depicting Bonnie jovially strumming a bright red guitar so shiny it looked like it was made from candy.

Charlie looked thoughtful for a moment. "Because we didn't come here first." She walked toward the posters. "If you were a little kid and you saw the cute commercials, then saw these posters and toys and all that stuff, then I think that's exactly what they would have looked like."

"Because you already have those images in your head," John said. He tore the Freddy poster off the wall and stared at it momentarily before letting it fall to the ground. "But we know better. We know they're monsters."

"And we're afraid of them," Charlie said.

"And so we're seeing them for exactly what they are," John concluded.

Clay went up to the arcade mascots again, his gun still

drawn. He walked back and forth in front of the displays, looking at them from different angles.

"How did you find me?" Charlie asked suddenly. "You showed up like the cavalry—just in time. How did you know I was here? How did you know any of this was here?"

No one answered right away. John and Jessica looked to Clay, who was casting his eyes around the room purposefully; he looked like he was searching for something specific. "We followed . . ." He trailed off.

Charlie looked at each of the three of them in turn. "Who?" she demanded. But just as she spoke, the closet door burst open, banging against the wall with a ringing clatter. The twisted Freddy who had taken Charlie came crashing out, his mouth still unhinged and swinging unnaturally. He was a nightmarish version of the Freddy they'd known as kids, with searing red eyes and the musculature of a monster. He turned his elongated head from side to side wildly, his jaw bouncing in place.

"Run!" Clay yelled, waving his arms and trying to usher them together toward the door. Charlie was rooted to the ground, unable to take her eyes off the maw of the beast.

"Wait!" Jessica cried suddenly. "Clay, these aren't possessed like the others—they're not the lost children!"

"What?" he said, momentarily stopping his frantic movement and looking thoroughly confused.

*"Shoot it!"* Jessica screamed. Clay clenched his jaw, then raised the gun and aimed at Freddy's gaping mouth. He fired once. The shot was only a few feet from Charlie's ear, and it was deafening. Freddy jerked back, the python-like jaw contracting, and for a split second his image blurred and distorted. The unnaturally stretched mouth began to close, but before it could, Clay fired again, three more times in quick succession. With each shot the creature seemed to glitch: it blurred, sputtering around the edges. Freddy's mouth curled in on itself, not quite closing but shrinking inward, as the bear hunched forward around its wounds. Clay fired one last time, aiming for Freddy's head. Finally, the animatronic toppled forward, a misshapen heap on the ground.

Freddy's image flickered like static on a television screen. The color faded from his fur, then everything that made him *Freddy* winked out, leaving only a smooth plastic figure in his place. It looked like the rest of the animals in the room, a blank mannequin stripped of its characteristics. Charlie approached the thing that had been Freddy cautiously. The ringing in her ears was beginning to fade. She crouched down next to the creature, tilting her head to the side.

"It's not like the other mascots from Freddy's," she said. "These aren't made of fur and fabric, they're made of us—by twisting our minds." The words came out with a revulsion she hadn't expected.

"Charlie," John said softly. He stepped forward, but she ignored him. She touched the creature's smooth skin. It felt like something between plastic and human skin: a strange, malleable substance that was a little too soft, a little too slick. The feeling of it made her nauseous. Charlie leaned over the body, ignoring her disgust, and plunged her fingers into one of the bullet holes. She dug around in the slippery, inorganic stuff of the chest cavity, pretending not to hear Jessica and Clay's protests, and then she found it. Her fingers touched the disc, which was bent in half, almost broken. Charlie pried out a second piece of metal that was wedged beside it.

She stood up and held it out to the others; a bullet rested in her palm.

"You shot the chip," she said. "You killed the illusion."


No one spoke. In the momentary quiet, Charlie was suddenly aware of the racket they had just made, in this place so accustomed to stillness. The silence was broken by a clicking sound: the noise of claws on tile.

They all whirled to see, and from what had appeared to be a dark and empty corner, a wolflike figure split away from the shadows and stalked toward them, upright but hunched forward, as if uncertain whether to walk as a beast or a human.

They backed away as one. Charlie saw Clay about to trip on Freddy's collapsed body. She shouted, "Look out!" He stopped, turning to see, and his eyes widened at something behind Charlie.

"There!" he cried, and fired a shot into the dark. They turned: an eight-foot, misshapen Bonnie, the rabbit counterpart to the creature on the floor, was blocking the doorway behind them. Its head was too large for its body, with eyes glowing white-hot in the dark. Its mouth was open, revealing several rows of gleaming teeth. Clay fired again, but the bullet had no effect.

"How many bullets do you have left?" John said, measuring up the two threats still in the room.

Clay fired off three more shots at Bonnie, then lowered the gun.

"Three," he said dryly. "I had three." From the corner of her eye, Charlie saw John and Jessica draw closer together, moving a little behind Clay. She stayed where she was as the others retreated, transfixed by the two advancing figures: the wolf and the rabbit. She started to walk toward them.

"Charlie," John said with a warning tone. "What are you doing? Come back!"

"Why did you bring me here?" Charlie asked, looking from one creature to the other. Her chest was tight and her eyes ached, like she'd been holding back tears for hours. "What do you want from me?" she shouted. They looked back at her with implacable plastic eyes. "What is this place? *What do you know about my brother?*" she screamed, her throat raw. She flung herself at the wolf, hurtling toward the gigantic beast, as if she could tear it apart with her bare hands. Someone caught her by the waist. Human hands lifted her up and pulled her back, and Clay spoke quietly into her ear.

"Charlie, we need to go, *now*." She pulled herself out of his grasp, but remained where she was. Her breath was unsteady. She wanted to scream until her lungs gave out. She wanted to close her eyes and sit very still, and never emerge from the darkness.

Instead she looked again from Bonnie to the nameless wolf and asked, her voice so calm it chilled her to hear it, "Why do you want me?"

"They don't care about you. I'm the one that brought you here." A voice spoke from the same shadowed corner the wolf had emerged from. The rabbit and the wolf straightened their posture, as if responding to the speaker's command.

"I know that voice," Jessica whispered. A figure began to limp forward, obscured by darkness. No one moved. Charlie realized she was holding her breath, but she didn't hear anyone else breathing in the silence, either, just the uneven shuffle of whatever was coming. Whatever it was, it was the size of a man. Its body was contorted, sloping to one side as it lurched toward the group.

"You have something that belongs to me," said the voice, and then the figure stepped into the light.

Charlie gasped and heard John's sharp intake of breath. "Impossible," Charlie whispered. She felt John move up to stand beside her, but she didn't dare take her eyes off the man who stood before them.

His face was dark, the color mottled, and it was swollen with fluid; cheeks that had been hollow were now distended with the bloat of decay. His eyes were bloodshot, the burst capillaries threading through eyeballs that looked just a little too translucent. Something inside them had gone bad, jelly-like. At the base of his neck, Charlie could see two pieces of metal gleaming. They extended from within his neck, rect-angular lumps standing out from his mottled skin. He wore what had once been a mascot suit of yellow fur, though what remained was now green with mold.

"Dave?" Jessica breathed.

"Don't call me that," he snarled. "I haven't been Dave for a long time." He held out his new hands: blood-soaked and forever sealed inside a rotting suit.

"William Afton, then? Of Afton Robotics?"

"Wrong again," he hissed. "I've accepted the new life that you gave me. You've made me one with my creation. My name is Springtrap!" The man who had once been Dave cried the name with a hoarse glee, then scrunched his gnarled face back into a glare. "I'm more than Afton ever was, and *far* more than Henry."

"Well, you smell terrible," Jessica quipped.

"Ever since Charlie remade me, set me free to my destiny, I've been master of all these creatures." He crooked his fingers and made a sharp gesture forward. Bonnie and the wolf took two steps forward, in unison. "See? All the animatronics are linked together; it was a system designed to control the choreography for the shows. Now, I control the system. I control the choreography. All of this belongs to me."

Springtrap shuffled forward, and Charlie shrank back. "I owe you both another debt of gratitude as well," he said. "I was imprisoned in that tomb beneath the stage, scarcely able to move, only able to see through the eyes of my creatures."

He gestured at the two who stood behind him. "But for all that I could see, I was trapped. Eventually *they* would have broken me out, but having you do it yourself was a delightful surprise." He met Charlie's eyes, and a muscle twitched in her cheek.

*Get away from me, don't come any closer.* As if reading her thoughts, he sidled nearer to her. She would have felt his breath on her face, if he still breathed.

Springtrap raised a bent hand. The fabric suit was ragged, revealing his human skin through the gaps. She could see the places where metal pins and rods had buried themselves alongside his bones and tendons, into a rusted shadow-skeleton. He touched the back of his hand to Charlie's face, stroking her cheek like a beloved child. From the corner of her eye, she saw John start forward.

"No, it's okay," she forced herself to say.

"I won't hurt your friends, but I need something from you."

"You have to be kidding," she said, her voice brittle.

His mouth twisted into something that grotesquely resembled a smile.

John heard a faint click, and turned just in time to see Clay loading one bullet quietly into his gun. Clay shrugged. "You never know when a corpse may wander out of the shadows wearing a rabbit suit." He raised his arm, steadied himself, and fired.

Springtrap recoiled. "Kids!" Clay shouted, "the door!" Charlie jerked her eyes away from Springtrap almost painfully, as if he had been exerting some hypnotic force on her. Bonnie had abandoned the exit, leaving it clear. Clay, John, and Jessica began to run. Charlie glanced back, reluctant to go, then joined the others.

They ran back the way they'd come from, Clay leading the way as they wound through the carnival games and looming, featureless mascots. He strode purposefully ahead, as if he knew the way. Charlie remembered her question that no one had answered. *How did you find me?*

They were chased by sounds: scraping metal and the clack

of the wolf's claws. In the open space, the noises echoed strangely, seeming to come from every side. It was as if an army pursued them. Charlie quickened her step. She glanced up at John, seeking reassurance, but his eyes were on Clay ahead of them.

They reached the room with the waterfall, and again Clay knew the path. He headed directly for the passage beneath the cliff, where the water emerged. They pressed through it one by one. Clay and John were too tall to walk through without bending over, and Charlie felt a quick pang of relief. *The monsters won't fit.* Halfway through the passage, Clay paused, standing motionless in an awkward position. He craned his neck, studying something just out of view. "Clay!" Charlie hissed.

"I have an idea," he said. Two shadows emerged from the far side of the room. Jessica glanced at the black-lit tunnel beside them, ready to run for it. But Clay shook his head. Instead, he guided the group backward, none of them taking their eyes off the monsters. All that shielded them now was the river that bisected the room. The animatronics were approaching the water hesitantly. The wolf sniffed at it and shook his fur, and Bonnie simply bent down and stared. "Don't run," Clay said sternly.

"They can't cross that thing, right?" Charlie said.

As if responding to her cue, the two mascots stepped unsteadily into the river. Jessica gasped, and Charlie took an involuntary step back. Slowly and deliberately, the anima-tronics continued toward them through the waist-high water. The wolf slipped on the smooth bottom and fell. It dunked completely under the water for a moment, before scrambling to the side, thrashing violently. Bonnie lost his footing as well but managed to grab the riverbank and steady himself, then continued forward.

"That's not possible," Charlie said. Behind her came a peal of laughter, and she whirled around.

It was Springtrap, his eyes scarcely visible, peering through the black-lit tunnel nearby. "Was that your plan?" he said incredulously. "Did you think *my* robots would be as poorly designed as your father's?"

"Well then, I'm sure you made them fireproof as well!" Clay called out. His voice reverberated in the cavernous, empty room. Springtrap frowned, puzzled, then looked at the water in the stream. It was glistening in the dim light, color dancing on its surface in gleaming swirls, like—

"Gasoline." Charlie turned to face Springtrap. Open gas cans lined the walls, some lying on their sides; all were empty.

Clay flicked a lighter and flung it into the water. The top of the river caught fire, a flame billowing up like a tidal wave, obscuring the animatronics in the middle. The creatures struggled to the side of the river, emitting guttural, high-pitched shrieks. They managed to crawl onto the bank, but it was too late. Their illusions deactivated. Their plastic skin was exposed, liquefying and falling from their bodies into little flaming pools on the floor. Charlie and the others watched as the dissolving creatures fell, writhing in agonized screams.

They all stood frozen, mesmerized by the gruesome spectacle. Then, from behind her, Charlie heard a quiet scraping sound. She whirled around to see Springtrap vanish into the mouth of the narrow, black-lit cave. She took off after him, running into the eerie light.

"Charlie!" Clay called. He began to chase her, but the flaming creatures had crawled across the floor—perhaps trying to reach their master, perhaps in mindless desperation—and now they blocked the mouth of the cave with their blazing remains. Charlie set her eyes on the path ahead. She couldn't afford to look back.

The passage was narrow, and it smelled damp and ancient. The floor felt like rock beneath her bare feet, but though it was uneven, it wasn't painful. The surface was worn and smooth. As soon as the dark of the cave closed over her, she felt a spark from her dreams: the tug of something so like her that it *was* her, blood calling to blood.

"Sammy?" she whispered. His name glanced off the cave walls, shrouding her in the sound of it. The absence inside her pulled her forward, drawing her toward the promise of completion. *It has to be you.* Charlie ran faster, following a call that came from deep inside her.

She could hear the distant echo of Springtrap's laughter at intervals, but she couldn't spot him ahead of her. Occasionally she thought she caught glimpses of him, but he was always gone before her eyes had time to focus in the disorienting glow of the black light. The cave twisted and turned until she had no idea which direction she was headed, but she ran on.

Charlie blinked as something moved at the corner of her eye, just out of sight. She shook her head and ran on, but then it happened again. An unnatural shape, neon-bright, slithered out of the wall and wriggled past her.

Charlie stopped, clapping a hand over her mouth so she wouldn't scream. The thing undulated up the wall, moving like an eel though it was climbing rock. When it reached the ceiling, it vanished, but she couldn't see a break in the rock where it might have gone. *Just keep going.* She started to run again, but suddenly more of them poured out of the seam at the base of the wall. Dozens of wriggling shapes swam and danced, moving along the floor of the cave like it was the floor of the sea. Three of them headed right for Charlie. They rippled over her feet and she screamed, then realized as they circled her, nibbling curiously at her toes, that she felt nothing. "You aren't real," she said. She kicked at them, and her foot passed straight through empty air: the creatures had vanished. Charlie gritted her teeth and ran onward.

Ahead of her, large glowing creatures like dancers made

of mist appeared and vanished one after another. They dashed across the passage, as if they were running along a path that just happened to intersect with this one. When Charlie was almost close enough to touch them, the one nearest sputtered and faded out. She ran on, listening for the sound of Springtrap's maniacal giggle, hoping that it was enough to guide her.

She turned a corner, then the passage angled sharply the other way. Charlie ran straight into the wall, catching herself with her hands at the last second. She spun around, looking for the way forward. The jolt had been enough to distract her. She couldn't tell which way she had come from. Charlie took a deep breath and closed her eyes. She could hear a soft voice in the air. *Left.* She started running again.

A burst of blue light nearly blinded her as a massive shape rose in the darkness. Charlie screamed, flinging herself back against the wall of the cave and throwing her arms up to shield her face. The thing before her was a gaping mouth full of teeth, all glowing blue. The enormous maw bore down over her.

"It's an illusion," Charlie whispered. She ducked and tried to roll away in the narrow space. Her shoulder struck a rock and her arm went numb. Charlie clutched it instinctively and looked up: nothing was there.

She pressed her back against the wall of the cave, taking deep breaths as feeling slowly returned to her arm. "It's another transmitter," she said quietly. "Nothing I see here is real." Her voice was thin in the rocky passage, but saying the words aloud was enough to make her stand again. She closed her eyes. The connection she had felt was growing stronger as she ran, the sense that she was running toward a missing piece of herself. It was unbearable, stronger than the urge to fight or flee from danger. It was greater than hunger, deeper than thirst, and it pulled at the core of her being. She could no more turn back than she could choose to stop breathing. She set off again, hurtling farther into the cavern.

Far in the distance, Springtrap's laughter still echoed.


"Charlie!" John called again, but it was hopeless. She was long out of sight, deep into the cave, and what remained of Bonnie and the wolf still burned in front of the opening.

"We have to go!" Clay shouted. "We can find another way!" Jessica grabbed John's arm and he gave in, following Clay toward the arcade entrance.

Just as they reached the door, the twisted Freddy lunged out of the shadows, almost falling to the ground. Jessica screamed and John froze, struck still at the sight of him. His illusion sputtered on and off in pieces. An arm flickered away, exposing the smooth plastic underneath. Then the fur returned and his torso went blank, revealing the gunshot holes, and the ugly, twisted metal beneath the plastic shell.

Worse was the face: not only was the illusion missing, but the material underneath. From his chin to his forehead, the left half of Freddy's face had been ripped away, revealing metal plates and gnarled wires. His left eye glowed red amid the exposed machinery, while his right eye was completely dark.

A noise behind them broke John from his horrified reverie. He looked back to see that Bonnie and the wolf had gotten to their feet, still smoldering. Their plastic casings had almost entirely melted away, still dribbling slowly off their bodies, but the robotic works beneath seemed intact. They approached steadily, moving into position, so that John, Clay, and Jessica were surrounded.

"Do you have any bullets left?" John asked Clay in a low voice. Clay slowly shook his head. He was turning in a cautious circle, shifting his gaze from one animatronic to the next, as if trying to gauge which would make the first strike.

Charlie ran steadily on, keeping her eyes on the path. She turned another corner and blinked. Something was glowing blue ahead of her. *It's not real*, she told herself. She paused for a moment, but the glowing shapes didn't move. She kept going, realizing as she drew closer that the passageway was widening, opening out finally into a small alcove where the blue glow became clear.

The floor was spotted with patches of mushrooms, their caps glowing an intense neon blue under the black light. She slowed her pace, went to the nearest grouping and bent to touch the mushrooms. She snapped her hand back in surprise when she felt a spongy substance. "They're real, sort of," she said.

"Yes," said a voice beside her ear, and then she was choking. Springtrap grabbed her by the neck, crushing her windpipe. Charlie only panicked for a moment before anger returned to her, giving her clarity. She reached her arm out forward as far as she could, then jammed it back, striking her elbow into his solar plexus with as much force as she could muster. His hands dropped from her throat and she leaped free, turning to face him as he clutched his injured gut.

"Things have changed since you died," Charlie said, surprised by the calm disdain in her voice. "For one thing, I've been doing sit-ups!"

"I think this is it," Jessica said quietly, spinning in place as the three monsters approached, leaving no avenue of retreat. John felt his chest clench, his body protesting the idea. But she was right. He put a hand on her shoulder.

"Maybe we can play dead," he said.

"I don't think we'll have to play," Jessica said resignedly.

"Backs together," Clay barked, and they backed up into a

tiny triangle, each facing one of the creatures. The wolf was crouched, ready to spring. John met its eyes. They were sputtering in and out: dark and malevolent, then completely blank. The thing drew back, and John steeled himself. Jessica grabbed his hand, and he clenched hers tightly. The wolf leaped—and then fell to the ground screeching as something knocked it viciously on its face. The figure, invisible in the shadows, grabbed the wolf's feet and yanked it backward, dragging it away from its human prey as it howled, scrabbling at the floor with its claws. It kicked its hind legs, freeing itself, and began its attack again. Jessica screamed, and John shouted with her, then watched, breathless, as the wolf was caught by its feet again. The thing that held it flipped it onto its back and jumped on top of it. The new predator paused for an instant, meeting their eyes with a silver glow, and Jessica gasped.

"Foxy," John breathed. As if spurred on by hearing his name, Foxy plunged his hook into the wolf's chest and began to tear at its exposed machinery. The screeches of metal ripping apart metal ground at their ears. Foxy continued to dig furiously, burrowing into the wolf as wires and parts fell from the sky. He snapped his jaws in the air, then tore at the wolf's stomach, wrenching out its insides and flinging them aside with a brutal efficiency. The wolf was overpowered, its limbs flailing helplessly before falling heavily to the ground.

Behind them came another inhuman scream. John whipped around in time to see the fire-ravaged Bonnie on its stomach, being dragged steadily into the shadows. Its eyes blinked on and off in a panicked, meaningless pattern. It screamed again as, with a horrible grinding sound, it was torn to pieces by whatever lurked in the shadows. Pieces of metal and shredded plastic scattered across the floor, skittering out in front of the prone rabbit, so that it could see the remnants of its own lower half. It screamed again, anchoring its claws into the tile in a last, futile defense, only to be pulled screeching into the dark as though through a grinder. In the shadows, four lights glowed. John blinked, realizing they were eyes. He nudged Jessica.

"I can see them," he whispered. "Chica and Bonnie! *Our* Chica and Bonnie!" Beside the river, Foxy had torn the wolf's limbs from its body. He leaped from the ravaged torso and took an attack posture toward the large, twisted Freddy, which twitched and flickered for a moment, then lowered its massive head and charged. Foxy leaped, hitting the twisted Freddy's face with full force and knocking it onto its back, then tearing into its head cavity, slashing at what was left of the twisted face with enthusiasm.

Something grabbed John and he snapped out of his trance. The twisted Bonnie grabbed him with an arm of exposed metal, but the eyes in the dark rose suddenly behind it. The original Bonnie grabbed the torso of the twisted Bonnie and threw it aside to where Chica waited; she grabbed the misshapen rabbit's head and wrenched it off in a burst of sparks.

John shielded his eyes. When the smoke settled, all that remained was the hollow, burnt corpse of an unidentifiable monster. Bonnie and Chica had vanished into the shadows.

Charlie ran for the mouth of the passage, but Springtrap leaped on her with preternatural speed. He knocked her to the ground and reached again for her neck with his swollen hands. Charlie rolled out of the way, and something jabbed her hard in the back. She snatched at it, and a mushroom cap came away in her hands. She leaped to her knees as Springtrap got to his feet, circling her, looking for an opening. She glanced down: a sturdy, metal spike had held the mushroom cap in place. She wrapped her hand around its base, blocking it from Springtrap's sight with her body.

Charlie looked up at him, meeting his gelatinous eyes, silently daring him to attack. As if on cue, he sprang at her, leaping with his arms thrust out, stretching again toward her throat. At the last moment, Charlie ducked her head and thrust the spike upward with all her might. It stopped with a jolt as it hit his chest, but she drove it in, ignoring his sputtering cries as he tried uselessly to beat her away. She stood, her hands shaking as she shoved the stake in as far as it would go. He toppled backward, and she knelt swiftly beside him, giving the metal spike another thrust.

"Tell me why," she hissed. It was the question that consumed her, the thing that kept coming back in her nightmares. Now he said nothing, and she rocked the stake back and forth in his chest. He made a gagging cry of pain. *"Tell me why you took him! Why did you choose him? Why did you take Sammy?"*

"Into the cave!" John shouted. "We have to get Charlie!"

They hurried to the opening, but from inside the cave came a strange, overwhelming clatter. They all stepped back as a horde of the balloon boys emerged from the cave, shaking back and forth on unsteady feet, their pointed teeth chattering loudly as they wobbled forward with staring eyes.

"Not again! I hate these things!" Jessica cried. Clay took up a fighting stance, but John could see they would be overwhelmed. There was something different about the children now, something coordinated. Though they shook and wobbled, it no longer seemed like a sign of weakness. Instead, John thought of warriors rattling their shields: the threat before the battle.

"We have to get away," he said. "Clay!"

Something shook the earth—pounding, even footsteps—as a shadow loomed above them. John looked up and saw a smiling Freddy Fazbear approaching, his hat at a jaunty angle and his massive limbs swinging. "Oh no! He's back!" Jessica screeched.

"No, wait! That's *our* Freddy!" John grabbed Jessica and shielded her with his arms. Freddy lumbered past them and into the crowd of balloon boys. With a single lunge he smashed both arms into the crowd, creating a deafening shatter of metal and plastic. The air was filled with arms, legs, and broken shrapnel. Freddy got to his feet and grabbed one of the balloon boys, lifting it up like it weighed nothing. He crushed its head with one hand. Freddy tossed the body to the ground and stomped on it, pursuing the others as they ran. They scattered, but Freddy was moving swiftly, and the room resounded with the noise of cracking plastic.

"Come on, into the cave!" Clay yelled over the din, and they ran for the passage. They hurried down the narrow path, Clay at the front and John taking up the rear, glancing behind to make sure they weren't being followed. Suddenly Clay halted, and Jessica and John nearly ran into him. Crowding up beside him, they saw why he'd stopped: the path split, and there was no trace of Charlie.

"There," Jessica said suddenly. "There's a light!"

John blinked. It was dim, but he saw it. Somewhere down the passage there was a blue glow, though it was impossible to tell how far away it was. "Come on," he said grimly, pressing past Clay to take the lead.

"*Why did you take Sammy?!*" Charlie cried again. Springtrap wheezed and smiled but did not speak. She grabbed his head with both hands, desperate with fury. She lifted his head and brought it crashing against the rock where it lay. He made another sharp grunt of pain, and she did it again. This time something began to ooze from the back of his head, running thickly down the rock. "What did you do to him?" Charlie demanded. "Why did you take him? Why did you choose *him*?" He looked up at her; one of his pupils had swallowed the iris of his eye. He smiled vaguely.

"I didn't choose him."

Hands grabbed Charlie's shoulders, dragging her up and away from the semiconscious Springtrap. She shouted and turned to fight back, only stopping herself when she saw that it was Clay. The others were behind him. She turned back, shaking with rage.

"I'll kill you!" she cried. She lifted Springtrap up by the shoulders and shoved him back against the rock. His head bounced and lolled to the side. "What do you mean you didn't choose him?" Charlie said, leaning in close to him, as if she might read the answers in his battered face. "You took him from me! Why did you take him?"

Springtrap's mismatched eyes seemed to focus for a moment, and even he seemed to have difficulty muttering his next words.

"I didn't take him. I took you."

Charlie stared, her fingers going lax, loosening on Springtrap's moldy suit. *What?* The rage that had filled her to the breaking point drained away all at once. She felt like she'd lost too much blood and was going into shock. Springtrap didn't try to get away; he just lay there coughing and sputtering, his eyes once more unfocused, staring into a void Charlie couldn't see.

Suddenly the floor rattled beneath them. The walls rocked inward as the whole cave shook, and something mechanical roared on the other side of the wall. The sounds of grinding metal filled the air.

"It's a battle royale out there!" Clay shouted. "This whole place is coming down!" Charlie glanced at him, and as soon as her head was turned she felt Springtrap slip from her fingers. She whipped back around, just in time to see him roll through an open trap door at the base of an enormous rock a few feet away. Charlie leaped up to follow him, but the floor quaked violently. She lost her footing, nearly falling as half the cave wall came tumbling down. She stopped, glancing around in confusion: real rock and dirt cascaded all around them. "It's not the fake cave that's collapsing!" she shouted to the rest. "It's the whole building!"

"Is everyone okay?" Clay shouted. Charlie nodded, and saw that John and Jessica were still on their feet. "We have to go!" Light shone through a crack in the wall ahead. Clay started for it, motioning the others to follow. Charlie hesitated, unable to take her eyes from the last place she'd seen Springtrap. John put a hand on her arm.

The walls of the fake cavern had almost completely fallen, and now they could see the actual interior of the complex.

"That way!" Clay shouted, pointing to a narrow maintenance hall that seemed to stretch off endlessly into the distance. "None of these things will be able to fit through there!" Clay and Jessica ran for the entrance to the corridor, but Charlie faltered.

"Charlie, we can deal with him another day," John shouted over the din. "But we need to survive this one first!" The ground shook again and John looked at Charlie. She nodded, and they ran.

Clay led them racing through the tunnel as the sound of its collapse chased them. The air was filled with dust, obscuring the path ahead. Charlie looked back once, but the ruins were lost in the haze. Eventually the rumble of falling rock was reduced to a distant thunder. The clean, narrow hallway began to feel removed from the madness behind them.

"Clay we have to stop," Jessica cried, holding her side like she was in pain.

"I see something up ahead. I think we're almost to the end

of this. There!" The hallway ended in a heavy metal door, partially cracked, and Clay beckoned John to help him open it. It squealed and protested, then gave way at last, opening into a simple room of dark stone. One wall of it had been knocked down, and the room gaped open, the cool night air pouring in.

John looked at Charlie. "We're out! We're okay!" He laughed.

"Don't you see where we are?" she whispered. Slowly, she walked the length of the room, gesturing to the four enormous pits in the floor, one of which contained a headless, half-buried robot. "John, this is my dad's house. It's the room we found."

"Come on, Jessica." Clay was helping Jessica through the gap in the collapsed wall. He paused and looked back to John.

"It's okay," John said. "We'll be right there." Clay nodded. He helped Jessica through and moved out of sight.

"What is this?" Charlie put her hand on her stomach, a sudden unease settling over her.

"What's wrong?" John asked. Something flickered all around them, a disorienting flash, too fast to even tell where it had come from. A thunderous crash echoed from the hall they'd just broken out of. "Charlie, I think we should go with Clay."

"Yeah, I'm coming." Charlie followed John to the gap in the wall as he climbed through it.

"Okay, come on," John shouted, holding out his hand to her from what had once been her own backyard. She started forward, then stopped as the lights flickered again. *What is that?*

It was the walls. The whitewashed concrete was blinking in and out of existence, shivering like a dying bulb. It was the wall Charlie had been drawn to the first time they came to this place. Now she felt its pull as she had in the cave. It was stronger here than it had ever been, even in the dreams that left her drained and aching. *I'm here.* She took a step toward the far wall and felt another pang in her stomach. *Here. Yes, here.*

"Charlie!" John cried again. "Come on!"

"I have to," she said softly. She went to the wall and put her hands on it, as she'd done before. But this time the concrete was warm, and somehow smooth despite the rough finish. *I have to get inside.* For a moment, she felt like she was in two places at once: here, inside the little room, and on the other side of the wall, desperate to get through. She drew back suddenly, taking her hands off the wall as if it burned. The illusion flickered, then died altogether.

The concrete wall was made of metal, and at the center was a door.

Charlie stared, blank with shock. *This is the door.* She'd been drawing it without knowing what it was. Approximating over and over something she had never seen. She stepped forward again and put her hands on the surface. It was still warm. She pressed her cheek against it. "Are you in there?" she called softly. "I have to get you out."

Her heart was pounding, blood rushing in her ears so loudly she could scarcely hear anything else. "Charlie! Charlie!" John and Jessica were both calling her from outside, but their voices seemed as distant as memory. She stood, not taking her hands from the metal but tracing her fingers along it. It felt like letting go for even an instant would cause her pain. She brought her hands to the crack in the wall: it had no handle, no knob, and no hinges. It was just an outline, and now she ran her thumb up and down the side of it, trying to find a trip, some trick that would make the door open and let her through.

She heard John climb back inside and slowly approach her, keeping his distance, as though he might scare her away.

"Charlie, if you don't get out of here, you'll die. Whatever's behind that door, it can't give you back your family. You still have *us*." Charlie looked at John. His eyes were wide and frightened. She took a small step toward him.

"We've lost enough. Please, don't make me lose you, too," John pleaded. Charlie stared at the ceiling as it trembled; clouds of smoke were pouring out of the corridor they'd come from. John coughed heavily; he was choking. She looked at him. He was terrified, unwilling to draw closer than he already was.

She turned again, and the world around her faded; she couldn't hear John behind her, or smell the smoke filling the air. She laid her hand flat against the wall. *A heartbeat. I feel a heartbeat.* Though she made no intentional movement, her body turned to the side. She tensed, committing to remain where she stood, without ever making the decision. Something began to hiss: the steady, gentle sound of air being released. From the base of the door came a rhythmic clicking. Charlie closed her eyes.

"Charlie!" John grabbed her and turned her forcefully toward him, shaking her out of her stupor. "Look at me. I'm not leaving you here."

"I have to stay."

"No, you have to come with us!" he cried. "You have to come with *me*."

"No, I . . ." Charlie felt her voice trail off; she was losing strength.

"I love you," John said. Charlie's eyes stopped drifting: she fixed them on him. "I'm taking you with me, right now." He grabbed her hand roughly. He was strong enough to pull her away by force, she knew, but he was waiting for her to acknowledge him.

She looked into his eyes, trying to let them bring her back. It felt like trying to awaken from a dream. John's gaze was an anchor, and she held it, letting him keep her steady, draw her back to him. "Okay," she said quietly.

"Okay," John repeated, heaving the words out in a sigh. He'd been holding his breath. He walked backward, guiding her as he went.

She climbed to the top of the broken wall and paused, bracing herself against the insistent pull of the door and what lay behind it. She took a deep breath—then was torn backward by a colossal force. She ripped back through the rocks, her arms pinned to her sides. Charlie screamed, struggling to get away. Dimly she heard John shouting close by.

As she whipped her body back and forth against its grip, Charlie glimpsed the immense thing that had caught her. The twisted Freddy stared blankly forward, or at least what remained of it. It held her with one arm; the other was gone, and wires hung from its shoulder like extra bits of sinew. Its plastic casing had melted away, and what remained were metal plates and stays, a skeleton with unnatural bulges and gaps in its frame where the collapse had mangled it. Its face was a gaping hole, spilling teeth and wire that hung in shapeless masses. Charlie couldn't see it legs, and after a second she realized they were gone. It had dragged itself, one-armed, through the rubble. Wires spilled out of its body like guts, and when she saw its stomach, Charlie went cold with terror.

Its chest had parted at the middle. Sharp, uneven teeth lined both sides. Charlie kicked at the animatronic, but it did no good: it forced her instantly into the chasm. The thing embraced her, pushing her deeper inside its chest as they toppled backward together. The metal rib cage snapped shut: she was caught.

"Charlie!" John was kneeling beside her, and she reached out through the metal stays. He grabbed her hand. "Clay!" he shouted, "Jessica!" Jessica was there in seconds; Charlie could see Clay struggling back through the narrow opening.

"Wait!" Charlie cried as Jessica tried to pry the chest open. "The spring locks, they'll kill me if you touch the wrong thing!"

"But if we don't get you out, you'll die anyway!" Jessica shouted. Charlie saw for the first time that the mouth wasn't finished closing. It was layered somehow, and metal plates began folding over her like petals of a horrid flower. John started to stand, but Charlie tightened her hand around his.

"Don't let go of me!" she cried, panicked. He dropped back to his knees and pulled her hand to his chest. She stared at him, even as the metal plates closed over her, threatening to seal her off. Jessica tried to jam them delicately, without setting off the spring locks. "John—" Charlie gasped.

"Don't," he said roughly. "I've got you!"

The plates continued to slide down and meet in the center. Charlie's arm was trapped in the corner of the strange mouth, protruding from the only gap where the plates didn't meet. She looked around wildly: another layer was closing. She was wedged into the suit haphazardly, her whole body crammed into Freddy's torso, and she could see nothing but dimming figures as more layers of metal and plastic closed over her. Above her, Jessica was trying to stop the next layer from emerging, and she felt Freddy's mutilated body lurch.

"Jessica! Look out!" she screamed at the top of her lungs. Jessica leaped back just in time to avoid Freddy's violently swinging arm. The animatronic was on its back, but it struck out randomly, beating Jessica and Clay away. Its body rocked back and forth, and Charlie eyed the springs and robotic parts all around her: she drew her knees up to her chest, trying to make herself smaller.

John let go of her hand, and she grabbed at his absence. She could no longer see outside. "John!"

Freddy's body shook, struck by a massive blow.


"Let go of her!" John screamed. Clay hefted a metal beam from the ground and struck at Freddy's head. The twisted bear tried to strike with its remaining arm. Clay ducked out of the way and hit it again from the other side, out of reach. Jessica was still at the creature's chest, trying to find an opening to pry at, but each layer melded seamlessly together. There was nothing to catch at. John moved in next to her, trying to help. Clay struck at the head over and over, making Freddy's whole body jolt with every blow.

"I can't get to her!" Jessica yelled. "She's going to suffocate!" She tried to steady Charlie's trembling hand. Clay hit

Freddy's head once more with a resounding crash, and they heard metal cracking as the head was knocked off the creature's body.

"Can we get her out through the neck?" John asked urgently. Freddy's arm continued to flail, but it had weakened, and was just rising and falling, seeming to swing without purpose.

"Clay, help!" Jessica cried. He ran to take over, digging his fingers between the plates to pry them open. Jessica continued holding Charlie's hand, which had gone limp. "Charlie!" Jessica cried. Charlie's hand closed over hers again, and Jessica gasped with relief. "John, Clay, she's okay! Hurry! Charlie, can you hear me? It's Jessica." There was no sound from inside Freddy's sealed chest, but Charlie held on tightly to Jessica's hand as the others grimly worked to free her.

Suddenly a single high-pitched click reverberated through the air. John and Clay froze, their hands still hovering above Freddy's chest. For a moment, the air stood still, then the metal body convulsed violently. It launched itself off the ground, and a ghastly crunch of metal pierced the air. All three pulled back instinctively. Clay and John jumped away from the thing, and Jessica scrambled backward, dropping Charlie's hand.

The suit fell again and was still. The arm was splayed on the ground at an awkward angle. The room was silent. "Charlie?" John said softly, then his face went white. He ran to the place where her arm was exposed, falling hard on his knees, and grabbed her hand in both his own. It was limp. John turned it over and tapped her palm with his fingers. "Charlie? Charlie!"

"John," Jessica said very quietly. "The blood." He looked up at her, confused, still holding on to Charlie. Then something wet dripped onto his hand. There was blood running out of the suit and down Charlie's arm. Her skin was slick and red, except the hand he held. He watched, unable to look away, as it dripped steadily from the suit, pooling on the ground and beginning to seep into his jeans. It covered his hand and hers, until his skin was slippery and he began to lose his grip. She was sliding away from him.

Sirens were suddenly nearby, and John realized vaguely that he'd been hearing them in the distance. He looked dazedly up at Clay.

"I radioed them," he said. "We aren't safe in here." Clay took his eyes off the suit and looked up to study the ceiling. It was bowed and cracking, on the verge of collapse. John didn't move. People were shouting outside, and flashlights bobbed up and down as they ran toward the crumbling building. Jessica touched his shoulder. Breaks and cracks resounded through the space.

"John, we have to." As if to mark her point, the floor shook again beneath them and something crashed loudly not far away. Charlie's hand didn't move.

A uniformed officer pressed through the crack in the wall. "Chief Burke?"

"Thomson. We have to get the kids out, now." Thomson nodded and motioned to Jessica.

"Come on, miss."

"John, come on," Jessica managed to say, and a thunderous clatter sounded from behind them. Clay looked to the officer again.

"Get them out of here." Thomson took hold of Jessica's arm and she tried to shove him away.

"Don't touch me!" she shouted, but the officer firmly pulled her up and over the rubble, half dragging her outside. John only half heard the commotion, then someone's hands were on his shoulders as well. He batted them away, not looking around.

"We're leaving," Clay said in a low voice.

"Not without Charlie," John responded. Clay took a deep breath.

John saw him signal someone from the corner of his eye, then he was grabbed forcefully by two large men and dragged toward the opening.

"No!" he shouted. "Let me go!" They shoved him roughly over the broken wall, then Clay struggled out behind them.

"Is everyone out?" a female officer called.

"Yes," Clay said hesitantly, but with the ring of authority.

"NO!" John shouted. He broke free of the officers holding him back and ran for the opening again. He had one foot through the gap, then stopped dead as a sweeping flashlight briefly illuminated the room in front of him.

A dark-haired woman knelt in the pool of blood, holding Charlie's limp hand. She looked up sharply and met his eyes with a piercing black gaze. Before John could move or speak, hands grabbed his shoulders again and drew him back, and then the whole house collapsed before them.

# CHAPTER FOURTEEN

**W**e don't know for sure," Jessica said, firmly setting down the fork she'd been playing with on the diner table. It made a disappointing click.

"Don't do this," John warned. He didn't look up from the menu, though he hadn't read a word since he picked it up.

"It's just, all that we saw was, you know, blood. People can survive a lot of things. Dave—Springtrap, whatever he wants to call himself—he survived one of those suits, *twice*. For all we know she might be trapped in the rubble. We should go back. We could—"

"Jessica, *stop*." John closed the menu and put it down on the table. "Please. I can't listen to this. We both saw it happen. We both know she couldn't have . . ." Jessica opened her mouth again, about to interrupt. "I said, *stop*. Don't you think that I *want* to believe that she's okay? I cared about her, too. I cared about her a lot. There is nothing I want more than for her to somehow have escaped. For her to drive up in that ancient car and get out all furious and say, 'Hey, why'd you leave me behind?' But we saw the blood: there was too much. I held her hand, and it didn't feel like anything. As soon as I touched her, I just—Jessica, I *knew*. And you know it, too."

Jessica picked up her fork again and twirled it between her fingers, not meeting his eyes. "I feel like we're waiting for something to happen," she said quietly.

John picked up the menu again. "I know. But I think that's just how this feels." From behind him, he heard the waitress approach for the third time. "We don't know yet," he said without looking up. "Why am I even looking at this?" John set the menu back down and covered his face with his hands.

"Can I join you?" John looked up. An unfamiliar, brown-haired young man slid into the booth next to Jessica and across from John.

"Hey, Arty," Jessica said with a weak smile.

"Hey," he said, glancing from her to John and back again. John said nothing. "Everyone okay?" Arty asked finally. "I heard there was some kind of accident. Where's Charlie?"

Jessica looked down, tapping the fork on the table. John met the newcomer's eyes, then shook his head. Arty blanched, and John looked out the window. The parking lot outside blurred as he fixed his gaze on the smudged and streaky glass.

"The last thing she said to me was . . ." John lightly touched his fist to the table. "'Don't let go of me.'" He turned back to the window.

"John," Jessica whispered.

"And I did. I let go of her. And she died alone." There was silence for a few moments.

"I can't believe it," Arty said, his brow furrowed. "We had just started dating, you know?"

Jessica kept her face smooth, and John turned his thousand-yard stare on Arty. The boy faltered. "I mean, we were going to. I think. She really liked me, anyway." He looked to Jessica, who nodded.

"She liked you, Arty," she said. John turned back to the window.

"I'm sure she did," he said evenly.

Random thoughts swirled through his mind. The mess of her room. The pang of concern when he saw her childhood toy, Theodore the stuffed rabbit, torn apart. *Charlie, what was wrong?* There was so much more he wanted to ask her. Those blind faces with their smooth, nearly featureless faces and their couplet word games. Something—everything—about them had disturbed him, and now that he pictured them again, he was bothered for another reason. *They looked like William Afton's designs—the blank faces with no eyes. Charlie, what made you think of that?*

Jessica made an indistinct cry, and John startled back to the present to see her racing to the door, where Marla had appeared. He got up more slowly and followed her, with a sense of déjà vu. He was waiting his turn as Marla hugged Jessica close, stroking her hair and whispering something John couldn't hear.

Marla released Jessica and turned to him. "John," she said, taking both his hands. The sorrow in her eyes was what broke him. He leaned in and hugged her close, hiding his face in her hair until he could compose himself. When his breathing had steadied, she pushed him gently back and took his arm. They all went back to the table where Arty waited, peering uncertainly over the side of the booth. They sat down again. Marla slid in next to John and looked from him to Jessica. "You have to tell me what happened," she said quietly. Jessica nodded, letting her hair fall over her face for a minute in a shiny brown curtain.

"Yeah, I want to know, too," Arty piped up, and Marla glanced at him as if only just registering his presence.

"Hi," she said, sounding slightly puzzled. "I'm Marla."

"Arty. Charlie and I were—" He glanced at John. "We were good friends."

Marla nodded. "Well, I wish we were meeting under different circumstances. Jessica? John? Please, tell me."

They glanced at each other. John looked to the window again. He was content to let Jessica do the talking but felt an obligation—not to talk to Marla, but to talk *about* Charlie. "Charlie was chasing something from her past," John said, his voice calm. "She found it, and it didn't let her leave."

"There was a building collapse," Jessica added. "Her father's house."

"Charlie didn't make it out," John said roughly. He cleared his throat and reached for the glass of water in front of him.

John vaguely heard Marla and Jessica exchanging words of comfort, but his mind was elsewhere. *The woman, kneeling in the pool of Charlie's blood, holding her hand.* He had only glimpsed her for a moment; she had looked almost as surprised to see him as he was to see her. But there was something familiar about her.

He turned away from the others again and closed his eyes, trying to picture it. *Dark hair, dark eyes. She looked severe and unafraid, even with the ground shaking and the building tumbling down over her head. I know her.* The woman he remembered looked different, younger, but her face was the same . . . Suddenly he had it. *The last day I saw you, Charlie, back when we were kids. She came to pick you up from school, and the next day you weren't there, and the next day, and the day after that. Then even us kids began to hear the rumors, that your father had done what he did. And that's when I realized I would never see you again.* John shivered.

"John, what's wrong?" Marla said sharply, then blushed. "I mean, what are you thinking?"

"Her aunt was there," he said slowly. "Her aunt Jen."

"What?" Marla said. "Where?"

"They hadn't spoken in months," Jessica said doubtfully.

"I know," John said. "But she was there. When I ran back, just before they pulled me away, I *saw* her. With Charlie."

The thought struck him like a blow across the chest, and he looked out the window again so that he wouldn't have to meet anyone's eyes. "Charlie's aunt Jen was there," he repeated to the dirty pane of glass.

"Maybe Clay called her," Jessica offered. John didn't respond. No one spoke for a long moment.

"I think it's best not to look for more mysteries," Marla said slowly. "Charlie was—"

"Are you all ready to order?" The waitress asked brightly. John turned to look at her with impatience in his eyes, but Marla cut him off.

"Four coffees," she said firmly. "Four eggs and toast, scrambled."

"Thanks, Marla," John whispered. "I'm not sure if I can eat, though."

She glanced at the rest of them. Arty looked briefly as if he wanted to say something, then he cast his eyes down at the table. The woman departed, and Marla looked around. "We all have to eat. And you can't sit around in a diner all day without ordering anything."

"I'm glad you're here, Marla," John said. She nodded.

"We all love Charlie," she said, looking at each of them in turn. "There's never a right thing to say, is there? Nothing ever makes it okay, because it's not."

"All those crazy experiments," Jessica said suddenly. "I didn't understand, but she was so excited about them, and now she'll never get to finish."

"It's not fair," Marla said softly.

"So what do we do?" Jessica said with a plaintive note in her voice. She looked at Marla like she must have the answer.

"Jessica, sweetie," Marla said. "All anyone can do is hold on to the Charlie that we all loved."

"It's over," John said hoarsely, turning away from the window abruptly. "That . . . that psychopath murdered her, just like he did Michael and all those other kids. She was the most fascinating, the most amazing person I have ever known, and she died for *nothing*."

"She did *not* die for nothing!" Marla snapped, leaning in

toward him. Rage flashed in her eyes. "No one dies for nothing, John. Everyone's life has a meaning. Everyone has a death, and I hate it that this was hers. Do you hear me? I *hate* it! But we can't change it. All we can do is remember Charlie, and honor Charlie's life, from the beginning to the very end."

John held her stormy gaze for a long moment, then broke away and looked down at his folded hands on the table. She mirrored the movement and placed one hand over his.

Jessica gasped, and he turned back to the table wearily. "What, Jessica?" John asked. Her nervous energy was beginning to exhaust him. She didn't answer, but gave him an incredulous look, and turned back to the window. Marla leaned past John, craning her neck to see. Reluctantly he looked, too, letting his eyes focus for the first time on the parking lot outside the window, and not the pane of glass itself.

It was a car. The woman driving killed the engine and got out. She was slim and tall, with long, straight brown hair that glistened in the sun. She was wearing a bright red, knee-length dress with black combat boots, and she strode purposefully toward the diner. They all watched motionless, as if the slightest sound might rupture the illusion and send her away. The woman was almost at the door. Arty said it first:

"Charlie?"

Marla shook her head. She leaped up and turned, calling from the seat, "Charlie!"

She ran for the door, and Jessica was quick on her heels, crying out after her. They rushed to the doorway to meet her just as she walked in.

John stayed where he was, craning his neck to see the door. Arty seemed confused, his mouth open slightly and his brow furrowed. John watched for a steady moment, then turned away decisively, facing across the table with a grave expression. He didn't speak until Arty met his gaze.

"That's not Charlie."

## About Scott Cawthon

Scott Cawthon is the author of the best-selling video game series Five Nights at Freddy's, and while he is a game designer by trade, he is first and foremost a storyteller at heart. He is a graduate of The Art Institute of Houston and lives in Texas with his wife and four sons.

## About Kira Breed-Wrisley

Kira Breed-Wrisley has been writing stories since she could first pick up a pen and has no intention of stopping. She is the author of seven plays for Central New York teen theater company The Media Unit, and has developed several books with Kevin Anderson & Associates. She is a graduate of Cornell University, and lives in Brooklyn, NY.

# A DEADLY SECRET IS LURKING AT THE HEART OF FREDDY FAZBEAR'S PIZZA...

Unravel the twisted mysteries behind the bestselling horror video games and the *New York Times* bestselling series.